Catherine Cookson was born in Tyne Dock, the illegitimate daughter of a poverty-stricken woman, Kate, whom she believed to be her sister. She began work in service, but eventually moved south to Hastings, where she met and married a local grammar-school master. Although she was originally acclaimed as a regional writer – in 1968 her novel *The Round Tower* won the Winifred Holtby Award – her readership quickly spread throughout the world and her many bestselling novels have established her as the best-loved of contemporary women writers. After receiving an OBE in 1985, Catherine Cookson was created a Dame of the British Empire in 1993.

Also by Catherine Cookson

NOVELS

Kate Hannigan
The Fifteen Streets
Colour Blind
Maggie Rowan
Rooney
The Menagerie
Slinky Jane
Fanny McBride
Fenwick Houses
The Garment
The Blind Miller
Hannah Massey
The Long Corridor
The Unbaited Trap
Katie Mulholland
The Round Tower
The Nice Bloke
The Glass Virgin
The Invitation
The Dwelling Place
Feathers in the Fire
Pure as the Lily
The Mallen Streak
The Mallen Girl
The Mallen Litter
The Invisible Cord
The Gambling Man
Miss Martha Mary Crawford
The Tide of Life

The Slow Awakening
The Iron Façade
The Girl
The Cinder Path
The Man Who Cried
Tilly Trotter
Tilly Trotter Wed
Tilly Trotter Widowed
The Whip
Hamilton
The Black Velvet Gown
Goodbye Hamilton
A Dinner of Herbs
Harold
The Moth
Bill Bailey
The Parson's Daughter
Bill Bailey's Lot
The Cultured Handmaiden
Bill Bailey's Daughter
The Harrogate Secret
The Black Candle
The Wingless Bird
The Gillyvors
My Beloved Son
The Rag Nymph
The House of Women
The Maltese Angel
The Year of the Virgins

THE MARY ANN STORIES

A Grand Man
The Lord and Mary Ann
The Devil and Mary Ann
Love and Mary Ann
Life and Mary Ann

Marriage and Mary Ann
Mary Ann's Angels
Mary Ann and Bill
Bill and the Mary Ann
Shaughnessy

FOR CHILDREN

Matty Doolin
Joe and the Gladiator
The Nipper
Blue Baccy
Our John Willie

Mrs Flannagan's Trumpet
Go Tell It To Mrs Golightly
Lanky Jones
Nancy Nutall and the Mongrel

AUTOBIOGRAPHY

Our Kate
Let Me Make Myself Plain

Catherine Cookson Country

WRITING AS CATHERINE MARCHANT

House of Men
The Fen Tiger

Heritage of Folly

CATHERINE COOKSON

UNABRIDGED OMNIBUS EDITION

THE FIFTEEN STREETS
COLOUR BLIND
THE UNBAITED TRAP

LOMOND

Typeset in 11 on 12pt Plantin by
Chippendale Type Ltd, Otley, West Yorkshire.

Printed and bound in Great Britain by
Mackays of Chatham plc, Chatham, Kent

THE FIFTEEN STREETS

CONTENTS

AUTHOR'S NOTE

The characters in this book are entirely fictitious and have no relation to any living person.

Although the setting is Tyneside and several place names have been used, 'The Fifteen Streets' are imaginary.

Owing to difficulty in comprehension by the uninitiated, I have not adhered to the Tyneside dialect.

CHAPTER ONE

THE BROTHERS

'Hannah, drop that an' come an' see. The O'Briens are at it again . . . blue murder! Come on. Come upstairs, you can see better from our top window.'

Wiping the soap suds from her arms, Hannah Kelly hastily lifted the lid of the wash-house boiler, scooped off the grey scum with an enamel mug, dabbed the contents of the boiler with a stick, then ran out of the wash-house and across the backyard, thinking as she did so, 'Eeh, I haven't got time for this . . . And our Joe warned me.'

She caught up with her neighbour as she was opening the stair door.

'Who is it this time? The old man?'

'Yes.'

'Who's he at? Dominic?'

'Aye.'

'Are they drunk?'

'Are they ever owt else!'

They scurried across the kitchen to the front room, and automatically took up their stations, one at each side of the window, bodies close to the wall, heads held slightly to the side against the mesh of the Nottingham lace curtains, their arms wound tightly in their aprons.

'My God, what a mess, Bella!'

'He must have thrown them two pictures out since I came down for you.'

'Eeh, God Almighty! It's a shame. Just as Mary Ellen was getting things pulled together again.'

'Look' – there was glee in Bella's voice – 'there they are at the window throttling each other. Christ!' she exclaimed as something came hurtling through the window into the street, 'which one missed that, I wonder?'

'Eeh! he's thrown the pot through the window. Oh, Bella, that'll bring the pollis. God Almighty, it's awful! It's enough to bring on the bairn . . . she's at the worst time, on eight months.'

'Best thing that could happen. Who wants a bairn at forty-five, I ask you? She should have been more cute. Anyway, she wouldn't listen to me. I told her I could get her a bottle of white mixture from our Harry's

Emma, who scrubs the wards up at the grubber; the nurses would have given it to her. It would have skited everything out of her.'

'Well, you know she wouldn't do that, she's a Catholic, Bella.'

'Catholic, be damned! They tell 'em to have bairns, but do they bloody well keep them? I'd like to see any priest tell me I must have bairns. Do you know what I'd say?'

Hannah chuckled. 'I've a pretty good idea . . . Look, there she is, there's Mary Ellen. She looks like death.'

They both became silent and watched the woman below picking up the two picture frames from the road. The loose glass splintered about her feet as she shook the frames, and as she shooed some children away from the broken chamber, Hannah remarked, regretfully, 'Pity about that. It was a boody one, too.'

Unblinkingly they watched the woman edge her way indoors, with neither a glance upwards nor to the right or left, although as they knew, she was fully aware of the watchers. Only the children were on the street, staring silently until the door closed, when they drew nearer, and some daring spirits, braving the glass, hitched themselves up on the high window sill to get their faces level with the hole. But as they did so the blind was dropped, and Hannah exclaimed, clicking her tongue, 'She shouldn't have done that – dropping the blind right down before dark – it's the sign of a death. It'll be the bairn, likely.'

'Damn good job too. Better if it was her old man though, in case he lands her with another.'

They turned slowly from the window, and Hannah said, 'By, that wouldn't have happened if John had been in; he'd have put a stop to that . . . Funny, isn't it, Bella, that the old man doesn't go for John.'

'Not funny a bit. He's afraid of him, if the truth was known. Old O'Brien and Dominic are both alike, full of wind and water. That's why they fight . . . By God! I wish I was in Mary Ellen's place for five minutes. I'd lay those two sods out with the poker! She's soft, that's what she is, soft as clarts . . . Are you going to stay for a cup of tea?' she added. 'I'll put the kettle on, it won't be a minute.'

'No, lass, I'm not half through, and it's getting on for dark.'

Bella glanced sideways at Hannah. 'Should you come across Mary Ellen – you see her more than I do – and she tells you what it was all about, knock up.'

'Aye, I will. But there's small chance. She's close, is Mary Ellen. You know that.'

'I know she doesn't like me. Thinks I can't mind me own business.'

And she's right there, thought Hannah.

'And anyway, I'm not the same colour as them,' went on Bella nodding her long horse-face. 'Me St Patrick's Day's colour's blue. Wait until next Thursday week when Dominic's wearing his shamrock. There'll be skull and hair flying then. The fifteen streets won't hold him . . . My God, remember last St Patrick's Day? That was a do, eh?' She laughed at the memory.

'Eeh, Bella, I must be off.' Hannah unwrapped her mottled arms, and banged out the creases in her coarse apron.

'Well don't forget to knock up if you hear owt.'

'I won't.'

Hannah went down the stairs, walking sideways in case she slipped, as the stairs were too narrow for her feet encased in an old pair of men's boots. By the time she reached the bottom she had also reached a decision: she wouldn't tell Bella Bradley what she heard, if she heard owt at all. Too nosey was Bella, by half. She'd rather keep in with Mary Ellen, narrow as she was. At least she minded her own business. And her Joe warned her only last night against Bella Bradley. He said he'd bash her face in if he found her upstairs again – he was nettled after hearing what she said about their Nancy not being all there. He knew Nancy wasn't all there, but it maddened him to hear anyone say it. More so now that Nancy was growing up . . . Hannah sighed. What would become of Nancy? She didn't know. And anyway, there was no time to think now, the washing had to be finished.

Across the road, in number 10 Fadden Street, Mary Ellen O'Brien worked in the semi-darkness behind the drawn blind. She adjusted the block of wood under the chest of drawers – the leg had been kicked off during the last row – and screwed in the knob of the top drawer. She picked up the grey blanket and patchwork quilt from the floor and spread them again over the lumpy bare mattress on the iron bed. She pushed the wicker table back into the centre of the room, and stood leaning on its weak support, breathing heavily. Her eyes, dry with the pricking dryness of sand, looked round the walls. They were quite bare . . . Well, they would remain so. The only two pictures in the house were now gone. Never again would she try to build up. She had told herself, if they went this time it would be the last.

She looked towards the closed door, which led into the kitchen. She knew that beyond, on either side of the fireplace, they'd be sitting, spent. Their rage and passion flown, they would be like the two halves of one body, accepting each other now that the conflict was over for a time.

She lifted her apron and wiped the sweat from her forehead. If only they weren't so big . . . like giants. She hadn't dared go between them this time because of the bairn . . . She put her hand on the raised globe of her stomach and felt a movement. It brought no sense of feeling to her other than that of apprehension. Why, oh why was she to have this all over again? Hadn't she been through enough in her time? During the twenty-six years of her married life she had given birth to eleven bairns, and only five were alive, for which she thanked God. What she would have done with thirteen in these three rooms only the Almighty knew.

A pain through her breast made her gasp, and she covered it with her hand, lifting up its weight. Last year this time they'd been flat . . . flat for all time she'd thought, for it was ten years since Katie was born. Practically every year since she was married she'd been dropped, but from Katie there'd been nothing. The pain shot through her again, and she remembered such a pain from the past. It was before John was born. She was as strong as a horse then, as small as she was, and she enjoyed the feeling of the pain, anticipating the tugging of the young mouth on the nipples . . . if it lived. It did live, and it was John . . . John, who had never given her any trouble. Oh, if they were all like John, and, at the other end of the scale, Katie. Funny that these two should be alike and the others so different from them. Dominic was different from the day he was born, the year after John. She had always been slightly afraid of Dominic, even when he was a child. It wasn't that he alone suffered from the O'Brien rages, for they all did, except Katie. It was rather that there was something fiendish about Dominic. It showed in everything he did, in his teasing, in his laughter, and especially in his good-looking face. Like John and Mick, he took after his da for his looks. But although they all took after their da Dominic and Mick were better looking than John. When she looked at her eldest son she had the feeling that the features which made the other two good looking made him ugly, and in some strange way this pleased her. To her mind it separated him entirely from them. It was his nose that made the difference, she supposed, with that funny little nob on the side of the nostril. He got that when he climbed the dock wall to get some coal that bad winter. He slipped and his nose was cut on the broken glass set in the top of the wall. The cut did not join properly and gave his face a quaint look from the side. But it wasn't only his nose; John's eyes were different from the others. They were large and brown too, but a different brown . . . dark and kind. That was it, they were kind, like Katie's.

She sighed and rubbed her hand gently round and round her breast. Then, hearing a shout coming through the kitchen from the back-yard, she moved her head impatiently – she never thought of Molly unless the girl made herself felt by sight or sound. Molly was . . . well, she couldn't place Molly. She was of a too apparent mixture of them all, and so had no individuality of her own. She was swayed, first one way and then the other; even her rages could be deflected by a stronger will. No, Molly would be no heartache, for she aroused no feeling.

Mary Ellen straightened her shoulders and refastened the top button of her blouse over her straining breasts before walking towards the kitchen door. It was no use standing here thinking; thinking got you nowhere. It was close on five o'clock and John would be in at half past. She'd have to get on with the tea . . . Thank God they fought in here and not in the kitchen. They might have knocked the pan of broth off the hob, and there was nearly fourpennorth of vegetables in besides a twopenny scrag end . . . Well, if you searched hard enough there was always something to be thankful for.

As she expected, her husband and son were sitting one each side of the fireplace, their brows puckered over half-closed eyes. Shane's grey hair was standing up straight in tufts; there was blood on the hair near his temple, and his high cheek-bones were showing blue under the tightened skin. At the first glance she saw that his rage wasn't entirely spent, for the muscle was moving in his cheek as he clenched and unclenched his teeth, and his limbs, as always, were jerking with the nerve tick. His knees, in their reddened moleskin trousers, were wide apart, and his feet were crossed below his hands, which were gripping the seat of the wooden armchair. His body looked as if it was still ready to spring . . . No, his rage wasn't spent yet, because he was sober. He'd had only two shifts in this week and had tipped the money up. But Dominic had a full week. For three weeks now he'd worked full weeks. Not that it made much difference to her – she was lucky if she got ten shillings out of him. She often had to meet him at the dock gates to get even that . . . or send Katie. But Dominic's rage was spent because he was drunk and happy.

She took Dominic by the shoulder and shook him. 'Here! Get yourself to bed.'

He lifted his head and smiled crookedly at her, cracking the dried blood on his mouth as he did so. He looked at her out of one merry, brown eye, the other being hidden behind a curling lock of light brown, youthful hair.

'All right, old girl.'

He rose obediently to his feet, and some detached part of her marvelled for the countless time at his docility towards her when he was in drink. Why was it she could manage him when he was drunk? She even found herself liking him in this state. She had no fear of him in drink, when he spoke civilly to her, often with a touch of affection. But it was strange that even in drink she could have any affection for him now, for she remembered the look in his eyes during these past weeks when they lit on her stomach . . . ridicule, scorn, and something else . . . a something for which she could find no word. She pushed him before her into the bedroom, her head coming just to the bottom of his shoulder blades. She always wondered, when close to them, how she gave birth to such great men.

Dominic sat down with a plop on the side of his bed and began to laugh. 'If he wasn't my old man I'd have knocked him stiff. But I'll break his bloody neck the next time he interferes with me. I didn't ask to be set on the ore boat – they want the young 'uns down the holds.'

He fell back on the bed and lifted up his legs, and Mary Ellen immediately swung them down again. She took off his boots and loosened his belt, then unbuttoned his trousers and tugged them off his legs, leaving these looking particularly ludicrous in their tight long pants. Never in all the many times she had pulled trousers off them had she yet been able to conquer the feeling of revulsion. Husband or son, it was the same.

She heaved him up by the shirt front and dragged off his coat. Then she let him fall back on to the bed. She threw the quilt over him and put his coat on top of it, and lifting his trousers quietly from the floor, she put them across her arm and went out, through the kitchen, past her husband, who now sat hunched up over the fire, and into the front room, where she turned out the contents of the trousers pockets on to the table.

There was a half-sovereign, two two-shilling pieces, and four pennies. The half-sovereign he would have to stump up for his board, so she put that back into the pocket again, together with a two-shilling piece. The other two-shilling piece and the coppers went into a little cloth bag that dangled from a pin fastened to the inside of her skirt. It already held tenpence. She had taken to this device of the bag when Shane came back from the Boer War, because he lifted every penny he could get his fingers on for drink.

She went back to the bedroom and quietly placed the trousers over the bed rail, and as she returned to the kitchen the window was darkened by a distorted bulk, and a gentle tap-tap came on the door.

Mary Ellen sighed. As inevitably as the calm which followed the storm would come this tap-tap on the door after any disturbance in the house. She often thanked God for an upstairs neighbour such as Peggy Flaherty. Many a one, placed as she was above the noise and fighting that was almost part of the weekly routine, would have done more than object, she would have brought the pollis; and after a number of such visits they would have been in court and likely turned out of the house. Peggy was a bit queer; still, as God knew, there were worse states than being queer. But today, Mary Ellen felt tired, and even Peggy's well-meant sympathy was an irritant. She opened the door, and would have smiled, if she could, at the quaint tact of this fat, dirty woman.

'I was after warming meself up with a mouthful of stew, Mary Ellen, an' I said to meself, "I'll take a drop below, it'll stick to Mary Ellen's ribs." ' She proffered the basin, full of a lead-coloured liquid, with darker pieces of matter floating about on its surface. 'Are you all right, lass?' She peered at Mary Ellen through her short-sighted eyes, looking for a black eye or other evidence of the fight.

'Yes, I'm all right, Peggy. And thanks for the soup.'

'Oh, that's all right, Mary Ellen . . . You'll drink it, now, won't you?'

'Yes, yes,' Mary Ellen hastily assured her, wondering whether Peggy was suspicious of the fate of her proffered balms. She would have to be very hungry, she thought, before she ate anything made by Peggy's hands in that menagerie upstairs. Before he died, Charlie Flaherty earned his living in many ways. At one time, he worked for himself as a tally man, and when payment was not forthcoming, took the equivalent in kind; so two of the three rooms upstairs were stacked from floor to ceiling with an odd assortment of things, not one of which Peggy would part with, ranging from a stuffed baby crocodile to a collection of books, out of which Peggy was wont to say 'she got the extinsive iducation' she possessed. She spread more false knowledge round the fifteen streets than it was possible to imagine. Many of the inhabitants would have sworn that Henry VIII was Queen Elizabeth's husband, and that England once belonged to the Irish before William the Conqueror came over and took it from them. For the sum of a penny she would write a letter; for a little more, give advice on how to deal with a summons, or a case of defamation of character, or assault. Often this advice, if faithfully carried out, would have got the worried seeker a sojourn in jail. It was strange, that although she was said to be odd and barmy, her advice was still sought. Perhaps it was because it was known that on these pennies she mainly relied for her existence. There was an unspoken feeling in these streets, which, if translated, would have implied . . . you save someone the workhouse and you'll never land there yourself.

'God and His Holy Mother preserve us this day, the trials we have! Is there anything more I can do for you, Mary Ellen?' went on Peggy.

'No, I'm all right, Peggy, thanks.' Mary Ellen looked at the basin in her hands, hoping to convey a hint that she would like to go in and make a start on the soup.

But Peggy did not notice this move; or if she did, she refused to take the hint; for she had something weighty to say. Leaning forward, she whispered, 'Did I ever tell you, Mary Ellen, Mr Flaherty's cure for all this?' She nodded towards the closed scullery door.

Mary Ellen, suppressing another sigh, said, 'No, Peggy.'

'Iducation! No man would fight, he said, once he had iducation. And he knew what he was talking about, for he got about among the gentry, you know, Mary Ellen. It was his theory that once a man got iducation he wouldn't raise a hand to his wife. He might, being a human being, get a bit irritated and say, "Retire to your room before I kick your backside!" or some such thing, but to lift his hand . . . no!'

'There may be something in it.' Mary Ellen again looked at the basin. 'Sure you haven't left yourself short, Peggy?'

'Not at all. Not at all. Anyway you go now inside, and don't talk any more; and get that down you, it'll put a lining on your stomach. And remember, if you want any advice you know where to come.'

She shuffled away, and Mary Ellen closed the door . . . Don't talk any more, and, Retire to your room before I kick your backside! If there was a laugh left in her she would have laughed; but she would

17

remember them, and some night by the fire she would tell them to John, and they would laugh together.

John came in at half-past five. He hung his cap and coat, together with his black neckerchief on the back of the kitchen door, then sat down on a box in the tiny square of scullery and loosened the yorks that bound his trousers below the knee. Before washing his hands in the tin dish that was standing on another box he looked into the lighted kitchen and smiled towards the three children sitting at the table. Only Katie returned his smile, her round, blue eyes sending him a greeting.

Mick called, 'Got anything, John? Any bananas or anything?'

And he answered, 'Not tonight; we're still on the grain boat.'

When John came to the table, his mother set a plate of broth before him, out of which a series of bare ribs stuck up, like the skeleton of a hulk. The smell was appetising, and the eyes of the three children focused on the plate.

Mary Ellen exclaimed harshly, 'Get on with your bread and dripping!' and almost simultaneously each bit into his own inch-thick slice of bread.

She placed another plate on the table and said to her husband, 'Your tea's out.'

Shane turned from the fire and stared at the plate, and from there to his son and the other three. His body started to jerk, first his head, then his arms, and lastly his right leg. His words too, when they came, were spasmodic and heavy with bitterness: 'Served last now, am I? It's a difference when you're not bringing it in. You've got to work or you don't eat . . . not till everybody else is finished.'

John put his spoon down and stared at his father: 'I'll wait until you're done.'

His mother signalled wildly to him from behind her husband, and pointed to the bedroom. John read her signal, but continued to stare at his father, until Shane's eyes dropped away and he growled, 'It's them young 'uns – I was never set down before me father.'

His head jerked to one side as if he were straining at a bit, and Mary Ellen said quietly, 'Don't be a fool! Get your tea.'

'You want to start, you do!' Shane sprang up from his chair, kicking it to one side as he did so. 'It only needs you to start. Belittling me before the bairns! That's a new tack.' He towered like a swaying mountain of rage over the short unwieldly figure of his wife.

Mary Ellen took no notice, but went on cutting bread on the corner of the oil cloth which covered the table, and the children continued to eat, their eyes fixed on their plates. Only John kept his eyes on his father, and Shane lifted his bloodshot gaze from the top of his wife's head to meet John's again. He stared at his

18

son for a moment, his compressed lips moving in and out. Then he swung round, grabbed his cap from the back of the door and went to go out: but as he reached the back door he paused and cast his infuriated glance back into the kitchen again: 'The next bloody thing'll be: There's the door . . . Get out!'

He kicked savagely at the box holding the dish of water. There was a clatter and a splash; the door opened and banged, and only the clink of his heel plates becoming fainter down the yard broke the silence in the kitchen.

When they could be heard no more, Mary Ellen moved. She went into the scullery and, bending down with difficulty, began to sop up the water from the hollowed stones.

Dimly, with a mixture of pity and understanding, her thoughts followed her husband . . . Dominic getting drunk on his earnings . . . John coming in from work. Both of them on full time, and him with only two shifts in. He was getting on and he couldn't work like he used to, and the gaffer picked the young and strong 'uns. His strength was failing – she'd noticed that. Drink and hard work and wet clothes that were often frozen to his skin were at last taking their toll. He seemed to retain his strength for one thing alone . . . if only that would slacken with the rest. It must sometime. Then God, let it be soon.

'I'll help you, Ma.' Katie was on her knees by the side of her mother.

'No! Get up out of that. That's the only clean pinny you've got!'

'Well I haven't got to go to school the morrer.'

'Doesn't matter. Get up out of that.'

'Here!' – John stood above her – 'let's have it.' He held out his hand for the cloth.

'Oh get out of me road, the both of you!' Her voice pushed them back into the kitchen, and she went on bending and wringing out the cloth. Who did they think did all the other work, the washing, the cooking, the scouring, the humping of the coal, bucket by bucket from the back lane into the coal house because now she couldn't throw the shovelfuls through the hatch?

She partly soothed her irritation by saying to herself: 'You know John's always telling you to leave the coal until he comes in. Yes, but how can I' – her irritation refused to be soothed – 'with people waiting to get their washing out!' She flung the cloth into the bucket. Oh, she felt so tired. If only she could see a way out of all this . . . if only the bairn was born! Yes, that was the main stumbling block. Once that was over everything would be all right; she would cope, as always.

She went into the kitchen again and said to Mick, 'Go and empty the bucket and wash it out, and bring some clean water . . . See you wash it out, mind!'

Mick's mouth dropped, and he muttered, 'Aw! Why can't she do it?'

He dug Molly in the side, and she cried, 'Look at him, Ma! Stop it, our Mick!'

John took the rib of bones from his mouth: 'Your mother spoke to you.'

'Me ear's bad' – Mick placed his hand over the side of his head – 'it's been running all day.'

'You going out to play the night?' John asked.

'Yes.' Mick scowled at the table.

'Then empty the bucket.'

John went on picking his bone, and Mick clattered from the table, while Molly sniggered into her pinny.

'You'll laugh the other side of your face in a minute, my girl,' said Mary Ellen. 'Get those dishes washed.'

'Then can I go out to play?'

'Who you going out to play with in the dark, you're not going to run the streets?'

'We're going in Annie Kelly's wash-house; her ma's had the pot on, and it's warm. Annie has some bits of candle, and we're going to put them in bottles and play houses and dress up.'

'Play houses and dress up,' Mary Ellen muttered to herself. Aloud, she said, 'And burn yourselves to death! . . . Well, and only half an hour, mind. And you can take Katie with you.'

'I don't want to go, Ma; I've got to do some homework.'

'What!' the mother and John lifted their heads and stared at Katie.

'You got your sums wrong?' asked John, in surprise.

'No.' Katie shook her head and tried to repress a smile, but her eyes grew rounder and her dimples deeper as she looked at their straight faces.

'Then why have you to do homework?' John asked; 'you never have before.'

'I've got to learn something. Miss Llewellyn asked me to . . . '

'She's Miss Llewellyn's pet, everybody says she is . . . I hated Miss Llewellyn. I was glad when I was moved up.' Molly wet the tip of her finger on her tongue, and in this way she secured a number of crumbs from the table. When she had put them in her mouth, she swung round on Katie, saying, 'You didn't tell me ma Miss Llewellyn gave you a penny the day for learning your poetry first, did you? Nelly Crane told me . . . so!'

The smile vanished from Katie's face, and Mary Ellen looked down on her daughter in surprise, the daughter who was the only one of the family to take after her. She could see this child, as she herself once was, plump and bonnie and open-handed. It was unusual for Katie to keep anything.

'Did she give you a penny?' she asked.

Katie neither moved nor spoke, but her eyes, as they looked back into her mother's, became glazed, and she cried out within herself, 'Oh, our Molly! our Molly!' Now it was all spoilt – the wonderful, wonderful thing she was going to do was spoilt. The Easter egg . . . the real Easter egg in a real box, tied up with a real silk ribbon, was lying in fragments about her! And the picture of herself handing it to Miss Llewellyn was lying with it.

That penny had brought her secret hoard to fivepence. For three weeks she had kept John's Saturday penny and the two halfpennies her mother had given her. Today's surprise penny had meant such a lot, for she had only another month or so during which to get the remainder of the shilling.

Her mother became blotted out by a mist; then she felt John's big hands drawing her to him and pressing her against his knees.

When he bent and whispered in her ear, 'Are you saving up to buy a present?' she experienced the feeling she had felt before that John was in some way connected with God and the priests, because he knew everything.

She nodded her head against the bottom of his waistcoat, and he whispered again, 'Your teacher?'

At this she gasped and pressed her face tightly against him. John exchanged a glance with his mother, and a smile flickered for an instant across her face.

'I think you must be the cleverest lass in the school,' John went on.

Katie brought her head up swiftly and stared at him. 'Why, that's what Miss Llewellyn says! She says . . . she says I'm advanced and I must work at nights and . . . and read a lot.'

'There you are. There you are. Miss Llewellyn knows. She knows when she's on a good thing. What have you got to learn the night?'

'Oh, I already know some of it, the end bit,' she laughed. 'Listen. A man named Shakespeare did it.' She stood back from his knee, threw her long black plaits over her shoulder, joined her hands behind her back, and said:

'There take an inventory of all I have,
To the last penny; 'tis the king's: my role,
And my integrity to heaven is all
I dare now call my own. O Cromwell, Cromwell!
Had I but serv'd my God with half the zeal
I serv'd my king, he would not in mine age
Have left me naked to mine enemies.'

John stared down on her face, which was illuminated by the feel of the strange words on her tongue, and Mary Ellen stared at the back of her dark head. Then their eyes met, reflecting the glow of her words, which were unintelligible to both of them . . . But Katie had said them . . . their Katie . . . the only one of them who had ever wanted to learn. With a swoop, John lifted her up and held her on his upstretched hands. Her head was within a few inches of the ceiling, and he laughed up at her: 'Will I push you through to Mrs Flaherty?'

'Eeh! No, John. Eeh, our John, let me down.'

She wriggled on his hands, anxious to get away from the ceiling and the proximity of Mrs Flaherty and her weird house.

As he lowered her to the floor John laughed, 'You'll soon be cleverer than Mrs Flaherty, and then everybody will be coming here and saying, "Please, Katie O'Brien, will you write me a letter?" and you'll say, "Yes, if you give me sixpence." '

'Oh, our John, I wouldn't! I wouldn't ask for sixpence.'

He bent down to her and whispered hoarsely, 'Oh yes you would, if it would get your teacher a present.'

She slapped his knee playfully, then turned her face away to hide the tell-tale glow.

Molly banged the mugs into the cupboard; she banged the door as she went out; then her voice came through the keyhole:

'Miss Llewellyn has a swellin',
An' I'm not tellin'
Where Miss Llewellyn
Has a swellin'.'

John turned quickly away from Katie's outraged face, rubbing his hand across his mouth. But he could not rub the laughter from his eyes, and Katie turned on him, her voice full of hurt surprise: 'Oh, our John, you're laughing! Our Molly's awful . . . Miss Llewellyn hasn't got a . . . She's lovely, she's beautiful. She wears a lovely white blouse with a frill at her neck, and her hair's brown and shines all over the place. And Mr Culbert's after her. Cathleen Pearson says he wants to marry her.' Katie's voice broke: 'She's beautiful . . . she's beautiful.'

John sat down by the fire and pulled her on to his knee, cradling her in his arms and soothing her: 'Of course she's beautiful, of course she is. And who's Mr Culbert when he's out?'

'He's . . . he's a teacher at St Jude's.'

'Is he? Is he? Well, he can be the Prime Minister for all I care. But you know what I'm going to do? I'm going to this Mr Culbert, and I'm going to say, "You going to marry Miss Llewellyn and take her away from teaching our Katie? You are . . . like panhacklety!!" '

'Oh, our John, you're awful!'

Laughing, she scrambled up and stood on his knees and flung her arms about his neck, endeavouring to strangle him with her small strength.

'Here! hold on.'

'Eeeh!' – she drew her face back from his – 'you haven't got to say that.'

'What, hold on?'

'Yes. Miss Llewellyn says you've got to say, "Wait a moment," or, "Stop a moment." '

'Do you hear that, Ma?' He winked at his mother, who was now sitting at the other side of the hearth mending a pair of moleskin trousers.

She gave a flicker of a smile and went on adjusting a patch. What was it about these two bairns of hers that brought her such strange joy? To see them playing together like they were now seemed to make up for all the heart scolds of life. She still thought of John as her bairn, although he was twenty-two and six foot one. He would always be her bairn, her first bairn. There were some who said you loved all you gave birth to. Fools! You couldn't love even two alike. Even those two opposite, she loved one more than the other, but she couldn't tell which.

Her mind returned to concrete things, and she said without looking up, 'The front window's out.'

John did not reply, but after a moment put Katie on the floor and, taking a box of matches from his pocket, went to the front room.

Katie was about to follow him, when Mary Ellen said, 'Get on with your homework, hinny.'

It was some time before John returned, and still he said nothing. He sat down on his chair again and took off his boots and put his stockinged feet on the fender, and sat staring at the kettle singing on the side of the hob. Presently he took a loose Woodbine from his pocket and lit it . . . Would it never end? Would life go on like this for her until she died?

He cast a glance at her bent head. The hair was grey, yet coarse and strong, springing from the centre parting and refusing to be drawn flat into the knob behind; but the face beneath was deeply marked with lines. They ran in puckered furrows across her forehead and bit deep from her nose to the corners of her mouth. The mouth in repose, as it was now, looked despondent, without hope. Could you wonder at it! And there was this other thing to happen. And her so little, not much bigger than a bairn herself.

He shifted suddenly in his chair. What could he do? He was helpless. If only he had a decent job, if only he hadn't been pushed into the docks. Well, where else could he have gone? If a lad wanted to make money at fourteen he had to give up all idea of being apprenticed to a trade. It was the same in all the places: Palmer's shipyard, the steel works, the chemical works. Now he'd be a dock labourer for the rest of his life; and he would never earn enough money to make any noticeable difference to her life. Did his father ever feel like this, feel this sense of frustration and helplessness? That's why he drank as he did. And Dominic? Ugh – he made an involuntary gesture with his hand as if wiping his brother away – that swiller!

He lifted his feet up to the side of the pan hob and sank deeper into his chair. Drink was a funny thing once it got you. He was drunk only once, and could still remember isolated parts of the feeling. It happened the first week he was on capstan work. He had been promoted from hatching at two-and-six a shift and now felt a man. After being paid off, he was walking out of the dock gates with the men when one of them, nodding towards the line of public houses filling the street opposite, said, 'Comin' over?'

He felt flattered, and went with them into The Grapes. He remembered the feeling of his stomach swelling and the continual belching of wind, and his mouth becoming fixed open in a wide grin. It was this grin that was partly the reason why he did not touch the drink again, for he brought the picture of himself over into his sober consciousness, and in it he saw the face of his father when in drink, as he had seen it since he was a child, with the large full-lipped mouth stretched wide, conveying not the impression of geniality but of imbecility. And his cure was completed by knowing, on waking up in bed undressed, that his mother had done for him what she did for his father. It was some time before he could entirely rid himself of the feeling of shame and humiliation when he thought of himself being undressed by her.

There were times when he wanted a drink badly – like today, when his throat felt clogged tight with dust – unloading grain was a dry job. He had gone across to the horse trough outside the gates and filled the iron cup four times. Some of his mates called, 'Cheap that, John.' 'Aye, and no headache the morrow,' he replied. They no longer asked him to join them.

A crescendo of snores came from the bedroom, and he shifted his position again. There was something he wanted more than a drink, and that was a mattress. Could he put it to her now? He looked towards his mother. She'd had enough for one day, he told himself, without anything more to worry about. But when a series of spluttering coughs terminated the snores, he said, 'There's a pitch boat due in shortly; if I get set on her, it'll mean extra. Could you . . . get me a mattress with it?'

'A mattress!' Mary Ellen stopped sewing and looked at him. 'A mattress?'

He turned his head to the fire again. 'I want you to put Mick in the bed; I'll sleep in the cupboard.'

'Oh lad' – she joined her hands together over the patch – 'you can't sleep on the floor. And anyway, the cupboard isn't big enough, it barely holds Mick.'

'I can leave the door open.'

The sadness seemed to sink from her eyes into her body, shrinking it still further. She turned her gaze to the fire, and her hands lay idle . . .

24

There was no way of getting another bed into the room, even if they could get one. And for John to lie in the cupboard! She shook her head, not knowing she did so.

The cupboard in the bedroom ran under Mrs Flaherty's front stairs; its total length was five feet, and he wanted to sleep in that! If the door was open, it was cold and draughty, even in the summer; if it was closed, it was naturally airless. She often worried about Mick having to lie there . . . but John! And his feet would extend over any mattress – they did through the bed rails, both his and Dominic's. But that wasn't the floor.

She looked at him and saw by the way his face was set that he meant to do it, and if she didn't get him the mattress he'd lie in the cupboard in any case, on Mick's bag of straw. She sighed, and her hands began to work again.

There was no sound in the kitchen except the sound of Katie's pencil and Dominic's muffled snores, until Molly rushed in the back door, crying, 'Ma! do you know what?'

'Make less noise!' Mary Ellen said.

'But Ma, there's somebody moving in next door the morrer.'

'Wash yourself and get ready for bed . . . Who told you that?' Mary Ellen asked.

'Mrs Bradley told Annie Kelly's ma, and Annie Kelly told me.'

'Then if Mrs Bradley said so, it must be right.' Mary Ellen rose, pulled the table to one side to get at the wooden couch beyond, and began to make up the girls' beds, one at each end.

'Get your things off, hinny,' she said over her shoulder to Katie.

The two girls undressed in the scullery, all except their boots and stockings. These they took off, sitting on crackets before the fire, chatting to each other now quite friendly. Katie sat next to John, her bare feet on the fender sticking out from under her patched, flannelette nightie.

John's fingers moved slowly through her hair. And when the bedroom door opened and Dominic lurched into the kitchen he didn't lift his eyes from the paper he was reading.

Dominic stood near the table, blinking in the gaslight. He yawned, running both his hands over his head; then pulled his belt tighter before coming to the fire. He shivered and sat down in the seat vacated by Mary Ellen, growling to Molly as he did so, 'Move your carcass!' He ran his tongue round his dry lips, shook his head in an endeavour to throw off the muzziness, and stretched out his hands to the fire.

'Any grub?' he asked, without turning his head.

'There's broth,' his mother answered from her bent position over the couch.

Katie looked past Molly to her brother's face. It looked huge and frightening, with the dark stubble around his chin and up the sides of his cheeks, and the darker marks of the dried blood standing out around his mouth. When he hawked in his throat and spat at the bars, she drew her feet sharply beneath her nightie, nearly falling off the cracket as she did so. John's hand, still on her head, steadied her, but he did not take his eyes from the paper.

Dominic saw her frightened glance, and a twisted grin spread slowly over his face. He leaned back in his chair, and after a while Katie's toes came from beneath her nightie again. Her feet were cold, for the steel fender was well below the bottom red bar of the fire. She lifted one foot up above those of Molly, to wriggle her toes in front of the lower bar. There was a hiss, a splatter, and Dominic's yellow saliva was running over her foot.

As she hid her face from the sight and pressed her mouth to stop herself from being sick, she felt John springing away from her. His chair was kicked back, and she flung herself to the floor by the bottom of the fender, lying along its length, pressing close to its brass bars to keep clear of the pounding feet. Molly had sprung to the couch, where she now sat huddled. And before Mary Ellen could reach them John's fist swung out and Dominic reeled backwards and crashed into the cupboard door.

Mary Ellen flung herself on John, crying, 'Lad! lad!' She beat his chest with her fists in an endeavour to push him back: 'John lad! John lad! For God's sake!'

John did not look at her, but gathered her flaying hands in one of his, and tried to push her aside. But she kept in front of him by pressing her body against his, calling beseechingly up to him, 'Lad! Lad! John, lad!'

His face was bereft of colour; his lips were drawn back from his teeth, and his eyes were like black marble. Through her body she could feel the waves of anger running through his; her breast was pressed against his stomach, which shook with the elemental forces demanding release.

'Holy Mary, Mother of God, Mother of God!' she cried. 'No more the day, lad!' She took no heed of her other son, standing with his fists at the ready behind her; Dominic, she knew, wouldn't fight John unless he had to, for in John he had more than his match. No, it was John she must stop. 'John, lad – John! I can't stand any more this day. Oh, Jesus, Mary and Joseph, you know I can't stand no more the day.'

She felt a great intake of breath coming into his lungs and the rumbling thunder of the words as they were released from his throat: 'I warned you what would happen if you did that again!'

Relief swept through her; he had spoken; she could manage him if he spoke.

He spoke again, and his words now brought a faintness over her; the child in her womb seemed to stop breathing. The words fell into

26

her inner consciousness, to be remembered as would those spoken by a prophet have been, for, like Katie, she felt that John was near the priests and God, for what he said was mostly true. And he said now to his brother, 'One of these days I'll kill you.'

There was no threat in the words, only a quiet certainty.

CHAPTER TWO

A DAY OF BONNY LASSES

Poverty is comparative. There were those who did not live in the fifteen streets who considered the people living there to be of one stratum, the lowest stratum; but the people inside this stratum knew that there were three different levels, the upper, the middle, and the lower. All lived in 'houses' either upstairs or down; but in the lower end each house had only two small rooms, and upstairs or down the conditions were the same – the plaster on the walls was alive with bugs. These might only appear at night, to drop on the huddled sleepers, but that strange odour, which was peculiarly their own, wafted through the houses all the time, stamping them as buggy. No-one went to live in the lower end unless he was forced. To the middle and upper fifteen streets the bottom end was only one step removed from the workhouse, for its inhabitants were usually those whose furniture had been distrained or who had been ejected from their former houses for non-payment of rent.

There were three nightmares in the lives of the occupants of the middle and upper fifteen streets. And these were linked together: they were the bums, the lower end, and the workhouse.

In the middle houses there were four rooms . . . boxes, generally, but boxes that were divided, giving privacy of a sort to one or two extra beings. The upper end had only three rooms to each house, and these were either up or down. Here, water was not carried from the central tap in the back lane but from a tap at the bottom of each yard. This stamped the area as selective, automatically making it the best end.

But even into this stratum of the fifteen streets no-one had ever been known to arrive with their furniture in a van. A flat lorry, yes, or a coal cart; at worst, a hand barrow, after dark. These were the three general modes of removal. But a van! a proper one, bearing the words 'Raglan, Furniture Removers, Jarrow-on-Tyne', never.

The street was out to watch with as much interest as if it were a wedding, or a funeral, or, what was more common, a fight. The three O'Brien children had a grandstand view: they stood in a row beneath their front window sill, and behind them, in the room, were the elders, Mary Ellen, Shane, Dominic and John. The sons stood one at each side of their mother and father. They were standing together as a family for

28

once, joined by the common interest, watching in silent wonder as each piece of furniture was carried into the house next door. They had not seen furniture like this before. There was the big, bright, round table, with the thick single leg and bunchy feet like claws; there was the suite of patterned plush, with ball fringe all round the bottom of the couch and chairs; there was the big clock, nearly six feet high; and there was the bed, a wooden one painted white, with pictures on the panels; there were two other beds, but these were of brass. Yet these were outstanding too, for they were neither chipped nor battered. That was not all. There were carpets, two of them, besides a load of rugs one man could hardly shoulder. And the road was strewn with all kinds of things that rent Mary Ellen through with envy; a feeling she thought she was past this many a year. But then, she had never seen owt like this before in the fifteen streets . . . or anywhere else: the mahogany plant stand, with its looped chains, the large china flower pots, the clothes basket full of coloured china, and the little mangle, which looked like a toy but which she knew wasn't. Who were these folks who could own such things, yet had come to live here? It didn't make sense somehow.

She glanced up at John to see what effect all this was having on him, and her eyes left him quickly and travelled down his gaze to the street again. He was looking at a lass who had just come out of the house. Mary Ellen wasn't sure if she was a child, a lass, or a woman.

John, staring at the girl over the brown paper that covered the hole in the window, was being puzzled in much the same way; the girl on the pavement was as shapeless in form as Katie, showing no evidence of either hips or bust. Judged on her figure, she could be a child; and her face too had something of the immaturity of the child in it. Yet it was old. No, not old – he rejected the word – wise, that was it . . . and bonnie too. Yes, she was bonnie, that pale skin against the dark hair. The hair was unusual in that it hung loose about her head. Cut short, boyish fashion, it was like a dark halo. He was curious to see more of her, and, as she turned to speak to the old man with the white hair, who was directing the unloading, he unconsciously bent forward.

Whatever she said brought a smile from the long, serious face of the man, and she smiled in return: and John knew them to be related; it was as if the same light shone from them. It illuminated their faces, and seemed to convey a ray of light even to himself, for he found his face relaxing into a smile as he watched them. He wondered who they could be. Was the man her da, or her grandda? And the little lad running to and fro was evidently one of them, for he had the same pale skin and dark hair.

As John considered the fine furniture and their fine clothes, his smile faded. The old man was wearing a suit and a collar and tie, as though got up for a do, and the girl, a blue woollen dress with a little woollen coat of the same colour. It looked neat and trim and was as unlike anything the lasses of the fifteen streets wore as John could possibly imagine.

The two removal men were struggling to get a chest of drawers through the front door. It was the biggest chest John had seen in his life; it was taller than himself. He could see only one of the men, who was bearing the weight of the bottom end and was stepping backwards and forwards under the other's directions. John knew what had happened. The front door did not lead directly into the front room, but into a tiny square of passage. The other man had got his end stuck in this passage.

The old man's assistance was to no avail; and John watched the girl glance about her at the dark, huddled figures blocking the doorways. Then her eyes came to the window and met his. For a second they looked at each other, and he noted the surprise and curiosity in her glance, and realised in a flash that to her he must appear as if he was standing on something to look over the brown paper. Humorously he thought: I'd better show her it's me all the way. I'll give them a hand with those drawers . . . and damn the tongues! He turned, to find Dominic, who was nearer the front door, looking at him with eyes full of mirthless laughter. Dominic slowly hitched up his trousers, buttoned his coat, then went out into the street.

With a feeling of frustration mixed with anger, John watched Dominic speak to the girl, and saw her look sharply from Dominic's face to the window as if to reassure herself there were two of them. Then she smiled on Dominic, and he bent his broad back under the chest, taking the weight off the men, and in a few minutes they all moved into the house.

John and Mary Ellen turned from the window and went to the kitchen. Nothing had escaped Mary Ellen; she had followed the desire of her son and felt Dominic interpret John's thought and use it against him. She said, 'Come and finish your dinner, lad, it'll be kissened up to cork.'

Taking three plates out of the oven, she called to her husband. Shane, looking mystified and his head jerking, came to the table. 'Must be bloody millionaires,' he said. 'Know who they are?'

'No,' she answered. 'I know nowt about them.'

The meal was eaten in silence. Once or twice Mary Ellen glanced at John, but his face was closed, telling her nothing. She got up to clear the table, and muttered impatiently when a face was pressed against the window and a voice called, 'Can I come in, Mrs O'Brien?'

Mary Ellen's brows knit together, but she answered pleasantly, 'Oh, it's you, Nancy. Yes, come in.'

A girl of sixteen sidled into the room. Her face was flat, almost concave, and her nose and eyes seemed to be lost in its centre, as though a force were sucking them in. The expression was serious and earnest, like that of a child struggling to be impressive. She began with quaint ceremony, 'Hallo, Mrs O'Brien.'

And Mary Ellen answered kindly, 'Hallo, Nancy.'

'Hallo, John.'

John turned from the table and said, 'Hallo, there, Nancy.'

'Hallo, Mr O'Brien.'

Shane growled something, keeping his eyes directed towards his plate. And Mary Ellen, thanking God that the rest of the family weren't in to lengthen Nancy's usual formal greeting, said, 'Sit yourself down, Nancy.'

Nancy sat down, and John said to her, 'Still like your place, Nancy?'

'Yes, John,' she answered; 'I've nearly been there a month now.' It was a curious defect of her speech that her mouth never closed; her lips refused to meet, so her voice sounded nasal, like that of someone with a hare lip.

John answered tolerantly, 'Yes, you have, Nancy,' knowing that the time she had scrubbed and cleaned in the Fitzsimmons outdoor beershop was nearer to four years than four weeks – time had no place in Nancy's mind. Her body gave the impression of uncontrolled strength; her long arms hung out from the short sleeves of her coat, a brown, faded thing, and her boots looked too small for her big feet.

John said kindly, 'You look very nice the day, Nancy.'

She smiled at him, stretching her face; then, preening herself and dusting down the front of her coat with her red hands, she said, 'This is a new coat. Me ma bought it. And these boots too. And I've got a silk dress, with a sash. And I'm going to get a hat with a feather in.'

Shane's chair scraped back and he went to the front room. Mary Ellen looked after him for a moment – he never could stand the senseless prattle of Nancy. She went into the scullery to wash the dishes, glad that John was in to cope with Nancy should she start laughing . . . Oh, Nancy's laughter! Mary Ellen shuddered. She thought she was afraid of nothing on earth as she was of Nancy Kelly's laughter – it put the fear of God in her. But John could manage her – he always had; he made her think she was like other lasses. She could sense John's pity for Nancy; it was like her own, but without the strain of fear that ran through hers.

She heard Dominic coming up the backyard, whistling. He was pleased with himself for outwitting John, she supposed. She hoped to God he did nothing more to aggravate John's feelings; the sick premonition of last night was still partly with her. She was more afraid of John's rages than of either Shane's or Dominic's, for his were stronger, being made more fierce through sober justification.

Dominic came in and surprised her by closing the scullery door and so shutting them off from the kitchen. He stood near her as she bent over the dish, and said softly, 'Any chance of you lending me the money to get me clothes out?'

She looked up at him, her hands still in the water. 'I've only got the rent. You put your suit in, you'll have to get it out.'

'I'll give it to you back next week.'

'I haven't got it; I only have a few coppers left for the gas over the week-end.'

Dominic's suit had been in pawn for more than a month, and he had made no effort to get it out, even on his full shifts. Without it he was tied to the house and spent his Sundays in bed, for by some unwritten law no-one went out of doors on a Sunday dressed in their working clothes. Even if a man possessed a shilling to 'get a set in', he never showed his face inside a public house unless he was 'tidy'.

Strangely enough, Mary Ellen realised it wasn't tomorrow Dominic was thinking of, but tonight, and that new lass next door; although how he'd had the nerve to ask such as her out, she didn't know . . . But then she did. Dominic had the nerve for anything if he wanted it badly enough. She said cuttingly, 'Why don't you ask one of your cronies for it?'

He cast her a sidelong glance, in which she saw the sharp, questioning look – he wondered how much she knew. She knew more than he thought she did, to her sorrow. There was a certain woman of the docks, Lady Pansy, so-called because of her style in her heyday when she entertained nothing less than a chief engineer. But times had changed, and with them Lady Pansy's figure and face. Although she couldn't claim big money now she still liked her men young and strong, and Mary Ellen knew that all the money from Dominic's full shifts was not spent on drink – the thought made her sick – and the woman was as old as she was, if not older!

If Mary Ellen's refusal dampened Dominic's spirits, he hid it successfully, for in the kitchen he was extra hearty, forestalling Nancy's greeting by giving an imitation of herself.

'Hal-lo, Nan-cy!'

'Hallo, Dominic.' Nancy wriggled on her chair.

Dominic went and stood over her: 'What's this I'm hearing about you, Nancy? They tell me you're courtin'.'

'Eeh! who told you that?' The girl wriggled in agitation. 'Eeh! I'm not . . . am I, John?'

John said nothing, but left the table and took a seat by the fire. He knew where Dominic's teasing would lead.

'Well, that's what I heard,' Dominic went on; 'I thought you were goin' to wait for me. Nice one, you are.' He pulled his belt tighter in feigned annoyance.

'Eeh, Dominic! I haven't got a lad, I haven't. I don't let them come near me. If they touch me, I yells I do.' Her face gathered itself into a troubled pucker.

32

John thrust the poker between the bars and raked savagely – he knew that Dominic's tactics were more to madden him than to tease Nancy.

Dominic laughed, and went on, with mock seriousness, 'Let's get this settled. When are me and you goin' out for a walk, eh?'

Mary Ellen came hurriedly into the kitchen: 'I think you'd better be going home now, Nancy, your ma will be wondering where you are.'

As Nancy stood up, Dominic said softly, 'I'll get another lass, mind.'

And Mary Ellen cried, 'That's enough of that! Get away home now, Nancy.' She turned to the girl and led her, trembling, to the door; but before they reached it, it opened, and Hannah Kelly herself stood there.

'Oh, this is where you are' – she looked unsmilingly at her daughter – 'I guessed as much. Go on, get yourself over home.'

Nancy slid by her mother, and Hannah came in and closed the door. Her manner was conspiratorial. 'Well, what d'yer think, eh? D'ye know who ye've got next door, Mary Ellen?'

Mary Ellen shook her head.

'My God! Ye'd never believe. They call this the Irish quarter, but what with the Jews and the ranters . . . and now this! Well, my God, I ask ye!'

'What are they?' asked Mary Ellen bluntly.

'Spooks!' Hannah's head came forward, impressing the word.

'What!'

'Spooks. He's called The Spook in Jarrow and Howden and round there. Remember a bit back when the Irish navvies burnt a hut down and the pollis had to get the man away? Well, that was him. He was givin' a service or somethin'.'

Mary Ellen turned and looked from one to the other of her sons, who were now both listening to Hannah Kelly with interest.

'Dorrie Clark knew who he was the minute she set eyes on him, and she was tellin' Bella Bradley that when she was delivering once in Jarrow, he came in and wanted to lay his hands on the woman. That's what she said . . . lay his hands on her! Did ye ever hear owt like it? To ease her labour, he said, because she'd been in it four days.'

Mary Ellen looked distinctly shocked. 'Did she let him?'

'Did she hell! Ye know old Dorrie. She said she kicked his arse out of the door. And she would an' all, full of gin or not. But my God, there'll be the divil's figarties around these doors before long! Mark my words; ye'll see.'

Mary Ellen was evidently disturbed. She looked from one to other; then she addressed John, 'What d'you make of it?'

John turned away, and went to the bedroom, saying, 'I don't know; they looked all right to me.'

Hannah laughed and called after John, 'Mind yerself, John lad, that she don't lay hands on you. They say the lass is as bad as the old man.'

Then turning to Dominic, she said, 'And you there, ye've soon got yer leg in.'

Ignoring her jibe, Dominic asked: 'D'you know what the old man works at?'

'Now that's another funny thing' – Hannah pointed her finger at him – 'he's the Mr Bracken that has the boot shop in Jarrow.'

The three of them looked from one to the other, and the same question was running through their minds: 'Why did a man who owned a boot shop come to live in the fifteen streets?'

In the bedroom, John pulled the wooden box from beneath the bed and took out his suit. It was too creased to wear, so he knew it hadn't been in the pawn; had it been in his mother would have pressed it ready for him. Taking a dirty raincoat from the back of the door, he stood pondering a moment whether he should change his black neckerchief for a white muffler, but decided against doing so. He would keep it for tonight, when he would be going to the Shields to have a look round the market and perhaps go to the second-house somewhere. Now, he was just going for a walk.

He did not bother to change his working boots, but went into the kitchen and finding his mother alone, asked, 'Will you put an iron over my suit?'

'Yes, lad,' she replied. 'Are you off for a walk?'

He nodded. 'Where's Katie?'

'Here she is, coming up the yard,' said Mary Ellen.

'Want to come?' he asked her.

'Oh yes, John. Yes!' In her excitement, Katie hopped from one foot to the other.

'Not with hands and face like that,' he said. 'What have you been up to?'

'Playing shops . . . I won't be a tick; wait for me.'

Mary Ellen was already pouring the water into the dish; and after a few minutes Katie, her face shining and a round straw hat lying straight on the top of her head, was walking down the yard with John.

He took her hand, and they went along the cobbled back lane to the main road.

'Where shall we go?' he asked her.

'Oh, the country, John. Up the country!'

'Simonside?'

'Yes. Oh yes, Simonside!'

The day was cold and clear, with the wind blowing straight in from the sea. The sky was high above the housetops and above the towering cranes, which reared up inside the stone wall edging the road opposite the fifteen streets.

John looked up at the white tufted clouds moving swiftly across the sky, and said, 'Look up there. They look like a fleet of white brakes off for a day's outing, don't they? I bet they're off to the country, too – Morpeth or some place.'

Katie chuckled. This was one of the many reasons why she loved going walks with John – he made up stories about everything. She glanced up at him, her eyes twinkling: 'I bet when they come back they'll be singing, like the people do on the brake trips:

"Aa'm back to canny auld Jarrer,
A hip, a hip hooray." '

She giggled, and John tilted her hat over her eyes, saying 'Saucy piece!'

They walked by the side of the wall for some way, until they came to the chemical works and the tram sheds. Then, further on, as they passed a narrow cut, bordered on one side by the end of the chemical works and on the other by the railings which fence in part of the Jarrow slacks, John asked her, 'Do you want to go down the slipway?'

Katie shook her head quickly and shuddered.

'What are you frightened of?'

'It's that black mud – it's deep, and if you fell in you'd never get out.'

'But the tide's up now, and there might be a little boat moored there . . . All right, all right,' he laughed when Katie shuddered again; 'but you never used to be afraid of the slipway.'

She didn't say that Mick had dragged her down there and pretended he was going to push her in. He had held her over the stone coping, and she had gazed, petrified, at the silvery black, slimy mud sloping away from just below her face to the narrow stream of water at the bottom, running slowly beneath its shot-coloured oily surface. She didn't dare tell her mother in case John got to know, for then he would have gone for Mick.

They came to the Jarrow slacks at the point where they were open to the road. The water was lapping just below the bank, a few feet from the edge of the pavement. The large, square stretch of water was covered with timbers, roped together in batches, right up to the gut.

There was a permanent way, starting below the pavement and reaching to the gut, running through the middle of them. It consisted of logs, a foot wide, lashed end to end and to each side of posts driven in at intervals over the stretch. In parts, the logs were black and rotten and looked as safe for foothold as a loose rock on the edge of a precipice. But children were playing on them with happy unconcern, jumping from them to the roped timbers. Some children were far away over the timbers, laying flat along the edges, trying to rake in pieces of wood that were floating by. And the sight of them brought back the past vividly to John. How many times had he perilously stood on the end timbers, near the edge of the gut, and waited for the tide to come in, bringing with it its drift wood. Often, for weeks on end, this wood was their only source of warmth, but often again, they had to do without the warmth whilst he hawked the sack of wood around, trying to sell it for twopence. He seldom succeeded; coke was the best sell. If he followed the coke carts from Jarrow right into Shields he could pick up as much as two bucketfuls each trip. Pieces would roll off the cart as it jogged along, especially when it crossed the tram lines. He'd get twopence for the coke, and if he could follow the cart three times, that meant sixpence. But he rarely completed the third journey, for his legs became so tired. He remembered the melancholy feeling that would settle on him as he followed the carts. It seemed to be worse when the sun was shining . . . That was an odd thing he hadn't entirely grown out of – he didn't like the sunshine. For years this feeling vaguely puzzled him. Then one day the reason was made known to him. The sunshine, he discovered, showed up his surroundings. It brought a queer kind of pain to him. On a dull day, the docks, the coal dust, the houses, the rattling trams, and the people all seemed to merge into one background; but when the sun shone, there they all were, standing out in relief, dirty, stark, tired; and in some odd way it hurt him . . . The feeling was coming on him now, and he tried to ignore it, for it always made him start thinking; and when he thought, he got mad at things. As his mother said, thinking got you nowhere.

Katie plunged him further into the trough by exclaiming, 'You know, when I grow up, John, I'm going to be a teacher.'

He squeezed her hand and said, 'I bet you will too . . . head-mistress!'

A teacher! Would Katie's dreams ever be fulfilled? He couldn't see it happening. She would go into a place at fourteen like the other lasses, and the bright eagerness would die. Her dreams, like his own when a lad, would be lost in the fight for food . . . It was funny, but that was all life amounted to . . . working life out to keep it in – working for food and warmth; and when the futility of this was made evident, blotting it out with drink. What did it all mean, anyway? What was living for?

When in this state of mind he always asked this question. The priests had one answer; but that had long ago ceased to satisfy him. Now he was asking himself another question: Had he to stay round these quarters until he died? He wasn't happy around here, yet when he moved out of this quarter, as he was doing now, up into Simonside, the lonely feeling became intensified and he felt lost, and some part of him wanted to get back again into the fifteen streets, into the docks, anywhere but near these grand houses that stood back from the Simonside bank, with their drives and large gardens. He couldn't understand why his sense of loneliness should be greater away from the life that was irking him.

He was being daft, he told himself – just daft. He should get himself a lass. That's what he needed. He was twenty-two and he'd never had a lass. He had never kissed a lass, not even in a bit of fun. Katie was the only one he kissed. He knew there were one or two in the fifteen streets who would come at his nod, but he hadn't nodded. His flingings and tossings in bed at night had equalled Dominic's, and many a time he promised himself to ask Jenny Carey or Lily McDonald to go out on a Saturday night; but with the light of day he forgot about them.

Lately, Dominic hadn't tossed so much. And once or twice John had been tempted to seek his cure; but then again, the temptation vanished with the light.

'Look, John,' said Katie; 'there's Father Bailey.'

The priest was coming down the drive of one of the big houses, and he waved to them, calling, 'Hallo, there.'

John stopped and said, 'Hallo, Father.'

He wouldn't have stopped had it been Father O'Malley; but then, Father O'Malley wouldn't have called 'Hallo, there.' At best, he would have inclined his head slightly. Not even if he knew you hadn't been to mass would he speak to you on the street; he would wait till he had you indoors, then raise the roof on you. But Father Bailey was different. Even when he was chastising you for not going to mass he was nice about it.

'Are you going for a walk, the pair of you?' The priest smiled, first up at John then down on Katie; and not waiting for an answer, went on, 'It's just the day for it. You know, John' – he took a step backwards – 'I believe you get taller.'

'It's the clothes, Father; they've shrunk.'

'Well, there may be something in that, but I've always had the idea I came up to your shoulder. It must have been just an idea.'

He turned to Katie. 'And now, Katie O'Brien, what honours have you been gathering on your head this week? Do you know we have a clever girl here, John? Every week I hear something about Katie O'Brien. She's the top of her class for this, that, and the other. It'll be teaching the teachers she'll be in the end.'

'Oh, Father!' Katie O'Brien lowered her head and blinked at her boots.

The priest patted her straw hat. 'I'm just on my way up to the fifteen streets; I'll look in on your mother. How is she, John?'

'Oh, just middling, Father.'

'And your da, and Dominic?' There was a question in the priest's eyes.

They held John's, and he replied gruffly, 'Things don't change.'

'Oh, you're wrong there, John; every minute of the day they're changing.'

'Yes? Well I haven't noticed it.'

Father Bailey patted Katie's hat again, but still addressing John said, 'We never do. But look ahead, John . . . Shall I be seeing you at mass tomorrow?'

'I don't think so, Father.'

'Oh! This'll never do. Not at all, at all! I'll have to come and have a crack with you soon. But I must be off now. Enjoy your walk, both of you. Goodbye. Goodbye.'

'Goodbye, Father.' 'Goodbye, Father,' they said, and continued their way up the Simonside bank, past the little school and into what was termed the country, a few fields with hedged lanes between. If you didn't turn round and look back you could imagine there were no docks, no pits, no drab grey streets; and if you could stretch your imagination you could visualise these fields with their straight rows of tender green going on for ever.

'Shall we walk to the Robin Hood?' Katie asked.

'It'll be too far for you,' said John.

'No, it won't. I could walk miles and miles.'

She skipped on ahead of him, leaving him with his thoughts – thoughts of the priest; of this lonely feeling; and of the lass next door. His mind dwelt on the lass: Would he like to take her out? Good God! he'd never have the nerve to ask the likes of her, even if she were free – she was different somehow . . . Then why was she living next door? . . . There was no answer to this. And Dominic, he wouldn't be backward in asking her. But no! surely he wouldn't have the cheek, the state he was in with drink, and that woman. Yet why did he go out and give them a hand? It wasn't with any idea of helping, but to speak to the lass . . . Anyway, why was he thinking about all these things that didn't matter a damn! Hadn't he other things to think about? His mother in her trouble; and the house with hardly a whole stick standing.

But the sun and the wind were changing his mood – he didn't want to think, he only wanted to wander here in this quiet road.

He took off his cap and let the wind play through his hair. He ran his hand through it, and felt the freedom of being uncovered out of doors. It was such a relief to walk with his cap off, and no-one would see him here so it didn't matter, for it was another unwritten law that a woman did not go out without a hat or a shawl covering her head, nor a man a cap.

Katie came running back to him, exclaiming, 'Oh, John, your hair looks just like Miss Llewellyn's with the sun shining on it! It's all brown and shiny.'

'What!' he exclaimed. 'Miss— Don't be silly.' He ruffled it more.

'It is though.'

'Go on with you!' He took her hand and pulled her to his side, and they walked on until they came within sight of the Robin Hood, then turned towards Simonside again. Katie sang hymns, school songs, and rhymes, one following on the other without pause, while John walked along in strange contentment, listening to her.

They were nearing the top of the bank, where it dipped to the docks, when her singing ended abruptly and he felt her hand tugging on his. He looked down on her upturned face. It was alight with pleased surprise – her eyes were wide, sending him a mute message. Wondering, he followed her gaze, and saw a woman coming towards them, a young woman. She was taller than average, and wore a brown cloth coat with a full skirt. It was nipped in at the waist and gave emphasis to her bust. She carried her head high, and her hat, which was green and had a brown feather curling round its brim, appeared like a crown set on the top of her head.

As she came nearer, John became aware of her hair. It fell over her ears in soft folds, and when he noticed the colour, he connected it with Katie's excitement and thrust his cap on his head. Good God! Miss Llewellyn – and she not much more than a lass. And he'd thought she was getting on . . . well, in her thirties. She was looking directly at Katie and smiling.

He looked beyond her, but to his horror she stopped as she came abreast of them and said, 'Hallo, Katie.'

'Hallo, Miss Llewellyn.'

John felt Katie's fingers opening and shutting within his palm.

'You are a long way from home.'

'Yes, Miss Llewellyn.' Katie was breathless.

John gave a sidelong glance at the bent head – he could dare this because she wasn't looking at him. He had never before been so close to such a face. Katie said she was lovely. Katie wasn't far wrong. The skin of her cheeks was a soft, creamy pink, the nose was short, and in striking contrast the mouth was wide and laughing.

When she turned her eyes on him, he switched his away; and he fumbled in the pocket of his coat for his red handkerchief as she said, 'You're John, aren't you?'

He felt his eyes forced back to her, to look her full in the face, and for no reason he could understand he began to tremble inside – almost, he felt, like the jerking of his father's limbs, only invisible. He was painfully conscious of the cap on his tousled hair, of his dirty raincoat, of his neckerchief, and of his big boots, with their leather laces showing numerous knots. His Adam's apple moved swiftly, and he swallowed, but no words came.

And she went on, 'I've heard such a lot about you.'

Her voice, too, was like none he had heard before. Like her face, there was laughter playing around it. Was she laughing at him? Very likely.

He knew she was, and though he felt it was kindly laughter the hot colour flooded his face when she said, 'I don't suppose you know, but you are a combination of Prince Charming and God to a certain young lady.'

He thought quickly, as he found himself doing at times, and spoke before he could stop himself: 'Neither of them would be flattered.

And if the last one hears of it there's not much chance of me getting up there.'

Her laugh rang out, joyous and infectious, and to his utter surprise he found himself laughing with her.

Katie stood looking up from one to the other. She did not join in with their laughter, her happiness was too profound – Miss Llewellyn laughing with their John!

When he thought of it later, he was surprised at her next remark – and her a Catholic and a teacher too – for she said, 'I don't suppose that will worry you very much. I should take the heaven you're sure of.' Her words seemed to confuse her slightly and the tinge of pink grew deeper in her cheeks.

He made no answer, thinking that if this life was her idea of heaven he'd bet on the one up there. The wind swirled about them, and she turned her back to it, leaning slightly back and holding her hat on with both hands. Then she terminated the meeting by saying, 'Well, I'll see you on Monday morning, Katie,' and to John, 'I'm glad I've met you in the flesh, for now when I listen to your sayings being recorded I'll be able to place them. Goodbye. Goodbye, Katie.'

'Goodbye, Miss Llewellyn.'

'Goodbye.' John did not turn immediately away, but watched her bending against the wind, the coat pressed against her legs. And he saw that she wore shoes and that her ankles were thin. He turned away, and Katie, walking close by his side, sighed. They looked at each other and smiled secretly, then walked on in silence, until John asked, 'You don't tell her all I say, do you?'

'No. Oh, no!' Katie lied firmly. And in the next breath she exclaimed, 'Isn't she lovely!'

He stopped and looked towards the docks, and Katie went on, 'And isn't it a lovely day!'

'Grand.' The word seemed to answer both her questions.

Far away in the distance he could see the masts of the ships, disembodied things, seemingly borne on air. He looked up at the sun, and for the first time in his life felt glad to be out and under it. He thought of the lass next door and of the lovely lass just gone, and he said, more to himself than to Katie, 'Yes, it's a lovely day; a day of clean wind and far mast-heads, and bonnie lasses.'

Katie stared up at him. Oh, their John was wonderful, the things he said! A day of clean wind and far mast-heads, and bonnie lasses! It was like . . . well, not like the poetry she learnt at school . . . and yet it was. Oh, and Miss Llewellyn had seen him! She had seen how wonderful he was.

Mary Llewellyn, walking briskly away in the opposite direction, was smiling no longer. Her face was thoughtful, and her eyes sad. So that was John. Poor soul! Poor soul!

CHAPTER THREE

ST PATRICK'S DAY

Mick led the Catholics, not because he was the eldest but because he was the biggest. At the top corner of Fadden and Blacket Streets he marshalled his gang, twenty-five in all, and saw that they were supplied with weapons. He made sure that the innocent-looking paper balls dangling from lengths of rope or string each had a good-sized stone in its centre. About twenty yards away, at the corner of Whitley Street, the Protestants were gathering, and their leaders were doing much the same as Mick. This was to be the climax to the day's badgering and cornering of individuals and isolated groups, of swinging the paper balls round the heads of victims, whether Catholic or Protestant, and asking the terrifying question, 'Are you blue or green?' Pity help the individual who had the courage to defend his colour to the opposite clan, for he was often hit until he was sick or rescued by some indignant passer-by.

Mick's gang were protesting loudly that it wasn't fair, for the ranters had three separate gangs – the churchies, the chapelies, and the odds, the latter group consisting of Jews, Salvationists, and a Quaker.

Mick exclaimed loudly that three lots were nowt, for they'd bash all their bleeding heads in. Adroitly he spread out his men in the form of an arrow, placing the bigger boys at the head.

He took a long time over this, for he was enjoying his momentary power and the admiration of the younger children swarming on the top of the stackyard wall that hemmed in the ends of the fifteen streets.

Someone began to sing the hymn:

'Oh glorious St Patrick, dear Saint of our Isle,'

and all the children on the wall took it up:

'On us, thy dear children, bestow a sweet smile;
And now thou art high in the mansions above,
Oh glorious St Patrick look down in thy love.'

The ending was the signal for the advance, both sides moving slowly towards each other. Then, with a rush, there was a swirling of balls,

41

and there were screams and cries of 'Long live Ireland!' 'Up the shamrock!' in which were mingled 'England for ever!' and 'God save the King!'

Hard blows were struck by the arrow heads. But they had learned no lesson from last year; so their balls became entwined, and many combatants had to stop and free them, and whilst doing so a number of them laughed, especially if their enemy happened to be a pal on the other three hundred and sixty-four days of the year. And so the fight became spasmodic, lacking the ferocity of the earlier battles; it became a mêlée of half-hearted punches and pushes. And the jeering from the mixed supporters on the wall became derisive.

Mick realised there was something lacking. He fell back with his side and engaged in a battle of vituperation!

'Protestant, Protestant, you dirty lot,
Yer backside's blue and yer nose all snot!'

to which the Protestants replied:

'Catholic, Catholic, ring the bell,
When you die you'll go to hell.'

It was all very half-hearted – the excitement seemed to have died in the completion of the preparations.

Mick felt a definite sense of disappointment and feared the flatness of the fight might be put down to his leadership, and that Big Geordie Flannagan might be picked to take his place. He looked round for some sign that would be the means of leading him to fresh applause. And like manna from heaven he found it. Standing solitary at the top end of his own back lane was the boy from next door . . . the spook's lad.

The boy was looking from one group to the other with evident curiosity. His face looked all eyes, and Mick was quick to detect a gleam of fear in them. With the true instinct of a leader, he first of all planned to cut off the enemy's retreat. So he called three of his best men to him, and in a few words told them what he intended doing, and despatched them down Fadden Street with orders to come up the back lane. A few more whispered words to other members of his gang, and they stopped yelling and stood looking towards the boy.

As soon as Mick saw the three outriders coming up the back lane he called out loudly, 'Look! There's the spook!'

After a moment's hesitation the word was taken up, 'The spook! The spook!' Those on the other side stopped their abuse and they too turned towards the boy, whose face had blanched. He did not turn and try to escape down the back lane, for he knew, from the laughs behind him, that that escape was cut off. Instead he tried to think of what his grandfather had told him to do when confronted with hostile thought, but terror swamped any thinking.

Fascinated, he watched the two opposing sides converging on each other and the children swarming down from the wall. They began to form a solid mass before him, and he listened to shouts that weren't new to his ears:

'His da's a spook!'

'Me ma says he's a divil.'

'Me ma says if you bless yersel' when you pass him he can't do you any harm.'

'Me da says the priest put a curse on him an' he was kicked out of Jarrer, an' he'll wither away.'

'Mr Roberts, our minister, says they're evil and we mustn't have any truck with 'em.'

On and on it went, not loudly or angrily, but steadily and defiantly, and in some faint way the boy detected fear of himself in their voices. Yet he knew what that fear would make them do. It wasn't the first time he had been in a similar situation, but he found that repetition did not make him more brave.

Mick too was aware of the fear. The crowd of them would do nothing, he thought, just call the spook names and perhaps throw a stone or two, until some woman came out from her backyard and scattered the lot of them. He wanted a chase, some life in the proceedings.

Again he gave instructions to others of his gang, who sped away to block the ends of the streets, all but the last one. Then he yelled out to the crowd, proclaiming himself leader and a man of fair play, 'Give him a chance . . . Let him away! Give him a start!'

Molly, who was standing near him, whispered, 'Where you goner chase him?'

'The gut,' he whispered back without looking at her, for his eyes were now fixed on those of the boy.

The boy was shivering in stark terror; he knew what this chance meant; it meant running, running, running until his whole body sobbed and his trousers became wet. And he knew that long after the fear would have passed the feeling of his wet trousers would remain. But it was either running or being stoned here.

A gap appeared in the crowd and Mick's voice yelled, 'Come on, spooky! We'll give you a start.' He was leading them all now, the Catholics, the Protestants, the Chapelies and the others. He kept yelling, 'Let him through! . . . Come on, spook. We'll give you ten for a start when you're through.'

There was a whirling in Mick's blood when he saw the boy begin to move, and a stream of saliva trickled from the corner of his mouth. The boy, his face the colour of dirty dough and his eyes stretching the skin, came abreast of Mick. He would never reach the gut, Mick thought – he was too small. They would drag him there.

Suddenly he threw his arms out wide, a signal that no-one must move and shouted, 'One!'

At the sound the boy became galvanised. He shot away, and Mick, when he noted the speed with which the boy ran, quickened his counting, almost choking with suppressed glee when he saw the boy's maddened terror on realising the exits of the streets and back lanes were blocked.

'Ten!' was a scream in Mick's throat. He was off, ahead of the milling, screeching children. They stumbled into each other, kicking and pushing to get a clear road. Some left the main chase and ran down the streets, knowing that this would be the quickest way and that they would pick up the chase again on the main road, the word had been passed, 'To the gut! To the gut!'

Among those who diverted was Molly. She sped down her own street, her hair and legs flying. And she almost cried with vexation when she saw her mother step from their front door.

'Here!' Mary Ellen caught at Molly's arm, almost unbalancing herself. 'Have you gone mad? What's all the screeching for?'

'Aw! Ma, let go.'

'Get inside!' said Mary Ellen.

'Aw! Ma, I'm goin' with our Mick.'

'With Mick? What's he doin'?'

'He's . . . he's . . . They're chasin' the lad next door to the gut.'

Mary Ellen brought her hand across her daughter's ear with a crack. 'Get yersel' inside – I'll gut you! A big lass like you running mad with a lot of lads!' She pushed Molly before her through the front room, calling, 'John!'

John came out of the bedroom asking, 'What is it?'

'It's our Mick . . . he's chasing the lad next door to the gut. There's dozens of them running mad!'

'Are you sure it's Mick?'

'Ask her.' Mary Ellen pointed to the snivelling Molly.

When John looked at Molly she hung her head, and Mary Ellen said, 'Go and see what he's up to, lad; for if the pollis catches him at anything down there they won't give him another chance, after catching him loosening the timbers that time.'

'Why are they chasing the lad next door, are they playing at something?' John asked Molly.

'No,' Molly muttered into her chest. 'It's because he's a spook.'

John hastily put on his coat and left the house; and as he went out into the back lane he bumped into the girl from next door. She was running, and gasped, 'I'm sorry.' She smiled faintly at him and ran on again.

He did not speak, but hurried after her. He guessed where she was going . . . someone must have told her. Children were straggled along the road; most of them, frightened by the thought of the gut, especially as it was getting dark, had given up the chase.

One bold spirit addressed John: 'Your Mick's goin' to push the spook into the gut, Mr O'Brien.'

John knew that between Mick and Dominic there was only the difference in years; the cruelty was already fully matured in Mick, and he was quite capable of doing what this boy said. He set off at a run and caught up with the girl before she reached the short cut leading to the gut. Shortening his step to suit hers, he said, 'Are you looking for your brother?'

She nodded, but did not speak; and John again had the impression of age. There was a similarity, he noticed, between her expression and that which was more often than not on his mother's face . . . This wasn't the first time she'd gone to her brother's aid – by God, he'd break that young rat's neck!

'You go back, and I'll see to them,' he said to her. But she shook her head.

As they turned down the cut, the shouting came to them, and John sprang away from the girl and ran on ahead.

With the intuition of the young, his coming was noted and the boys crowding round the disused boathouse on the edge of the gut gave the cry, 'Look out! Scatter!'

The size of John looming out of the gathering dusk and the fear of being caught and held responsible gave aid to their legs. They made for the opening near the boathouse, and like dots of vapour they disappeared across the disused ground adjoining the slacks.

John pulled up at the slipway. There was no sign of the boy. Likely, he had taken refuge on the wall round the corner. The wall supporting the slipway turned sharply at right angles, bordering the gut for a considerable distance, and ended abruptly where the gut was deepest, for the swirling tides had by slow degrees loosened its large granite stones, and many of these now made only a row of pin-points in the mud. The wall was just above ground level and was eighteen inches wide on the top, but from its back edge arose a six-foot fence of stout sleepers.

John walked sideways along the wall, pressing his back against the sleepers, and as he turned the corner he saw the boy and Mick.

The boy was standing up against the last sleeper of the fence, Mick was lying flat along the wall; and there was no sound from either of them, except the whack of the stick as Mick hit at the boy's legs, trying to dislodge him into the black, oozing mud. So lost was Mick in the relish of the moment that he did not hear John's approach. The first he knew was the sound of harsh breathing over him; then he was whipped to his feet and for one sickening second he was hanging in mid-air over the mud. John brought him to his feet and shook him until his head rolled on his shoulders.

'Get home and stay there! If you're not in when I get back it'll mean twice as much when I find you.'

Mick clutched at the sleepers to steady himself, and growled, 'You hit me and I'll tell me da.' Then he retreated hastily along the wall, and John went on to the boy.

In the dim light the white face shone at him, and he said soothingly, 'It's all right, sonny, it's all right.'

The boy did not answer, and John said, 'Come on, give me your hand.'

But the boy still did not move; he seemed petrified into dumbness, and his fingers held on to the sleeper as if glued to it. The wall ended directly below this sleeper, and the rising tide was already creeping towards its fallen stones.

As John unbent the boy's fingers he saw that they were bleeding, and he wished for the moment he would have Mick under his hands. When he picked him up the boy lay stiff across his arms like something frozen hard. The girl was standing at the corner, her face as white as her brother's, and she clutched at them both, saying, 'Is he all right? Oh, David, are you all right?'

'Steady!' John said. 'Let's get off here.' And she went before them along the wall to where it met the ground.

As John put the boy down she drew David into her arms, crying, 'Oh, my dear, what have they done?'

The boy shuddered, and his body fell against hers, and she soothed him, saying, 'There! There! . . . We'll go home – Grandfather will soon be in and everything will be all right.'

But when she took his hand to walk him up the bank his legs gave way beneath him, and he fell forward. John picked him up again, saying, 'You'd better get him to bed.'

As he strode up the road with the girl trotting by his side and holding on to her brother's ankle, he thanked God that most of the people were indoors having their tea and that the corners of the streets were deserted by their usual batches of men, for he felt self-conscious in doing this rescue act.

The door was open and the house lighted just as she had left it; and as John passed through the front room and into the kitchen he had the impression that his home next door was a hundred miles away. He became conscious of his big, dirty boots on the carpet, and when he laid the boy in a chair, drawn up to the fire, the comfort of it was conveyed to him by his hands sinking beneath the boy into the upholstery.

The girl ran into the bedroom, and returned with something in a glass. David drank it, then asked, in a thin, small voice, 'How long will Grandfather be?'

'Not long, darling.'

The girl was kneeling by the chair, and John, looking down on her, repeated to himself, 'Not long, darling.' Never before had he heard

46

the word spoken, except in derision. How strange these people were.

He was turning to go, saying, 'I hope he'll be all right. My brother will be dealt with,' when the girl sprang to her feet.

'What are you going to do to your brother?' she asked. 'Thrash him?'

'What else?'

'Oh please!' her words tumbled over one another – 'Please don't do that! It won't do a bit of good . . . not the slightest, just the opposite.'

John frowned down on her in perplexity: 'What do you expect me to do? Let him off? He might have killed the lad there—' He nodded towards the chair.

Her eyes, set deep in her white face, looked black and enormous, and she began to plead with him as if her life depended on it: 'But he didn't! You must talk to him, point out where he was wrong . . . Will you? . . . Please. But don't thrash him; you'll only thrash it into him.'

'Thrash what into him?' John's brows drew closer together.

'The fears, the inhibitions . . . all the things that drove him to do what he did.'

John stared at her. What was she getting at? Was this part of the spook religion? She was strange, not in sayings alone, but in her looks; her curveless body, like a lad's, was as attractive as any bulging bust and wobbling hips.

He turned away from her and went towards the kitchen door, but she hastily blocked his exit: 'Please! . . . Oh!' – she closed her eyes and moved her head from side to side – 'if only Grandfather was in he'd explain so much better than me . . . But you mustn't thrash him.'

Looking down into her strained face, John saw that for the moment, the thought of Mick being thrashed had entirely eliminated the worry for her brother – she was like no-one he had met before . . . she was really in earnest that Mick should be let off. But he knew Mick, and she didn't, so he said, 'Do you think he would understand a talking-to? No. The only thing Mick and his like understand is the thick end of the belt across their . . . ' Somehow he couldn't say 'arses' in front of her, so he ended lamely, 'You see. You don't know them.'

'Oh, but I do,' she said, smiling faintly, trying to override his last remark; 'I've known dozens of Micks. Look—' She put out her hands and caught hold of the lapels of his coat. The gesture was almost childish in its naturalness, and he looked down at her hands, then at her face close beneath his own; and an odd sensation passed over him . . . Hannah Kelly said, 'Mind she doesn't lay hands on you, lad.' But this wasn't the kind of laying on she was referring to. If a lass of the fifteen streets laid hold of him, there would be a particular meaning to it; they would lark about a lot before she did this though, and afterwards his arms would go round her. He had seen the process

47

enacted at the corner ends and in dark places in the back lanes. Often, when a lad, he watched the climax with an envy that dissolved into loneliness. And now here was this lass with her hands on him, and the sensation he was experiencing was almost one of reverence, similar to that which he at one time felt for the Virgin . . . But he didn't want to feel reverence for her, or any other lass. She was fetching and he wanted . . . He lifted his hand and covered one of hers – it wasn't much bigger than Katie's, but it was different. His blood began to warm with the feel of her, and he smiled slowly. Her soft, curving mouth was just below his, and as he watched it move, it fascinated him. He wasn't fully aware of the words it was forming until she stepped away from him, taking her hand from his and saying, 'If you had to treat a dirty wound, you wouldn't rub more dirt into it, would you?'

Still on about Mick . . . He came to himself, and said thickly, 'I'm sorry; I'll have to deal with him as I think fit.' A feeling of bewilderment and frustration, mixed with annoyance was filling him; and he passed her, saying gruffly, 'He'll have to take what's coming to him.'

It was with relief he entered his own kitchen. Here were people and things he could understand . . . and manage. Going straight to the wall by the side of the fireplace he unhooked the razor strop.

'Is the lad all right?' Mary Ellen asked.

'Just,' John answered briefly. 'Come on' – he motioned with his head to Mick.

'I'm not comin'. I'll tell me da!'

'Go canny, lad,' Mary Ellen said to John.

Go canny. Here was another one. 'Go canny!' he rapped out at her with unusual irritation. 'Do you know he nearly killed the lad! As it is he's practically sent him out of his mind. It's as well for you you got hold of Molly when you did, or you'd have something more than a thrashing on your plate the night. Go canny!' He flung round from her and pointed to the door.

Mick began to snivel and cried, 'Ma! Ma, don't let him!'

Mary Ellen turned from Mick to the fire, and John seized him by the collar and pulled him to the door, there to meet Dominic coming in.

Dominic looked from one to the other before eyeing John through narrowed lids: 'What you at? Playin' boss of the house again?'

'You mind your own damn business. If you'd had a little more of it there might have been an improvement in you!'

Mary Ellen hastily broke in, addressing herself to Dominic, 'He's nearly killed the little lad next door.'

After a moment, during which he glanced from one to the other, Dominic stepped aside, and John pushed Mick before him down the yard and into the wash-house.

Mary Ellen found herself staring at Dominic; she couldn't quite take it in; he was sober, solid and sober; and it St Patrick's Day!

And added to this surprise was another; for when he took his cap off she saw that he'd had a haircut . . . a proper one; his thick, brown, curling hair was neatly trimmed up the sides, making him, even with the dust of the ore on him, look more attractive. He hadn't come in to tea and she imagined him to be in the bars; but he must have been having a haircut!

She went to the oven to take out his tea, a plate of finnan haddock, but he said, 'I don't want that yet.'

With further amazement she saw him wash himself quickly, take off his yorks and change his coat. He was banging the dust from his trousers as he hurried past her to the front room.

'Where you off to?' she asked.

Dominic paused a moment, and the expression she hated, a mixture of scorn, cocksureness and craft, came over his face. His eyes flicked over her, and her throat contracted with dislike of him. He said heavily, 'Where d'yer think?'

She stood still, listening to him going out of the front door, and between Mick's howls out in the backyard, she heard the knocker of the next door banging. Her fingers moved nervously back and forth across her lips . . . How would it work out? Candidly she wouldn't care if Dominic left home tomorrow and she never set eyes on him again, but there was no such luck as that happening; he was here and he was going after that lass. It would have been bad enough had she been a Protestant – that was something you could lay your finger on – but what these people next door were was something beyond her ken, something dark and mysterious, something not far removed from the devil; for whoever heard anyone connected with God daring to say they could cure people! Even the priests wouldn't dare. And then another strong point proving their ungodliness was all their fine things. God didn't shower gifts on those He loved – He pointed out the road of poverty to them. Father O'Malley could be hard, but he was right in some things; if you got your reward here, then you could make sure it wasn't from God.

From last Saturday, when they moved in, she had made up her mind to have no truck with them. At odd times she had stopped working and found herself listening to the girl singing. The first time she had heard her she was shocked; she felt it was indecent somehow, almost as bad as if she had seen her walking naked, for it wasn't like a woman singing to a bairn, nor yet over her poss-tub, but was high and clear and without restraint. And the morning she heard the singing before breakfast she was bewildered; for even if you had something to sing about you wouldn't do it before breakfast, unless you were prepared to cry your eyes out before supper . . . No, she wanted no truck with them. Yet here was John saving the lad and braying their Mick, and Dominic in next door pouring sympathy over the lass in his best manner. And he had a best manner, Mary Ellen knew; but she also knew it was an impossibility for him to keep it up. Well – she again fastened the errant button of her blouse and momentarily lifted the weight of her body – that was as far as things were going, if she could help it . . . not one of them would darken this door!

She crossed herself swiftly and murmured, 'May the Lord bless us and preserve us from all evil, and bring us to life everlasting. Amen.'

CHAPTER FOUR

THE CONFLICT

Mary Ellen's temper was fraying thin. The weather was bad enough with the rain pelting down and the wind howling as if it was December, but to have them all in the house except Mick and Molly, who were at school, was too much. Neither John nor Dominic had been set on this morning; a mail boat had come in with a cargo of fruit, but the gaffer had given the work to the men who had not been set on the recent boats. It was bad enough that they were off work, but to have them all stuck round her like this was too much of a good thing. And what was more, she was feeling a little sick with the heat of the oven and the smell of the dirty working clothes put to dry all round the kitchen . . . If only this other business were over. She was tired of it all – her body was so bairn-weary. She was feeling now that things were getting beyond her.

Even Katie could draw no kind word from her, and she pushed her to one side to get to the oven, saying, 'Get out of me way, bairn.'

Katie was home from school because her boots leaked; and her eyes were streaming, not only as the result of a cold but with crying. She hated to be off school, more so now than ever, for Miss Llewellyn had said that if she worked hard she could sit for an examination, which might be the first step on the road to her becoming a teacher. She had tried to tell her mother, but Mary Ellen snapped at her, and even John did not seem interested.

She looked towards him now. He was sitting in the corner on the far side of the fireplace mending her boots. He had put odd pieces of leather on the soles and was now cutting up an old boot to get enough leather to sew across the slits. She returned to her book, the only one she possessed, a Grimm's Fairy Tale, and she knew each word by heart.

The front-door knocker was suddenly banged, and without waiting she went to answer it. It had been knocked twice already this after-noon, once by a tally man and once by a man begging. The beggar wasn't pleased when she brought him a slice of bread. He bent it up and put it in his pocket, and her mouth watered, for it was new bread from a flat cake just out of the oven; it was a long time till tea-time, and she had got out of the habit of asking for bread between meals for she remembered times when they all had bread at tea-time except her mother, and she was frightened that this would happen again.

It was Mrs Bradley at the door, and she asked, 'Is yer ma in?'

Katie said, 'Yes.'

'Then tell her we're gathering for poor Mrs Patton's wreath . . . Here, take her the paper.'

Katie took the paper and went into the scullery to her mother. 'It's Mrs Bradley – she's gathering for flowers, ma.'

Mary Ellen's lips set in a tight line as she read down one side of the list and half-way down the other . . . shillings, sixpences . . . only two or three threepences. She gave a sigh, and lifting up her skirt took fourpence from the little bag and handed it to Katie, together with the list.

As Katie passed John he asked, 'What's that for?'

But before she could reply, Mary Ellen called, 'Go on, you, Katie,' and Katie went on to the front door. Mary Ellen knew that John didn't hold with gathering for wreaths, but what could she do . . . and that Bella Bradley collecting!

John knew what he would have done . . . the gathering for wreaths had always irked him. They would collect as much as two pounds and spend the whole lot on flowers, when the widow, if it was a man who had died, was more often than not destitute, and within a week the bairns would be crying for bread. They knew this only too well, the women who took it on themselves to gather, yet they still bought flowers to show respect for the dead. He snorted and banged the hammer on the last, sending a pain through his knee. It made him mad! He knew that, even if there was no insurance money, besides collecting for the flowers they would collect for cabs, to make the dead look decent. They didn't collect for the hearse. No, that could be ticked, to be paid off at so much a week. But the undertakers weren't so ready to tick cabs. And if it was for one of the Irish, the relatives would pawn, beg, borrow or steal, but they would have a bit of a wake. It was all crazy! And yet he understood from his mother that the funerals were nothing like they used to be, for in her young days, she told him, she longed for the Irish to die so she could go to the wake with her mother and have a good feed.

What had she put on the list, he wondered. Whatever it was, by this time next week they would be glad of it; for if they were not set on there wouldn't be a penny in the house.

Many things were beginning to make him wild. And on a day like this, tied to the house, he had nothing else to do but think. Lately he had been feeling the desire for someone to talk to, someone who could answer questions. Once or twice he tried to talk to Father Bailey, and endeavoured to have the material in his mind formed into concrete questions; but when he was with the priest he found it was no use – he knew what he wanted to say but couldn't get it out.

52

His mother was always saying thinking got you nowhere; you must have faith and rely on that. Faith! He looked at her now, pounding a great piece of dough, the second batch of bread she had baked today. What had faith done for her? She could hardly get her arms into the bowl for the roundness of her stomach. He took his eyes from her. Where would they put the bairn when it came? He'd have to try and rig up something out of boxes – the clothes basket that had served them all as a cradle was done long since. He pulled his legs up hastily as Dominic made to pass him on his way to the bedroom.

Mary Ellen called after Dominic, 'Don't lie on that bed with those boots on, mind!' but the only answer she received was the banging of the door.

John settled himself back against the wall: he always felt easier when Dominic was out of the room. He had finished one boot and was preparing the thread by rubbing it with tallow for patching the other when he heard his mother give a startled mutter. She was looking out through the kitchen window, and she exclaimed, 'I don't want them in here!'

As she rubbed the dough off her hands, there came a knock on the kitchen door. Katie was about to open it, but Mary Ellen said, 'Hold on. I'll see to it.' When she opened the door, there stood the old man and the girl.

'Good afternoon, Mrs O'Brien.' It was the old man who spoke, and his voice was as kindly as his smile; but Mary Ellen would not allow it to make any impression on her. She didn't reply, but stared at them fixedly, the door held firmly in her hand, while he went on, 'I thought we would just come round and get acquainted. And also ask you to thank your son for helping my boy last night.'

Mary Ellen's eyes darted to the girl. She was wearing a waterproof coat with a hood attached, and from under it she smiled at Mary Ellen, like a child who was asking to be liked. They were barmy, Mary Ellen thought. Their Mick had nearly done for the lad, and here they were, coming to thank John! They weren't all there, either of them – they couldn't be. She wanted no truck with them. She was aware that the old man was becoming drenched, but that was his look-out; they weren't crossing the doorstep.

She was saying abruptly, 'That's all right. It was our Mick's fault, anyway,' when she felt her hand taken from the door, and John stood there, saying, 'Won't you come in?' It wasn't often she got angry with John, but now it took her all her time not to turn on him.

The old man said, 'Thank you. Thank you. Are you by any chance the Mr O'Brien I owe so much to?'

Pushing two chairs forward John said, 'Take a seat.' He did not look at the girl, but went on, 'It's us should be doing the thanking. Not many people would be taking it like this.' Then he turned to Shane: 'This is my father.'

Shane reluctantly took the proffered hand and muttered something, and his head, which had been still, began to jerk.

The old man, seeming not to notice the lack of cordiality, said, 'My name's Peter Bracken. And this is my granddaughter, Christine.'

Shane nodded, and after a short silence that was broken only by the scraping of chairs, he turned to Mary Ellen, now vigorously pounding the dough, and said, 'I'm off to see if there's anything in.' He pulled his steaming coat off the rod that ran under the mantelshelf, and with a final nod towards Mr Bracken, he went out.

Mary Ellen watched his huge figure slumping down the yard. Off to see if there's anything in at this time of the day! It was just to get out of the way; he hated to talk to strangers at any time. There was a faint wreath of steam still hovering about the shoulders of his coat as he disappeared into the back lane. It brought a tightness to her breast, and she murmured to herself, 'Shane, Shane,' as she was wont to do years ago when her pity was mixed with love. And the feeling made her more resentful towards the pair sitting behind her. Now he'd be wet to the skin, and his twitching would go on all night.

She knew she was being very bad mannered standing with her back to them, but she couldn't help it; yet she found herself listening to the girl talking to Katie. They were talking about the book, Katie's voice sounding broad in comparison with the girl's, which was quiet and even and without dialect. And then she found herself listening to John. He was talking more than she had heard him do so before. He was talking to the old fellow about the docks and the kind of boats that came in and what they brought . . . iron ore from Bilbao, black fine ore from Benisaf, the heavy ore from Sweden that made the steel, esparto grass for paper, prop boats from Russia, with the cargo stacked from one end of the boat to the other to make the tonnage. As if the old fellow would want to know all that! She had never heard him talk so much about the docks before. He went on to speak of the unloading as if he had been down the holds all his life, instead of just two years. What had come over him? Perhaps he was doing it because she was offhand with them. Well, he knew she wanted no truck with them; and they were a thick-skinned pair to sit there knowing, as they must know, that they weren't wanted.

'I suppose you are always kept busy, Mrs O'Brien?'

She started, and was forced to half turn her body and look at the old man, and to answer him civilly: 'Yes, most of the time I'm at it.'

'You must find it very hard looking after such a big family. And I mean big,' he laughed.

'Well, you've got to take what God sends.' Immediately she felt she had said the wrong thing, giving him an opening to start his ranting, but to her surprise he didn't take it.

He stood up, saying, 'Well, we mustn't delay you – I just felt I would like to make your acquaintance, Mrs O'Brien.'

Mary Ellen turned from the dish, again forced to respond, this time with a smile. It was funny, but they seemed all right. Was this spook business just an idle rumour? People were in the habit of making a lot out of nowt.

She returned the girl's smile too, but when she saw John, silent now, looking at the lass, the smile froze on her face. She didn't want any of that kind of truck, not for John she didn't . . . Dominic could do what he liked.

There was another knock on the front door, and this time she had to tell Katie, who was hanging on to the girl's hand, to go and open it.

Christine spoke directly to Mary Ellen for the first time. 'Will you let Katie come in to tea, Mrs O'Brien? It's rather a special occasion, it's Grandfather's birthday.'

She cast a smile, full of light, on the old man, and he said, 'Sh!'

She answered, 'No, I won't. Do you know how old he is?' She was speaking to John now, looking up into his face.

John's eyes twinkled, and he answered seriously, 'Twenty-six.'

They all laughed, except Mary Ellen.

'You're just sixty years out!' said the girl.

'You're not eighty-six!' Amazement brought the words out of Mary Ellen.

'Yes, that's what I am, Mrs O'Brien.'

Mary Ellen stared at the straight, lean body of Peter Bracken, at his unlined face and deep-set eyes, shining like black coals. The only sign of real age was the white hair, and he was eighty-six. Fear of him overcame her again. You didn't reach eighty-six and be like that, not naturally you didn't. Shane was fifty-seven, and he was old. She had known men live to eighty, but they ended their days in bed, or on sticks. No, her instinct had been right at first . . . there was something funny about them, something beyond her understanding; and she wanted no truck with them.

She was brought from her fear by the sound of footsteps accompanying Katie's through the front room. Who on earth could Katie have let in now!

The small, black-clad figure standing in the open doorway soon informed her. She gasped at the sight of Father O'Malley. His presence always meant a rating for something or other. Today it would be Katie off school and Mick being kept from Mass last Sunday. Oh, she'd had enough for one day! And there were these two still standing there, not smiling now but staring at the priest as if they were struck.

'Good afternoon, Father. Will you take a seat? It's dreadful weather; you must be wet.' Mary Ellen was doing her duty. At the same time, she noticed the half-inch thick soles on the priest's stout boots, and chided herself for thinking: It'll take some water to get through them.

John spoke next: 'Good afternoon, Father.'

'Good afternoon,' said Father O'Malley, in his thin, tight voice; but he looked neither at Mary Ellen nor at John, for his eyes were fixed on those of Peter Bracken.

Noting this, John said, 'Mr Bracken's a new neighbour of ours, Father.'

The priest did not answer, and Peter Bracken said, quietly, 'Father O'Malley and I already know one another.'

'What is this man doing in your house?'

Mary Ellen knew the priest was addressing her, although he did not look at her. She shivered and said hesitantly, 'Well Father . . . '

'Order him to leave at once! And forbid him the door in future.'

Mary Ellen twisted the corner of her apron and turned towards Mr Bracken and the girl. But before she could get the words out, John broke in sharply, 'Hold your hand a minute! Me da's not in, and next to him I'm head of this house, such as it is, and I'm telling no-one to get out, Father.'

The priest swung round on him, his eyes almost lost behind their narrowed lids and the double lenses of his glasses: 'So you are head of the house, are you? And you will take the responsibility on your soul for associating with this man?'

'I know nothing against the man.' John's face was as set as the priest's.

'You don't?' Father O'Malley raised his eyebrows. 'Then you're about the only one in these parts who doesn't. I will enlighten you. This man is an enemy of the Catholic Church . . . '

'That is not true! I'm an enemy of no church . . . '

Father O'Malley cut short Peter Bracken's protest, and went on: 'Why, I ask you, is a man of his standing living in a quarter like this? Because he makes it his business to live among Catholics so he can turn them against the Church.'

'I live wherever there is fear and poverty, and try to erase it.' The old man's face was no longer placid; it was alight with a force and energy that gave the impression he was towering above them all.

'Do you know what this man has dared to say? Only that he has a power equal to that of Christ!' Father O'Malley's eyes bored into Mary Ellen's and then into John's. 'In fact, he says he is a Christ!'

John, his eyes wide and questioning now, looked to Mr Bracken for denial. But none came.

'You know you are twisting my words!' cried the old man. 'What I maintain is we all have the power to be Christs. If we are made in God's image and likeness, then it stands to reason we are part of Him; our spirit is pure God material. The only difference between my spirit and God's is the size of it – the quality is exactly the same. That is what I preach. And the more I become aware of my spirit, the more I get in touch with it, the more God-like things I can do . . . And I have done God-like things—' Mr Bracken pointed at the priest: 'You know I have! And it is this very proof that upsets your slavish doctrine.'

'Silence!' Father O'Malley's voice was like deep and terrible thunder.

Mary Ellen clutched at the neck of her blouse, and Katie hid her face in the folds of her mother's skirt; the bedroom door opened and Dominic came into the kitchen, but no-one took any notice of him.

The priest's voice dropped low in his throat. He addressed himself to John. 'Are you asking for any more proof than that?'

Before John could answer, the girl spoke, 'My grandfather will give him proof – he will show him his own power, and free him from you and your like. It is not God's will, as you preach, that he or anyone else should live in poverty and ignorance all his days. If they were made aware of their own power they would throw all this off.' She flung her arms wide and took a step towards the priest. 'You would stop them from thinking – for once they think, they question. And they mustn't question, must they? They must accept! It wouldn't do for them to realise there's no purgatory or heaven or hell but what they make themselves!'

Before John's eyes there rose the picture of Miss Llewellyn leaning back against the wind, saying, 'Take the heaven you are sure of.' Then his mind was brought back to this slip of a girl facing up to a man like Father O'Malley; not only facing up to him, but attacking him. What she was saying was quite mad, but she had courage.

The thought saddened him; it might be the courage of fanaticism, and she looked too sweet and girlish to be imbued with fanaticism.

The old man drew her back to his side, saying, 'Be serene, Christine. Remember, anger poisons.'

Father O'Malley's voice cast a deadly chill over the room as he said, 'The day is not far hence when you will rot in hell for your blasphemy!'

'The day is not far hence,' took up Peter Bracken, 'when your sect, if it does not throw off its dogmatism and learn toleration, will be fighting for its life; for there are seeds in the wombs of women, at this moment, that in thirty, forty or fifty years' time will shake the foundations of your preaching. The minds of people are moving. They are searching for the truth – they are reading. And what are they reading first? – the very books that are forbidden by your Church, for the first question the groping mind asks is: Why have these books been forbidden?'

Father O'Malley looked as if he was about to choke – black anger swamped his face. After a silence, tensed to breaking point, he addressed Mary Ellen, 'I leave you and your conscience to judge. And remember, I am warning you . . . disaster and damnation follow this man. If you wish to save your immortal soul and those of your family, throw him out as you would a snake!' His eyes burned into Mary Ellen's for a second, and then he was gone. And the banging of the front door shook the house.

It occurred to John that Father O'Malley had ignored him because he stood up to him; it was noticeable that the priest concentrated on his mother because she was afraid. He looked towards her. She was leaning on the table with one hand; the other was held under her breast tight against her heart. And she was shivering.

Dominic spoke for the first time: 'Don't take any notice of him; he thinks he's still in Ireland.' His words weren't spoken to his mother, but to the girl. But she did not return his glance, or answer him, for she was staring at Mary Ellen.

Into this tense atmosphere came Mick. He entered the kitchen, his head on one side and his hand over his ear. 'Ma, me ear's runnin' and it's ach . . . ' He stopped short at the sight of Mr Bracken and glanced quickly from him to John.

No-one moved for a second until Peter Bracken exclaimed in an exalted voice, 'Mrs O'Brien, I will show you! Your boy has earache, probably an abscess. I will cure it. Through the great healing power of God I will cure it.'

He made a step towards Mick, and in a moment the kitchen became quickened into life. Mary Ellen flung herself between them, intending to grab Mick to her, but Mick, thinking of last night and taking Peter's cure to mean much the same thing as when his mother boxed his ears, saying, 'I'll cure you!' sprang away from them both. Mary Ellen made a wild grab at the air, overbalanced and twisted herself to clutch at John's hands that were outstretched to her but missed them and fell on her side on to the mat.

Mary Ellen knew, almost as she fell, what had happened. The blinding pain, like a red-hot steel wire, starting in her womb and forcing itself up through her body and out of her head, blotted out even itself in its transit. When next she felt it she was lying on the bed – the pain was filling all her pores and forcing out sweat. She opened her eyes and looked up into John's face. She wanted to say to him, 'Don't worry, lad. Don't worry,' for his face was like death, but she could utter no word.

The hot wire was boring again, identifying itself from the other pains by an intensity that no previous labour had brought to her. It left no room even for fear when she realised that that Bracken man was near her; nor did she feel any element of surprise when she heard him saying, 'I'll go in and work at her head through the wall. Take her hand and don't let go.'

Mary Ellen felt her hand being taken between two soft palms, and she did as she was bidden when his voice came directly to her, as if through a thick fog, saying, 'Hold on to Christine, Mrs O'Brien, and the pain will go.'

As the pain forced her knees up and her head down into her chest, Mary Ellen gripped the girl's hand. And when she next regained consciousness she knew she was not on the bed but above it, lying on a sort of soft platform, and the girl was still by her side, while Hannah Kelly and Nurse Snell were working on somebody lying on the bed. And then the doctor came, not the shilling doctor, but Doctor Davidson from Jarrow, and she wondered vaguely who would pay him. He reached up and took her hand and tried to unloosen it from the girl's, but as he did so Mary Ellen felt herself dropping down into that contorted mass below her, and she clung on like grim death to the soft hand. She heard him say, 'You're Peter Bracken's grand-daughter, aren't you?' There followed a silence. Then his voice came again, 'Well, there are stranger things in heaven and earth than this world dreams of; and I won't despise your help, because I'm going to need it.'

She lay for years on the platform with queer sensations passing through her body, and the next voice she heard was that of Shane, muttering, 'Mary Ellen, lass, Mary Ellen.'

She knew he was crying, and she wondered at it. She thought of the time when he loved her and she loved him – it was all so long ago. What had happened since? Nothing. He still loved her, but she loved Katie and John. But they didn't love Shane – he had no-one but her. What would happen to him when she died she didn't know – and it didn't seem to matter.

It was odd, but rather nice, lying here thinking untroubled thoughts. She hadn't to get up and see about the baking or washing or meals, or, what was more important, money. She had an ache somewhere, but she couldn't lay her finger on it. And she was conscious of smiling when the doctor reached up and, lifting her eyelid, exclaimed, 'Odd, very odd.'

The next voice that came to her was Father Bailey's. It was nice to have Father Bailey near; he brought a feeling of comfort. And as he made the sign of the cross and touched her lips, she felt a great happiness. She saw him standing at the foot of the platform and smiling, not at her, but at Mr Bracken, who, she felt, was standing just behind her head. Father Bailey was saying, 'God's ways are many and mysterious. He has made these ways and only He can judge them.' She heaved a great sigh and fell into a kind of sleep, thinking, 'Yes, we are all one.' It was the answer Christine Bracken had given to Father Bailey.

The gas in the kitchen was turned low. It flickered up and down and spurted out of a little hole in the bottom of the mantle. In the dim light John knelt before the fire, taking out the ashes. He raked them slowly and quietly, and was glad of their warmth on his hands, for in spite of a good fire, he felt cold. It was the chill before the dawn, he thought. Was it only twelve hours since all this started? It seemed many lifetimes to him. And what it must be like for Christine, sitting in that one position by the bed, he could not imagine. He thought of her now as Christine – the night had joined them in a relationship that seemed to him to be stronger than any blood tie; he had wrapped a blanket about her and taken off her shoes, and put on her slippers. He had been next door for them, and had to find them himself, for the old man was sitting facing the wall and appeared to be asleep. He had taken her cup after cup of tea, and when, stiff with cramp, she could not hold the cup, he held it for her. Once she leant against him and he supported her with his arm. And an hour ago, he had tried to withdraw her hand gently from his mother's, but the result was the same as when others had attempted to do this – Mary Ellen's fingers became like a vice around those of Christine. His mother had been on the point of death, he knew, her life reduced to a mere flicker, yet whenever her hand was touched it held all the strength of vital life in its grip on Christine's. The doctor had said it was touch and go: 'I've done all I can,' he said. 'I'll be back first thing in the morning.' And looking hard at John, he asked, 'Do you believe in spiritual healing?'

John answered simply, 'I'm a Catholic.'

'So am I,' said the doctor. 'And I'm dead against it professionally and otherwise . . . yet . . . ' He had stopped abruptly, buttoned his coat, and said, 'Good night. We'll know more in the morning.'

Father Bailey had left the house without saying anything, his face set and thoughtful.

Shane's reactions when he saw the girl sitting there were surprising to John. He had come back into the kitchen and stood looking down into the fire, his body strangely still. 'I don't care who keeps her alive – it can be the divil himself,' he said, 'as long as she doesn't leave me.'

He had turned and looked quietly at his son, and John realised that beyond the drinking and the fighting there still remained in his father a deep feeling for his mother. It surprised him and at the same time brought him closer to this man, whom at times he almost despised. A little while ago he had managed to persuade him to lie down – Dominic was already in bed, having retired there shortly after twelve. He had stood with the others round his mother when they thought she was breathing her last, but when she continued to breathe he said there was no point in the lot of them staying up, and anyway he'd have to be out early to see if he could get a start.

John knew that he, too, would have to be at the docks by six o'clock. There was a prop boat due in, and he might get set on – not that he liked prop boats, for there was no piece work – you received four shillings a day, and no overtime; but that would certainly be better than nothing, for with his mother bad, money would be needed now more than ever before.

Although he'd had no rest he did not feel tired; the training of working forty-eight hours at a stretch as a young lad when on tipping had hardened him. He thought nothing of working all day and all night to discharge an ore boat, and the men liked him in the gang. He could set the pace, and the pace meant everything when the quicker the discharge was done the sooner the men were paid. He looked at the clock . . . half-past four. There were many things that should be done before he left the house; so he proceeded to tidy the kitchen, shaking the mats and sweeping the floor – his mother would want them to be dependent on neighbours as little as possible, kind as they might be.

He was setting the table for breakfast when Hannah Kelly came from the front room.

'I'll go over home a minute, lad,' she whispered, 'and get our Joe up. Then I'll be back.'

He thanked her, and asked, 'Do you think there's any change?'

'I don't know . . . perhaps there's a little – she seems to be breathing easier. Funny about that lass, isn't it?' She looked questioningly at John. 'Mary Ellen hanging on to her like that after saying she wanted no truck with them.'

John made no reply.

And after a moment she whispered again, 'She's had me scared stiff, sitting so still. 'Tisn't natural. What d'ye make of it? And what are ye going to do if it goes on any longer?'

'I don't know,' he said.

Hannah shook her head: 'It's rum. Makes ye put yer thinking cap on, don't it?'

He nodded slowly, and she said, 'Aye well, there's queer things happen in the world. We'll know this time the morrer, likely.'

After Hannah had gone, he stood staring before him. What would happen to them all if his mother should die? She was the axis around which they revolved. Molly would soon be leaving school, but she would be less than useless to run this turbulent house. He looked down on her, lying in the corner of the couch. Her mouth was open, and even in sleep she looked what she was, feckless. Now if Katie were older . . . What! The thought shocked him. Katie work and slave after the lot of them! No. Let her have a better start than that, even though it be only in service. But his mother wouldn't die. Somehow they wouldn't let her die.

He classed Mr Bracken and Christine as 'they' when he thought of them in their strange and eerie capacity of healers; but as Mr Bracken and Christine, he thought of them as kindly folk, and in Christine's case, as bonnie and taking.

When he went quietly from the kitchen into the front room to replenish the fire, he saw them as he had seen them last – his mother, lying straight and still and curiously flat, with one arm outstretched to that of Christine, who was sitting close to the head of the bed; only this time there was a difference – inches separated Mary Ellen's hand from Christine's.

Christine smiled faintly. The smile seemed forced on to the chiselled whiteness of her face, her eyes looked vacant, like the hollowed sockets in a sculptured head.

John bent over her, whispering anxiously, 'Are you all right?'

She tried to broaden her smile, but the effort seemed too much, and she fell against him. He glanced at his mother. She was breathing evenly now, and a faint tinge of colour had crept into the greyness of her face.

Christine whispered, 'She's asleep . . . it's over.' She sighed, and her body pressed with gentle heaviness against him.

'Come into the kitchen,' he said.

'I can't yet. I've . . . I've got cramp. I'm stiff. In a little while.'

She sounded sleepy, and for a moment he thought she had fallen asleep.

Hannah Kelly came into the room again, and exclaimed softly, 'She's let go then.' She peered at Mary Ellen. 'She's better. Ye'd better get away to bed, lass,' she said kindly to Christine.

Christine, in an effort to rise, almost lost her balance, and John put his arm about her and supported her to the kitchen, followed by Hannah's quizzical glance and raised eyebrows. 'Aye, well,' she soliloquised, 'ye never can tell where blisters light. But my God, won't Mary Ellen go mad!'

John sat Christine on a chair by the fire, and stood helplessly watching her as she slowly started to cry. It was a gentle crying; the tears welled up from their source, spilling over the dark, thick fringe of lashes on to her cheeks, then down on to her clasped hands.

'You're all in,' John said. 'Come on, I'll take you in home.'

Like a child, she placed her hand in his, and he drew her to her feet.

'The cramp . . . it's still there' – she tottered as she stood – 'my legs don't seem to belong to me.'

In the flickering light of the gas, she looked up at him and smiled through the tears. 'It's been a strange night, John.'

He nodded silently. He wanted to thank her for what, in the back of his mind, he felt that she and her father had done, but to say 'Thank you for saving my mother's life' would be to accept the strange and terrible power that was assuredly theirs, and some part of him was afraid. It seemed ridiculous that this slip of a lass could be anything but what she looked . . . a fetching, boyish-looking girl.

Christine sighed and said, 'Everything would have been perfect if the baby had lived. Will your mother be very upset?'

He couldn't answer for his mother . . . nor for himself, for he felt she would be shocked at his thankfulness that it was dead.

She swayed, and again he put his arm about her and led her to the door. Her legs gave way beneath her, and she clung to him saying, 'It's only temporary. In the morning I'll be all right, but now all my strength has gone.'

Stooping swiftly and saying, 'This is the best way then,' he lifted her up into his arms. She offered no resistance, but sank against him, her head on his shoulder. One of his hands was under her breast, and he saw the curve of it as her blouse and petticoat pouched, small, not much bigger than Katie's, and the sight of it brought no more excitement to his blood than the tiny mound of Katie's would have done. Some part of his mind wondered at this. His other hand was below her knees, and his face, as it bent above hers, was close enough for kissing. He could have dropped his mouth on to the lips and told himself it was in gratitude. And she too perhaps would have accepted his excuse. And it would have been a start. It would also have fixed Dominic. But he did nothing, not even press her close. Perhaps it was because he was worried about his mother, but he might have been carrying Katie, for his feelings were not aroused above tenderness. Vaguely, he was irritated by this. The night had brought them together in one way, a way that was deep and would be lasting, he knew, but it wasn't the way of a fellow getting off with a lass; it was a way that had missed his body and touched something beyond.

As he carried her into her own kitchen, she stirred and opened her eyes, and her hand came up and touched his cheek. And she whispered, 'You're so nice, John . . . so good.' And he knew that he would have started something had he kissed her, because she liked him in a way perhaps that hadn't gone past her body.

CHAPTER FIVE

THE COMIC

Katie moved the parcel on to her other hip. It was heavy; but not as heavy as the weight inside her; the weight was leaden. To go to the pawnshop with any parcel filled her with shame; to walk up the dock bank, under the knowledgeable stares of the men idling there against the railings caused her throat to move in and out; and to meet any of her schoolmates on the journey made her want to die; but when it was John's suit she was carrying every tragedy of the journey was intensified a thousandfold.

When her mother asked, 'Will you go down to "Bob's", hinny?' Katie had stared at her, speechless. She wanted to say, 'Our Molly should go, she's bigger,' but she knew from experience that Molly always got less on the clothes than she did, and generally too, she lost something, the ticket, or worse still, a sixpence. And because her mother looked so thin and white when she asked her she remained silent, and watched Mary Ellen go to the box under the bed and take John's suit out.

It seemed such a shame that it was John's, because he had started work only that morning. They all had, after being off weeks. But there was nothing in the house now to make them a meal, and although they would get subs, her mother was relying on these to pay the three weeks' back rent. Katie felt that once the rent was paid, her mother would look less white.

Going through the arches into Tyne Dock she met Mrs Flaherty.

'Oh, ye're not at school the day?' Peggy greeted her.

'No, I was sick.' Katie stared up into the half-washed face, criss-crossed with wrinkles, and her tone defied disbelief.

'Oh, that's a pity, it is. Ye shouldn't miss your iducation. Some day, when ye're old enough, I'll lend ye one o' me books; they'll iducate ye like nothing else will. When ye're old enough that is.' She snuffled and caught the drop from the end of her nose on the back of her hand.

'Thank you.' For as long as she could remember Katie had been promised one of Mrs Flaherty's books, and the promise meant nothing to her now. She said, 'Ta-ta, Mrs Flaherty,' and walked on, the parcel now pressed against her chest and resting on the top of her stomach.

Although she thought impatiently that Mrs Flaherty was always on about education, she wished her mother was a bit like her. She had almost given up talking to her mother about the examination and what Miss Llewellyn said, for her mother didn't believe Miss Llewellyn meant what she said – last time, she had stopped her talking, saying, 'Oh, hinny, you mustn't take so much notice of things; your teacher's only being nice. The examination she's on about is likely the one you have every year.' And when Katie had sat quietly crying, Mary Ellen said to John, 'Look, lad. I can't go down to the school and see what she keeps on about, I only have me shawl; will you go?'

'What! Me? Not on your life. Now that's a damn silly thing to ask me to do, isn't it! What could I say to the headmistress?'

'Well, will you go and see her teacher, then?'

John had just stared blankly at his mother, then picked up his cap and walked out of the house.

Katie thought the only one who understood was Christine. She liked Christine nearly as much as she liked Miss Llewellyn, but not quite. Life had taken on an added glow since Christine came into it; for Christine made her pinnies and dresses out of her own old ones. She gave her and Molly nice things to eat, too; and she had even given them money, real money, half a crown each. But only twice, for when they took their half-crowns into their mother the second week she made them take them back.

Katie could not understand her mother's attitude of not speaking to Christine and her grandfather. She allowed her and Molly to go next door, but Mr Bracken and Christine had never been into her house since that terrible day some months ago when their mother was taken bad. John and Dominic, too, went next door; and she often sat on John's knee while he and Mr Bracken talked. They talked about funny things, one of which stuck in her mind: Mr Bracken said you could have anything you wanted if you only used your thoughts properly . . . There were so many things she wanted, but she wanted above all to be a teacher. Should she do what Mr Bracken told John, lie on her back with her arms outstretched and think of being a teacher until she felt herself floating away? Eeh no! she'd better not, for there were some people who said Mr Bracken was the devil. He wasn't; but anyway, she'd better not do it.

She always had a queer feeling when Dominic was next door when she would wonder if he were trying to do what he was doing that night she went in unexpectedly. He had Christine pressed in the corner and was trying to kiss her. Her blouse was open, and the ribbon of her camisole was loose. Katie knew that Christine was frightened, for she held on to her until Dominic went out. Then she told her not to mention to John what had happened; and Katie only too readily promised.

At last she reached the dark well of the pawnshop, and listened, her eyes wide and sad, as Bob said, 'Only three-and-six, hinny. It's getting a bit threadbare.' He turned to a woman and asked, 'Will you put it in for her?' And the woman nodded, taking the penny Katie offered her. Katie wished she were fourteen, then if she had to come to the pawn she wouldn't have to pay somebody for putting the stuff in – a whole penny just for signing your name! It was outrageous, and she disliked the woman intensely for being so mean as to take the penny.

As she was leaving the shop with the money tightly grasped in her hand, Bob said, 'I've got something here that might interest one of your brothers. It'll fit nobody else round these parts. It's a top coat, and it's a bobby-dazzler. Ten shillings, it is. And I only wish I had what it cost when it was new. Tell one of them to have a look in.' Katie said she would.

She went on to the butcher's, and from there to buy a gas mantle. In Mr Powell's, she stood waiting while he hunted for the box which contained the turned down mantles. His search took him into the back shop, and Katie was left alone standing before an assortment of comics. They were arrayed on a sloping counter: *Rainbow*, *Tiger Tim's Weekly*, *Comic Cuts*, and others. Her eyes dwelt on them longingly. It was weeks and weeks since she was able to buy a comic. She would likely get a penny off John on Saturday. But Saturday was as far away as Christmas, and there stretched before her the rest of the afternoon and the long, long evening. And she daren't ask her mother for even a ha'penny out of the suit money. On the front of *Rainbow*, the Bruin boys were up to their games again: the tiger, the parrot, the elephant, and others, were playing one of their naughty pranks on Mrs Bruin. And inside the comic, Katie knew, would be the story of the little girl who was really a fairy and worked magic. Her eyes darted to the back shop. All she could see was Mr Powell's feet on the top of a pair of steps. Her hand went up and touched the *Rainbow*. It hesitated for a second, then with one swift movement, the *Rainbow* was inside her coat, and for the first time in her life she found herself wetting her knickers. The combined horror was too much for her. She ran out of the shop, down the dock bank to the arches. She did not stop to look inside her coat; her sin had already obliterated the joy of the comic. She was a thief! She had stolen! Mr Powell would miss the comic and put the pollis on her track; her mother would be taken to court and her face would become white again, and all at school would know . . . Miss Llewellyn would know!

Standing over the gutter, under the high, bleak arches, she vomited, and the comic slipped down from beneath her coat and became fouled with the sick.

There was a long row of boys and girls waiting to go into confession, for tomorrow was the first Friday in the month, on which day they all attended communion. They nudged each other and fidgeted whilst bending over in grotesque positions in supposed prayer. They whispered and passed sweets, and showed one another holy pictures; yet there was no noise at all, so practised were they. It was three weeks since Katie was last at confession, the longest period between her confessions she could remember. Although the chill autumn air was filling the church she felt hot and sick. She had been sick a number of times since the day she took John's suit to the pawn – she refused to think of it as the day she stole the comic. But now she had to think of the comic, for she was about to make her confession.

A teacher, not Miss Llewellyn, came and moved a row and a half of children down to the pews opposite Father O'Malley's box, which were singularly bare of penitents. This left Katie the next to go to Father Bailey. She was filled with a mixture of relief and fear, relief that she had escaped Father O'Malley's judgment, and fear that her turn was upon her.

A small, dark shadow emerged from one door of the confessional box, and Katie stumbled in. But for the faint gleam of a candle coming through the mesh from the priest's side the box was black dark inside.

'Please, Father, give me the blessing for I have sinned,' she began. 'It is three weeks since my last confession.'

'Go on, my child.' Father Bailey's voice was like a soft balm falling on her.

'I have missed Mass once.'

'Through your own fault?'

'No, Father. It was me clothes; me ma wouldn't let me come.'

'Go on, my child.'

'I have spoken in church and I have missed me morning and night prayers.'

'How often?'

'Three times . . . no, four . . . perhaps a few more, Father.'

'Why?'

' 'Cos the lino's all cracked and it sticks in me knees when I kneel down.'

The priest made a noise in his throat and said, 'To strengthen your soul it is important that you say your prayers – prayers are the food of the soul like bread is the food of the body . . . You understand, my child?'

'Yes, Father.'

'Then under no circumstances should you starve your soul.'

'No, Father.'

'Go on.'

But Katie couldn't go on. Her clasped hands, pressed against the elbow rest on a level with her face, were stuck together with sweat. The confessional box seemed weighed down with the smell of incense and mustiness.

'Is there anything more?' the priest asked.

'Yes, Father.'

'Well then, what is it?'

Silence followed his question. And after a moment he went on: 'Don't be afraid, my child; there is nothing so terrible that God won't forgive.'

'I stole.'

The priest's hand was taken away from his cheek and his face turned towards the mesh, and Katie looked up into two white bulbs. Then the hand was replaced again.

Katie shivered during the silence that followed; she felt her sin had been a shock even to the priest.

'What did you steal?'

'A *Rainbow*.'

'A what!' The hand was dropped again.

'A comic.'

The priest coughed. 'Now, my child, you know how it hurts our Blessed Lord when you do anything like that.'

'Yes, Father.'

'And will you do it again?'

'No, no. Never, Father.'

'No, I know you won't. And if you could find a way to pay the shop-keeper for the comic it would put everything right, wouldn't it?'

'Yes, Father.'

'Now, for your penance say one Our Father and ten Hail Marys, and tell Our Lord that never again will you hurt Him; and He will forgive you. And don't forget to kneel when you are saying your prayers, in spite of the lino; for remember the nails in the cross.'

The priest made the sign of the cross and said the absolution, whilst Katie murmured, 'Oh, my God, I am very sorry I have sinned against Thee, because Thou art so good and by the help of Thy Holy Grace I will never sin again.'

'Good night, my child, and God bless you,' said Father Bailey. 'And worry no more; He understands.'

In a holy daze, Katie walked out of the box, and in the same state she said her penance, kneeling in the corner of the dark church, straining her eyes up to the statue of the Virgin and the Child, knowing that her sin was wiped away. And on walking out of the church, there was John, standing under the lamp. It all seemed part of God's Grace. She ran to him and flung her arms about him, crying, 'Oh John! Oh John!' as if she had not seen him for years. Then she asked, 'Are you going to confession?'

'No,' John said; 'I was passing and I thought I'd wait for you.'

She knew this wasn't true; he never had to pass this way; he had come to meet her because she was crying when she left home. She seemed to have been crying for weeks. She knew that her mother and John were worried about her, for she couldn't tell them why she cried. But now she was free again – the dreadful weight was lifted from her.

John, looking down into her bright face, wondered what had wrought the change. He said teasingly, 'Has Father Bailey given you a pair of wings?'

'Eeh, our John!' She shook his arm as she walked by his side. 'But Father Bailey is nice, isn't he? He's so nice he makes me want to cry.'

'Well, in that case, I'll tell him to go for you the next time I see him, for you've done enough crying lately to last you a lifetime.'

Katie did not speak for a time. And then she said softly, 'I won't be crying any more, John.'

'You won't? Well, that's something to know. Why have you been crying so much lately, anyway?'

There was a longer silence before she replied, 'I stole.'

Her statement came as a shock, stunning him for a while.

'You what, Katie?' he asked.

'I stole, and I was frightened. It was a comic from Mr Powell's. And now I've been to confession and Father Bailey says it's all right.'

'You stole a comic from Mr Powell's?' There was incredulity in John's voice . . . Mick and Molly could thieve; Dominic and himself could lift things from the dock, although his own lifting was a fleabite compared with Dominic's – Dominic filled his trousers from the yorks up with grain, and sold it to anybody who kept hens; the only thing in that line he himself brought home was a few green bananas for the bairns, or an odd bit of fruit from burst boxes. Nevertheless, they all did it; but that Katie should lift anything seemed monstrous to him. It might only be a comic, but everything needed a beginning. 'Have you done it before?' he asked.

'No, only that once!'

'Why did you do it?' The question was ridiculous; as if he didn't know why she had done it!

'I hadn't had a comic for weeks, and I hadn't a ha'penny.'

'If you want a comic, ask me. Don't ever do that again, will you?' He stopped and looked down on her.

Katie couldn't see his face clearly, but she knew by his voice that he was vexed, more vexed than Father Bailey had been. 'Oh no, John, I'll never do it again . . . never.'

Yes, she could say that now, but there would be times, many times, when she would be without a ha'penny . . . and he too. What would happen then?

They walked on in silence, and he told himself it was only a kid's trick . . . Yes, it might be . . . any kid's, but not Katie's. It was this blasted, soul-shrivelling poverty, where a bairn was driven to steal because she hadn't a ha'penny! The thought persisted that because she had done it once she would do it again, and that by the time she

left school and was ready for a place she'd be a dab hand at lifting. And
then there'd be more scope. Nothing big perhaps; just a few groceries,
an odd towel, or a hankie . . . Oh, he knew what would happen . . .
Well, it mustn't; not to Katie, anyway. He must try and get more work,
or different work, or something. He must see that never again would
she be short of a ha'penny. But would that solve the problem?

He slowed his pace, and Katie, silent and apprehensive, glanced up
at him. Suddenly he stopped again and said, 'What about this exam
your teacher's on about? What have you got to do?'

She peered up at him. 'Miss Llewellyn says that if I pass this
examination I can do pupil training after I'm fourteen; and do another
examination, and perhaps then I may be able to . . . to go to . . . a
college.' The last word was whispered, and John whispered back, 'A
college?' He sighed, and they walked on again. It was fantastic . . .
College! Yet why should it be? What did Peter Bracken say, not only
say but lay down that it was a law? Anything to which you applied
your thought you could bring into being. Peter had urged him again
and again to put some of his methods to the test, but he had laughed
at him, saying, 'No, Peter, I'm a Catholic; a poor one, I admit, but
nevertheless that's my religion, and I'm trying nothing else.'

But Peter had said, 'This has nothing to do with religion, John; it's
merely using your thought in a proper way.'

Well, here was a test . . . Could he think Katie to a college? It
sounded as daft as if he had said he would think her into being the
Queen of England. Yet hadn't Peter given him proof of his power
of concentrated thought? His mother was living proof. And she was
aware of it too; that was why she never spoke of it, or to Peter; to her
simple mind it was something too terrible for probing.

Peter said that once you set your mind and heart on something
and concentrated on it day after day, things came to your aid in
what seemed a mysterious way but which was simply your positive
thought reaching out into the realm of all thought and making contact
with its own kind.

John did not profess, even to himself, to understand half Peter's
words, let alone their meaning, but this much he could, perhaps,
believe . . . if you wanted a thing badly enough you could get it.
But as Peter warned, beware of what you want, for sometimes that
which you felt you wanted most could, in the end, wreck you.

Well, it would certainly be to Katie's good if she became a teacher,
and he couldn't see that wrecking anyone. It was a wild and almost
impossible dream, yet he would will it. But first he must know what
he was up to. He would go and see Miss Llewellyn.

For the third time he stopped. Was he mad? Go and see that lass!
She'd scare the yorks off him. Well, he wouldn't wear yorks. No, he
wouldn't. To Katie's astonishment, he hurried on again, and now she
had to run to keep pace with him.

70

Only Mary Ellen was in when they got home, and Katie stood listening to John with an astonishment equal to that of her mother's as he said, 'Look, Ma, there's fifteen shillings' – he placed the money on the table – 'I was saving it up towards a suit. I want you to pay the seven-and-six off that top coat and get me a new shirt . . . one with a collar.' He did not look at Mary Ellen when saying this, for never before had he asked for a shirt with a collar; it had always been a striped flannelette one and a new muffler. 'Get a good one,' he added, 'about five shillings. And get me a cap too, a grey one, darkish.'

'What's up, lad?' Mary Ellen asked quietly when he had finished.

'Nothing much.' He turned and smiled at Katie, and punched her playfully on the side of the head. 'I'm going to see her teacher about that examination, as you asked me, and I want to be decent.'

CHAPTER SIX

THE VISIT

John stood sheepishly before Mary Ellen: 'Now if you tell me I look like the silver king I'll not set foot outside the door.'

Mary Ellen didn't proffer to tell him anything, she merely continued to stare at him. Who would have thought that a coat and a collar on his shirt would have made such a difference. He looked like a . . . well, like one of those adverts in the *Shields Daily Gazette* . . . no, better; there's never been a coat like this in Shields, she was sure. And anyway, the name inside the pocket said London. He was big enough, God knew, but the coat made him look even bigger. It was not shaped like those she was used to seeing, but hung full and was as thick as a blanket, with a check lining of fine flannel. A thrill of pride surged through her. Why, he could pass for a 'big pot'. His boots were shining as they had never done before, and the grey cap matched the dark, heather colour of the coat. She said, with a poor effort of offhandedness, 'You'll do. Mind, don't forget to take your cap off when you go in.'

'Now what do you take me for! I'm not a numbskull altogether.'

'No, lad, I know,' she said apologetically. 'Anyway, you'll likely not find her in . . . Saturday night and all. Why you couldn't go in the daylight, I don't know.'

'You know fine enough. Imagine me going down the street like this; the place would be out.'

Breaking the silence of her admiration, Katie burst out, 'They would have thought you were going to a wedding and shouted, "Chuck a ha'penny out." '

'Yes, they would that,' he laughed. 'Well, here I go. And if that Miss Llewellyn doesn't fall on me neck and say, "Oh, John, you look lovely," I'll skelp her face for her.'

He left them both laughing, Katie rather hysterically, her face buried in the couch.

Now he was outside in the dark street the jocular ease of manner he had assumed before his mother fell from him. He walked swiftly, passing people he knew but who failed to recognise him, and of whom he felt one or two turn as if puzzled and stare after him.

When he reached the dark stretch of road beyond the sawmill, he slackened his pace and, like a child, fingered the coat. He brought the lapel up to his nostril and sniffed. There was a faint aroma of tobacco mingled with another smell . . . not scent . . . he couldn't place it. He could only think it was a swell of a smell anyway. But now he must forget about the coat and think of what he would say to Miss Llewellyn. God, what an ordeal! Would he be able to speak to her alone, or would her family be there? Had she a family? He supposed so. Anyway, as his mother said, being Saturday night she might be out. Likely with that Culbert fellow. But it was early, not six o'clock yet, so there was a chance he'd catch her. If he didn't he could try again on Monday, which would give him another chance to wear the coat. He chuckled to himself: 'I'm like a bit of a bairn, and as frightened.'

Katie had told him where the house lay on the outskirts of Simonside. She said he would know it, for it had a lawn in front and two gates, and that one of the gates had a wooden arch over it. He found it all too soon; it stood by itself, lying well back from the road. There was a light in an upstairs window, and the only light downstairs came through the stained glass of the front door. He stood at the gate looking towards the house until the sound of approaching footsteps, which had the ominous tread of a policeman, gave him the impetus to walk up the short drive.

His ring was answered by a maid, a little slip of a thing, all starch and black alpaca down to her feet. Very much like Katie would be if this didn't come off, he thought.

The maid spoke first, after having peered at him. 'Mr Llewellyn's not in.'

He almost laughed. They could titivate her up, but they couldn't titivate that accent; it was the broadest of Tyneside.

'Neither is Mrs Llewellyn,' she said, and was on the point of closing the door on him when he found his voice.

'It's Miss Llewellyn I want to see.' He smile at her; he could be at home with her, anyway.

'Oh.' Her eyes grew wider, and she opened the door further. 'Well, you'd better come in. She's upstairs; she's just got back.'

John stepped past her into the hall, and she went to open a door to the right, then changed her mind, saying, 'Eeh no, you'd better wait in here.' She crossed the hall, passed the foot of the stairs and went down a short passage. And when he followed her she ushered him into a long, narrow room, at the far end of which a fire was burning.

She left him, only to return before he had time to look round. 'I forgot. What's your name?' she asked.

A great desire to laugh came over him. It could be Katie . . . no, Molly; Katie wouldn't have forgotten to ask the name.

'O'Brien.'

'O'Brien,' she repeated. Then, seeing the twinkle in his eye, her face refused to be uniformed like her body and she smiled broadly. 'I'm

73

new, I've only been here a week.' She hunched her shoulders. 'I'm always putting people in the wrong rooms. This is Miss Mary's.'

She disappeared, and he stood, cap in hand, looking around him. Well, he was inside, in Miss Mary's room. So she was a Mary, like his mother. And she had a room to herself . . . not a bedroom either. He thought the Brackens' furniture wonderful. Then what could he say of this room?

As he gazed about him, the room took away the ease and self-possession the little maid had momentarily given him. It was a melody of colour. He had never imagined colour as part of a room – good, strong furniture, yes, but the colour never got beyond a shiny brown. Here there was russet and green, gold and white. The room was carpeted to the walls with green. Green curtains hung across the entire wall at the further end of the room, and a russet-covered chair and couch were standing cross-wise before the fire. Half of one long wall was taken up with a low bookcase, on top of which stood a number of china figures, gentlemen in ruffles, ladies in crinolines, their delicate colourings reflected in the dark surface of the wood, on which they endlessly danced or bowed. The yellow tone was supplied by early chrysanthemums, rearing with frosty elegance from a tall glass vase standing on a round table . . . And then the white tone. He found his eyes drawn to this, and he walked a few steps towards it. It was a statuette of a woman, dead white and completely nude. The trailing hair covering part of one breast and falling across her stomach and over her womb only emphasised her nakedness. She was standing on an inlaid box by the side of the green curtains and reached just above his waist. She was about two feet tall, but she filled his entire vision, seeming to become alive before his eyes. In the back of his mind, he knew that she was indecent and should not be in a good Catholic home, especially a schoolteacher's.

As he heard the quick, muffled footsteps descending the stairs, he almost sprang back away from her into the centre of the room again, and faced the door. Mary Llewellyn came in smiling, and as he looked at her he wondered at his nerve in daring to come and see this woman. Never before had he come into contact with anyone like her, and he was struck dumb. She seemed to move in a radiance. Did it emanate from the softness of her eyes or from the tenderness of her lips, or from the quick movements of her hands as she spoke? He did not know – he knew only that she was different.

'Hallo, Mr O'Brien.' Like her eyes, her voice was warm; and a slight catch of huskiness in it added to its charm. 'You wanted to see me? Come up to the fire and sit down.'

He followed her, his eyes fixed on the piled coils of her hair, and his inarticulateness was passed over in the process of sitting down.

He sat, half in the big chair, his cap in his hand, and she sat on the couch, across the hearth from him. She was wearing a blue dress with a dark red belt . . . she was like her room, full of warm, embracing colour.

'I suppose you've come to talk about Katie?' she smiled at him and waited.

'Yes.' The voice didn't sound like his own; it was as if he were shouting in a large, empty hall.

'I'm so glad you have, for I should like to know your plans for her . . . Would you like her to become a teacher?'

'Yes.' Damn! Couldn't he say anything but yes! She would get the impression he was nothing but a numbskull.

'I'm glad of that. I know what to do now – I'll speak to the headmistress about her. Even if she only becomes an uncertified teacher, it would be something, wouldn't it?'

'Yes. Oh yes.' Was he a fool altogether? Yes, yes, yes. Why couldn't he be himself and say something, badly as he might express it?

There followed a silence, during which their eyes met and held. Hers were the first to drop away, and he felt she was embarrassed by his staring . . . perhaps annoyed. She leant forward and stirred the fire, and he suddenly began to talk – to straighten matters, as he put it to himself.

'I'm a poor envoy.' He wasn't sure if this was the right word, but he liked his placing of it; and he went on, 'There is so much I want to say about Katie, and so much to ask you. There's nothing I want more in the world than for her to become a teacher, but . . . Well, it's like this. You can guess how we are . . . ' he substituted the word 'situated' for 'fixed' – 'You can guess how we are situated. It's no good pretending, is it?' Without being aware of the transition, he was at his ease, talking frankly as he would have done to someone who knew all there was to know about him. 'There won't be any money to help her as far as I can see. If it's going to mean money, well, I'm afraid . . . ' He lifted his shoulders expressively. 'If it was left to me and I could earn it I would, but I'm rarely on full time.' This was coming down to earth with a vengeance, he thought. So much for his coat.

Mary was leaning back against the couch now, and she too, as she listened to him, was thinking about his coat. Remembering how she had seen him before, she had expected to find him dressed in much the same way. The coat so altered his appearance that she hardly recognised him as the same person; he looked rather handsome. Well, not handsome. There was something too rugged about his face for it to be handsome. Attractive? Yes, he looked very attractive. His eyes, particularly, were nice, especially when he smiled. It was strange what a difference clothes could make, outwardly at any rate. Yet the first time she saw him, she remembered imagining how he might look if he could dress like Gilbert. It seemed odd now that she should have met him the day she refused Gilbert . . . Suddenly she thought, I like him; he's nice – he's like Katie in a way.

75

She stood up hastily, saying, 'I haven't had any tea. Perhaps you'll have a cup with me, and then we can talk the whole thing out. Excuse me a moment.'

She gave him no time to refuse, but hurried away; and when she reached the door she turned, saying, 'Would you care to take off your coat? . . . you'll feel the benefit of it when you go out; it's nippy tonight.'

John stood up, staring down the empty room. This was a contingency for which he hadn't bargained. Against the coat, he knew his suit looked cheaper and shabbier than ever . . . Well, she was no fool to be taken in by the coat – no doubt she had guessed he had come by it second-hand. He took it off and laid it with his cap over the chair. Then he stood on the hearth-rug looking down at his suit, and a determination was born in him: this was the last suit he'd ever get from a tally man. The coat had told him one thing: there were clothes that were made to fit a man. And he'd have them. How? He didn't know; but have them he would. If one rig-out had to last him a lifetime; he'd be dressed decent for once.

And she had asked him to stay and have a cup of tea . . . tea with Miss Llewellyn! It was fantastic.

He ran his finger round the inside of his collar; it felt tight against his neck. He glanced into the mirror over the mantelshelf, and hardly recognised himself; the soft glow of the light seemed to make him look different. Or perhaps it was the collar . . . And that was another thing . . . never again would he wear a muffler at the weekends, and perhaps not at nights either.

He had just sat down again when she came in with a tray; a silver one, with a teapot and jug on it. As he would have done to relieve his mother from carrying anything, he got up and took it from her. She smiled her thanks, and brought a little table, and set it between the chair and the settee, and he placed the tray on it.

The maid came in carrying another tray, which Mary took from her, saying, 'All right, Phyllis, I'll see to it.'

With a sense of unreality, John watched her pour out the tea. She had set a little table at his hand and told him to help himself. The bread and butter was so thin he could have put the plateful in his mouth at once. He watched Mary double her piece in two, and followed suit, refusing her offer of jam, for that would mean too much palaver.

And so, like one in a dream, he took tea with Miss Llewellyn, and listened with only half his mind while she talked of Katie. He was thinking of this room and of her and of the strangeness of the whole thing . . . They were sitting here alone together, having tea, just as if . . .

He was startled back to the full import of what she was saying by hearing her repeat something he had said weeks ago: 'A day of high winds and far mastheads, and bonnie lassies.'

She laughed at his startled expression, and said, 'Now, when I find phrases like that in Katie's composition, although I know she's a clever child, I don't think she's that clever. Nor when she writes this: "The morning sky was massed with white clouds, like brakes ready for a day off." '

He felt the hot colour flooding up from his neck, and she asked, 'Have you tried writing these thoughts down and working them into something?'

'Writing them down?' he repeated. 'Me? Good Go . . . lord, no.'

'Why not?' she said. 'Burns did, and many others. I think you should. I was sorry when I had to make Katie scrap the composition in which she stated that ore on her tongue and sweat in her hair and bleeding nails meant gold on a Saturday and roaming round the market, hemmed in with the smell of tallow and the flapping of skirts.'

Now his face was scarlet, and he said, 'I'll have to be more careful of what I say . . . You see, we go for walks—' He stopped.

'You should write them up, you know,' she put in; 'a lot of what Katie repeats has poetry in it. Why don't you try?'

He had been leaning back in the chair, quite at ease. He still leant back, but he was no longer at ease. His face drooped into a sadness, which conveyed itself to his voice, together with reproach and stark frankness as he said, 'I can't even speak properly.'

'Oh, please don't say that!'

It was Mary's turn to flush now. She stood up, and taking his cup, refilled it. 'You don't speak differently from anyone else. And that has nothing to do with putting your thoughts to paper.'

'I've been told there's such a thing as grammar.' There was a touch of bitter sarcasm in his voice.

'Yes, but that comes . . . you learn as you go.'

He made no reply, and she, too, became silent, furious with herself for being a tactless fool. He had been so at ease, with quite a charming naturalness, and she had to bring up such a suggestion as him starting to write, of all things! But on the other hand, she was perfectly sincere in all she said, for some of the things Katie repeated were surprising in their poetical content. But be careful of what you are about, she warned herself. Don't put into his head ideas that will make the life he has to lead more obnoxious to him. Remember, you are not talking to Gilbert.

She glanced at the clock . . . half-past six. She hoped Gilbert wouldn't put in one of his friendly visits; visits that were, she knew, manoeuvred by her mother.

John, noting her glance, said rather flatly, 'Well, I'll think over what you've said. I'd better be going now . . . Saturday night isn't a very convenient time to call.'

'No, no' – she put out her hand as if to press him back into his chair from the distance – 'you haven't finished your tea yet, and I'm not going out again. And anyway,' she laughed in a renewed effort to put him at ease – 'there are many things I want to ask you. Who, for instance, are Mr Bracken and Christine? Oh, Christine's wonderful!' She gave an imitation of Katie, closing her eyes and screwing up her face. 'You see, I get them every morning – while Katie is walking with me to school.'

John laughed with her. 'Our Katie's a chatterer. They are the people who live next door.'

'And Christine has a wonderful house, and cooks wonderful food, and has wonderful clothes . . . Oh, she's wonderful!'

John's laugh rang out, free and unrestrained now – her imitation was so like Katie when describing anyone. 'I'm afraid Katie thinks a number of people are wonderful. Not that she isn't right,' he added hastily, realising that sitting before him was, to Katie, the most wonderful of them all.

Mary, looking intently at him, wondered if he was in love with this Christine, about whom she heard so much. Katie talked of only two people, John and Christine; before, it was only John . . . Our John said this, Our John said that . . . and the child had managed to convey a picture of someone quite out of the ordinary. Mary knew that the O'Briens were poor; not just clothes-poor, but of the poor who did not always eat well, which was a different and more potent kind of poverty; but the child had made this John emerge as someone untouched by poverty, an independent being, living with yet not of them. Then lately, to this worship was added that of this Christine . . . Christine and John, Christine and John.

How was it, Mary wondered, that some girls got men like this to love them, big kind men with a sense of humour as he had. At their first meeting, she'd thought he was to be pitied, but now she saw that she was wrong – he was intelligent and entertaining, the latter without making any effort to be so. He was certainly better company than Gilbert, even if he lacked Gilbert's taste in literature and art . . . or perhaps, because of it. Being a big man, like her father, was he attracted to small women, she wondered. This Christine, according to Katie's description, was apparently small. So was her own mother, small and helpless. Helpless! The word brought a cloud over Mary's eyes, for she had come to recognise that beneath her helpless exterior her mother was pure granite; and to live in peace with anyone like her meant submerging oneself entirely. When she was young, her happy, loving nature did not question her mother's tyranny, and it was easy to accept 'Mother knows best'. How different her life would have been had she stood against her; for now her art study would have been finished. And who knows where it would have taken her – London – even Paris. Because her mother considered it wicked to draw bodies with no clothes on, she obediently put clothes on them.

And again, when her mother said she would never make an artist . . . and anyway, artists weren't nice people . . . she subdued her natural talent becoming a schoolteacher, not through necessity, but because her father insisted she should have an occupation. But during these last few years had come a change, until now a state of undeclared war existed between her and her mother. The request to have a room of her own began it, and the refusal to be pushed into marriage with Gilbert Culbert, the son of her mother's old friend, widened the breach. And when, answering some inner urge, she bought the statue, and her mother demanded that it be removed from the house, the breach was further widened.

Lost in her thoughts, she did not notice that they were sitting in silence. How strange. She could never sit in silence with Gilbert. She lifted her gaze from her hands and found John looking at her, not intently, but rather reflectively. She smiled, and he blinked and roused himself.

'Are you interested in boats?' she asked. 'I mean the building of them.'

'Well, I know nothing about the building of them. I only know I get certain feelings when working in them. A feeling of friendliness for some and dislike for others. I suppose it has a lot to do with their cargo . . . and,' he laughed, 'the sweat in my hair.'

She laughed with him and asked, 'Would you like to see some models my father has made?'

'Yes, I would, very much.'

'Come into his workshop, then.'

She rose and went down the length of the room, and John followed her towards the green curtains. Before she drew them aside she gently moved the box and the statue. He watched her steady the statue with her hand, and it occurred to him as being strange that the statue no longer looked indecent but rather lovely . . . very like what she would be . . .

He was red in the face when she looked up at him, and she said hastily, almost apologetically, 'I came across it in an antique shop in Newcastle. It's an octoroon. I don't suppose you know any more than I did what an octoroon is; but, on looking it up, I found that she is the offspring of a quadroon and a white person, and a quadroon is one part negro and three parts white. Sounds very complicated, doesn't it?'

They were standing regarding each other now. Her hand was on the curtain and her face was unsmiling, and in her eyes he fancied he detected an appeal. For what exactly, he didn't know. But he said, 'I think it's very beautiful.' He, too, was unsmiling. And when she answered simply, 'Thank you,' it almost appeared as if the compliment had been meant for her. She turned swiftly and opened the french window, and stepped into the conservatory. He followed, going through a door close by and into the workroom.

It was in darkness, and she said, 'Just a moment. There are matches here, I'll light the gas.'

She gave an impatient exclamation as the box fell from her hand, and when, instinctively, they both stooped to retrieve it, causing them to collide and she to overbalance, his hands naturally were thrust out to steady her, and in the darkness he supported her . . . for one brief second his hands held her arms, and in that second the thing was done – the fuse that might have smouldered and died was fanned.

When the room was plunged into stark light from the double burner, John was still standing near the door. Mary did not speak for a moment, and when she asked, 'What do you think of them?' he moved slowly into the room and began to look round. There were dozens of models of small craft, set in stocks, on the shelves. In amazement, he asked, 'Your father made all these?'

'Yes. And most of them he's built full-size and sold. Do you recognise Mary, the tug?'

It was with genuine astonishment that he exclaimed, 'Your father's Llewellyn the boatbuilder then!'

'Yes. Didn't you know?'

He shook his head. He had never associated Llewellyn, the boatbuilder, with Miss Llewellyn the teacher. He knew Llewellyn by sight, as most of the dock men did. He had a little boat-building yard, tucked away on the side of the river. It still went under the name of Haggart's Yard, and it was known that Llewellyn worked in it as a lad by the side of his father. But that hadn't suited young Llewellyn; and he and his father built a boat on their own and sold it. It was said they built it in their backyard. That was a start, and eventually, when old Haggart died, and his own father too, Llewellyn bought the yard. He was known as a rising man . . . And he was her father!

With this knowledge, she again assumed to him the unapproachableness of an hour ago. How had he the nerve to come here!

When she spoke to him, smiling over her shoulder and saying, 'Come and look at this little yacht, my father hopes to build her some day,' he went to her; but the ease had left him, and he held the model in his hand without making any comment. Her nearness made him uneasy. He suddenly wanted to get away from her and her politeness . . . she would act like this towards anyone, a beggar on the road, even . . . she was made that way, courteous, easy of manner.

'What do you think of it? You have seen lots of boats, but have you seen anything like her?'

She was looking up into his straight face, trying to draw him out again, when a voice from the doorway said, 'Hallo, Mary.'

They both started at the sound of the quiet, even tone.

'Oh! hallo, Gilbert,' she said, and after a pause, added, 'Come in a minute . . . This is Mr O'Brien. Mr O'Brien, Mr Culbert.'

Neither of the men made the usual gesture to shake hands, but inclined their heads . . . John in an abrupt nod, and Culbert in a more leisurely movement. John knew that he was under Culbert's scrutiny, and after his first concentrated stare, he did not look at the man but at Mary; for he was asking himself how anyone like her could take up with a fellow like Culbert, a weed of a man, narrow all the way up, right to the pointed head, over which his thin hair was meticulously brushed.

When Mary led the way back into her room John made straight for the chair over which his coat and cap lay, and she said nothing to delay his departure.

He nodded again to Culbert in farewell, and Mary escorted him to the front door. The feel of his coat about him did nothing to allay his renewed feeling of gaucheness.

'Well, thanks,' he said awkwardly. 'It's been kind of you to . . . to help me about Katie.'

They stood regarding one another, and she too seemed to have lost some of her ease of manner. 'I'll do all I can for Katie, I'm very fond of her. And she's a clever child . . . Good night, Mr O'Brien.'

She held out her hand, and after the merest hesitation he took it. Firm and cool, it gripped his, conveying a sense of breathlessness and urgency. The feeling hung between them; even when their hands parted and he passed through the doorway it was there . . . a breathlessness.

He walked away down the path with her parting words acting like an opiate to his brain. 'If you feel there is anything you would like to know, at any time, please come and see me again.' It was odd, he thought, but she was the kind of person he could ask questions of.

But once out in the cold night air, the old brake of 'Steady your keel' thrust its reality upon him, and he said to himself, 'Well, that's that! It went off all right; Katie's set.'

As he reached the bottom of the Simonside bank, he deliberated whether to go into Shields and the market or walk slowly back home. If he did the latter it would mean thinking and going over every second of the past hour. No. He would go into Shields where there were lights and people . . . But what about being seen in this coat? Well, what about it? It seemed that within the past hour he had lost and regained his self-confidence a number of times, but, each time he regained it, it was stronger, for now he didn't mind being seen in the coat; it was the portent of things to come . . . he would have things . . . his mother and Katie would have things. How, he didn't know; but they would.

His decision to seek company in the shape of crowds did not immediately have the desired effect, and he found himself again thinking of Mary Llewellyn, but with a forced detachment. Fancy a lovely lass like her going to marry that . . . skinnymalink! Well, it was certainly no business of his. She had been very nice to him, more than nice; and she would help Katie; that was the only thing that mattered.

As he entered the first arc of Tyne Dock a well-known figure, shambling towards him, brought him back with a bump to his own world. It was Nancy; and he could hear her snivelling when she was still some distance away.

'Hallo, Nancy. What's the matter?' he asked her.

She hesitated, shuffled off the pavement in uncertainty, then shuffled back when she recognised him. 'Eeh, John. Eeh, John.'

'What's the matter?' he asked again.

'It's our Annie. She left me in the market – she run away, and she had me tram fare. An' me ma said she had to look after me and put me on the tram for me place.'

'Have you walked all the way from the market?' he asked her gently.

'Yes . . . It's our Annie. She run away, she did. An' me ma'll skelp me when I get in, she will, cos Mrs Fitzsimmons said I had to be back to clean the shop out when they closed. An' me ma said our Annie had to put me on the tram.'

John put his hand in his pocket and gave her threepence. 'Now stop crying. You'll be back in plenty of time. There's your tram fare and a penny to buy some bullets. Stand over there' – he pointed back towards the bottom of Simonside Bank – 'the Jarrow tram will be along in a minute.'

'Eeh! I can't get on the tram there, John. There's a bar there an' me ma says I've got to keep away from bars, cos the men come out.'

John could see the tram in the distance swaying towards them. He held out his hand to her: 'Come on, I'll put you on it.'

The tram jolted to a stop, and he helped her up, saying to the conductor, 'Put her off at the corner of Ferry Street, will you?'

As the conductor rang the bell, a figure leant forward from the end of the long wooden seat: 'Why, is that you, John?'

He recognised Mrs Bradley, and answered rather shortly, 'Yes, it's me.'

'Why lad, I hardly knew you . . . Well I never.'

The tram rumbled away, and the last John saw was Nancy showing the coins in her hand to Mrs Bradley. The picture did not remain in his mind an instant, but he was to remember it, and, unimportant as it seemed, it was to assume such proportions that although it happened on this day of emancipation, when he had first worn a fine top coat and taken tea with Miss Llewellyn, its ugly significance was to blot them out.

CHAPTER SEVEN

CHRISTMAS EVE

Mary Ellen hummed softly . . . it was many, many Christmases ago that she felt as happy as she did now. The morrow was Christmas Eve and she was really looking forward to it. She worked at the table in the middle of the kitchen, cutting out pastry for mince pies. Above her head hung a large, honeycombed paper ball, suspended from the paper chains crisscrossed under the ceiling. The kitchen was quiet and warm with an unusual air of cosiness about it. As she worked she planned for the morrow. She'd get up earlier than usual and blacklead the stove before lighting the fire; and then, after she'd got them all off to work, she'd get done and put everything shipshape; then she'd get the dinner ready, and have the afternoon clear . . . to go and get the coat.

Aye, it was a long time since she'd had a coat, a new shawl would have done her; but no, John had a bee in his bonnet, and she was to have a coat for Christmas . . . What had come over him lately? He was the same lad to her, yet somehow he was altered. It wasn't only the new suit he had, although that made him look fine; no, it was in some other way he'd altered. Well, never mind, he was still her lad, and the best on God's earth. If only the other one was like him.

The thought of Dominic caused her to stop humming. Why hadn't he gone away, as he'd been hinting of doing for some weeks past? Then Christmas would have indeed been grand. She knew he had been enquiring after jobs in both the Liverpool and London Docks; anywhere, he had said, to get away from this hole.

When she came to think of it, Dominic too seemed changed. It was all that lass next door she supposed – he was set on her; but he didn't seem to be making much headway. Was John his stumbling block? This was another thing which puzzled her. John was always in next door, and often she heard his laugh joined with that of the girl's. But there it seemed to end. If he were courting her, he was doing it in a funny way; for he never took her out. Pray God he wouldn't either. No, no, that would be terrible if John really took up with her. Well, she wasn't going to think about it; she was going to enjoy this Christmas. She already had a piece of brisket and an aitchbone, and if John went down to the market last thing the morrow he might pick up a duck or something cheap. They sold them off for next to nothing rather than have them left on their hands. By, it'd be grand if he could get a duck! And on Christmas Day they'd have Christmas cake and the rice loaf she'd made. Nobody knew yet, but she was going to put icing on the cake. By, they'd have a grand do.

A tap on the door broke in on her thoughts and she called, 'Come in,' and Peggy Flaherty, after kicking her boots against the wall, stumbled into the kitchen.

'Oh God above, it's enough to freeze your liver! It's at it again, Mary Ellen – won't be able to stir hand or foot outside the door shortly.'

'It hasn't started to snow again, surely?'

'It has so, Mary Ellen. As if it wasn't bad enough with everywhere frozen solid. God's truth, I've never seen anything like it! We'll have to be after watching the tap in the yard, Mary Ellen, or it'll be a dry Christmas in one way we'll be having. Oh, ye're lovely and warm in here, lass' – she wriggled her fat inside her many coats – 'and the smell's good enough to eat. And did ye ever see such a picture of a kitchen, with all those bonny chains!'

'Sit down and warm yourself, and have a pie,' said Mary Ellen.

'I will an' all, for I'm chilled to the bone. I'm just back from Shields. Look' – she pulled three small packages from her bass bag – 'some bits of things for the bairns' stockings.'

'Now, Peggy' – Mary Ellen compressed her lips – 'that's madness, that is! You know you haven't got it to go and buy presents.'

'Why haven't I then? I haven't got a bite of sup to buy for Christmas or Boxing Day, because out of the goodness of your heart ye've asked me down . . . so why haven't I? There they are' – she laid the packages on the mantelpiece – 'we'll say no more about them. There's only one thing I regret, and that is I haven't got it to buy you all something. But business isn't what it used to be; divil the pennorth of advice I've given out this past three weeks. What's the matter with people, Mary Ellen? 'Tisn't as if there were no rows; God alive, they followed each other like flies down at the bottom end last week? If it wasn't for running me clubs I'd be hard set at times; but as long as I get my rent I'm all right. And God's good. There was last week-end I didn't know which way I was going to turn, when, coming up the yard, that blessed lad of yours slipped me sixpence. By, Mary Ellen, I think if ye lost everything in the world and ye'd only him left, ye'd get by . . . Is he courting, Mary Ellen?'

'Courting?' Mary Ellen turned and with a blank face looked at Peggy. 'Not that I know of. Why do you ask?'

'Only I've seen him a number of times, three to be exact, and the last no later than this dinner-time, talking to the same lass. And a bonnier piece I've never seen. And mark ye, she wasn't from around these doors either. Today she had a fur coat on, and the tails hanging from the collar alone must have left a number of poor animals feeling cold around their backsides.'

'A fur coat?'

'The same. Tall she was, and strapping looking. And a voice like the gentry, for I heard her as I passed. And it's me that knows how the gentry talk – ye know that, Mary Ellen – for Mr Flaherty spent his life rubbing shoulders with them. And it's the same process, ye know: as ye can't touch pitch without becoming defiled, so ye can't mix among the gentry without picking up their lingo.'

Mary Ellen surveyed Peggy. 'You must have made a mistake.'

'Not a bit of it, Mary Ellen. John called out to me himself. "Hallo there, Peggy," he said, as true as I'm sitting here.'

Mary Ellen turned back to her baking board . . . John talking to a lass with a fur coat on. Who could it be? And three times. He wasn't a one to stand talking to lasses at any time, only that one next door. She turned to Peggy again: 'It wasn't—' she nodded her head towards the fireplace.

'No. I may be short in the sight, but I'm not that bad. This was a big lump of a lass, in fact she was a woman; and twice the size of that scrag end next door, bless ye.'

Mary Ellen could question Peggy no more at the moment, for there was another knock on the door; it was Hannah Kelly.

She had a coat over her head, and she shook the soft snow off it before coming into the kitchen. 'What weather! The only ones enjoying it are the bairns. Hallo, Peggy. Is this where ye are? By! they smell good Mary Ellen.' Hannah nodded towards the pies.

'Help yourself, lass,' said Mary Ellen.

'Not now. Thanks all the same. I only came over to see you a minute . . . about something.'

Peggy, taking the covered hint with the abundance of her good nature, said, 'I'll off up, Mary Ellen, for I must make a start; I'm up to the eyes upstairs.'

'She never said a truer word,' said Hannah, when Peggy had gone. 'How she lives among that junk, God alone knows. I came over to tell ye about our Nancy, Mary Ellen; but I couldn't do it with her sitting there – she'd be offering me advice, and I'm not in the mood to take Peggy's advice the day.'

'Is anything wrong, Hannah?'

'It looks like it; I've had a letter from Mrs Fitzsimmons about her. She says she's getting more queer every day, and she's getting that way she won't work; she just stands staring at her and says she can't. Ye know, Mary Ellen, that isn't like Nancy. As bad as she is she can do the rough work of half a dozen. Mrs Fitzsimmons says I'll have to bring her home if it keeps on . . . Oh, Mary Ellen, there'll be hell to pay again with our Joe if she's in the house all the time.'

'I'm sorry, lass. But perhaps you'll get her in some place else.'

'Not if she won't work. Ye don't mind me coming across and telling ye, Mary Ellen? Ye've got enough on your plate, I know, without my troubles stacked on top, but ye're the only one I seem to be able to talk to about her.'

'Why, lass, I only wish I could help you.'

Hannah sat down by the side of the fire and stared into the glowing coals for a moment. 'It's an awful thing, Mary Ellen, to know that a bairn ye've given birth to isn't all there.'

Mary placed her hand on Hannah's shoulder. 'We all have our loads, lass; if it isn't one thing it's another.'

Hannah gnawed at her lower lip. 'You and John are the only two who treat her like a human being. I know I don't. Sometimes I can't stand the sight of her. Oh, ye don't know, Mary Ellen, it's awful. But then, when I hear Joe going for her, I get a sort of feeling and want to protect her somehow.' She shook her head sadly. 'Well, the only thing I hope is she doesn't come home till after the new year. Joe's banking on a little bit of a do on New Year's Eve, but it'll be knocked completely on the head if she's home; he'll do nothing then; likely stay out most of the time.'

'She'll be all right,' Mary Ellen persisted, 'don't worry. Look, let's have a cup of tea.'

Mary Ellen bustled about making tea. In the face of the tragedy of having a partly imbecile daughter her load seemed very light. She had poverty and drink to put up with, but not that, thank God. Hers were all right up there.

The two women drank their tea and talked on . . . about Bella now. Hannah wasn't speaking to Bella, for whenever she did Bella made some excuse to come downstairs and ferret out her business. And Bella's constant presence in the house maddened Joe. Mary Ellen could well understand this, for she had no use for Bella Bradley, who was never happy unless someone else was in trouble . . .

As the snow thickened and the light vanished earlier than usual the kitchen was lit only by the glow of the fire – through necessity the gas was never lit until it was almost impossible to see, and Mary Ellen worked on, after Hannah had gone, more by feel than anything else. She began to sing softly to herself – her mother and grandmother had sung the song before her – the simple words expressing the tragedy of at least one phase of their love:

> Love, it is teasing,
> Love, it is pleasing,
> Love is a pleasure when it is new;
> But as it grows older and the days
>   grow colder
> It fades away like the morning dew.

Mary Ellen wasn't thinking of the words, or how they applied to her own life, but that she had much for which to be thankful: Shane had not been really drunk since she was bad that time, and his twitching had eased. There had been no row in the house for months either. Well, they said it was a long road that had no turning, and hers had turned.

On these pleasant thoughts the kitchen door was thrust open again. She turned towards it, but could not distinguish who was standing there. It could have been John, Shane or Dominic; but she was expecting none of them for another hour.

'Why can't you light the bloody gas!'

Mary Ellen groped for a piece of paper, which she lit in the fire and put to the mantle, then turned and looked at Dominic. She had seen his face portraying many moods, contorted with passion or anger, drawn tight with cunning; but his expression now was one she had never seen; his eyes were wide and hard, and to her mind, had the thick, dull shine of a beer bottle. He seemed to be spread in a new kind of anger, wide and high with it.

'I want me tea now. I'm going out!'

'Well, get in first, can't you! It isn't ready yet. Can't you get changed and have it with the others?'

'No, I can't! And anyway, you wouldn't expect God Almighty to sit down with me, would you?'

She stared at him. Had he gone off his head? She watched him fling his cap across the table on to the couch, pull off his coat and fling it after the cap. The coat, in its flight, whipped a number of pies on to the floor and sent a cloud of flour off the board.

'Here!' Mary Ellen cried, 'what's up with you?'

He did not answer, but grabbed the kettle from the hob and emptied it of hot water. He also emptied the pail of cold water, and proceeded to wash, the water splashing over the side of the dish and up the wall as he did so.

Mary Ellen cleaned up the mess from the floor; then picked up the kettle and pail and went cautiously down the backyard. The ashes on top of the ice were already covered with a layer of snow. The tap was running in a thin trickle and she stood on the fringe of ice and water, steadying herself against the wall as she filled the pail . . . Always something to spoil things. What was it now?

She hunted around in her mind, but could find nothing. Whatever it was was connected with his work, for he was home early. And him saying, 'You wouldn't expect God Almighty to sit down with me.' Did he mean John? She couldn't fathom it.

When she returned to the kitchen, Dominic was in the bedroom, and she hurriedly cleared the table and set some bread and dripping and mince pies out.

When he eventually came to the table he stared down at the food. 'That's a fine meal for a man, isn't it!' His voice seemed to be torn from his throat.

'Well, you wouldn't wait. I'm going to fry.'

'You're going to fry!' he mimicked raspingly. 'Well, see that you do plenty of it; the big pot'll need it to fill his swelled head.'

Then his anger had to do with John. But how? What could have happened at work?

After having eaten all Mary Ellen had placed before him, Dominic left the house by the front way. As soon as the door banged behind him Mary Ellen went hastily into the room, and stood listening. Then, as she expected, came the muffled knock. He was next door.

She sang or hummed no more but, filled with the old dread, waited for John coming in – she had spoken too soon about her road turning. There was something afoot, and from the appearance of Dominic it was bad.

Katie and Molly rushed in, their hands blue and their noses red. 'Oh, Ma, is the tea ready?' 'And, Ma, our Katie's dirtied her knickers,' cried Molly.

'What!'

Both Katie and Molly burst out laughing at their mother's expression. Molly bringing her head down to Katie's and the two of them pressing their faces together in their mirth.

'Not that way. She slipped on a slide and ended up in some broken ice and slush,' Molly giggled.

'Are you wet?' Mary Ellen asked Katie.

'No, Ma, it dried.'

'Tea won't be for some time yet,' said Mary Ellen. 'Here take a bit of bread and get yourselves out again.'

Mary Ellen pushed a slice of bread at each of them. 'You can stay out for another half-hour or so. Hunt up Mick and bring him back with you.' It would be better, she thought, if she had the house to herself when John came in.

When at last she heard the clanking footsteps in the yard, she stood still facing the door. It might be Shane. The feet kicked against the wall, and the door opened. It was John, not with brows drawn and lips tight, but with an almost childish expression of pleasure on his face. He wasn't smiling – with an effort he was keeping his face straight – but the light in his eyes danced at her. She turned from him, puzzled. It couldn't be that lass with the fur coat. No, how could that affect Dominic?

'Is it still snowing?' she asked, as she bent over the pan on the fire.

John didn't answer, but came and stood by her. 'Anybody in?'

'No,' she said.

He took her by the shoulders and pulled her round to face him, so close that her head had to go back to look up at him. 'I'll give you three guesses . . . What do you think's happened?'

'Why, lad, how should I know?'

'Go on.'

'You've been set on the Benisaf boat.'

John flung his head back and laughed out loud.

'Aye, lad, how should I know? Tell us.'

He stepped back, thrust his thumbs into the lapel of his coat, drew himself up to his fullest height with mock dignity, and said, in the deepest tones of his voice, 'Mrs O'Brien, behold . . . a gaffer!'

A gaffer . . . Mary Ellen could make no comment. Had he gone mad too? A gaffer. Her lad, and him only twenty-two. Why, there was something wrong somewhere. There was only one gaffer over the boats, and he must be a man steady in his years. The old gaffer had died a couple of days ago, she knew, but they couldn't have picked John. It was fantastic. Her face expressed her feelings, and John laughed and said, 'You don't believe it?'

'Well, lad . . .'

'Yes, I know it's hard to take in.' He was suddenly serious. 'I haven't taken it right in meself yet. I couldn't, for the life of me, believe they meant it.'

'Did the men pick you?'

'Yes, they voted for me to take old Reville's place.'

It was customary for the dock men who unloaded the boats to choose their own boss. They also paid him so much a head out of their wages. Most of the unloading was paid on tonnage, and the gaffer's job was to select men for the boat and at the end of discharging collect the money from the dock office, subtract his due and pay out the men. But this alone did not cover his duties, which often entailed taking off his coat and fighting it out with any man who thought he was not getting a square deal, and who said so forcibly. Another thing expected of the gaffer was to provide subs for men who were out of work and advances to those just being set on again.

This was in Mary Ellen's mind when she said, 'But lad, how can you do it? . . . The subs.'

'I've got over that. You know McCabe in the dock office. Well, when I went to tell him he seemed to know how I was fixed, and offered to lend me a few pounds to make a start . . . I'll be able to pay it back in a few weeks. And I won't forget him for it.'

'Lad, don't start on borrowed money. There's the twenty-five shillings for that coat. I don't need a coat; I've made . . .'

'Here . . . that's enough. You're getting that coat.'

'Were all the men for you?' She gazed up into his face; she was smiling now and her heart was racing within her breast. To think her lad had been picked for a gaffer. Oh, the road had turned all right.

'Not all. But the ones that mattered were.' He turned away and took off his coat. She knew he was referring to Dominic, and perhaps Shane.

'Does your da know?'

'Yes. He took it all right.'

She heaved a sigh of relief. Now perhaps Shane would get set on more often. No. She could quieten her hopes on that score – John would more likely be fair to the other extreme.

'Was none of the others after it?' she asked.

'Yes. But none of them were steady.'

Her eyes became misted. They had picked him, despite his years, because he was . . . steady. Her John a gaffer. And Katie set on the road to be a teacher. Oh, God was good.

The tears, gathering in her throat, threatened to choke her, and she turned away and put her apron to her face.

'Here! Here!' John pulled her round, and as his great arms pressed her gently to him a dam burst within her. No sorrow could have broken it; but this happiness was overwhelming, and she sobbed it out, leaning against him.

An hour later, when John saw Christine, he knew that she was already aware of what he had come to tell her; and after she exclaimed, 'Oh, John, what wonderful news! And at Christmas too,' he looked at her closely and asked, 'What's the matter? Aren't you well?'

'Yes. Yes, I'm all right,' she said hastily.

'No you're not, you're as white as a sheet. Has . . ?'

She turned away and picked up a half-dressed doll from the table. 'Dominic's just gone. He told me about you being made a gaffer,' she said.

'Yes, I bet he did; and he'll likely be the first one I'll have to take my coat off to. But that didn't make you look like this.'

Christine sat down by the fire with the doll on her knee, and proceeded to pull a frilled silk dress over its head.

'Look. If he's been up to any of his tricks . . .'

Christine cut him short with unusual curtness: 'He asked me to marry him.' She said it while looking John full in the face; the look was almost a challenge, and he experienced a feeling of guilt. Why, he couldn't fathom; but it was so strong that it swamped his indignation at Dominic's audacity.

'He wants me to go to Liverpool with him; then perhaps abroad.'

'Abroad?'

'Yes.'

'Are you going to marry him?'

'No.' She was still looking at him, the dress was only half over the doll's head. He blinked, and looked away from her down at his feet; and she sighed faintly and resumed the fitting of the dress.

John looked at her again. She was so sweet sitting there dressing the doll; why couldn't he go to her and put his arms about her and kiss her, just as often before he'd had the desire to kiss her? But he knew that, whereas for him it would merely be a kiss, to her it would be the absolute symbol of love. How he became possessed of this knowledge he didn't know, for, as he had asked himself on previous occasions, what did he know about lasses? If she were Jenny Carey or Lily McDonald he would perhaps have kissed her by now and let things take their course, but with Christine he couldn't, it wouldn't be fair. Was it even fair to come in so often? He supposed not, but he liked talking to her and Peter.

The strain that had fallen on them was relieved by David appearing. After glancing round, he asked, 'Has he gone then?'

'If you're staying in take your coat off, dear,' said Christine.

John knew to whom David was referring, he also guessed that Dominic had shooed David out.

'I'm getting a sculler for Christmas, John . . . a real one.'

'No!'

'Yes. Aren't I, Christine?'

The boy's large, dark eyes, glowing in his pale face, always aroused a tenderness in John. He was so thin, and almost girlish in his fragility.

John asked Christine, 'He doesn't mean a real one?'

'Yes. Grandfather has already bought it – it's at the quay corner. David's going to paint it himself and get it ready for the fine weather. Aren't you?'

The brother and sister smiled at each other. John realised that this was another of Peter's ways to eliminate yet another fear from his grandson. The child was highly strung and nervous, and had never quite got over the shock of seeing his parents killed in a collision between a tram and a cab when he was five years old. The episode at the gut no doubt added the fear that the boat was to erase. And the thought came to John, as it had often done lately, that Peter was a splendid man. How could anyone mock at him? By! he wished he'd been there when that crowd of hooligans burnt his hut down. They would have gone along with it.

He looked at the boy standing by Christine's side watching her put the bonnet on the doll . . . They were like a little family of saints, tender with each other, kind to everyone, and forgiving beyond his power to understand. He sat for a while longer watching Christine finishing the doll. Then he said he must get indoors and give a hand, for there were still more decorations to be hung around the walls.

Christine smiled at him as he left: 'I'm glad about your job, John.'

'Thanks. I knew you'd be . . . Tell Peter, will you?'

Christine nodded; and David cried suddenly, 'I'm going to stand at the corner, Christine, and wait for Grandfather.'

The boy chattered loudly as he and John walked down the yard, but outside, in the back lane, he pulled at John's arm and whispered, 'John, can I . . . I want to tell you something.'

'Yes, what is it, David?' John stooped to him.

'It's Dominic – Christine's frightened of him . . . she's always frightened of him. He made me go out and he said to Christine you wouldn't get her, but he would, some way. You won't let him, will you?'

John remained silent for a moment, looking at the blur that was the boy's white face, which stood out even against the newly fallen snow. It was straining up to him, appealing, pleading. 'Don't you worry, David. Christine will be all right; I'll see to that.'

'Will you, John? Will you?'

'Yes—' John patted David's hand, and the boy seemed satisfied and ran off in evident relief; and John turned thoughtfully into the backyard, to meet Katie coming out of the lavatory.

'Come in here a minute,' he said to her, drawing her into the washhouse and closing the door; 'I want you to do something for me.'

'Yes, John?'

He knew by her voice that her face was eager. 'Look; whenever you hear Dominic go in next door, you run in the other way, will you?'

'Yes, John. But if me ma . . .?'

'You can tell her you are going to return something of David's, a picture book or something.'

'Yes, John.'

'And no matter what he says, don't leave him alone with her. If he makes you and I'm in, come and tell me. You've got that now?'

'Yes, John.'

'Has he ever chased you out?'

Remembering Christine's warning, Katie merely answered, 'Sometimes.'

'Have you ever seen him . . ?' John stopped. 'Well, never mind. You know what to do, don't you?'

'Yes, John.'

Neither Katie nor Molly could remember a Christmas Eve like this one. They had faint memories of being excited at the prospect of hanging up their stockings, and a memory, not so faint, of disappointment at the meagreness of their contents when they opened them; but tonight was different. In the cupboard at the side of the fireplace were parcels, some that John brought in last night, some from Christine, and others. Katie and Molly would make running dives at the lower door of the cupboard, calling, 'I'm gonna open it, Ma! I am! I am!'

Apart from saying, 'You dare,' Mary Ellen took no notice of them. Her face wore a faint smile and her body seemed settled in contentment as her needles flew on the toe of a sock. They were the last few rows of a pair she was knitting for Shane. Why had she thought of knitting him socks for Christmas she didn't know – she could not remember ever giving him anything at Christmas, except the first Christmas they were married. She wouldn't, of course, say that these were for a Christmas box; she would just put them out with his change of clean underclothes. Perhaps he would notice them, perhaps he wouldn't.

She glanced up as John came out of the bedroom, and she had to say to Katie, 'Leave John be, hinny, he's got to go out . . . Stop clambering! you'll dirty his suit.'

'Give me a shuggy before you go. Come on, John, just one,' Katie coaxed.

'Well mind, just one . . . that's all.'

'You're worse than she is,' said Mary Ellen as John sat down and crossed his knees and stuck a foot out.

Katie clambered on to the foot, and he held her hands as he hoisted her up and down. And she giggled and shouted, 'But say it! You're not saying it!'

'Give over, Katie, John's got to go out! You'll be packed off to bed, mind . . . Oh, what's the good! You're worse than she is,' Mary Ellen exclaimed, as John began to chant with each movement of his foot:

> Father Christmas soon will come
> Laden with all treasures.
> I would like a boat to sail,
> A rocky horse with a bushy tail,
> A farthing or a spade and pail;
> Katie wants a big, fat . . . dol-ly.

After the final heave, Katie fell off his foot, laughing, and John's eyes were drawn, for a moment to Molly. She was standing to one side, smiling, yet wistful. He suddenly realised he'd never had much time for Molly, and, scatterbrain as she was, she felt it. He saw it in her face now as she stood there. Impulsively, his hand went out and he pulled her to him, saying, 'Come on, you big soft lass,' and, laughing and giggling, she sat on his foot.

'Well I never. What next, I wonder!' Mary Ellen's tone was half laughing, half derisive.

Molly wasn't so easy to lift as Katie, and before John was half-way through the rhyme she had tumbled off on to the floor, where she lay, clasping Katie, helpless with laughter.

Mary Ellen, trying not to allow her gaze to linger on this son of hers, who was looking so grand, said, 'Get yourself away, lad, or else I'll not get them to sleep the night. And if you should see Mick, send him in.'

John put on his coat, saying, 'Well, expect me when you see me – I may have to follow the men to Newcastle to get the ducks. It's six you want, isn't it?'

He left the house with his mother joining in with the laughter of the children. The sound made him happy. There was something different about this Christmas . . . Well, so there should be. A gaffer! He breathed deep of the icy air. But it wasn't that alone. There was a difference both inside and outside the house. Perhaps the difference lay in himself; life at last seemed to be opening.

He walked briskly to Tyne Dock, and stood waiting for the Shield's tram. The snow plough had been out, and the space opposite the dock gates had the appearance of land on which the grab had been at work; pale grey mounds lined the pavement, and the hurrying figures, passing in and out of the lamplight and the light from the bars, looked jet black against them. Some iron ore men, still in their working clothes, came out of a bar and hailed John: 'Why, man, you look as if you've had some money left you. Pinched our wages already? Or has the North-Eastern left you a prop boat?'

'Aye, they offered me one for Christmas, but I told them what to do with it: "A Benisaf or nothing" I said.'

There was loud laughter at this. 'I bet you did too! Well, a happy Christmas, and many of them,' they called as they moved away. 'And see we have full shifts for full bellies next year, mind.'

'Many of them,' John answered.

As he watched their unwieldy figures disappear into the darkness, he felt a thousand miles removed from them. They were good enough fellows in their way, but with one thought dominating them all . . . plenty of work, which meant plenty to eat and drink, or the reverse process. But somehow he didn't feel of them. It wasn't just since he had been made a gaffer, he had been feeling like this for some time past. Was it since he had got this coat? He didn't know; something had changed him . . .

The aisles of the open market were congested with buyers, and the shouts of the stall-holders were deafening. John saw that it would be hours yet before the stuff was sold at anywhere near his price. Ten or eleven would be the time to come back. So he walked down King Street, debating whether he should go to the second house at the Empire or the Tivoli. To whichever place he went, he couldn't go in the threepennies, not in this rig-out. It would mean the sixpennies, or even the ninepennies. That was one drawback of being dressed-up.

'Hallo, Mr O'Brien.' Mary Llewellyn stood in front of him, her arms laden with parcels.

'Good evening, Miss Llewellyn.'

They were blocking each other's path and that of the other pedestrians as, after the greeting, they stood mutely surveying each other, surprise showing in both their faces, as if this was the last place one would have expected to find the other.

'Did you ever see such a crowd?'

'No, I never have.'

John hadn't noticed the crush before, but now they seemed to be hemmed in on all sides.

'Are you doing your last-minute shopping?' she asked him.

'No . . . yes . . . Well' – his eyes twinkled – 'I'm hanging around until they give the ducks away in the market.' And as he said it, he wondered why it cost him nothing in pride to admit such things to her.

They laughed together, and one irritated shopper exclaimed, 'If you want to stand laughing your heads off clear off the flags and let people pass.'

They pulled long faces at each other, and Mary said, 'I suppose she's right.'

'Can I carry some of your parcels to the tram?' John asked.

'Well, I wasn't going home yet. But it would be a help if you'd relieve me of some of them for a time; I have a little more shopping to do.'

He took the boxes from her and stacked them under his arm. Then they turned towards the market again, John walking slightly ahead of her to make a way.

Laughing gaily, she left him outside while she went into a linen shop, and he stood gazing into the window, seeing nothing. He knew that this night was different. There was magic about it; in the cold and the snow, in people's faces, and in meeting her. Strange, up till a few months ago, he had never set eyes on her. But since that night he had been to see her they had run into each other a number of times, mostly when he was coming from work; yet she didn't seem to mind his working clothes. The first time they met, it was she who stopped and talked, just as if he were all got up instead of being covered from head to foot with splatters of wet clay. He had been working on a boat from Sweden, and the ore was embedded in lumps of clay, which made the digging and picking heavy and dirty.

After these meetings, he never allowed himself to think, using his mother's formula . . . thinking got you nowhere. She was interested in Katie, and through Katie, kind to him. That was that. But this meeting, like everything else on this Christmas Eve, was different. She had asked him to carry her parcels, and he was standing waiting for her as if he was her . . .

'I won't ask you to carry this one.' She was standing by his side, and he stared at her, not speaking; her face, under her fur-trimmed hat, shone at him like a star. For one brief second, the street and the hurrying crowds vanished, and she was alone in a vast emptiness, shining, and for him.

His face was unsmiling and his voice deep in his throat as he asked, 'Have you time . . . would you care to go to a variety show or the pantomime?'

He waited, tense and unthinking as her smile faded. The expression in her eyes changed a number of times in as many seconds, but not once did they portray annoyance or amusement.

'I should love to.' She turned away from him, and he fell into step by her side, thinking now, as he had never thought before: Had he gone mad? What of the Mr Culbert? It was Christmas Eve and perhaps she was expected at home for a party or something. What in the name of God had made him ask her! And what about money? He had five shillings of his own . . . would that do? . . . Yes. Somehow, he knew she wouldn't expect too much. But again, what in the name of God had made him do it! It was the last thing on earth he would have thought of doing . . . Or was it? Hadn't he often wondered what it would be like to take someone of her stamp out? Yes, but just as one dreamt dreams, never for one moment expecting them to happen. The funny thing was she hadn't refused. She hadn't been merely polite, either; she seemed quite sincere when she said, 'I'd love to.' Well, now he must put his thinking cap on. They would have to go in the very best seats, and she'd have to have some bullets. Bullets! he repeated scornfully . . . chocolates. Get a little box . . . A box! No need to go mad altogether. She wouldn't expect it anyway. He pushed his shoulders back. Expected or not, he'd get a box.

'Do you think there's time for me to make a telephone call?'

They were standing outside the Empire, and for a moment she drifted from him into the class that made telephone calls.

'Where do you have to go? The post office?' he asked.

'Yes; I won't be more than five minutes.'

'Of course. Come on.' He shouldered his way through the crowd. Class or no class, she was going out with him, this once anyway. And he'd do the thing properly; it would be something to remember.

In spite of her fur coat and rinking boots, Mary shivered as she waited in the telephone box. It had happened as she hoped it might. But where would it lead? . . . There was time enough to ask that later, she told herself. What she had to do now was to smooth things over with those at home.

She gave a gentle sigh when she heard her father's voice say, 'Yes. Who is it?'

'It's me, Mary.'

'Mary? Why, where are you? What's up? You should be home by now; we're nearly ready.'

'Look, dear. I won't be home . . . not until . . . quite late.'

'But where are you? You know you can't do that, Mary; we're going to Gilbert's! Look lass' – he cut her short as she was about to speak – 'it's Christmas, and we want things to go peaceable like. Where are you, anyway?'

'Shields Post Office.'

'What's made you change your mind?'

'I . . . Well, I met a friend.'

'But it isn't right. You know what a state this will put your mother in.'

'I never wanted to go. I've told her so all along. She shouldn't have accepted for me . . . Look, Father, can't you see what Mother is trying to do?'

'Yes. I know, I know.'

'Well then, why should you want me to go? And anyway, it isn't fair to Gilbert. She's giving him the idea that I can be coaxed round, and I can't.'

'Who's your friend?'

'Oh, you . . . you don't know him.'

'It's a man then?'

'Yes, it's a man.'

'Well, this is going to be a lovely evening for me.'

Mary laughed softly. 'It's yourself you're thinking about.'

'Well partly.' There was a chuckle. 'You'll be for it tomorrow, mind. And somehow I did think this was going to be a peaceful Christmas.'

'It's the loveliest Christmas I've ever known. Goodbye, dear.'

'Here! Mary . . . look, who's this fellow?'

'We may talk about him later.'

'Mary . . . you'll go to Midnight Mass? For God's sake don't miss that, or there'll be hell to pay.'

'We'll see. Goodbye. Wait. Do you want to know something?'

'What is it?'

'I like you, Mr Llewellyn.'

Laughing, she hung up the phone, and almost ran to join John.

Mary Ellen yawned. She wished John was in, and then she'd go to bed. She leaned back and glanced up at the clock . . . ten-past eleven. Had he managed to get a duck?

She sat with her chair drawn up close to the fire, her feet on the fender, her skirt tucked up on to her lap, exposing her short legs to the dying ashes. The house was quiet, only Shane's and Dominic's snores alternating with each other's from the rooms. Behind her, the girls lay curled up under the thin brown blankets and a heap of coats; and, at each end of the mantelpiece hung their packed stockings, together with one for Mick.

As she yawned again, she heard the muffled pad of footsteps on the yard, and, pulling down her skirt, she got up to open the scullery door as John quietly lifted the latch of the back dor.

Stupefied, Mary Ellen gazed at him; then, in a whispered exclamation, said, 'In the name of God! have you bought the market?'

John laughed softly as he lowered a great parcel on to the table, followed by a stone brown paper bag and a square box. 'You'll never guess what it is . . . it's a turkey! And this is a bag of fruit. And there's bullets in that box.' He spoke softly and rapidly.

'A turkey! But where'd you get the money, lad?' Mary Ellen looked closely at him. If she didn't know differently she'd have thought he'd had a drop – his eyes were shining, like coals . . . Perhaps it was the frost.

'We . . . I waited till the last thing, and I got him for four bob.'

'But what's all this other?'

'Fruit.'

'A stone bag of it!' Mary Ellen looked amazed. 'Are they specked?'

'No, I should say not.'

John did not look at her. He had taken off his cap and was combing his hair. 'Miss Llewellyn sent them for the bairns.'

Mary Ellen stared silently at his profile. Miss Llewellyn.

John turned to her, putting on his cap again. 'I'm going to Midnight Mass at Jarrow. I'm getting the last tram up.'

Miss Llewellyn and Midnight Mass. Her lad going to Midnight Mass with Miss Llewellyn! It was funny but she'd been thinking about Midnight Mass earlier on this evening, feeling the need to give thanks for all her good fortune at this Christmas time. It was years since she had been to Midnight Mass, and in spite of her tiredness, she'd thought: For two pins I'd go to Midnight Mass if John was in. She would have worn her new coat, although it wouldn't have mattered about going in her shawl; there'd be mostly shawls and mufflers there anyway. And she'd imagined herself kneeling as she used to do in the aisle, or even on the altar steps, wrapped about in the thick, incensed air, full of hushed rustle, so full would the church be. And for a brief hour she would really feel the Child was being born and be one with Mary in her travail.

But John was going to Midnight Mass, and he was going with Miss Llewellyn. She knew now the reason for the light in his eyes.

John tried not to show undue haste, but there was only a few minutes before the tram would pass the bottom of the street, and she would be on it. Already it was late, and perhaps they'd not get in the church. He did not want this to happen, for he had the desire to kneel at Mass with her, not only because it would mean being with her another hour or more, but because to go to Mass with a lass had a subtle meaning, which neither needed nor could be defined by words.

The four hours they had been together seemed to spread back down his lifetime. There seemed no moment when he had not watched the expressions dancing over her face like shadows in a garden, nor a moment when he had not been carrying her parcels or buying her chocolates, or when he was not sitting with her in the dark and laughing with her at a pantomime; or when there was a second in his life when she did not urge him to remain quiet while the stallholder, in desperation, brought his final and unmovable price of eight shillings a turkey down to four shillings! or when had he not watched her taking her choice of fruit, bananas, pomegranates, oranges, apples, pears and nuts. And now they were going to Midnight Mass, and there would be no tram back. They would have to walk all the way from Dee Street, in the centre of Jarrow, to the heart of Simonside. It would be a long way for her, and difficult walking, for the pavements were sheets of knobbly grey ice; and it would be a long way to walk without touching each other. She might have to take his arm – he thought of it as 'link' – Miss Llewellyn and him linking!

A surge of feeling that demanded some form of expression swept through him, and, stooping, he kissed Mary Ellen swiftly on the side of the brow. Without a word, he was gone. And Mary Ellen stood fingering the place his lips had brushed . . . Her lad had kissed her . . . for the first time since he was a tiny bairn. And because he was in love.

She had been worried lately, thinking he was struck on her next door, and had wondered where it would lead, for she doubted, if he took her, there'd be much happiness for him; not that she had anything really against the lass, only that terrifying religion of hers. God knew there was no happiness came out of a mixed marriage. With a Church of England one it would be bad enough, but with a Spiritualist! . . . And yet, as awful as that possibility seemed, he would have had a little show of happiness in a way, whereas now there was none for him that she could see. For what was the obstacle of religion compared with the obstacle of class? Had he gone mad? And that Llewellyn lass, too? Where did they think it would lead? Her da was a boatbuilder; and a docker, even a gaffer, would be so much midden muck to him. They had a fancy house, with even a lavatory inside, so Katie said, and kept a parlourmaid and a cook. Was the lass mad? There was no-one better than her lad, no-one in the wide world, but he was a docker and from the fifteen streets. And that lass must know nothing could come of it . . . She was struck by his size and his ways, and she would shelve him when the novelty wore off. And what would it do to him? She thought of his eyes when he had come in, and slowly she sat down by the fire again and stared into its rose-grey embers.

CHAPTER EIGHT

NEW YEAR'S EVE

It was a good thing New Year's Eve fell on a Saturday, John thought, for it meant one day less holiday. They would start work on Tuesday, the ones, anyway, who were sober enough. He wanted work, and more work. If he had his own way he'd carry on, night and day, for three parts of the week; he'd make them throw the stuff out of those holds as it had never been thrown out before. He wanted money. God, how he wanted money.

He sat before the fire, dressed in his working clothes, tense with thinking. Shane sat opposite him, sober and sullen; he'd been drunk only once during the holidays. This was a record. Was he turning over a new leaf? John wondered, or was it because he was forced to realise that the more he drank the more he twitched? But twitching or not, tonight he'd likely have a skinful. What would she say to this house and the lot of them? Would she take them as she took him? That was too much to ask. Whereas last Saturday night he thought he'd never known a moment in his life without her, now, across the vast space of time since he last saw her, he could not even recall her face clearly. Again and again he tried to visualise her; but always her face ran into a blur. Even when he attempted to recapture the wonder and the ecstatic feeling of achievement as, with her on his arm, he walked past the fifteen streets, huddled and sleeping under the star-carpeted sky, the feeling would slither away. It was strange, too, but he could not actually remember how he left her. What did they say to each other? Nothing much. They were quiet on the journey back; all the laughter and fun had been left in Shields market. As they walked up Simonside Bank, he had asked if she were tired, and she had replied that she'd never felt less tired. Yet she sounded sort of sleepy when she said it . . . But there must have been more than that said. One thing he knew he hadn't said: 'Can I see you again?'

Why hadn't he, when it was foremost in his mind during those last few minutes with her? But foremost, too, had been the thought of money. He couldn't really ask her out unless he intended taking her somewhere. Well, he could have taken her out tonight.

All this morning he was hoping he would run into her as he came home from work. And when he didn't, he told himself it was the best thing that could have happened; there were many things he could do with those extra few shillings – his mother would know what to do with them. So perhaps it was all for the best – he moved impatiently in his chair. Perhaps . . . there was no perhaps about it. What was he aiming at, anyway? Was his brain softening, just because of that one night? If he were to see her again, what would it lead to? So intense was the urgency of the question that he almost spoke aloud. You are going stark, staring mad! Look around, and ask yourself what you and she can ever be to each other . . . even if she does like you . . . He was on his feet, staring down into the fire; she likes me all right, I know it. She more than likes me . . . she feels the same as I do.

Mary Ellen could remain silent no longer; John's drawn, twisted face was wringing her heart. Shane was dozing now, and she whispered, 'What's up, lad?'

'Nothing. I'm going to have a wash.'

He went quickly into the scullery, and as he washed himself Mary Ellen gazed sadly at his back. She knew this would happen – she knew there'd be no happiness in it for him. She wanted to go to him and in some way comfort him; but her mind was lifted from him to Molly.

Molly's screeching voice came from the back lane, and Mary Ellen knew she was fighting again, for she was hurling rhymes at someone's head:

Annie Kelly's got a big fat belly,
And her belly wobbles like jelly.

My God! that lass nearly fourteen and yelling things out like that. Mary Ellen pushed past John and opened the back door.

'You, Molly! come in here!'

Molly was having her last word: 'You wouldn't do much for God if the divil was dead, Annie Kelly. You're mean, so you are. Poor Nancy!'

'Come in here!' Mary Ellen hauled Molly over the step. 'You can thank your lucky stars your da's dozing,' she whispered fiercely, 'or I'd bray you!'

'Well, I was only sticking up for Nancy,' Molly snivelled. 'She's been sent back from her place, Mrs Fitzsimmons won't have her. And Annie wouldn't let her play with us; she punched her.'

'Sent back from her place,' Mary Ellen repeated to John. 'That means the do's off.'

'Damn good thing, too,' John answered shortly. 'They'll be yelling out for the money before the new year's in a week.'

'It'll likely be spent now, lad, in any case.'

The door opened again, and Katie rushed in breathless.

Mary Ellen hushed her: 'Be quiet, hinny! And close that door, the cold's enough to cut you in two.'

'Ma, can I go with Christine? And Molly too? There's a big stretch frozen hard, past Cleveland Place, and everybody's going there to slide . . . proper sliding. Christine's got proper sliding skates with knives on the bottom. And there's a man there with a fire selling roast taties . . . Oh, Ma, can we go?'

'Go on, Ma, let's.' Molly joined her plea to Katie's.

'What about it cracking?' Mary Ellen asked John. 'Will it be deep?'

'It won't crack in this frost.'

He was drying himself, and asked Katie, 'How does Christine know there's skating? Has she been?' He hadn't seen Christine since Christmas Day, and then only to wish her a happy Christmas and to thank her rather sheepishly for the tie. He knew now why he hadn't kissed Christine, and the knowledge made him strangely embarrassed in her presence.

'Yes,' answered Katie. 'She was there yesterday, her and David. She says they're going to have a big fire on the bank the night to light the ice up.'

'How far past Cleveland Place is it?'

'It's in Roper's Field.'

'You'd better give it a miss,' said Mary Ellen; 'you'll slide the boots off your feet.'

'Not any sooner than with sliding in the streets,' said John.

'But it's them falling through I'm afraid of.'

'Don't worry,' he said; 'I'll take a walk up and have a look.'

He went into the bedroom and started to change hastily. Roper's Field . . . off the Simonside Road. There was just a chance she might be there.

In the kitchen of Cumberland Villa, the two maids were standing near the partly open door, straining their ears.

'Hear anything?' asked the cook.

'Not a word,' replied Phyllis. 'And the way the missis looked I thought she was going to explode. I bet you anything you like though she'd heard about that fellow.'

'I wouldn't believe a word of it,' said Cook. 'And I'd be careful what I was saying if I was you. Miss Mary walking out with one of the O'Briens! Huh! I'll believe that when I see it.'

'I tell you our Doris saw them in the market, and our Doris knows them both as well as I know you. She was standing behind them, and she said they were laughing and talking together like . . . well, like a couple who was walking out . . . Sh! Listen.'

Phyllis's elbow stopped the cook's retort. 'There!' she hissed. 'Get an earful of that. Have you ever heard the missis go off like that before? What did I tell you?'

In the drawing-room, James Llewellyn was appealing to his wife: 'Look, Beatrice, leave this to me.' He spoke gently and soothingly;

the jocular brusqueness, which was his usual defence against her, was gone from his tone.

'Too much has been left to you, and look at the result!' She turned from him, and again addressed her daughter, with quiet tenseness now. 'No wonder you wouldn't tell me who you were with on Christmas Eve! It is to your credit that you were ashamed.'

Mary stood with her elbow resting on the mantelpiece; her face was half turned from her mother, and she stared unseeing into the fire, her attitude belying the anger that was filling her body.

'You must have lost every spark of decency. You never, at any time, had a proper sense of what is correct. But this! Have you any idea how I felt when Florence Dudley told me they saw you in the Empire with a . . . docker?' Beatrice Llewellyn spat out the last word, her thin nose and delicately chiselled mouth almost meeting over it. Her large pale blue eyes showed depths of purple, and her expression was weighed with actual hate as she looked at this girl whom she had come to think of as being by her but not of her. This last disgusting episode proved only too conclusively from which side she had inherited her qualities. 'Will Dudley says he comes from the fifteen streets and the family are notorious,' she ended.

Mary faced her mother, and her tone was infuriatingly quiet when she said, 'Of course they are. Anyone within a three-miles radius of the fifteen streets knows that. If you didn't shut out every unpleasantness from your life you would have heard it before . . . One of the main things for which they are notorious is hunger. Dwell upon that the next time you're preparing for the Dudleys coming to dinner.'

Beatrice Llewellyn stood aghast – never before had Mary dared to address her so. 'They are poor because they drink and gamble. And you! You are a slut! You were out with that man until three o'clock in the morning. Do you think it won't be all round Jarrow and Shields by now?'

'I hope so.'

Mary's stillness seemed to lift the tension to breaking point. Her father cried, 'Here, lass! Here, that's enough!' and Beatrice Llewellyn perpetrated what was to her mind unforgivable . . . she screamed. 'You low creature!' The words seemed to emerge from the top of her head. 'You're utterly debased. I shall have Father O'Malley to you. Yes. Yes. I shall . . . Leave me alone!' – she tore her arm from her husband's soothing hand, and flung like a small tornado out of the room.

During their twenty-six years of married life, James Llewellyn had never seen his wife lose control; this was the first show of sincere passion he had witnessed, and it left him, not only shaken, but worried. Usually she tried gentle tears and studied silences, alternated with the persistent reiteration of her point. But for Beatrice to lose her dignity meant this affair had indeed struck home.

'You've done it this time.' He came to the fireplace and knocked out his pipe against the bars. 'You know, lass, it was a bit of a shock.'

'To you too?' Mary asked sharply.

'Aye . . . yes. It's no good saying one thing and thinking another. But when Will Dudley got on about seeing you with one of the Big O'Briens I could have punched him in the face. Although he put it very nicely, I could tell it had afforded them a good topic of conversation all the week, and that was why Florence Dudley was so anxious for us to drop in this morning. When your mother came downstairs with her I thought she'd collapse . . . How long has it been going on, lass?'

'It hasn't been going on, as you call it; that was the only time.'

'Oh . . . Well' – there was a measure of relief in her father's voice – 'and are you . . . Well, is it finished?'

'I don't know.'

'You don't know! What do you mean, lass?'

'I mean that if it rests with me it won't be finished.' Mary turned towards him, nervously rubbing the palms of her hands together. 'I haven't seen him since, because he never asked me.'

James Llewellyn stared at his daughter. His lass, who was the best-looking lass for miles, and who could have her pick, was in love. Even had she not practically put it unashamedly into words, he could see it in her eyes. She was in love with this dock worker, John O'Brien; and not in the light-hearted way that lassies fell in love, but in an earnest, stubborn, painful way, a way that would leave a mark on her, however things went. Well, he wasn't going to stand by and see her make a hash of her life, and say nothing. This was one time her mother was right. 'Now see here' – he planted his feet firmly apart and pointed his finger at her – 'you know which side I've always been on, don't you? You know that life would have been much easier for me if I'd taken your mother's part all along.'

As his fingers wagged at her, Mary thought: he's nearly as big as John, and he has the same clumsy movements, a sort of endearing gaucheness. All the money in the world won't polish him. Anyway, he was once a dock worker himself, so why can't he understand about this?

'But I want you to understand, lass,' James Llewellyn went on, 'that I'm with your mother in this.'

'You'd rather see me married to Gilbert then?'

'I don't want you to marry anyone you don't fancy . . . But yes' – he thrust out his head – 'yes, I'd rather see you married to Gilbert than carrying on with this business. At least you wouldn't starve . . . Oh, Mary' – his large leathery face crumpled – 'stop while there's time. You don't know what you're running yourself into. Lass, I hate to say it, but I've seen those O'Briens rolling from one side of the arches to the other. I even remember the mother, years ago, a little body, standing outside the bars with the bairns clinging round her, trying to get a few shillings out of her man before he blued the lot. I tell you, lass, they're noted.'

'He doesn't drink.'

'That's what he says.'

'He doesn't, Father.' There was a fierce ring in her voice. 'And he's not just a docker either; he's been made a gaffer.'

'What! Did he tell you that? How old is he?'

'Twenty-two.' Her head was thrust up in defiance, daring him to say, 'So he's younger than you.'

But what he said was, 'He's a damned liar! There's no fellow could be made a gaffer at twenty-two. Thirty-two would be more like it. He's stuffing you, lass. Can't you see?' He was angry for her.

'No, he's not. Anyway, it should be easy for you to find out.'

'Yes. Quite easy. But even so, if he is a gaffer, what's that?'

Mary did not reply but stood looking at him, her eyes wide and sad, for she too, was asking herself the same question . . . He was worth something better than that.

To James Llewellyn, she looked at this moment pathetic, and he could never remember his joyous, laughter-loving daughter looking this way. Taking her by the hand, he said, 'Hinny' – using the endearing word that was banned in the house because of its commonness – 'I only want your happiness. What do you think I've worked for all these years? To leave you comfortable. Look, my dear, tell me you'll drop this.'

The tears gathering in her eyes obscured her vision. Why, oh why, did they think money could buy off or replace a feeling that was made of intangible stuff? Money and love were on two different planes . . . Yet were they so divided? Love needed money for its existence. Without it, more often than not it died, as the body, wherein it was housed, fought and struggled for life. Yet if the chance were given her, would she risk the survival of this love that seemed to be eating her away? Oh yes, yes. The tears spilled on to her face. 'I can't. If he asks me out again, I'll go.'

She watched her father leave the room and close the door after him with painful slowness . . .

Mary was sitting in her own room, crouched over the fire, when the dinner bell rang. She made no move to carry out its summons. Nor, as the time went on, did anyone come to enquire why. Never before had she felt so unhappy, and she couldn't see the unhappiness lifting; it stretched on and on into the future, for the only person capable of dispelling it was as class-conscious as her mother. She felt now that Christmas Eve had been merely a lapse of John's, and that during the quiet walk back from Jarrow he was already regretting it; he had left her with scarcely a word. Every dinner-time and teatime of this past week she had fought with herself not to stroll casually down through the arches, presumably on her way to Shields, in the hope of encountering him. But some hard core of pride said no . . . she wouldn't scheme to trap him into asking her out; if he wanted to see her he would find a way; and there was always the post.

What a New Year's Eve! She got up and wandered about the room. If only she could see him for a moment, run into him accidentally, as she had done last Saturday night . . . But wouldn't it have been better had they not met at all – not last Saturday, but in the first instance. He attracted her that first night he sat in this room, and she had been unable to get him out of her mind since.

The memory of that meeting brought back the niggling envy of Christine . . . Was that girl something to him? Was she the reason why he hadn't asked her to repeat the evening? She didn't know . . .

She went upstairs and put on her outdoor things, for she felt that were she to stay indoors any longer she would scream, as her mother had done this morning. Remembering her mother's voice and look, she realised that whether she pursued this business to its height or it merely fizzled out, the last supports of the barrier that had been erecting itself for years between them were hammered home today, and their combined lifetimes would not be long enough to break it down.

Standing on the bank at the edge of the field, John looked down in amazement on the scene. He had witnessed nothing like it before. The field, which dipped into a shallow valley, had every appearance of a lake, and there was scarcely a yard of its surface which had not its moving figure. Very few had skates; the main sport seemed to be concentrated on the long single and double slides. On the double slides young men and girls crossed hands, skimming away with enviable balance towards the centre of the ice. Children had their slides nearer the edge, and were watched by spectators, who outnumbered the skaters. Some of the young lads were already getting the bonfire going. The air was filled with laughter and shouting, the smell of burning wood, and the thick, comforting smell of roasting potatoes. The faces of the crowd seemed alight with a newborn joy.

The feeling of mass gaiety puzzled John. It was this whiteness; it had gone to their heads and caused a madness. The drabness of life was lost under the spell of its gleaming sparkle, and the people seemed to be deluded into thinking this clean, white world would remain – their house roofs were white, their window sills, their doorsteps. The docks and the ships, too, lay buried under the clean illusion – even on the top of the highest mast there was a virgin white cap of snow, fast and secure and promising to remain for ever. There would be no tomorrow, or the next day, when the gutters would be choked with brown slush, the roads become rivers, and the houses grey again, and they themselves grey and blue, feet wet, bodies shivering. It was cold now; but this was a dry cold, which quickened the blood, freed the perception and brought all the instincts to the surface, giving to each person an awareness of his existence, which demanded of the body that it be used, now, at this very time.

As he stood there John began to feel something of this mass joy. The whole scene, which seemed to have been dropped from another world, where only light laughter existed, bewildered him, and part of him realised that it was out of place in the realistic grimness of this area.

He watched Christine gliding gracefully in small circles near where Katie, Molly and David were sliding with other children. She looked little more than a child herself, a dark, elfin, slip of a child.

Christine caught sight of him, and waved and beckoned him on to the ice; but he shook his head and waved his hand in refusal. And after a while, she glided to where he stood on the bank.

'Isn't it wonderful! Come on . . . I'll pull you.'

'Not on your life,' he laughed.

He was relieved that there was no stiffness in her manner, for it must have been evident to her that he had avoided seeing her during this past week. She looked very fetching, standing below him with a red tam-o'-shanter on the back of her head, and for a fleeting second he felt a regret that it was not she who was filling his mind and body at this moment, for then things would have been plain sailing.

'A big thing like you afraid of the ice!' she called up to him, teasingly.

'You'd be more afraid if you got me on there and I fell on you.'

'I'll risk it. Come on. Come on, John' – the pleading was in her eyes and voice.

He shook his head: 'I've a number of other ways of making a fool of myself besides that.'

Christine saw that it was no use trying to coax him; nevertheless, she stood for a time gazing up at him. Then, without further words, she turned and skimmed away again.

John continued to watch her and the children, but between times his eyes would search the field. Although the light was fading he could still see the further bank, and he thought it would have to be very dark to prevent him from picking her out from the crowd. He noticed Katie leave the long line of sliders and walk quickly towards him.

'What's the matter?' he asked. 'Are you tired, or after a hot tatie?'

'Our Dominic's along there, John. He's watching Christine.'

John remained silent, and did not turn to the spot Katie indicated but looked to where Christine was still whirling unconcerned. 'Is he all right?' he asked; which meant, was he sober.

'Yes, he looks it . . . and . . . and he's got a collar and tie on too.' Katie's eyes fell to John's collar and tie, then to his new coat; and she added, with awe in her voice, 'He's got a new coat an' all, John.' Her eyes were round in amazement – the advent of any new clothes in the house was something to dwell upon, for in most cases their approach was awaited for weeks. As late as last night Dominic had no new clothes, yet here he was, all dressed up.

John's mouth moved into a twisted grin. Dominic wasn't to be outdone then. The buying of new clothes would be all to the good if it kept him off the drink; but John knew only too well that someone would have to whistle for the money for the coat. He glanced casually now in Dominic's direction. Yes, there he was, practically head and shoulders above the crowd, and even from this distance and the little John could see of him, the difference in his appearance was noticeable.

Momentarily John's attitude towards his brother softened, and he wondered if Dominic's feeling for Christine was anything like his own for Mary. But his wondering was definitely only momentary . . . He would have gone about it in a different way if it was . . . and he still paid visits to 'Lady Pansy'. Moreover, his love for Christine, if it could be called such, had instilled her with nothing but fear.

He bent down to Katie: 'Don't forget what I told you about keeping with Christine.'

'No, John, I won't.'

'No matter what he says on the way home, don't you leave her, mind.'

'No, John.'

'Go on then, on your slide; I'll be here for some time yet.'

Groups of lads and lassies on the banks had started singing. 'Keep your feet still, Geordie, hinny' vied with 'Cushy Butterfield', and 'Bleydon Races' with 'Auld Lang Syne'. But now the careless mad pleasure of the scene was dispelled for John, for Dominic was there. His presence acted like a pressure forcing out the ease from his body and the quietness from his mind, and replacing it with antipathy, which was the only true bond between them.

As the daylight of the last day of the year faded, the twilight seemed to urge on the gaiety. The bonfire was well alight now, sending up showers of sparks through the grey dusk into the far-reaching blue beyond. John found that after looking towards the fire for a time the skaters on the ice appeared like dark, scribbled lines on a white canvas. He closed his eyes and pressed his eyeballs with his fingers. And when he opened them, there she was, standing not a yard from him.

When he was a child, his mother, if she had a piece of toffee for him, would say, 'Shut your eyes and open your mouth and see what God will send you.' He had shut his eyes, and look what God had sent him.

He took a slow step towards her – Dominic and all he stood for was gone, and the magic and madness of the scene was upon him fully now. No subterfuge need be used on a night like this; truth was easy, and desirable.

'I wondered if you would be here.'

At his words, her face, which had been set and strained, fell into a smile; not her usual, light-flashing smile, but one holding a tinge of sadness.

John did not detect the sadness . . . sadness and this girl were as apart as the earth and the sky. To his mind, she spelt radiance, to his body, magnetism; she was ecstasy and joy. But he had only plain words with which to speak: 'Have you ever seen anything to equal this around these parts?' He did not take his eyes from her face, but indicated the ice with a movement of his head.

'Never. It's like something you'd see in Switzerland.'

Her eyes, playing over his face, made him drunk with feeling; all the barriers between them were being swept away on a swift moving tide. The need was upon him to touch her, if only her hand.

'Have you been sliding?' he asked.

'I haven't any skates.'

'What about using our feet? It seems popular.'

'Here?' She pointed to the entwined throng below them.

'No. Let's go round to the other side; there are fewer people there, and if we fall there'll be less to laugh at us.'

Mary made an almost imperceptible motion with her head. The action was more pointed than words in its acquiescence.

They turned together. Then stopped. It was the red tam-o'-shanter that brought itself to John's notice. Without it, Christine, at that moment, would have been merely another face – even Katie was just part of the crowd.

Christine and Katie stood hand in hand below them, silent and staring.

'Why! Hallo, Katie.'

'Hallo, Miss Llewellyn.' Katie's fat, rosy cheeks were very like the proverbial apples as she smiled.

'Are you having a lovely time?'

'Yes, Miss Llewellyn.'

'And did you have a nice Christmas?'

'Oh yes, Miss Llewellyn. Oh, lovely! And thank you, Miss Llewellyn, for the presents and all the lovely fruit.'

Mary's eyes were forced from Katie's to the girl in the red hat. The girl was staring at her; her eyes, dark and enormous, seemed to glow with a purple gleam. Even in the dusk, their light was penetrating, and Mary felt it stripping her. It was an odd sensation. It was almost as if the girl was looking into the very depths of her heart and finding there things of which even she herself was not aware.

When John said, 'This is Christine,' the girl, with a lightning movement, whirled Katie round and away, and in a moment they were lost in the moving figures and the dimness.

The situation had suddenly become awkward. Why had Christine dashed off like that? He knew fine well why! His neck became hot.

Then a surge of relief swept over him . . . thank God he had never made up to her! He was free in that sense, anyway . . . free for Mary. Oh, the daring, the audacity, the madness of it!

He turned towards her again, and this time the sadness in her face was clear to him. She too then had seen how Christine felt. He must make it clear to her that there was nothing in it.

'What about the slide?' he said.

Without answering, she turned from him, and they threaded their way among the crowd.

'Christine's a nice girl,' he began lamely.

'Yes, she looks it.'

They were forced to step apart to make way for a group of running children, and when they came together again, he continued, 'I don't think she'll ever grow up though. She's . . . well, she's just like Katie.'

She looked at him and smiled, a small, understanding smile. He smiled back at her, and they walked on in silence.

The far bank was almost deserted, the crowds having been drawn to the light of the bonfire and the man with the brazier and the roasting potatoes. The ice, too, was not so smooth here, for tufts of grass broke the surface.

'Shall we chance it?' He held out his hand, and she took it and stepped from the bank on to the ice. 'Single or double?'

'Single I think, for a start . . . You go first, I haven't been on the ice for two years.'

'Two years! It must be at least eight since I was on a slide . . . Well, here goes.' He ran and started to slide; wobbled, steadied himself, and wobbled again; then, with a suddenness that found every bone in his body, he sat down on the ice with a heavy plop.

With a sureness that spoke of past schooling, she reached him as he was getting to his feet. He was laughing, and said, 'Good job you weren't behind me.' And when he felt her hands gently dusting his shoulders he prolonged his own banging of his clothes to shake off the loose snow.

'Shall we try again?' he asked.

'If you like,' she said; but there was little enthusiasm in her voice.

'Do you want to slide?' He was facing her now, their breaths were mingling and their eyes holding. The words were a question that did not mean what it asked, and she answered with a candour that seemed to be of the very essence of the day.

'No.'

He reached out and took her hand, and they walked carefully towards the bank again.

'Would you . . . would you like to go for a walk? Or what about Shields?'

'Not Shields. Let's go for a walk.'

They walked down the narrow lane and on to the main road without speaking. Being a country road it was unlit, and in spite of the snow covering it, it appeared black after the glare of the fire-lit field. The darkness gave him courage, and he unclasped her hand and drew her arm through his, entwining his fingers through hers and holding them close to his coat. They walked on in step, and as he felt her hip moving against his he became conscious of the stillness between them, a stillness that seemed to be waiting only for the right moment to burst into sound . . . sound that would bewitch and delight him, because it would be her voice telling him what he wanted, above all things, to know. But as they walked on, it seemed to him as if the silence would never be broken.

When, of one mind, they turned down a side lane and stopped and faced each other, he told himself that never before had any man felt for a woman as he felt for her. But now the moment had come he seemed paralysed, and even the potency of his feeling could not lift him over the barrier to her. It was she who opened the way, with such words that flung barriers, prejudices and classes into oblivion: 'Oh, John, if you don't tell me I won't be able to bear it.'

There was a second of wonder-filled time before his arms went about her, not gently, as he had imagined them so often doing, but savagely, crushing her into him until he could feel her racing heart pounding against him. He did not kiss her immediately. His lips travelled the whole surface of her face before they reached hers, but when they did, their bodies merged and rose, above the snow and ice, above their separate lives, away from this earth to some ethereal place where time is not. When, swaying together, their lips parted, it seemed to them both as if they had actually fallen into another era of time, so much did they know of each other.

'Mary.'

She did not answer but leaned upon him, moving her face against his.

'I love you.'

Her arms tightened about him.

'I'm mad . . . I shouldn't say that.'

'Oh beloved.'

Beloved . . . a woman had called him beloved . . . him! This beautiful woman, this girl, this . . .

'How is it you can care for a fellow like me? Mary! Oh, Mary!'

Her reply was smothered against him. And when he would have again begun deprecating himself her fingers covered his mouth. 'You're the finest person I know – there is no-one to come up to you.'

She cut short his protest: 'John, let nothing ever separate us, will you?' Her voice was earnest. 'Nothing, nor no-one. Promise. Never.'

The urgency in her voice stilled him – it was almost as if she was pleading with him. That she should be asking to let nothing separate them seemed fantastic.

Taking her hand gently from his lips he said, 'It's me should be putting that to you. What do you think will be said when this gets about? Will you be able to stand it?'

Her answer was the covering of his mouth by hers with such passion that all the longing, all the loneliness of his life, all that was drab and tawdry, vanished. Her love for him raised him to a new level of self-esteem.

'Oh, Mary, my love . . . my dear . . . do you know what you mean to me? Do you know what you stand for?' He was gentle now, holding her face between his large hands, peering at her, seeing each feature in his mind's eye: 'You're beautiful.'

'I couldn't be too beautiful for you.'

Her words were like notes of tender music, borne on the white wings of the snow. He shook his head slowly at the wonder of them. 'I don't know how you can love me . . . you who have everything. I'm ignorant, and I'm ashamed of it. Mary' – his voice was shy – 'will you teach me?'

'Oh, my dear, you don't need . . .'

He stopped her, 'Yes, I do need. And you know I do. I never want you to be ashamed of me.'

'John . . . John, don't.'

His humility brought the tears to her eyes, as he went on, 'And there's my folk. It isn't that I'm ashamed, only . . . well, I suppose you've heard of our family. There hasn't been much chance for any of us; my mother slaved all her days, and . . . and my father and brother . . .'

'Sh!' She leaned gently against him, stroking his cheek as a mother would soothe a child.

She murmured something, and he whispered in awe, 'What?'

And she repeated, 'It's a case of Ruth and Naomi.'

But still he did not understand, yet although the words held no meaning for him, her tone conveyed a deep humility, and he was filled with wonder.

CHAPTER NINE

NANCY

The home-made paper chains lay in a jumbled heap on one side of the table, the three bought ones lying neatly concertinaed by themselves together with the honeycomb ball. These would do for another year, Mary Ellen decided, if she could hide them somewhere. She had never before been so late in taking down the decorations; it was 5th January, and she was just escaping bad luck by taking them down today, the morrow would be too late. But it had been nice to leave them up till the last minute, for they carried on the feeling of this wonderful Christmas and New Year. By! – she stopped in her work to look out of the kitchen window to the roofs beyond, where the last of the snow was sliding in a grey mass into the gutter – she had never known such a time. The stuff they'd had to eat! And Shane being sober, even on New Year's Eve; and no rows in the house. There was Dominic's surliness, of course, but she was used to that and had not allowed it to spoil things. And anyway, he was out most of the time . . . all night, once.

This business of John's troubled her at times; but what could she do, for he said nothing. He was going about looking like a cat with nine tails. She hoped to God something would happen to make it last. But how could it – him and Miss Llewellyn! Where would it end? . . . Well, she wouldn't worry – everything else was going fine; the coal house was full of coal and the bairns were rightly set up with clothes, the last, thanks to them next door – the thought of thanks took shape before she could stop it – well, anyway, they had been good, no matter what they were. She'd wished time and again she could go and thank them, but she was unable to bring herself to do so. The fear of them still held her, and she couldn't face them, so she had sent her thanks by the bairns and John. The fear had strengthened in an odd way too during these past weeks, for Mick's ear had stopped running for the first time in two years, and Shane . . . Why was it, after all these years, Shane had eased off the drink and his twitching had lessened? Did he find himself lying on a platform above the bed with Peter Bracken's hands moving over him? My God! She shuddered. It was the first time she had admitted to herself the influence of Peter Bracken on her the night the child was born. She put her hand inside her blouse and felt for her rosary, which she had taken to wearing round her neck of late.

Staring out of the window, she said her beads: Hail, Mary, full of grace, the Lord is with thee. Blessed art thou amongst women, and blessed is the fruit of thy womb, Jesus . . . She had gone through two decades, when she saw the backyard door open and Hannah Kelly enter the yard.

Hastily, she fastened her blouse.

What did Hannah want so early in the morning? . . . There was something curious about her walk: she couldn't have had a drop already, surely. She watched Hannah fumble with the latch of the kitchen door, and when she came in and closed the door, and stood with her back to it, Mary Ellen exclaimed, 'Why, lass, you're bad! Come and sit down.'

Hannah shook her head and murmured, 'Oh, Mary Ellen!'

'What is it? Is it Joe?'

Hannah again shook her head. She tried to speak but the words refused to come, her mouth opening and shutting like that of a fish.

'What is it then? Nancy?'

Hannah's eyes drooped and her head fell on her chest.

'Tell me, lass. What is it?'

'Dear God, dear God,' Hannah said, and her voice sounded small and lost, and she looked like a bewildered child in spite of her long, bony frame. 'I may be wrong. Will you come over with me, Mary Ellen, and see? I came the back way, for Bella Bradley's on the lookout.'

'Is Nancy ill?' Mary Ellen asked, taking her shawl from the back of the door.

Hannah made no reply but went out, and Mary Ellen followed closely after her . . .

Nancy was in bed, lying well down under the clothes, and Mary Ellen, as she entered the bedroom, could see only her eyes. They held an odd look, a mixture of wariness and cunning, an expression not usual to their dullness.

'Hallo, Nancy,' said Mary Ellen.

But Nancy did not reply with her usual normal address; she just stared from one to the other.

Hannah, stripping the clothes from her, said, 'Lift up your nightie!'

With her eyes still darting from one to the other of the two women, Nancy complied. The nightdress was short and tight, and she had to drag it over her hips.

Mary Ellen gazed at Nancy's stomach. She knew now what Hannah suspected, and she exclaimed to herself. 'Oh, Jesus, don't let it be.' Nevertheless, to her eyes there was nothing really to justify Hannah's suspicions, and she looked across the bed to Hannah: 'Lass, what makes you think . . ?' she said.

'She's past her time, and I've seen nothing; and I think that's what Mrs Fitzsimmons twigged. And her being sick and not working.' She spoke as if Nancy wasn't there. 'Stand up!' she said harshly to her daughter.

Nancy lumbered out of the bed, still with her nightdress held above her stomach. And now Mary Ellen thought she could detect a small rise. But still she would not believe this thing possible; nobody in their right senses would dream of taking a lass like this.

'Look, lass' – she turned to Hannah – 'it may only be wind. Or perhaps a growth,' she said hopefully.

Hannah, her eyes dead in her large, round face, turned away and walked into the kitchen.

'Put your clothes on, hinny,' Mary Ellen said to Nancy; and the girl immediately pulled her nightdress over her head and began to dress.

In the kitchen, Hannah was sitting dejectedly at the table, and Mary Ellen said, 'Get her to the doctor's lass. Take her now. It may not be what you think, and it'll set your mind at rest . . . Anyway, it can't be that.'

Hannah, in dismay, turned and stared into the distances beyond the kitchen walls: 'It's that all right. I'll take her, but I know.'

'Have you asked her anything?'

'Yes, I asked her if a man had touched her, and she wouldn't answer. And that's a funny thing in itself, for she always says right away, "No, Ma, when men speak to me I run away." And then again, twice last week she disappeared. I had Annie out looking for her for three hours on New Year's night, and she found her round by St Bede's Church. She had come across the salt grass, but she wouldn't say where she'd been . . . Oh, Christ . . . Christ Jesus!' Hannah burst out. 'What's going to happen? Joe will kill her. And if he finds out who it is there'll be murder done. Oh, Mary Ellen, what am I going to do?'

'Here, steady yourself, lass. Come on, get up and put your coat on and take her now.' She pulled Hannah to her feet. 'You'll catch him if you go now.'

While Hannah was putting on her coat, Mary Ellen went into the bedroom where Nancy was still laboriously dressing: 'Hurry up, hinny, your ma's waiting.'

Mary Ellen found she couldn't look at the girl . . . If she were going to have a bairn and had kept quiet about the man, then there was some part in her that was sensible, Mary Ellen reasoned. Unless, of course, she was too afraid to say anything. But now that she came to look at her, the lass looked less afraid than she had ever done.

She bustled Nancy into the kitchen: 'There you are then, lass' – she was addressing herself to Hannah – 'get yourself off . . . And remember, whichever way it goes, don't worry. You can't help it; the blame can't be laid at your door, you've done your best.'

She watched them walking down the street, wide apart, like strangers, Nancy humped and shuffling, Hannah as stiff as a ramrod;

and a sadness settled on Mary Ellen, the beginning of a long, long sadness.

John hurried out of the docks . . . Friday night and the first week of the new year over, and six boats discharging at the same time. He had just come from the weigh beam after paying off half the men. It was a strange sensation standing at the weigh beam with his pockets full of money and handing each man his due, and feeling that although he was young enough to be a son to three parts of the men they liked him, and trusted him to give them a square deal. As he left the last arch and passed the bottom of Simonside Bank he glanced through the darkness to the curving incline, and the thought that within the next hour he would be hurrying up there brought a leaping and tingling to his blood. The nights of the past week had been like glimpses of paradise – was there anyone in the world as beautiful and as sweet as her? Where was there a woman of her standing who would take him as he was? He had no notions about himself. Eight years in the docks had not filed him down, but roughened him. The only saving grace, he told himself, was that he was aware of it and would do his best to remedy it. He would have to if he were ever to feel worthy of her, even to the smallest degree. Moreover, another thing he would have to do was to find a better job. It was impossible for him to remain in the docks . . . even as a gaffer, for it would take more than a gaffer's wages to support her in the way to which she was used. Almost every night of the past week, after he had left her, his main thought had been that he must better himself; and he had worked it out that there was no chance for him in the North, nor yet in England . . . America . . . the Mecca of the Tyneside Irish loomed before him like a lodestar. If she would have him he would go there. Perhaps she would go with him right away . . . No; not for a moment would he consider that. When he had made enough money he would send for her. Not for one day of her life would she live differently because of him . . . And then there was his mother and Katie. If he went to America he'd be able to send them money too. For look at the wages you earned out there! And it wasn't all moonshine. The Hogans from High Jarrow were doing fine, he'd heard; the father and four lads all in regular work, and sending for the rest of them this year. And there was that young Stanley Tapp, who went out and had his lass follow him. So why shouldn't he, with his strength and fitness, make a go of it! There was no job he couldn't tackle. Yes, that's what he'd do. But he'd have to wait a while before he put it to her; he couldn't ask her anything yet; it was too soon. Had he been loving her for only a week? It seemed now as though it had been going on for years. And each time they met the knowledge grew stronger that she loved him with an intensity that almost matched his own. This coloured his life, and lifted him to the heights whereon he saw himself wrestling a mighty living out of the world and giving her, not only the things that she was used to, but such things to which even she had not aspired.

He was whistling as he walked up the backyard, but stopped before he entered the house; his mother wouldn't have whistling in the house, it was unlucky. She was standing by the table, and before her, on the mat, stood his father and Dominic with their bait tins still in their hands. Shane's lower lip was thrust out, and he was saying, 'The swine should be crucified!'

'What's up?' asked John, loosening his muffler.

'It's Nancy,' said Mary Ellen, looking down at her feet.

'Nancy? What's wrong with her?' John took off his coat and rolled up his sleeves before reaching for the kettle from the hob.

'She's going to have a bairn.'

John's hands stayed in mid-air. 'She's going to what!' His brows met over the exclamation.

'It's true. Hannah's had her to the doctor. She's nearly out of her mind.'

Turning slowly, John looked from his father to Dominic, and back to his mother again. Nancy Kelly going to have a bairn! It was utterly incredible. He thought of her face as it really was without the veil of his pity covering it . . . the loose, repulsive mouth, the beady eyes, and the pushed-in nose. How could any man touch her, unless he too 'wasn't all there'.

Mary Ellen was saying, 'And the funny thing is, she's gone . . . odder' – she couldn't say 'brazen' to the men – 'I can't keep her out of the house.'

Although Mary Ellen was filled with pity for Hannah and the girl, she had found the day trying beyond description, for when Nancy wasn't standing leaning against the stanchion of her own front door, staring across the street towards the house, she was knocking at either the back or the front door. Mary Ellen felt she could not say anything to Hannah as yet, for Hannah was distraught, not only with her daughter going to have a child, but at the change in her. It was as if now, with life moving within her, some part of Nancy had become activated into normality . . . a crude and shocking normality to the women, for she seemed proud of her achievement and was determined to show it to her world. Subconsciously through the years, she must have taken in, with perhaps a feeling of envy, the arrogance of the pregnant women standing at their doors, their arms folded across the bulks of moving life. And she may have laughed unknowingly at their jokes as they patted the tiny flutterings of their aprons, saying with raw wit the old, threadworn joke, 'Lie down, yer father's not workin'!'

Whatever had happened, she was now . . . brazened, and Mary Ellen's pity was turning to irritation.

Dominic sat down by the fire – he hadn't spoken – and Shane and John still stood regarding Mary Ellen.

'This'll send the little bantam clean off his head.' It was Shane who spoke, and he was referring to Joe.

As Mary Ellen was about to make some reply, the back door opened and Nancy sidled in.

'Look, Nancy!' Mary Ellen exclaimed sharply; 'get yourself away home.'

But Nancy, who never to Mary Ellen's knowledge had disobeyed a command in her life, simply ignored her. Instead, she came well into the kitchen and stood looking from one to the other of the men. They all stared at her, Dominic out of the corner of his eye. And when Nancy met his gaze, she flung herself round from him, showing him her back, like a child in the huff, and amidst silence, she walked towards John, and smiled her grotesque smile as she placed her hand on his sleeve.

'John.'

Tears almost came into John's eyes as he looked at her: God, but it was awful! Yet above his pity there arose a feeling of revulsion against her. Some subtle change in her was making itself felt – she was no longer the child.

She said again, 'John;' and he was about to say something to her when his head was jerked up by the sound of choking.

It was Dominic; he had risen from his chair, his body quivering with waves of shut-in laughter. Mary Ellen and Shane were staring at him. He lumbered past them and threw himself on to the couch, where he sat leaning back, facing them, his face working with glee.

Staring wide-eyed and questioningly at her son's contorted face, Mary Ellen was wondering what in the name of God had come over him.

Suddenly Dominic could control himself no longer, and his laughter filled the house. Bellow rolled on top of bellow. But as he rocked himself back and forth his eyes never left John's, and the implication was lost on none of them. He waved a helpless hand, encompassing Nancy and John. And John's voice rose above Dominic's laughter, almost deafening them, as he cried, 'You bloody swine!'

With one movement he flung Nancy aside and sprang for Dominic. At the same moment, Shane and Mary Ellen threw themselves on him. Dominic got up, his laughter gone now: 'Let him fight, the dirty bastard! Come on!' He tore off his coat and made for the back door.

John's rage sent Shane and Mary Ellen spinning away from him, and he was after Dominic; but as he crossed the step, Dominic's fist shot out and caught him full in the face: yet so little did it affect John in his rage, it could have been Katie's hand.

After the light of the kitchen, the backyard appeared black, and for a time they struck at each other blindly. But soon their fists met the other's body with quickening and sickening thuds.

'For God's sake, stop them!' Mary Ellen cried to Shane. She tried to push past him into the yard, but he barred her way, saying, 'Let them have it out.'

'No! No! He'll kill him. John'll kill him! For God's sake stop them!'

A small crowd was now gathering at the yard door, and the windows on the far side of the back lane were being thrown up – the cry had gone round, 'The O'Briens are at it.'

The one showing the least concern was Nancy; she stood against the kitchen table her arms folded on her stomach and a silly smile flicking her face.

The sight of her thus was too much for Mary Ellen. She darted back into the kitchen, and taking Nancy by the shoulders, pushed her through the front room and out into the street shouting, 'Go on! Go on, you young trollop, you! And don't darken these doors again!'

Back in the kitchen she tried once more to push past Shane, for blood was flowing freely now. It was running from John's mouth and from Dominic's eyebrow, and their shirts were wet with it.

Peggy Flaherty's voice came from the upstairs window, crying, 'Stop it! Stop it, you lads! Stop it, the pair of you. John, where's your sense gone? Do you want to break your mother's heart? Behave like a gentleman, can't you! Oh, if only Mr Flaherty was alive!'

Mary Ellen, through Shane's arm, could see the dark bulk of Peggy hanging half out of the window.

Peggy cried down to her: 'Mary Ellen, are you there? Will I throw some slops over them?'

Mary Ellen made no answer, for she was now staring at the lass from next door. Christine had come into the suffused light, paused for a moment near the battling figures, then walked right between them.

John's fist was travelling towards Dominic's body, and Mary Ellen closed her eyes tightly, for the girl's face, as she confronted John, was in line with it.

Only the sound of gasping breaths came to Mary Ellen. She opened her eyes slowly, and they were apart, with the girl standing untouched between them.

Christine lifted her hands and pushed John towards the kitchen door, where Mary Ellen pulled him over the threshold.

Then Christine turned to Dominic. He was leaning against the washhouse wall now, wiping his face with his shirt sleeve. He paused and looked at her, and said pointedly, 'This is one time I'm fighting in the right.'

'Fighting was never in the right.'

'No? Huh!' – he spat out some blood, then went on wiping his face – 'not even when your wonderful John gives Nancy Kelly a bairn?'

There was a rustle among the crowd about the yard door. The whispers linked, forming a wave; then broke again, as one person after another darted away into the blackness . . . John O'Brien had given Nancy Kelly a bairn!

When John at last arrived at their meeting place, Mary wasn't there, and his feelings became a mixture of sick disappointment and relief . . . relief because of the uncertainty of her reaction when she saw his face. She would, he knew, be full of sympathy, but would she think that he was indeed one of the 'Fighting O'Briens', fighting for fighting's sake? – he'd be unable to explain why he had fought. So he walked towards her house, keeping on the far side of the road, and when he came opposite the gate he stood well back in the shadow of a hedge, and waited, wondering what construction she had put on his non-appearance.

The house was lit up, and occasionally a shadow darkened the blinds, but the shadow could have belonged to anyone.

How long he stood there he did not know, but a clock somewhere in the distance, struck the hour, and he guessed it was nine o'clock. And as he was making up his mind to move away, the front door opened, and she was there, silhouetted against the light. But not alone; a man was with her, and from his thinness, John knew him to be Culbert.

John's nerves tensed as he watched them standing talking, and his teeth grated when he saw Culbert's hand take hers. But she remained still and Culbert moved away, and the door was closed.

After standing for a while longer, John walked slowly away. He was cold, and his eye was paining, and the whole of his face was stiff and sore. Now the import of Dominic's wild laughter rose to the fore of his mind again; and with it came a paralysing sense of fear. Fear was the least of John's emotions – he could not remember ever having known real fear; he had been scared, but being scared had no connection with this weakening feeling of fear. What if it got around, what Dominic had suggested? God! he couldn't stand it. Anyway, people wouldn't believe it. Him take Nancy Kelly! . . . But wouldn't they? The lot around the fifteen streets would accuse Jesus Christ himself of it, if they were in the mood to do so. At times, it would appear they were utterly devoid of reason or sense, the rumours they believed and passed on.

As he neared the corner of Fadden Street, the huddled darker blur standing out against the wall told him the men were there. It was usual for them to gather at the corner and crack, and it was their voices which generally proclaimed them. But tonight they were quiet. And as he passed them he knew a mounting of his fear, which almost reached the point of terror when he realised the rumour was already let loose.

A figure stepped from the group and walked for a few steps by his side, then stopped. John stopped too, and the two men peered at each other.

'I want a word with you,' said Joe Kelly.

John did not answer him, for the fear was drying his mouth. He waited, and Joe seemed to be waiting too.

Then Joe brought out thickly, 'What have you got to say?'

'What about?' John parried.

'Come off it, you know bloody fine!'

John made a desperate effort to bring reason and calmness to the fore: 'Look, Joe,' he appealed to the little man, whose face, even through the darkness, conveyed its trouble to him, 'do you, for a moment, think I would do such a thing? For God's sake, man, have some sense! Nancy's always made a set for me because I've been kind to her . . . What do you think I am? I mean no offence, Joe, but I'm not that hard up for a woman.'

'Then why did you take her up the country?'

'Take her up the country? Me?'

'Aye, you! And give her money . . . You might be big, John O'Brien, but I'm going to kick the guts out of you!'

Before Joe could spring to carry out his intention, John's hands gripped his shoulders and pinned him against the wall, while he kept his body bent out of reach of Joe's legs.

'Listen here, Joe Kelly: if there's any guts to be kicked out, I can do a bit of it myself. But before we start that, let's get this straight. The whole thing's a pack of damned lies from beginning to end. You bring me the one that saw me up the country with Nancy; and let's get Nancy herself and ask her.'

'That's the ticket,' said a voice from the group of men; 'give him a fair crack o' the whip. I told you you were up the pole to believe it. Now, if it had been the other big sod . . .'

Another voice was added to that of the first: 'Aye, Joe . . . Ask your lass, and get Bella Flabbygob to face him and tell him herself.'

Joe's writhing body was stilled. 'All right then,' he growled. 'If you've got the face, come and clear yourself.'

John, walking swiftly and tensely by Joe's side, said, 'I don't need to have any face, I've done nothing that I'm ashamed of.'

Thrusting open his back door, Joe cried to the startled Hannah, 'Get her up!'

After one bewildered glance towards John, Hannah went into the bedroom, and in a few minutes returned, pushing Nancy, half awake, before her.

Nancy had a coat about her shoulders, and her long, thick legs stuck out, like mottled props, below her short nightgown. Her feet were bare and not very clean, and the whole picture of her was revolting to John . . . That anyone should imagine he could touch a thing

121

like this! The thought made him angry, and momentarily banished his fear. He confronted Nancy.

'Look, Nancy. Have I ever taken you up the country?'

Still only half awake, she blinked at him.

'Have I?' he persisted.

'No, John.'

John cast a quick glance at Joe.

'Now,' he went on, 'have I ever given you money?'

She blinked again. She was a child once more; her new-found self was lost in bewilderment and sleep. 'Yes,' she answered simply.

Joe scraped his feet on the floor as John said, 'Listen carefully now. When did I give you the money?'

She thought a while, then said, 'Up Simonside.'

They all stood silent. Simonside was the country. It was the place for lovers and courting. Hannah drew in her breath, and Joe bit out, 'Want to know any more?'

'Yes. How much did I give you?' John bent towards Nancy.

'Threepence.'

'And what did I give it to you for?'

'For being a good girl.'

Joe snorted and John turned on him. 'I know the night I gave it to her. I met her crying under the arches. Annie had left her in the market and she hadn't her tram fare. She was afraid to stand outside the bar, and I put her on the tram, and' – the face of Bella Bradley peering at him came back to John – 'Bella Bradley was on that tram. It was her who put this into your head.'

'I've no use for that 'un,' Joe said, indicating Bella with a lift of his eyes towards the ceiling, 'but she said she saw you coming down the Simonside bank with her.'

'How the hell could she,' burst out John, 'if she was in the tram and it black dark!'

Joe had no answer to this. He turned from John to Nancy, his look indicating his detestation. Then he flung a question at her that made Hannah cry out and John wince.

Nancy stared back at her father, unmoved by the question itself. She was wide awake now, and she wriggled and flung her head to the side with a new defiance. As Joe, all restraint gone, went to hit her, she screamed and jumped aside like a grotesque animal.

Hannah caught her husband's arm, crying, 'Leave her be, man!'

Then Joe, Hannah and John were struck speechless, for Nancy, standing in the corner, her coat lying at her feet, her long neck thrust forward, was yelling at Joe: 'Leave me alone . . . see, you! You hit me if you dare, see! I'm gonna have a bairn, I am, an' be married . . . Yes, I am. I'm gonna be married when the bairn's born I am.' She tugged her tight nightgown back and forward around her hips, then turned her face towards John: 'Aren't I, John?'

122

John stood gazing at her; he was dumb and sick. Had she remained the half imbecile child he could have dealt with her, but this new Nancy, full of craft and cunning, filled him with horror. When she came boldly towards him, her hand outstretched, he yelled at her, 'Take your hands off me!' and like someone possessed, he rushed from the house and started to run, with Joe's voice bellowing after him, 'You won't get off with it like that!'

CHAPTER TEN

MARY LLEWELLYN

Her home had always appeared a place of warmth and comfort to Mary, but not up to now had she looked upon it as one of the tentacles of her mother's possessiveness. Mary knew that, in her gentle way, her mother clung like a leech and sucked at one's individuality; and one of her sucking tentacles was the creating of comfort . . . good food, warmth, even the seductive fire in one's bedroom.

After Mary's victory of claiming a room to herself the creature comforts were diminished for a time; if she wanted a fire in this room she had to light it. Yet after a while, Beatrice Llewellyn saw that by pandering to her daughter's ridiculous idea of privacy, a new tentacle could be affixed. But since New Year's Eve, much to Mary's discomfort, this tentacle had been released. No fire had been lit in the sitting-room for a fortnight, let alone in the bedroom, and Mary's enquiry of Phyllis had been answered by, 'The mistress says there are fires in the drawing-room and dining-room, Miss Mary.'

For the first week of the new year it had not irked her, for her evenings were spent with John; and the fireless room was merely something that showed up her mother's pettiness. But for six days now she had seen John only once, and that under such circumstances, she would rather not have seen him at all. Added to this, the striking cold of her fireless rooms seemed to have brought her up against life with a vengeance.

Last night, after having gone fruitlessly to their meeting place, she wrote John a letter . . . a letter bare of pride. She had thrown pride over from the first night he failed to keep their appointment, for each dinner-time since, she had taken a roundabout way home, walking slowly through the arches, hoping against hope to meet him. Then today she saw him; but unfortunately only after she had met her mother and father almost at the dock gates. After her father's kindly greeting and her mother's fixed stare, they were walking on abreast, past the gates themselves, when John came out. His abrupt stopping brought them all to a halt; but before she even had time to speak, he was gone, across the road and into the Jarrow tram.

It was only by using all her control that she did not follow him. In the brief moment of meeting she could see something was wrong. He was in trouble, and he had been fighting. His eye was discoloured, and there was a scar across his lip. But it was the look in his eyes that shocked her. They were not the brown, kindly eyes of her John, they looked haunted . . . even frightened.

It was disastrous that her mother should see him like this. Mary knew, by her mother's tilted chin and stiff profile, that she recognised him and was showing her disgust. And her father's repeated short coughs spoke, too, of his embarrassment.

Mary stood now in her bedroom, recalling the incident. There was another hour and a half before she would know if her letter had broken this estrangement for which she could find no cause. She pulled her fur coat tighter about her as she sat down by the window and looked out into the black garden. If he did not come tonight what would she do? Her life seemed barren and futile without him, and he had toppled her standards overboard. Up to a few months ago she was sure she knew what she wanted from life: culture, travel, and of course a lovely home. It was true she had never loved Gilbert Culbert, but it was his profession, she thought, had weighed her feelings against him; for she could not see herself going out to work when married, and thirty-seven shillings a week wasn't going to enable her to do the things she had planned, although she knewsif she were to make this match there would be considerable help forthcoming from her mother. Yet, compared with John, Culbert was a man of means. But here she was, willing to forgo everything shu valued for this man, who would hardly be able to feed her, as her father had so strongly pointed out, apart from supporting her in the smallest comfort.

She was helpless before the power of her feeling. No clear thinking would touch it. Nor did she want it to be touched, for she realised she had found something given to few, a love strong enough to defy convention. And not in the ordinary way; but to defy convention by living under its nose. For that's what it would mean if she, Nary Llewellyn, the boat-builder's daughter, married John O'Brien, the docker.

'Miss Mary!'

Mary started. 'Yes?'

'Your mother says she wants . . . she would like to see you in the drawing-room.'

'Very well.'

Mary turned from Phyllis, whose bright eyes were greedy for more scandal. Mary guessed her own doings were the high spot of conversation in the kitchen, and knew that, because she was associating with one whom they considered to be below their class, she was unworthy of their respect. It showed covertly in their manner, and she upbraided herself for being hurt by it. For this, she told herself as she went downstairs, was nothing to what she would have to put up with – she mustsget used to scorn, and the scorn of the poor was scorn indeed.

Her mother was sitting in her wing chair to one side of the large log fire, the heat of which met Mary as she entered the room. Beatrice Llewellyn looked smaller and younger and more fragile at this moment than ever before.

'You wanted me?' Mary halted in the centre of the room.

'Yes.' Beatrice Llewellyn paused, adjusted the lace cover on the arm of her chair, then went on, 'I would just like to ask you, Mary, to conform to the rules of this house if it is your intention to stay in it.'

Mary remained silent; it was like the ultimatum to a lodger.

'You know your meals are served in the dining-room! If you do not deign to have them there with us, then I'm afraid you'll have to eat out, for I'm not having them taken to your room.'

Anyone but Mary would have been deceived by her mother's tone into thinking that behind its evenness lay forbearance and toleration, but to Mary its studied calmness, in itself, was a danger signal.

'Is that all you wanted me for?' she asked.

'No, it is not all I wanted you for.' Beatrice Llewellyn lifted her eyes from the contemplation of the lace cover and looked straight at her daughter. 'You astound me, Mary. I cannot begin to understand you . . .'

'No?' Mary raised her eyebrows slightly and waited.

'I can't think that one, even with your liberal tastes, can have sunk so low as to continue to associate with a man who is the father of an imbecile girl's child!'

The words glanced off the surface of Mary's mind. She was prepared to hear something against John, she hadn't thought her mother would speak otherwise, and at this moment she was feeling sick with cold and worry; so until, like a boomerang, their meaning rebounded back at her she just continued to return her mother's stare. There was a cause then for the six empty nights and his avoidance of her at dinner-time . . . there was a reason; someone was going to have a baby by him.

What! – her mind jumped clear of its numbness – her John who was clean and loving and kind, whose love, so full of desire, was yet restrained, whose hands, even in their loving, were not the probing, groping hands of Gilbert . . . her John going to father a what!

She repeated aloud, 'What! What did you say?'

'You heard what I said.'

'And you expect me to believe you?'

'No' – her mother's voice took on a note of resignation – 'No, all Tyneside could believe it, but not you. You are so obsessed by that . . . that man, that individual with the brutalised, battered face, whose licentiousness drives him to take a poor imbecile . . .'

'Be quiet! How dare you!'

'Don't speak to me like that, Mary!'

'I will! You sit there taking a man's character away . . . damning him . . . you, who know nothing . . . !'

'I take his character away! Can a man have any character who would touch that dreadful Kelly girl?'

'Kelly. You mean Nancy Kelly?'

'Yes, I mean Nancy Kelly.'

'You're mad! No man would . . . would go with that girl.'

'She's going to have a child, and you don't for a moment imagine it's an immaculate conception, do you?' Her mother was being unconsciously funny; if only the implications for John were not so terrible Mary would have laughed.

There was scorn in her mother's smile and maliciousness in her voice when she said, 'His exalted position of being a gaffer is in jeopardy too, I understand. For even certain dock men have standards of morals.'

The desire of her mother to hurt her was so palpably evident that Mary was stung to reply, 'Yes, for your sake, I should hope so, seeing that my father worked in the docks until he was twenty. You seem to forget that, don't you. I, in my way, am doing exactly what you did . . . taking up with a dock worker.'

Beatrice Llewellyn rose swiftly from her chair – she was no longer calm; Mary had touched a vulnerable spot, and she hated to be reminded that her prosperous husband had ever been other than what he was now. 'There's a coarseness in you, Mary, that disgusts me,' she said sibilantly. 'Your father was never a dock worker; he was apprenticed to a trade, as you well know.'

'What difference does it make?' Mary found she wanted to argue, to keep talking, so that she would not have to think.

But her mother ended the interview by leaving the room. She walked past Mary, her face tight and her blue eyes flashing with vexation, causing the air seemingly to vibrate with her displeasure. Mary did not move – she stood nervously tapping her lips with her fingers . . . Nancy Kelly was going to have a child . . . that dreadful-looking girl who was no more than a child herself. And they were saying John was responsible. So that was why he looked as he did. And that, too, was why he had been fighting. How had he come to be accused of such a thing?

The old saying: There's no smoke without fire, came to her. But she refuted it with her mind and body; and she swung round and rushed upstairs. Yet the thought persisted; why had he been named?

Mary reached their meeting place half an hour before the appointed time. In the darkness of the lane she waited, each moment dragging itself out into seeming hours, filled with dread and anxiety. Twice she heard footsteps on the main road, but they didn't turn into the lane.

When at last she heard the heavy tread of feet coming towards her, she pressed back into the hedge, fearing lest it was not him. But as the dark bulk drew to a halt, she whispered softly, 'John.'

No answer came to her, and she moved slowly forward, and again she said, 'John.'

In the centre of the lane, he stood out against the starlit night, and she could feel the tense unhappiness holding him down. She reached out her hands and again spoke his name. This time he answered her. His arms went about her, and she was lifted into his embrace and held tightly against him in an unhappy silence. He did not kiss her, but bent his head and buried it against her neck; and his mental anguish engulfed her.

'What is it, my dear?' She purposely asked the question, for she felt he must tell her himself, and in the telling perhaps the strain would ease.

But he said nothing. And so they stood, wrapped close in an embrace that was full of questioning and stress. Then, as if his words had journeyed through many doors before finding a way out and were now tremulous in their release, he asked, 'Mary . . . would you marry me if I had enough money?'

The proposal was so unexpected – it was the last thing she had thought of hearing at this moment. She had imagined he would give some reason for their separation, if not speak of this dreadful other thing. For perhaps a second she remained still. Then she gently took his head between her hands and raised it. His face was indistinguishable in the darkness, but so well did she know each feature that his expression seemed at this moment to be outlined in light.

'Oh, my dear, I'd marry you now, just as you are.'

The question of Nancy Kelly flashed like a falling star across her mind, only to disappear into nothingness; its dreadful import could not possibly touch this man.

'No, no. Never that.' John's arms fell from her, but she held his face tightly, saying, 'Why not, my darling? Why not?'

'Because' – his head moved restlessly between her hands – 'I'll never take you while I'm in the docks.'

'But, my dear . . .'

'It's no use.'

He gently released his face from her hands, and held them tightly: 'I couldn't do it . . . Mary, I'm going away. Will you wait for me?'

'Where are you going?'

'America.'

'America! But John! Oh, my dear' – she pulled him towards her – 'I can't let you go . . . not all that way, not without me . . . John, take me with you. Let's start together' – she was pleading as if for her very life – 'if we are together nothing matters.' She had her arms about him now, and he stood still within their circle, steeling himself against her offer, which for the moment had lifted him out of the terrifying depths of despair and revulsion to life that had almost overwhelmed him during these past few days, and which during that one brief moment had erased the picture of Nancy Kelly from his mind, so that he could no longer see her waiting for him at the corner of the street, or watching the house from her door or front window. His whole life had been coloured darkly by her. He would see her face reflected in the expression of the dock men's covert glances and in the too friendly overtures of a section of the men, who wanted him to know they didn't believe the rumour. The house that, during the holidays took on a semblance of happiness, was now a place of dread, and his mother seemed to have become bent under the load of it. Time and again he had found her watching Nancy from behind the curtains as she, in her turn, watched the house . . . What would his mother do when he was gone?

He jerked his head as if to throw off this additional worry, and answered Mary, rejecting her offer, as he knew he must, but crying out internally at the necessity that drove him to it: 'No, it wouldn't work. I've got to go there and get a start, and make enough money to set up.'

The term set up and all that it implied lifted him back to a week ago, when there was no fear in his life, only the ecstatic feeling of loving her. He pulled her to him blindly and kissed her, and so was lost for a time, until she murmured, 'John . . . listen to me. Now don't get wild at what I'm going to say. But I've got a little money . . . only a little' – she felt his withdrawal and clung on to him – 'Listen, darling, don't be foolish. It isn't much, for I've never bothered to save. It's what my grandfather left me. There's two hundred pounds. We could . . .'

'Mary . . . do you love me enough to wait a year, perhaps two?'

It was as if she had never made her offer. She answered, 'Yes . . . for as long as you wish.'

'That's all right then.'

He kissed her again. Then said, 'I've been making enquiries; I'm going as soon as I can. I went up to see some people called Hogan in Jarrow last night. They've told me what to do.'

'Oh, John' – the huskiness of her voice was deepened by the catch of tears – 'why . . . why all this rush?' And as she asked the question, Nancy Kelly came back into her mind. It was because of this he was going more than anything else. He was running away.

'John, what is it? What's worrying you? Tell me.'

He remained quiet, and she felt the stiffening of his body again. Then he put her thoughts into his own words: 'I'm running away . . . I've been accused of something, and I can't face it . . . Mary' – the muscles of his arms hardened against her soft flesh – 'if you heard something bad about me would you believe it? I can't prove to you that I'm innocent, I can only tell you I am . . . It's about . . . I'm . . .'

He stopped and a shiver passed through his body. He could not bring himself to say, 'I'm accused of giving Nancy Kelly a bairn,' nor could he say, 'I'm as innocent as Christ himself, for I've never had a woman; nor will have until I have you, be it in two years or twenty.'

The cold dark bleakness of the night pressed down on them. They stood slightly apart, and Mary waited for him to go on and voice his misery. But he remained silent. The silence seemed to fill the lane and to widen the distance between them. At last she could bear it no longer, for now she was with him she knew without doubt that he was incapable of committing that of which he was accused, and she cried out, 'You would never do anything bad. Never! Oh, my dear, don't let this thing cause you to make hasty decisions. Don't let it drive you away. Stay and see it out.'

'You don't know what it is they are saying.'

'Yes, I do. I know all about it.'

The silence fell on them again, softly now, filled with reverence.

She knew all about it and she was here! He whispered, 'You know about Nancy Kelly?'

'Yes.'

The wonder of her love and faith coursed like a mountain stream through him, sweeping before it the fear and dread that had been intensified by the thought of her revulsion towards him should the rumour ever reach her. Her name burst from him on a broken laugh that could scarcely be identified from a sob.

She was in his arms, crushed tightly against him, and he was pouring words over her: 'Nothing matters now. I can face anything. I'll make money. We'll start a new life together . . . Oh, Mary, my love, I'm as innocent of what they say as . . . as Katie is. I've always been sorry for the girl. I used to mind her when she was a bairn, and she would come to me when she was frightened . . . She's changed; she's different now. But somehow, I think she's still frightened, and that's why she's made a dead set for me. And it's made them think . . . But what does it matter now? Nothing matters, only you. We'll start life in a new land; and you'll teach me, as you were going to, and make a new man of me.'

She tightened her arms about him . . . She teach him! What could she teach him but the superficialities, whereas he could teach her all there was to know of life.

CHAPTER ELEVEN

ASK AND YE SHALL RECEIVE

The February storm had raged for three days, during which hail, snow and rain was driven against the houses with such force as to almost penetrate the walls. It succeeded through many windows, and some of the people found it as dangerous to stay indoors as to go out and risk the flying slates and toppling chimney pots. But today the storm was lashing itself out. The streets were dry and the sun shone fitfully through the racing clouds.

It shone now on Nancy standing in her doorway. It showed her up vividly to Mary Ellen as she watched from behind her curtains. For the past three days Mary Ellen had seen Nancy only dimly, and appearing more grotesque than ever through the two rain-streaked windows. But now, there she was, as vivid as the picture that was seared on Mary Ellen's mind.

The girl, Mary Ellen knew, was possessed of a devil. This was the only way to account for her laying the blame of the bairn on John without actually saying so, and for her turning on Hannah and standing up to Joe. Mary Ellen knew that she, too, had become possessed of a devil. It entered into her the night Dominic and John fought, and when John stayed out all night, wandering the streets, after Joe Kelly had followed him into the house, demanding to know what he was going to do about supporting Nancy. The devil had frightened Mary Ellen, for he urged her to do Nancy a physical injury, and she prayed constantly to be relieved of all temptation. But from the night her lad told her he was going to America, she prayed no more, and the devil took full possession of her. She watched Nancy at every available moment, and there were times when she actually lifted the sneck of the front door with the intention of making a dash at the girl and tearing her limb from limb.

Nancy stood now scratching her head. She was doing it systematically, working over first one section then another; and Mary Ellen wondered for the countless time how anyone in their right senses could imagine her lad touching that thing . . . But they not only imagined it, they voiced it. Since Bella Bradley had set the ball rolling, at least half the fifteen streets would swear to having seen John with Nancy Kelly in some questionable place.

She could have borne it all, Mary Ellen thought, if only it wasn't driving her lad away. What would she do without him? The day he left the house, it would be as if she were laying him in his coffin, for she would never see him again. It was all right him saying he would send her money . . . he'd want all his money if he was going to marry that lass. And anyway, she didn't want money, she only wanted him. What would life be like when, cooking, washing and mending, she wasn't doing it for him?

She moved from the window and leaned against the wall, and pressed her nose tightly between finger and thumb, meanwhile taking great gulps of air – she mustn't start crying now, it was close on twelve o'clock, and John and Shane would be in soon, it being Saturday. Dominic was already in, sitting over the fire, picking his toes.

In spite of her efforts, tears started to flow. Unless Dominic got that job in Liverpool she'd be left with him and his beastly ways. John never sat over the fire, picking his toes . . . he washed his feet in the scullery. But not Dominic; he'd sit picking at the hard skin on the soles of his feet, or lifting the dirt from his toenails with his fingernails. There was nothing so ugly, Mary Ellen thought, as feet, and none so repulsive as Dominic's, big and broad and well-shaped as they were. She knew, with an overpowering certainty, that once John was gone and she was left to suffer Dominic, the devil would have his way. And there would be no door standing between her and Dominic, as there was between her and Nancy, acting as a deterrent to her uplifted hand. And the devil alone knew what she would have in her uplifted hand. Oh, if only her lad wasn't going to that America. Oh, God, if only something would happen to prevent him! She groaned and rocked her body . . . Ask and Ye Shall Receive. Yes, but there were so many things she had asked of God, and had she ever received them? Perhaps she hadn't asked properly. Or she may not have wanted them as she wanted this one thing. If there was only somewhere she could be alone and kneel down, she'd pray to Him and ask Him. But the minutes alone were few and far between, especially at the week-end . . . But she was alone now. She moved swiftly to the room door and closed it. Self-consciously she knelt down close by it so that she wouldn't be taken unawares if Dominic made to enter, and should anyone happen to glance in the window through the narrow aperture of the curtains it would look as if she were scrubbing.

Almighty God, she began, Almighty Lord of Heaven and earth, grant me this one prayer and I swear unto You that never until the day I die will I miss Mass. Almighty and powerful God, grant me this plea . . . She did not at once voice the plea, even mentally, but searched about in her mind for other words to denote power with which to adorn the name of God. But she could think only of Great and Almighty. She discarded the set prayers – she wanted something more powerful with which to contact Him. So she began again . . . Great and Almighty God, Ruler of our lives, You who can do all things, do this for me I beseech Thee . . . don't let my lad go to America. Make something happen to stop him. Only You can do this, Almighty God . . . only You.

Her joined hands were pressed tightly between her breasts and her chin above them quivered with emotion. As she rose trembling from her knees, Katie's voice called from the scullery, 'Ma! Ma, I want you.'

Mary Ellen smoothed down her hair and rubbed her face over with a corner of her apron before going into the kitchen. She knew Katie must have seen Dominic and would not pass him, fearing lest his fingers were pushed beneath her nose.

Katie was standing in the scullery, trying to tidy her windblown hair before replacing her hat.

'What is it, hinny?' Mary Ellen asked heavily.

Katie whispered, 'Sh!' and pointed towards the kitchen. She pulled the door to, before going on in hushed tones, 'I just wanted to tell you I'm going to the slipway with Christine.'

'The slipway?' said Mary Ellen. And Katie again cautioned her. 'Sh! Ma.'

'What are you going to do there?' asked Mary Ellen softly.

'The boat's there . . . Mr Bracken had it fetched from the quay this morning on a cart. It's all painted up. David did it all himself. Oh, it looks lovely, Ma.'

'It's too windy, hinny, you'll get blown off the wall.'

'I won't go on the wall, Ma. The boat won't be on the wall' – Katie chuckled at her mother's ignorance – 'it'll be in the water!'

After a pause during which Mary Ellen adjusted Katie's hat, she asked, 'Who'll be there?'

'Only Christine and David.'

'Not Mr Bracken?'

'No.'

'Then you'd better not go, hinny. There should be no messing around with boats unless a man's knocking about.'

'But Christine knows all about boats . . . she can row! But anyway, Ma, it's tied up, and Christine's not going out in it, she says it's too windy. She says, maybe the morrow if the wind goes down we'll have a sail . . . there's a sail in it too, Ma!' She looked up at her mother with a mischievous smile. 'We'll take you out for a sail, Ma . . . right to where the big ships are. And the boat'll rock, and you'll be sick.'

The picture of her mother being seasick tickled Katie, and she leaned against her, and put her arms round her mother's ample waist, and shook with laughter as she moved her from side to side, imitating the rocking of a boat.

'Stop it, hinny!' Mary Ellen felt far from laughter, but she smiled at this canny bairn of hers, and she had the desire to fondle her. She took off Katie's hat again and reached for the broken comb lying on the scullery window-sill, and began to comb the top of her plaits.

Katie made a protest, 'Ma, Christine's waiting!' But she still leaned against her mother, and the pressure of her arms tightened about her.

When Mary Ellen replaced the hat she patted Katie's cheek. Then, awkwardly, she stooped and kissed her. Katie's arms came up swiftly about her neck, and she returned the kiss with an ardour that seemed strange in one so young. Kissing was an uncommon ritual in the house, and Mary Ellen said, 'There, there. Now off you go.'

But although she told Katie to go, she still held on to her, buttoning her coat, lifting her plaits from off her shoulders, and yet again straightening her hat. When at last she closed the door after Katie, she stood for a time thinking of her, and the thoughts brought her a modicum of comfort . . . she'd always have Katie. For years and years yet she'd have Katie, and they'd cleave together even more so when John was gone . . . That was another thing . . . Katie had to be told that John was going. What would her reactions be, for John was to her as a god?

A new fear entered into Mary Ellen . . . Would it create an aim in Katie's life, and that aim to be to go to America to join John? She shook herself. This was going too far . . . this is what came of thinking . . . Let God's will be done.

She steeled herself to go into the kitchen and to the oven where a hot-pot was cooking, for Dominic would be still on with his poking – she knew he prolonged it merely to tantalise her. But when she entered the kitchen he wasn't there; and further to her surprise, he came out of the bedroom, pulling on his old mackintosh. He had changed his trousers and was wearing his good boots. And he passed her without a word and went out, slamming the door after him.

Where was he off to in such a hurry? Surely he couldn't have heard what Katie said. If he did hear, he was off now to corner the lass at the slipway. It was quiet there, and nobody to stop him . . . only Katie. Well, Katie was as good as any.

Dominic's chase of Christine had aroused little interest in Mary Ellen of late. Under other circumstances the fact that Peter Bracken had forbidden him the house would perhaps have aroused in her a feeling of shame that a son of hers should have acted in a way to merit such treatment. At times, she did wonder at Dominic's persistence, and wondered too what it was about the lass that made him half demented for her. These past few weeks he had been drinking more than he had done since the Brackens came to live next door; not getting blind drunk, but just enough to arouse his temper and make him more detestable still. He was close on that stage now, having spent the best part of the morning in the bars.

Shane came in, and to her surprise spoke first.

'Lashing itself out,' he said gruffly.

It was some time before she answered, 'Yes, and about time too.' There was a change in Shane that bewildered her; he had almost dropped the drink, and he sat with her at nights instead of going to the corner. It began, she felt, when she was ill . . . or was it when John was made the gaffer? She knew that in his own way Shane was proud of that. And the change was more evident still since this trouble of John's. She felt dimly that he was trying to comfort her for what she was suffering on account of the lad, and dimly also, she felt a bigness in him for doing this, for it was John who had the affection that should have been his.

'Will you have it now or wait for John?' she asked, indicating the dinner.

'I'll wait.'

It was strange that she should ask him this and that he should comply. Not long ago he would have bellowed, 'Who the hell's boss, him or me?'

When John came in she did not glance towards him, for she knew how he would look – his face would be straight and lean; the flesh had dropped from the bones these past weeks; the brown of his eyes would be darker, and in their depths would be a look she could not bear to see.

Mary Ellen's heart lifted towards Shane when, seated at the table, he said to John. 'We got her out in time all right, didn't we?' He was referring to the unloading, and her emotion almost choked Mary Ellen as she realised that her husband was trying to get on a friendly footing with his son; for never before could she remember him speaking in such a way, not only acknowledging John as an equal, but as his superior . . . it was how a man spoke to his gaffer; it was also how a father tried to convey his faith in his son.

John looked hard at Shane, then said quietly, 'You did that.'

They ate on in silence, and Mary Ellen went into the scullery to try to suppress the choking in her throat. As she stood, her hands pressed tightly against her neck, Molly's voice came screaming from the back lane. 'Ma! Oh, Ma! . . . Ma!'

What could she do with that lass? Would she never grow up?

'Ma! Ma!' Molly's voice came nearer.

Was she mad, screaming like that! By, she'd box her lugs for her when she got her inside.

Molly's cries effectively suppressed Mary Ellen's emotion, and she pulled open the back door with an angry jerk . . . She'd give it to her; she'd swipe the hunger off her!

'Ma! Oh, Ma!' Molly tore up the backyard and flung herself on her mother, ignoring the upraised hand: 'Ma! it's Katie . . . Katie and Christine.'

She stopped and gasped for breath as Mary Ellen gripped her shoulders.

'What's happened?' Mary Ellen asked with strange quietness; then called over her shoulder, 'John!'

As John reached the door Molly was gasping out, 'They're in the boat; they haven't any oars . . . It's going round and round down the gut. It was our Dominic; he tried to get in the boat with Christine, and she pushed him back and Katie loosened the rope . . . I was behind the railings watching. Katie wouldn't let me go with her, but I sneaked down, and I saw our Dominic come. Oh, Ma! and David's screaming in the slipway.'

John was running down the yard with Shane on his heels, calling, 'Make straight for the slacks; don't go down the slipway, it'll be in the main gut by now.'

Mary Ellen, with Molly at her side, followed them, whispering as she ran, 'What is this now? What has come upon us now?'

On the main road, passers-by stopped and gaped at the two great men in shirt sleeves tearing along as if the devil was after them, the old man behind the young one, and the little woman and the lass behind the old man.

Someone called, 'What's up? Is it a fire?' But the running men took no heed, and one after another, the passers-by appealed to the woman and girl. And sometimes the girl answered, 'It's me sister . . . she's in a boat an' being carried down the gut.'

Children tacked themselves on to Mary Ellen and Molly, and men turned in their tracks to run back down the road towards the slacks.

When John came to the open space of the slacks his heart almost stopped. Without looking towards the gut he knew the boat was there, for the bank was lined with people. At this end of the slacks was the double tram line, where one tramcar had to wait for the other to pass. They were both standing empty, and their drivers were calling to the people, 'We'll have to go'; but none of the passengers attempted to leave the bank.

As John ran down the pavement towards the middle of the slacks where the gangway of timbers led from the bank to the edge of the mud, he had to push his way through the people now pouring out from the streets known as the New Buildings that faced a part of the slacks. He thrust at them with his arms, knocking them aside and calling forth hot exclamations. Those standing on the gangway jumped clear of him, and he took the timbers four at a time. The noise from the bank died down and there was only the wind, on which was borne thin wails, and the squelch of the water between the timbers beneath his pounding feet. Automatically he paused at the cabin, which was mounted on a platform of lashed timbers in the centre of the great square, and grabbed up a long pole with a hook on its end that the timber man used for pulling the timbers together. Now the race was to reach the end of the timbers bordering the gut before the boat came abreast of him. He could see it was being held stationary at the moment; but by what he couldn't tell. If it was stuck on the other side of the gut on the great mud flat that extended to the river then it was almost a certainty that it would be sucked into this oozing morass.

Arrived at the end of the roped timbers, he had to take to the narrow planks that formed a precarious gangway to the gut. Here, he couldn't run, but had to pick his way over the green slimy wood. The pole impeded him still further; and once he slipped and the water swirled about his thighs before he could pull himself up again. He had managed to retain his grip on the pole; and as he regained his footing a great 'Oh!' came to him from the bank. The sight of the boat speeding towards him lent wings of sureness to his feet, and within a matter of seconds he reached the gut.

Clinging to the great post that was the last support of the foot timbers he shouted madly to the approaching boat, 'Grab the pole!' But the wind tore at his voice, carrying his words away from him and them.

The boat was now making swift circles; one second, he would see Katie's face over the gunwhale, her eyes staring in terror, the next he would be looking at the back of her head, her hat still on it. Christine was sitting in the middle of the boat, her arms stretched taut, her hands gripping the sides in a pitifully vain endeavour to steady the tiny craft. She had seen John, for each time she fronted him her eyes held his for the second before they were torn away again.

It was not the wind that was driving the boat down the gut so much as the tide which was in full ebb; the locked waters between the floats of timbers were rushing madly back into the gut to meet the water draining from the mud flat beyond. Added to this, the suction of the cross channel, bordering the sawmill on the far side of the slacks, made the main gut a frothing, boiling mass of water.

As the boat came abreast of him, John bellowed, to the very limit of his lungs, 'Catch the hook, Christine!'

Perhaps she heard him and was afraid to loosen her grip on the sides of the boat, or perhaps his voice became only part of the wind, for when he cast the crooked end of the pole towards the boat it fell close to it, and anyone on the alert could have grabbed it; but the fraction of time during which this could have happened was lost. The boat gave another mad turn and was away, past him. He saw Katie stand up. She seemed to stand perfectly straight and still, and he experienced the odd sensation that her face was floating to him . . . imagination! But it was not imagination when he heard her voice coming to him against the wind . . . 'John! Oh, John!'

137

The boat was now flung into the vortex of water where the channels of the gut crossed. It heaved and whirled. Then like a ball, held by some mighty hand, it became still, and John saw clearly the two figures, their arms wound tightly about each other, crouched together; the hand was lifted, and the boat like a ball, was thrown up and over.

As John raised his arms to dive, two hands clawed at him and grabbed his belt. He half turned, screaming at the man behind him, but in wrenching himself free he overbalanced and toppled into the water. When his head broke the surface Peter Bracken grabbed his hair, and Peter's agonised voice screamed at him, 'It's no use! It's no use! They've gone. Don't make another.'

Two more hands stretched out and, gripping John's braces, they hauled him on to the plank again, where he lay still with Peter Bracken bending over him. A great stillness was pressing down on him. It was the stillness of the dead of all time. In it there was no regret, no pondering, no desire, no recrimination, no feeling whatever; it was void, because it held no thought.

He looked towards the upturned boat; he watched Katie's hat, mounted on a crest of frothing bubbles, rise and fall, bobbing round and round the swirling boat, like the earth round the sun. Peter Bracken's tearing sobs came to him, and he did not wonder at them. Nor, when he turned towards him was he surprised to see a very old man. Time passed and the receding tide showed the shining mud about the planks on which they stood.

Men were walking cautiously along the planks now. First, Peter Bracken was helped back, and when the men said, 'Come, lad,' John allowed himself to be led back to the timbers, one going before him and one behind, steadying him as though he were a child.

The timbers were thick with men, soundless men. John walked alone now, and they made a path for him. Closing in again after him, they followed him to the bank, where the sobbing and wailing rose and fell like the waves of the wind.

Three people were standing apart at the foot of the bank, and when John stopped and looked at them, the stillness began to lift from him. The first impression to penetrate it was that his father had his tick back worse than ever. This was followed by the painful realization that his mother was a little old woman, and her not yet fifty, and that Molly would never be Katie. They looked at him, and the sobbing on the bank seemed hushed.

Then from the middle of a group of women, David's voice rose, crying, 'Christine! I want Christine!' and the stillness was lifted completely from John; and a name passed through his brain like a tearing flame . . . Dominic!

He threw up his head as if sniffing a scent, and his eyes swept the crowded bank from one end to the other. But from where he was standing below it, it was impossible to seek out anyone from the broken front line of the crowd.

A path was miraculously cleared for him when, turning suddenly from the agonised stare of his parents, he rushed up the gangway. Across the main road was a rise of grassy ground bordering the New Buildings. He made straight for it. Now he was looking down on the congested road, and there in the far distance, on the very outskirts of the crowd, he saw Dominic's head. It was hatless, and the fitful sunshine was turning the hair to gold. Whether Dominic had seen him John did not know, but as he tore along the comparatively clear ground Dominic's head disappeared; and when John reached the spot, Dominic was gone.

To a woman of the fifteen streets, John said only one word, 'Dominic?' and she pointed to the disused workmen's hall: 'He went round by the back of there, lad.'

When he reached the back of the hall John caught sight of Dominic . . . he was running across the middle of the field used by the chemical works as a dumping ground for their foul-smelling residue. The field was a mass of small mounds, and Dominic was leaping like a kangaroo over them.

As John raced over the field the distance between them lessened appreciably, and when he came out on to the Cleveland Place road, there was Dominic, not twenty yards ahead, disappearing round the corner of the tram sheds.

They were both on the main road now, and the people struggling back to the fifteen streets called to John, 'Stop lad! . . .' 'Give up, lad! . . .' 'What's done's done . . . think of your mother.' And when men's arms went out and tried to hold him he brushed them off like flies.

As they neared the fifteen streets Dominic was lost in the dense crowd awaiting news from those who had been down to the slacks. But John knew that Dominic would make for the stackyard at the top of the streets; here, in the maze of stacked timber he would hope to escape. He was right; he saw Dominic mount the wall and disappear.

John did not jump the wall, but stood on its top – his desire was teaching him cunning. He could not tell which way Dominic had taken, and once on the ground it would be like searching for a needle in a haystack; but from up here he should see Dominic's head as he moved between the stacks.

It was some minutes before John detected it, for Dominic's hair was in tone with the seasoning wood. Dominic had paused to glance behind, and John was off the wall, running swiftly and noiselessly, not in Dominic's direction but to the right of him. Dominic was making for the railway line at the end of the yard and he'd get him there.

John reached the end of the stacks and waited, his eyes darting back and forth to the last three openings – it would be from one of these that Dominic would emerge. He came out of the middle one, running swiftly; and pulled up a few yards from John. His mouth was open and his jaw was moving from side to side. The brothers surveyed each other, John's eyes sending out streams of diabolical hate, while in Dominic's the hate was mixed with fear.

John did not say, 'You killed them . . . Katie and Christine, and now I'm going to kill you,' nor did Dominic say, 'It was an accident'; without any word they closed, and John, like a raving bull, smashed his fists into Dominic's face. From the start, Dominic was handicapped by his raincoat, but fear made him hit back desperately. It also made him aware that he could not stand up to the blows being levelled at him; so he used his knee. Bringing it up sharply, he rammed it into the lower part of John's stomach, and as John bent double Dominic ran back down the opening through which he had come, only to be brought to a stop by the cries of men coming through the jumbled stacks. Assuming that the men were after him, he decided to carry out his first intention of taking to the railway. But when he turned once more there was John, at the opening of the stacks.

Blindly, Dominic rushed at him, using his fists and his feet; but it was as if John had set up a guard of flaying hammers, and soon all Dominic could do was to protect his face with his crossed forearms. He was pinned against a stack, and long after he ceased to fight John's fists pounded him, and he seemed to be kept on his feet only by the succession of lifting blows At last, Dominic's knees gave way and he slid on to his side. John stood above him, gasping; then, using his foot, he pushed Dominic on to his back, and only then did he become aware of the crowd gathered about them.

Exclamations came from all sides. 'My God!' 'Leave him be, lad; he's had enough.' 'God Almighty, I think he's done for him!'

On hearing the last remark, John wiped the blood from his face with a sweep of his hand, and stared down on Dominic . . . Was he dead? No, he mustn't be dead . . . Not this way, this easy way. He was going to die in the gut. He would drag him there, to the spot where they went down, where Katie's straw hat went round and round. The tide would be low, so he'd throw him down the steep incline of mud. He would be conscious and would claw at the mud as it slowly sucked him in. But – he looked up from Dominic and stared glassily at the faces of the men – they would stop him. Yes, if he attempted to do it now. Well, he would beat them; he would take this thing home. He moved Dominic again with his foot . . . He wouldn't let him out of his sight, and in the night he'd get him to the gut. If he had to drag him every inch of the way he'd get him to the gut.

The exclamations came to him again, more shrill now, for the women had joined the men, after forcing open the stackyard gates.

'Oh, Jesus, have mercy on us! he's killed him. God Almighty, it'll be a hanging job!'

It'll be a hanging job! . . . The cry reached Mary Ellen, standing on the outskirts of the crowd, surrounded by a group of women, all with tear-stained faces, and all urging her, in one way or another, to return home . . . 'You can do no good, Mary Ellen.'

'You must think of yourself and Shane.'

'Yes. Shane's lying back there bad, the shock's been too much for him . . . Come on, lass.'

Mary Ellen stood quiet in the centre of them. She wasn't crying, there was no liquid left in her body to form tears. Her body was dry, it had been burnt up, and the flame was now going to her head . . . If these women didn't get out of her way, she'd scream. She must get to her lad. He had killed Dominic, so she must be with him. To her, this seemed to be the end of a long waiting – Katie was gone; Dominic was dead; and there was only John . . . He had done what he said he would do – John always meant what he said. Now there was nothing else to wait for.

Mary Ellen knew that the agony within her was screaming to be set free. The agony was wide and deep, reaching into the bowels of the earth. In an odd way, she felt herself one with the earth . . . the dirt, the mire, and the richness. The scream of agony was tearing around in the dry emptiness of her body, and swiftly, in a spiral, it was mounting to her head. Once it was there, she would be free, for when it escaped from her lips she would feel no more . . . at least, not with any feeling she would recognize; once she screamed, she would be changed for all time, for madness would possess her.

As her mind ran to meet the scream, she heard it. It seemed to lift her and the women from the very ground. But it wasn't her scream; it was Nancy Kelly's. And it was mixed with laughter . . . the terrible laughter. The women covered their ears, but Mary Ellen stood listening. Then she thrust wildly at the bodies hemming her in, and forced her way through the men to the space where John stood, and Dominic lay with Nancy Kelly kneeling by him, pulling at his torn and bloodstained clothes, and crying, 'Dominic! Dominic! Don't be dead! I've kept me mouth shut, Dominic . . . I did what you told me.' She pulled at him, trying to shake life into him again. 'Dominic, you must marry me when the bairn's born . . . I've been a good girl, Dominic, I did what you told me.'

Nothing but her screeching voice could be heard; the crowd was as silent as the stacked piles of wood.

The blood pounded into John's head. Dominic, the father of the bairn! The swine! The god-damn, dirty swine! Reaching down, he grabbed Nancy and flung her to one side. Then he was on top of Dominic, crying out as he beat his fists into the inert, blood-covered face, 'You dirty swine! And you put the blame on . . .'

His words were lost as the men tore him aside. Fighting, they bore him to the ground, and so many held him that only his eyes were free to move.

As one of the men shouted to the others, 'Look slippy there! Get him away, can't yer!' John heaved in an effort to free himself . . . If they got Dominic away they'd hide him. Why didn't he finish him off when he had the chance! He writhed and struggled until the uselessness of his efforts was borne upon him, and he suddenly became still. Well, wherever they took Dominic he'd find him! Oh, Katie! Katie! – he closed his eyes to shut out the men's faces as sorrow overwhelmed him.

When the men released him and he got to his feet, he saw his mother. She was picking at a button of her blouse, her eyes, dead in her white face, staring at him.

When he said, 'I'll find him,' she remained silent; then she turned and walked slowly away, and he followed her; and the crowd closed in behind, like a gigantic funeral procession.

CHAPTER TWELVE

THE AFTERMATH

There was no door in the fifteen streets that was closed to John; for three days he had walked in and out of the houses, into bedrooms, some tidy in their bareness, some a mass of jumbled old clothing and mattresses, and some indescribable in their squalor. He saw nothing of the conditions, he looked only for a concealed form; under beds, in cupboards, in rooms where the sick were lying, and where weary hands would reach out in a vain effort to give him comfort. He spoke to no-one, and he trusted no-one; he knew that in this time of trouble the people of the fifteen streets were united in one huge family to protect him, as they thought, from himself. So he did not search systematically, but after searching the houses at the lower end, he would suddenly double back to the top or middle streets, and houses he had searched but a short time before would be gone over again. No harsh word met him; even if he stalked in on a family eating he would be greeted soothingly.

He had one assistant in his search: Peggy Flaherty. Her fat, wobbling body hugged by coats, she would accompany him at odd hours of the day, most of the time talking away at him: 'Never give up, John. We'll get him yet. By God! we will an' all . . . He needn't run off with the idea he can escape you, can he lad? And he'll not get out of these buildings.'

Often, in his darting from one place to another, he would leave her behind; but she would be guided to the house where he was. And again she would tag along after him, nodding knowingly to the groups of people gathered in the street. Only at night did she leave him alone for any length of time, for then he paraded the main road.

John knew that Dominic would be in no fit condition for days and that it was practically impossible for him, up to now, to have made his escape by the stackyard, for since the breakthrough, the gates were doubly locked, and there remained only the wall as a means of exit that way. So for two nights now he had watched from the main road. The night policeman, on his beat, would stop and talk to him, the darkness wiping away his officialdom: 'Is it worth it, lad? You know what will happen, don't you? You'll get time, if not the other. Anyway, how do you know he's not already gone? By what I hear, he's likely in hospital.

If it hadn't been for your sister saying the little lass loosened the boat, we should have been on to him ourselves. And you can count yourself lucky, you know, one of us wasn't on the scene when you got at him. So don't look for trouble, lad, and get yourself home to bed.'

No words had penetrated John's mind since those spoken by the men when they were holding him; and it might have been that he did not hear this advice, for he made no reply. It was as though his mind, so packed with the weight of his sorrow and hate, could take in nothing more. During the first two days he did not actively think of Katie and Christine, nor yet of Mary, whom he felt to be part of his sorrow for all time, for she, in some strange way, was a partner in the guilt he was laying on himself. Because he had allowed the madness of his love to possess him, he ignored the danger in which Christine stood, and did nothing to protect her beyond ordering Katie to act as a buffer to Dominic's advances.

On this, the third day of the search, when the strain was telling on him, in the leaden weight of his limbs and his unsteady walk, and in his burning eyes that would close whenever he stood still for a moment, his mind, strangely enough, was beginning to sort itself out; thoughts were separating and presenting themselves, as it were, before him. He was standing leaning against the wall on the waste ground at the top of one of the streets, where he had paused for a moment during his search; and his hand moved over the three days' growth on his face. His body felt dirty, his inside empty, and his head light. But the thoughts came, one after the other, isolated yet joined: I must stop sometime . . . if only they find them before they're carried out to sea; if I could see Katie once again it might not be so bad. Oh! Katie! Katie . . . My father's done for, he'll not work again. Why am I not with my mother, she needs me? But she understands I've got to find him. She wants me to find him; she hates him as much as I do . . . Why doesn't Peter Bracken look for him instead of yapping, 'Forgive us our trespasses'. Father O'Malley says Peter is the cause of all this, and if my mother and me had done as he commanded this would never have happened.

As if his thoughts had conjured up the priest, Father O'Malley, accompanied by Peggy Flahetry, appeared before him.

'Oh, there you are, lad,' Peggy said. 'And here he is himself, Father . . . Away with you now!' she added to the children who were following them.

Father O'Malley confronted John: 'Come into the house,' he ordered. 'I want to talk you.'

John blinked slowly and made no reply.

'Did you hear me?' demanded the priest.

And after a short silence, during which Father O'Malley waited, and the children sniffed, and a few women added themselves to the group at a respectful distance, the priest went on, 'This has got to stop! Who are you to take God's work into your own hands? He will seek vengeance without your help. He has already shown you what He thinks of you going against His Holy Will – I cannot repeat too often, that had you kept that man Bracken from your house this state of affairs would never have come about.'

'It's hopeless,' Peggy Flaherty broke in. 'Time and again I've told him to give up the search. Oh! it's no use at all.' She proceeded to rattle on, in spite of the priest's gimlet eyes demanding her silence and John's blurred and bewildered stare as slowly the fact forced its way into his mind that she, and she alone, had urged him in his search.

There were murmurs from the women: 'The priest's right. There's been no luck about the doors since that Bracken man came.'

'No! nor will there be!' Father O'Malley threw at them, effectually drowning the more considerate comment: 'Aye, but he's lost his lass too.'

'Come!' Father O'Malley commanded John.

John stood for a while longer . . . the priest and Peggy, and the women, were becoming blurred: he must rest and have something to eat if he intended going on. And so, in the eyes of the women and children, strength was added to the priest's power when John turned and obediently followed him . . .

In contrast to John's ceaseless moving Mary Ellen sat almost immobile in the kitchen. At odd times she would go to the front room and attend to Shane; but she cooked nothing, nor cleaned, and, like John, she did not speak. And if at times she stared at Molly, her face did not show any surprise or wonderment at the change in this daughter of hers; for Molly was 'running the house'. She had screwed her plaits into a tight little bun at the back of her head and she wore her mother's holland apron, rolled up at the band. Overnight, Molly threw off her prolonged childhood; she was not now a girl, but a little woman. And she was spurred on by the praise of the neighbours: 'That's it, hinny, you be your mother's right hand. You must take Katie's place now.' They talked as though Katie had been an elder sister.

Sometimes Molly would stand in the scullery and cry for Katie, while at the same time experiencing a feeling of relief that Katie was gone; for she would never have been needed had Katie still been here; and she was needed – they couldn't do without her. Why, she told herself, she was the only one in the house who hadn't lost her mind . . . except Mick; and he was no help, one way or the other. All he could do was to stand among awe-struck groups of lads, bragging that he knew where Dominic was hiding . . . He didn't! She tucked her apron more firmly about her as she thought that, of all the youngsters, she was the only one who really knew – Dominic was taken into a house at the top of the street when they carried him from the stackyard; but when John started to search they moved him. It was Peggy Flaherty's idea. They did it in the night and John hadn't found Dominic yet.

Thinking of John, Molly looked again at the screwed piece of paper in her palm . . . After attending her father, the doctor had said, 'Look, my dear; take heed of what I'm going to say to you. Now do you think you can make your brother John some tea when he comes in and put these two tablets in without him seeing you? Be very careful of them; they are strong and will soon put him to sleep.'

She felt very proud it was she who was asked, for her mother was sitting there and he never asked her to do it. So there was a rising of excitement on Molly when she saw John and Father O'Malley coming up the backyard. She'd make the tea now, and offer a cup to the priest; and perhaps he would bless her and say she was a gift of God to her mother and them all at this time.

But the priest did not bless Molly, nor speak to Mary Ellen, but continued to talk to John, who was sitting with his elbows resting on the table and his hand covering his eyes.

Mary Ellen listened while she looked into the fire. Did he never tire? Would he never stop? Why did he persist that the Bracken man was accountable for all this, when it was she herself who had brought it about? Hadn't she prayed on her bended knees to God, and asked Him to make something happen to stop her lad from going to America? Well, He had made something happen . . . John would never go to America now. God was laughing out of the side of His mouth at her, she felt, and He was waiting for the climax between John and Dominic. The regret she felt in the stackyard when she knew that Dominic was not dead had soon changed to a dread that John would find him. By now, he must have been in every house in the place bar one, and if he were not half demented, that one would surely soon present itself to him. She cast her eyes towards the ceiling . . . How much longer would Dominic remain there, hidden amongst the old furniture, the crocodile, and the poss tubs? She felt like his jailer, sitting outside the prison door, protecting him from a vengeance that hunted him. Had the hunter been anyone but John she would have let him in to do his work.

She turned to look at the priest drinking his cup of tea, and she wondered what she would do if he should propose that they kneel down and say the Rosary, for she was feeling hostile towards a God who had done this to her . . . using her own prayers to bring her to grief! Her eyes moved slowly to John – he was drinking his tea at one go. Soon he would be asleep, if Molly had done what the doctor told her. How long would he sleep? Long enough to get the other one away? And when would he go back to work? There would be only him to work now, for it was doubtful whether Shane would do a hand's turn again . . . No. John would never now go to America.

She turned to the fire once more, and her old dominant self made an effort to oust the apathy . . . Get up and see to Shane! it ordered.

And that lass is wasting the food trying to cook it. You can't expect neighbours to go on bringing stuff in . . . But the apathy lay heavily on her and she allowed it to settle about her again as a protection.

The priest's voice was going on and on, and she was listening again. He was saying, 'You've been godless for years, and then you wonder why tribulation like this comes upon you. Can't you see, man, you can't defy God and get away with it; the ignoring of His Holy Mass Sunday after Sunday brings its tribulation. Make up your mind to turn over a new leaf . . . Throw off all undesirable companions, and come to Mass.'

The priest's voice was falling to an almost sympathetic tone, it was quiet and even; and, as Mary Ellen listened, the wonder was born in her that he could be capable of such gentleness. As his voice became slower still, she turned to look at him. His eyes half closed, he was leaning across the table, for all the world like someone drunk, and he was emphasising each laboured word with a wobbly shake of his finger.

Mary Ellen rose sharply to her feet, staring at the priest, her eyes wide and her mouth open. As Father O'Malley lifted his head and slowly comprehended her astonished look, he pulled himself upright . . . What in the name of God had come upon him! This great, great tiredness. He shook his head in an endeavour to throw it off. Holy Mother of mothers, had he caught something? . . . But what could he have caught? Where had he been today? . . . The Flannagans . . . and the child with the suspected sleeping sickness . . . In the name of God, it couldn't be! God wouldn't let his faithful servant suffer such a thing. But he had surely caught something – never before in his life had he felt so tired.

As Mary Ellen began to laugh, the priest rose slowly to his feet. These people! What were they? Ignorant hooligans, who could be driven to do the right thing only by fear . . . Oh, God, don't let this thing fall upon me! he appealed. By the use of my strong will I will bring these people to You . . . Only take this from me . . . that woman laughing! She was mad! . . . He must get home and to bed. He turned and staggered through the front room, with the terrified Molly behind him and Shane, half raised up in bed, following his erratic course in bewilderment and Mary Ellen's laughter becoming dimmer in his ears.

Mary Ellen had no power to stop the laughter; it swelled inside her, like the fire did a few days ago . . . or was it years? It shook every fibre of her body. She held one hand tightly against her stomach and a forearm across her wobbling breasts. John was standing over her, his glazed eyes blinking, and saying, 'Stop it, Ma! Look; steady on.' He was holding her by the shoulders, and her wide-open mouth and grimacing face were doing more to bring back his mind to normality than all the reasoning in the world. It only wanted his mother to go mad to complete the whole thing. 'Look, be quiet!' His voice cracked hoarsely on the words.

'I . . . I can't, lad.' She moved her hands to her sides, where the pain of her laughter was tearing at her. 'The . . . the pills! she p-put them in the wrong . . . c-cup.'

John could not understand what her words were meant to imply. He shook her again: 'Ma! Ma! Stop it, I tell you!'

Shane's voice came weakly from the front room, calling, 'What is it? What is it out there? Why are you laughing? For God's sake!'

Slowly Mary Ellen's laughter subsided, and she gazed up into John's dirty, stubbly face, and for a second her own smoothed out into an expressionless mask before crumpling under the release of her tears; and her broken words, 'Oh, me bairn! me bairn! me bonnie bairn!' cut through John, and completed his awakening.

He put his arms about her, holding her tightly, and her emotion rocked its way through him, and the burning of his eyes became unbearable. Like the rush of water when the main dock gates were opened to admit a ship, the tears came to him too. Silently flowing, they fell on Mary Ellen's brow; and their raining, more than her own, restored her, and set her once again in her rightful place as pivot of the house. And so, as always, they balanced each other.

Mary Ellen's body still shaking and her tears still falling, she drew away from John, and taking his arm, saying, 'Come, lad,' she led him to the bedroom. When he sat on the bedside she lifted up his feet, and as she unloosened his boots he groaned and, turning his face into the pillow, sobbed, with the tearing, heart-rending sobs that only a man in sorrow can cry.

As Father Bailey hurried up Fadden Street he kept telling himself that this was not the time to be amused; tragedy had stalked this street, and was still doing so. But, nevertheless, only the darkness hid the twinkle in his eye and the quirk on his lips. The story the child Molly had brought to him was fantastic . . . giving Father O'Malley the tea with the drug in! And him staggering out into the street to be confronted by Peter Bracken, of all people. And then to be taken into Bracken's house! Oh, it was the limit of limits. In the wildest stretches of imagination, Father Bailey could not see his pastor allowing himself to be even touched by the hand of Peter Bracken, apart from being led into his house.

When Peter Bracken opened his door, Father Bailey said, 'You sent for me?'

'I did,' said Peter. 'Will you come in?'

Nothing more was said until they reached the kitchen, and even then not immediately; for the sight of Father O'Malley stretched out on the mat, with his head on a pillow and a blanket covering him, was almost too much for Father Bailey. Father O'Malley looked less prepossessing in sleep than he did awake. He looked, Father Bailey thought whimsically, as though he might be dictating to the sender of dreams as to their type and quality.

Father Bailey suppressed his mirth and left till later the relish this situation would provide, particularly for those times when his superior would be most overbearing . . . Oh, the laughs he would get from this would last him a lifetime!

'How did it come about?' he asked Peter, without daring to raise his eyes from the floor in case this man who was also in sorrow, should detect his mirth.

'I happened to be coming up the street,' replied Peter, 'and found him slumped against the wall near my door. Molly was with him and she told me what she had done. There was no-one about at the time, but I knew that should anyone see him it would be said immediately that I'd put the evil eye on him.'

Without looking up, Father Bailey nodded.

'Or should he have been seen staggering about,' went on Peter, 'some people would have said . . . well, that he was drunk. People only need to see a shadow to create the substance.'

Father Bailey slowly brought his gaze up to this man . . . How many terrible substances had been created from shadows for him! And not a few by the priest at his feet. And yet he had endeavoured to save Father O'Malley from the stigma of drunkenness!

'You can get a cab and take him home,' Peter Bracken went on: 'Or you can leave him here till he wakes.'

Yes, he could get a cab, Father Bailey thought, and take him home. But then again, should he be seen being carried from the house, this man would be blamed for putting some 'fluence on him . . . No; he would leave him here. And please God, he'd be here to see him wake . . . he wouldn't miss that for a bucketful of sovereigns.

'Would it be putting you out,' he asked, 'if he stayed?'

'Not at all,' said Peter Bracken quietly.

'And myself too?' added Father Bailey. 'I have some things to attend to, but I'll come back later if I may . . . And I'd better look in on the doctor who issued those tablets.'

'There's something I'd better tell you,' said Peter . . . 'It was important that John should have taken those tablets' – he nodded down at the sleeping priest – 'for tonight it is arranged that . . . that' – he couldn't bring himself to speak Dominic's name – 'the other one is to be got away.'

'You know where he is then?' said Father Bailey, with interest.

'Yes. But he can't remain there much longer. John will shortly regain his senses, and he will surely guess; for he's upstairs above him in the only house he hasn't searched.'

'Good God!'

'John is too good a man to suffer . . . for him. He must be got away!'

The priest nodded again, and asked, 'Where is he going?'

'I can't tell you that. I can only tell you he'll be put aboard a tramp steamer.'

'Will he be fit to work his passage?'

'Not for a time; but that has been arranged.'

Peter Bracken said no more, but Father Bailey knew that sick men weren't taken, even on tramp steamers, for nothing. And the man before him was the only one around these parts who could supply the money and arrange the whole thing. He shook his head . . . Here, indeed, was a good Samaritan; and under such circumstances as to make the act heroic. He looked at Peter's shrunken figure and at the face, which during the last three days had drooped into deep lines of age, and he said: 'I think you're a very brave and forgiving man.'

The old man turned away, his lips trembling: 'I am not brave; it is that I can bear my sorrow easier than the others, for my child is near me. Death to them' – he nodded towards the wall – 'even with their religion, is a severance that only death can join again. But to me there has been no parting, the main part of her is still with me.'

For the moment, the priest experienced a tinge of envy for this man's faith . . . Here was faith as it should be. Would any Catholic think like this? No, he thought regretfully. Christ Himself was in the blessed sacrament of the altar for them, but their faith was so limited that it could not reach over the boundary to Him . . . so there were few miracles. They prayed to God to come to them, instead of boldly going to Him.

'Can I help in any way?' he asked. 'Is there anything I can do?'

Peter turned to the priest again: 'You can, if you will. John wouldn't suspect you. You could get more tablets and see that he takes them. If the men don't get the other . . . this done tonight, there may not be another chance for days. And then it may be too late.'

Father Bailey looked steadily at Peter Bracken: 'Why are you taking all this trouble over someone who has done you such a terrible injury?'

Peter's eyes closed, and his face set in lines of pain. He had lost the mainspring of his life and hopes, for Christine would have carried on his ideas. She had been brave; more so than him in some ways, for he was vulnerable to jibes – how many deaths had he died these past three days because of the attitude that had been taken towards Christine. It was as if his girl did not count . . . as if she too had not died the same death as the child, even the blame for the tragedy, in some subtle way, had been laid on her, while the perpetrator of it had even come in for a modicum of sympathy from a section of the people, and he himself was more hated and feared than before . . . and his heart was sore within him.

But he answered the priest calmly: 'Because I believe in the Great Plan of Life. I believe all that has happened had to happen. What I am doing I must do, for I feel also that it isn't in the Plan for John to commit a crime and suffer for it. There are other things for him, he has begun to think, and nothing can stop him evolving.'

As if expecting some deprecating remark, Peter's eyes held those of the priest for a moment before he went on: 'I believe he will eventually do something for the betterment of his people . . . I know he will, for Christine has told me; and she knows, for, you see, she loved him.'

Father Bailey's gaze was almost tender, as he looked at this old man, who, strangely enough, held views which were in exact keeping with some of his own; did he himself not always say that the path was all mapped out for each one of us from the day he was born, that the great Creator knew the shape of every pebble to be trodden by our feet. This man was a thinker, and was possessed of a spirit that wasn't un-Christlike. He preached that he was part of Christ in his understanding and in his power, and although the doctrine he taught was divided by insurmountable barriers from his own, nevertheless the essence was very much the same. And he must talk to him; for whether he knew it or not, at this moment his need was great. Father Bailey knew that to extend to Peter Bracken the hand of friendship would be a herculean task; the main stumbling block would be, not so much the difference of their religions or opinions, but the priest now lying on the mat between them; and not him alone, but others of his breed, who with a little learning packing the narrow channels of their minds, set up theories bred of their own enlarged egos and used them under the stamp of the Church . . . Well, this was one time he was going to make a stand. If this man and he could never see eye to eye, they would have gone far if each could respect the other's point of view . . . A flash of enlightening candour through the priest's mind told him that the trying would be his work alone, for this man in his humility was advanced far beyond him.

He put out his hand and touched Peter Bracken's sleeve: 'I'll fix up that lad next door; then perhaps we can have a talk.'

After Father Bailey had gone, Peter, his eyes bright and head raised, stood by the side of the sleeping priest. He spoke as if to someone near: 'You were right, my dear; your going had a purpose. Never could this have come about otherwise. Will you ask all the guides of tolerance to help this man here? I, too, will work on him, that he may become more like him just gone.'

While Peter Bracken was sitting at the head of Father O'Malley the priest jerked violently – it was as if his spirit was up in arms at this outrage. From time to time his lips and cheeks would puff out and emit sounds like 'Pooh! poo-pooh!'

Peter did not smile – it needed Father Bailey to appreciate the humour of the situation.

The tin alarm clock on the mantelpiece showed twelve-thirty. Father Bailey sat looking at it, and from time to time he wondered whether it had stopped. But as he stared, the hand would give a slight movement, and once again he would tell himself that these were the longest three hours he had spent in his life . . . and the oddest. Was there ever such a situation! Here he was, sitting in this kitchen, after midnight, with this toil-worn woman opposite, so still she might be dead; and three cups on the table, the largest holding the white powder already mixed with the milk. And there on the hob was the teapot, stewing its inside out. They would likely all die from tannin poisoning if they were to drink the stuff. Well, pray God there would be no need. Less than half an hour now, and the men would be here and gone, and John could remain asleep or wake up just as he pleased, and no harm done . . . And for himself, he would go next door, where at least there was a comfortable chair to recline in while waiting for the grand awakening, as he termed it, of his superior . . . Was there ever such a situation! There next door was lying the man who was the sworn enemy of all spiritualists, and of Peter Bracken in particular and being tended gently by the man himself.

Father Bailey felt his eyes closing and he was thinking sleepily that it was many years since he enjoyed a conversation like the one this evening . . . a very enlightened man that. Of course, God help him, he was entirely wrong in many of his opinions, but there were some which tied up amazingly with those of the Church. Peter Bracken's idea, for instance, that the spirits, termed guides, and through whom the healing was done, were the good people who had gone on, whom he and all Catholics termed saints. Now that was an interesting point . . . He was awakened, startlingly, by a gasp from Mary Ellen.

They exchanged glances and looked towards the bedroom door; the bed was creaking heavily. There was a shuffling, a short silence, and John appeared at the open door.

It was only two days since Father Bailey last saw John, yet the change in him hurt the priest; he looked gaunt and twice his age.

But now was not the time, Father Bailey told himself, to waste on useless pity. Of all the times John could have chosen to wake up this was the worst; even if he drank the stuff this minute, as strong as it was, it was doubtful whether it would take effect before the arrival of the men.

John shook his head and ran his hand over his forehead. Then he looked dully but enquiringly at the priest.

And Father Bailey said promptly, 'Your father's not too good, John. Your mother called me in.'

John accepted this, and looked at his mother; then from her to the clock . . . twenty minutes to one! The pain of his existence flooded back to him . . . he had slept for hours! They would have got him away then. Well he had to sleep some time. But, oh God, why couldn't he have got him first, then this agony would have been appeased. Now it would go on for ever.

'Have this cup of tea, lad.' Mary Ellen was pouring the black tea into the cup with shaking hands.

John ran his hand round his face and shook his head: 'I'll have a wash first.'

'I could do with another, myself, Mrs O'Brien. Have a cup with me, John, it'll pull you together.'

The priest took the cup from Mary Ellen's hand and stirring it vigorously, passed it to John.

Without demur, John took it and drank a mouthful of the hot tea. He pursed his lips before replacing the cup on the table. Huh! the taste . . . his mouth was dry and thick!

Going to the hearth, he picked up the kettle. It was empty; and the occurrence was so unusual that he shook the kettle, then glanced at his mother. It seemed a symbol of the new life . . . nothing would ever be the same again.

Mary Ellen took the kettle from John's hand, whilst he went to the table and finished his tea. The priest sighed and sat down heavily, saying to John, 'Sit down, lad.'

Docilely, John sat down, as if his being knew nothing of hatred and the craving impulse to destroy.

Mary Ellen passed between him and the priest and placed the kettle on the fire. Then she too sat down, and the silence became heavy; until Father Bailey exclaimed, 'Well, Mrs O'Brien, I must soon be making my way home.' But he didn't move; and into the renewed silence came a soft padding. It bore no relation to footsteps. Mary Ellen and the priest exchanged quick glances, but John went on looking at the kettle, which had begun to hiss softly.

The padding which came from the wall at John's back now passed on to the ceiling. The priest turned his gaze from Mary Ellen and stared into the fire . . . Well, if they made no more noise than that, it would be all right – the old stockings round their boots were quite effective. Another two or three minutes, and it would be over.

The minutes passed, and John stood up and lifted the kettle from the fire, forcing back into himself the urge to be going. What was he idling here for, anyway? In another few minutes he'd be asleep again. And there was still the chance he might find him; for how did they know how long he would sleep. They might have been afraid to risk getting him away. This time he would stay at the bottom end of the streets; it was ten to one he was there, for his cronies were in that quarter.

'That water isn't hot,' Mary Ellen broke in, getting to her feet – in the scullery he would be standing under the staircase and the padding had started again.

'It'll do.'

As he made to pass her, he was brought to a halt by the sound of something falling on to the floor above. It could have been a chair or a box, or any piece of Peggy Flaherty's ménage. Perhaps John would have let it pass as just that had he not looked at his mother and from her to the priest. The apprehension in their exchanging glances was like a revelation to him . . . 'The bitch!' The words were forced out through his clenched teeth – at this moment he wasn't thinking of Dominic so much as Peggy Flaherty. It was as clear as daylight . . . her trailing round with him to throw him off the scent of that swine! What a bloody fool he was! He almost threw the kettle on to the hearth; but when he turned to dash out of the back door he found the priest barring his way.

'Get by!' he said grimly, towering over the tubby figure of Father Bailey.

'Listen, John. I'm not going to get by . . . Now you listen to me!' – the priest stared up at John with as much aggressiveness as was in him to portray – 'you can do nothing . . . you're as helpless as a new-born babe. Get that into that big head of yours. You've just swallowed an excellent sleeping draught, one that would put a horse to sleep. And that's where you'll be in a very few minutes.'

John stepped back and glared at his mother. Mary Ellen, her hands clasped, her eyes dumbly pleading, said nothing. He remembered her laughter, earlier on, and her jumbled words about Molly and the pills, and the queer turn of the priest . . . Now Father Bailey sitting there waiting, with that tale about his father. Why, they'd all hoaxed him like a child! But he wasn't asleep yet. No, by God! not by a long chalk.

He swung up the bucket of water standing by the tin dish and bending, poured it over his head; then towelled himself vigorously. And before Mary Ellen and the priest were aware of his intention he was through the front room.

In the street, he ran as he had never run before, round the bottom corner and up the back lane. But when he reached the backyard he found only Mary Ellen and Peggy there. They were standing by the kitchen door, an epitome of the conspiracy against him and of its successful close.

In the moment of his pausing he was made aware of the effects of the drug, for he had the desire to push past them into the kitchen and to sit down. But the desire was swept away and he turned and ran again, for the main road now. However they tried to evade him, eventually they must make for the main road.

A cold drizzle was falling, and already his shirt was wet; but this would keep him awake. There was no-one in sight, as far as he could see, and he stood in the shadow of the wall, scanning the openings to the streets. There was a lamp at each corner, but so far did the streets seem to stretch away into the darkness that he realised he must keep on the move if he hoped to discern any movement from the lower streets.

His lids felt heavy and drooped slowly over his eyes. He stretched them and swore grimly to himself. They had only to play a waiting game . . . they were in there somewhere still, he was sure. How much longer could he fight against this increasing drowsiness?

He had to lean against the wall. Gradually his anger died in him, and all he wanted to do was to lie down . . . Blast them! He started to walk, briskly as he thought, but soon stopped again and leaned against a lamp post. His head was throbbing to the rhythm of approaching horse's hooves. Soon the black shape of a cab rocketed towards him, and ahead of it, on the pavement, he made out the scurrying figure of Father Bailey.

Panting, the priest came alongside John and laid a hand on his arm. He murmured something, but John did not hear what it was. He was looking at the cab, which was now abreast of him . . . and there was Dominic's face! His eyes were turned towards the window. They were sockets of darkness in a white blur. Time seemed to stand suspended, giving the brothers the opportunity to exchange their last looks of hatred. Then something sprang from John and leaped upon the sneering face of his brother. But whatever it was it had no effect . . . the cab rolled on, the bandaged face disappeared. And John, like a child, allowed himself to be led gently away by the priest; he was thinking dimly that all his life there would be a want in him . . . something uncompleted.

CHAPTER THIRTEEN

RENUNCIATION

The under-manager of the sawmill watched John jump the wall; he was waiting for him on the pavement of the main road.

'You know, that's a punishable offence,' he said evenly.

John straightened his cap. 'I suppose so.'

'Well, I don't want to seem stiff' – the man was almost apologetic – 'but it's got to stop. I shouldn't mind if it was just one doing it, but it only needs a start you know, and we'll have everybody living in Jarrow coming out this way, and I leave you to guess what'll happen to the timber . . . It's got to stop, you see.'

John merely nodded before moving off; and the man, looking after him, thought 'poor devil'. It was right what they said, he had gone a bit queer. What other reason could there be for him not using the dock gates – for though the sawmill yard might be a short cut to Jarrow, it was difficult of access. Perhaps the lad thought he was still chasing his brother. Well, whatever he thought he was doing now, he'd have to find some other way of doing it but by this wall . . .

John realised this as he strode homewards. But there was no other way to avoid meeting Mary; if he used the main gate sooner or later they would be bound to meet. For four weeks now he had come out by the wall; it cut off the arches and the length of road past the Simonside bank. It did not cut off the gut – no deviation could cut off the gut. At first, he was determined to avoid Mary only until he should feel strong enough to face her; but with each passing day he became weaker, and told himself that in the silence between them the madness would fade and he would not have to see her. Then her letters started to come. Every day for the past three weeks there had been a letter. They were all neatly stacked in his box under the bed . . . and all unopened. With the coming of the first one he knew he must not open it, for the words it held would break down his reserve.

In the long stretches of the night he would think of the letters and what they held, and it would seem as if their substance created Mary herself, bringing her into the room to him . . . at times, even into the bed. He would feel her there, even smell the faint perfume that was hers, and his arms would go out to her, and in pulling her to him he would come to himself and, getting up, would stand on the cold floor, staring out of the window into the black square of the backyard, or up at the piece of sky visible between the houses, and know that Mary and the magic world that she alone could make was not for him – this wherein he stood was his world, this his night view for all time . . . this was his far horizon; this was the limit to all his wild hopes; here in this house he would have to work out his salvation. Sometimes he would lean his head against the window frame and murmur, 'Katie, Katie,' as if asking her forgiveness . . . If only he had never had the idea of making her a teacher! It was his fault, for she was a child and would have forgotten about it. Then he would never have got dressed up to go and see . . . her. And not seeing her, he would have come to love Christine; and the issue between him and Dominic would have been finished earlier, and his Katie and Christine would have been alive today . . . Again, had the Brackens not come next door, and, like a disciple, he had not sat at Peter's feet, lapping up all his mad ideas about the power of thought, this would never have happened.

Well, he was finished with thinking . . . his mother was right – it got you nowhere. There would be no more wild imagining for him. The road he was on held no space for flights of fancy. He had been mad in a number of ways. Between her and Peter he had gone crazy for a time. She even made him believe that the quaint thoughts which came into his head were unpolished gems, holding poetic qualities . . . and Peter, that life held something gigantic for him, that one day he would lead men, not into battle, but out of it . . . out of the battle with squalor into brighter and better conditions. Peter even egged him to take on the job of being a delegate to the Labourers' and General Workers' Union . . . God! how far above the earth he had walked; until that business of Nancy Kelly's! Even then he saw his Mecca in America. But now it was all over. He knew where his Mecca lay . . . in this house, in the fifteen streets and in the docks, working to feed his mother and father and Molly and that other growing Dominic.

Yet as he walked up the road, he knew that it wasn't all over; the hardest part for him was yet to come. He would have to see her and finish it. Far better to make a clean cut than try to keep dodging her. Once it was done, he would feel better; he could not feel worse.

Saturdays were like the opening afresh of a wound; the week-ends altogether were a torture. And now another was upon him. Since jumping the sawmill wall, he knew how he must spend this one . . . he must read the letters! . . .

When he entered the kitchen, his eyes, in spite of himself, were forced to the mantelpiece. There was yet another letter against the clock. He thrust it into his pocket, then washed himself before sitting down to dinner. Shane was already at the table, and John, out of the pity growing in him for his father, answered his questions patiently . . . Yes, the first boat of the year was in from Sweden with Lulea ore, and it seemed heavier than ever . . . yes, there was one due in on Monday from Bilbao.

'That'll mean piece work,' his father said . . . 'five shillings a shift.' He shook his head and looked down at his trembling hands. 'Perhaps if I made a start I would steady up . . . eh, lad?'

'Give yourself time,' said John, knowing that all the time in the world wouldn't put his father back in the docks.

'Yes. Another week then,' said Shane, with pitiable relief.

Silently, Mary Ellen moved between the oven and the table. Into the love she held for this son of hers was creeping a feeling of awe. The letters were creating it. The lass was writing to him every day, yet he was standing out against her. If ever a lad was in love, he was. But he was renouncing her . . . and for them. Where did he get his strength? She recognised him as a man with a man's needs, and her humility ignored the origin of his strength in herself. If only in some way he could have the lass . . . But it was impossible, the house depended on him; they could only live by him.

Here was another Saturday. How she dreaded and hated Saturdays! She seemed to spend her weeks gathering strength to face the Saturdays. Yet life went on. Round the doors, it was back to normal. Already the incident was being referred to as something long past, in remarks, such as, 'That was a Saturday, wasn't it?' or, 'That day the two bairns went down.' The only ones outside the house who still felt the weight of that day were Peggy Flaherty and the Kellys . . . Peggy, because John, as she said, wouldn't look the side she was on. He wouldn't forgive her for duping him, and her fat was visibly disappearing through the worry of it. Her simple soul felt that until she was on speaking terms with John again nothing would be right. The Kellys were affected because now there could be no redress for Nancy. They would be saddled with her child and their scraping to live would become more difficult, while the possibility of yet another Nancy would be growing under their eyes. Mary Ellen, too, often thought of this. In a short while now, the child would be born, and she would be a grandmother. And always there would be Dominic across the street from her . . . from behind the curtains, she would look for the traits to show. She could see herself doing just that all down the years, for there was no possibility of her ever leaving the fifteen streets. Nor did she want to now; all desire for a change had long since left her, and she knew she must see life out to its close here. This did not worry her, but what did was that her lad would have to do the same. She hadn't wanted him to go to America, but that wasn't saying she wanted him to be stuck in the fifteen streets all his life . . . Dear God, no . . .

The meal was over, and while Molly cleared away Mary Ellen, taking Mick's shirt from the top of the pile of mending, cut off the tail and pinned it across the shoulders, before sitting down opposite Shane and beginning to sew.

John came from the bedroom, and looking hard at Molly, asked, 'Did someone call here a while ago? You know who I mean.'

Molly, after staring back at him for a second, hung her head and answered, 'Yes.'

'Why didn't you say?'

Molly turned her head a little and stared down to her mother's lap . . . How could she say to him, 'You were all mad when she came'? She recalled going to the door on the Sunday afternoon and seeing Miss Llewellyn standing there. She had asked to see her mother or father, and Molly had said she couldn't, they were both bad. It felt nice, at the time, to deny something to her one-time teacher, a teacher who had never taken any notice of her; and when she was able to deny her John, saying that he was out and she didn't know where he was, she experienced a definite pleasure. There was no room in her to feel sorry for Miss Llewellyn, who looked pale and bad. She didn't want her here, anyway. She guessed that Miss Llewellyn had clicked with their John, and she was puzzled, yet made bold, by sensing the come-down it was for anyone so swanky to click with their John. And so, after Miss Llewellyn had gone, she forgot about her. And now here was John blaming her, and she didn't want him to be vexed, for the daily aim of her life was that he and her ma would come to like her as they had liked Katie.

When she gave him no reply, John went back to the bedroom. He picked up the letter he had been reading . . . 'Dearest, I felt I must come and see you. Judged by my own sorrow, yours and your people's must be unbearable . . .' She had come here, to this house. Through the open door she must have glimpsed the conditions from the bareness of the front room, yet it had not put her off; nor the fifteen streets themselves. Nothing would put her off. She would go on believing that when he had accepted his sorrow he would come again to her.

He picked up another letter . . . 'Beloved, I understand. I will wait patiently. Each night I go to the lane, and I know that if you are not there there is always the following night, or the one after, or yet the one after that . . .' He ground his fist into the palm of his hand, and getting up, began to pace the floor in his stockinged feet . . . How much could a man endure! Of all the millions of women in the world, this one, who stood out above them, had to offer him a love such as this, a love men dreamed of, and died with it still but a dream. And it was his, it was being offered to him, John O'Brien, of 10 Fadden Street, of the fifteen streets. Yet he must renounce it, and do so now, this day. He must tell her in words that the mad dream was over. He must do it quickly and cleanly; the cut must be made without sentiment; there must be no tender goodbyes, and no holding out hopes for the future. He knew what the future held for him . . . he was a gaffer, and he'd remain a gaffer; and there was not even the remotest chance of her even becoming a gaffer's wife.

John caught sight of Mary before she saw him. She wasn't in the lane but on the main road, walking slowly with her back towards him, and the setting sun cast an aura of white light about her as she moved. He paused and drew in to the side of the road. The sight of her back had taken all the strength and determination out of him – what hope had he then to stand firm when he faced her. It was easy to be brave in a room talking to oneself. There you asked the questions and fired the answers; there were no eyes to bore into your heart and no touch to set the blood racing. In the bedroom he had been brave enough to don his old style of dress; with a grim defiance he had knotted the muffler ends around his braces, put on his old trousers and heavy boots, and lastly his mackintosh and cap. This, he told himself, was getting back to what he really was, and it would make things easier for her; she would have less regret at what she imagined she was losing. But now he wasn't so sure. His decent clothes would at least have left him free of thinking of himself. Fingering his muffler he could only think of her reaction when she saw him like this – well, wasn't that what he wanted? He continued to watch her for some minutes, and his heart defying his head, cried out, 'Mary – oh! Mary!'

As if the voice of his longing had become audible, she turned, and John, knowing that the time had come, stepped into the centre of the path and walked slowly towards her.

Mary remained still, gazing over the distance towards him. She did not see his clothes, only his face. Even from a distance it sent out its lostness to her, and she murmured aloud, 'My dear! my dear!' and with a little cry she picked up her skirts and ran to him. John halted before she reached him, and the resistance needed to stop the automatic gesture of holding out his arms became a pain.

'Oh John! – my dear!' Her hands were on his chest.

He swallowed as if ridding himself of a piece of granite, and said, 'Hallo, Mary.'

'Hallo, my dear,' she smiled at him gently; 'how are you?'

'All right.' He could not take his eyes from her face. She was pale, but she was more beautiful than he had ever seen her, and the tenderness in her eyes caused him to groan inwardly.

'How is your mother?' she asked softly.

'All right.'

'And is your father better?'

'Yes.'

Her eyes fell from his to her hand. Her fingers were softly stroking his muffler. 'I've missed you, dear.'

It was unbearable. No flesh and blood could stand it. He moved brusquely away from her and began to walk; and in a second she was by his side with her hand in his arm. 'What is it, John?'

He did not reply, and she went on, 'Shall we go up the lane?'

He turned into the lane without speaking, his arm hanging straight and stiff under her touch. The action was boorish, but he knew that if he allowed himself one tender move he would be finished. They stopped by the field gate, where they had been wont to lean and watch the moon and make love. Beyond, the after-glow was tinting the field of young wheat with sweeping strokes of pastel colour. John did not lean against the gate but stood staring into the field.

'Talk about it, my dear. Katie would want it so. It will make you feel better.' Mary had withdrawn her hand from his arm, and now she stood by the side of him, waiting.

'No talking would make any difference to that,' he replied tersely; 'but there's something else I've got to talk about.'

She remained silent, and he went on, swiftly now, 'I am not going to America – that's finished. This business has put paid to my father. He'll never work again. And Molly and Mick are still at school. There's no money coming in, only mine.' He turned now and looked at her; the afterglow which was mellowing the world around had no softening effect upon his face. 'Nothing can come of it now – it's no good going on. You understand?'

'No,' she said, 'I don't.'

He moved his head impatiently: 'How can I? What will there be to live on?'

'We could wait . . . you asked me to wait while you were in America.'

'That was different. What could there be to wait for now?'

'Molly leaves school this summer, and your brother will soon be fourteen.'

'And what about my mother and father?'

'There are ways and means. You could always manage to keep them.'

'Out of what?' he almost shouted. It was as if he were fighting her now, and some part of him was shocked; but he went on, 'Where would we live, and on what? – just tell me that.'

She made no answer. And his head dropped, and he murmured, 'I'm sorry.'

'There's no need to be sorry.' She took a step nearer to him, but did not touch him. 'John, look at me.' She waited until he raised his head before going on: 'We love each other. There won't be anyone else for either of us – we know that – so don't let this happen. There is a way out, there must be – there is a way out of everything.'

Peter's words – 'There is a way out of everything. Use your mind and it will give you the solution.' Peter's reasoning, added to the appeal of her voice and the entreaty of her eyes, broke the tension of his body for the moment, and he allowed his mind to clutch at a fleeting hope – could there be some way out? Could the madness be resurrected? Oh the joyful bewilderment of touching her again! Her face blurred before his eyes, and her voice became blended with the evensong of the birds.

'If you'll only listen to me, darling – I don't mind where I live or how I live, as long as I'm with you. We could be married and I'd go on working. John – I'll come to the fifteen streets . . .'

The blur cleared. The mention of the fifteen streets held the power to betray dreams for what they were. No longer did he see the pleading in her eyes. He saw only her well-cut costume, the gold wrist-watch, the ring on her finger with the large amber stone in the centre, the patent leather of her narrow shoes, and the glimpse of grey stockings, which were of silk; and covering all, the perfume which emanated from her was in his nostrils, the perfume whose ingredients lay not in any bottle but in a sequence starting from a scented bath to fresh linen – and she said she would come to the fifteen streets! He laughed inwardly, harsh, bitter laughter, and said sharply, 'Be quiet! You don't know what you're talking about. Have you ever been inside a house in the fifteen streets?'

'No.'

'It's a pity you haven't.'

'There's no disgrace in being poor.'

'No? I used to think that at one time, but I don't any longer – it's a crying disgrace, but one that I can't alter. But I can do this – I can save you from yourself. You shall never come to the fifteen streets through me.'

'John, darling, listen.'

'I can't listen, I've got to go.' He stepped back from her outstretched hand.

'John, please . . . Oh, don't go like this – John, I love you . . . Don't you see, I can't go on without you?'

The stillness of the field settled on them. Outwardly they appeared lifeless things, fixed in their staring. Then, in spite of himself, he spoke her name, 'Mary.' And like a caress it touched her. But the caress was short-lived, for he went on, 'This has got to be – it's got to finish right now. It's no use going on – no – no!' – he silenced her quietly and with upraised hand. 'All the talking in the world won't make it any different. You'll forget – time will help.'

'It won't – I know that deep within my soul you'll remain with me for ever; I won't be able to forget you – John, oh, John – please! Please let us try to find a way out.' She held out her arms to him, and the humility in their appeal probed a fresh depth of pain in him. But he did not touch them, and Mary made a desperate final effort: 'Katie would have wanted it – she loved to think that we . . .'

'Don't! . . . Goodbye, Mary.' For a second longer he allowed his gaze to linger on her. A lark in the field beyond suddenly rose, singing, from the grass and soared into the dusk of the closing evening. When he saw the mist of tears blinding her eyes, he turned from her and went down the lane.

It was done!

CHAPTER FOURTEEN

WHITHER THOU GOEST

Mary Ellen was puzzled by her own emotions. The sorrow of Katie's loss had not died or faded – it was as poignant as the hour when it happened – but she could bear it now with equanimity because of use. What puzzled her was that it seemed to have moved aside to make room for the sorrow she was feeling for John. Daily she watched him closing up – life seemed to be dying in him. He was becoming the kind of dock man he had never been, even before he had taken to wearing collars and ties. He had not yet taken to drink or lounging at the corners, but he never seemed to get out of his working clothes, and he never moved from the house once he came home from work. Nor did he sit in the kitchen, but spent hours in the bedroom – wrestling, Mary Ellen thought, with himself.

It was a fortnight since the letters ceased, and in some strange way their cessation had brought an added emptiness to her days. With their daily arrival, there remained the hope, however faint, that things would come right for her lad. Now hope was dead, and with it the part of him that had survived Katie's loss was dying too.

What was there to live for now? Mary Ellen asked herself, as she banged the poss-stick up and down in the tub, full of clothes. With no possibility of happiness for her lad and nothing she could do about it, her usual incentive to 'cope' was gone – if only an act of God would finish them all off and leave John free! But God never did things like that – nothing with any sense or reason in it . . . There she was, going again. Her bouts of defiance against God brought her hours of fear and remorse in the night, yet mixed with her fear was a tinge of admiration at her day-time audacity at facing up to Him, and strange, too, was the contradictory feeling of late that she wanted to go to church – not to Mass, so escaping Father O'Malley's censure, but just to sit quietly in church, with no-one there, and perhaps come to terms with God. She did not actually think of it like this – she had not advanced so far in her bravery to do so – but the feeling in her urged that should she go to church and sit quiet she would feel better. The feeling was strong in her now, and she stopped possing and whispered aloud, 'I'll go – I'll go now!' She rubbed her wet arm across her forehead and shook her head, and muttered, 'For God's sake, what's come over you? Have you gone completely up the pole? There's another two hours washing in front of you yet!' She stooped, and lifting the clothes from the tub, began running them into the mangle. There was a series of groans, squeaks and loud jolts, as garment followed garment.

The tub empty of clothes, she dragged it into the yard and poured the water down the sink, and she made no effort to move as the dirty foam swirled about her feet. Rolling the tub back into the washhouse again, she happened to glance up, and met Shane's eyes on her. He was standing at the kitchen window and his face bore the look of despair that covered them all. Although he had made no mention of it for weeks now, she knew that he, too, was continually crying out inside himself for Katie, and also that he was suffering because of the knowledge that through his dependence things were not right with John. She stood leaning over the empty tub for a moment, her eyes gazing down at the water-worn wood. Then, as if she had found a command written there, she hurriedly left the washhouse.

In the kitchen, she dried her arms and combed the top of her hair. Shane watched her silently. Even when she put her coat on he did not question her. With her face turned from him, she said, 'I won't be long.' Then, as if compelled to expose her madness to him, she added, 'I'm going to the church.'

That any woman could leave her washing at two o'clock in the afternoon to go to church must prove, she thought, to a man like Shane that she was mad; but he made no comment on her extraordinary behaviour. Not until she was going through the front room did he speak.

'Mary Ellen.'

She turned: 'Yes?'

He was groping in his trouser pocket. 'Will you light me a candle?' He handed her a penny and their eyes met over it; and perhaps for the first time in their married lives they felt joined in thought and purpose.

As Mary Ellen opened the front door a pantechnicon passed and stopped at Peter Bracken's, and she saw Peter himself standing on his doorstep. For a space they looked at each other, and she knew that she should go to this man and say some word, for her son had been the means of killing his lass; yet through his lass she had lost Katie. With his very coming here, tragedy had entered her life. Peter's eyes were asking her to speak, but she found it impossible. It was strange that only once had this man and she exchanged words – that day in the kitchen, the day the bairn was born. Before she turned away she tried to send him some kindly message; but whether she succeeded or not she couldn't tell. She hurried away down the street, knowing that she had looked her last on Peter Bracken – he was leaving the fifteen streets and never again would they meet. Why had he come here in the first place? To relieve poverty and ignorance, he said. Oh, God, how happy she would have been in her poverty and ignorance had she still Katie. Yet she could feel no virile bitterness against him, which was strange. Instead, she felt they were sharing the same sorrow, and she wasn't troubled at her manner towards him, knowing intuitively that he understood . . .

The day was dull and the sky low. Inside the church the light was as dim as if it were evening, and the air, as usual, was different from that outside – thick and heavy with the weight of stale incense. At the top of the centre aisle, Mary Ellen, her head bowed, made a deep genuflexion. She did not look towards the altar, where always and forever reposed Jesus in the Blessed Sacrament; somehow she wanted no 'truck' with Him; It was His mother she needed. She went down the side aisle walking softly, as if trying to escape the notice of the Holy Ones standing in their niches with flowers at their feet.

There were no candles burning on the half-moon stand to the side of Our Lady, and she stood in shadow until Mary Ellen lit her candles, one for Shane, one for John and one for herself. Then The Virgin was illuminated, smiling down on Mary Ellen, half holding The Child out to her.

Mary Ellen knew she should kneel and say a prayer, and ask The Virgin about Katie and tell her about John, but she felt very tired and all she wanted to do was to sit. She sat in the end of the front pew, as near as she could get to The Virgin, and gazed at her, preparatory to speaking about her lad. But as she sat on, her feet resting on the long wooden kneeler and her hands joined in her lap, she found she couldn't think of John. It was as if he and his troubles had shrunk, her mind groping for them in vain. As the flame of the candles lengthened, the smile of The Virgin deepened, and it seemed to Mary Ellen that she moved and hitched the Infant higher up on to her arm as she herself used to do with Katie. The light of the candles grew brighter and brighter as she stared at them, and the church outside the ring of light became darker. A great peace swept over Mary Ellen. It started in her feet with a tingling warmth and coursed through her body, flooding her being with a happiness she could never remember experiencing before, or ever imagined possible. So great was her happiness that it left no room for fear when she saw The Virgin move and gently push someone towards her.

When Katie stood at the end of the pew and, smiling shyly, said, 'Oh, Ma!' Mary Ellen felt no surprise. She leaned forward and gripped Katie's hands. 'Why, hinny, I thought you were – gone.' She wouldn't say 'dead'. And when Katie answered her, saying, 'It was only for a few minutes, Ma. Things went black and then it was over,' Mary Ellen took it as a natural answer, and went on, 'You're not out there then, hinny? – not out in the sea?'

Katie's laugh tinkled through the church, and she glanced back at The Virgin, and The Virgin's smile broadened. 'We never went out there, did we, Christine?'

166

Katie turned her head and spoke into the shadows, and Mary Ellen asked, 'The lass, is she with you?'

'Why, of course! We're waiting together – it's nice waiting.'

'Waiting?' repeated Mary Ellen. 'For what, hinny?'

'For the time to come when we should have died, and then we'll go on – we went too soon, Ma.'

'Yes, hinny, you did.'

Now death had been mentioned, a sweet contentment was added to Mary Ellen's happiness – she felt she was with death, and it was a pleasant thing, not only pleasant, but strangely exciting. Her bairn was in it, and was happy. 'How long must you wait, hinny?'

'We don't know; but once it's over we'll start growing again – a different growing, getting ready to come back – won't we, Christine?'

Mary Ellen peered into the shadows but could see nothing, and Katie went on, 'Before we go, I'll come and see you again – and Ma . . .'

'Yes, hinny?'

'Don't worry about John; he's going to be happy, so very happy.'

'How can you tell, hinny?'

'We know about those we love. Go home now, Ma.'

Katie's lips rested on Mary Ellen's and the sweetness of them pressed down into her being . . . the sweetness like a gentle perfume was in her nostrils when she opened her eyes.

'Katie, hinny—' She put out her hand, gropingly. She could not see Katie, but something stronger than reason told her she was there. She whispered again, 'Katie, hinny,' then looked towards The Virgin. She was as she had first seen her, yet different, for her face seemed to hold the knowledge of all eternity.

Katie and Christine were all right . . . they were with her. It did not enter Mary Ellen's head to question how Christine – the spook's daughter – could be with The Virgin, who, above all others, was a Catholic first and the Mother of God after.

Smiling gently to herself, Mary Ellen left the church. Katie was happy, oh indeed she was happy – and everything was going to be all right for her lad. Katie had said so.

The ghoulish picture of Katie floating in deep water that had filled her mind for weeks had gone – Katie wasn't there – she knew where Katie was . . .

Going homewards Mary Ellen walked with a lighter tread; there was an urgency in her to reach the house and tell Shane, although how she was going to tell Shane about Katie without him thinking her completely mad she didn't know. But Shane needed comfort, and if she could tell him in a sensible way that she had seen Katie she had no doubt that he would feel as she did now. She hurried up the backyard, ignoring the dead fire under the washhouse pot and the mounds of unfinished washing, and entered the kitchen. Shane was there, sitting in his armchair beside the fireplace, while opposite him sat the lass. Mary Ellen had never met Mary Llewellyn, but there was no need for anyone to tell her who this was.

Bright spots of red burned in the dull colour of Shane's cheeks: 'I told the lass to stay – you wouldn't be long.'

Mary rose to her feet and watched the little woman unpin her hat and hang her coat carefully behind the kitchen door. She had not spoken, and Mary began, 'I hope you don't mind, Mrs O'Brien . . . I wanted to talk to you.'

'Sit down, miss,' said Mary Ellen with strange gentleness, 'you're quite welcome. Can I offer you a cup of tea?'

'Please; I should like one.'

Mary Ellen pressed the kettle, which was standing on the hob, further into the fire. At the same time Shane rose, saying, 'I'll be lying down for a while.' He left the kitchen without glancing at Mary – it was as if she had been there always and was likely to remain. The room door closed behind Shane and the two women were left alone.

Mary Ellen, filled with a growing awe and wonder, silently placed the teapot to warm, and unhooked the cups from the back of the cupboard and put them on the table. Oh, Katie, Katie. Can this mean what you said about John's life? She dare not look at the lass in case she should disappear as Katie had done.

'How is John, Mrs O'Brien?'

Mary Ellen was forced to stop in her trotting to and fro and look at this woman, whom her lad loved. She said simply, 'He's not too grand, miss.'

Mary turned her gaze towards the fire, and after a moment asked, 'Do you agree with his decision?' Then before Mary Ellen could make a reply, she turned to her again and went on rapidly, 'Please believe me . . . I understand . . . I know that you have only him now to look after you, and I want him to do that always. But that is no reason why we should be separated – is it, Mrs O'Brien? We care for each other – very deeply, and there is a way out if only he would listen to reason.'

'You can't marry without money, lass.'

'Did you wait until you had money?'

Mary Ellen shook her head. 'This is different . . . you're different. He'd want money to give you a home.'

'I don't want that kind of a home, Mrs O'Brien' – Mary leaned forward and took hold of Mary Ellen's hands – 'the solution is for me to come and live here. I must show him that I can do it. There are always empty houses going, and I could continue my work. Even if I didn't, I have a little money, enough to keep us a couple of years, living simply . . . How much is the rent of these houses?'

'Four and tuppence.' Mary Ellen, her hands locked in the soft firmness of Mary's, was trying to measure the cost it had been to her lad to give up this lass, whose charm was already telling on her . . . Aye, but it wouldn't work out. She would never be able to stick it here; it would strip her of everything but the capacity to regret . . . Yet why should she stick here? Wouldn't John fight with every fibre of his being to take her out of this? That is, if she persisted in coming here and persuaded him to marry . . . Peter Bracken's gone, the house next door is empty . . . It was almost as if Katie was at her elbow – the voice in her head was Katie's. She remained still, listening to both Katie and the lass.

'Will you help me, Mrs O'Brien? I can assure you that you'll not suffer for it. Please, Mrs O'Brien, do help me. I want to come and live here, somewhere near. He will know nothing about it until it's done. I must show him that I can live here successfully . . . will you?'

'There's a house empty right next door, lass.' It was as if Katie had nudged her. 'It was the Brackens' you know . . . the lass . . .'

'Yes, yes, I know . . . Oh, Mrs O'Brien, tell me what to do. Who do I see about it?' In her excitement Mary stood up, and Mary Ellen, her mind suddenly filled with doubt, turned away and mashed the tea. Would John want to live in a house where the lass Christine had lived? . . . She seemed to hear Katie's laugh tinkling again as it had done in the church. Now it was deriding her superstitions, and Mary Ellen set down the teapot, and turning back to Mary, said resolutely, 'I'll do anything to see my lad happy; although I'd better tell you, lass, it'll be hard for you . . . at the very best it'll be hard going.'

'You doubt that I'll be able to stand it?'

'No, somehow I don't. If you care for him enough it'll keep the iron out of your soul.'

With a sigh that swept the tenseness from her body, Mary sat down again. As she took the cup of tea from Mary Ellen, they smiled at each other and a quietness settled on the kitchen as they sat drinking and thinking, their thoughts in different channels but flowing the one way.

The flat cart was at the door – a clean, respectable flat cart, but the sight of it and its import had prostrated Beatrice Llewellyn. She lay on her bed, faint with rage and self-pity. There was rage, too, in James Llewellyn's voice as he talked to Mary from the doorway of her room, moving from time to time to allow the removal man to pass. He only spoke in the man's absence, talking rapidly to get in all he had to say.

'You'll regret this to your dying day . . . do you hear me?'

'I hear you.' Mary, with her back to him, went on lifting books from the shelves and packing them into a tea chest.

'You don't know what you're doing – you can't! Why, woman, the scum of the earth live in the fifteen streets – he's not a man! No man who could lay any claim to the name would ask anyone like you to go there.'

'He hasn't asked me, he has refused even to see me.'

'And you have so little pride you are going to live there and push yourself on him?'

'Yes, I have so little pride I am going to do just that.'

The man came in and as he lifted the tea chest asked, 'Is this the lot, miss?'

'Yes . . . except the two trunks and the cases in the hall.'

James Llewellyn threw a murderous glance at the unfortunate man as he lumbered past him with the box. 'Have you got the place furnished?' he barked the question at her.

'No.'

'No? You mean to say you are going to live there with those few odds and ends?' He nodded towards the hall.

'I have bought a bed and a table . . . just the necessary things.' Mary kept her face turned from her father. She thought of the problem the buying of the bed had caused – whether to be modest and buy a single bed, or to be true to herself and buy what she hoped would be necessary. She had not asked Mary Ellen's advice about this. It was something she had to decide for herself . . . And was she brave enough to face the comments of her future neighbours? for she did not delude herself into thinking it would escape their notice; and she could practically hear their comments on a single lass buying a new double bed. She knew already that the hardest thing to bear in the fifteen streets would be her lack of privacy.

She had ordered a double bed and by now it would have been delivered. She glanced for the last time round the room, her eyes avoiding her father's. He was standing, black and massive, filling the doorway. She did not mind her mother's censure, but his cut deep into her. She would have gone happily to the fifteen streets had he given her some kind word.

'You'll be the talk of the town – a laughing-stock!' He barred her way, and she waited, eyes cast down, until he would move aside.

'I'll not be the first, or the last.'

'Your mother's ill.'

'My mother isn't ill . . . she's merely angry, and you know it.' She lifted her eyes to his. His face was mottled with his emotions, and she could not bear to witness it any longer.

'I must go . . .' She stepped towards the door, but her father did not move. He stood staring at her, his face working, fighting against the softening emotion that was breaking him down – his lass going to live in the fifteen streets! His Mary, who loved colour, and light and laughter, who was so close to him, closer than his wife, who could reason like him and laugh at the same things. She was going to live in one of those wrecks of houses, just to be near that big docker . . . God Almighty! it was unbelievable . . . Yet he had given her credit for being able to reason like himself. Then could she be so far wrong? . . .

Was there something worthwhile in the fellow? Worthwhile or not, she had no right to be doing this. She was mad.

'Mary, lass, don't go . . . I'll try to fix something . . . a job or something, for him.' His face fell into pitying lines of entreaty.

She shook her head slowly and put out her hand to him, speaking with difficulty.

'It wouldn't work . . . he'd refuse. This is the only way, to take whatever he has to offer, however small, and make it do . . . Perhaps later—'

'Oh, lass' – he pulled her into his arms – 'oh, Mary, lass!'

They held each other for a moment, tight and hard. Then, thrusting her from him he went hurriedly down the passage, and Mary, trying to stem the flood of tears, listened in amazement to him barking down the drive at the carrier.

'Come in here, and give a hand with these things.' He came back, followed by the man, whom he bewildered with his torrent of orders.

'Get that china cabinet out, and that bookcase. And the couch and chair. Then up with this carpet.'

'Father – no, don't. Listen to me,' she protested, 'I don't want them . . . I must go as I am. It will only make it more difficult. He wouldn't want . . .' She stopped. Her father wasn't listening; he was in a frenzy of action. He passed her, carrying one end of the heavy bookcase, almost pushing the man off his feet, both with his confused orders and force, and she knew she must let him do this for her. However more difficult it would make the work ahead, she must accept these things.

When the room was at last bare, she walked down to the gate, her father at her side. In deep embarrassment they stood facing each other.

'Well, good luck, lass. I dare say I'll find my way to see you . . . what's the number?'

'Twelve Fadden Street.'

'You can always come back, you know.'

'Thanks, my dear.'

'Goodbye, lass.'

'Goodbye.' It was impossible to say more. Blindly she went down the road. The cart on ahead was a blur, and it remained so until she came within sight of the fifteen streets.

All afternoon they worked. They cut the carpet, and it covered the floor of the front room and bedroom. The kitchen boards were bare except for two rugs, which to Mary Ellen's mind were far too bright and grand for such a room. The things the lass had brought were lovely! She was glad the lass's father had made her take them, for now one of the main problems to the marriage, as she saw it, was removed . . . they were set up. But her happiness in this new turn of events was marred, and it was the statue that was responsible . . . that great white, bare woman, as naked as the day she was born, and standing on a box where anyone at the front door would get an eyeful of her. The lass was respectable, she knew that, and apparently to her mind this naked woman meant nothing except what she was, a statue. But let them about the doors get a glimpse of it, and Mary Ellen knew the result as if it had already taken place. The women would dub the lass 'a loose piece', and from the start her life in the fifteen streets would be suspect. They would conjure up the men she'd had, and her lad would become an object of pity for having been caught, and never would the lass be able to pass the corners of the streets without hungry eyes and low laughter following her. If only she could explain to her . . . but it was a hard thing to explain. Mary Ellen knew she wasn't at her best with words, but actions now . . . yes. If she were to knock the thing flying accidentally . . . She stood looking at it. There wasn't much time left, for John was due any minute now. Molly was on the watch for him at the corner, and the lass was in the kitchen getting her first meal ready. Well, it was now or never. She lifted her hand and swiped the naked woman to the floor. As it crashed, she heard a gasp, and there, standing in the doorway, her face white and shocked, was Mary.

Across the debris they stared at each other. Mary Ellen, her face working, tried to explain. 'I had to do it, lass . . . they would think . . . the women would say . . . They wouldn't understand around these doors . . . I want you to have a good start.'

Mary gazed down on the fragments of her expression. The statue had been a symbol of truth to her; a figure indeed of her emancipation from cant and hypocrisy; a symbol of her growing freedom. But now it was gone. Never until this moment had she fully realised what coming to the fifteen streets would mean. She imagined at worst it meant living meagrely. Now she saw that was but a small part of it. To live happily, her life would not only have to be altered from the outside, but from within. Not only her actions, but her thoughts, must be restricted. This little woman had not broken the statue from malice, but from a desire to help her. Some deep knowledge of her own people had urged her to its destruction, and it might be only one of the many things which must be destroyed if she were to suffer this life. Could she suffer it?

'Lass, I didn't mean to hurt you.' Mary Ellen's face was pitiable, and her fingers, as always when she was in distress, picked nervously at the button of her blouse. Had she, with her mad action, destroyed what she wanted most? Happiness for her lad. The lass looked hurt and bewildered. She wanted her off to a good start, but she had achieved just the opposite. She bent her head in an effort to hide the raining tears . . . was nothing ever to go right?

When she felt the lass's arms go about her, she leant against her, faint with relief, and felt herself almost a child again as Mary patted her back, saying, 'There, there! It's all right. I understand. I should have had more sense than to bring it. Please don't cry! Just think' – she gave a little laugh – 'if Father O'Malley had seen it!' They both began to shake, small, rippling tremors, which mounted into laughter; quiet, relaxing laughter such as Mary Ellen never thought to laugh again. Oh, the lass would get by. She knew what to laugh at.

They both stopped abruptly when a knock came on the front door, and Mary Ellen opened it to Molly.

'He's coming up the road, Ma.'

'All right,' said Mary Ellen, 'you know what to do. Tell him I want him to come in the front way.'

Without looking again at Mary, she said, 'Well, lass, I'll get myself away in,' and she went through the kitchen and out of the back door.

In her own backyard she paused a moment. Within the next few minutes she would have lost her lad, for she had no doubt that once he stepped inside that door he would be gone from her and another woman would have him. She wanted his happiness didn't she? Yes, above all things she wanted his happiness. But with it she hadn't thought to feel this added sense of loneliness. Well, she'd have to turn her mind to the others. Shane, for instance, who needed her as never before. And Molly, who seemed to have been born when Katie died. And Mick, who'd need two steady hands on him to keep him from Dominic's path. Yes, she still had a lot to cope with. And her lad would be next door for some time yet – Rome wasn't built in a day.

Left alone, Mary felt unable to move. There were a dozen and one things she wanted to accomplish before seeing him; among them to change her apron and do her hair. But now she could only stand rooted. A few minutes ago she had asked herself if she could suffer this life. What a ridiculous question to ask, when her whole being told her she could suffer no life that did not hold him.

The heavy tread of his steps reached her, and she lifted her head to the sound. All the colour of life, all the essence of the music she had heard, all the beauty she had seen and felt with her soul's capacity, rose in her, and she moved towards the door. Not until she heard the sound of the knocker on his own door did she lift the latch.

It was some time before he turned his head towards her, and then he did it slowly as if afraid of what he would see. She held out her hand, and he moved towards her but did not touch her. It was she who took his arm and drew him over the threshold and closed the door behind them. Walking ahead of her into the room he looked about him, and his face was drained of its colour. He brought his gaze from the fragments of the broken statue lying by the fireside to her face, and he said grimly, 'No, Mary. You can't do it . . . that's how you'll end, like that – broken.'

'Some things are better broken.'

'I'll not let you do it.'

'You can't stop me, dear . . . it's done. Here I am, and here I stay until you have me . . . and after.'

His eyes travelled again around the room, and she smiled gently at him. 'Do you like it?' He made no reply, and she said, 'Come and see the kitchen.'

In the kitchen he stared at a table set in shining whiteness for two. The kettle, startlingly new, was singing on the hob. It caused something to break in him. He closed his eyes, striving to fight the weakness. 'You don't know what you're doing . . . you'll regret it . . . your father should—'

He could say no more. She was leaning against him, her arms about his neck. The oval of her face was lost in light. 'Hold me, John.'

His arms, telling his hunger, crushed her to him. The faint perfume of her body mingled with the acrid smell of iron ore, and in the ever increasing murmur of his endearments and the searching of his lips her words were lost:

Whither thou goest, I will go: and where thou lodgest, I will lodge: thy people shall be my people, and thy God my God: Where thou diest, will I die, and there will I be buried: the Lord do so to me, and more also, if ought but death part thee and me.

THE END

COLOUR BLIND

AUTHOR'S NOTE

The characters in this book are entirely fictitious and have no relation to any living person.

Although the setting is Tyneside, and several actual place-names have been used, the fifteen streets, Casey's Wharf, and other parts of Holborn are imaginary.

Owing to the difficulty in comprehension by the uninitiated, the Tyneside dialect has not been adhered to.

In this story I make no effort to solve a problem. The solution, if there is one, for the living conflicts, the half-castes, would seem to lie in the far, far future.

CONTENTS

PART ONE

PART TWO

PART THREE

PART FOUR

PART ONE

CHAPTER ONE

ME DAUGHTER BRIDGET

'Glory be to God and his holy Mother. Well, well I never! And it to happen on me birthday an' all! . . . Did y'ever now.' Kathie McQueen threw her great head back and opened wide her full-lipped mouth and let the resounding waves of her laughter free. Her huge breasts and hanging stomach wobbled with it, and her feet, encased in the remnants of a pair of slippers, slapped at the bare floorboards alternately.

The boy, standing at the side of her chair, holding a letter in his hand, smiled up at her. He did not laugh with her, although his heart was racing and leaping inside his narrow chest. Having lived with the McQueens for four years he was used to their laughter, and perhaps it was the extravagance of it that subdued the laughter in himself, for his face rarely stretched beyond a smile. The McQueens frequently chipped him about this, saying, 'Go on, Tony, stretch your gob. Go on, give your face a day off, lad. Go on, forget about your leg; the inch you've lost on that you've got in your napper.' They meant it kindly. All the McQueens were kind to him, even Matt. But no matter how kind they were, or what they did for him, he could never laugh with them. For there was something he didn't understand about their laughter; at times it even brought a fear to him.

Into the sound of the laughter came a dull thumping on the back door, and the boy, raising his voice, shouted, 'There's someone at the door.'

'What?' Kathie brought her streaming eyes down to his. 'Someone at the door? Away then and open it.' And in the next breath she called, 'Come in, there.'

Before the boy had limped half-way to the door, it was opened, and a small girl with a coat over her head came into the kitchen.

'Me ma says can yer lend her yer gully, Mrs McQueen?' The black coat, forming a hood about her face, emphasised the pinched cheeks and hungry eyes, and the voice, too, sounded thin and hungry as it issued from the shadows of the coat. 'She won't keep it a minute. We've got some bread and me ma's got a ticket to get some groceries. But we've got the bread now . . . and . . .' Her voice trailed off.

'Yer ma got a ticket? God be praised! But I thought ye got yer gully out last week,' said Kathie, reaching across the table and picking up a long bread-knife.

'It had to go back with the fire-irons so as to get the bread.' The child's voice seemed to come from more remote depths of the coat.

'Ah well, times like these won't last much longer.' Kathie handed the child the bread-knife. 'Yer Da's bound to get set on now . . . cough, spit an' all. They'll be taking the blind and the deaf soon, they'll take owt during a war, God bless the Kaiser!'

Kathie's head was again thrown back, and the boy and girl stood regarding her solemnly, fascinated by the great pink and grey cavity of her mouth.

Her laughter seemed to remind her of the previous bout, and its cause, and she stopped suddenly, saying, 'It's good news we've got the day . . . what d'ye think? Me daughter Bridget's on her way home . . . Tell yer ma, Milly.'

'Brid coming home? Oh, I will, Mrs McQueen.'

'An' tell her she's married, at that . . . Me daughter Bridget's married, tell her, to a seafaring gentleman. Now what d'ye think of that? Go on now, tell her. And let me have that gully back!' she shouted to the departing child; 'they'll all be in in a minute, and I want it for the tea . . . Eeh, Tony lad' – she turned once more to the boy – 'read it again. No . . . give it me here.'

She took the letter from his hand and held it at arm's length, and, pulling her chin into the rolls of fat on her neck, she said slowly, ' "Dear Ma, I'll be home on Friday night. You will be surprised to know I am married. He goes to sea. My name is Mrs Paterson. Ma, there's something I should tell you, but I can't write it down. I'll have to come home. Love, Brid." '

The boy looked at her in admiration. He knew she couldn't read a word . . . she couldn't even write her own name. But her grotesque, fat body seemed to be the storage house for everything she heard; she had only to hear a thing once to remember it for ever.

'I know what she's afraid to tell me, Tony lad.' She leant towards him and whispered with a natural frankness, 'It's a baby she's goin' to have, ye know.' She joined her arms together and rocked them as if a child lay on them. 'Ye know, like my Eva upstairs. Now there's no disgrace in having a child if ye're married and the priest's blessing on ye, is there, Tony? Now is there? But me Bridget was always the shy one.'

The boy regarded her in silence. Women with protruding stomachs were a common sight to him; he had only to walk down the back lane any time of the day to see one. In the summer he looked down on great cones of flesh hanging out from open blouses as the women sat on their front doorsteps suckling their babies. Eva upstairs had always appeared ugly to him, with her young fat and her red hair, but when her stomach had bulged she had been repulsive. And when her babies were born – for they were twins – they, too, were repulsive; and had grown more so, with their skinny bodies and rickety legs.

Yet here was Mrs McQueen classing Bridget, his beautiful Bridget, with Eva. If Bridget had a baby, it would be beautiful, like her, and its hair would be fair, and the grey of its eyes would dance at you. But it wouldn't laugh all the time, for Bridget was the only one of the six McQueens who didn't laugh all the time.

Tony blinked his eyes in startled surprise as Kathie McQueen's hand brought him a playful slap across the face. 'It's a solemn puss ye have on ye. But ye like me Bridget, don't ye?'

He nodded but made no answer. Liking was a poor word for the feeling he had for Bridget. She was the star that had filled his dark sky since the day his mother died and an aunt, his only living relative, had refused his claim on her. It was the McQueens who came forward, and without any preamble took him into their already full house. But only the fifteen-year-old Bridget brought him comfort. When they sat round the fire at night, huddled close to its often small embers, but always shouting and laughing, it was she who would sit next to him, with her arm about him. And when the lads called after him 'Hoppy on the Don!' it was she who would walk by his side, and at times fill him with curious pain when she affected to limp slightly, saying she had a pain in her hip. She championed him until he reached twelve, when he suddenly started to grow. But from then Matt had taken notice of Bridget's attentions to him. If she brought him some little tit-bit from her daily place, Matt would say, 'Stop making a blommin' fool of him. Why don't you give him a dummy?' At times there would be fierce rows, and he felt he was the cause. And the rows always took place in the wash-house, where Matt would push Bridget, and their voices, low and thick with rage, would filter into the house. One thing Tony noticed was that Matt didn't corner his sister when their father was about. And it was after one of these rows, which seemed to mount with the years, that Bridget suddenly went away. And for weeks afterwards Matt hadn't laughed.

And now Bridget was coming back, and she was married. This fact did not touch Tony's own feeling for her, but into his mind there crept a fear – a fear of Matt's reactions when this knowledge should be made known to him – and he thought, I won't look at his face when he reads the letter.

Cavan McQueen was the first to come in, his laugh in the back yard heralding his approach. The booming of his voice and the depth of his laughter were in striking contrast to the short, slight body. And his shortness was emphasised as he stood by his wife. He threw his bait tin with a clatter on to the table before bringing his hand with a resounding whack across Kathie's buttocks.

'We're set, lass. The war's only been on three days and the sods are begging us to do overtime.'

He was lifting his hand again to repeat the slap when she yelled, 'Stop it, ye little rat, ye!' Then her voice dropped to a thick caressing tone. 'Cavan lad . . . guess what. Ye'll never guess in a month of Sundays . . . read that.' She pulled the letter out from her blouse, then stood with her arms folded on the shelf of her stomach watching him. She saw the smile follow after the laughter, to leave his face wearing the blank, stiff look she hated.

When he made no comment she cried angrily, 'Ain't yer pleased? What would ye be wanting? The child's coming home an' she's married. Ye're wearing a look as if ye'd heard she'd been dropped with a bairn and no-one to father it. She's married, man, an' all respectable – they call her Mrs Paterson. And what's more, she got him herself. She hadn't to drag him to the altar rails like Eva had that miserable swine up there.' She flicked her eyes towards the ceiling.

Cavan rubbed his greasy hand over his moustache and said dully, 'Aye, there's that in it,' and handed the letter back to Kathie. Then, turning slowly, he went to the corner of the room, took off his coat, and proceeded to wash himself in a tin bath of hot water which was standing on a low shelf attached to the wall. He dried himself on a piece of sacking that had been hemmed into a square, and which still bore the sugar manufacturer's name across it. He took no heed of the upbraidings of Kathie as she pounced round the kitchen; he could stop her effectively whenever he wished, and she knew just how far she could go. His mind was trying to grasp the fact that his lass . . . his own lass . . . was married, and him not knowing. Of his four children, his heart laid claim only to one. In varying degrees he liked Eva, Matt and Terence, but Bridget he knew he loved.

He scrubbed himself more vigorously with the sacking to cover up the thought. Bridget had the knack of making people love her. All men seemed to love Bridget, even those that shouldn't . . . His thoughts swung to his son . . . That had been the trouble: Matt hadn't let Bridget live any life but that which he chose. If it hadn't been for Matt, Bridget would never have left home, to go all that way to London to work; and then to Liverpool.

Cavan stopped rubbing himself and stared down into the bath of dirty water. He was trying to see through his thoughts, but they were as opaque as the water. Yet this much he could see: if Bridget had not got married away, she would never have got married at home . . . not as long as Matt was alive.

Kathie's voice, raised in laughing greeting to their younger son, brought Cavan's mind from Matt, and he turned from the contemplation of the water and threw his greeting to the lad who was a replica of himself. 'How's it gone?'

'Oh, champion.'

'Was it hard?'

'Aye, a bit. But I'll get used to it. The stink of the chemicals made me sick at first, and you get covered all over with white dust. Most of them have overalls . . . can I have a pair of overalls, Ma?'

'Ye can have owt ye like, lad, if ye bring the money in.'

'Well, I'll be doing that. A pound a week, and me only sixteen!'

'Aye,' his father put in, with unusual seriousness, 'you'll be a millionaire shortly. But look out, and don't let on to anyone, for when the Government get wind you're having three meals a day they'll find some bloody way of bringing them down to one, or nowt.'

Terence took no notice of this, but said, 'Da, you said if we all got set on you were going to try for a house in the middle or top end.'

'Aye, I did.'

'Well you'd better look slippy then, for they're being snapped up; the men coming to work in the Barium are looking round. They want to live as near as they can.'

'Oh, there'll always be plenty of houses if ye've got the money to pay the rent. But we'll stick where we are till we see how long this war's goin' to last. It might only hang on a few weeks, and then where'll we be if we move, eh? Best forget moving for the time.'

But as Cavan sat down to his tea he was thinking as much about the possibility of moving as he was about Bridget's coming. They were both entwined in his mind; for hadn't he always promised Bridget that one day they'd move back into the middle of the fifteen streets . . . or, with a bit of luck, perhaps the top end. It was a great pity they couldn't have moved before she came back, but he had learned too much from life to take a step like that without being sure the present flood of work would last. Here they had a roof over their heads. And it wasn't a workhouse roof, although he knew that the latter contingency had only been avoided by his wife's laughing tenacity and Matt's pilfering, and the pulling in of his own belt to let what food there was go to the others. But God was good, and had showered his special Providence over them, when all around, weeping women and grim-faced men had watched their last sticks of furniture being carried out by the bums before wending their heart-breaking way down the Jarrow Road to East Jarrow, through Tyne Dock and down Stanhope Road, to where Talbert Road showed the grim gates at the far end, which, once entered, a family was no longer a family but merely segregated individuals, with numbers on each of their garments. When this happened the McQueens had stood close together, defying Life's blows with their laughter. Bridget and the boy Tony hadn't laughed much, but the others made up for them.

It was said that only the scum of the earth lived in the fifteen streets, but Cavan would have considered himself one of the fortunate of the earth if he could have moved into the middle section, where the houses possessed four box-like rooms, and you went upstairs to bed; and where you were the proud possessor of your own back yard, and what was more – a netty. There you hadn't to stand waiting for your turn until your bladder nearly burst, or see the bairns doing the wet dance while they waited, for he would allow none of them to foul the yard.

Here, in these two rooms that dared to flaunt the name of a downstairs house, the lavatory had to be shared with the family upstairs, although since Eva had come to live above them the situation had eased considerably. Before the previous tenant had taken the long trek to the iron gates there had been nineteen of them sharing the yard and its amenities.

When Cavan heard his quarter referred to as the 'stink-pot' or the 'buggy-boxes' his laughter would disappear, and he would yell at the offender, asking how he could expect anything else. During one of his angry spells he started a campaign against the bugs and enlisted a number of the neighbours. Paper was stripped off the walls, which were soaked with carbolic. This was quite effective if both upstairs and downstairs co-operated. But poverty dulls incentive, and the war against bugs needs to be wholesale, so many were soon back where they started. But not 42 Powell Street; for Cavan became almost a maniac with the carbolic, the smell of which permeated their clothes and food.

Cavan's thinking had reached a point where he was asking himself if it was the living conditions as much as Matt that drove Bridget away from home when Matt came in.

Matt seemed to spring into the kitchen – there was a spring in his every step. If he laughed when he walked, the combination became a beguilement, bringing the children after him and the eyes of the girls on him. His body, like his father's, was thin; but he had height with it, and a steely sinuation that spoke of arrogant maleness. His face was narrow and overhung by a thick mop of sandy hair, growing low on his brow. It was his eyes that were the most noticeable feature of his face; they were like large jet beads, and not even his laughter could lift the brooding veil from them.

Kathie's greeting to him was shriller than ever, and her laughter caused Tony to fix his eyes on his tin plate; it was the kind of laughter that frightened him, for somehow he didn't think it was meant to be laughter at all.

'I'll give yer a month of Sundays, Matt,' Kathie was yelling, 'to guess what's happened. Go on: Jesus in Heaven, ye'll never guess it.'

Matt look questioningly at his father; and Cavan returned his look, but said nothing.

'What is it?' Matt turned to his mother.

14

Still laughing, she said, 'Get the grease washed off yer, and come an' have yer tea – I've a steak as thick as a cuddy's lug for yer. Oh, ye'll never guess.' And her laughter and chattering filled the time until he came to the table.

'Let him have his tea,' said Cavan.

Kathie stopped her laughing and said soberly, 'Yes. Yes, I will.'

'I'm not having any tea till I know what's up.' Matt stood by his plate looking at his mother.

She looked at Cavan, and when he nodded his head she put her hand inside her blouse again and handed the letter to her son.

Tony did as he had promised himself: he didn't look at Matt while he read the letter. With great deliberation he wiped up the last of the gravy from his plate with a piece of bread, going round and round it until the tin shone with a silver gleam. Under his lowered lids he saw the letter flung on to the table. He saw Mr McQueen, too, wiping his plate clean with his bread.

Then Mrs McQueen's fist banging the table made him jump, and her voice nearly deafened him as she yelled, 'That's the last damn time the Cullens will get a loan of me gully. I've sworn it afore an' I'll swear it again! Here's me having to tear me own bread while those hungry hounds are lording it with me gully.'

Tony saw Matt's legs moving with unusual slowness towards the door. When he heard it close he lifted his head and watched Matt disappear down the back yard and into the September dusk. Mr and Mrs McQueen with one accord left the table and went into the other room; and Tony was left with Terence, who, taking advantage of the situation, cut a piece off Matt's congealing steak and motioned to Tony to do likewise. But Tony took no heed; he was tense with the feeling of nervous expectancy, longing for, yet dreading the time when Bridget would be in the kitchen again.

As Matt walked out of the fifteen streets into the main road he turned the lapels of his coat across his chest to hide his dirty shirt, for he had come out without his muffler. The air was soft and close, but he shivered, and a girl crossing the road called to him, 'Hallo there, Matt – you look as if ye'd seen the Kaiser. Have they called yer up?'

The sound of his laugh was sufficient answer for her, and she went on her way, laughing too.

Laughter was easy – when everything else failed you could always laugh. Then why hadn't he stayed in the house and laughed this off? No, he'd had to make a bloody fool of himself and come out! It was the shock. Bridget married! Well, he knew she'd marry sometime, didn't he? He knew that once she got away on her own some fellow would get her. He twisted the torn lining of his coat pocket round his fingers, tearing it still farther. He'd thought that in the months following her surprising departure he had worked the whole thing out; he'd imagined he had got her out of his system, for life, although emptier, became easier without her. The tearing, mad feeling of possessiveness faded, and he lost his hate of all mankind because she was not near to bestow her smile on it. He had been mad – he could see that now. But he could also see now that he would be mad again. What possessed him? Why was it he should feel like this about her? All his life he had suffered and enjoyed the torment of this feeling for her. He could remember himself as a tiny child holding her and knowing that she was his; still a baby himself, he had washed and dressed her; no-one was allowed to take her to school but himself; he had even stolen for her. He knew he would have let the others go hungry to death, and they would have done, or else to the workhouse, if Bridget's grey eyes hadn't told him that there was a gnawing in her stomach . . . And now she was married, and was coming home to flaunt her catch – the bitch! She was just doing it to torment him, By God, he'd kill her! No, no! . . . He wiped the moisture from his lips with the back of his hand. Whatever was the reason for her coming back, it wasn't to torment him. He would give her her due; she would never do that intentionally. Then why was she coming?

It was dark now, and he walked on through Tyne Dock, down Eldon Street and into Shields. If it had been light, he would have cut through the Deans into the park. He had been taking walks in the park often of late; to get away from the grime and muck of the fifteen streets, he had thought. Yet up to Bridget's going away he had never noticed their grimness. Vaguely he knew that to make his life bearable he needed something. Her personality, in such contrast to his, and her strange beauty had supplied that something. Now he was searching blindly to replace it. The park, in the minutest way, brought Bridget back to him. Was it its colour and cleanness? – for Bridget had always been clean. Or was it just some quiet place where his thoughts could move around her without the perplexing agony of her presence? He didn't know.

She would likely be home now, and they'd all be about her, laughing at the tops of their voices, and she would be smiling at them, that lovely wide smile. He turned abruptly and walked towards Jarrow again. After she had quietened them all, as she had the power to do, she would look around her and say, 'Where's Matt?' Yes, she would ask for him, for she knew as well as he did that some part of her belonged to him. And she could never rob him of it, husband or not.

When he passed the dock arches and reached the quiet stretch of road joining Tyne Dock to East Jarrow he started to run swiftly and lightly, with the loping grace of some forest animal. He kept on running, past the slacks where the water flapped at the bank to the side of his feet, past the Barium chemical works, where Terence had started that day, past Bogie Hill, and on to the fifteen streets.

He was panting when he reached the back yard, for it had been a long run, and as he paused behind the closed door of the yard, looking towards the gas-lit blind of the kitchen window, he was at once struck by the odd quiet that prevailed. He knew, as if he could see her, that Bridget had come. She was there, in the kitchen. Then why was there no laughing, no yelling? He looked to the upstairs window. It was alight, and he could see Eva moving back and forth with the unwieldy bulk of a child on her hip. Why wasn't she downstairs with the rest?

He turned the lapels of his coat back and straightened his shirt neck, and walked slowly up the yard. His hand hovered over the latch of the door; then he thrust it open, and with his usual spring entered the kitchen.

They were all there except Eva: his mother and father, Terence and Tony, and Bridget. They all stared at him, and the almost audible pleading in Bridget's eyes was also in those of the others. But he looked at none of them, not even at Bridget; for his eyes were riveted in stupefied amazement on the massive Negro standing behind Bridget's chair with his hand possessively covering her shoulder.

CHAPTER TWO

A SEAFARING GENTLEMAN

'Oh, it's ye, Mrs Cullen – did ye want to borrow something?'

Jane Cullen knew it was a danger signal when Kathie addressed her as Mrs. She stood within the door, hugging her shawl about her, and looked in envy at this neighbour whom no sorrow or tribulation could affect. She guessed Kathie was a bit upset about the black man, but nothing to speak of – if it had happened to one of her lassies she would have died with shame. She said gently, 'I was wonderin', Kathie, if ye'd lend me yer boots. I've got to go into Jarrow and it's pourin', and there's not a sole on mine. If he gets the job of night-watchman I'll get meself a pair.'

'Ye've been saying that for the last year, Mrs Cullen. If it isn't me gully, it's me boots!'

Jane looked at Kathie for a moment, then turned silently to the door.

'Here, take them.' The boots were thrust against Jane's arm, and as she took them with a low murmur of thanks Kathie remarked grandiosely, 'I'll soon be able to pass them on to yer altogether, for me daughter Bridget is buying me a new pair. She's able to buy anything she likes now she's married such a well-set-up gentleman. Did yer hear that she's setting up in the middle streets? Four rooms she'll have at that. They're down in Shields this very minute getting the furniture, and for the whole house, mind yer . . . there'll be no beg and scrape for me daughter Bridget.'

Jane nodded her head and smiled weakly. 'I'm glad for her, Kathie.'

For a second longer the two women stared at each other, then Jane sidled out, and Kathie, turning to the fire, stood grinding her strong teeth together until her jawbones ached. She'd let them see; no-one would pity her. She had laughed longer and louder these past few days than ever before, and she had made the others laugh too, saying, 'If ye laugh, they won't pity ye, and if they don't pity ye they'll envy ye.' Cavan, Terence and even Tony had done as she bid. But not Matt . . . Matt seemed to have been transfixed into silence from the moment he saw the Negro. And Eva – that big daft slobbery bitch. Kathie turned up her eyes and their venom was enough to penetrate the ceiling. Playing the respectable married woman! And getting all virtuous like – the silly sod, when her belly was full of Harry McGuire before she'd dragged him to the altar rails!

Eva had always envied Bridget; and rightly too, Kathie thought; but now she refused even to speak to her sister. And so Kathie had taken Bridget's marriage lines and held them under Eva's nose. But Eva, with an air that nearly drove her mother mad, had pointed out that a Registry Office marriage was no marriage; so besides the awful disgrace of having a black man, Bridget was also living in sin, and she'd soon have Father O'Malley on her track. And, blast her, she was right, too . . . about the priest, anyway, for he had never been off the doorstep since he'd got wind of the affair.

He had managed to corner Bridget but not him . . . Kathie couldn't bring herself to call her son-in-law James. To his face she addressed him as 'Mr Paterson'; and time and again she wondered at the ordinariness of such a name for such an extraordinary man, and wondered too what in the name of God made her Bridget marry him. She couldn't get a word of explanation out of Bridget. When she asked her, Bridget just drooped her eyes and clasped her hands on her lap, and sat still and tense, until Kathie cried, 'Then why did ye come back?' And to this Bridget answered simply, 'I wanted to be near you all when he's away at sea . . . and the bairn coming.'

A bairn coming. Kathie held her head between her hands. A black bairn. For it would be a black bairn, she was sure; there was too much of him in comparison with Bridget's whiteness. The child would be black both inside and out, and her Bridget would have to push a black bairn around the streets. Mother of God! How could a daughter of hers stand up under the shame of it? She rocked her head with her hands. But Bridget didn't seem to be ashamed: there she was, away now in Shields, walking openly with him in the broad daylight! Hadn't she watched her go down the street with never a look to right or left, her head held high as if she had something to be proud of? What had come over her? Why had she done it? Kathie beat the top of her head with her fist. Would the good God tell her why she had done it?

Something of the same question was passing through Bridget's mind as she faced the look of ill-concealed scorn in the eyes of the shop assistants. She had watched her husband put down the five pounds deposit and sign his name with a proud flourish on the form which was an open sesame to a choice of oil-cloths, of beds and bedroom suites, of half-sets of china and Nottingham lace curtains. Never had she dreamed that she would be able to set up house with thirty pounds' worth of furniture. She should be mad with the joy of it; but there was no spark of joy in her, only pain and pity, and gratitude and abhorrence – the pain and pity and gratitude were the feelings that the bulk of towering blackness evoked in her; the abhorrence was for herself and the thing she had done.

When they left the shop it was her husband who showed her out. Taking the door from the hand of the shopwalker he stood aside to allow her to pass. But the closing of the door did not shut out the tittering from the shop, and its sound brought an angry flush to Bridget's cheeks, and a higher tilt to her chin. They laughed at her because he treated her like a queen! If she had married one of them she would have been made aware of her inferiority for the remainder of her life, and if she had married one of her own class never would she have known the meaning of worship – not to speak of consideration; never would she have known what it was to be loved as this man loved her. Then why was she ashamed of him? Why did it take all the rallying of her forces to brave the streets with him at her side?

When they were together, closed in by four walls, with no eyes upon them, the shame would fade, and then a strange tenderness for him would fill her. Even at times a feeling she thought might be love for him would sweep over her. This often happened in the night when he woke her with his loving, for even with his passion, which lifted her into realms hitherto unknown, his love-making never lost the adoring quality that gave to it a gentleness. But she wished again and again that he would not show this gentleness to her in public, for it was this as much as anything that brought the guffaws and smiles of ridicule upon them. She wanted to tell him, but she could not bear to hurt him. She had soon found that she could hurt him with a look or a word; and she knew that she must never do this . . . she must never hurt him more than she had done by marrying him. She did not blame him for marrying her – if she had been in her right senses it would never have come about – Matt had always warned her . . . Matt . . . She shuddered. She had Matt to face yet. Oh God, give her strength for the day when Matt would speak to her, and drag from her the reason why she had done this thing.

Her husband's hand in her arm pulled her closer to him, and his thick bell-toned voice, speaking his short-cut English, fell on her head. 'You cold? . . . You shivering? . . . Me, I'm big selfish beast. I take you home right away, eh?' He bent down and looked into her face. 'Eh, honey? We go home, eh?'

She smiled at him. 'I'm not cold – someone was walking over my grave.'

'Someone on your grave? . . . Sh!' He pulled her still closer. 'You don't talk of graves; you make me have creeps too. No grave will get my Rose . . . By way, your mam don't like me calling you Rose, do she? But you Rose all through . . . Bridget, it is hard sound – like – like a swear, eh?' He laughed, his head thrown up and his massive shoulders shaking.

His laugh was infectious, but the passers-by did not join in as they would have done had he been alone . . . a black man and a white girl was something not to be condoned in any way. In the unmoving depths of his mind James Paterson knew this, but in the conflicting groping layers nearer the surface, where his thoughts jumped and clung to anything that would bring him a level nearer to the white man, he told himself that the looks of the women were jealousy of his Rose's beauty, and those of the men, envy of himself for his luck in possessing her.

He believed in luck . . . he believed he was born lucky. Had he ever starved like other black men? No. Hadn't he been to school? Couldn't he read and write? . . . By God, yes! And hadn't he always had any woman he wanted? Again, by God, yes! There were times when he had to push them off . . . white women liked black men; and they weren't all women of the bars, either; no, by God, they weren't. But one thing he never had until he took Rose; and that was a virgin. He knew then that Rose must belong to no man but him. It had been hard work getting her, and he'd nearly lost his boat. It would have been the first time he had missed a trip, either through drink or women, but he had been prepared to do it for Rose . . . The nagging thought came again . . . would she have married him had she not discovered there was a baby coming? . . . Yes; yes, she would. For his Rose loved him; and the colour of his skin meant nothing to her.

He pulled her even closer to him until he bore her weight on his arm. He wanted to lift her up and carry her through the streets; he wanted to show all men by some definite sign that she was his; he wanted to touch her and caress her. He said softly, 'We call at our own house – what you say?'

She consented readily, for anything was better than going home when Matt would be in, and have his eyes avoid hers and his silence beat at her.

As they turned into Dunstable Street James spoke a cheery 'good evening' to a small group of men standing at the corner. They answered him in low growls, turning their heads away and becoming engrossed in each other's conversation.

And Bridget felt a desire to stop and shout at them, 'He's as good as you – he's better than you. He wouldn't let his wife trail round the bars after him to get what was left of his pay; nor yet have his beer if the bairns went naked – you lot! What are you, anyway? . . . Scum . . . scum.'

She was shivering again when they entered the empty house; and James, all concern for her, said, 'I know you got chill, honey – come, we go to your home – there's big fire there.'

'No, it's all right; I want to stay here awhile.' She smiled at him. 'We'll plan where we'll put the furniture.'

He responded to her, as pleased as a child: 'Oh, my, yes. Tomorrow when it all come – my!' He shook his head. 'We have our home – my Rose has a beautiful home . . . And me . . . between watches I sit on deck and think of you sittin' here thinkin' of me – eh?' He took her chin in his great black hand and tilted her face up to his. Her grey eyes were moist with the pity that was foremost in her mind at that moment, and he said, 'You not sad?'

She turned from him and went into the little bare kitchen, and he followed her in concern. 'You not like the house and the pretty furniture?'

The expressive, appealing gesture of his outstretched arms wrenched the words out of her! 'Oh yes, yes – it's only that I'm happy.' She sniffed and blew her nose. 'I always cry when . . . when I'm happy.'

As his laughter resounded from the bare walls she knew that in a way she had spoken the truth, for she would be happy in this house with all her lovely furniture. She would have four rooms all to herself, and a back yard to herself, and she could bolt the door and be shut away from people. Apart from those looking down on the yard out of the windows opposite, no-one would see her if she did not wish it. And she would have the added comfort that her people were near if she wanted them. Oh yes, she would be happy. She was happy. She could believe it; for now they were alone together.

The soft light that had been the magnet that first drew him was in her eyes, and he pulled her away from the window to the dark corner near the fireplace.

'You love me, Rose?'

She nodded.

'Always?'

She nodded again.

'No other man, ever?'

She shook her head.

'Not when I'm away at sea, like some white women?'

'No, no, never that!' Her protest was vehement.

His enormous lips slowly traced the outline of her face. The moving black blur filled her with such conflicting emotions that she became faint under them. His unfinished words ran into one another, forming a lulling drawl. 'Rose love . . . my beautiful Rose. No other woman in world like you . . . You marry me 'cause you love me. You don't mind colour, and our baby . . . my baby, she be a girl; we call her Angela, eh? like angel . . . Rose Angela.' His fingers moved down the waist-band of her skirt and pressed gently on her stomach. 'I feel her heart-beat . . . she'll be like you, Rose . . . white and beautiful with long limbs and . . .'

The sound that checked his words was of someone breathing. The both remained still, pressed close against each other for a second

22

longer, listening to the hiss of the indrawn breath. James turned slowly, but Bridget almost jumped into the centre of the kitchen at the sight of the priest standing in the front-room doorway.

If it had been an ordinary man, James would have demanded 'What the hell you up to, eh?' before, perhaps, whirling him through the air into the street. But a priest to him was not a man, so he said with laughing irony, 'Why, sir, you near scared me white.'

The priest looked from James to Bridget, and the expression in his eyes bore down her courage. Her head drooped and the old childhood fear of him overcame her.

'I told you to bring him along to the vestry.' Father O'Malley might have been speaking of an animal, and his words seemed to have been pressed thin in their effort to escape his tight lips.

'I . . . I didn't tell him, Father.'

James looked enquiringly from one to the other. Although he didn't like the tone the priest was using to his wife, nor the way he was looking at her, the smile still hovered about his face. Bible-punchers were funny; all bible-punchers were quaint men.

Father O'Malley again addressed Bridget. 'You have told him what must be done?'

She shook her head, her eyes still directed towards the floor. 'No, Father.'

The priest adjusted his thick glasses and brought the pin-points of his eyes to bear on James. 'You must be married; and you must take instruction.' He separated each word, and the effect was very much that of James's stilted English. 'I will marry you on Saturday morning at eight o'clock.'

'Marry? . . . Me? . . . We be married?' James looked in perplexity at Bridget's bowed head. The smile had left his face, and his body was stretched to its fullest height, making the small priest appear like a dwarf in comparison. 'What you mean, married? I got paper all signed – we married.'

'Not in the eyes of God. A Christian marriage cannot be performed in a Registry Office; and you must take instructions to become a . . .'

'But me am Christian.' A patient smile began to hover around James's lips; he felt he knew now why the priest was so concerned. 'Why, sir, I was baptised – yes, yes, I know all about Christ Jesus . . . Mr Edwards, he very good missionary – splendid fellow, he learned me Jesus Christ all through, and what those bloody Jews did for him. A good man, Jesus Christ . . . Yes, me Christian all right.' James's smile widened, spreading the corners of his mouth to meet the expanse of his broad nostrils. 'You no need worry 'bout me.'

'The missionary wasn't a Catholic – it isn't the same. This is your fault!' Father O'Malley hurled the accusation at Bridget.

'Here, here! You no speak to her like that.' James stepped to his wife's side and placed a protecting arm around her shoulders. 'You man of God all right, but you no speak like that, please. You mean me isn't Christian 'cause me not Catholic-Christian? Christ Jesus all kinds Christian. The Catholic Father he came and play chess with Mr Edwards, and laugh fit to bust over jokes. They both Christian men. Once Catholic Father say to me I am name same's Christ's brother, and I should be fisherman. Always that stay in my head. An' one day I leave my home for the water. Me was never fisherman, but me always on water . . . That Catholic Father was good man. He know me Christian all right.'

'Be quiet!' The sharpness of the command whipped the returning smile completely from James's face, and his scalp moved, shifting his mop of wire curls from side to side. The priest went on, looking now with open contempt at Bridget, 'This is no marriage and you know it. You have sinned enough already, and naturally as night follows day retribution will come upon you. Your only atonement can be to ensure the safe keeping of the soul of your child; and God knows it will need that to be in safe keeping. Be at the church at eight o'clock on Saturday morning; and I will take him for instruction whenever he is in port.'

'You what, by God!'

James made to follow the priest as he went through the front room, but Bridget clung on to him, crying, 'Please, James . . . James. Don't for my sake . . . James, we will see Father Bailey . . . he's different . . . he'll explain to you.'

James became still. His eyes were puzzled and sad as they looked down into hers. 'You no want us do this thing – to go be married again? If we do this, no dignity left. Mister Edwards always say "Keep dignity", and here I feel' – he pointed to his chest – 'dignity be gone if we do this. We married all right in here' – he pressed his hand on his heart – 'I know we'm married all right . . . Very much married. But him, he say we not married at all.'

Bridget's mind suddenly cried at her, Oh God, if only Father O'Malley was right, and it was no marriage! But it was a marriage all right. The night she had slept with James hadn't made it a marriage; but when a man with a greasy collar had mumbled some scarcely intelligible words over them and they had written their names in a book, that had made it a marriage. Why? but why? The cry against man's social order that had rung through unhappy unions down the ages found only one answer in her mind, You've made your bed and you'll have to lie on it.

She said to James, repeating the formula that had been drilled into her at school, 'The Catholic religion is the only one true religion.' Then she added, 'You've got to be married in the Catholic Church before – before it's all right with God.'

24

It was a bright Saturday morning and the streets were warm, and women, the respectable ones, were kneeling on the pavement washing their steps. Some were covering a large half-moon of the pavement with bath brick, taking care to get a smoothness in the distribution, regardless of the fact that within an hour, perhaps less, the feet of the children would have stamped it black; clean patches seemed to draw children like magnets. But this morning the women turned from the daily sign of their respectability to stare at Kathie McQueen and her man Cavan, all dressed up . . . and Kathie in her funeral coat too! One after the other, after answering Kathie's loud greeting, they knelt back on their heels and stared after her swaying figure encased in the tight black satin coat, and at Cavan, who from the back appeared like a boy walking with his mother, and silent, too, like some boys who are forced to walk with their mothers on some disagreeable errand, for he gave no greeting to the women, nor yet cast a glance at them.

'We are off for a jaunt with me daughter Bridget and her man.' Kathie threw this information to the last remaining women in the street, before they turned into the main road.

'And what better morning for it, eh?'

And the women answered back, 'None better.'

In the comparative quietness of the main road Cavan, still looking straight ahead, said, 'Ye're foolin' nobody but yersel'.'

And after a moment's silence Kathie replied, 'That's as may be; but I'll not have their pity . . . see?' She turned her head aggressively on him. 'They'll think as ye want them to think, in the long run . . . I've seen it afore . . . it's always the way.'

They walked on in silence again, and Kathie adjusted her large satin-covered hat that had once been black but was now a variety of shot greens, then hitched her coat into an easier position under her breasts, and hoped as she did so that the button wouldn't give way; and she cursed Father O'Malley at the same time. If he had to marry them again he could have waited a bit; and with Cavan in work she might have got herself a coat, for this one had seen its day. Eighteen years it had been on the go, and it second-hand when she got it. She'd had her nine-and-six worth out of it, and many a proud moment it had given her, for hadn't it come from a big house and been worn by a lady? You only had to smell it to know that. But she never thought she'd wear it to go and see her daughter married a second time to a nigger. The humiliation weighed her down and caused her greetings to the step-washers in Dunstable Street to be even louder. And when she knocked at Bridget's door the satin of the coat was rippling and changing its greasy hue with her laughter.

The door was opened instantly, as if Bridget had been waiting for her knock, and Kathie was unable to keep up her laughter to cover her annoyance when Bridget, without a word, stepped into the street, and James, looking more massive and black than ever because of the stiffness of his body and the sombreness of his face, followed her. He, too, gave them no greeting; but locked the door; then, taking his place by Bridget's side, walked down the street, Kathie and Cavan following.

Kathie yelled at Cavan; she yelled to the step-cleaners again; she yelled to no-one in particular; and some of her words, even to herself, were unintelligible . . . To be turned back at the door like that; not to be asked in and given a drop of something to help things along a bit. God knew that at ordinary funerals and weddings you needed something; and this was no ordinary wedding; yet not a drop of anything. What were things coming to, anyway . . .

The church was empty when they arrived, and self-consciously they filed into the back seat after genuflecting towards the main altar; all except James, who did not bend even his head; nor did he follow the others' example and kneel down, but sat with his arms folded across his chest and his cheek-bones making tight the skin of his face with their pressure.

Presently an altar-boy, trying hard to cover his amusement, came with an order from the priest; and they rose and filed down the aisle to the altar-rails. They had barely reached them when Father O'Malley appeared on the other side, his face as stiff as his vestments. With a peremptory finger he motioned James and Bridget to kneel down. And so the service began.

The priest's voice was not even audible. There was a hurried guttural mumbling of words, the flicking over of leaves of the prayer-book, the passing from one hand to the other of a penny, then the flinging of the words at James, 'Will you have this woman to be your lawful wedded wife?'

James flung the responses back in a voice that made the priest start in spite of his grim control; but so low was Bridget's 'I will' that the priest accepted it without having actually heard it.

It was over, and Cavan and Kathie followed the couple to the vestry. Cavan's face was the colour of chalk and Kathie's so red as to appear on the verge of apoplexy.

Once the register was signed it was as if Father O'Malley couldn't get rid of them quickly enough. Scrambling up the aisle ahead of them, he led the way to the church door, and without a word watched them file past him into the street, his eyes, like rapier-points, piercing each one of them in turn. James was the last to leave, and the door was allowed to swing behind him, almost catching his heels.

'Of all the rotten holy Joes in this world, he's one!' Kathie could contain herself no longer. 'I hope he finds himself dead in his bed one of these mornings, and God forgive me for sayin' such a thing; but that's me curse.'

'Shut up!' Cavan's voice was deep and angry. He was hurt to the very soul with the indignities his daughter had brought upon herself. 'We've reached rock-bottom when you curse the priest; we've had enough bad luck; hold your tongue!'

'I'll not hold me tongue; one of these days I'll tell him me opinion of him to his face, and chance Hell's flames for it, ye'll see.' Kathie talked at her husband all the way to the fifteen streets; but she did not laugh; nor did she address her daughter or son-in-law; she allowed them to walk well on in front until they reached their own street, where they stopped and waited for her. Then all she said was 'I'll see ye later.' Her laughter had failed her.

Bridget and James entered their house in silence, and as Bridget made to go upstairs James pulled her to him and stared at her fixedly; and Bridget was hurt by the look on the usually laughing face of her husband. Compassion for his bewilderment overcame her, and she laid her hand on his cheek. 'I'm sorry, James; it had to be done. Perhaps you'll understand later when you've had instructions.'

His face softened, and she was surprised at the relief she experienced with the sound of his voice; but for his answers at the altar-rails he had said no word to her since leaving the house; it was as if he were striving to keep the dignity he prized so much.

'Now you feel we married?'

She nodded dumbly.

'That's all right then.' He drew her into his arms and held her gently for a while in silence. Then holding her away from him, he smiled at her, saying, 'Now we can be happy; for two more days we can be happy. You sorry I'm sailing Monday, Rose?'

'Yes.'

'Truly?'

'Yes – yes.'

'You don't want me to leave you?'

'No.'

'You know I don't want leave you. I don't want leave you ever.' He sat down and drew her on to his knee and, taking off her hat, ran his hands over her hair. 'Most beautiful hair in the world. My Angela have hair like this . . . Rose—' He buried his face between her breasts.

'Yes?'

'I want ask you something . . . If German get my ship and I not come back, you not let her forget me . . . you tell her about me?'

'Please, Jimmy, don't say that. Never fear, you'll be all right.'

She felt the strong conviction within herself that God would make her suffer all her life for her mistake, and that James would be immune from danger so that her punishment might be meted out to her. She repeated, 'Never fear.'

27

The broad sweep of his eyebrows lifted, showing more white to his eyes. 'Me? I don't fear nothing or nobody – not for me I don't. But for you, yes. I won't tell no lies 'bout what I fear: two men I fear for you, 'cause they both make you afraid. One is that goddam priest, and the other is . . .' He stopped; then went on slowly, '. . . your brother. He like me worse than the others. When I am here he can't touch you, for he knows I would break him like that.' He clenched his huge fist until the knuckles showed pink beneath the black skin. 'But when I'm gone, you very afraid of Matt.' The last was a statement.

'No – no I'm not – I won't be; he's all right.' She avoided his eyes and screwed nervously at the bottom of his waistcoat.

'No lie, Rose. Your brother mad because you marry black man – your brother like you very much. Me, I know. Your mother, da and others all right, but Matt . . . he black inside. Me, I know men. From twelve years I work with men – all kinds of men – down stokehold. Eight years I been in same ship, and the Chief he say to me, "New bunch this trip, Jimmie. What you make of them?" The Chief, he think lot of me. I would have been his donkey-man many times over but for this.' He tapped the skin of his hand. 'Chief ask my opinion of men, not 'cause he don't know men. He big Geordie fellow. But he like talk with me, and he know I know men . . . Oh! you no cry. Rose. Please you no cry.'

She leant against him and her sobs mounted; and he beseeched her, 'You no cry. Me, I am sorry, Rose; but I am full of fear for you – don't – don't. Why you cry so?'

She continued to sob and he swung her up into his arms; and as he rose to his feet with her she gasped out, 'Don't go, James; don't go away.'

'I got to go, honey, you know that.' He smiled down on her. 'But I mighty glad you don't want me go. And you no worry any more; I see that brother and I fix him 'fore I go. We go upstairs now, eh? And you put on pretty dress and new hat with feather, and we go out and make everybody look at my Rose, and fellas turn and say, "Him lucky fella . . . him marry twice same girl." '

He smiled down on her; then opened the stair door with his foot and walked sideways up the stairs, hugging her closer to him.

CHAPTER THREE

MATT

James had been gone three days and Bridget was feeling strangely lonely. After the first flush of relief she began to miss him and his deep broken speech telling her how wonderful she was; she missed the feeling of strength and protection he gave her; she missed him at night, and this caused her to feel wicked. In the night she lay tossing and turning, fighting the feeling of wanting him; in the night she never thought of him as black, for the night made all colour one. It was in the daytime, going about the work of the house, that the barrier of his colour would loom up and terrify her. She knew that in marrying James she had committed a sort of outrage, and that this had lifted her in one sweep off the plane of her people; but it had not dropped her on to the plane of James's people; it left her in a no-man's-land where, as far as she could see, there was only herself.

As hour added to hour, she felt less inclined to leave her house, for she knew she was vulnerable to the hostile looks of the men and women of the fifteen streets, and for once she felt thankful and glad that the war was on, for in the excitement and sudden rush of prosperity they would, she thought, have less time to give to the scandal she had created; not that they would miss taking some action should the worst among them give tongue. So, for the time, she stayed within the precincts of her own four small rooms, and some part of her was rested with their sanctuary.

That she must soon face the people and even work among them she knew, for James's monthly half-pay note of two pounds fifteen shillings would scarcely keep her for four weeks and pay the rent, coals and light, which came to eight shillings a week. Then there were the instalments of five shillings per week to pay on the furniture. Although James had provided for this by leaving with her the remainder of his fortune, fifteen pounds, she had the desire not to touch a penny of what was to her a vast sum, but rather to add to it. She knew that he must have spent a great part of his earnings on women and drink, but the habit, started by the missionary, of saving a little of his earnings had stuck, and not a penny James had put into the Post Office in eighteen years had he withdrawn; until he met her. Thirty-five pounds he had saved, and the feeling of the growing wealth, Bridget felt, had in no small way added to the dignity he so greatly prized.

Only once during the past three days had Bridget visited her mother, for Matt was on night shift and she was afraid of encountering him without the shield of James. She sat now beneath the gas mantle that sported a pink porcelain shade, sewing at a minute flannel petticoat. Her expression was a mixture of tenderness and apprehension, and unconsciously her lips moved as she repeated the prayer that was never long out of her mind; and now it was almost audible; and as she murmured 'Please God, make it all right!' the knocker of the front door banged once, and after a moment's hesitation she rose slowly and laid the petticoat on the table; then stiffening her body she went through the front room and opened the door.

Her relief made her exclaim in an unnaturally high-pitched voice, 'Why, Tony! Come in . . . I'd been wondering when you were coming.'

Tony limped over the step and into the dark room, and Bridget, her hand on his shoulder, guided him to the kitchen. 'Come and sit down; have you had your tea?' She pulled a highly varnished wooden chair towards the glowing fire.

'Yes.' He sat down without taking his eyes from her face.

She sat opposite to him and for a while they smiled at each other. Then she said awkwardly, 'It's funny me having a house, isn't it?'

He nodded, and the broken peak of his cap jerked further down his brow. He pushed it up and continued to stare at her.

'Do you like it?' She made a small motion with her hand around the room.

Reluctantly he took his eyes from her face, and screwed round on his chair to take it all in. 'Eeh, it's fine, Bridget.' Stretching out his hand he shyly touched the fringe of the green chenille cloth covering the table. 'It's lovely!'

'Come on, I'll light the gas and show you the front room.'

She ran from him, and he followed more slowly, his grey eyes wide with wonder, for she appeared to him now like the girl he saw when he first came to their house.

In the front room she pulled down the new cream paper blind, with its edging of imitation lace, and lit the gas. Tony looked from one piece to the other of the suite: four single chairs, two armchairs and a couch, each one defying comfort with its stiff back and red plush seat. He looked at the bouquets of flowers forming large diamonds on the linoleum; at the plant-stand before the window, holding a fuchsia which was actually in flower; then at the mantel border, an elaborate piece of black satin on which were pen-painted three large and unreal birds, and there was genuine admiration in his voice and in his eyes when he said, 'I've never seen anything like it, Bridget; it's beautiful.'

'Come on upstairs.' She was as eager as a child. 'Wait until you see the dressing-table.'

On the way upstairs he stopped and touched the corded stair-carpet with his hands; but his wonder was suddenly covered with embarrassment when he entered the bedroom. He had to walk close to the great iron and brass bedstead to get to the dressing-table, and as he did so he realised for the first time that Bridget was no longer the Bridget of the McQueens' laughter-filled kitchen; she was married . . . she was a married woman, and she was married to a nigger.

'Look,' Bridget was saying, 'it has three mirrors, and the two side ones swing back and forward – like this. Have you ever seen anything like it?' And when he made no answer, Bridget turned to him and looked down on his lowered eyes, and his embarrassment reached her.

They went down the stairs in silence, and now Tony knew that in some way Bridget was aware of what he was thinking, and there was an agitation in him to reassure her. Bridget mustn't be hurt – she mustn't think he was like the others. He said suddenly, 'I like Jimmy – I like him better than anyone I know.'

She smiled sadly, and his heart twisted inside him as he saw the wet mist cover her eyes.

He began to talk with unusual rapidity. 'I've got a job, Bridget . . . I'm starting at Crawley's grocer's shop the morrer – I'm going in the back first, weighing up spuds and flour. He's giving me five shillings a week, and I'll soon get a rise if I do all right, he says. I would have got more if I'd been able to go out with the orders, but it's me . . . Anyway, I'll soon be serving in the shop. I'm glad the war's on; I wouldn't have got it if the war hadn't been on.'

'Oh, I'm glad for you, Tony – oh, I am!' Bridget was mashing the tea. 'We'll have a cup of tea . . . you'd like a cup, wouldn't you?'

'Yes, Bridget. Yer ma's going to get me a pair of long trousers . . . new ones . . . as soon as I get a pay.'

'Oh, that'll be grand.'

'I'm dying to get into long trousers . . . Bridget, you know in six years and ten months I'll be twenty-one; and you'll be twenty-six. You'll only be five years older than me then.'

She turned to him, puzzled and wondering at the odd turn of his thoughts. 'But I'm five years older than you now – I'll always be five years older than you.'

'Yes, yes, I know' – he wrung his cap between his hands – 'but I'll be grown up then . . . I'll be able to do things . . . if people . . .' He took his gaze from her, and his dark lashes cast a long shadow on to his thin, pale face, giving to it an almost girlish delicacy.

Bridget, looking at his bent head, read his unfinished words wrongly. 'Nobody will ever say anything about you, Tony – your limp isn't really noticeable, and you're growing now. Why, you are nearly as tall as me. And, you know, you're nice-looking – yes you are.'

As he gave an impatient shake with his body, saying, 'Oh, it wasn't that,' Bridget exclaimed, 'Hush a minute!' and they both stood listening to the rattling of the backyard door-latch.

'Is it locked? Will I go and open it?' he asked.

'No; drink your tea.'

He drank it, standing near the table, his eyes watching her listening as she moved about the kitchen. When the front door-knocker banged he put down his cup and asked, 'Will I go home, Bridget?'

She answered him on her way to the door, 'Yes, Tony, you'd better; but come again – come often.'

Matt stood on the pavement, the distant light of the street lamp emphasising the piercing blackness of his eyes. He did not even glance at Tony sidling past him, but stepped into the room and closed the door.

With the first sight of him Bridget had returned to the kitchen, where she now stood, staring down into the fire, her hands gripping the brass rod. She waited for him to speak until she could wait no longer, and she turned to where he stood just within the kitchen door, surveying her.

'You needn't think you're coming round here to frighten me, our Matt, because you're not . . . James told you – I know he told you what would happen if you did anything.' Her voice trembled with the fear she denied, and she went on, throwing her words at him, 'You always wanted everything your own way – well, you can't run my life. I would never have left home if it hadn't been for you.' She had said all the things she had told herself she wouldn't say.

'Why did you do it?' Each word was thin and had a piercing quality that cut deep into her.

She shivered, but rapped out, 'That's my business.'

'You were drunk, weren't you?'

Her bust and shoulders lifted in an attempt at denial, but no words came. Their eyes fought each other's; then her head drooped and she flung round to the fire again.

'I warned you, didn't I, to keep off it . . . I always told you it made you a sloppy, dribbling sot. You can't carry it . . . I told you, you bloody young fool.' Every syllable dripped with his contempt of her.

'Well, you nor nobody else will have to pay for my mistake.' Her head was resting on the rod now, and her voice was flat and quiet.

'Won't we?' He took three rapid steps forward which brought him to the table. 'We're just the laughing-stock of the streets, that's all! Our street was raised yesterday, with Cissie Luck making

32

that fat swine of hers stand aside to let her into her front door; he put his toe in her backside and she screamed up the street, "Now me next bairn'll be khaki." '

Bridget winced as if in physical pain; and Matt went on, 'And then Pat Skinner linked with his seedless piece when they were passing the corner, and the chaps nearly cracked their sides with laughing. They were yelling, "Give her the Paterson touch, lad" . . . Nobody paying for your mistake!' He spat past her into the fire. 'By God! We're all paying for it, every damned one of us. And let me tell you this – we've only just started. As for you, you can thank your lucky stars there's a war on. If there hadn't been, they would have hounded you out of the place; and they'll likely do it yet. Some of the men in the Barium were throwing their quips at Terry yesterday; they were saying why should black swines have the houses when they've got to travel across the water each day.'

He was standing behind her now and the gusts of his breath were on her neck: 'Do you know what me ma heard that Dorrie Clark say? Do you?'

Bridget remained silent and still.

'She was spouting in the shop that you should be sent down to Holborn, among the Arabs. And do you know what the others said – that the Arabs wouldn't allow a dirty nigger among them.'

Bridget swung round on him, almost knocking him over. 'Shut up you, shut up! Don't you dare call him a dirty nigger. He's better than you or any of them around these doors – he's too good for me. Yes he is, yes he is.' She was screaming now. 'He knows how to treat a woman, that's more than the men here do. If they bring in their wages they think they're gods, and the women have to wait on them hand and foot from the day they marry them; and even when they are giving them bairns and wearing them out they are pawing at whoever will let them. They've got room to talk – they have, the men around here! And the women too, for that matter – dirty-mouthed lot.'

'At least they have white bairns.' As always when he had succeeded in arousing her anger, his own subsided. He spoke quietly now, but his mild barbed words had more effect on her than had his rage.

Bridget put her hand up to her throat and tore at it; and moved her head from side to side as if trying to free herself from some fearsome grip. Matt saw the colour drain from her face; and when she staggered and groped for a chair, he stood watching her, fighting the torrent of feeling that was pouring back into his veins now that they were together again, and as she slid from the chair on to the floor he sprang to catch her, crying, 'Bridget! . . . here, Bridget! . . . what's up?'

33

For a few minutes she lay lifeless on the mat, while he gripped her bloodless face, still entreating, 'Bridget; here, come on – what's up with you?'

It was strange, but never before had he seen a woman in a faint; women of his knowledge didn't faint, even when carrying bairns. So he kept calling to her, and when at last she opened her eyes his voice was soft with his anxiety. 'Brid, what's up? Are you all right? Can I get you something? Have you anything in the house – a drop of anything?'

The shake of her head was almost imperceivable.

'Come on, get up.' He lifted her into a chair and supported her with his arm, and she pointed weakly to the tea-pot, saying, 'Give me a drink.'

The tea did nothing to revive her, and he stood over her, his voice harsh again, yet threaded with his anxiety. 'You take the damn stuff when you shouldn't, yet when you need it you haven't got any. Will you be all right till I go and fetch you something?'

'I don't want anything.'

The weakness of her voice only strengthened his determination. 'You've got to have something to pull you round. I won't be a minute. Lie on the mat if you feel bad again.'

He was gone and she was left alone. The fear of him, too, was gone: it was ousted by the fear he had brought to the surface, the fear that she would have a black baby. Her mind was sick and her body shivering with the fear . . . and all because she had got drunk.

She had known Matt knew how she had come to marry James and would make her admit it. The twice he had seen her drunk was at New Year parties. The first time, when she was seventeen, she only took two glasses of whisky, but those were enough to make her throw her arms around Len Bryant and kiss him in front of everyone. She could never remember doing it, as she disliked Len Bryant because he was always trying to touch her, and she wouldn't believe Matt; but she believed her father when he told her.

It was the following New Year's Eve before she again touched whisky . . . her previous reaction to it having faded from her mind. She only knew that the smell of whisky held a fascination for her, and she liked the cutting taste, and in spite of – or perhaps because of – Matt's scowling eye she took a proffered glass. This time she lifted up her skirts and danced, and Frankie Flanagan, whose house the party was in, lifted her on to the table. . . and his wife punched him in the face; and she herself had been slapped sober in the wash-house by Matt.

It was after this she swore to herself never to touch whisky again, for she knew she couldn't carry it. But looking back now she saw that the chain of circumstances that led to her next being drunk could not have been foreseen by even the most wary of individuals; for who would have thought getting friendly with another house-parlourmaid in London would have been the main link? This girl's sister had recently married a man who was managing a public house in Liverpool, and they had written asking her to work for them. Soon Bridget herself received a letter from her friend, with a glowing account of the highly paid jobs to be had in Liverpool; and it was no time at all until she found herself in such a daily post; and getting half as much money again as she had been receiving in London, but paying out much more than the half for an attic room above a stable attached to the public house; and it was the simplest thing in the world to grant the request of the sisters to help in the rush-time on a Saturday night; also the simplest thing to get merry in the back room afterwards with a few of the regular seafaring clients – the honour of being called into the back room being an inducement to the men to empty their pockets again at the end of the next trip. There she met James . . . but she couldn't remember taking him to her room, she could only remember the horror of her awakening; and from then till now seemed but four hours instead of four months.

Her mind raked up again the humiliations that attended her marrying James; the scorn of her one-time friends; the order to get out by the supposedly outraged sister; the expressions on the faces of the many landladies; until she felt she could bear it no longer and that she must brave the shock that James would be to her people and go to them. She had imagined, too, that once inside the fifteen streets she would find a measure of peace and protection among her own kind; but when she thought this, the enormity of her crime in all its entirety had not been brought fully home to her . . . it needed the return to her own class to do this.

'Here, drink this.'

She had not been aware of Matt's return. The smell of the whisky from the glass held close to her face brought her to herself, and she turned her head away, saying, 'I don't want that.'

'Don't act the goat – here, get it down you!'

'I tell you I don't want it . . . Matt, I don't want it!' She gazed up at him pleadingly. 'I promised I wouldn't . . .' She broke off and shook her head. 'I'll be all right; this'll pass.'

Matt stood staring down at her, his lower lip pressed out. Who had she promised? That dirty black swine? She had promised him she wouldn't drink, had she! . . . after he had dropped her! Well, the nigger had got her through drink; then, by God, it would be through drink that he would lose her! He gripped the back of Bridget's head; then, putting the glass to her lips, forced the whisky between them.

CHAPTER FOUR

THE BIRTH

In such communities as that of the fifteen streets there is often found an outstanding personality, a personality that is respected for its self-sacrificing and good qualities, or one that is held in awe or fear for some power it is credited with possessing – mostly evil. Such a personality was Nellie Milligan. She was known as a fixer. Despairing women, realising that once again they had fallen, would immediately turn their thoughts to Nellie Milligan and wonder how the sovereign could be raised; but raise it they would, even to the extent of pawning every bit of bedding a pawnshop would accept, to enable them to pay for having the burden removed.

The days of the twelve or fifteen in a family were past; but to see up to half a dozen children with hungry eyes was more than enough for some of the women; so, ironically, many called God's blessing on Nellie Milligan, while here and there a woman, trailing out the remainder of her life only half alive, cursed the day she had seen her.

No-one knew Nellie's age . . . some of the old women said she was 'getting on' when they were young. She was known to possess various powers; she was a wart-charmer and she could also mix a concoction that would remove hair from the faces of women suffering 'the change' – that the new growth was stronger only called for a stronger potion; she was also known to possess powers which could overcome sterility; but these supposed powers she was chary of using. Apparently the most propitious time for using these powers was after she had fixed somebody; and when, some years ago, Maisie Searle, who had never shown the sign of one during the ten years of her marriage, found she was carrying, and that after going to see Nellie who had just fixed Mrs O'Leary of her ninth, Nellie's reputation was itself fixed, and both the priest and doctor were powerless against her.

Nellie never did anything straightforward . . . all her jobs were surrounded by mystery. Even when she told the cards, it would be behind drawn blinds and before a coke fire, winter or summer; and all her fixing jobs were attended, at least on the patient's part, by drinking bottles of evil-smelling liquids. Most of the women did not mind this, as after drinking the prescribed doses they had little or no recollection of what followed.

It was rarely a woman went to Nellie with a first child; although sometimes a bride, finding herself flung into the maelstrom of life and seeing herself fast becoming like the child-weary women about her, would become fear-stricken; and she would pay Nellie a visit on the quiet.

Of all her jobs it was really only the first 'uns that brought Nellie any satisfaction; and nearly always she was cheated out of these. If it wasn't a young outraged husband threatening to strangle her for attempting to deprive him of the visible evidence of his manhood, it would be the older women themselves threatening to split on her if she did it. They would remain blind and dumb should she help one of them; but with a first, almost to a woman they would be against her. But none of them knew about Bridget Paterson. Nellie herself hadn't thought about it until a week ago, when she had been telling Kathie McQueen her cards . . . and then with no intention of fixing it . . . that had been Kathie's idea. Never before had she been called upon to do a job like this, not when the bairn was just on being born; and she wasn't quite easy in her mind about it.

She made her way now up and down various back lanes on her way to Dunstable Street. She was thankful that it was snowing, for other than a few stray children playing there was no-one about . . . but even if she were seen, who would dream she was going to fix a nine-months one. She reached Bridget's back door, and like a thin black shadow on the white snow she sidled up the yard and tapped on the kitchen door.

The door was opened with the utmost caution, and Kathie peered at the black-shawled figure standing in the yard. She held a warning finger to her lips before pulling the old woman over the threshold into the scullery.

'Not a sound above a whisper out of ye, for God's sake, Nellie.'

Nellie let the shawl fall from her head, to disclose an almost bald scalp, and she stared at Kathie with small, bird-like eyes, while her toothless jaws champed together as if she were munching something tough.

'Have ye got everything?'

The old woman nodded.

'Oh my God, I hope ye know what ye're doin'.'

The small figure bridled, and her jaws stopped their munching. 'Ye want it done? And anyway, is she the first I've tackled?'

'No; I know.'

'Are ye sure she's for havin' it away? She's late in the day in thinkin' about it.'

'Of course I am . . . only she's too proud to say so. What do ye think she's been on the bottle these past months for? She's scared of the thing being black.'

'But I thought it wasn't due for two or three days yet?'

37

'So did I, but ye know what first ones are. I wouldn't have known she was even bad, but the boy Tony was here, and he came back and told me she had gone to bed. So I sent him straight to you.'

'Ye think it's near?'

'As near as makes no odds . . . have ye got the stuff?'

'Aye.'

'But how'm I gonna get her to take it, all in a hurry an' all, like this?'

'I've bought a bit of horse-flesh.'

'Horse-flesh! What in the name of God for?'

'To burn . . . there's nothing smells like burnt horse-flesh. Fry it in the frying pan till it burns and waff it up the stairs, then run up with the drink to her. She'll be so parched she'll gulp down anything. And by the way' – she knocked a drop off the end of her nose with the back of her hand – 'it's a drink we'll be needing ourselves, to get through . . . have you got owt?'

'I've got a wee drop of rum. But will the stuff knock her off?'

'Enough for me to do what I've got to do.'

'Ye won't use the crochet hook on her, Nellie? Ye won't hurt her?'

'I've told you before, there'll be no need . . . it isn't an abortion you want.'

'And ye won't do owt to it, Nellie, if it's white, will ye?'

'No; but haven't I told ye? I saw it in your cards as plain as the nose on your face . . . it's black it'll be, like night.'

'Aye.' Kathie rolled her head on her mountainous chins. 'Aye, ye did tell me, and I've never known a minute's rest since. And it won't look as if it had been . . . ?'

'Not a sign . . . it'll be stillborn.'

'But if she knows it's you up there—'. Kathie wrung the corner of her apron. 'She hasn't been near me since she saw us together a week past.'

'She'll not know a thing once she takes the stuff; and if she does, she'll think it's a doctor fiddling about with her . . . Now come on and get me the pan.'

As Kathie watched Nellie bring a thick collop of horse-flesh from under her shawl she shuddered. 'God protect us! Where d'ye get it?'

'Never ye mind . . . it'll cost ye a shilling . . . And, Kathie' – the beady eyes closed still farther – 'it's a pound, mind, when the job's done!'

'If it's dead.'

'It'll be dead all right.'

'But mind, not if it's white, mind, Nellie . . . don't touch it if the colour's all right.'

As Nellie was about to place the pan on the fire she turned to Kathie, saying, 'Look, before I start: ye're sure she hasn't sent for the doctor, or the nurse or somebody? I've me name to think of, and it's late in the day.'

'How could she? I was round here within five minutes of the boy telling me. And she hardly knows what it's all about, anyway . . . it's her first, isn't it? No, she couldn't have sent for anybody; and she's never been one for making neighbours, thank God for that! She's kept herself to herself for months now.'

The horse-steak sizzled on the hot pan, and Nellie stood silently watching it. For a moment the terrible cold menace of the shrivelled old woman was borne home to Kathie, and she had the urge to fling her out of the door; but the dread of being a grannie to a black bairn was too strong. So she, too, stood silent and waiting, until the stench began to fill the kitchen, forcing her to go to the back door. As her hand went to the latch Nellie's fingers, like cold steel, gripped her arm, and without a word she was drawn back into the kitchen again, choking and spluttering. And Kathie's fear of Nellie increased when she saw that the choking fumes were having little or no effect upon the old woman.

'Here, take the pan up on the landing and waft it about while I get the stuff ready.'

Kathie, her eyes streaming and her apron held across her mouth, took the pan and groped blindly for the stair door. Never before in her life had she smelt anything like this, and she had smelt some smells. God, why had she got herself into this? She crept up the stairs, the pan held at arm's length, but before she reached the top Bridget's voice came to her.

'What's that smell, Ma? What are you doing? Oh, what's that smell?'

'A bit of steak . . . it dropped in the fire.' She coughed and spluttered. 'It'll be all right in a minute, I'm gonna open the window.'

Not being able to stand any more herself, she went hurriedly down the stairs again, and as she burst into the kitchen she let out a squeal like a trapped rabbit, for standing in front of Nellie, like some threatening giant, was Dr Davidson. The pan tipped in her hand and the charred steak fell on to the mat.

'So it's you, is it?' The doctor's eyes struck fire at Kathie. 'Giving her a hand, are you? . . . My God! Now listen to what I am saying.' His finger stabbed her in the chest. 'If anything goes wrong with that child up there, I'll see you both behind bars.'

For a moment Kathie was unable to utter a word, and her head rolled as if it would drop off her shoulders; then, sick with fright, she began to bluster. 'Behind bars, is it? And what, may I ask, am I goin' behind bars for . . . for burning a bit of meat?'

'Burning a bit of meat . . . !' The doctor turned his attention to Nellie again. She had not uttered a syllable, but her eyes, stretched to their small wideness, had never left his face.

'You . . . you fiend of hell! I've wanted to catch you red-handed for years. And now I've got you . . . with your' – he coughed – 'damned incantations.'

Still Nellie said no word; but her eyes slid to the table; his followed, and he said, 'I'll relieve you of that.'

His hand reached out to the unstoppered bottle, but, as quick as lightning strikes, Nellie was there before him. She grabbed up the medicine bottle; and whether by accident or design, Kathie, stooping in front of him to retrieve the steak, blocked his way; and Nellie, minus her shawl, escaped through the front room.

The doctor bestowed a look on Kathie that should have shrivelled her, but with relief filling her she faced him boldly. 'What's got into ye, Doctor, may I ask ye? What's got into ye?'

Doctor Davidson took a deep breath and almost choked. 'As long as something hasn't got into your daughter you'll be safe, Mrs McQueen . . . this time! But I'll see to it that your friend has killed her last child around these parts.'

He was forced to stop and cough into his handkerchief, and Kathie, regaining her confidence and belligerence, broke in, 'What do you know about it all? . . . You with your belly well fed. Nellie Milligan has saved many a poor soul from destruction around these doors. You and the priest between you are the ruination . . . the priests keep on tellin' yer, ye must do yer duty as a wife, and ye do it, from sixteen to sixty; and yer belly's full of bairns every year. And who's to feed and clothe them, and pay the doctor? . . . Aye, pay the doctor, eh? Nellie Milligan has been a godsend, I tell ye, to many a poor soul. Ye like bringing bairns into the world, because, given half the chance, ye cut them up so as ye can see their insides and try to find out where ye went wrong with the last one ye knocked off . . . Oh, I know all yer tricks.'

Dr Davidson stood surveying Kathie for a moment after she had finished. Then, between short coughs, he said, 'Well, if you've had your say, Mrs McQueen, I'll go upstairs; but for your information I'll tell you that your daughter wants this baby, black or white. Perhaps you didn't know that?'

He left Kathie, her mouth half open and her hands on her hips, staring after him.

So the girl had suspected her mother was up to something, and rightly, too, Dr Davidson thought as he mounted the stairs. Sending that strange, urgent little note to him, which told him nothing in the actual lines, but volumes between.

As he entered the bedroom, Bridget, in her nightdress, rose from the side of the bed, one arm hugging her waist. She showed evident relief at the sight of him, and said, 'I've got the pains, Doctor.'

'And what do you expect to have, eh?' He laughed as he placed his bag on the wash-stand.

'What's that dreadful smell, Doctor?'

'Oh, that . . . Your mother's been doing some fancy cooking and tipped a steak into the fire.'

'A steak? . . . But why should she?'

'Come; get into bed.'

As she slowly got back into bed he picked up a bottle from the wash-stand and looked at it curiously. It was a bottle of disinfectant, and next to it were two neatly folded hand towels, while on a chair nearby stood a number of sheets and clothes; and before the fire in the small grate was a towel-rail with baby clothes arranged upon it. She certainly had everything ready. And disinfectant, too. He was surprised and pleased. The nearest they ever got to antiseptic in the fifteen streets was carbolic soap; and even the old hands rarely had everything ready and neat like this. Marrying that Negro had seemingly done her little harm. But hadn't he heard something about her taking to drink? Must have been idle rumour, for the house didn't look that of a drunk.

'You've got everything ready, I see,' he said, smiling down on her. 'And a very nice little place you've got here, too . . . haven't seen better.' He knew she was pleased, and he continued to talk to her as he examined her. 'You've sent for Nurse Snell?'

'No, Doctor.'

'Oh, but you should have done. And, you know, you should have come and seen me before . . . Who's going to look after you?'

'My mother.' Her tone did not reveal her fears, but she made no protest when he said, 'I think we'd better have the nurse, just for the first few days, eh?' He patted her shoulder, saying, 'It won't be long . . . it nearly got here before me. How long have you had the pains?'

'Since early this morning.'

'Oh, you're going to be lucky, it's coming quick . . . When is your husband due back?'

'Tonight or tomorrow.'

'Good . . . good. Here, pull on that . . .' He tied a piece of sheeting to the bed-rail and left her gripping it while he went downstairs again, where, without any preamble, he said to Kathie, 'You know where Nurse Snell lives? Go and tell her I would like her to come along here at once. If she isn't in, leave word to that effect. And don't give the wrong message.'

'Nurse Snell, is it?' cried Kathie. 'Look ye here, Doctor, if I want a nurse I'll get Dorrie Clark. In any case, I can do as good as either of them; and I don't charge seven and six or fifteen bob! I can see to me own daughter.'

'Yes, you very nearly did see to her! Now get yourself away this minute; if you're not gone on that errand before I reach the top of the stairs, I'll inform your daughter what the smell is she's so anxious about, and what her mother and Mrs Milligan were up to . . . Now what do you say?'

'Blast ye for an interfering swine! That's what I say.' Kathie snatched her shawl off the door. 'Don't think you'll frighten me . . . you! . . . nor a battalion like you. You and Father O'Malley would make a fine pair.'

God forbid, thought Dr Davidson, as the door banged behind Kathie.

When he again entered the bedroom it was to find Bridget crying. 'Oh, come now. Come now,' he laughed, 'you'll forget all about the pains once the little nipper's here.'

Bridget shook her head. She could not tell him it wasn't the pain that was making her cry, but the dread of its result. For days now the child had lain comparatively quiet within her, and she had soothed herself by thinking that if it was black it would be full of vigour and life, and be making itself felt. Then despair would seize her, and she would imagine the baby's stillness was because it was black and content and good-tempered like James. But whatever she imagined its quiet movements to mean, she did not imagine the baby to be dying. Not for a moment did she want the movements to stop altogether and signify her release . . . no, she wanted this child, as something that James might have for his own. But oh, Jesus, Jesus, she didn't want it to be black!

Soon the pains, gathering on themselves, formed a mountain that she must climb, and in the climbing there was no place for worry about colour. She was aware, as time went on, that the nurse was with the doctor, and when the child left her body all anxiety and worry flowed out with it. It was over. Whatever colour it was could not be altered; she should have realised that from the very beginning. She had been silly to worry.

When she heard the doctor chuckling, a deep rounded chuckle, she thought, he's laughing because it's quaint; all black babies are quaint.

The baby was twenty-four hours old when James got in. He came in like a wind, a hot driving wind. Kathie cast startled eyes on him when he flung open the kitchen door, then turned her back to him; but Cavan rose from his seat by the fire and there was understanding and sympathy in his look. James, his eyes holding a depth of emotion and anxiety, uttered one deep-belled word, 'Well?'

'It's what you was wantin'.'

Before Cavan finished speaking, James pulled open the stair-door. He took the stairs in three leaps, but pulled up for an instant on the landing. It might be what he wanted, but was it what Rose wanted?

Bridget's eyes were closed when he neared the bed; he did not know whether she was asleep or not. Although his attention was riveted on the blanket-wrapped bundle lying on the far side of her, he stopped before going round the bed, and stooping, gently laid his face against hers. Because she made no movement whatever, he knew she was awake, but he said nothing, and going round to the other side he reverently picked up the bundle.

Through half-closed, sleepy lids, two brown eyes looked up at him, so like his own that a leaping, choking happiness that was almost an agony tore through him; but it was nothing to the ecstasy when the wonder was borne in on him that his child was white, with skin the colour of thick cream, and hair that was straight; it was as black as his own, but it was straight. The lids widened and the child gazed at him in fixed concentration, as if, he thought, she knew him. And when her hand wavered from the folds of the blanket and plucked at his finger his joy mounted, passing out of him and flying in thanksgiving to the God he was aware of, and to others dimly sensed. He raised his eyes to the ceiling and struggled to find words adequate to this feeling, but only one word came to his mind. He had first heard it outside the bars around the Liverpool docks, when, rain or shine, abused and laughed at, the Salvation Army had beaten its drums and tinkled its triangles in praise of God. He threw back his head and his voice resounded through the house, startling all but the child as he cried, 'Alleluia! Alleluia! Alleluia!'

PART TWO

CHAPTER FIVE

A MUCH-RESPECTED MAN

The fog-horn, blasting from a tug, seemed to carry its force through the grey drifts of mist right into the forecastle without losing any of its strength. James, pulling the cord of his white sailor-bag tight, unconsciously screwed up his face in protest. There were few things he hated about the sea, but he hated the sound of the fog-horn; its melancholy note seemed to search out an answering chord within himself.

'You're not losing much time, Jimmy?' An old fireman, lying in his bunk, rolled on to his side and stared at the great black head level with his own.

'Not much time to lose.'

'Lucky for you we came to the Tyne to load this trip.'

'Yes, lucky for me.' James thumped his kit-bag on the floor to give him a better hold of the top, pulled his cap firmly down on his head, turned up the collar of his blue reefer jacket, then, thrusting the bag up the companionway, climbed on to the deck with the voice of the old man shouting after him, 'Don't forget me, Jimmy, when your wife's givin' out that new bread, mind.'

The deck was abustle, the hatches were off, and the men, working by the light of naked gas jets run by piping from the jetty to the holds, were grabbing at the tubs from the swinging cranes and tipping the coal into the hatches as if the devil was after them.

The voice of the chief engineer spoke from out of the mist, 'Just off, Jimmy?'

'Yes, Chief.'

'Dirty night.'

'Yes, 'tis, Chief.' Jimmy turned towards the wavering outline of the engineer. 'If old man changes his mind, you let me know, Chief?'

'I will, Jimmy; but you know as well as me that it's no good. I told you what he said; and we are off as soon as she's loaded; he's been at the gaffer to stir those dock tykes up.'

'She out of breath with running, she catch her barnacles on the bottom one of these days. Good night, Chief.'

'Good night, Jimmy. Make good use of your time, and remember me to the nipper.'

Jimmy's smile wasn't evident to the engineer, but he could feel it in the voice as it came to him. 'I will. Sure I will, Chief. She always talks of the engineer-man; she never forgotten you bought her that doll, Chief . . . and that near two years ago. Yes, I tell her 'bout you.'

The massive bulk of Jimmy was lost in the fog before he reached the gangway, but the chief continued to gaze in the direction he had taken. He felt uneasy in his mind about the man; he had done so for a long time now. At one time, Jimmy used to talk to him, especially about his white wife. At first, this association with a white woman had sickened him, but then he had asked himself why should it; Jimmy was a better man than some of the whites on the ship. Of course he was an exception, for most niggers made him sorry the old overseer's whip was out of fashion; but Jimmy was a good type, and there was no need to feel sorry for his wife. In any case, Jimmy was likely a damn sight too good for the type of woman who would marry a black man; any pity that was to be thrown about should go to him. Something had been wrong this long while, and it had to do with the wife, for he rarely spoke of her now; all his talk was about his child, his Rose Angela . . . highfalutin name, that. She was an unusually bonny child. A pity, though, there was evidence of the tar-brush in her. The Chief stood for a moment longer looking in the direction James had taken; then, shaking his head, he turned towards his cabin to take comfort in his bottle. What could you expect, anyway? The sins of the fathers left their mark . . . or was it the mother in this case? . . .

As James passed the dock-policeman's little stone office by the side of the main gates the policeman on duty peered at him. 'Oh, hullo there, Jimmy. Why couldn't you bring better weather with you? In for long?'

'All the weather they would give me, boss,' James laughed. 'No, it tip, fill and run trip . . . same as ever.'

'Good night, Jimmy.'

'Good night, boss.' He squeezed sideways through the small door in the gate and sprang across the road to the Jarrow tram and threw his bag on to the platform just as the tram moved off. He pushed the bag under the stairs and stood on the platform until the conductor said, 'Inside; there's a seat there.'

James took the seat – the corner one next to the door.

He gave a greeting to an old woman sitting opposite, who smiled at him, saying, 'You got back again then, Jimmy?' And he was about to answer her when the evident recoil of a young woman at his side froze his reply. He became still inside as he realised she was withdrawing her skirt from contact with him by tucking it under her hip. Slowly he turned and looked at her, but her eyes were staring straight ahead.

The old woman again spoke, her voice, loud and strident, filling the tram. 'Ye've just missed the Victory teas, Jimmy . . . they've had 'em in nearly all the fifteen streets. Eeh! they've had some do's

. . . tables the length of the street, and the stuff to eat you wouldn't believe. And sports for the bairns; an' dancin'.' She rattled on, but James was not listening to her; he was conscious only of the inch of brown wooden lathe that separated his clothes from the girl's. It was many years since an incident like this had happened to him. He liked to think that the war had wiped all this feeling away, in England anyway, and he wanted to turn to the girl and say, 'I'm a steady, sober man, miss. I've worked to be respected, and I am respected. The people hereabouts know me and like me . . . you should have heard how dock pollis spoke to me, same as white man. And on my ship they call me Lucky Jim. I have a wife and a child, and money in bank. I do nothing bad . . . I keep my dignity . . . I'm much respected man.'

But he said nothing to the girl, he just sat staring, like her, ahead, reassuring himself that he was a . . . much-respected man, and a very lucky man. Any man who had a daughter like his Rose Angela was a lucky man, wasn't he? And Rose, wasn't he lucky to have Rose? He refused to answer himself this question, but instead asked, 'How she be this time, I wonder? Will she be in temper or crying fit to burst?'

The thought of his wife overshadowed for the time the hurt he was feeling, and as the tram jogged along he sat brooding, as always now when his thoughts touched on Bridget. What was wrong with his Rose? What had come over her? It started right back before the child was born. His home-comings then found her irritable, but he excused that because the child was heavy on her. But after it was born she became worse; and once, looking at her unusually puffed face, he said seriously, 'Rose, you drinking!' Her fury had silenced further accusation, and for a time he believed his guess was wrong, until his reason told him he had seen the results of drink on too many women not to know that she was drinking, and drinking heavily. But what he could not make out was why she never took it when he was home. The longest he had been home during the past four years was a fortnight, and he remembered it as a period of stress. He also remembered her passionate crying when he was leaving, her begging him not to go – to get a shore job. But he needed the sea, and, what was more, the war was on, and the sea needed him. But now the war was over, and, big as the wrench would be, he was going to look for a shore job. He had tried to tell the chief during this trip, yet somehow he had been unable to bring himself to it; but next trip would be his last, he had made up his mind. This docking for only twenty-four hours had decided him; he'd thought they'd be in for at least a week, as the old tub needed her bottom scraping.

At the corner of the fifteen streets he rose from his seat, and he looked once more at the girl. And this time she returned his look, and the hostility in her eyes hurt him. She would have a

49

separate tram-car for coloured people, he thought, as they did in some countries. And he wondered, as he had often done before, why one adverse look could outweigh, even totally obliterate for a time, the acceptance of the majority.

The old woman, lumbering off the tram, called, 'You'll be glad of something inside you a night like this, comin' off the water an' all . . . Bridget'll have the old broth pan goin', I bet.'

'She don't know me coming; but all the same she have broth pan going. Good night.'

'Good night, Jimmy.'

He strode along the main road towards his own street, his mind heavy with the feeling of uncertainty now that he was nearing home. How would she look at him? If only that soft light of old would be in her eyes. She was sorry she had married him . . . he knew that . . . and yet she wanted him . . . he knew that too. Life could be heaven, and life could be hell; but it had been mostly hell lately. He shifted his bag from one shoulder to the other, stiffening his back in the process.

He was nearing his door when the thick silence of the street was split by laughter, loud, high laughter that checked his step. It was Rose's laugh, but he had only once before heard her laugh in such a way – that night in the back room of the bar in Liverpool. He did not knock on the door, but stood listening, and he knew she was drunk again and that she wasn't alone. He became still; no anger filled him, only a questioning, and he began to reason with himself quietly, Now you find out . . . now you know what it all about . . . take things quietly . . . go round back: she not drinking alone. This thing happen before to other men . . . why you think it not happen to you? Into the stillness within him bored a pain, twisting the muscles of his chest. Not Rose . . . she not bad. He wiped the moisture from his face with his hand. You go find out. You don't be fool. You soft you know in some way . . . you been clarts where Rose concerned, she got you on a string, she know it. No . . . you no knock – it was as if something stayed his hand – you go clear this thing up. Gone on long enough it has. You don't know what matter with her half the time. You not coward 'bout other things, don't be coward 'bout this.

When he left the door, Rose's laugh followed him; it seemed to add weight to his legs, slowing his steps as he went round the bottom corner and up the back lane. Gently he tried the latch of the back door and found it locked, so, placing his hands on the top of the wall, he drew himself up and over, and, softly withdrawing the bolt, lifted his bag into the yard; then he re-bolted the door again.

Now, inside the yard and only a few feet from Rose and whoever was with her, the reasoning stillness was deserting him, and his muscles were knotting themselves. For a moment he hated Rose for being the cause of this undignified creeping up his own back yard.

When he reached the kitchen window her voice came to him, thick and fuddled, 'We'll have a tune – Sister Susie – eh?'

James bent down and put his head level with the bottom of the blind. He could see nothing, but the slow wail of a man's voice came to him:

'Pad-dy wrote a letter
To his Irish Molly-oh,
Saying if you don't receive
Please write and let me know.'

Into the wailing broke a voice which brought James upright; it was saying, 'That's Tipperary, you fool! It's on the other side. Wind the damn thing up, and empty that glass.'

Before the last word died away James had thrust open the door and was in the kitchen. Bridget, her mouth open and moving in a vain effort to voice her surprise, was leaning back against the dresser, and the glass half full of whisky she held in her hand was spilling in a steady trickle to the floor. Matt, who had been in the act of pouring some beer from a tin can, placed the can on the table with an abruptness that caused the froth to shoot up in a spray and cover his waistcoat.

In one sweeping glance James took in every detail of the kitchen: the untidy hearth with the ashes filling the pan, the dirty dishes on the table, Rose Angela's clothes lying in a heap by the side of the fireplace, and the order of drinking. There was one beer glass and one whisky glass, and Matt had the beer glass. A hot fury swept through James, opening his pores and bringing the sweat in large greasy beads on to his face! Here was the answer to all his bewilderment . . . Matt! Matt, who had always hated him for marrying his sister. Here was the explanation for the mirthless sneer in Matt's eyes.

Matt and he met seldom, but when they did the sneer was there, not only in his eyes but in the curl of his lip. Never had James encountered Matt in the house before, all their previous meetings having taken place in the McQueens' kitchen; but here was a man, James saw, who was very much at home, so much so that he himself was the intruder.

Matt, kicking his chair to one side, backed towards the little dresser, and his eyes, black with hate, never left James's face. James, throwing up his head, sniffed loudly in an unconscious primitive gesture, then, tearing off his coat, he cried, 'You not try get away; we settle this in yard. You pay for this, you dirty louse!'

'Jimmy, no! . . . look, I'll tell you.' Bridget thrust out a wavering arm to him, but it was knocked to one side as Matt's hand flung back to grab at a knife lying on the dresser top.

'Who's trying to get away?' As Matt brought the knife forward Bridget screamed, and James, with a lightning stroke, swung up the flat iron that was standing on the pan hob and whirled it across the narrow space, just missing Matt's hand but striking the blade of the knife and sending it spinning into the air. Bridget screamed again; and she clasped her hands over her face as the knife scattered dishes to the floor. With a shove of his hand James thrust the table aside, and Matt and he were facing each other.

Matt's mouth was square, and his venom was ground from beneath his clenched teeth. 'You black swab! Why couldn't you stick to your own breed? You took her when she was drunk; well, you can have her now. She's so whisky-mad that you nor nobody else can stop her. So come on!'

James's fist almost covered Matt's face as it struck him, sending him crashing back against the dresser. His strength could have finished off any ordinary man with a single blow, but Matt was no ordinary man. He was possessed of a hate for the black man that gave him the tearing power of a lion. With a shake of his head he recovered from the blow and bore right into James, bringing both his fists and feet into play.

The gramophone and the little table on which it stood were whipped into the hearth, sending the pan off the hob in their flight. The soup spluttered into the fire and a shower of ash and steam filled the kitchen, and Bridget's screaming mingled with the hissing. She wrenched open the kitchen door and yelled, 'Help! . . . My God! Help, somebody . . . help!' She turned, still screaming, and saw Matt and James locked together as if in a passionate embrace: then she saw James free himself with a heave from Matt's entwined arms, and with one hand thrust him away and with the other deliver a blow under the chin that lifted him from the floor and sent him crashing on to the fender.

Bridget's world became very still; in the kitchen, in the yard, and all beyond there was no movement; the only sound was James's heavy breathing. She stared from the doorway in petrified horror at the still, limp figure of Matt, with the long gash in his cheek and the blood gushing from his temple. She lifted her eyes to James. His face seemed no longer black, but grey, and he was standing motionless, staring down at Matt. She moved slowly towards him and stood by his side. 'My God! What've you done? . . . Oh, Holy Mary!'

He said nothing; and she stooped and touched Matt's wrist, and, with her hand still holding her brother's, turned her face up to her husband and whispered a terrified whisper.

She dropped Matt's hand; and as she stood looking at James with a startled look as if she had never seen him before, the stair-door opened and a voice whimpered, 'Ma.' She did not look at her child, but spoke her thoughts as they came to her. 'They'll hang him . . . it was my fault, but they'll hang him . . . Oh my God, what have I done?'

James did not move or answer her, but he screwed his head slowly round and looked at his daughter. She was crying and biting her knuckles, and, as a tiny smile for him broke through her tears, a fear never before experienced swept over him . . . If Matt was dead, then he, too, would soon be dead, and never again would he see his Rose Angela, nor she him.

As a curl of fog came into the kitchen, seeming to bear on its grey tendrils the enquiring cries from the back lane, James shook himself, first his head and then his shoulders . . . they'd hang him for sure . . . no black man could hope to get off after killing a white; he'd seen the result of that more than once. It would be no use telling them he hadn't meant to kill Matt, that he didn't kill him, it was the corner of the steel fender that had done it . . . it would be no use talking at all; there was one justice for the white and one for the black. He was no fool, he told himself; all his steady living would be forgotten in the face of the crime he would have to answer for. But he didn't want to die. He lifted his head, listening now to the yelling from the back lane:

'Are you all right, Bridget? What's up? Open the door there. Come on there, open up!'

If they once got hold of him there'd be no escape, he'd die all right. But he wasn't going to die, he'd get away. If he could reach the ship he'd be all right – yes, that was the way out. He must get to the ship and see the chief. He wouldn't be the first the chief had got across the water. The chief held his own ideas on justice. The thumping on the back door told him that the time he had to accomplish this was very limited. He grabbed up his coat from the floor, but stopped in the act of thrusting his arms into it; if he went now there would be no return, he would never see his Rose Angela again. He looked from her to Rose, and at this moment there was in him no feeling but bitterness for his wife. She had brought him to this, to running away, to hiding for the rest of his life, and to separating him from his daughter. Even if he lived he might never see his child again. Suddenly he knew that this would be unbearable. He could suffer anything but to be separated for ever from his child. Where he went, the child must go, for she was all his; Rose did not need her as he did. Intuitively he knew that Rose resented the knowledge that their child held more of him than her, despite its looks to the contrary.

Bridget, shocked into soberness, watched her husband stoop towards Rose Angela. She knew that his intention was to escape, and she thought he was about to embrace the child. Even when he swung her up and into the shelter of his coat she did not for one moment imagine he would attempt to take her with him. Only when, clutching Rose Angela to him, he ran through the front room did it dawn on her, and then she screamed louder than she had done before, 'No, James! . . . Jimmy! Jimmy! No! Don't . . . leave her be.'

When she reached the front door there was no sign of James and she stood on the road with the fog swirling round her, crying like a child herself. 'Jimmy, come back . . . bring her back . . . bring her back.'

Once clear of the streets and running along the main road, James's mind began to work, planning out a way to evade the pursuers he knew would soon be following him. In between his planning he soothed the child, saying, 'You no cry, you with your da; you all right.' He would make straight for the ship, for they wouldn't expect him to be mad enough to go back to her. But he couldn't get to her through the dock gates, so he would have to enter the docks by way of the river. This would be no easy task in the fog, but if there was a sculler lying at the slipway, he'd chance it. If there wasn't, he'd climb the sawmill wall and thread his way to the jetty where his ship lay. Of the two ways, he preferred taking the sculler and running the risk of being rammed, for if he went by the wall he might be spotted by someone inside the docks.

Rose Angela was crying again, her cries jerking out of her with his running, and as he spoke to her a voice shouted through the fog, 'Why, Jimmy, is that you? Is that you, Jimmy? What's up?'

Although he recognised the voice, he did not stop, not even when he heard the uneven hop of Tony's run following him. But coming to the slipway, he paused and listened. There was no sound other than his own harsh breathing and the quiet whimpering of the child, so he judged that Tony had gone back to the fifteen streets; and as he ran down the narrow path leading to the water he felt a regret that he had not given Tony some last word, for he knew that the lad's liking for him was sincere.

There was no sculler tied to the wall at either side of the narrow slipway. He splashed frantically through the rim of the tide, feeling for one, but his hand encountered only the iron ring in the wall, and he cursed. There was nothing for it now but to climb the sawmill wall. Running up the path to the road again, he went more carefully, keeping to the grass verge to deaden his steps. Rose Angela was quiet now, as if asleep, and as he left the lane and came into the main road again the pale blur of the gas lamp showed him the slight figure of Tony. He knew it was him before he heard the voice asking again, 'Is that you, Jimmy?'

'Yes, it's me!'

'What on earth's up?'

Between deep gulps of air James answered, 'I row with Matt. He dead. I got to get away, Tony.'

'Matt dead? My God!'

'I no mean to do it, Tony.'

'But, Jimmy, why've you got the bairn with you?'

'I take her with me . . . she mine.'

'You can't do that, man.'

'Yes, she go with me . . . she all mine.'

'But, Jimmy, what about Bridget?'

'Sh!'

They both stood silent, listening. The sound of pounding feet and shouting came through the fog, and James started to run again, with Tony hopping unevenly by his side.

'I get over sawmill wall to my ship.'

'You're mad, man, you'll never be able to get over that wall with the bairn. They'll be on you before you can do it.'

'You hand her to me . . . yes, you do that.'

'Listen, man, can't you hear them?'

James could hear them, and the voices were almost paralysing his legs. His body was wet with sweat, yet he was cold with the fear that penetrated to the core of him. He had seen black men collared before by angry whites.

'Jimmy, for God's sake don't get caught! If you keep running, they'll get you – if not here, at the docks. Look, I can't keep up . . . Jimmy, look, it's your last chance.' Tony grabbed at his arm. 'Drop down here beside the slack bank and let them get by, then you can make your way to the sawmill wall keeping under cover of the bank.'

Whether it was Tony's reasoning or his own fear that made him follow the boy's advice James didn't know, but he dropped down the bank and lay on his side, pressed close to the wet seaweed-tangled grass, with Tony lying alongside him and the child lying as still as death between them. James pressed Rose Angela's face close to his own, but she made no sound, seeming to know that his life depended on her silence.

The men were passing them now, calling to each other as they ran:

'The dock pollis will nab him.'

'The trams and roads'll be watched.'

'They'll get him. The bairn will be the finish of him, anyway, the black swine!'

The black swine . . . James stared into the chilling darkness. It didn't take long for a black man to jump from a damn good sort to a black swine . . . you were given no benefit of the doubt if you were a black man.

'You see? You can't go on the road, Jimmy. There'll likely be more coming as it gets round the streets. You'll have to keep under cover of the bank and get into the sawmill yard from the gut side; and you'll have to plodge into the mud and water for a way.'

James made no answer. He knew that Tony was right, and that that was the only means of escape now. But he could only get that way on his own; it would be impossible to take the child. He pressed her closer to him, and Tony, guessing his thoughts, whispered urgently, 'Jimmy, man, you can't take her. And anyway, you could never keep her on the ship, can't you see? Get away while the going's good. Go on, man, for God's sake don't let them catch you! Matt's not worth swinging for . . . he's bad, right through. I've been wanting to tell you for some time what he was doin', but I couldn't.'

After a space, during which only the lapping of the water could be heard, James's strangled whisper came through the grass to Tony. 'No comin' back, Tony – if I go without her, she forget me.'

'No she won't, Jimmy . . . I won't let her. I promise you, man. I'll tell her what a fine fellow you are. I promise on my oath, Jimmy. And when she's older perhaps there'll be some way of her comin' to you . . . I won't let her forget you, Jimmy, I won't, only for God's sake get away.'

As fresh footsteps passed above them Tony felt the quivering of James's body. He put his arms about the child and drew her from James's clinging hands. 'She'll be all right, Jimmy, as God's my honour. I'll see to her.'

'I come back, Tony . . . some time I come back.'

'All right, Jimmy, only go on now . . . hurry, man.'

As James's hand moved over his child's head Tony knew he was crying, and as he felt the Negro's hand pressing for a moment on his cap he turned his face into the grass to stifle his own emotion.

It was Rose Angela's whimpering, 'Da! I want me da,' that brought Tony up the bank and on to the road.

Not wishing to encounter anyone from the fifteen streets, he walked on the pathless side of the road, and in this way he brought Rose Angela home without being stopped.

There was a crowd around Bridget's door, silent, weird, misshapen bulks, all so intent on watching the stretcher being carried from the house to the vehicle standing in the road that they took no notice of Tony and the child. The sight of the workhouse ambulance puzzled him . . . why were they taking Matt away? Would they bring the ambulance just to take him to his mother's to be laid out? He felt not the slightest touch of sorrow for Matt being dead. In fact, as he made his way to the back door, he knew a great surge of relief that Matt would no longer be Bridget's evil genie.

When he entered the yard Kathie's shouting came to him. 'He'll swing, what's left of him when Sam Luck and the lads get hold of him; they'll leave the print of their hobnails on his face, God speed them, the murderin' swine!'

Tony pushed the open door wide and entered the kitchen. It was crowded with the McQueens, and Eva was crying noisily. Only

Bridget was seated, and Tony noticed that the last vestige of the girl was gone. Drunk or sober, he would never see the girl Bridget again. She was a woman with the stamp of sorrow on her. She became blotted from his gaze as the family surged round him. 'In the name of God where'd ye find her? Have they got the swine?'

'Have they got him?'

In Mr McQueen's moderate tone Tony seemed to detect an odd anxiety, and as he pushed his way through them all to Bridget he answered, 'No, he was well on the road to Newcastle the last I saw of him.'

'Have you told the pollis?' screamed Kathie.

'No.'

'Then somebody off and tell them. The Newcastle road, go and tell them!' Kathie threw her order from one to the other, but no-one obeyed her . . . they were looking at Tony as he faced Bridget, who was standing now, leaning heavily on the table with one hand. The child was still clinging to him, and he said to Bridget, 'I promised Jimmy I'd look after her.'

'You what? Christ! Listen to him!' cried Kathie.

'Shut up yer mouth!' said Cavan.

Tony stared steadily at Bridget. He, too, in the past hour, seemed to have left his youth behind and become a man, so much so that he voiced his first and only criticism of Bridget. 'You can't blame Jimmy for this . . . you asked for it.'

Bridget's head drooped, and for a space there was an uncomfortable, startled quiet in the kitchen. But it was soon shattered by a squeal from Kathie. 'Blame him be damned! If my Matt dies it'll be a rope's end for him. As it is, when they get him he'll get ten years for what he's done. Blame him, the . . . !'

'What?' Tony swung round on her. 'He isn't dead, then?'

It was Mr McQueen who answered. 'It's touch and go; he may not last the night. We've got to go down in an hour or so. Terry's gone in the van. It was Mr Steel on his motor bike that got them here so quick. He brought the pollis back an' all.' Cavan stopped and looked about him with a helpless air. 'I'd better go and tell them we've got the bairn.'

Matt wasn't dead, then, and there was the chance he would go on living. Although Tony knew that Matt's survival had lifted the dread of hanging from Jimmy, at least for the present, a sense of disappointment enveloped him, and he experienced a feeling of shock that was not unmixed with horror when he realised that Mr McQueen felt the same with regard to his son.

As Bridget took the child from his arms he wondered why, loving her as he did, he did not mind her being married to a black man, yet had always hated the fact that she spent a moment alone with her brother. If Matt didn't die and Jimmy couldn't come back, what would happen? There would only be him to stand between Bridget and Matt. And he would stand. He was eighteen and he was no longer a boy. Matt laughed at him because he was skinny and had a limp; they all either laughed at him or were sorry for him; well, he would show them. He struck Kathie speechless for a moment by saying, 'You want to get yourselves all away home and let Bridget and the bairn get some rest.'

Eva let out a laugh, then checked it abruptly and stood for a time looking somewhat shamefaced, until Cavan said, 'He's right; come on. Some of us must go down to the hospital, anyway.' Then she said, more to herself then anyone else, 'Well I never did. What next!'

Kathie took up Eva's words. 'What next! Aye, God Almighty, I wonder what next!' She stood behind Tony and her wavering forearm told of her desire to 'land him one'. But Cavan said authoritatively, 'Come on, the lot of you . . . I'll see you later, lass.'

He went out, followed by Eva and her docile husband, but Kathie stood for a moment longer glaring at the uneven line of Tony's shoulder. Cavan's voice calling, 'D'ye hear, you?' broke the concentration of her gaze, and she swung up her coat from the chair and flung it about her, saying, 'Some people are getting too big for their boots and they'd better watch out.' Her voice broke as she remembered her trouble, and she went on, 'As if I hadn't enough to put up with, me lad bein' battered to death an' all, without ye trying to be cock o' the midden.' She went out, shouting warningly, 'I'll see ye later, me lad!'

As the door banged Bridget sat down again, holding the child tightly to her. She looked vacant, as if her mind was emptied of thought, and when Tony said gently, 'Put her to bed Bridget, and go yourself, and I'll bring you up a cup of tea and clear up here,' she looked up at him, saying, 'If they catch him before the pollis they'll beat him up.'

He took her elbow and raised her to her feet. 'Don't you worry, they won't catch him.'

As he led her to the stairs, she said, 'I can't go to bed, Tony, I'll get her to sleep and come down. And Tony' – the tears flooded her swollen eyes again – 'will you stay with me until I know?'

'As long as you want me, Bridget.'

He watched her going up the stairs, lifting one foot slowly after the other as if they were weighted, and he knew a queer feeling of possession. So surprising was it that it caused him to flush, and he turned sharply and started to clear the kitchen.

The McQueens had made no effort to straighten the upturned articles of furniture; even the broken crockery had been kicked under the dresser to make room for their feet. The fireplace was still a shambles, and for a moment Tony looked around helplessly, not knowing where to start. Then abruptly he took off his coat and hung it behind the door. The act of doing this made him pause, and his hand rested for a moment on the nail . . . his coat hanging behind Bridget's door! It held a significance.

In his wideawake dreams of the night he imagined wild, wild things, such as something happening to make Bridget lean on him. Lean on him! That was laughable and fantastic. He knew this in the daytime, but in the night it was feasible. He had even pictured himself doing just what he had done this minute . . . hang his coat up . . . for when a man hung his coat up in a house . . .

What was he thinking, when there was poor Jimmy running for his life! If they caught him he'd be gaoled; if they didn't catch him he would come back some day, as he said. So wasn't Bridget still married? Slowly he dropped on to his knees and started to clear the fireplace.

CHAPTER SIX

ROSE ANGELA

All the children in the class knew that Miss Flynn didn't like Rose Angela Paterson; and when Miss Flynn got at Rosie, all their attention would be riveted on Rosie's face. They would screw round from their various positions to watch her, and they would wonder if her eyes could possibly become any larger, and how long she could stare at Miss Flynn without blinking. A day seldom passed without their being entertained in some way; but today Miss Flynn had been at Rosie twice . . . this morning because she hadn't danced the way they all did, and this afternoon because one of her long jet-black plaits had come undone.

As Rosie stared at her teacher she knew that she must remain silent, for it was no use trying to answer the question of how she lost her ribbon; if she said, 'Ribbons won't stay on my hair,' Miss Flynn would say she was insolent. She had long since learned that silence was the best defence, although she knew she would be punished for this too.

'Come out here!' Miss Flynn's voice was as thin as her body; the combination of her prominent boned face and thinly-covered scalp had justifiably earned her the name of 'Scrag-end' among the children.

Even the motion of Rose Angela's walk was enough to arouse a deep feeling of resentment in Miss Flynn. As she watched the child thread her way among the desks towards her she wanted to dash at her and shake that quiet, maddening poise out of her. She did not question herself as to her reason for hating this child; consciously she told herself that the child was the outcome of a sinful union; she was a half-caste, and looked it, with that thick olive skin and those great eyes. She didn't need to have thick lips and a pug nose for anyone to see that her father was a black man. That's what came of sinning. All men were sinful. She was glad, oh God, she was glad, that never once in her life had she done anything wrong or impure; she had never been out with a man and she never wanted to. She stared down on Rosie and wet her lips, one over the other, as she arched the cane back and forward between her two hands . . . she'd knock some of the sin out of her.

'Hold your hand out!'

Rose Angela held out her hand, trying not to think that when the cane lashed her palm her heart would leap. She kept her eyes on the piece of cabbage fixed firmly between Miss Flynn's front teeth, but when the cane descended for the third time she closed her eyes tightly.

'Now perhaps you'll keep your hair plaited. No-one wants to see the length of your hair. If I had my way I'd cut the lot off and relieve you of your vanity.'

If a pair of scissors had been at hand at that moment, Miss Flynn would not have been accountable for her actions. Of all the things she disliked about the child she disliked her hair most of all. She also resented the fact that this half-caste, with a runaway bully of a Negro for a father and a mother who was a daily servant, should be cleaner and better dressed than the other children. But of course there was that other man – that cripple. He was, she understood, the mother's fancy piece. That's where the money came from to dress the child like this . . . oh, the sins of some people!

'Get yourself to confession tonight and ask God to forgive you for your pride, for the proud can never enter into the Kingdom of Heaven,' she threw at Rose Angela's unsteadily retreating figure; and she added, 'Your road to Heaven, in any case, is going to be long and thorny . . . if you ever get there.'

After this outburst Miss Flynn felt curiously better, and for the rest of the afternoon peace reigned; but the children's minds, as porous as sponges, absorbed the feeling Miss Flynn had given out, and when school was over four of the girls who were usually Rose Angela's travelling companions to and from the fifteen streets dashed away and left her.

Walking alone out of the school yard, the sadness that this wholesale desertion always created settled on her. Although she knew that tomorrow they would be pally with her again, she could never understand why Florrie Tyler, her best friend, should leave her and go with the others, when they hadn't quarrelled in any way. This had happened before. She found she was either with them all or she was standing alone, facing something that she could feel but as yet could not fathom.

Turning the corner of the school wall, she came face to face with her schoolmates. They had formed a blockade across the pavement, faces strained to keep from laughing, eyes wide and hands joined.

Janie Wilson, who lived next door to the McQueens, was the spokesman. 'We ain't goin' to let you play with us any more, are we?'

The other three shook their heads vigorously.

'An' we don't want a loan of your schoolbag. An' you can keep your Saturday penny and stick it, can't she?'

Again there was vigorous nodding of heads. Then in silence they waited for some response.

The quietness with which it came left them at a loss, and aggravated them more than any shouting would have done. 'All right, it doesn't matter.'

Rose Angela watched them as they formed a ring and whispered together; then, with one accord, they broke from each other and ran some way along the road before turning and shouting, 'Rosie Paterson, you'll never go to Heaven. Even if you get up there they won't let you in, 'cause you ain't white.'

The startled expression on Rosie's face amply repaid them for her previous lack of response, and Janie Wilson's voice came above the others. 'Miss Flynn's got it in for yer . . . you ain't white and you can go to confession, but you'll not get to Heaven. I asked me ma, and she said yer da was a blackie, and you'd never get into our Heaven. You'll go down' – she pointed her thumb violently towards the pavement – 'and be pitched into the fire.'

For a long time now it had seemed to Rose Angela that she had been gathering to herself different kinds of fear. There was the fear of going home and finding her ma crying, sometimes with her head on her arms on the kitchen table, sometimes lying across the bed upstairs. At these times the fear would paralyse her limbs and she would want to be sick. The fear would disappear if, as sometimes happened, her mother put her arms blindly about her and there was no smell of whisky from her.

Then there was the fear that Uncle Tony might die . . . that he would fall under a tram, or that on a dark night he would slip into the water of the slacks, for if anything happened to Uncle Tony who would she have to talk to? or, what was more important, listen to? What would happen if a Sunday should pass and he didn't take her for a walk and sit or stand at the same spot on the slack bank, and tell her what a grand man her da was and that she must never be ashamed of him, for one day he was coming back? She knew why they stood at the same spot, for when she stood there a voice, deep and thick and melodious, echoed through her mind, murmuring words that were only intelligible by the feeling of warmth they created in her.

Then there was that other fear, the fear that caused her to wake up, trembling and sweating, in the night, and cry for her mother, but being aware as she cried that her mother could lift this fear from her did she so wish, that hers was the power to say to Uncle Matt, 'Don't come into this house any more!' In her Uncle Matt Rose Angela saw her idea of the devil; the jet-black eyes in the white face, with one end of the long scar on his cheek pulling down the corner of his eye while the other end pulled up one side of his mouth, were terrifying to her. When her Uncle Matt stood looking at her without blinking she wanted to scream. She had done so once, and her mother turned on Matt, saying, 'Get out!' But he didn't go, he just stood with his head bent, muttering, 'That's it . . . you turn on me too. The lasses go in their back doors when they see me comin'. And who's to blame, eh? I didn't start this.' Matt's voice sounded to Rose Angela as if he were crying, but his eyes remained dry and hard. Her mother had sat down and beaten her fists slowly on the corner of the table . . . that had been terrifying too.

So because of her Uncle Matt Rose Angela had a great desire to qualify for Heaven, for in the other place there'd be a man like him. And now here was Janie Wilson saying that she wouldn't go to Heaven.

She stood still, watching the girls hitching and skipping into the distance, and, try as she might, she could not stop her tears. As they rained down her cheeks she reassured herself: she would get to Heaven – she'd be good and she would go to Heaven. She wouldn't miss Mass and she'd go to Communion every week. Jesus, Mary and Joseph, say she would get to Heaven . . . Her tears threatened to choke her. Why was everyone so nasty? Miss Flynn and the girls and Uncle Matt, and even Granma. What had she done? . . . She made her way with bowed head along the road. She'd go into church, it'd be quiet there and she would get over her crying. She couldn't go home like this.

In the empty church she knelt out of habit in her class pew, and endeavoured to pray. But as her thoughts, dwelling on Janie Wilson, would form no set prayer, she made a mental note that she must confess the sin of 'wilful distractions at prayers' when she next went to confession. She knelt until her knees ached and her head swam; but her tears had stopped, so she rose, genuflected towards the main altar where Christ stayed, and left the church.

She was standing in the porch blowing her nose when the door opened behind her, and Father Bailey came through. Startled, she looked at him, wondering where he had sprung from, for the church was empty. She dropped her head as he said, 'Hallo there, Rosie.'

'Hullo, Father.'

'Have you been paying a visit to the Blessed Sacrament?'

'Yes, Father.' She began to breathe more evenly; he hadn't heard her crying or he'd surely be saying something.

'That's a good girl. Always keep a devotion for the Blessed Sacrament and you won't go far wrong in life.' He placed his hand on her hair and felt its silkiness. 'By, it's beautiful hair that you have, Rosie; it has the sheen of the starling on it.'

Forgetting her tears, she gazed up into his round, red face and her heart swelled. It wasn't wrong to have nice hair then. Here was the priest saying it was nice . . . she wasn't sinful, then, as Miss

Flynn made out, because she kept her hair nice. But what was the good of having nice hair if you were destined for Hell? Suddenly Rose Angela knew that she couldn't bear the indecision – to go on all tonight and all the morrow, and perhaps for ever, knowing she mightn't be going to Heaven was unbearable. But here, standing right before her, was Father Bailey, and if anyone could tell if she were going to Heaven he could . . . he could even send her there if he liked, for he knew so much about it.

'Father, could I ask you something?'

The pleading in her eyes that always affected the priest brought him a step nearer to her, and he whispered jocularly, 'Anything you like, Rosie. But mind, I'll charge you tuppence for it.'

A smile appeared for a moment on her face, but was gone again as she asked tentatively, 'Father, will they let me into the white Heaven?'

'The white what?'

'The white Heaven, Father.'

'Are you getting mixed up? You don't mean Heaven, surely. Are you meaning the public on the Cornwallis Road, The White Heather? Now what would you be wanting to get in there for, might I ask?'

'I do mean Heaven, Father . . . God's Heaven.'

The priest straightened his stubby figure and tugged at the bottom of his waistcoat with both hands. 'Now what makes you ask such a question? Of course you'll go to Heaven, providing you're a good girl.'

'But they said . . .'

'Who said?' he asked sternly.

She hung her head again. 'The girls said, Father . . . because me da was black I won't get into the . . . proper Heaven.'

The priest remained silent, staring at the bowed head of this eight-year-old child who was already feeling the weight of 'man's inhumanity to man'. The tears in the church were the forerunner of many she would shed. God help her. Although he smiled at her there was an unsteadiness in his voice as he said, 'Look at me, Rosie, for I have something to tell you. You're a very ignorant child, you know.' He shook his head with a hopeless gesture. 'Has no-one ever told you that God is colour-blind?'

'Colour-blind . . . ? No, Father.' Her eyes were stretched to their widest.

'Haven't they now? Are you quite sure?'

'Yes, Father . . . is he?'

'He is so . . . as blind as a bat where colour is concerned . . . of course, mind, he can make out the flowers, but not people; he doesn't know a black from a white, nor a yellow from a red . . . God help him.' Father Bailey threw back his head and laughed; and

64

with a mixture of appreciation of his wit and profound relief Rosie joined him.

'Ah! Rosie' – Father Bailey wiped his eyes – 'the good Lord appreciates a joke, even against himself. Now away home you go. Good night and God Bless you.'

'Good night, Father.' Rose Angela paused in her turning from him. 'And I'll get in, Father?'

He patted her head gently. 'You'll get in, Rosie. You of all people, I should say, will get in. And remember what I've told you about God being colour-blind, for it's the truth – one of the great truths.'

'I will, Father – I'll always remember.'

'That's it. Now let me see you smile – you don't smile enough. Ah, that's better. Now off you go.' With a push he helped her on her way, and she ran the whole distance home, her feet just skimming the pavement, so light was her body with relief.

Arriving at the corner of the fifteen streets, she again met Janie Wilson, accompanied by a new crony this time. Janie had acquired a large slice of bread, and she almost choked herself in gulping a mouthful when Rose Angela, with a hitherto unheard of assurance, said, 'You were wrong, Janie Wilson, I will get in, Father Bailey said so . . . so there!' And with a lift of her head she was about to walk on when a violent push landed her against the wall.

'Who're you settin' your old buck up to?' Janie's face was purple with indignation and the dry bread wedged in her gullet. 'Take that, you cheeky bitch. And that!'

Rose Angela took the smacks on the face, and instead of the blows, as usual, frightening her, they aroused a strange exhilarating feeling in her, the feeling of wanting to strike back. She knew she could never hope to stand up to Janie, so she used her schoolbag. With a swing of the long strap she brought the bag in contact with the side of Janie's head. The manoeuvre was very effective, for Janie screamed and kept on screaming. Rose Angela did not stop to enquire why she screamed, but ran off, thinking, I'm glad I hit her . . . I'm glad . . . I'm glad.

It was a strange feeling; never could she remember standing up to anyone before. She had always been aware that the other children made use of her, and imposed on her; somehow she knew that because her colour was not exactly like theirs she qualified for all the dirty work of their play. She always allowed them to make her the finder in 'Deady-one', and when broken bottles and jars and other glassware had to be smashed still further to provide the imaginary contents of sweetshops it was she who had to sit before a stone, with another in her hand, breaking the glass, often with bleeding fingers. They liked her when they could use her; and she hadn't minded being used, for it made them happy, and she wanted people to be happy and laughing. But now she was going to stick up for herself: she was as good as them. The priest had said so hadn't he? Well . . . he said she would get into the same heaven as them, and that was the same thing, wasn't it? But her mind refused to dwell on this point; it didn't matter, anyway. If anyone hit her again she would hit them back, and if Miss Flynn got at her she would say . . . What she would say to Miss Flynn she never told herself, for as she reached her back-yard door she heard her grandmother's voice, shouting as usual. It slowed her running to a walk, and she entered the house unsmiling and serious.

Her mother and Uncle Tony and her grandmother all turned and looked towards her. Rose Angela's eyes came to rest on Tony. Why, she had forgotten it was Wednesday and his half day – fancy forgetting that!

'Go on, stare at him!' her grandmother rapped out at her. 'Go on, worship him. If ever there was a mean sod in this world it's your Uncle Tony. But go on, stare at him and put him to shame.'

Rose Angela looked swiftly from one to the other. Her mother was ironing at the table and didn't raise her head; her Uncle Tony was staring at her grandmother, and, as always when he was angry, his nose was twitching.

Kathie was sitting entirely obliterating a wooden armchair, and each movement of her body was creating still more bulges of flesh. Her eyes, nestling in two full pouches, fastened themselves on her grandchild, and she went on, 'What would ye say if I told ye yer Uncle Tony had come into a house and a fortune?'

'It's no fortune, I'm telling you, it's forty pounds.'

Kathie, dismissing Tony's protests with a wave of her hand, went on addressing herself to Rose Angela. 'What's forty pounds but a fortune in these times? And a house, mind, a grand house with six rooms. And an estate around it.'

'Oh my God!' Tony held his head. 'A bit of a garden . . . look here . . .'

'An estate, I said, with trees and flowers and vegetables – taties and cabbages an' everything an' all.' She thrust her finger into Rose Angela's chest. 'He could sell the house, and get God knows how much for it . . . but will he? Be God, no! And will he let us go there to live in it? Eh?' Her eyes rolled sideways to Tony, and he, using her full title as he had done from a child, cried, 'Look, Mrs McQueen! I'm going to have no more of it . . . I've told you . . . and don't keep on.'

'There we are, five grown-ups stuck in two bug-ridden boxes, and never a sight of a big tree for miles, as ye well know yerself, child. And him that I brought up and treated as me own refusing to give us house-room. I could understand him not jumping at Terry's scheme to start a grocery business, but to refuse us house-room, packed as we are . . . !'

'Well, I'll soon alter that!' cut in Tony. 'I can make one less any day.'

'That's it, threaten to walk out on us.' She turned her attention from Rose Angela. 'The fix I'm in, with only Matt workin', and him on half time, and not knowing where the next bite's coming from. That's gratitude for you.'

Although Kathie still shouted, her eyes were wide, and showing in them was anxiety. Tony saw it, and blamed himself, but, oh God, if she'd only give over! She would try the patience of a saint. Why, oh why, he asked himself, had he not moved at the end of the war when they were all working, and she had money to squander but never to save. He was heart-sick of sharing the same room with Matt and Terry and of eating with them all, for now there was Eva and her growing brood to share the table.

When he received the letter three weeks ago asking him to go to Denver's, the solicitor in King Street, and there being told that his mother's only sister, she who refused to have him as a boy, had died, leaving him the money and the house, his first thoughts were, I don't want anything of hers, the upstart; she would have let me go into the workhouse! On reflection, however, he saw that this could be an answer to his unspoken prayers. Hadn't he longed for enough money to buy a special boot? Time and again he had saved the few pounds that would be necessary, only to hand them to Kathie 'just as a loan' to pay the rent, or the coals, or the tally man, or, more recently, to buy food. When asking for fresh loans, Kathie's conscience never seemed to trouble her about the dozens of unpaid ones, and Tony had come to think that all his life he would have to pay for her past kindness to him. But with regard to the unexpected legacy he was standing firm. When he had bought his boot, and perhaps a suit of clothes, and rigged Rosie out, then he'd see to Mrs McQueen, but he'd be damned if he was going to let her get her hands on the whole of the money. He knew what it would mean – a grand bust-up to show off to the neighbours, clothes for them all . . . so that when the money was gone there'd be plenty to pawn!

Kathie was still talking, addressing her remarks once again to Rose Angela . . . How wonderful it would be not to hear her voice ever again . . . Well, the choice was his . . . he had a house now, all his own, packed with good furniture and linen, and a little garden, the like he had not even dreamed of. He could go there and live, there was nothing to stop him. Of course it would be a long way to travel to the shop, right from High Jarrow to yon side of Harton village, but he would soon get used to that.

He stared at Bridget's hands moving the iron back and forward, back and forward, into the gatherings of Rose Angela's dress . . . What was he thinking about? Why was he playing games with himself? He could no more leave the vicinity of Bridget than he could walk without limping. There was only one way he could live in that house, and that dream was as impossible as . . . He was recalled sharply to Kathie again.

'Yer Uncle Tony thinks the world of ye. Then why don't he let ye and yer ma rent his fine house; and then she can let us have this un.'

Bridget, putting her iron quietly down, looked at her mother. 'I've told you before, Ma, I'm not leaving this house.'

'No.' Kathie jumped up with surprising agility. 'Ye're as mean a swine as he is. Four rooms for ye and the bairn . . . ye could let us share this and we'd all have lived as happy as larks. But no. What ye keeping it for, may I ask? Hopin' for yer black man to come back? Well, God speed him to ye! And it's meself that'll escort him to clink, and make sure that he gets ten years for making my lad look like a beast . . . As for you' – Kathie turned her venom on Tony – 'standing there like a weakly bull gaping at a cow – whatever ye're keeping yer house for, remember . . . what God has joined together let no man put asunder . . . she's married till she knows the nigger's dead!' The door banged and she was gone.

After a moment of surprised silence Tony hopped for the door, crying, 'She's not getting off with that!'

But Bridget checked him, her voice quiet and even. 'It's no use, Tony, the less said the better.'

He turned to her, his face scarlet, and Bridget, picking a fresh iron from the heart of the fire, spoke to Rose Angela, 'Go upstairs and change your pinny and wash yourself up there . . . there's water in the jug in my room. And your tea'll be ready in a minute or so.'

Without a word Rose Angela went upstairs; and Bridget, testing the iron by holding it near her face, said, 'Don't worry, Tony; you know my mother doesn't mean half what she says . . . she never stops to think.'

He stood watching her across the table. He was as tall as her if he supported himself on the toe of his short leg, and now he wanted every centimetre of his height. He squared his shoulders to give him breadth. In the next few minutes she must see him as other men. He said slowly, 'She did mean it, she's not blind . . . I supposed nobody is blind enough not to notice how I feel about you, Bridget.'

There, it was out; and with the voicing of what seemed to him the feelings of a thousand lifetimes his courage grew. 'She was right. Your mother's no fool; she knows that the only one who'll get that house will be you and the bairn.'

'Tony!' Bridget stopped moving the iron. Her calmness was probed and her face now showed her concern. 'Don't be silly; you're no longer a boy!'

'I'm glad you've noticed that, anyway.'

She flicked her head impatiently. 'Well, act like a man and have some sense . . . Look, Tony; use that house, and use it now. It's a gift from God. Don't sell it.' She leant across the table towards him. 'Tony, there's Molly Cullen; she's a nice girl and she dotes on you. Now here's your chance. Be sensible, and get away from here. Molly's a cut above the rest; she'll live up to Harton, given the chance, and . . .'

He waved his hand at her. 'Bridget, save your breath, there'll be no Molly Cullen nor anybody else for me, and you know it.'

'And you know nothing can come of this' – her voice was harsh – 'so why do you keep on? If you think I'll go and live with you in your house . . .'

'Who asked you? There'll be plenty of time to refuse me when I ask you. I'm offering you the house, with no tags to it.'

As they stared at each other, the look in her eyes and the excited churning of his stomach told him that at least she regarded him as a man.

Bridget resumed her ironing again. 'Have you forgotten Jimmy?' she asked quietly.

'No.'

'And you still believe what you've told her for years?' She indicated the stairs with a nod.

There was a slight pause before he answered, 'I used to; but now I don't know . . . Bridget, look at me . . . If there wasn't Jimmy, would you have me?'

She remained silent, her eyes fixed on his.

'Answer me.'

'I don't know . . . I've never looked at it that way, because . . . Anyway, I'm so much older than you. Oh, it's all so mad. Don't let's start any of that talk. All I want is peace and quiet; I've had enough.' She turned abruptly away from him and the table.

'Listen here!' His voice compelled her to stop. 'You've got to look at it that way! Jimmy might come back the morrow, and he mightn't come back for years . . . or never; but one way or the other I've got to know how you feel. Do you want Jimmy to come back?'

The direct question startled her, and she stood gripping the rod and staring at the maker's name on the iron front of the fireplace: Greave & Gillespie, Jarrow-on-Tyne. Over the years the blackleaded words had formed a focus point for her thinking. Did she want James to come back? At times, yes. At times she longed for him, and had she known where he was she would have gone to him. But when these times passed she knew that the longing had been mainly of the body; most of the time her mind was filled with recrimination of herself for the trouble her folly had wrought. Father O'Malley foretold that retribution would fall on her for making such a marriage. It had fallen, and was still falling. Each day she paid. At first it was the stigma of the colour; but when James removed that with his flight he saddled her for life with Matt, with his twisted face and mind.

The first sight of Matt's face and the knowledge that his hold on her was greater than ever had made her resort again to the refuge of the bottle. But half a dozen glasses of whisky were not enough to shut out all her trials and to give her a brief feeling of gaiety; whereas before, two had done so. Rather, the effect of the whisky was to accentuate her troubles. But even though she knew its numbing effect was gone, she still retained the desire to drink. The habit was strong, and it needed an independent fight to conquer it. And only during the past few months had she known any real respite. She had never blamed Matt for making her drink, for it was her belief that no-one could make you do anything you didn't want to do. And because of this opinion, she had also pointed out to herself time and again that some part of her must have wanted James enough to have married him. The only question she had been unable to answer was: would she have done so if she hadn't been afraid of having a baby? . . . And likely as not in the workhouse, for she would never have come home.

And now Tony was asking did she want James back. If it would mean living quietly, as they had done during the first few months of their marriage, yes – even if it meant bearing the stigma of his colour again. But should he come back, her mother and Matt would see that his liberty was short; and knowing he was in jail would be worse than not knowing where he was . . . But she must not go on thinking of James, she must answer Tony. If she said she wanted James back, would Tony go away? She turned quickly and looked at him, as if to assure herself that he was still there, and in a revealing moment she knew that life without him would become unbearable. Up till now she had not known how much she relied on him, on his kindness and his patient devotion and steadfastness; and on the buffer he made of himself and placed between her and Matt. And in this moment, too, she realised that the feeling he bore her was no ordinary one; it had stood the iron test of witnessing her maudlin drunk. Her head drooped at the thought. Not once had he seen her drunk but many times, and yet here he was offering her his house, and all he was asking in return was to know she cared for him. If need of him meant caring, then she realised he was her life. For the first time she saw him, not as Tony, the boy, but as a man who loved her. She looked at his deep-set eyes, at his mop of light-brown hair, which seemed too weighty for the delicacy of his face, at the uneven slope of his shoulders that did not mar his bearing but lent to it an air of nonchalance, and she wished from the depths of her being that they had been of the same age. Then, in spite of Matt, she might never have left home; for at this moment she knew it would have been an easy thing to love Tony. But now it must not come about, it was too late. She had made her bed and she must lie on it alone; she must not drag him into the mire of her life. He must get away from the fifteen streets and all that they stood for. If he could not see Molly Cullen now as a mate, perhaps he would later, or find someone else; but under no circumstances must he remain invisibly tied to her. At least she would do this decent thing.

She watched the pain come into his eyes as she said harshly, 'Isn't it natural I should want him back? I married him, didn't I?'

She returned to the table and proceeded to force out the creases from her blouse with a partly cold iron, knowing that his eyes were on her.

'It's all right, Bridget, it makes no difference' – the quietness of his voice brought a smarting to her eyes – 'the offer still stands. If you don't take the house, it'll stay there. I'm not selling it – nor living in it.' He turned towards the door. 'Tell Rosie I'll be round for her after tea.'

She could not restrain her tears as she watched him limping down the yard. She was filled with relief, while at the same time despising herself. He wasn't going . . . he wouldn't go, no matter what she said. Oh, it was wrong, all wrong, but – oh God – she was thankful that he felt as he did. He was like an anchor to which she could tie herself to stop the drift towards drink and, she sometimes thought, towards madness.

Rose Angela came quietly into the kitchen. 'Has Uncle Tony gone?'

'He's coming back for you after tea . . . I won't be a minute, I'll just finish this. The kettle's boiling.'

Rose Angela stood looking at her mother. She saw that Bridget had been crying; but it hadn't been the kind of crying that was caused by the whisky bottle, so she was filled not with fear and revulsion but with a feeling of blinding love, which caused her to go to Bridget and shyly put her arms about her waist. As she hid her face under her mother's breast Bridget slowly placed the iron on the flat tin lid. The feeling from her child seeped into her, and, putting her arm about Rose Angela, she said gently, 'What is it, hinny?'

Rose Angela moved her face against her mother, and the action was so like that of James that Bridget took a deep breath to steady herself.

'It doesn't matter if we don't go and live in Uncle Tony's house . . . I love you . . . I love you, Ma.'

Bridget pressed the child to her. Her emotion, a mixture of remorse for having withheld her love from this child and the tenderness now flooding her, was almost unbearable. She was searching in her tear-flooded mind for appropriate words to express this tenderness when a commotion in the back yard caused her to push Rose Angela from her.

From between the curtains she could see Sarah Wilson striding up the yard, dragging her Janie with her. She knew that Sarah Wilson was no friend of hers, and now her raucous voice, louder than usual, was proclaiming that something was wrong. But what, and why was she coming here?

Bridget did not move towards the door but hastily dried her eyes and stood waiting until Sarah, peering into the kitchen between the gap in the curtains, called, 'You there, Mrs Paterson?'

Mrs Paterson! Something was wrong . . . only when you were in the black books did you receive your full title. Bridget opened the kitchen door, saying 'What is it? What's wrong?'

'What's wrong? Ah, ye might well ask. Here' – she pulled the straining Janie towards her – 'hev a look at this.' She tried to force Janie's hand, which was holding a bloodstained cloth, away from her face, but Janie cried, 'Aw, don't Ma . . . don't; it'll bleed again.'

'Take yer blasted hand away and let her see!'

'Don't shout like that, Mrs. Wilson!' Now Bridget was on her dignity. 'Come inside if it's got anything to do with me.'

'Don't shout!' cried Sarah, pushing Janie into the kitchen. 'Don't shout! Wouldn't you shout if yer bairn's eye was nearly put out?'

'But how . . . ?' began Bridget in perplexity.

'Aye, how? By that 'un there.' She pointed to Rose Angela, whose face was almost comical in its amazement.

'Rosie?'

'Aye – Ro-see.' There was definite mimicry in Sarah's tone. 'Let her see.' She tore her daughter's hand down, and Bridget saw an ugly cut about half an inch long to the side of Janie's cheek-bone.

She looked from Janie to Rose Angela. The child was staring in horror at Janie's face. 'Did you do that?'

Rose Angela shook her head slowly, and Janie cried, 'Yes you did. You did it with your schoolbag.'

'Aye, with her schoolbag,' added her mother. 'She can't fight with her hands, like other bairns.'

As Bridget stared in amazement at Rose Angela, whose meekness was sometimes a source of irritation to her, she was conscious of the back door opening, but she didn't turn round. The whole incident so bewildered her that she just stood staring at her daughter and listening to Sarah.

'She used the buckle side deliberately, didn't she?'

Janie nodded at her mother. 'And what's going to be done about it? That's what I want to know. Marked for life, my bairn'll be, all through that one's wickedness . . . through her not having proper control. Spoilt, that's what she is, decked up to the nines . . .'

'That's got nothing to do with you, Mrs Wilson.'

'Ain't it? Ain't it though? If she wasn't spoilt, this wouldn't have happened. Wild she is, and dangerous, like him that was her da was.'

'You never said a truer word.'

Bridget swung round to find Matt surveying them from the doorway.

'Aye, you've had some of it. Look at my bairn's face, Matt.' Janie's face was turned up for Matt's inspection, and from it Matt's eyes travelled to Rose Angela, and their expression needed no translation. The hate was plain for all to see, so much so that Sarah said, 'Aye, well, it's enough to make anyone turn on their own kith and kin what you've had, lad. But it should be knocked out of her before it gets any worse. That's all I say, Matt, it should be knocked out of her.'

Matt, with his eyes still riveted upon Rose Angela, muttered, 'Aye, it should be knocked out of her.'

'If there's any chastising to do, I'll do it.' The sharpness of Bridget's tone brought Matt's gaze away from the shrinking child.

'Aye, you will, like hell,' he said. 'Soft as clarts you are with her, because she puts on her mealy-mouth to you – butter wouldn't melt in it, but I know her; I've watched her outside. This doesn't surprise me' – he pointed to Janie's face – 'I've seen it coming.' His voice gathering deep in his throat, he went on, 'For two pins I'd take the buckle-end of me belt . . .' His hand moved as he spoke to his trousers.

'Just you try it and you'll see who'll get the belt,' cried Bridget, blocking Rose Angela from Matt's sight by standing in front of her. 'And now clear out, the lot of you. And Mrs Wilson, if you take Janie to the doctor right away he'll put a stitch in it, and I'll pay – it'll heal all right if it's done now.'

'Aye, it'll heal . . . like this.' Matt slapped his distorted cheek with his palm.

'Get out, I've told you!' Bridget's eyes blazed at her brother.

Mrs Wilson went out, pushing Janie before her, crying, 'You haven't heard the last of it, by a long chalk.'

Matt, pausing at the door, spoke with chilling quietness, 'The buck nigger will never be dead as long as she's alive, and I hope she lives long enough to pay for this.' He again slapped his face. 'And she will pay, and with her physog too. I'll fix her one of these days so she won't mark anyone else.'

He was gone, and the kitchen was filled with dark premonition. It chilled Bridget, turning her faint and weak. She looked at Rose Angela. The child was leaning against the wall, and her face, pallid with stark terror, seemed more beautiful than ever before. She was too beautiful, Bridget thought – such looks brought nothing but trouble. And it was her face that enraged Matt – it always had – and given half a chance he would destroy it. My God! If he did anything to spoil the bairn's face! As if his intention was imminent, she pulled Rose Angela to her, and held her tightly, saying, 'It's all right, don't be frightened – your Uncle Matt won't do anything. Why did you hit Janie Wilson?'

She could feel the tenseness sinking out of Rose Angela's slight body while she waited for an answer. And when it came, it was in whispered gasps. 'Janie slapped my face, 'cause I told her I'd get to Heaven. She said I wouldn't 'cause . . . 'cause my da's a nigger. And I asked Father Bailey and he said I would . . . 'cause God's colour-blind, he said.'

Bridget's arms became stiff, and her eyes, staring at James's fretwork pipe-rack on the wall, were fixed in their pity.

'I didn't mean to hurt her . . . I just swung my bag at her . . . Ma! . . . Oh, Ma!'

'Sh! Sh! don't cry, hinny.'

'Ma, will Uncle Matt—' She was stiffening again.

'No, no.'

'But he said . . .'

'Sh . . . I'll not let him. Don't worry, don't cry.' As Bridget's arms tightened around the sobbing child she knew that only constant vigilance would save her from Matt's hands.

She had always known that there was something odd about Matt. When she was a girl she had been able to ignore it for long spells during which he was 'just like any of them', but when unintentionally she aroused his anger by laughing or joking with one of the lads she would be brought into painful awareness of the oddity. Even when, her own rage aroused, she was fighting him, she would be wondering all the time why he should be like this. She knew no other brother who treated his sister as he did her – sisters generally came in for scorn and derision.

She had expected her marriage to alienate him from her; but it hadn't, and the result was his twisted face. Nor did this, contrary to what she had imagined, direct his bitterness towards her. Instead, he used the disfigurement to bind her to him, to draw on the affection he could get in no other way. That he hadn't vented his venom and bitterness on her wasn't, she knew, because he didn't feel bitter; she was only too well aware that every fibre of his being was corroded with bitterness. It was towards the child that it was directed, and it always would be. Bridget, looking ahead down the succession of coming years, realised that she would always have to watch Matt in order to protect the bairn, just as her da and Tony watched him to protect her.

PART THREE

CHAPTER SEVEN

THE WORKLESS

The cancer of unemployment was eating the country, and the Tyneside in particular. It was eating into initiative and hope, and doubling despair. A man, becoming unemployed, went on the dole; and he would sign on each day before vainly doing the round of the shipyards. And in the evening he would stand at the corner with his pals, who were in the same predicament as himself, and they would hide their feelings in jokes. If he lay in bed at night and wondered what was to become of him and the wife and bairns once the dole was finished, he gave little sign of it during the day.

It is said that man can get used to any condition if he is in it long enough, and it would seem there was truth in this, for, as the years went on and the dole bred the Means Test, most of the men on the Tyne had forgotten how it felt to carry a bait tin – in fact they doubted whether there had ever been a time in their lives when they had worked. The younger men didn't have to wonder about this; those born just prior to or during the 1914 war never knew what it was to be employed. Even those apprenticed to the few small firms still in existence were stood off immediately they reached the age of nineteen.

It was strange, too, how stark poverty changed the flavour of the jokes from sex to food.

'Well, I'm off for me dinner.'

'What's it the day, lad?'

'Chicken.'

'Chicken agin?'

'Aye . . . I'm so bloody full of chicken I've got the urge to gan an' sit on a clutch of eggs.'

And so it went on. Here and there a man suddenly ended the struggle, and the effect on his mates, oddly enough, was such as to stiffen their fibre. 'It's no use taking things like that,' would be their attitude; 'things can't get any worse; the bloody Government will have to do something if they don't want trouble. Hang on a bit longer.'

There were protests, mass meetings, marches, but no perceptible change. In many houses the furniture was sold bit by bit, until only the table and mattresses remained. The sight of the bairns standing

77

around the table to their meagre food hurt a man, but when the wife sat on the boards to feed the youngest, blazing anger would fill him; and so there would be more shouting at meetings, more protests. But even anger cannot be sustained on an empty stomach, and it would fade, except in the case of the few, in whom injustice burned as a fuel. These carried the fight in London – even to 10 Downing Street itself; but their sincere cries were lost in the noise of the rabble they gathered to themselves on the march.

The slump had long been with the McQueens – Cavan's last full week's work was in 1922, and his last work of all in 1926. Terence, too, had early joined the band of unemployed. Only Matt found work, odd days here and there. The McQueens seemed to think that Matt would always have work, however small . . . for life owed him this. But latterly, even Matt had failed to achieve even a day a week; and now Tony was the only one to go out at a regular hour.

Although most shops sported a sign 'No more credit given' and the windows showed more and more empty cartons, Mr Crawley's two shops still managed to keep their heads above water. Tony for some years now had been managing the second business, a small one-windowed shop in a side-street, and the fact that he was in the glorified position of manager and had never been out of work, added to which he was receiving the great sum of ten shillings per week rent for his house, surrounded him with an atmosphere of unwilling respect and thinly veiled resentment. If he had not been the asset that kept the wolf from the door, Kathie's spleen and Matt's venom, together with Terence's jealousy, would have been openly hurled at him. Only Cavan was grateful to him. It infuriated Kathie to know that for years now Tony had stayed in her house because, by doing so, he was helping Bridget . . . He'd had the nerve to tell her he'd cut down the extra five shillings he had been giving her each week if she sponged on Bridget. Sometimes Kathie thought she hated Tony worse than she had the nigger . . . for, give the devil his due, the nigger had been good for a few bob or so every trip, with no conditions attached.

And another infuriating thing was that her daughter Bridget, her that had been the apple of her eye, her who she had brought up like a lady, had withdrawn herself from them all during the years. Only Cavan seemed welcome in her house . . . and, of course, her fancy man. It was the desire of Kathie's heart to hurl this latter accusation at Bridget, but fear of the consequences kept her tongue in her cheek. If Tony should go, God knew how she would manage. As it was, with such a lodger, she appeared to be in comfortable circumstances compared with those of her neighbours, and to shine in any way helped to make life bearable. It was good to be able to say to Jane Cullen, next door, 'It's a stone of flour I'm after bakin', and two dozen fresh herrin's I've got in the oven this minute. Oh, it's a tea they'll have the night,' for it gave her a queer sense of satisfaction to see Jane unconsciously moving her tongue over her blue lips whenever food was mentioned. On baking days she would open her back door and window wide to allow the smell to waft into the Cullens' hungry house.

The Cullens were meek, and Kathie despised them. Most of all did she despise Mollie, who had grown hollow-eyed and grey-faced waiting for Tony to take up with her. At this moment Kathie was thinking of the Cullens as she banged her oven door on a shelf of baking potatoes . . . 'Gutless lot!' There were the scrap-ends of bacon Tony had brought home at dinner-time to be fried; she'd kick up such a stink of food that the smell would knock them all out.

Phew, it was hot! As she wiped the sweat from her neck with the oven rag Eva's youngest boy called through the open door, 'Grannie, Rosie's home. She's got her case an' all.'

'What?' Kathie swung round on the boy. 'When?'

'Just now.'

'My God, she's lost her job again.' Kathie turned abruptly to Cavan, who was sitting on the edge of the bed and peering over the top of a pair of wire rimmed spectacles at the boy.

He closed the book he was reading and asked quietly, 'Are you sure?'

'Aye, I am – she give me a ha'penny.'

Taking off the spectacles, Cavan placed them in an old black case, and put them in his waistcoat pocket.

As he slowly took his coat from the back of the door Kathie said, 'Three weeks she's been in that job . . . my God!' and as he went out of the door she called after him, 'Mind, if she gives you owt, you stump up.'

Cavan threw an angry glance back at her, but said nothing. He turned into the back lane, dusting the front of his greasy coat as he went. What was it this time? It couldn't be the same thing again . . . surely to God not. What was the lass going to do? If only she could get married or something. But there would be small chance round here – the fellows would be willing enough, God knew, but their mothers and sisters wouldn't be. It wasn't only the bit of colour in her that turned the women upon her, but something else – what, he didn't know – he couldn't lay a finger on it – it wouldn't go into words. Was it the proud way she walked that maddened them? or the quietness of her? or her voice, so like her father's, him that must be dead these many years? or was it her face? Aye, it was likely her face, for it did something to men, particularly married ones.

How many times had she been given a week's money in advance and sent packing? He had lost count. And it was bad that she should be out of work at this time, too, with Bridget off an' all. He doubted whether he'd come in for anything at all the night. She was always liberal with her bit pocket-money – rarely did she see him without slipping a sixpence into his hand. And he always made the same protest, 'No . . . no, lass, ye've got little enough'; but she would smile and say, 'Get yourself a bit baccy, Granda.' Aye, she was good; both her and Bridget – his pipe would have cracked many times during the past years had it not been for them. It was strange, he thought, that he felt no humiliation in taking from either of them, yet if Kathie threw him tuppence his stomach bridled.

Funny what life did to you; funny how people changed. Time and things that happened made you change. And many things had happened to him during the past ten years. But more so during the past two; for who would have thought the desire to work would go completely from him, that it would be sent packing by this other strange desire that filled him?

He walked slowly, taking the long way round to Dunstable Street . . . He was sixty-two, and it was only during these last two years of abject poverty that he had become aware of living. It happened in an odd way, so odd that he trembled when he thought that but for a fight about St Patrick's nationality, and being laughed into spending his last threepence on buying a hundred books that he didn't want, he would never have known this new world.

He remembered the night that Kathie bullied him into making a barrow out of a soap box and a couple of old bicycle wheels so that he should go to the tip and pick cinders. The barrow would hold twice as much as a sack, and he had been given the ultimatum of picking more cinders or going without food, for she couldn't buy both coal and food. His protest that the tip ripped the soles from his boots brought the retort from Kathie that he wrap old sacking about his feet and leave his boots at home. He had done this, but, like a great number of other men, not until it was dark.

Part of the tip burned continuously, and this saved many of the men from their death, for in the chill, often mist-ridden dawns they would huddle together as near the blazing parts as was safe. It was during one such dawn that the row began. A big Irishman was expounding, half in fun and whole in earnest, on the merits of being Irish, when a quiet voice from among a little group of men said, 'If it's such a grand country, why don't you go back there?'

'By me patron saint! Are ye meanin' to be insultin'?' the Irishman had demanded.

'Not necessarily,' went on the voice, 'but it's odd that you lot who are so bigoted about your country couldn't pick an Irishman for your saint.'

'What! In the name of God what is St Patrick but the most Irish of the Irish?'

'English . . . St Patrick was English.'

That did it. The men had all their work cut out to keep the Irishman from throwing the man into the blazing tip. When the row subsided, Cavan, taking up his barrow, urged the young fellow to leave and come along with him.

Half-way home Cavan burst out laughing. 'It was funny the way you got him on the raw, joking about St Patrick being English.'

'I wasn't joking – he is.'

'You're funning.'

'No, not a bit of it – he was English, all right.'

'How do you know?'

'Oh, I read it.'

'Well, you can't believe all you read. Was it in the paper?'

'No, of course not.'

They went on pushing their barrows; and Cavan looked through the drizzle of rain at this young fellow, tousle-haired, dirty and thin, as they all were, whose calm assurance was making even him have his doubts as to St Patrick's nationality. But he felt he must warn the lad of making it an open statement, particularly around these quarters.

'I shouldn't repeat it too often, lad.'

'Why not?'

'Oh well, you know.'

'Aye, I know . . . for the same reason that folk don't like to remember that Christ was a Jew. They like to think he was an Englishman, or God, which amounts to the same thing with some of the bloody church-going lot.'

Cavan was aghast. 'But why, man, he was God!'

'All right, if you think so. He may be to you, but he isn't to me; nor is he to two-thirds of the world. I think he was the greatest man who has yet lived, but I don't think he was God.'

Cavan stopped pushing his barrow.

'You serious, lad?'

'Yes, why shouldn't I be?'

The positive tone silenced further questioning. Cavan had never heard anyone talk like this.

It wasn't until Cavan was leaving him to continue his journey alone to Jarrow that the young fellow said, 'Do you read much?'

Cavan rubbed his sleeve across his face. 'Not in my line, lad. Although, mind' – he gave a superior nod – 'I've got some books – stacks of them – nigh on fifty. There was nearly a hundred, but the wife stuffed some up the wash-house flue.'

The young fellow put the handles of his barrow down on to the road. 'What kind of books?'

'Oh, all kinds; some in foreign tongues; but some of the English ones are as bad – I can't make head or tail of them. Some are about science and some are about the Middle Ages. Some've got one pound marked on 'em. Fools and their money, I say. They all belonged to an old wife who died, by the name of Peggy Flaherty. The bums sold up the house to meet the back rent, and I went along 'cause I'd now't better to do, an' when they put the books up, just for a lark I said threepence . . . and be hanged, I got them. Laugh – the place was razed. And there was me and all the bairns in the neighbourhood carrying the books home in a long procession, and Kathie raised Cain and made me dump them in the wash-house. Still they've come in handy.'

'Can I see them?'

'Why, aye, lad.'

And that had been the beginning. Ted Grant saw the books and convinced Cavan of their value, not in money but in knowledge. He was absurdly grateful for the dozen that Cavan gave him, and he persuaded Cavan to take the rest into the house, which he did, and stacked them under the bed; and so impressed was he by Ted's praise of them that he threatened to annihilate Kathie if she stuffed any more of them up the flue.

Ted was a married man, with three children all under six. He was also an embittered man, because, having won a scholarship to the High School, his parents were forced by circumstances to take him away at fifteen. He was further embittered through having been so weak as to marry while on the dole, for he became dependent on his wife. He was still dependent on her, for she went out to work, leaving him to see to the house and the children. His trek to the tip was made mostly from choice, for it helped him to keep his self-respect – he was doing work of a sort, and among men.

Cavan's conversion to reading seemed to happen overnight. From Ted Grant, who was young enough to be his son, he learned, sitting half the night listening to him, being guided by him, step by step, until now he could read his own books with understanding. And there was rarely a day passed but he did not quote his tutor's words to the joking yet admiring men at the corner, 'They can starve your bellies, but only you can starve your mind.' So although there was little or no prospect of work for Cavan in the next few years, after which he would be really too old to bother, there were times now when the thought of sudden prosperity, returning life to its normal routine of the war years, was actually frightening to him. He wanted nothing to interfere with the orderliness of his days and nights – his sitting on the tip, except in very severe weather, from ten at night till five or six in the morning, his sleeping for six hours, and the rest of the day being taken up with his reading and keeping his eye on Matt. The only part of his present life which he resented was this trailing of his son – this casual shadowing of Matt whenever he thought he was making his way to Bridget, and his sitting in Bridget's kitchen in his endeavour to outstay Matt – wasting precious hours of his reading time in shielding Bridget from . . . From what was he trying to shield Bridget? Cavan had never put it into words; but the feeling that he was preventing something happening never left him; and it was being strengthened as he watched his son's face becoming even more twisted, and his step losing its spring and beginning to slither, and his fingers plucking the front of his coat. This last habit was a recent addition to his queerness. Cavan noticed it first when Matt, Bridget and he were in the kitchen, and Rosie unexpectedly came in. Matt, his black, gimlet eyes fixed on the girl, who never looked at him if she could help it, began to pluck his coat like a woman plucking a hen.

Cavan began to dread the times when Rosie would be at home. It was one thing keeping his eye on Matt where Bridget was concerned, but he felt utterly inadequate to stand between Rosie, the girl, or the woman as she now was, and Matt. He had formed one point of the protective triangle in which she had stood as a child, the other points being Bridget and Tony; but as soon as she went into service the triangle became useless. And now here she was home again. He turned into Dunstable Street's back lane and into the house, and found Bridget alone in the kitchen.

'Well, lass?'

He took off his cap and hung it on the knob of the chair.

'She's back again.'

'Aye, I heard.'

'Somebody's been quick.' Bridget's tone was sharp.

'It was Johnnie.'

'It isn't her fault.'

'I never said it was, lass.'

Bridget doubled her fists and beat her knuckles together, betraying her worry. She stood gazing unseeingly out of the kitchen window, and as Cavan looked at her straight back he felt a stirring of pride that he, a little shrimp of a man, was father to such a fine, upstanding figure as Bridget. Here she was, on forty, with no grey hairs and a body as straight as a die. The only part of her showing the stamp of her trials was her face, which had a stiffness about it that at times he likened to enamel. He cleared his throat and spat into the fire.

'It's no use taking on, lass.'

'But this is the third place she's had in two months.' She swung round and faced him. 'Why in God's name can't they leave her alone?'

Cavan rasped his hand across his chin, and gazed down on his boots so covered with patches that there was no sign of the originals left.

'And she hasn't given her a reference.'

Cavan's head jerked up. 'That's bad . . . what'll she do?' Bridget turned to the window again, saying, 'God knows . . . where can she get without a reference?'

In the silence of the kitchen Cavan sat pulling his lower lip in and out between his finger and thumb; and when Bridget turned from the window and thumped the kettle on to the fire he said, 'Don't worry, lass, something'll turn up – she'll drop into a good place one of these days.'

'Where?' asked Bridget harshly. 'Oh, I could kill them all!' She ground the kettle into the cinders . . .

Upstairs, Rose Angela, too, asked herself where she could go now – no decent mistress would take her without a reference. She sat on the side of the bed and looked at the reflection of her face in the little mirror of the dressing-table, and not for the first time she told herself how she hated that face – it had brought her nothing but misery. The brown of the eyes, in the depth of which lay the pain and mystery of her father's race, were deepened still further by the sweep of the long, black lashes, which shadowed the skin until it reached the cheek-bones, changing its colour from a creamy tint to that of deep olive.

It was this face which laid her open to men like Mr Spalding – oh, Mr Spalding and his hands – she shuddered and closed her eyes – waking her up in the night, moving over her in the dark. She had wanted to scream, but she knew it would bring his wife, so she had pleaded, 'Leave me alone . . . please leave me alone.' But she did scream; even with his hand over her mouth she screamed. But apparently not even the scream convinced Mrs Spalding that her husband was at fault – Rose Angela had enticed him, and would have to leave. But such was Mrs Spalding's mentality that she said nothing the next morning, and allowed Rose Angela to continue with her usual routine of doing the washing; but when this was finished she handed her three days' wages and told her to go. Rose Angela did not even protest that she was entitled to a week's wages in lieu of notice; she packed her things and went, tired, and slightly dazed, and burning under the humiliation of yet once again losing her place and having to go home.

What was she to do? She saw her head shaking in the mirror. Should she try to get into some shop? But there were so many trying, and one stood little chance because of the married women, who pleaded a family to support. She could perhaps go into the working-man's café . . . No! She stood up and began to unpack her case, stacking her uniform neatly in the drawers of the dressing-table, her morning pink prints and big white aprons, her black afternoon dress and little frilled caps. No! She would first try to get a place somewhere.

She began to move about the room, straightening things out of habit. Always on her return from the big houses her home seemed smaller and the fifteen streets more grim. She paused in her moving and looked down into the street. The children as usual were filling the pavement, more so immediately below the window. When they were chased from other doors they invariably settled outside twenty-eight, for Bridget never shooed them off. Rose Angela watched them with the yearning that had never left her. How often had she stood as she was doing now and watched their play. The longing to join them was past, but the hurt of being ostracised by them still remained.

This being cast out was not due entirely to the tint of her skin, but because, since the day she marked Janie Wilson, she had become suspect . . . there were two people now in the fifteen streets scarred, and by a Paterson; and mothers warned their children, 'Keep clear of that Rosie Paterson, mind,' and the children, ever anxious to create bogies, fed their inherent cruelty on this ready-made one. The spark of courage Rose Angela had felt after hitting Janie Wilson had been crushed, and had never risen again. More and more she began to sit by the fire, sometimes thinking and wondering why her thoughts hurt her, sometimes listening to Bridget reading stories. But very seldom did she hear a story right through, for when her Uncle Matt came in Bridget would send her upstairs. There had been a period of stark fear, she remembered, after she hit Janie, when she was afraid even to go to school, and would walk with her head bowed and her arms ready to shield her face. Her fear, she knew, was not unwarranted, for her mother would often be at the school gate to meet her, and if this were impossible she would tell her to go along to her place and wait there. The years did little to lessen the fear.

Directly below her a group of children were taking turns at kicking the bottom of a broken bottle into chalked squares. They were doing this while standing on one foot and with their hands behind them. Rose Angela looked at the smallest among them, a child of five, Janie Wilson's child, and thought how like her mother she was. A boy was manipulating a piece of tin, through the centre of which were drawn two pieces of string. As he pulled the string the tin whirled, making a sawing noise, and he dashed among the girls, working it against their faces. There were screams and yells, and they scattered and ran, all except Janie's child, who stood fixed and screaming. Rosie was about to knock on the window when a big girl pounced on the boy, crying, in a very good imitation of her elders, 'Get out of it! Do you want her to be marked for life, like her mother?'

Rosie turned sharply from the window. Marked for life! The mark of the buckle had shrunk until now it wasn't a quarter of an inch in length. It had not spoiled Janie's looks, for she had none to spoil. Rosie had long suspected that this lay at the core of Janie sustaining the hate over the years. Oh, what did it all mean . . . She sat down on her bed again. What did living amount to? Fear and hate, fear and hate, that's what her living amounted to. It always had and it looked as if it always would. She could count on one hand those who had never caused her to be afraid – her mother and Uncle Tony, her grandfather, Father Bailey and Mrs Kent. If only Mrs Kent hadn't died – she would still have been with her, and happy. Mrs Kent had made her feel as if she was different; and not because she was a half-caste, either. She would come to the kitchen at nights and talk about her husband, who had been killed in the war. But more often she would talk about Rose Angela herself. Frequently during the two years they were together she had said, 'Don't you worry, my dear, you won't always be doing this. You'll see . . . you'll marry, and marry well, and I'll live to see it.' But she was dead, and Rose Angela often thought that if those two comparatively happy years could have gone on she would have been content to let Mrs Kent's prophecy of a happy marriage go forever unfulfilled.

Her mother's voice came to her from the foot of the stairs, 'Rosie, there's a cup of tea . . . your granda's here.'

'I'll be there in a minute, Ma.' She straightened the coils of her shining black hair and smoothed down her grey print dress; then she went downstairs.

'Hallo, Granda.'

'Hallo, lass – how are you?'

'Oh, all right, Granda.' She smiled at him, and took a cup of tea from her mother's hand, then sat down near him; and Cavan, returning her smile, thought, You can't blame the chaps, really. God in Heav'n, but she's bonny! While he was thinking this he felt that the description was not quite right, but how could anyone find words to fit the effect she had on a man? He could well see her driving a fellow crackers, and doing so unconsciously, because he knew she was unaware of her power. Her movements were so natural and unaffected, yet in them was the sensuousness that tore at a man's control . . . God help and protect her! Where would she end?

'How's your reading going, Granda?' There was a faint twinkle in her eye.

'Oh, fine, lass.'

'And the professor?'

'Oh, Ted's still goin' strong.'

'Has he unravelled any more mysteries?'

'My God, yes.' He hitched his chair nearer. 'Do you know something, Rosie?' He stopped and pinched his lip and nodded to himself before going on. 'I'd like to be letting on to Father O'Malley about this – aye, well, I might an' all some day – Well, do you know there's not a bit of truth in this Adam and Garden of Eden business – never has been.'

Rose lifted her eyebrows.

'Yes, it surprised me, but there's been books written about it . . . do you know it's the belief – and that of men of great learning – that we come from . . .'

'Monkeys!' put in Bridget, endeavouring to forget her anxieties by joining in her father's pet pastime.

'Not a bit of it. Life in the first place was nothing but slime. Now can you take that in? Slime. And another thing; do you know why a snake's the length it is, eh?'

'No, Granda.'

'Well, because it wanted to be that long.'

Both Bridget and Rose Angela remained silent during his impressive pauses, knowing that it gave him great pleasure to expound the knowledge gathered from his books and Ted Grant.

'And do you know why a bull has horns?'

'No. Granda.' Rose Angela shook her head.

'Because it thought them up.'

Here Bridget and Rose Angela laughed.

'Ah, you can laugh, but it's a fact. It's all in a book by a fellow called Lemarck . . . the bulls and cows and such had only their heads to fight with, and they wanted something hard there so much that it affected their glands and things, so horns started to grow out of the tops of their heads.'

'They weren't made by God, then?' The twinkle was evident in Rose Angela's eyes now. 'Where does he come in, then, Granda?'

'Ah, ye've asked me something there. Where does he, lass? It makes a fellow think. It made me think a bit, I can tell you, 'cause, as Ted says, he could've made the slime in the first place; but that does away with this business of making the world in seven days. But then again Ted says it was only them Romans who chopped time up into days. A day could've been the word that meant a million years, for all we know. And then, as Ted says again, who's to know how long he took over making it? That's if he did. He's never told anybody, for Ted says half them prophet fellows, if they were about the day, would be shut up as loonies. People believed them in bygone times 'cause they was always frightened of what they couldn't understand. Aye, and that's another point. Have you ever thought of how our lives are ruled by what other people say? They say God wants you to do this or that, but how does anybody know what God wants of them, other than what the good part of their hearts tells them, eh?'

'Don't you believe in God then, Granda?'

'I don't know, lass; I just don't know.' He stroked the bare part of his scalp with two fingers. Then, looking from one to the other, he laughed. 'Be damned, it's funny, but I just don't know.'

Bridget, getting up to refill the cups said, 'Then I wouldn't let on to Father O'Malley about it.'

And while they were all laughing together Rose Angela thought, This is nice, just the three of us here. If only there could be more times like this. She listened to her Granda with only half her mind – she was thinking how strange it was that he should have become so altered by the reading of a few books, and him an old man. Perhaps when she was old she would get to love books, too; but now she only wanted to look at things, and listen. If only she could go to far-away places, where there was colour – lots of colour – earth colours and water colours and sky colours. And if only she could sit and listen to music. Oh, if only she had a wireless, a wireless all her own, so she could listen to music – any kind of music, for any music was better than none.

'Do you believe in God, Rosie? Do you believe Jesus Christ was God?'

'Of course, Granda.'

'That's right, then, that's right. Stick to your belief. But I wonder, would you still believe if I was to lend you some of my books? Now there's one by that fellow called Darwin – a right stink that fellow kicked up at one time . . .'

Cavan's voice went on, getting more excited, and Bridget rose and cleared the cups away, and Rose Angela, her eyes intent on her grandfather, followed her own thinking. She would always believe in God – life would be unbearable without this belief. How often, when a child, had Father Bailey's words 'God is colour-blind' soothed and comforted her. And how often now did she turn to that saying for comfort. Should she lose her belief in God, then she would be lost indeed, for she had come to know that He alone in all the world was . . . colour-blind. Even her mother, whom she loved with a deep, unshakable love . . . she wasn't colour-blind. Rose Angela knew that when Bridget stared at her without seeing her she was seeing her husband. She looked at Bridget now, and not for the first time realised just how lonely her mother's life was. She had been alone for years. Even loving Uncle Tony hadn't filled her life.

Rose Angela could look back to the day when she first discovered that her mother loved Uncle Tony. It was a Sunday, and Uncle Tony came to take her for the usual walk. As they were leaving Bridget said, 'Don't tell her that any more.' And she had watched her mother and Uncle Tony stare at each other; and when they were outside Tony looked happy, and suddenly he laughed. But from that day he never again told her that her father would come back. Was her father dead? Sometimes she thought he was. At other times she was strongly convinced he wasn't. Now and again she experienced an odd feeling that he was speaking to her, in a sort of pleading way, as if he were asking her not to forget him. There was no fear of her ever forgetting him – he was too much a part of her, too deeply buried in her being, to ever throw him off, even if she desired to. And never once had that been the case. Even as a child, realising he was black, she did not want him to be other than he was; for it was the man himself she loved, not in the way she loved her mother, but in a protective way. The term seemed silly to apply to the great black man she could still remember with astonishing clearness . . . but would she know him now if she saw him?

She was recalled to what her grandfather was saying by him tapping her knee. 'And did you know there is a fly that flutters about in a horse's stomach and drives him mad? Did you know that?'

'No, Granda.'

'Well, there is. And can you explain this? When the horse sees that fly buzzing around him, trying to find a sore patch to lay his eggs on, he nearly goes mad and no-one can hold him. Off he dashes, hell for leather. Now how does the horse recognise that fly? And how does he know what it will do to him? 'Cause if he'd already had a dose of him, he'd be dead . . . Now can you explain that?'

'No, Granda.'

'No, nor nobody else . . . And here's another thing that'll surprise you . . .' What the other thing was Cavan didn't explain, for the kitchen door opened and Matt entered. And the harmony of the kitchen was immediately shattered. Cavan spat into the grate and said, 'I'm sorry, lass, I've marked yer hob.'

'That's all right.' Bridget took up a paper, and, folding it, began to swat flies vigorously.

Rose Angela, after one startled look at Matt as the door opened, remained still. It was difficult to sit still with Matt's eyes on her, but lately she had told herself she must run no more – she must show him by her stillness that he could scare her no longer. If only she could make a pretence of not being afraid it would be something, for inside of her, always and forever, she knew she would fear Matt and what he might do. Her voice sounded a little cracked as she said, 'You were telling me about the horse, Granda.'

'Aye, aye, I was.' Cavan, now slowly and laboriously, went on talking, while Bridget banged the paper against the walls, on the table and against the window pane.

No-one spoke to Matt, nor he to them. He had moved into the kitchen and was standing leaning against the cupboard door, picking his teeth with a broken match-stick. The years had brought a stoop to his thin figure, and his face had grown two different kinds of skin – the puckered side was faintly blue, with the scars showing silver, like a winding river seen from a great height, while on the other side the skin was of a deadly whiteness and unrelieved by a trace of colour. His hair was sparse over his pointed head, and his eyes seemed to have narrowed to slits, from which jets of red light darted. For a time his gaze followed Bridget and her banging; then it again became focused on Rose Angela. The match-stick worked up and down the crevices of his teeth as his eyes swept their menacing light over her. They came to rest at length on her face, and forced her eyes to meet his. And when, despite her efforts, he saw the fear in their brown depths, his lip curled and he said, 'Been at your whoring again, eh? And got the . . . ?'

Before he could finish speaking the newspaper struck him across the mouth. 'I've warned you, haven't I?' Bridget's face was livid.

Matt made no answer, but stood looking at his sister. The red light from his pupils seemed to have diffused itself into his skin, for the top part of his face was pink-hued. Dead flies from the swatter were sticking to the stubble of his chin; and their squashed bodies, adding to the terribleness of his face, together with his accusation, were too much for Rose Angela. Pressing her hands over her mouth she fled upstairs.

Cavan, too, felt a great sickness rising in him as he looked at his son, and not for the first time he wished with all his heart that the nigger had done the job properly, for he knew that Bridget's blow had been in the nature of a caress to him – Matt did not mind what Bridget did as long as she noticed him. Why should this be? Cavan asked himself. Why should he have bred a man with this unnatural feeling? He could find no answer within himself, nor would his books be able to provide him with the reason, as they did for so many things; and it wasn't a question he could ask of anyone, so he would never know the answer.

CHAPTER EIGHT

THE JOB

The night had been exceptionally close, and Rose Angela lay waiting for the light to break. She had slept hardly at all. The heat of the past few days had made the houses like ovens, and the nights were not long enough to allow them to cool before another day dawned and their bricks were re-baked. As she lay listening to a baby crying in a house across the street she knew that she should be everlastingly grateful for having a room to herself, when all around her four to a room was privacy. Yet she could feel nothing but a great anxiety – what was to become of her? For three weeks now she had walked the streets of the towns on both sides of the river, but when there were girls with good references what chance had she? To every place she went she had to admit that her last mistress wouldn't be likely to give her a reference. When asked why, she could only say, 'We had words.' She would offer the name of her previous mistress, but with the women practically lining up for jobs why should a mistress bother herself about this person, who dared to 'have words', and who was undoubtedly a half-caste – it would be inviting trouble. Rose Angela could read the thoughts of prospective mistresses as their calculating eyes surveyed her. Now, after weeks of tramping, her mind and body were tired and a despair was settling on her. It would have to be that café – he said he would always set her on – the manager with his big red hands, and his fat body which seemed to have been poured into his greasy suit. And there wouldn't be him alone, but the riff-raff of the waterside, with whom, in comparison, the men of the fifteen streets were gentlemen. But she must have work of some kind, things were getting desperate. Her mother had only been able to secure two half-days a week for some time now, and so she was afraid the necessity might arise when her Uncle Tony would stop the extra he now gave to her grandma to give to them. And this would mean more bickering, more rows, with her grandma yelling for all the world to hear. Oh, what would it be like to really live in one of the houses in which she had worked, where you couldn't hear what the people in the next house were saying? . . . Or in Uncle Tony's house, that little red house all by itself? Why had he never gone to live there? Was it because of her mother? If only he had taken them away from the fifteen streets years ago when he had first come by it. In that quiet, sheltered house she would have been free from her Uncle Matt's eyes, and the fear of him would have died. Why had her mother stayed on here? Was she waiting for her father to come back? He would never come back now after all this time. Anyway, what would she do about Uncle Tony if he did come back?

She turned restlessly over and lay on her stomach, and one long black plait hung down by the bedside and brushed the floor. The light through the blind began to change, and she lay waiting to hear the sound of the barrows as the men passed the street corner. This was usually her time-signal, a signal without pain now, for the men would be dry and warm. But in the winter the creaking of the barrow wheels filled her with pity and despair . . . there they were now, the wheels on the bricks. She could hear a man singing . . . 'Oft in the Stilly Night' . . . the song of reflection,

> *The eyes that shone,*
> *Now dimmed and gone,*
> *The cheerful heart's now broken.*

Oh, why must they sing? And that song with the heart-breaking words. She thrust her fingers into her ears, shutting out the unquenchable spirit of man, but almost instantly she released them as the unusual sound of the front door-knocker being banged came to her. Who on earth could it be at this hour of the morning?

She was on the landing pulling a coat round her when Bridget, opening her door, said, 'Wait, I'll go.' She had forgotten it might be her Uncle Matt. So she stood aside and let her mother go downstairs; but when Cavan's voice came to her from the kitchen she ran downstairs and asked, 'What's wrong, Granda?'

'Wrong? Nothing, lass.' He wiped the dust and sweat from his face with a piece of rag. 'I've just been telling your mother if you're lucky you'll be getting a job this mornin'.'

'A job?'

'Aye, lass. You know Ted's wife was in a good place in Shields? Well, she's ricked her foot.' He tried to cover his excitement and to appear sympathetic. 'Bad job altogether. Poor Ted's proper cut up about it, and he doesn't know what's going to be done now.'

He wiped his face again and sat down, while Bridget and Rose Angela watched him, waiting for him to go on.

'It'll likely be weeks before she can go back there again, for it takes a young 'un to climb over them sleepers and such like to get to the house; and then there's the stairs; and with him a bit cranky – he has the house cleaned every day.'

'What you talking about, Da?' asked Bridget impatiently. 'I thought you said it was a good place.'

'It is.'

'Well, what's this about getting over sleepers? . . . And who's the mistress?'

'Where is it, Granda?' asked Rose Angela. 'I don't mind how much work there is.'

'Off Holborn, hinny.' Cavan rubbed the back of his hand sheepishly under his nose.

'Holborn!' Both Bridget and Rose Angela spoke the name together.

'Off, I said. Look, give me a chance to tell you. Do you know Cassy's Wharf? No, you don't. Well, it's by a cut off the Mill Dam bank afore you get to Holborn proper. It's never been used for years as a wharf, but long ago – God knows how long – somebody built a house there. By all accounts the builder must have been as cranky as the chap who lives there now – great windows it has. Anyway, there was once a field all round the house. That was God knows how long ago, too, but it was gradually surrounded by sidings. Then the field became the graveyard for all the old bogies and wagons. But the house still stands there, and this painter fellow has it done out white twice a year, and everything's to be cleaned every day. And he hardly ever sees it, 'cause he's always up top painting. Ted says Bessie used to get tired going up trying to get him to come to a meal. When he's the mood on him, he'll paint night and day, then sleep for days and get up roaring for something to eat and go for her if it isn't ready.'

'But, Granda' – Rose Angela's voice was quiet – 'there isn't a woman there? He's not married?'

'No, lass, that's what I was going to tell you. You see' – he looked apologetically from her to Bridget and back to her again – 'you see, you won't need to fear him – Ted's Bessie says he dislikes women. He never paints owt but men and boats, and they've both got to be on their last legs afore he'll do either.'

'Is he mental?' asked Bridget.

'No, he's just cranky. But cranky or not, he makes money; and he must spend it, 'cause he gave Bessie a free hand. And she makes quite a bit, so Ted says, out of the housekeeping. So, lass, if you get a place like that . . .'

'If she gets a place like that, we won't depend on anything out of the housekeeping,' said Bridget, stiffly.

'Well, I was only saying, lass,' said Cavan, getting up; 'I was trying to do me best.'

'Look, Granda,' Rose Angela said soothingly, 'sit down a minute and I'll make you a cup of tea. And go on, tell me more about it. When did this happen to Mrs Grant, and what's the man's name?'

'Just last night, hinny. She tripped over a sleeper, and a bloke found her and went for the painter chap; and he put her in a taxi-cab and sent her home. Ted says all you've got to say is you've come in Mrs Grant's place until she's better. But mind, hinny' – he nodded cautiously at her – 'you'll have to give it up when she's better. Ted was clear about that.'

'Oh yes, Granda, I understand – that's only fair. But what's the man's name?'

'Stanhope. It's easy to remember . . . like Stanhope Road in Shields. Mr Michael Stanhope. And there's another bloke; but he's away most of the time. He's in Austria now, in a place called Teeroll or some-such. He's another painter. Although he's madder by a week than this one, Bessie says, you can have a laugh with him, where you can't with the Stanhope bloke. I think Bessie's just a bit scared of him.'

'Are you sure he's not mental?' asked Bridget again.

'Not as far as I can make out, lass.'

'I'll soon find out when I get there, Ma.' Hope had almost made Rose Angela gay. 'And I don't care if he is a bit mental, I'll look after him.'

'You'll have nothing to do with the place if he's not all there; you'll go and get yourself—' Bridget was about to say 'murdered', but she feared the word, so she substituted 'in trouble'.

'There's always been trouble down there,' she went on. 'Look at that Saturday a few years back, when the Arabs rioted around the shipping office and stabbed them three policemen.'

'You couldn't only blame the Arabs for that,' Cavan put in sharply; 'it were our blokes agitating them not to sign the P.C.5 form that did that, together with those bloody Arab boarding-house masters who bleed them dry. Look what them masters did a while back . . . sent the Arabs in droves up to the workhouse. Blackmail it was, just to compel the town to give them outdoor relief, so as the poor skinny scabs could tip up their dibs to them again. It was the white agitators and the black masters who caused that shipping trouble, I'm telling you . . . Anyway' – he turned towards Rose Angela – 'you won't be near them. As I've told you, Cassy's Wharf cuts away from Holborn.'

'What time did Mrs Grant start, Granda?'

'Eight, hinny.'

'All right, I'll be there at eight.' She touched his stubbly cheek. 'Thanks, Granda. You know, it's a good job for me that you read.'

'How do you make that out, hinny?'

'Well, if you hadn't got interested in books you wouldn't have had Ted Grant for a friend, and he would likely have given someone else the chance to fill his wife's place.'

The deduction pleased Cavan, and he laughed. 'Aye, there's that in it.' And when Rose Angela handed him his cup of tea he raised the cup to her, saying, 'Here's to Bessie's slow recovery. Not that

94

I'm wishing her any harm, mind you, but—' He chuckled and winked at her. 'Good luck, lass.'

Rose Angela took the seven o'clock workmen's tram into Shields. The appellation was a mere courtesy title – now only a sprinkling of miners and odd workmen occupied it. She alighted by the slaughter-house, where the piteous bellowings of the beasts were already to be heard. She had left the tram earlier than was necessary in order that she might ask the way of some 'white person', for beyond the Mill Dam lay Holborn, and Arabs. And strange though it appeared, her dislike of Arabs exceeded that held by most white people. When on one or two occasions an Arab had spoken to her, his very approach had seemed an insult. Yet it was this feeling of revulsion which gave her the insight into how the Negro was viewed by a white, and helped her to understand a little the white man's deep dislike of the Negro who was penetrating his preserves. But her understanding did not make her situation easier to bear, even though the touch of colour in herself, at least outwardly, was slight.

She reached the top of the Mill Dam bank without meeting any women, so she stopped an old man and enquired of him the whereabouts of Cassy's Wharf.

'Cassy's Wharf? Aye, I know where that is, but it's a job to get at. Why d'ya want to get there?'

'I'm after a job.'

'Funny place for a job – a lot of queer characters around this quarter, you know, lass – although it isn't as bad as it used to be in my young days, except for the bloody Arabs. They're swarming like flies here. But now let me see, which is your best way.' He ruminated for a moment. 'Aye, look. Go down that street there – it's the only street you need touch if you follow where I tell you. At the end of it you'll see a narrow cut between two warehouses. Go down there, it'll bring you to the river bank; then turn right and keep straight on . . . well, you won't be able to keep straight on, for you'll have to dodge between trucks and things, but keep as near the river as you can and you can't miss the wharf. They tell me there's still a house along there. Is that where you're going?'

Rose Angela said it was, and, after thanking him warmly, followed his directions. All the doors in the street were closed; the blinds of the windows were still drawn, and the bright morning sun intensified the blackness of the passageways separating every other house. The place seemed entirely dead; the only live thing was herself, and the only noise the heels of her shoes on the pavement. She came to the cut between the warehouses, and this was as dark as the passageways, for the towering buildings seemed to meet above the narrow slit. She couldn't see the end of the cut, only where it curved in the dim distance. But as she rounded the curve she saw coming towards her a man with lowered head. He was walking slowly and was merged in the duskiness of the passage. It was well he wasn't fat, she thought, for the breadth of the cut was hardly wide enough to allow two people to pass. It was with an inward shrinking she realised that the approaching man was an Arab. She could see him peering at her across the narrowing distance. He stopped, and, standing with his back to the wall, waited for her to pass. She did not look at him or alter her pace, but as she passed him her coat brushed him and her heart thumped in agitation. He did not speak, but she knew his eyes were fixed on her, and as she walked on she was conscious of his gaze on her back. She wrinkled her nose in distaste – that sweet-scented smell peculiar to most Arabs hung in the air. When as a child sitting in a tram she had first smelt this heavy aroma she had wondered if her father too had that kind of smell, only to dismiss it as impossible.

Immediately beyond the passage she came to the river, and turned right; but as the old man said, she was unable to keep straight on for long – the banks seemed a graveyard for old trucks, some wheel-less, some on their sides. An old railway carriage, also without wheels, and sunk in coarse sea grass, attracted her attention, and she glanced through a window, only to hurry quickly on again, for two men fully dressed were lying in huddled positions on its floor.

Climbing over piles of stacked rails, walking in and out of the maze of wagons, she felt she was entering a sort of waking nightmare, and this feeling leapt into certainty when she saw the house. The jumble of debris stopped suddenly, and there ahead of her was a clear space of about thirty feet, with a narrow red-brick house at the end of it, the windows and door shining startlingly white. She stopped, and for no accountable reason a surge of happiness welled in her. She knew she had never seen this house before, yet it was familiar. It was as if she had known it, and through knowing it had been happy. She entered the clearing and began to walk slowly towards the house . . . Would he be up? It wasn't yet eight. She had better find the back door.

As she turned round the side of the house the river, too, turned, seeming to follow the line of the bright golden beach pathway; and when she came to the back she stopped again in pleased surprise. There lay the wharf not eight yards from the house, with the sun thick and warm on the fawn-coloured planks of the landing and lining the black water-marked piles of the jetty with silver streaks. A vivid splash of blue moving gently on the sparkling water drew her to the jetty edge, and she looked down almost tenderly on a little boat with a white furled mast lying down at its centre . . . how lovely! If only the man himself turned out to be all right and she could work here.

'Well, and what do you want?' The deep grunt of the voice, and the unexpectedness with which it came, nearly caused her to topple into the water. She gripped the jetty post, and, turning, looked towards the house. Her first jumbled impression was that the whole back of the house was made of three huge panes of glass, the widest being the top one, out of which was thrust the wildest looking head she had ever seen. She opened her mouth to explain her presence, but his next words halted her, and she experienced a faint tingling of pleasure at them.

'I don't want a model – I have more than I can cope with.'

She looked at his eyes sweeping over her, but felt not the slightest embarrassment. She could not name the expression they held; she only knew they were without that look she had come to fear in the eyes of man.

'I don't do women, anyway.'

'I am not a model, Mr Stanhope – I came to take Mrs Grant's place until she's better . . . that's if I'll be suitable.'

He blinked down on her as if recalling who Mrs Grant was.

'Oh yes, the blasted woman hurt her foot. Well, come in.'

Breathing quickly, she moved towards the door, set back in a little porch, and entered the house. If only he would take to her! Oh, Holy Mother, let me get this place.

She stood waiting for him in the most beautiful kitchen she had ever seen. The woodwork, she noticed, wasn't white, but of the palest blue. There were cupboards all along one side of the room and the little fireplace was blue-tiled, and never made for cooking, she thought. She turned to the window. The wharf and a large stretch of the river was framed in it like a picture. She had never imagined the Tyne looking like this . . . and the sight of a boat moving swiftly, with the grace of a dancer, across the middle of the pane intensified her prayer; Dear, dear God, let me get this place.

'What's the matter with your legs?' The bellow, coming from somewhere inside the house, startled her.

Was he shouting at her? Who else, if he lived here alone? She moved towards the half-open door and stepped into the hall, which for all its whiteness appeared dark after the sun-filled kitchen. Before her was the side of the staircase, and she looked up, but could see no-one, so she asked softly, 'Were you calling for me, sir?'

'Yes. Are you deaf?'

Quickly she mounted the stairs, her steps making no sound on the thick dark-blue carpet, but when she came to the landing it was empty. She looked at the four closed doors, then at the second flight of stairs, and went hurriedly up these; and there he was, standing in the doorway of a room, seeming to fill it not with height so much as with breadth. He was not much taller than she, but his solidness made him appear like a giant to her. Her eyes went to his hair, which looked like a tangled matting of coarse rope. She couldn't tell what colour it was, for the light behind him made it a mixture of red and brown, while the piece hanging over his brow appeared black.

97

'There's nothing the matter with your legs, is there?' He looked at them with close scrutiny, but his gaze did not offend her.

She shook her head slightly; and he turned into the room, saying, 'All the women I had before Bessie had legs – bad legs, swollen legs, stiff legs. They had a job to get here, and when they did the stairs were too much for them. Are stairs too much for you?' His voice was staccato and his eyes held an angry look, as if he was indulging in a row.

'No, I'm used to stairs.'

She was now in the room, and the scene bewildered her. From floor to ceiling the walls were covered with paintings. The sun, pouring through the great window, merged them into one rainbow whole, but apart from the window-seat there was not another fixture or article of furniture in the room – not even an easel stood on the bare floor. He walked to the window and turned there, his back to the light; and she stood in the centre of the room, facing him. The sun was dazzling her eyes and he became indistinct, only the vivid blue of his eyes remaining clear.

'How long is Bessie likely to be? Can you cook?'

'I don't really know – yes, yes, I can do . . .'

'Don't say it!' He held out a hand, short-fingered and square, in protest. 'Plain cooking! Floating cabbage and fries!'

She smiled, in no way offended. 'They tell me I'm a good cook.'

'What wage do you want?'

She was nonplussed at the question – to be asked what wage she wanted! She'd be sleeping out, so dared she ask for . . . twenty-five shillings? No, she'd better make it a pound. But then he might come down.

'Could I ask a pound?'

'A pound!' His face was wrinkled in the light.

Now she had done it. She began, 'Well, I . . .' when he cut in, 'Bessie got thirty-five shillings; you'll have the same if you suit.'

Thirty-five shillings! She could only swallow and say, 'Yes, sir.'

'What's your name?'

'Rose Angela Paterson – I'm called Rosie.'

'Well, all right.' Half turning, he blinked into the sun, and stifled a yawn. 'I'm hungry and I want a meal. But listen' – he swung round on her again, his manner more aggressive than before – 'I don't want my breakfast at nine, and dinner at one, and tea at six. If you don't think you'll like that arrangement, say so now. And I knock down when I want a meal – I don't have bells, I don't like them. And when I say I don't want to be disturbed I mean it. When I want you I knock, you understand?'

Still she said nothing, knowing he wasn't finished.

'And I want the rooms dusted every day, not with a duster but with a wash-leather. Why do I want unused rooms done every day? Because I hate dirt and muddle. Get rid of the idea that any old thing or condition does for an artist. Another thing – I don't mind being robbed, but I don't want it overdone.' He paused, waiting for some response; and when none came he went on, 'Why don't you bridle and say that you're an honest woman and don't touch anything that doesn't belong to you?'

She regarded him steadily, and said, 'Because I know it's done.'

'Oh, you do?' He nodded his great head at her. 'Well, you're honest about it, anyway, that's more than most of them are. Where were you last?'

Dear Lord, here it came!

'At Mrs Spalding's in Paddington Road. But that was three weeks ago – I haven't been well.' Would he ask for her card? If he did she would tell him the truth and chance it.

But he didn't ask for the card.

He said, 'We'll try it a week and see how it goes. And now I want a meal – a big meal, a dinner. And strong coffee. You'll find plenty of stuff downstairs. I'll have it in the drawing-room.'

'Yes, sir.'

She turned quickly away, only to be pulled up by his next words, 'And take that frightened look off your face, there's nothing to be afraid of here.'

She wanted to say, 'I'm not afraid of you,' but after a pause she went on her way without saying anything. Her body was feeling inflated and light with relief. She had got the place, and he was nice. Her mind questioned how anyone so abrupt and who said such unorthodox things could be nice, but he was, and she knew she would like working for him in this lovely, quaint house.

She ran down the last flight of stairs to the kitchen. He wanted a dinner. What would she make him? Something tasty and quick. She tore off her coat and opened one door after another. The cupboards in the kitchen were well stocked, and in the larder was a half chicken and a piece of cooked fresh salmon – a salad, yes – but something hot before – soup. Lentils, an onion and a little curry powder. After searching at frantic speed she found all that she required.

The soup was simmering and the fruit pie baking, and she was standing at the table by the window arranging the salad when her hands became still and her eyes widened . . . her master, for she thought of him as that already, was walking, practically naked, towards the end of the wharf, his body looking even broader without clothes. His hair was still on end, and as she watched him she had a great desire to laugh. When he dived he became lost to her view, and she resumed her hurried preparations. But when the squat lumbering line of a tug ploughing up the centre of the river caught her eye, she stopped again, for in line with it she saw the shining lift of an arm cutting the water with regular precision. A figure leaning over the side of the tug waved, and a hand from the water answered the salute, and a faint call that could have been a greeting came to her. The atmosphere was homely, and she felt a warmth growing inside her . . . he must swim often, the tugmen knew him. And he'd be hungry . . . If only he liked the dinner . . .

Half an hour later she was standing dropping little squares of bread into boiling fat, to serve with his soup, when she heard his footsteps in the hall. Oh, if only he didn't bang or call for a minute, and then everything would be ready.

There was neither bang nor call, and when she took the soup in to him her knees were trembling so much that she felt her body was about to fold up, the consequences of which would be disastrous.

He was lying fully dressed on a divan; his eyes were closed, and as she said quietly, 'Your dinner, sir,' he opened one eye and looked at her.

'Dinner?'

For one moment she thought that his order had been a joke, for his tone was full of surprise, so that when he got up at once and went to the table her sigh of relief was almost audible. But if she expected any word of praise for her quickness or the quality of the meal she was disappointed.

She left him with his coffee and prepared herself a cup of tea, for she could eat nothing – excitement being her food at this moment.

She had barely finished the tea when his voice came to her, not from the drawing-room but from the upstairs window. Was he calling her? She sprang up, but stopped on her way to the open door, for there, in the middle of the wharf, looking upwards, were two men, one tall and thin and the other a dwarf, whose head was sunk deep into his shoulders and whose features were so strong and shapely as to give the impression of a sculptor's cast.

'I told you I didn't want you till three o'clock!'

'Yes, guv'nor.' It was the tall man who spoke.

'Well, what the hell're you nosing round for?'

'Just takin' a walk, guv'nor.'

'Walk be damned! Then walk some place else – this is my back yard, or front yard. It's private, and you know it.'

'We were just thinkin', guv'nor . . . we were just wondering—' The man broke off. He was still looking up, and the stretched sinews of his neck cast their own deep shadows. The silence continued until the man raised his hand and grabbed at the coin flashing through the sunlight. He touched his brow with his finger, saying, 'Thanks, guv'nor – we'll be here at three.'

There was no response from the upper window, and Rose Angela watched the men shambling off, ludicrous in their different heights, and pitiable in their crumpled threadbare clothes. Why hadn't they come and asked for a bite or something? She guessed these were the two men who had been lying in the railway carriage.

As she returned to her cup of tea her master's voice again startled her.

'Pete! You, Pete!'

The dwarf reappeared from the side of the house. He did not speak but stared up at the window.

'Seen anything of that fellow yet?'

'I asked him. He won't come.' The dwarf's voice was guttural and the words strangely clipped.

'Why not?'

'He says he don't want to be painted.'

'Did you tell him I'd give him two shillings an hour?'

'Yes.'

'Where does he live?'

There was a slight pause before the dwarf answered, 'I dunno.'

'You're a liar – you do.'

The dwarf remained silent, gazing upwards.

'Murphy!'

As if being produced from a gigantic hat, the tall man sprang round the corner. 'Yes, guv'nor?'

'Where does that fellow live?'

Murphy dropped his gaze from the top window to the dwarf's face, then he lifted it again. 'I dunno, guv'nor.'

'You're a liar, too.'

'Yes, guv'nor.'

'Look, I'll give you a pound if you get him here.'

'A quid!' Again Murphy dropped his eyes to the dwarf, but whatever he saw there wasn't reassuring. 'I'll try, guv'nor, but I ain't promising owt.'

'I'll make it two.'

They both stared upwards in silence, then turned slowly away; and once again it was quiet on the wharf.

Offering them two pounds just to get a man to come and sit for him! He must be made of money. Rose Angela went into the drawing-room to clear the table, and as she looked about the room she thought again, He must be made of money.

In her various places she had come to recognise good furniture from shoddy imitations, and although her knowledge of antiques was limited she knew that every piece in this room had been specially picked, for here, with the air of age and elegance, was comfort. The main tone of the room was brown, a deep patina brown, relieved in the upholstery by a shade of green that was almost blue. The window of this room, which ran the whole length of the house, looked out on to a white trellis, constructed to shut off the jumble of debris beyond. She would have liked to linger and examine the room further, but the desire was checked when she remembered what still had to be done with the wash-leather.

By mid-day she had finished the ground floor and the four rooms on the first floor. One of these had taken very little doing, as it was another studio belonging to the 'other one', whom her grandfather had referred to as being 'madder by the week' than her master. In contrast, the bedroom adjoining this studio was, to Rose Angela's mind, more like an overcrowded sitting-room, and unlike her master's, which was practically bare, without even a carpet on the floor, a large orange rug being the only covering on the bare polished boards.

She did not venture to the top of the house, and as the afternoon wore on she began to await anxiously the summons for another meal. It was close on three o'clock when it came . . . a dull thumping from above. With fast-beating heart she mounted the stairs and knocked on the studio door, and entered, only to find it empty. Staring along its length, she saw a crumpled rug lying on the boards by the window. Had he been sleeping on the floor?

Her conjecturing was interrupted by his voice coming through a partly-opened door to the right of her. 'Rosie!'

It was as familiar-sounding as if he had used her name every day for years. There was none of the harshness of the morning in his tone.

'Yes, sir.' She went into the room and saw him standing at a table, stretching some canvas over a frame. He did not lift his eyes from his work, nor speak further, until he had taken some tacks from his mouth and hammered them home.

'I'll have a pot of tea. Make it strong. Nothing to eat; but you can make me a meal about six. You needn't stay to clear – do that in the morning.'

'Is there anything particular you would like, sir?'

He walked to an easel, with a full-length empty canvas set on its pegs, and moved it to the side of a dais which ran the breadth of the room.

'No – as long as it's nothing hashed up, it'll do . . . I like fresh food.'

'Yes, sir. About the ordering, sir – do I do that?'

'Yes, yes, of course. Bessie always did. But mind' – he swung round and faced her, and his tone took on the edge that she associated with him as natural – 'sixteen pounds a month's my limit – not a penny more.'

'Sixteen pounds a month for food!' Her expression carried further the surprise of her voice.

'Yes, for food.' His eyes narrowed and their blueness became intensified. 'What do you think? It's not enough?'

Sixteen pounds a month to keep one man and a daily maid in food. Was he a fool? No, she dismissed the idea. Had Bessie been charging him all that? If so, it was absolute robbery. It was understandable her wanting to make a bit extra, with the family to feed, but four pounds a week for food! . . . Yet Bessie would be coming back, she must be careful what she said.

His narrowed, concentrated gaze remained fixed on her, and she met it. 'It will be more than enough, sir.'

'I'm glad of that.'

He turned to his easel again and she went out. Was there a touch of sarcasm in his voice? One couldn't blame him if there was – as he had said that morning, he knew he was being robbed. But four pounds a week!

She had just reached the bottom of the stairs when his voice came again. 'Rosie! Tell those two men to wait for a quarter of an hour or so. I'll shout when I want them.'

'Yes, sir.'

As she reached the kitchen there was a tap on the open door, and there stood Murphy and Pete . . . she thought of them immediately by their names. On closer inspection they looked more disreputable than they had looked on the wharf.

'You can come in and sit down. Mr Stanhope will knock when he wants you.'

'Thank you, miss. You're new, aren't you? What's happened to the other one?' It was Murphy who did the talking.

'She's hurt her foot.'

She made the tea, conscious of the men's eyes gravely watching her movements, and as she went out of the room with the tray she said, 'I'll make you a cup when I come back.'

But when she returned to the kitchen Murphy spoke again, hesitantly and sadly. 'I'd better tell you, miss – he doesn't like it, the guv'nor don't. He don't like us getting anything.'

'Has he said so?'

'Aye; at least he told Mrs Grant we weren't to come begging here or he'd stop us sitting.'

'Has he ever said anything to you himself?'

'No.'

Would a man who knew he was being robbed by his servants begrudge a bite and a cup of tea to these half-starved men? If Bessie wouldn't give them anything, it would be for reasons of her own.

'He hasn't said anything to me, so until he does you can have what's over – he doesn't like things hashed up.' And with a feeling of one in authority Rose Angela went to the pantry, and Murphy's long furrowed face gazed down on Pete with an almost angelic smile. But Pete did not return the smile. His eyes were riveted on the door, waiting for Rose Angela's return; and when she motioned them to the table his gaze did not flicker from her.

As hungry men will sometimes do, they began to eat the food in small bites, with a seeming finickiness – it was the habit of making a little go a long way; and they were only half-way through their plates of food when a hail from above brought them to their feet.

'Look, miss, we are much obliged. Could we put it in a bit paper and take it with us?'

'Yes, go on, I'll see to it.'

Murphy went into the hall rubbing his mouth vigorously, but Pete, standing in front of Rose Angela, asked abruptly, 'What's your name?'

'Rosie.'

'Your other name – full name?'

'Rose Angela Paterson – why?'

The dwarf did not answer, but hurried after Murphy; and about a minute later, when passing through the hall, Rose Angela was amazed to see them still standing halfway up the stairs. They both looked silently down on her and she up at them.

'What the hell you doing down there, Murphy?'

At the bellow from the upper landing they turned and sprang up the remaining stairs, and Rose Angela went on her way to the drawing-room, wondering if she had been wise, after all, to break Bessie's rule. For what were they up to, she wondered, looking at her like that and whispering on the stairs?

CHAPTER NINE

THE AWAKENING

It was eighteen days since Rose Angela came to Wharf House, and she knew now that one of the main things she wanted from life was the opportunity to manage a house; not just to work in one, but to control it – to be able to say, as she was doing now, 'I'll order this today,' or 'I'll make that for dinner the morrow.' Never could she remember being so happy; yet the eighteen days had not been without their worry.

She disliked fighting or arguing of any kind, and, on such occasions, had always found herself strangely backward with her tongue; yet the way she had stood up to the grocer had been gratifying, even if the meeting with Mrs Grant had still to be faced.

The barefacedness of the twisting that Mrs Grant and the grocer's man worked incensed her – four pounds' worth of groceries, fowl, meat and fish were certainly bought, but only half the amount was delivered to the house. The rest was divided between the two of them. She had wanted to change to another shop, but was afraid of doing so in case this particular shop had been the master's choice; but she was firm in her ordering, and with ham at sixpence a pound and streaky at threepence, and eggs a penny each, while cooking ones were twenty-four a shilling, not to overlook the fact that one pound of steak with a rabbit thrown in was little more than a shilling, a great deal of food could be bought for two pounds. She knew her refusal to co-operate with the man would make it awkward when she met Mrs Grant, but she could feel no regret. In any case, Mrs Grant would likely return to her own system, for it was doubtful whether the master would notice any difference, since so far she had given only one order of her own and perhaps she would not give another, for only yesterday Cavan had regretfully told her that Mrs Grant's ankle was considerably better.

Slowly she crumpled the pastry in the bowl as she looked out of the window towards the wharf. The sun had gone in and the river was lead-coloured and choppy, but it was still beautiful. Soon she would no longer be able to look at it, in either sunshine or shadow. As she was staring at the water the blue boat ran alongside the wharf, and for the moment Mrs Grant and her impending return were put aside. The scones would be done –

perhaps he'd like one with his coffee; it would have been cold on the water.

As he entered the kitchen she trembled a little, as always when in his presence; yet she wasn't afraid of him.

'There are some scones just out of the oven, sir. Would you like one with your coffee?' She turned her head towards him, her hands still rubbing the pastry.

'Yes . . . yes, I would – nice smell.'

He sniffed the air, and she said, 'I won't be a minute, sir, I'll bring it up.'

She was clapping the flour from her hands over the bowl when he said, 'I'll have it here.'

He pulled a chair to the table and sat down, and so great was her surprise that she stood with her palms pressed together and stared at him.

'You don't mind?'

'Oh no, sir – no.'

'Cold on the water.'

'Yes, sir.'

In spite of his abruptness, she knew he was trying to be pleasant, and a little whirl of happiness went through her.

'How old are you, Rosie?' The question was brusquely put, as were all his enquiries.

She turned, and for a flash of time looked directly into the blue eyes surveying her before answering. 'Twenty, sir.'

'You look older.'

'Yes, I know I do, sir.'

He pulled off his top boots and placed them by the side of the hearth, asking as he did so, 'What have you done all your life? This kind of work?'

'Yes.'

'What have you wanted to do?'

'Just this, sir – look after a house.'

'My God! Nothing more?' He twisted round and looked up at her incredulously.

'It isn't everyone who's lucky enough to do even that these days.'

Her voice was serious, and he answered more curtly still, 'Yes, I know all about that; but you . . . haven't you wanted something different – to be a dancer or get on the films? or be a mannequin, or an artist's model? . . . you'd make a good model, you know – not that I want to do you.' He raised his hand as if pressing her away.

'No, no; but there are plenty who would.'

She waited until she returned from the scullery with the coffee before saying, 'I can't see myself getting such work around the Tyne, sir.' And she smiled ruefully as she placed his coffee on the table.

'The Tyne! You don't want to stick around here all your days, do you? Get up to London and you'll be snapped up.'

'You think so, sir?' Her voice held no belief, but her smile broadened and she gazed for a moment on his bent head as he stirred his coffee briskly. London, and mannequins and artists' models! Who would want such things if they could work in a house like this, with the river flowing by and him up there painting away and thumping occasionally on the floor, and the peace that prevailed even when he was bellowing down the stairs. And now him sitting here talking to her! She experienced a feeling of satisfaction as she watched him bite into one of her scones – his mouth was full-lipped, and wide, like the rest of him; his hair still bore its numerous partings, and even without the sun's misleading light was of different colours. She often tried to guess how old he was, for on different days he looked a different age. Today he looked youngish, about thirty. Tomorrow, painting like mad, his hair standing up on end, he would look anything up to forty-five. She couldn't tell what his age was.

A knock on the kitchen door checked something further he was about to say, and Rose Angela, opening it, found Murphy there.

'Can I see the guv'nor, miss?'

'What do you want?' Stanhope called.

Murphy sidled into the kitchen, cap in hand and his long body swaying.

'Well? What you after?'

'I've got him, guv'nor.'

'The fellow?' Stanhope rose to his feet, his excitement evident.

'He'll come the morrow.'

'Why not today?'

'Well . . . ye see . . . he's been bad.'

'Bad! – Pah! You're just stalling to push me up a bit, like you've done all along . . . I'm not rising, Murphy.'

'No, guv'nor, honest to God! Just when he said he would come, he took bad – week afore last he was took bad.'

'Well, I'm giving you nothing on account this time . . . I want to see the fellow first.'

'Yes, guv'nor.' There was disappointment in Murphy's voice.

Stanhope sat down again and looked at Murphy, at the long, shambling length of him – By God, he had got him on to that canvas – every undernourished pore. And the little fellow too. It should shake them up, there . . . but he wouldn't send it until this other fellow was done . . . Now he should make a picture, especially if he could get him to look as he had done that day when he first saw him gazing across the river. He'd get him all right; he'd work on him night and day.

His attention was drawn to Murphy's working mouth and the saliva at the corners of it. 'I suppose you could squeeze a cup of coffee into that fat carcass of yours, eh? Well, you'd better get round Rosie – she makes quite good coffee . . . or perhaps you know that?' His eyes were crinkled at the corners and he threw a quick glance towards Rose Angela, and as a tinge of colour mounted her cheeks he laughed and scraped his chair back from the table, but his rising was checked by the abrupt opening of the door. He turned, with Rose Angela and Murphy, and stared at the young woman surveying them. The door in her hand, she looked from one to the other before coming into the kitchen; then she advanced with such a proprietary air that even Stanhope for the moment seemed in a subordinate position.

Rose Angela, strangely enough, had never met Bessie Grant, but the faintness in the pit of her stomach told her who this plump, fair woman was. She wasn't much older than herself, but she had all the assurance in the world.

'Good morning, sir.'

'Oh, hallo, Bessie. You're better then, I see.'

'Yes . . . yes, I'm better.' The look she threw towards Murphy said plainly 'and not before time'.

Stanhope rose and walked towards the hall saying, 'Come upstairs a minute, Bessie, will you?' His voice had lost the harsh note usual to it – it was now soft, and even pleasant. Perhaps he was glad to have her back, Rose Angela thought, with an accompanying pang.

Bessie, in the act of unbuttoning her coat, stopped. She looked at Rose Angela, and Rose Angela managed to smile at her and say, 'I'm glad you're better, Mrs Grant.'

To this pleasantry Bessie made no rejoinder, but with the same air of being in command she followed Stanhope.

Rose Angela turned to the window. She was finished, then. She hadn't thought it would be like this, like a bolt from the blue – she had imagined there would be a little warning, such as her granda saying, 'Bessie's better. I think she intends starting next week, lass.' But this suddenness, and coming at a time when everything was so wonderful . . . him sitting there drinking his coffee at the kitchen table, much the same as her Uncle Tony or her granda would have done . . . and poor Murphy and Pete – there'd be no more bits and pieces for them . . . and herself – there would be the round again – the humiliations, the despair. He said she could get a job as a model any day in London. Should she try? She knew it was a stupid question to ask herself, for she had not the courage to leave the small security of her home, and Bridget, Tony and her granda, for a life she thought would be just as hostile towards her as this one was, together with added dangers.

'I'm sorry, miss.'

She turned towards Murphy. 'Well, I was only temporary, you know, Murphy.'

'You'll be goin' right away, then, this mornin'?'

'Yes.'

'We'll miss yer, miss.'

'I'll miss you, too, Murphy, and Pete . . . I'll miss everything.' She turned blindly towards the window again. It would have been better if she'd never got the job . . . oh, a thousand times better.

'Look, miss' – Murphy came up behind her – 'could ye pop this way the morrer? Round about eightish.' He was whispering now. 'Pete and me – we've got something for ye – a surprise, like. If ye could come just to the carriage, round about eight, miss – could you?'

'Oh, I don't think so, Murphy . . . it's very kind of you . . . but—' She turned to him and her refusal was checked by the look of utter disappointment on his face. 'All right,' she added listlessly, 'I'll come.'

It would be a chance to see the house again, even if only from the outside, and she'd have to be out early going the rounds, anyway.

As Murphy, turning to go, muttered, 'I'm dead sorry you're going, miss,' she remembered the drink she had been about to get him, and she said, 'I forgot your coffee, Murphy. Just a minute; I'll get it.' But as she went into the scullery the sound of a door closing overhead reached them, and Murphy whispered, 'Never bother, miss. Thanks all the same, but I'd best be off.'

'No – wait.' If it was the last drink Murphy was to have here, he should have it, in spite of Bessie.

Suddenly Rose Angela found she heartily disliked Bessie. She had disliked her before she met her, because of her blatant robbery and her meanness towards these half-starved men.

She listened to the quick, soft padding on the stairs, and as she handed the cup to Murphy her eyes turned towards the kitchen door, awaiting Bessie's entry. But it didn't come. Instead, the front door banged with such violence that the window panes rattled, and Murphy almost dropped the cup.

Rose Angela and he stared at each other; then Murphy, putting down his cup, went quickly out of the house. He was back again in a minute, his body jangling with excitement and his enlarged Adam's apple jerking inside the loose skin of his neck.

'She's gone, miss . . . in a tear too – like the divil was after her. What d'ye make of it?'

What could she make of it? She shook her head and watched Murphy gulping the coffee, his face crinkled and happy – she dared not think of what she could make of it.

Murphy, wiping his mouth with the back of his hand, beamed on her. 'It looks as if ye might be set, miss.'

He left her, and from the window she watched his shank-like legs running across the wharf . . . Her being set would mean a lot to Murphy and Pete, but what would it mean to her?

She worked on in a daze, awaiting a summons upstairs, but none came. His dinner was ordered for two o'clock, and when she took it into the drawing-room he was there waiting. But he did not speak until she was leaving the room; then, quite briefly, he said, 'Bessie isn't coming back. Would you like to stay on?'

After a moment of silence, during which he turned his head and looked at her, she said quietly, 'Yes, sir, thank you.'

That was all; but as usual after any nervous strain she wanted to be sick, and she stood in the closed scullery, retching and asking herself what had happened. What could have happened? Surely Bessie hadn't come to give her notice in. She dismissed the idea – when Bessie came through that door it was into 'her kitchen'. Every particle of her declared it. Whatever had happened, she would likely have to wait until Ted told her granda before she knew.

At half-past six she closed the kitchen door – her kitchen door now – and went home. She had never felt so gay in her life before, nor so free. She had a job that she could see stretching on for ever; she could look ahead and say, 'I'll save up and buy things . . . I'll save up for Christmas and buy things for me ma and granda, and Uncle Tony. And perhaps some day I'll be able to buy a fur . . . Oh to have a fur!' She'd always wanted a fur – a long one . . . As she hurried over the sleepers and around the wagons she kept her mind from the man who had made this possible. Later tonight she would think of him and the events of the day, but now to get home and tell Bridget, and talk of the things she'd buy in the future.

Coming out on to the piece of clear ground before she entered the passage, she saw the Arab. He was standing as usual leaning against the broken wall surmounting the river bank, and as usual on her approach he took a step or two from the wall and awaited her coming. She had ceased being actively afraid of him; and now she wondered curiously if he was dumb, for since their first meeting in the passage she had encountered him both morning and evening, rain or shine, and always in the same place – against the broken wall. And never had he spoken, but tonight, adding to the events of the day, he said, 'Good evening.'

Her present happiness held down her fear of him, and she answered, 'Good evening,' but quickened her step as she did so.

'Excuse me . . . please don't be afraid. Can I walk with you?'

His hand came out to check her flight, but she swerved aside, saying, 'No – no thank you.'

'It's all right.'

The words reached her as she entered the passage. He was making no attempt to follow her, and she breathed more easily. She could even smile to herself about it. It was like something one read in a book – 'Good evening – may I walk with you?' Not . . . 'Goin' my road?' or 'Who's tyekin' ye hyem?' His precise English was surprising, for the Arabs one heard talking in the trams jabbered, and he looked so different from any of the others in his tight blue suit, except perhaps a bit taller. All Arabs looked the same to her, of medium height and extreme thinness.

But if, at any time, he should attempt to walk with her, what would she do? There was plenty of time to meet that when he tried it. Anyway, all she'd have to do would be to tell Mr Stanhope. Yes, she'd tell Mr Stanhope, for he didn't like the Arabs, and one bellow from him would scare a dozen Arabs. She laughed to herself – it was like a child saying, 'I'll tell me ma, mind!', or 'I'll tell me da, mind' – only she had never said the latter.

The journey to Jarrow seemed interminable, and when she alighted at the fifteen streets the sight of Matt standing with a group of men at her Grannie's street corner did not, as usual, stiffen her with apprehension. She would be afraid of nothing or no-one today . . . she was happy . . . she had a permanent job, and what a job! The sound of someone spitting followed her. She knew it was Matt, and that it was meant for her, but what did it matter? She walked on, her head high, her step free and swinging, and her face alight, but the moment she entered the kitchen the light was quenched, for there, sitting facing her, was Bessie Grant. On the other side of the hearth sat her Uncle Tony, it being Wednesday, and her mother sat by the table. They were all three quiet, but it was a quietness that any moment could have snapped with extreme tension.

Bridget rose and said, 'I suppose you know why Mrs Grant's here?'

'Oh, she knows, all right.' Bessie uncrossed and recrossed her thick legs.

'Wait a minute.' Bridget put out a gently suppressing hand towards Bessie. 'One story's good till another one's told. We'll take one thing at a time. Rosie – did you tell Mr Stanhope about the – the grocer? . . . You know . . . about Mr Pillin?'

'No, not a word. He knows nothing about it. I only cut down one week, and he hasn't seen the bill.'

'Hasn't seen the bill!' repeated Bessie, with utter scorn.

'He hasn't,' said Rose Angela heatedly, 'for it's in my bag. I've kept it here all the time.'

'Sh!' said Bridget, silencing them both. 'Then how was it, Rosie, that Mr Stanhope could tell Mrs Grant that she had been . . . well . . . getting a bit too much stuff?'

'Not through me. I tell you I've never said a word to him, and he couldn't have heard what I said to Mr Pillin because he was out. He was up the river at the time.'

'Then,' said Bessie, emphasising each word with a nod of her head, 'it's merely a damned excuse, as I said it was.'

'You'd better be careful what you're saying, Mrs Grant.' Tony rose to his feet. 'You can be made to pay for such statements.'

'Made to pay!' Bessie rounded on him. 'What with, eh? When she's even taken the bread out of me bairns' mouths because she's low enough to supply Mr bloody Stanhope with something that I wouldn't! I might have known – but that's what you get for helping people.'

At this moment Bessie was cursing her husband for persuading her, as she liked to think, to let her job to old McQueen's girl, who had been up against it. She was forgetting that at the time she thought it was a good idea, for had she asked any of her friends to take over, they would have known a little too much of her business – and Mr Pillin's, and she didn't want that. But she had considered McQueen's grand-daughter would be so grateful she'd keep her mouth shut. Yet what had happened? Yes, what had happened? It was as plain as a pikestaff – she knew now why this young bitch couldn't keep a job with a mistress. It had been easy going for her with no mistress at Wharf House. The Stanhope bloke was supposed not to like women, but he was a man, and that type of bitch would soon let him know how much of a man he was.

She looked at Rose Angela, and said with insinuating quietness, 'I wouldn't do what you're doing, not for thirty-five bob a week, I wouldn't. But perhaps you've come to some arrangement, eh? You can call the piper now. The lot of you here'll be decked out soon, and be moving, for he's rotten with money.'

Bridget, with set, white face, moved towards the door. 'You'd better be going, Mrs Grant.'

'Aye. I'll go . . . but mark you, don't think she's heard the last of this. Oh no, I'm not taking this lying down – I'll see me day with her, if it's the last thing I do.' She nodded, emphasising her threat as she passed Bridget.

The door closed, and Bridget turned towards Rose Angela, saying quietly, 'Now let's hear what you've got to say.'

'You don't believe her – do you?' Rose Angela stood supporting herself against the table edge.

'I don't know what to believe.'

'Ma!'

'Well, why has he kept you on when she's been with him over a year, if he knew nothing about her doing him? She's known to be a good, clean worker.'

'He didn't know from me.'

After a moment, during which Bridget's eyes bored into her daughter's, she turned to the fire, and took up her attitude of staring at the grate, her hands moving slowly back and forth along the rod. Her voice sounded muffled as she murmured, 'Mrs Grant said she found him in the kitchen with you this morning – you were having coffee together, and laughing; and all the time she was there he never came into the kitchen half a dozen times – he always used the front door.'

Through the righteous anger that was rising in her against Bessie Grant and her mother, and anyone who should think this of her, streaked a feeling of pleasurable surprise that he should have altered even slightly his habits since she had come to live in the house. But the pleasure vanished as quickly as it was born, for here was her mother half-believing Bessie Grant's implications. If Bridget believed this, what could be expected of others?

'I'd rather you left there,' said Bridget softly, 'rather than get yourself a bad name.'

Leave the house, and the river . . . and . . . and him . . . leave such a job, all because of Bessie Grant's spite. 'I'll not leave the job . . . I'll not leave there until he sacks me. As for what people believe – who's going to stop them if I leave tomorrow, when you believe what she said.'

Bridget turned in surprise at Rose Angela's tone. 'I don't want to believe it; but can't you see yourself it looks fishy? Why has he kept you on?'

'I don't know . . . I only know I've found a job I like, and I'm going to stick to it. And you can all think and say what you like.'

So finishing the most forcible words of her life, Rose Angela swung round and went upstairs, leaving Tony and Bridget staring after her.

Nothing could have confirmed her guilt so much in Bridget's eyes as this bold stand . . . her shy, timid Rosie to speak out like that! She could have come to such courage, Bridget reasoned, through one thing only – she was no longer a girl, she had been with that man. Bessie Grant had been right. The Rosie upstairs now was a different Rosie from the one who had returned so often from other places. A great sadness settled on Bridget . . . it wouldn't even be her own case over again, for such a man as the artist was, with money an' all, he wouldn't marry her. And if there was a bairn . . . Bridget was unaware of wringing her hands together until she felt Tony's hands gently unloosing her fingers. Impatiently she pulled them away from him. Here she was blaming her girl for what, all things considered, it was a wonder she hadn't done years ago, for even as a child she must have been aware of what was going on in the house between Tony and herself. Bridget dropped into a chair and bowed her head, saying dully, 'I'm to blame for this.'

Tony looked down on the beloved head and his face fell into lines of sadness. 'You mean, because of us, Bridget!' She did not answer the appeal in his voice, nor raise her eyes to his, and he went on, 'She could have been brought up a thousand times worse. You have nothing to blame yourself for – any blame there is rests on me; I badgered you into it. But I'd do it again and again if need be . . . Bridget, look at me.'

When she did not raise her head he took her face gently between his hands and lifted it to his. 'Don't worry, love' – he smiled down on her the gentle, comforting smile that had warmed her heart for years – 'she's your girl – she'll be all right. Do you know' – his smile broadened – 'looking at her just now I had the feeling she's coming into her own, somehow – she's been awakened.'

His artless words had other than the desired effect – Bridget groaned. 'Aye, she's been awakened all right!' she said.

CHAPTER TEN

THE RETURN

There was a wind blowing from the river, a cold, damp wind. It seemed to fill the cut with a solidness that had to be forced apart. Rose Angela pressed against it, head bent, and her coat hugged tightly to her. She was so cold that she felt she would never be warm again. All night she had been cold – the only warmth that was in her life had been wrenched out last night, not by Bessie Grant's accusations but by her mother believing it so rapidly. How could she? was the question she kept asking herself. Hadn't she left place after place to avoid that very thing? Her name now, she knew, would be so much dirt in the fifteen streets, not because she was suspect of being 'thick' with her boss so much as of having done Bessie Grant out of her job by it. What if the rumour should reach her master's ears? She shivered, imagining the violence of his reaction. Thank God the fifteen streets were miles away. To her knowledge he had never been there, nor was he ever likely to go.

Why was life like this? No little joy or happiness lasted; only the fears and hurts lasted, and the feeling of inferiority. And now the old tormenting questioning was upon her again: why, being a half-caste, were you credited with inheriting the lowest traits of both parents? The injustice had been hard to bear before, but now, since her mother, of all people, was holding her suspect, life looked black and hopeless. She could, of course, prove to her mother that she was wrong by giving up the job; but that would be madness – it was the best place she'd had since Mrs Kent's, and she knew, anyway, that now the job was hers she would never leave it until he sacked her.

After passing through the cut she again saw the Arab standing, sheltering from the wind, close against the wall. He made no move towards her, but said, with a strangely pleasant smile, 'Good morning; the wind is cold.'

Here was a coloured man in a foreign land who likely felt very much as she did. It should be natural to feel in sympathy with him, but all she felt was revulsion, yet so courteous was his greeting that she could not but answer him civilly, 'Yes, it is cold.'

'Can I speak with you a moment?'

'No, I'm late.'

'I won't keep you a minute. Don't be afraid – I mean you no harm.' He moved from the wall. 'Won't you let me talk to you?'

'No!' she shouted back at him, her walk on the verge of becoming a run.

Talk to an Arab! She had only to be seen doing that and . . . Once your name was coupled with an Arab you were . . . taboo. The word was associated in her mind with two girls she knew of who had 'taken up with' Arabs. One had married an Arab and gone to live in Holborn, the other wasn't married but just lived there – they were both taboo. Having heard the word connected with the disgrace of going with an Arab from her childhood, she now put no other construction on it; and she had plenty of fears in her life, she told herself, without a taboo being realised. To be accused of having a 'fancy man' was bad enough, but it was an entirely separate and pure thing compared with having your name coupled with that of an Arab. For a moment she thought of her mother, and, knowing the temper of the fifteen streets, she wondered at her ever being allowed to stay there with a black man. And she had been married.

Pete was outside the railway carriage, protecting a fire built in a hollow scooped out of the earth – he was kneeling, his back to the wind, holding the sides of his coat about it. He glanced up at her, but gave her no greeting, nor did the sombre expression on his face alter. Yet she knew he was very much aware of her, and had been before he glanced up. If, like Murphy, he was pleased she was being kept on he certainly didn't show it. He was a strange man, she thought, for only once had he spoken to her – the time he asked what her name was.

She wished that Murphy was about, for she felt that if she told him about the Arab he would walk with her to the Mill Dam each night, especially as the nights were cutting in. She remembered now he had asked her to be here at eight o'clock; yet he wasn't here. But when she reached the wharf she saw him talking to the guv'nor. They both turned at her approach and she shuddered at the dripping nakedness of 'the master' – he had just come out of the river and was pressing the water out of his hair with both hands. And once again she had the impression of immense strength. Her eyes barely touched him, yet in their flicking she was more acutely aware of Bessie Grant's accusation than she had been before.

His tone was unusually gay as he called to her, 'Breakfast, Rosie; and plenty of it.'

She surmised he was excited about this man coming, who must be even worse than Murphy and Pete to arouse his interest like this. Murphy had been strangely reticent about the new model when she questioned him shortly after her coming here, so she had not brought up the subject since. Doubtless she, too, would have been interested in the man's coming, but for last night – and her mother's reaction.

At nine o'clock the breakfast was over and the dishes washed, and the master was upstairs waiting for the man. She had orders not to leave the kitchen until he came. At quarter past nine he had not arrived, and Stanhope came into the kitchen, his good humour decidedly strained.

'Nine o'clock sharp he was to have been here. No sign of him, eh?' His laughter of yesterday was as if it had never been.

'No, sir.'

'I'll break that blasted Murphy's neck – he did this to me once before. It's my own damn fault – I shouldn't have given him a penny until I had the fellow here.'

Rose Angela made no comment, and he looked at her, his eyes narrowed and scrutinising. 'What's the matter? You all right?'

'Yes, sir.'

'Not bad or anything?'

'Oh no, sir.'

'Did you . . . have you come across Mrs Grant?'

Rose Angela replaced three plates on the delf rack before answering, 'She came to my home last night.'

'Ah!' The sound was expressive. 'Well, don't let her worry you – her notice was coming to her anyway. I was only waiting. If it hadn't been you it would have been someone else.'

She could find nothing to say, and as he left the kitchen muttering to himself about Murphy she thought that even the knowledge that Mrs Grant would have been dismissed in any case wasn't going to be much consolation to her now, for her mother wouldn't believe it.

Stanhope couldn't have reached the top of the stairs when a tap came on the back door. With hardly any interest, and with not the slightest emotion that could be indicative of a premonition, Rose Angela opened it.

The man confronting her was tall; he could at one time have been described as massive. He was still big, but it was merely the framework of bone. He was hatless and his frizzy black hair was greying to a whiteness about the temples. His neck, chin and the lower part of his cheeks were badly disfigured with deep pock marks; and one ear was distorted out of all semblance to an ear, and was twice its normal size. Rose Angela saw all these things at a glance – they were part of the dreadful and pathetic whole – yet her ready sympathy and pity was not touched by them, for she was filled with an incredible emotion. It had not come into her being at this moment at the sight of the man; it seemed to have been born when her body was born and to have lain waiting, to be touched into life on looking into this Negro's eyes. For the eyes resembled those she saw when she herself looked into a mirror.

She was conscious that her mouth was agape, and she felt dazed and stupid as if she had received a blow. She drew slowly aside and allowed him to step into the kitchen, and in his moving his eyes never left hers and hers became fixed in their amazement. She closed the door and stood with her back pressed to it and her hands gripping the sides of her apron. She was aware of the Negro's mouth working and his lips forming words that gave no sound. She saw his eyes glaze and a tremor pass down his body; then, outside herself, she heard the quick padding on the stairs again, and part of her mind shouted at her, 'Be careful!' But she still stood where she was, even when Stanhope entered the kitchen. He, however, did not notice her, for he was looking at the Negro, and when he spoke his voice was quiet, almost tender.

'There you are, then. So you got here.' Stanhope's eyes were devouring the Negro, moving over him with an ecstatic look such as a dealer would bestow on a rare gem.

'Yes, sah.'

The sound of the voice lifted Rose Angela immediately to the slack bank; the darkness was again around her, and she was smelling the rough smell of the jacket, a mixture of tar and mothballs and brine, and the voice that had lived in her mind only by the feeling of warmth its memory aroused was in her ears, speaking now, 'My Rose Angela – she mine.' She had never been able to remember one word from that night, but the simple 'Yes, sah' was the unlocking of the door, closed all these years, on the dim yet cherished memory. This was her da . . . the eyes had told her, and the voice wiped all doubt away.

'Come this way.' Stanhope held an arm out as if to guide the Negro, and added, 'Have you had anything to eat?'

'Yes, sah, thank you.'

He did not look at Rose Angela again, but went into the hall, guided by Stanhope's hand, and Rose Angela leant against the door, repeating stupidly to herself, 'After all these years . . . after all these years. It can't be. And to come here!' She could think of nothing clearly, her thoughts were racing and tumbling about. Only one impression stood out in the jumble of her mind – she was shocked at the sight of this man. If he was her da, and she had no doubt about it, he could not look more unlike what she had imagined. Only his eyes remained true to her picture of him, the picture her Uncle Tony had kept bright for years by saying, 'Your eyes are the same as your da's.' Her Uncle Tony . . . oh, her mother and Uncle Tony! What would her Uncle Tony do if her mother went back to her father? But would she go back? This wasn't the man she had married, not with all those pock marks and that ear. But the eyes must be the same as those her mother knew – gentle, with the gentleness lying deep in their warm brown . . . He mightn't look the same, but he was the same. Somehow she knew this. She looked up to the ceiling – up there was that great battered man who was her da. A faintness overcoming her, she groped her way to a chair and sat down. Mr Stanhope was painting him. What would he say if he knew? Would he look into his eyes and notice the resemblance? No, she doubted it. He would see the Negro as a whole . . . she shuddered . . . or what was left of the whole. The master was only interested in one thing, she thought – getting on to his canvas the last dregs of life. Yet Murphy had seen . . . or was it Pete? Yes, Pete's eyes saw everything. But he must have had something to go on. What? She would likely know later. Was this Murphy's surprise? He had asked her to come back this morning. What must she do now? Her thoughts raced again. What would happen when her Uncle Matt got to know? There'd be murder, for her Uncle Matt would surely overpower this great shadow of a man.

She sat on, her hands stretched out before her on the table and joined as if in prayer, until she was startled by two simultaneous sounds – the hall clock striking ten and a thudding from above. As she mounted the stairs she had to hold on to the banisters for support, and after she had tapped on the studio door she was thankful for the pause before Stanhope's voice called, 'Here!'

She went in, telling herself not to look towards the dais, but immediately her eyes were drawn to it. There he was sitting on the platform, his legs slightly apart and his hands lying palm upwards, one on each thigh. His back was supported by a cunningly contrived rotten hulk of a boat, kept in place by packing-cases; and the double effect of decay was such as almost to make her cry out.

Stanhope was standing before a full-length canvas, and as he softly called her to him his hand, moving the charcoal in swift, broken lines, did not stop, nor did his eyes stray from their darting back and forth to the platform.

'Make some coffee, Rosie, and bring some brandy up. And about twelve o'clock make a meal – something good. I'll have it up here. Bring enough for two.'

His voice stopped and she moved away without emitting the usual, 'Yes, sir.' As she reached the door she knew the Negro's eyes were following her, yet he was apparently gazing straight ahead. It was like the picture of the nun she had in her bedroom – wherever you moved the eyes followed you.

In the kitchen the old feeling of sickness threatened to overcome her, and it took all her will-power to conquer it. When she took the coffee up, Stanhope stopped work, and, pouring a generous amount of brandy into the cup, handed it to the Negro, saying, 'Drink this and have a break. How're you feeling?'

'All right, sah.'

The sound of the voice sent a pain through Rose Angela, and she knew a sudden longing to be alone and to cry. She stumbled uncertainly downstairs, and in the kitchen she had to upbraid herself, saying, 'It's no use going on like this . . . pull yourself together – he wants a dinner for twelve o'clock, and when he says twelve he means twelve; you know that.' But the upbraiding did little good and she commenced the preparations like a sleepwalker.

Once, going to the corner of the house where the dustbin was, she saw Murphy and Pete. They were standing looking speculatively towards the house from the edge of the clearing. She withdrew sharply from their gaze, for she wanted to talk to no-one yet about this thing . . . not until she had first talked to him. How long would the master keep him? As long as he could sit or stand, she supposed.

She made three journeys in all when she took the dinner up, but never once did she allow herself to look towards the Negro; yet when he rose and slowly stretched himself she was conscious of his every movement. Nor did she look at the master, for part of her was daring to question his gay mood – did this man's presence call for gaiety and bantering jokes?

As the afternoon wore on she wondered when she would get a chance to speak to him – she shied from using the word da, even to herself. Would she manage it when he came downstairs?

But she did not speak to him when he came downstairs, for Stanhope was with him, shepherding him as if indeed he was a precious jewel. He even walked out to the wharf with him, solicitous to the last moment, saying, 'Now are you sure it hasn't been too long? We'll cut it down tomorrow if it has.'

His gentleness and consideration sounded strange, this manner being utterly unlike that which he showed to Murphy and Pete. The Negro seemed to have adopted the tone Stanhope had set, for his voice sounded quite gay as he replied, 'No, sah. No hard work 'bout that – jus' settin'.'

'Well, I'm glad you think so. You'll be here the same time tomorrow?'

'Yes sah, same time.'

Through the window Rose Angela watched him walking away until he disappeared round the corner of the house. Stanhope, too, watched him until he disappeared from sight; then he came slowly into the kitchen, rubbing the palms of his hands together as if savouring his day's work.

'Well, what do you think of him? Marvellous specimen, isn't he?'

She turned towards her master – that's all he was to him, a marvellous specimen. For a second she felt a strong feeling of resentment against this man who saw misery only as something to paint; then it was replaced by a feeling of dread which his next words evoked.

'Poor devil, he's not long for the top . . . he'll be lucky if he sees the winter out.'

She put her hand up to her lips and closed her eyes, and his voice, for a moment, receded from her.

'What is it, Rosie? Are you ill? Come and sit down.' He placed a chair for her and she walked unsteadily towards it. His hand hovered uncertainly over her shoulder as if about to touch her. 'What's upset you today? Are you still thinking about Bessie?'

She gave a slight nod, and he went on, 'You're a silly girl. Look here, go and lie down on the couch in the drawing-room for a while, and go home as soon as you are feeling fit again.'

'I'm all right, sir.'

She rose to her feet, and he said harshly, 'You're not all right, but you'll do as you like, I suppose. You want to get this into your head – your life will be one long hell if you take notice of what the other fellow says – in this case the other woman.'

'Yes, sir.'

'Oh, for God's sake, don't agree with everything I say. And don't keep saying "Yes, sir".'

She marvelled at her own audacity when she asked quietly, 'What do you expect me to do – contradict you?'

His lips twisted into a smile that brought a boyishness to his face and his eyes twinkled at her. 'That would stagger me, wouldn't it?'

As he laughed she thought how she would have enjoyed this little exchange yesterday, or more probably the day before, but now she could think of nothing but what he had recently said. When she gave no reply to his bantering he went out abruptly, saying, 'Do what I tell you and get off home.'

He's not long for the top . . . he's not long for the top . . . the phrase kept repeating itself. Her da was not long for the top. She had scarcely met him, yet already she knew he was marked for death by the words that had always created pity in her – old so-and-so's not long for the top. Now pity for this great, battered, grotesque man began to rise in her; it obliterated the disfigured face – all she could see were the eyes, looking at her with love and pleading in their depth, and all she wanted now was to meet him and confirm the certainty of the kinship.

At six o'clock, as usual, she gave a last look round, adjusted the cloth cover on the supper tray and went out, closing the kitchen door behind her. She tried not to hurry, and her step was un-usually slow as she entered the chaotic jumble of wagons. She felt he would be waiting for her somewhere along here . . . but where? She must not miss him.

He was sitting on the step of the railway carriage; and at the sight of her he rose, and she went towards him, still walking slowly. When within a few feet of him, she stopped, and they took their quiet fill of each other.

'You know me, Rose Angela?' The appeal in his voice brought a pain to her heart.

'Yes.' She wanted to say 'Da', but she felt shy of the word.

'Long time, Rose Angela.'

'Yes.'

'You remember me, way back?' His voice was deep, yet had a hollow ring.

She nodded.

'All the years I want to see you . . . I think of you. But you more beautiful than I think.'

His voice cracked and the wet mist was in his eyes again, and she could bear no more. Her arms went out, and with a sound that was forced out of the suppressed depth of him he flung out his own, and they held each other. Their tears mingling, they stood pressed face to face, and as her lips touched his pock-marked cheek he let escape a cry as he had done on the day of her birth, but this time there were no words to it. After a time, during which neither of them spoke, she began to feel the shaking of his limbs as if the bones beneath his skin were jangling, and she said anxiously, 'Sit down.'

Like a child he obeyed her and sat down on the step again. 'You're cold,' she said, bending over him. 'Go inside.'

'No, I'm all right. Inside not very clean, but they not help it. Them good fellows . . . good fellows,' he repeated. He put up his hand to her. 'Sit down here, close by me, and you talk. All years I wait to hear you talk, Rose Angela.' His voice slurred over her name, making it sound like a caress.

She sat below him on the block of wood that formed the step, but she could not talk. Her feelings could not be interpreted into speech, but she bowed her head and pressed it against his knee and held his hands tightly with her own; and slowly the feeling was born in her that although she looked like and loved her mother, she was not of her, she never had been . . . she was of this man. Were he ten times as black, it would be the same.

He's not long for the top. As Stanhope's words came to her she sat up and looked into James's face. 'You're not well, you haven't been well – what's wrong?' she asked gently.

'Oh, that.' He shook his head and gave a laugh that was punctured by a little clicking sound in his throat that couldn't be called a cough. 'I was sick for time . . . but now me get like fighting cock.'

'What were you sick with?' she asked with concern.

He pointed silently to the pock marks on his face; then said, ''Fore this I was big fine fellow, go round with fair and boxed twice a day – twenty rounds I could take. But you wait' – he held her face lovingly between his hands – 'you wait. Now nothing stop me getting fit again.' So convincing was his tone that she believed him . . . She would look after him and get him well; she would spend on him the ten shillings a week she had intended saving to buy Christmas presents and clothes; she would feed him and feed him.

She asked suddenly, 'How did Pete and Murphy know who I was?'

He said again, 'Them very good fellows – them best fellows.'

'But how did they know?'

He turned his head away and looked across the river. 'I been in lower part of town three months, but I been sick. I want to go to fifteen streets, but no know how land lie. Pete, he scout for me; he talk to men around docks.' James paused, then looked at his daughter again. 'Matt still bad . . . still hate me . . . I no want to go to gaol before I see you little time.'

'Oh, Da!' the word escaped her.

'Long time I wait to hear that.' He stroked her cheek and went on, 'You no worry, I not go.' He touched the corner of her eyes with a gentle trembling finger. 'Pete, he say he knew you by your eyes – they like mine. When he think you my girl he ask your name, then Murphy, he make sure and follow you home. Me, I near mad 'cause I not come right away – I laid up with little cold.'

Not one word had he said about Bridget, and as Rose Angela gazed up into the eyes so like her own she knew why, and a hot flush covered her body. Murphy, in his scouting, would have heard more than just how her Uncle Matt felt – he would have heard, too, of the relationship that existed between Tony and her mother. That relationship would now have to end – her mother must be told. Her da couldn't return to the fifteen streets as long as Matt was there, but her mother could come to him here – he must want to see her so much. She forced herself to mention Bridget's name. Gently she said, 'My mother will get a shock, but she'll be glad.'

James looked away again to the river: 'No tell your mother, Rose Angela. She might come down here, and Matt, he guess. No tell anyone I here.'

For a moment she believed the reason he gave, and unwittingly said, 'But Uncle Tony . . . I could tell Uncle Tony; he would be safe.'

By the stillness of him she knew she had made a mistake, and she murmured, 'I'm sorry.'

He turned quickly towards her, reassurance in his tone. 'You no worry; I have all I want now I have you. We not be parted again, eh?'

The question had a timorous sound; and he inhaled deeply and slowly when, shaking her head, she said, 'Never again.'

123

After a silence, during which they each seemed to be savouring the other, James went on, 'Tony always good boy . . . him quite a man now.'

There was no bitterness in his tone, so she could say, 'He's always been very good to me.'

'Yes . . . that's what he promise: Me, I look after your Rose Angela, he said. Me, I tell her what a fine fellow you are . . .' His smile took on a piteous twist.

'He did – every Sunday for years he took me to the slack bank and talked about you.'

'He did?' There was some amazement in James's voice.

'Yes, for years; until I think he thought I was too big.' She did not even admit to herself that the Sunday walks had stopped from the time she happened upon her mother and Tony in the front room in each other's arms.

Again a silence fell between them; until James said sorrowfully, 'Me, I never thought I'd come back to you like this; always I dream I have pots of money, and always I see myself decking you out . . . I think I make so much money I even square Matt.'

As Rose Angela listened, her throat tight with tears, she knew that in a thousand lifetimes James could never have made enough money to placate Matt's hate – that was something beyond the bounds of bargaining or reasoning.

'You know I try and take you with me that night?'

He watched her nod.

'Yes, and I always mad I not do it. I could have got you away all right – not even old man know I was on board, and you were good child, quiet and making no trouble. You would have been all right in chief's cabin till ship got clear; then old man if he did find you not do nothing. Things been different perhaps if you with me.'

He shook his head musingly towards the river, and Rose Angela asked, 'What became of the chief?'

James straightened up on the step. 'Him die on next trip, when boilers bust. Sometime I tell you 'bout it . . . not now. Now we just talk of us, eh? Rose Angela' – he bent above her – 'will you take your hat off?' The request was humble, as if asking her to confer on him a great favour, but as Rose Angela's hands went readily to her head he stopped her with a warning movement of his hand, 'Sh! we got company; I hear somebody.'

Rose Angela had heard nothing, but, bending forward, she glanced between the wagons, and then saw the Arab.

'It's an Arab,' she said uneasily; 'he's always about here. He stands by the wall at the bottom of the passage nearly every day.'

James was in no way perturbed; in fact his expression showed pleasure. 'Oh, then, that be Hassan. He all right. Like me, he like river. Every day he come to river. He quite good sort, not like some.'

'Do you know him?'

'Yes – I work for him 'fore I was sick. He got eating-house . . . he quite rich man. But him not like some . . . him like the river and talk 'bout places and other peoples.'

She turned her head and watched the Arab coming into view, and she saw the blank look of astonishment appear on his face when he saw her and James together. James raised his hand to his forehead in salute, and after a moment, during which he stood stock still, the Arab, too, raised his hand; then came forward.

'You courtin' river again?' said James.

The Arab nodded and smiled, but his eyes rested on Rose Angela; and James, standing up, said with deep pride, 'This my daughter . . . you never believe I had white daughter that time I tell you, did you?'

The Arab continued to smile, and shook his head slowly. Rose Angela did not return his smile, but as she looked at him she thought, Now he will speak to me; if I meet him in Shields he will speak to me, and people will see us, and that will be the end of any name I have left. But this thought did not fill her with the usual fear and apprehension, and she wondered at it. Instead, she felt a new strength flowing through her veins, bringing with it courage. She looked at James. She had a da, and she was going to look after him and keep him safe. She had a feeling of belonging, of moving out of the inbetween world in which she had lived her life into another, more steady, planet. In this moment she experienced a sense of exhilaration in which she feared nothing or nobody . . . no – she made her mind gather the words together and present them to her – not even her Uncle Matt!

PART FOUR

CHAPTER ELEVEN

THE BOOKS

'Go ye down now and put yer spoke in and she'll do it.' Kathie leant across the table towards Cavan, who was sitting, his hands clenched on the arms of the chair, gazing stonily at her. 'She's got to do it. And why not for, I ask you? To let her brother sleep in her house a few nights. If it was her fancy man there wouldn't be two ways about it.'

Still Cavan said nothing, and Kathie went on, 'Christmas soon upon us an' all, an' ye know, none better, how we are fixed for coppers. It's worse I'm off since they put Terry on that job, with his tram fares and him eating like a ravenous loon, and wantin' pocket-money an' all . . . and now this to happen – to bring Matt up for a means test! God in Heaven, don't ye see it's less than nothing he'll get when they know Terry's bringing a penny in, an' us havin' a lodger an' all? But if he says he's sleeping out, for there's no place to sleep five of us in these two rooms, then he'll likely stand a chance of getting his full seventeen shillings. Don't you see?'

'Aye, I see.' Cavan's voice rasped like a jangle of steel filings. 'And he's not sleeping there! He can get a bed anywhere around for five bob or so a week.' As he glared at his wife he wondered if she was being purposely blind to Matt's feelings for Bridget – or was she just a fool?

'Five bob or so a week! Will ye listen to him! Five bob or so – the Virgin stand by me side and guide me. We have so much, sure we have, that we can throw five bobs about! Listen to me, Cavan McQueen. My Matt's goin' into nobody's house while his sister sports two rooms with not a soul lying in them.'

Cavan stood up. 'If she had ten empty rooms, he's not going there.'

'An' who the hell are you to say he's not goin' there?'

'I'm the same bloke who used to give you a hammerin'. It's a long time since you had one, but you're asking for it now.'

'Go on, ye little bantam, ye try it on.' Kathie stepped back from the table and rolled up the sleeves of her blouse.

'Oh, away to hell!' Cavan waved her off with a deprecatory move of his hand. 'Don't tempt me . . . only listen to this! We've heard the last of Matt goin' to Bridget's – do you hear that?'

Kathie was almost black in the face with the torrent of mixed emotions filling her great bulk – her thoughts moved from Matt and the means test to a more personal trouble – more than anything at this moment she desired that Cavan should hit her; his refusal to do so was like an insult. She watched him move towards the door, and so great was her feeling that her usual flow of invective was checked, and she stammered and stuttered, 'You . . . you . . . sod! I'll get even with you. Ye won't lift a finger to help yer own kith and kin, but I'll get even with ye – by God, I'll get even with ye before many hours have passed over yer head.'

The door banged and she was left yelling at the walls. 'I'll see me day with ye. Like me fine daughter Bridget ye are, getting too big for yer boots – with her loose piece of a girl giving her twenty-five shillings a week. And I know where that-'un'll end, too. And she's another mean sod, for not a penny has she given me since she started. But you' – she flung herself to the window and yelled fruitlessly – 'yer Rosie gives you a backhander, don't she!' The sound of her voice echoed around the walls, and the words seemed to fall about her and hurt her. She turned into the room and beat the table in her rage. He hadn't lifted a finger to her, and she had gone at him like that! Years ago, when the bairns were young, he often landed her one, and then he was sorry and she cooked him a good feed after; but now . . . now, nothing. Her head swung from side to side. Bridget and Matt were entirely forgotten, only her own failure confronted her. She could no longer rouse her man; nothing she did could touch him. How long was it since he last slapped her a wallop across the backside? Years; not since he had started that reading business. She no longer meant anything to him – she was just a fat hulk that he even turned from in bed at night. He wasn't always like that – by God, no! At one time she could say yes or nay, but not since he took to that reading. Her head stopped swinging . . . It was them books that had made him different . . . he wanted nothing but them books. Pity for herself turned to rage again. She looked towards the shelf that held eight books, all brown paper-backed and stacked according to their size. Cavan had made the shelf and hung it above the bed. As she stared, her fingers cupping one great breast began to twitch, and the fire dropping in the grate sent a glow into the darkening kitchen and showed up her mouth and eyes, stretching in their portraying of her thoughts. Who said she couldn't touch him? Didn't she say she'd get even with him? And what better way? She'd let him see she wasn't dead yet. Scorn her, would he? Sit there, hour after hour, reading and never a word out of him, never a laugh, never a joke? Well, she'd finish all that.

With three steps and a sweep of her hand the books were scattered over the bed and on the floor, and as she stooped to pick one up the enormity of her intention stilled her hand for the moment. Then with a growl which seemed to emerge from some dark depth, even beyond that of her enormous body, she gripped the pages and wrenched them out; and she threw them on the fire. But the dull glow of the cinders seemed to hesitate before sending even a small flame to lick their edges, and Kathie, taking a poker, scattered the pages, the more readily to catch the flame; and when they were alight she threw on the mutilated book cover. One book after the other followed until the fire was banked high with smouldering cardboard and blackened paper. And when there was no more to tear she thought of the box under the bed – she'd make a clean job of it. Scorn her, would he? She'd make him sorry he had ever imagined he could live without her. Once his books were burnt he'd be finished, for he'd never have the face to go into Shields to the library; even if he had the nerve he'd never go because he wasn't decently put on. And whichever way he went – Jarrow or Shields – it meant walking miles there and back; and he hadn't the boots, anyway. No, she had him right enough. Like some unwieldy animal she went down on her knees and dragged the tin box from under the bed.

Still kneeling, she went on working in a frenzy, pulling and tearing at the books and telling herself that no-one would slight her and get off with it; least of all that little rat who had chased her for months before she'd look at him. He'd thought nothing about reading in those days, nor did it matter a damn that she could neither read nor write.

That it was forty-five years ago Cavan had pursued her did not enter into her reasoning; nor had her illiteracy troubled her in the least until recently, when she imagined that part of Cavan's indifference was bred by scorn of her ignorance. She knew that the days of love-making were long past, and she herself was past wanting them renewed, but there had been little acts of endearment between them which, with the years, had taken the place of passion – such as him bringing her a wallop across the backside after being supplied with a good feed, or his feet searching and twining around hers in the night. But during the past two years even these had ceased.

Deaf to all sound but that of her rage, she did not notice the opening of the door; and so astonished was Eva's Johnnie at the sacrilege being perpetrated that he could not speak. For a time he remained still, watching his grannie; then silently closing the door, he ran off to tell his granda, whom he had just left standing at the corner of the street.

'Granda! Granda' – he flung himself against Cavan's legs – 'me grannie's gone off her chump – she's throwing your books on the fire!'

Cavan had not run for years, but now his running had an arrow's swiftness to it that far outstripped Johnnie's youthful legs; nor did his speed slacken until he reached the kitchen door. Still in his stride, he flung it open and was brought up sharply by the sight of the fire piled high with his treasures. Kathie turned and confronted him, pieces of charred paper clinging to her hair and face, which, with her frantic exertion and the heat, was looking like a great red balloon. For perhaps a moment Cavan stared at her, his mouth and eyes stretched wide; then rushing forward, he plunged his hands into the smouldering mass, and flinging handful after handful on to the floor, began to stamp on it, seemingly unaware that they were no longer his books, but small pieces of paper, most of them charred.

Standing amid the smoke and the paper, Kathie taunted him as he thrust his hands again and again into the now flaming jumble; and when, as if at a given signal, he stopped his vain efforts, her voice faded away in her throat, and she stood slumped, watching him looking helplessly down at the debris. He lifted his head and stared at her through the smoke, and she saw how useless had been her effort. Not even this would make him lift his hand again to her, for in his eyes was only sorrow and pain. Her flesh seemed to shrink from her bones as she watched the tears gathering in his eyes – never had she known her man to cry. She watched him stumble to a chair and sit down, and spread his burned hands out before him on the table; and when he dropped his head between them and began to sob, she, too, groped for a chair and sat down; and the knowledge that Cavan was not made hers again by the loss of his books but gone from her for ever made her great body tremble. Entirely forgotten now was the cause of the row, and she began searching her mind for a reason, asking herself what had led her to do such a thing. A surge of emotion she was unable to understand and had no power to control rushed upon her. Like a penance, it filled her with sorrow and regret; feelings that were both new to her, so new that they made her fearful – of what, she didn't know. She only knew that she was sorry and she must cry . . . she, who had laughed so much in her life, must cry as if for the first time. Slowly and painfully her sobs mingled with Cavan's; and the sound and the sight scared Johnnie, who was standing staring through the window; and since his mother wasn't in he ran to tell his Aunt Bridget.

Bridget was standing in her favourite position, hand gripping the brass rod and her eyes resting on the words 'Grieve Gillespie, Jarrow-on-Tyne' on the stove. How many times during the years had she faced a problem standing thus, and mostly about the man behind her now? She stood listening to his voice, soft and whining, and she thought for the countless time, Oh, if he were only dead! and for the countless time she was shocked and grieved at her thoughts.

'Just for a little while . . . I won't be in your way.'

'Matt' – her voice, too, was soft – 'I've told you. You can't stay here . . . Look, don't let's have any more rows over it – I've told you what I'll do – I'll give you a few shillings towards you getting a room for a week or two.'

'But why should I, when you've got two rooms doing nothing? And what'll folks say? They'll think it funny, I'll tell you, when me own sister won't take me in for a night or two.'

Bridget sighed. 'It's immaterial to me what people say.'

'Is it?' There was a challenge in his tone.

Bridget did not reply, and he went on, 'If your great managing director was to ask, he wouldn't be refused – he never has yet.'

'You know that's a lie!' She swung round on him. 'He's never stayed here at nights.'

'No, he gets what he wants before that.'

She raised her hand and dropped it helplessly. 'Matt – you're not staying here, and that's final.'

Bridget's rage was always more bearable to Matt than her indifference or her reasonableness. Now she was trying to be reasonable, to put him off with soft words, and it maddened him. Why was she trying to put him off? He knew why – because of that dirty half-caste. It was strange that although he hated Tony, the feeling was as nothing compared with that which even the thought of Rose Angela could rouse in him. Rose Angela still stood as a symbol of the thing that had taken his Bridget away from him; every part of her reminded him of the man whom he held responsible for his distorted face and the frustrations of his life.

Years ago he would have taken what he deemed his just revenge on Rose Angela's face, but for the knowledge that in doing so he would be cutting himself off for ever from Bridget. The hate of Rose Angela the child had been bearable because he knew that Bridget bore her no real love, but from the time he sensed the change in Bridget's affections his hate, when Rose Angela was present, often made it almost impossible for him to restrain his urge to destroy.

He would not admit to himself that the reason Bridget was refusing him was because she didn't want him in the house – he could not face the fact that his Bridget did not want him. She was, in his mind, the only one who did want him. And were it not for that 'un she would take him in like a shot; it was because of her he was being refused.

'I know why you won't have me here.' He addressed Bridget's back as she took a table cloth from the dresser drawer preparatory to laying the table. She did not answer him, and he went on, 'It's because of that 'un, isn't it?'

Still Bridget made no rejoinder.

'Well, it looks as if that reason will soon be moved.'

Bridget swung the cloth over the table.

'She's changed her fancy man. The funny thing is, the other bloke must be in the dark, as she's still working for him.'

'What badness are you concocting now?' Bridget's mouth was grim as she jerked round and faced him.

'I'm concocting nothing – it's the truth. She's picked up with one of her own kind.'

The muscles of Bridget's face sagged, and her voice shook as she said, 'Matt, be careful – I can only stand so much.'

'You'll have to stand this sooner or later; if not from me from somebody else.'

'Go on.'

'She's thick with an Arab.'

Bridget remained still.

'You don't believe me? Well, get on to Jack Rundall. He was with me the first time I saw them. She was standing talking to an Arab in the open near the ferry, as brazen as brass she was, and he eating her with his eyes.'

Matt was quiet now, both inside and out, for he had roused Bridget not to anger but to fear. Her face was stiff with it.

'No!' Her whisper was scarcely audible, but Matt heard it and said, 'It's true. And then there was last night, I watched her. The same Arab was waiting for her near the river, at the end of the cut that leads into Holborn. I saw them under the lamp. She gives him her hand and they start talking, then off they go, right into Holborn . . . into a café affair; and you don't have to be told what those places are.' His voice had assumed an almost sympathetic tone.

Bridget whispered again to herself, 'No, oh no, Rosie.'

Last night she was late – it was nearly nine o'clock when she came in. She had been late other nights, too, because, she said, there were some people staying with Mr Stanhope and she had to cook a late dinner. It sounded so feasible, and she had tried not to think there might be another reason for the lateness . . . and all the time she was going with an Arab. Oh God! Bridget folded her arms about her waist and began to rock herself . . . Not that, not an Arab. Yet could she be blamed? What example had she to follow? What had she thought all these years about her mother marrying a black man, not to speak of what she knew of Tony? . . . But an Arab! James had been handsome in his way, but the Arabs were like weeds. And then, what about her master?

Bridget had just said she cared nothing for people's gossip. For herself, she could bear it; but when it touched her daughter, it tore at her. Because of Bessie Grant, people had for months looked askance at Rose Angela, but now she would be stamped 'a real loose piece'; and she wasn't bad, somehow she wasn't bad. Lately when Bridget covertly watched her daughter's face she was forced to say to herself, 'If she's bad, then there's no good in heaven or earth.' No, she wouldn't believe it – Rose Angela would never go with an Arab, she had always been afraid of them. This was

134

another of Matt's tricks. He was evil – she stopped her rocking – but strangely enough he wasn't a liar. This fact forced itself on her mind and she muttered to herself, 'Oh my god, there must be something in it, somehow.' And Matt said Jack Rundall had seen her and all. If that was so, then most of the fifteen streets knew about it by now. Suppose they did to Rose Angela what they did to Rene Batten a few years ago . . . pelt her out of the streets. Oh Holy Mary, don't let this happen to my lass!

As Bridget sent up this fervent prayer Johnnie's voice came screaming up the yard, 'Aunt Bridget! Aunt Bridget!' And Bridget turned sharply as he burst into the kitchen, crying, 'Stop that yelling, you!'

'But Aunt Bridget' – he stood panting, the saliva running over his loose lower lip – 'there's hell on at me grannie's; she's burnt all the books an' me granda kept putting his hands in the fire and he's crying.'

'What! What you talking about?'

'They've been fightin'. Me ma's not in . . . oh, come on Aunt Bridget!' he pleaded. 'I tell you me granda's cryin'.'

Momentarily Bridget's personal worries were thrust on one side; but she looked suspiciously at her nephew, and, remembering his tendency to practical jokes, said, 'You're not having me on, Johnnie, are you, for I can't stand your games the day.'

'No, no, Aunt Bridget, strike me dead. They were rowin' and me granda went out and me grannie threw his books on the fire, and now she's cryin' an' all.'

Her ma crying! Bridget ran up the stairs for her coat, and when she returned to the kitchen Matt said, 'It'll be a damn good job if she has burnt the lot of them; he's been dotty since he got them books.'

If what Johnnie said was true, Bridget realised it would be nothing less than a catastrophe for her father, and as she hurried through the streets, Matt shuffling at her side, her own trouble was obliterated for the moment. If her da's books were gone, life would be finished for him. There were thousands of other books, she knew, but the motley assortment with their fund of varied topics were his books, even though sometimes she had been a little scornful in her own mind regarding his attitude towards them, thinking that he showed signs of senility in his treating them like children.

As they neared the back-yard door Matt exclaimed, 'By God, she must have done it . . . smell that?'

The yard was full of the smell of burning and Bridget's uneasiness grew; and when she entered the kitchen she was appalled at the sight of her parents sitting one each side of the table in utter dejection amidst the chaos of the room, but more so was she shocked by the look of her father. His already small body seemed to have shrunk and he now looked a tiny old man; and her heart was wrung when, lifting his brimming eyes to her, he said with the simplicity of a child, 'She burned me books, Bridget; she's burned all me books, lass.' It was as if he had said, 'She has burned all I hold dear in life; I am finished; there is nothing more to live for.'

That his dejection should then cause a slight irritation to assail her surprised Bridget. She knew her mother had done wrong in taking her spite out on him by burning his books, but need he take it like this? It wasn't as if he'd been a great reader all his life, and she doubted whether he understood one quarter of what he read. He remembered interesting facts and outstanding episodes, and delighted to relate his knowledge, also to pass on that which he gleaned from Ted Grant. But then again Bridget recalled that he had been happier during the past few years than she had ever known him to be, and her irritation vanished – he'd be happy no more.

She looked at her mother, pitiable with age and slobbery fat. She hadn't laughed so much lately. Strangely, in contrast with Cavan, she had seemed less happy these past two years. Was this why she had destroyed the books, because they had brought him happiness? But she was old, and she shouldn't feel like this. Yet, as Bridget continued to stare at her mother, the thought came to her that age brought no respite – there still remained the worries, the fears and hurts . . . the tearing of one human being to shreds by another. Life was ruled by emotion, and when emotion was frustrated this was the result – people died while they still breathed. And although, of the two, Bridget liked her father best, her sympathy at this moment went to her mother.

Rose Angela had been at Wharf House four months now. At times she could not believe this; it seemed like four years, or even fourteen, for the events before she came here were dim and dream-like in her mind, and no day up till today had been long enough for her. She wanted the hours to spread themselves so that she could savour the two great things that had come into her life – her father's return and their nightly meetings; and this other great thing, which she would not admit openly to herself but which made her days joyous and coloured her dreams at night with what might be if miracles could happen. But this latter had been thrust into the background and now only the thought of her father filled her mind. For last night she had left the house as usual at six o'clock and made her way to the spot where she always met James, near the railway carriage. But he was not there.

It was their custom, if it was dry, to walk along the river bank, but if a gale was blowing they shared the shelter of the railway carriage with Murphy and Pete. The railway carriage had been turned into winter quarters, the windows being covered at night with pieces of sacking nailed on to frames to hide the light of the fire in the home-made stove, and more recently, the light of a little lamp supplied by Rose Angela. Into the company sometimes came the Arab, Ali Hassan; and the contrasts of the men gave Rose Angela food for thought as she sat, silent mostly, listening to their individual tales – the Arab, the Negro, the dwarf who was half-Russian, and Murphy, born of an English mother and father unknown and brought up in the workhouse. And she often marvelled that never once in all the talks she had sat through was a swear word used in her presence. The courtesy with which they each treated her often brought a lump to her throat. It was as if she were someone of note – even a queen, she sometimes thought, could not receive more respect than she did. And the many sore places in her heart were soothed.

But last night her father was not waiting for her, nor was there any sign of Pete or Murphy, and she was filled with panic.

Hassan, waiting at the entrance to the cut, quiet and patient as always, seemed to her, at that moment, like a comforting angel, and she ran to him, crying, 'Oh, Hassan, where's me da?'

And he replied soothingly, 'Don't worry; he's a little sick and can't get out, but I'll take you to him.'

When she asked where Murphy and Pete were he said he understood they had gone that morning across the river, where, they'd heard, lay the chance of some odd work.

Rose Angela did not know where her father lodged. On this he had been firm. When she had asked him to tell her in case an emergency such as the present one arose, he had laughed and said, 'Me, I be ill no more now.' Nor did she know exactly what was wrong with him, for he would not talk about himself.

Hassan had called into his eating-house and collected some food, and as he led her along narrow streets and through short, black alleyways where she could see nothing but felt that in the thick depths figures were standing, she began to understand why her father had refused to bring her here; and on reaching the house, his firmness on the matter was made absolutely clear to her. The house was one of a number which led out of a yard, and the yard was approached by a passage from the street. The ground floor was in darkness and silence, but on the first landing pale shafts of light came from beneath numerous doors, and voices in strange tongues came to her. They passed another landing and mounted yet another flight of stairs, and the air, after the freshness of the river, almost stifled her. The prevailing smell was of dirt, dirt such as she had never yet encountered even in the worst part of the fifteen streets. Even before she followed Hassan into the room she was sick at heart for her father, but when she saw him in the rusty iron bed, his back supported against the bare rails, pity and love overwhelmed her. He grasped her outstretched hand, but he did not speak, for he was holding a rag over his mouth.

The beating of her heart stopped for a moment as she saw the red streaks on the cloth – consumption! Oh God! Yet he had no cough, just that little tickling sound in his throat. She imagined all consumptives coughed and spat, like that man who travelled on the Jarrow tram and spat into a bottle. She could never make up her mind which was the worst, spitting on to the floor or into a bottle. But her father to have consumption . . . and spitting blood with it! As his eyes looked into hers with unbearable love and tenderness she knew what she must do – she must come and live here and look after him.

During the past four months she had grown to love him with a love so deep it amounted to worship; and each day she was made more poignantly aware of what she had missed by being brought up without him, and of the unnatural load of fear that had been bred in her because of his absence. But now, the knowledge that he was near was building up in her a courage that had already ousted much of her fear. Yet there were always new fears waiting to be born. She had imagined he was getting better, for he looked better and talked as if whatever was wrong with him was now cured; but this – she knew what consumption meant, especially bleeding from the mouth.

They mustn't be separated again . . . for the time that was left to him she must be with him, even in this house.

She drew his head to her, and as he leant against her she felt him sigh, and a fresh surge of strength, like the strength that had once been his, flowed into her, and she knew she would need this strength if she was to stick to her decision. First, her mother must be told. To face Bridget and say 'I am leaving home, I am going to sleep in' would be the final confirmation in her mother's mind that she had 'gone wrong'; but far rather let her think she was living with Mr Stanhope than she was living in Holborn.

The simplest course for her, she knew, would be to tell her mother the truth, but there the simpleness would end, for she felt she knew her mother enough to know that even were there no Uncle Matt to be considered the return of this gaunt Negro into her life would fill her with nothing but pain and embarrassment, to say the least. It would also deprive her of what happiness she had with Tony . . . Rose Angela felt a separate pang of sorrow for Tony; he had been so good; he had lived his life just to serve her mother and her. No, things must remain as they were. Her father was wise – he knew the situation was only bearable as it was now. She could not tell whether he harboured any bitterness towards Bridget, for he never spoke of her, but she guessed there were a number of reasons why he did not want her mother to know of his whereabouts.

After a while, when she told James what she intended doing he became agitated, saying, 'No, Rose Angela, me better tomorrow. She not do this, Hassan, eh?'

Although Hassan said no and that it would be unwise to do so, his eyes were telling her that above all things he wanted her here, not in this house, but in Holborn.

Rose Angela was well aware of Hassan's feelings towards her, but so well had she come to know him that she no longer feared him, or resented the fact that he should love her; and at times she thought it a waste and a pity that he should care for her as he did, for never could she return a spark of such feeling. Even if this other great love had not come into her life, she would have never considered Hassan.

To soothe James she had complied with his wishes of last night and had gone home, but she had been borne down with anxiety. This morning she'd had to wait until word was brought to her regarding his condition for she could not have found her way to the house alone. Murphy came in the middle of the morning, and his words 'I'm afraid, miss, he'll soon kick the bucket' had decided her. She told Murphy that as soon as she was finished work she would go home and get her things, and she asked if he would meet her at the cut and take her to the house. She also asked him if Hassan had sent for a doctor, and Murphy said he had.

There were still two more hours before she could leave. She longed intolerably to get away, yet she shivered at the thought of facing her mother.

She was brought from her thinking by her master entering the kitchen. He had not 'thumped' for his afternoon tea – at least she didn't think he had. 'You didn't knock, sir?' she asked.

'No – I thought I'd have it down here – it's warmer. Not in your way?'

'No, sir, of course not.'

She began immediately to get his tea, thinking that if only she hadn't so much on her mind she could enjoy this moment. Twice before during the past few days he had taken his tea with her and talked to her, and she had lain awake at night thinking over the things he had said. She looked at him now, sitting in the basket chair by the little blue stove, and it came to her that he seemed lonely; and another phrase was added to that feeling which she thought could not be enlarged.

He startled her by turning his head suddenly and holding her gaze. 'You look pale today, Rosie. Are you over-working?'

'Oh no, sir.'

'You don't still take notice about that wash-leather business I barked at you when you first came, do you? I always used that technique on the types they sent me from the agency. You see, I was a lone man and I found they always wanted to run me as well as the house; that wash-leather was a very good way of putting them off.'

She smiled and said, 'You mustn't have been fierce enough, sir; it had no effect on me.'

'I'm glad of that.'

She turned from his eyes and began to set the tray; and he looked into the fire again, and a quietness that was weighed with peace filled the kitchen; and Rose Angela forgot for the moment what lay before her this evening.

'Rosie, would you mind coming in on Christmas Day?'

'Not at all, sir. I expect to.'

'If Mr Collins is here I won't ask you, for then we'll go out somewhere.'

'It won't matter in the least, sir. I'll come in.'

'Rosie' – he was still looking into the fire – 'what do you want most? Is there something that you've longed for and never been able to have? Tell me – I want to give you a Christmas present.'

She stopped in the act of pouring his tea out. What did she want most? That her father should be better. He couldn't give her this; but the other great desire he could fulfil, and him only. Her face began to burn and although his eyes were not on her she turned away in case he should look up and see what madness she had come to. It was one thing to surrender her soul to him in the deep privacy of her being, but it would, she thought, destroy itself through exposure.

'I've . . . I've never wanted very much, sir; I have all I want – a job, a very good job,' she added.

'Oh, Rosie, for God's sake don't be so humble.' He was aggressive again, his jaw thrust out and his eyes glinting. 'You shouldn't be humble; there's nothing about you to create humility. Why, you could—' He paused. 'Look; tell me truthfully; is there anything you've ever dreamed about?'

What words he used! She pushed the little trolley up to the fire, and now she was near him, looking down into his face, into those startlingly blue eyes. What could she say? Could she say a wireless? But that would be so expensive. A fur? Oh no . . . some little thing – a brooch.

'Perhaps a brooch, sir.'

'A brooch!' His tone ridiculed the word. 'You're a disappointment, Rosie.'

'Yes, sir.'

'Sit down and have some tea with me.'

She hesitated for a moment, and he yelled, 'Go on, sit down, woman! There, you've got me bellowing again . . . you shouldn't cross me.'

As she sat down on the opposite side of the hearth to him she caught the glimmer of a twinkle in his eye, and her own was forced to respond, and they laughed together.

'You must think me a funny old man.'

'I don't think you old, sir.'

'Well, I am; I'm nearly twice your age. I'm close on forty.'

'You don't look it, sir.'

'Nice and polite of you. Why are you not married, Rosie?'

The abruptness of the question caused her to stammer, 'Well . . . well . . .'

'I suppose you're waiting until you have enough money.'

'No, I am not waiting.' To herself her voice sounded cold and unemotional, giving no indication of the inner turmoil. She was conscious of drawing herself up, as if to defend her pride, as she went on, 'I've never been asked.'

He continued to look at her for a time before saying softly, 'There are more damn fools in the world than I thought.' Then he returned to his previous question. 'Now, tell me the truth, what would you like for Christmas? . . . Besides a brooch, that is. By the way, I hate brooches, and I can't stand women who plaster themselves with jewellery.' He looked so aggressive as he said this that she was forced to smile again, thinking it was well she knew him.

'There's nothing really, sir.'

'Well, I'm not buying you a brooch. I'll give you the money and you can get what you like.'

'That's very kind of you, sir.' She turned to the table to hide her pleasure at this, for above all things at the present time she needed money.

'You know, Rosie, you are the most formal individual I have ever come across. Tell me, are you afraid of me?'

'Oh no, sir.' Her assurance was so sincere that there was no doubt that it was true; but he went on, 'Then if you're not afraid of me you are of someone or something.'

Rose Angela looked down at her plate and broke her cake into small pieces. 'I have been afraid of many things in my life, but lately they have all gone, or nearly so.'

She said no more, and he did not press the question, but continued with his tea in silence until she rose and went to the oven; and he asked, 'What have you in there? It's a lovely smell.'

She called back to him from the scullery, 'It's your Christmas cake, sir'; and he repeated laughingly, 'It's your Christmas cake, sir.'

When she returned to the kitchen he was standing by the table, and as she readjusted her apron and straightened her cap he nodded towards her head and said, 'It still isn't straight.' There was a quirk to his lips.

She flushed and said, 'It's my hair, nothing will stay on it.' And she again attempted to straighten the cap.

'That's another thing I detest – caps. Take it off and never wear it again.'

She paused, her hands raised to her head, and at his next words her feelings almost suffocated her.

'You are very beautiful, Rosie.'

As her hands brought the cap from her head she forced her eyes from his in case she should betray herself, and the wisdom of this was given to her as he went on, his tone brusque again, 'Don't worry . . . I am merely paying you a compliment.'

He went out in his quick, bustling way, and she sat down by the table, the cap still held in her hands. 'You are very beautiful, Rosie . . . I am merely paying you a compliment.' Was that the artist speaking or was it the man? She sat quiet until the chimes of the clock from the hall told her that soon it would be time to go, and there were other things that she must think of; and she wondered why everything should have come into her life at once . . . her love for this man, and the coming of her father . . .

Rose Angela's nervous system was like a highly tensed wire. The fears of her childhood and teens had played on it with such regularity that it responded with a feeling of acute sickness and anxiety when anything of a worrying nature affected her. Now, as she faced Bridget, she felt so sick that it was as much as she could do to stand. She had told Bridget that Mr Stanhope had people staying and that she was going to sleep in for a little while. She had managed to face her mother's blank stare as she said this, but under Bridget's silence her new-found courage was failing her. She knew that her mother did not believe a word she said, yet she forced herself to go on bluffing. 'It'll only be for a little while. I'll still let you have something each week . . . perhaps it won't be so much for the time being, as . . . as I'm living in.' It would have been difficult enough to lie if Bridget had believed her tale, but under the circumstances she was finding it almost impossible.

'Are you going to live with your master or the Arab?' Bridget's voice was without tone or colour. It seemed like the voice one would expect to hear from the dead, could the dead speak.

Rose Angela mouthed 'The Arab?' without any sound coming from her lips, and Bridget said, 'Yes, the Arab . . . you are going to live in Holborn, aren't you, where you've spent a good many of your evenings these past weeks?'

Rose Angela could only stare at her mother. It was Hassan she was meaning . . . someone had seen her with Hassan. But who? It had always been dark when she saw him, except that once by the ferry, and then there had been no-one about . . . Oh, this was worse than anything she had ever imagined. Her mother mustn't go on thinking this. Oh no, she couldn't let her think this. She must tell her about James, no matter what it entailed: Matt's vengeance and Tony's unhappiness; she must tell her. She could have allowed her to go on thinking she was Mr Stanhope's mistress, but not this. To have married an Arab would have been bad enough, but to casually live with one . . . no, she would be foolish to allow anyone to think this, most of all her mother.

Relief flooded her with the knowledge that she was about to straighten things out, and she put out her hand to Bridget, saying, 'It's true I'm going into Holborn, but just to – well, lodge there.'

Bridget did not take the proffered hand, and as Rose Angela, knowing that she was about to give her mother a shock, said gently 'Sit down a minute, Ma', there came to her the sound of stormy voices from the back yard, and one at least brought the sickness over her again.

Within a second Matt and Tony were in the kitchen, and Matt, not pausing from his battle of words, directed the onslaught of his bitterness against the thorn that was forever in his flesh. 'That's the cause of all the trouble – there!' He thrust out his arm and pointed his finger at Rose Angela.

'Don't be so daft, man; she wasn't here when your ma and da were rowing.' Tony, too, was angry and his nose was twitching rapidly.

'She didn't need to be, but it was through her. She's at the bottom of everything. If me ma goes off her head I swear to God I'll kill her.'

'It'll take a lot to knock your ma off her head,' said Tony, scathingly.

'What is she, then, but nearly daft, running round the streets begging folks to give her books for me da?'

'That's remorse for the thing she did to him, and it'll do her good to feel like that, but it'll take more than that to knock her off her head . . . It's your old man you should be worrying about, not her. She's burned more than his books the day.'

Matt was not in the least concerned about his father, but his dauntless, laughing, loud-mouthed mother had always held his respect, and during the last few hours she had shocked him by going soft and begging the silent Cavan to forgive her, promising to get him all the books he could ever read. To Matt, her final humiliation was her actual begging for books, and it was all because Bridget wouldn't put him up for a night. And why wouldn't she? Because of that Arab whore.

'If she has,' he answered Tony, 'who's to blame but that dirty Arab supplier? Whites don't suit her now, she must get herself an Arab.'

Before Tony could bring out a startled exclamation and the sound of Bridget's groan escaped her lips, Rose Angela's voice rang through the kitchen louder than it had ever been raised in that room before. 'How dare you say such a thing! You're a liar! Do you hear, a liar!' There was no sign of fear in her as, for the first time in her life, she faced up to Matt. 'You and your filthy mind! You're like a sewer.' She turned from him and confronted Tony. 'Uncle Tony, do you believe I'm going to live with an Arab?'

'No, lass. I'd never believe that, never.'

'Then why,' put in Bridget beseechingly, 'are you going to live in Holborn, lass? Tell us that.'

The three stared at her, hanging on her reply.

Rose Angela looked from one to the other, and as her lips opened her eyes came to rest on Matt. She had only to say 'because James is there' and she would be clear; yet in doing so she would be handing him over to this maniac. She couldn't do it. She knew from the look in her mother's face that she believed the worst of her, and now even her Uncle Tony's expression was showing bewilderment and doubt at the mention of her going to live in Holborn. She looked at her mother again; then dropped her lids to shut out Bridget's tortured gaze and turned away, saying flatly, 'No matter what I said, you wouldn't believe me. Think what you like, I'm going to get my things.'

Matt hadn't spoken since she had called him a liar. To say the least, her bold front had startled him, and it was strange that he, who in the first place had accused her of going with an Arab, was now the only one to believe her when she denied it, even in spite of having with his own eyes seen her talking to one. He was astute enough to know that it had taken a very powerful emotion to arouse that outburst against himself, for he knew that he could instil the fear of God, as he put it, into her. He stood, his eyes fixed on the staircase door, awaiting her return and asking himself the question 'Why should she be going to live in Holborn, if not with somebody? And if it wasn't the Arab, then who was it?'

The gas began to flicker, and Bridget, moving heavily towards the mantelpiece to get some coppers from the toby jug for the meter, shoved him aside, and in putting out his hand to steady himself he touched the fretwork pipe-rack on the wall, the hated relic of the damned nigger! His whole instinct was to whip his hand away as if it had come in contact with molten steel, but his hand remained still as something clicked in his brain, and his widening eyes seemed to draw from the pipe-rack the answer to his probing. Slowly his fingers began to move into the holes, until they hung like talons from the rack. God Almighty! Could it be? Who else?

The gas went up with a plop and Bridget came back into the kitchen, and Matt turned from the pipe-rack and looked from her to Tony. Who else. Who else? They didn't know, they suspected nothing. Nobody knew, only that half-black rat up there. Hadn't she nearly given the game away to clear herself, just a minute ago? She had pulled up only just in time. No, nobody knew but her . . . and now him. God Almighty!

Slowly he began to rub the scar on his face. How long was it? Sixteen years . . . sixteen years! His fingers nipped the flesh about the scar at the corner of his mouth. Sixteen years he'd carried this, sixteen years of nights he'd lain tossing and turning. He looked back to the days when he had laughed with the lasses. He had wanted nothing from them but to laugh with them, not even to touch them. There was only one woman he had wanted to touch. Yet from when they laughed no more with him a desire to extract something from them had arisen, adding to the torment of his days and the agony of his nights; and now he who caused all this was back. He must be . . . that was the only answer to that lily-livered rat up there having the spunk to face him. Perhaps all these years she had been on the look-out for the nigger – she'd had it ground into her enough as a bairn by that blasted fool Tony that her da would come back. He'd heard him at it time and again before he got thick with Bridget. A pain like a knife twisting in his bowels went through him, and his fingers moved up the scar, nipping the silver flesh into momentary redness . . . Well, if his surmise was right, Master Tony would soon have the tin hat put on him; he knew his Bridget well enough to follow her reactions to the nigger's return.

He turned his eyes to the staircase door. She would get brave, would she? By God, she'd need to be brave before he'd finished with her. Stand up to him, would she? He'd see about that. He'd plaster her name with the Arab's so thick about the fifteen streets that she wouldn't dare put her nose inside them, much less come home again to live. If her own mother and Tony could believe she was thick with an Arab, how much more gullible would be the neighbours. And what about the painter bloke? Aye, what about him!

And if she was willing to forgo what was left of her good name to cover up for the nigger, it would be the crowning thumb-screw on her if he nabbed him – and by God, nab him he would, or die in the attempt.

CHAPTER TWELVE

THE END OF THE WAITING

Rose Angela would have laughed to scorn anyone who would have told her a fortnight ago that there were many worse places to live in than the fifteen streets, and that there would come a time when she would miss them, miss the privacy of a house, of going upstairs to bed, of walking from one tiny room to the other, and miss the streets themselves, and the greetings and conversation thrown carelessly across their narrow widths; for in Holborn the tongues were many and varied, and she never could make out whether the neighbours in the rooms around were rowing or merely talking.

She saw very little of her neighbours, or of Holborn itself, for she went out in the dark of the morning and returned in the dark of the evening, yet the atmosphere pressed down on her and was as strange as that of a foreign country. But her days were too full to allow the change to penetrate farther than the fringe of her mind. What did penetrate and cast a shadow over her days was the rift between Bridget and herself. She wondered if anyone before had experienced so much happiness and unhappiness at the same time; there was James's love and this other love, but they were unable to ease the separation from her mother. She did not much care now what the people of the fifteen streets or of the town thought about her, but she still cared very much what Bridget thought. But for this, she felt there could be no-one happier; her da was so much better – it seemed as though her presence had given him a temporary lease of life; and then this impending thing; for she did not hide the fact from herself that something was impending and that she was waiting for it, waiting with her heart racing so fast at times that she thought such emotion could not be borne and that something within her was bound to give way.

What would happen when at last her master spoke? She knew what would happen – she would become his mistress and so qualify for the name the fifteen streets had already given her. If this thought brought with it a sadness, she told herself she'd rather be his mistress than any other man's wife. Two weeks ago she would not have allowed herself to dream of becoming his mistress, for to her mind he had given no indication that he thought of her other than as a very good servant; but from the night he told her she was beautiful there had been a decided change in his manner towards her. For the three days following he almost ignored her, never looking at her, and when he spoke his voice was harsh and more clipped than usual; nor did he stay in the kitchen either for his morning coffee or for his tea, but used it merely as a passage from the hall to the wharf. Although the weather was at its worst, he spent most of his time on the river, and after one severe day he developed a cold. It was the cold that broke down his defence. He remained indoors the following day, and Rose Angela, without being summoned, took up a hot drink to the studio. He was painting on a small canvas, and on her entry he took the canvas off the easel and laid it face upwards on the table in the corner of the room, saying, 'I didn't knock.'

'I know, sir, but I thought you needed this.'

For the first time in days he looked at her. 'What are you thinking, Rosie?'

'That you should be in bed, sir.'

'That all?'

'You have a nasty cold.'

'I know I have – and I'm annoyed. I've never had a cold for years, and you're to blame.'

She didn't ask the inane question 'But why me?'; she just looked at him, her skin growing pink and the brown of her eyes deepening, and he turned from her, saying, 'You are either so full of humility, Rosie, that you are not quite woman, or you are so full of the wisdom of the serpent that you are laughing at me.'

She did not at the moment try to unravel his references; only one thing was clear to her and that was she was not laughing at him – whatever feeling he had for her could not arouse her laughter. He said no more, and she went downstairs.

Although, since then, his manner towards her had been gentle, he did not resume his habit of sitting in the kitchen; and she knew he was fighting her, and at times this knowledge filled her with glory and she waited, doing nothing to precipitate the moment yet longing for it to come about.

He was out now, in Newcastle she thought, for he had said he might not be back before she left. Only twice before had she seen him 'dressed', as she put it, and today she thought he looked very grand; and she knew a qualm of fear – his heavy tweeds and large trilby seemed to remove him from her – he looked too grand. Could anyone like him think of her in the way she was imagining? Yet she thought of his words as he left the house. 'Don't wait for me, Rosie, I may not be back before six,' and it seemed to her that he wanted them to convey the opposite meaning – it was as if he were saying 'Wait for me'. It would have been nice to have waited, on the pretext of giving him a hot meal, but she knew how much her da longed for her return, and she never kept him waiting a minute longer than she could help.

It was now half-past five and she went around the house doing the final touches of the day, building up the drawing-room fire, taking the counterpane off the bed and turning back the bed clothes; and as she left his room she glanced towards the flight of stairs leading to the studio. How empty the house was without him up there . . . even if she never heard him for hours his presence would seep down to her. The feeling to be nearer to the things that were part of him now enveloped her and she went slowly up the stairs and into the first studio. She did not switch on the light but passed through into the other, the room where he spent most of his life. She pressed one of the switches on a board near the door and the light appeared high up in the far corner of the ceiling. This was part of the system of lighting by which he worked at night. A reflector directed the light on to an easel, on which stood the small canvas he had been working on for days. She had not seen this picture, for his breadth always obscured it, and once she remembered him taking it down when she was in the room. Now she moved towards it and saw it was hidden behind a covered frame clipped to the top of the easel and leaving only a narrow strip of the canvas visible. Gently she lifted up the frame and stood staring at the picture . . .

Had she known this was what she would see? Was that why she was drawn up here? Did she really look like that, her mouth half smiling and her eyes sad? But were her eyes as sad as that? And her hair . . . did the coiled plaits appear like a silver and black halo where the light touched them? Surely she didn't look like this. No, this wasn't meant to be the picture of the self that she saw in the mirror, it was rather the picture of what she knew herself to be inside. The little things she laughed at were there in her lips, but the fears of her life were in her eyes. She unhooked the frame from the easel and the light fell full on the picture. And now she was confronted with another aspect . . . she looked superior, or, to use the fifteen streets' term, 'stuck up'. But she wasn't stuck up – no-one could be less stuck up – for what had she to be stuck up about? Nevertheless, there it was on the canvas. Was this how he saw her? She moved back and sat down and stared at the portrait, her hands gripped tightly in her lap. No matter how he saw her, he had painted her, and hadn't he said, 'I never paint women?'

'Well, what do you think of it?'

She swung round on the stool, her hands clutching the front of her dress. He was standing in the doorway, still in his outdoor clothes, and the sight of him made her dumb. She was afraid of having been found here, for this was his sanctum sanctorum, and it was an unwritten law that it would always be held as such.

As he walked towards her she turned to the canvas again; and when he stood behind her and she felt his coat against her shoulders a painful stillness filled her.

'Do you like it?' His voice was unsteady.

Still she could utter no word. His hand came down on her shoulder and moved slowly to her chin, and as her head was tilted back the stillness vanished; the waiting was over, and wave after wave of trembling happiness washed through her as she looked up at his great tousled head.

Now his other hand was on her face, cupping it. 'You know, Rosie, don't you?'

She closed her eyes against the light in his and felt herself swung round and to her feet.

'You know I love you. For God's sake say something! Stop me making a fool of myself. I know I'm a damned fool, but I can't help it. God knows I've tried.' He pressed her clasped hands into his chest. 'Tell me I'm not a fool . . . tell me, Rosie.'

Still she could release no words; it was as if her happiness had locked all expression of itself within her; but she leant towards him and all that her being held was in her eyes, and he kissed her, kissed her with a fierceness that met and satisfied the deep demand that lay hidden beneath her calm exterior. She stood crushed in his arms, pressed into him, almost crying from sheer happiness.

'Rosie; Rosie; Rosie—' With each murmur of her name he rocked her gently. 'How I've longed to do that. For months and months I've longed just to do that . . . even from the very first day. Do you know you've driven me nearly mad?' He held her from him. 'I'd sworn never to paint another woman, and you see what I had to do?'

Dimly she registered the fact that he had at one time painted women; and a woman was likely the reason why he had stopped. But what did anything of his past matter? He was hers now . . . hers . . . hers.

She was in his arms again and he was murmuring into her hair, '"What's your name?" I asked you that first day. Do you remember? "Rose Angela Paterson", you said. Rose Angela. There has never been anyone more like their name, half flower, half angel.'

She lifted her head and laughed at his flowery exaggeration, such a gay, happy, free laugh that she could not believe it came from her; and with a naturalness as if she had spoken it instead of merely thinking it every day she said his name . . . 'Michael.'

'Say that again.'

'Michael.' Her lips shyly framing the word seemed to hold it while she drew fresh joy from the utterance. As she was borne away on his emotion, part of her questioned the reality of what was happening. But reality or dream, it did not matter as long as she remained in this state.

'Come' – he took her by the hand and led her to the door – 'I've something to show you . . . something that you asked for.'

149

But at the door he stopped; and there was laughter in his eyes. 'What do you want most, Rosie? Tell me. But this time I want the truth, mind.'

And when she gave him the answer she had wanted to give him that night in the kitchen he swung her off her feet and up into his arms and carried her down the stairs.

She made no protest, but lay against him; and as he sat her down in the drawing-room, saying like a boy with his first love, 'I'll never let you walk up or down those stairs again – it will be an excuse to hold you,' she dared to say teasingly, 'Even when you bellow for me?'

His face became serious. 'To think I ever bellowed at you!'

Diffidently she put up her hand and touched his cheek. 'I used to long for you to bellow so that I could come up to you.'

He was on his knees, his arms about her again. 'You love me, Rosie?'

'Yes . . . oh yes. I've always loved you, right from that first day when you looked down on me from the window and said, "I don't want a model." '

'And all the time you put me off, by looking either frightened or aloof . . . You'll never look afraid again; from now on I'll make your life such as no fear will touch it.'

She moved her hands through his hair. 'It all seems too good to be true.'

'Nothing will be too good for you . . . I'll take you travelling – I'll show you the world. Not that I think much of the world at the present moment, but you must see places. We'll go through France to Germany, and through the Black Forest . . . you'll like that.'

She answered slowly, 'Yes, perhaps . . . but I don't know. I can think of no better life than to stay here in this house with you.'

'Rosie, your humility is painful, but I love you for it. Where's that damn box?'

He patted his pockets and dragged the greatcoat that he had flung on to the carpet towards him. 'There' – he thrust the small parcel into her hands – 'that's what you asked for.'

She undid the wrapping, and she flashed him a look of gratitude before opening the black box lying in the palm of her hand. It would be the brooch. It was the brooch, but such a one as she had never seen before. In an oval of finely wrought silver lay a rose worked in stones glinting with red and purple lights. She had no knowledge of precious stones, but she knew that in this exquisite setting lay something of great value, something that she was afraid to accept.

'Well, what do you think? You asked for it, you know; though what you want a brooch for God alone knows. You shouldn't wear jewellery – you have all the jewels you need.' He moved his fingers round the circles of her eyes.

'It's beautiful; but it's too much.'

'Too much!' he scoffed. 'Rosie you are the only beautiful woman I have met . . . in fact the only woman, beautiful or otherwise, who didn't think she was worth the earth. You must put a greater value on yourself.' He pressed her face tightly between his hands. 'After you've lived with me for a while you will – I'll make you know your own value . . . Oh, my love!' He laid his head on her breast; and his voice took on a touch of sadness. 'You don't know what you've done for me. I never thought I'd allow a woman into my life again. Years ago I received a nasty knock and it turned me against all your kind, but from the moment I first saw you, you changed that. And then to find you possessed a sense of fair play – you seemed too good to be true.'

He lifted his head, and she looked down into his eyes, the blue now dark and soft, and her mind was awhirl with the wonder of him and his love for her that was making him tremble. At last. At last life was coming right. You only had to wait and be patient and happiness came to you. Oh, Holy Mary! She felt she wanted to go down on her knees and pray. But the thought of praying brought a self-consciousness with it; if he didn't mention marriage – and she was sensible enough to know that there was very little likelihood of him doing so – and she went to him, as she knew she would, what about praying then? It didn't matter . . . nothing mattered but him. What was marriage and religion, anyway? Look at the lives the married people led in the fifteen streets . . . good Catholics, too! She would let nothing come between them. She would take this love whichever way it was offered and stand the consequences. But the consequences could only be good. And as she listened to his voice she felt the certainty of this.

'That day you told our enterprising Mr Pillin what you thought of him, you didn't know I was in the boat alongside the wharf, did you?' She shook her head. 'I had started up the river, but found there was some gear missing, and when I came back you were in the thick of it. You did something for me that day, Rosie: you more than saved me nearly two pounds a week; you gave me back my faith in human nature – the female side, anyway. It was surprising to know that a woman could be honest – a beautiful woman – and just for the sake of honesty, with no ulterior motive behind her action. Oh, Rosie, Rosie, I love you for so many things.' He gazed at her tenderly. 'What are you going to do about it?'

The onus was on her, and it brought the colour flooding to her face. She shook her head and swallowed, and he asked gently, 'Would you . . . would you come and live with me, Rosie?'

Her eyes fell away from his and she said simply, 'Yes.'

'Rosie! Oh, Rosie, my dear!'

He held her gently, and a silence fell on them that was not entirely devoid of embarrassment.

He rose from her side, saying, 'We'll have a drink, then dinner, eh?' But he hadn't reached the cabinet before she was on her feet, protesting, 'Not tonight! I'd forgotten the time . . . I must go home.'

'What! Now?' He turned in surprise. 'But you can't, Rosie.' He came towards her, his heavy brows gathering into a furrow. 'You don't mean to go yet.'

'I'll have to. Look, it's quarter to seven. He . . . they'll be worrying.'

'Surely not for an hour or so? Stay and have something to eat with me, and then I'll take you home. I've always wanted to take you home . . . next to keeping you here.' He stood close to her, not touching her, but his eyes tracing each feature of her face.

'Oh, I'd love to stay . . . you know I would.' She took his hand and held it to her cheek.

'Then why don't you?' He covered the hand that held his with his own.

'Because they're expecting me.'

He remembered it was Friday and she had been paid, and he surmised it was for this they would be waiting.

'All right, then, but I'm taking you home.'

At this her mind whirled into a panic, and saying she must get her things she turned from him . . . He thought she was going to the fifteen streets. What would he have to say to her living in Holborn? And what further would he say when he knew the Negro was her father? He would have to be told, but not tonight. Anyway, she must hurry. What on earth would her da be thinking? He'd be lying worrying. But how was she going to put Michael off?

'It's raining, and you've still got that cold . . . don't come out again.' Even to herself, her effort sounded feeble.

'Don't go out; but let you go alone, and over that road too?' He was his bustling self again. 'I don't know what I've been thinking of all along to allow you to go alone in the dark through that jumble of debris. God knows what might have happened to you.'

She was forced to smile at his solicitude. For months now she had walked through the debris and she doubted if he had even thought of it.

But his next words brought a tenseness to her body. 'I would have seen you to the tram, in any case, tonight, for I had to warn off one of those damned Arabs as I came in. I found him standing at the edge of the clearing, apparently surveying the house. Have you had any trouble with them coming here when I've been out?'

'No.'

As he was shrugging himself into his coat again he said, 'I'll break the first one's neck I find with his foot on my ground – I can't stand the oily blighters.'

Poor Hassan. At one time she had felt that way too. She still did towards most of the Arabs, but towards Hassan she felt nothing but sympathy. But she guessed this feeling would be hard to explain to this love of hers, who in many ways was a law unto himself. She would explain her acquaintance with Hassan after she told him about her da – it really shouldn't come as any great surprise to him to know that her father was a Negro, for he must see she had coloured blood in her veins. It was always a matter of amazement to her that the likeness in the eyes had escaped him. Yet her da had sat for him every day for a week, and he hadn't noticed.

As he insisted on buttoning a mackintosh of his over her coat she probed his feelings on the matter of her colour by asking shyly, 'Michael, do you mind about me being . . . coloured?'

'Coloured? Oh, my dear, I wouldn't mind if your father was an orang-outang as long as you were you.' He drew her to him. 'Never mention that again. I adore you . . . I always shall. Right from the day I first saw you I knew what would happen to me. Coloured! Where you are concerned I'm colour-blind.'

She laughed. 'Oh, how funny. You're like God, then.'

'God?' His eyebrows shot up into his hair. 'Me?'

'Well, I think you must be the only one besides him in all the world who is colour-blind. Our priest told me when I was a child that God was colour-blind; I've never found anybody else who is. Oh, and I love you for it. Oh, Michael, Michael!'

She kissed him with a fervour that prolonged the departure and made him plead again, 'Stay a little while . . . just a little while.'

'I can't. Tomorrow night I will, I promise.'

Yes, she would stay later tomorrow night. She would tell her da and he would understand.

As soon as they were outside she began to talk, as a warning to Hassan, whom she knew would be waiting. Stanhope held her by the arm, her elbow pressed into his side and her fingers laced tightly through his own; and going up the dark bank towards the market-place he pulled her into the deep shadow of a wall and kissed her, a silent, wordless kiss. But as they walked across the steel-glistening empty market-place to the tram it took all her gentle persuasion to counter his voluble insistence that he should accompany her home, and she did not feel safe until she stood on the platform of the tram as it jogged out of the market-place, watching him receding into the distance, the blueness of his eyes seeming to pierce the darkness until he was lost from her sight.

The tram stopped four times before she alighted; then she stood, uncertain for a moment what to do. She must give him time to get well out of the way before she ventured back to the Mill Dam again.

When she did come to the bank she kept to the shadow of the wall until she entered Holborn and, although she now breathed more freely, her steps became slower, for she had never before traversed these streets alone in the dark.

She had hardly covered the first deserted street when she heard quick padding footsteps behind her and a well-known voice call softly, 'Rose Angela.' She stopped in relief and laughed into the darkness, 'Oh, Hassan! I am glad to see you!'

Hassan made no reply, but walked quietly by her side; and because of his silence she knew that he was aware of what was between her and Stanhope. He would have seen them; perhaps he had followed them. Thinking of the dark bank leading to the ferry, she blushed and decided to bring the matter into the open. It would be the best way.

'Mr Stanhope set me to the tram tonight, he doesn't know that I'm living down here.' It was difficult to go on, for Hassan's displeasure was as visible as the wet darkness, and as cold. 'You wouldn't believe it, but he doesn't know James is my da. After painting him, too! It's odd, isn't it?'

Still Hassan made no comment, and they walked in awkward quietness until they reached the house, but in the darkness of the hall he spoke softly and rapidly, holding her gently by the arms as he did so. 'Rose Angela. You know I have a great love for you. No, don't say anything yet . . . I am not as others. I want one woman and one only, and that woman is you. I have money – much money. I can take you and your father away from here and send you both to Switzerland, where the healing air will prolong his life. But above all things I want to make you my wife . . . I want to marry you. The painter will never marry you – he comes of a class that scorns any colour but their own.'

She said nothing. The darkness hid his face from her, but she was filled with pity for him.

'Think it over. I don't want to hurry you, Rose Angela, but . . .' He did not finish, and they stood in silence again. He was waiting for her to speak; and as they stood it was brought to both of them that their silence was part of an unusual quietness that pervaded the whole house. Usually at this time of night the house was alive with clatter and noise. Only when danger threatened the inhabitants or something unusual was afoot would there be this silence.

Hassan drew closer to Rose Angela and whispered, 'Something is wrong. Go up and stay in the room, I'll be up later. Don't come downstairs again, not until I've found out what the trouble is.'

He gave her a gentle push towards the stairs, and she ran quickly from him, and each door she passed showed no light, nor gave forth any sound. Only from the bottom of her own door did a light shine. She paused, and the ecstatic happiness of the evening became submerged under the weight of a dread. Reluctantly her hand went to the knob, and she turned it slowly and went in.

For the past hour James had lain watching the door. Soon she would be here, and his day would begin. His days for the past two weeks had started at half-past six in the evening, when his Rose Angela came through the door, and ended at half-past seven in the morning when she left him. All day long he lay quiet, reserving his strength for her. He had little to say to Murphy or Pete, or even to the generous Hassan, while they sat with him giving him the news of the river. Only when they commented on the change Rose Angela had wrought in this room did he allow himself to be roused. Yes sir, by Jove . . . she wonderful.

He looked now to the corner where her shake-down was curtained off with a piece of gay chintz, and at the window to the side of him where the same material shut out the sight, if not the sound, of the torrential rain; even the rusty bedrail was removed from his gaze by her neat draping. His hands, long and bony, with the nails startlingly pink, moved lovingly to the glass jar of yellow chrysanthemums on the bamboo table by the bedside . . . she thought of everything. Flowers for him! And the food she brought him, food that now he couldn't eat. Two years ago he could have eaten it; how he could have eaten it. If he'd had food then there might have been a chance for him. Or if he had waited a little longer and hadn't sailed in that hell ship, with short commons and rotten boilers that sweated the flesh off a man. But hadn't he waited too long, years too long, always hoping that he would strike the money and come back and shower gifts on his Rose Angela?

It was strange how the thought of his once beloved Rose had been thrust into the background by the love for his child. Had he always known that Bridget wouldn't wait for him? He supposed so. Yet it came as a shock when he knew it was Tony she had chosen . . . Tony, the boy who had taken Rose Angela from his arms that night long ago; Tony, who had always liked him. He did not blame Tony. Women were the devil – they had always been the devil, all except his Rose Angela. Yet she played the devil with men, too, tenfold more than her mother had been capable of doing. Hassan . . . Hassan was mad about her. But he was glad she no want Hassan. He was good fella and kind, but he was not for his Rose Angela. He did not want her to marry any coloured man. No sir. She was mostly white and he wanted a white man for her. If she married coloured man all her life she'd be in trouble, inside of her and outside, whereas if she marry white man she be protected by his colour alone. The painter man he like his Rose Angela, there were many signs of that. He bellow a lot, but not at her; he look at her when she not looking, and his voice soft and kind when he speak to her. But would he marry her? Liking and marrying were two different things. And him a swell . . . And his Rose Angela. How did she feel about the painter man? She no say nothing, not even last night when he noticed strange light in her eyes when she came in, and he say to her, 'You happy?' and she replied, 'I'm happy to be back with you.'

'Who bring you?'

'Murphy, and he's practically drowned, but he wouldn't stay – it's blowing a gale.'

Murphy had not brought that light to her eyes, but as yet she did not wish to tell him who had, so he had turned the conversation.

'It blowing great guns all day – river'll be in a temper. I no like wind much. You like wind, Rose Angela?'

'No, I don't.' She touched his brow with her lips. 'That's another thing I've got from you, you know.' She looked lovingly into his face. 'You look heaps better today.'

'Me? I'm fine.' And to prove it he had hitched himself up and talked to her as she emptied the basket and set about preparing the evening meal. 'Me? I never like wind, 'cause I don't understand him, how him come about. Harvest – it no mystery; you put seed into earth. You can see the earth and see the seed, but you no can see wind. Only things that it touches you can see. Me, I see it touch one part of tree, other part still as death; and I see it wave one blade of grass – just one. Clever fellow on boat, he say it was worm or insect at bottom. Wasn't worm or insect on the tree. No, I no like wind. I hate fog and I no like wind, yet I love the water. And water and wind are cousins, they say. Strange. Me, I can never understand it. You like fog, Rose Angela?'

'No, I can't stand it either – it makes me afraid. I always expect something strange to loom up out of it.'

He nodded understandingly. 'Me same.'

The tie of kinship seemed to be stronger because she had inherited his fears, and he became silent, content just to watch her.

Later she told him she had seen a little house they could rent, not actually out of Holborn, but away from this quarter, and it pained him to witness her disappointment when he said, 'I no move from here, Rose Angela; Matt not get down this part. If I no sick I not mind, but . . .' He left the sentence unfinished, then went on, 'I be able to get up next week, and you go back home.' He hung on her reply, and it was like new life pouring into his veins when she said, 'You are my home.'

Was it any wonder he lived only when she was near him? But would he live enough days to make up for the years they had been separated? With the hope that is the heritage of the consumptive he thought he would and longer . . .

He was lying now, still and unmoving, his great eyes watching the door, but at half-past six she did not come. Nor yet at seven o'clock, and the fear of the wind became lost under the weight of apprehension filling his wasted body. And when half an hour later the noise and clamour of voices that always filled the house became gradually still and into their place came a scuffling of feet on the stairs as if someone was being dragged up them, he hitched himself up in the bed and waited, the sweat pouring down his body; and he fell back almost in a faint when the door was pushed open and a man was thrust into the room by Murphy and Pete.

Across the bedrails James and Matt surveyed each other, and both for the moment forgot all else but the terrible change that time had brought to each face.

Then the years fell away, and the hate that had reached its destroying climax in Bridget's kitchen sixteen years before filled the room. Matt's body jerked spasmodically with it; he made sounds in his throat but did not speak; only his eyes, riveted on James, spoke for him.

Murphy and Pete released their hold on him but remained threateningly close, and Murphy said to James, over the bed-rail, 'We had to bring him up – the Greek tipped us off he was watching the house. We couldn't nab him in the street, we had to wait until he got into the yard.'

Matt growled again, and Murphy, raising his forearm, warned, 'Mind yersel'.' Then he repeated, 'We had to bring him up; he knew you were here, Jimmy. He would have come up on his own or got the polis.'

James made no comment, but lay returning Matt's stare, and Murphy asked, 'What's to be done with him?'

The ominous question brought Matt's gaze from James and he glanced from Murphy to Pete, then swiftly around the room.

'Aye, have a good look,' said Murphy. 'The only way out is the way you come in.'

As Matt's eyes darted to the door the sound of running footsteps, intensified by the quiet of the house, came to him; and the other three men also turned their eyes to the door and waited. When it opened, Matt looked at Rose Angela standing there with her hands over her mouth, and a flash of his old power wiped out for the moment his own fear. Where was her bravery now? His eyes held hers as she came into the room and backed towards the bed, and when, without looking at James, she groped for his hand, Matt growled, 'Thought you were smart, didn't you? Well, you weren't smart enough, were you?'

'Shut yer gob, else I'll shut it for yer!' Murphy lifted his hand threateningly, and James interposed in a surprisingly calm voice, 'Let him talk, Murphy. There lots he wants off his chest.'

The sight of Rose Angela's fear seemed to restore Matt's courage, and he cried, 'There's one thing I'm gonna say, you needn't think I was fool enough to come down here without lettin' on to anyone,

157

so you can tell these two tykes of yours they better be careful what they're up to.'

'Why you come, anyway?' James asked.

'You know bloody well why I came . . . to get you!'

'You too late.'

'I don't know so much about that.' Matt's eyes darted to Rose Angela. 'I'll never be too late as long as that-'un's about.' Matt's sense of power mounted as he saw James's calm vanish and the hand holding his daughter's visibly shake. 'One of you'll pay for this.' Matt jerked his chin to indicate his scarred face.

James said, 'You no blame anyone but me . . . you asked for what you got, you try to ruin . . . my wife.' The word wife had a stilted sound, as if stiff for want of use.

'Your wife! A bit of a lass you took down when she was drunk. Your wife! I wonder, if she could see you now, what she'd think of her great, swaggering nigger. You made a mess of me, but, by God, it's a flea-bite to what you look like! That's why you didn't send for her on the quiet, eh? Didn't want her to see what a fool she'd been.'

The jerking of James's fingers within her palm told Rose Angela that Matt's surmise was one of the reasons why her father hadn't wanted to see Bridget; and when Matt went on, 'She knew she'd been a fool all right, long before you went, and you weren't gone five minutes before she had another bed-warmer,' she cried out, 'Don't believe him; he's lying! It was years after, years and years.'

She looked pleadingly down on James, and he, calm once more, reassured her. 'You no worry; that no matter . . . makes no difference.' He lay back and, staring at Matt over the bed-rails, said quietly and pointedly, 'When Bridget took other man I not know, but you did. Must have been very devil for you that!'

The words, like a knife-thrust, turned Matt's face to the colour of dirty silver. 'You black swine!'

He drew his body up as if to spring, and Murphy cried, 'I wouldn't if I was you.' And as he said this Murphy stepped a little to the front of Matt to prevent any movement he might make towards the bed, leaving exposed to Matt's right the little kitchen table, on which stood a lamp, an old-fashioned affair with a painted iron stalk and an oil container in the shape of a round flower surmounted by a tall lamp-glass.

In this tense, passion-filled atmosphere, Matt's mind was attuned to take advantage of any opening, and in the lamp he saw the weapon to his hand. Like a cat he sprang sideways, and in an instant he was at the far side of the table with the lamp in his hand. For a second, surprise made the others still. They stared at him, unbelieving, as if he were some demon capable of conjuring up separate selves. It was Murphy who made the first move, and Matt yelled, 'You stir from there and I'll hurl this on to the bed!' Slowly his eyes ranged from one to the other, and he said softly, 'Now who calls the tune?'

As Murphy made to move again Rose Angela cried, 'Don't Murphy, don't . . . he's mad . . . he'll do it.'

'Yes, I'll do it . . . you know your Uncle Matt, don't you?' He spat across the table at the term 'uncle'. 'But before I do it I'll do something else . . . come here, you!'

'You no move.' James was sitting upright, his voice hoarse with fear. 'I go.'

'I don't want you yet, I want her. I'll deal with you later. You come here. If you don't, you know what I'll do with this lamp.'

Wild-eyed and staring, as if her eyes were already fixed in death, Rose Angela loosened James's fingers from her coat, and pressed him back into the bed; and skirting Murphy and Pete, slowly walked towards the table.

'Not that side . . . this side.'

Like a marionette she obeyed him, until she was standing less than an arm's length from him, with the table at her back. Now she knew the summit of all fears . . . the total fears of her childhood and her teens were one minor tremor compared to the emotion now paralysing her. She felt that all her years had been a waiting for this moment. In the ecstasy of Stanhope's kiss she hadn't told herself, like most girls would, that all her life she had been awaiting such a moment . . . that this was what her thoughts and dreams had promised her, but now, standing fascinated under Matt's diabolical stare, she knew that this was the moment she had been awaiting, this moment in which he would destroy her face. Every atom of feeling in her was transformed into fear; it was shaking her limbs as if with ague.

'You're sick with fright, aren't you? Go on spew – you always spew when I frighten you.'

Without taking his eyes from her face Matt spoke to Murphy. 'Stop that dirty nigger from getting out of that bed, and you two listen to me. I'm gonna do something, and if any of you as much as move a finger when I'm at it I'll hurl the lamp into her half-breed face, d'you hear me?'

The desire to destroy both James and Rose Angela was burning its way through Matt like an acid. Inside his tortured mind he sensed that, whichever way things went, this was the end for him, but end or no end he was going to do things in his own way. For the first time in his life the desire for Bridget was lost under a greater desire – he would crash the lamp into her face if it was the last thing he did! But first there was something else he would do. For how many years had he wanted to feel the contact of his fist between those eyes? He could not remember a time when this urge had not swayed him. As he glared into Rose Angela's blanched face he realised that his hate of the daughter exceeded a thousand-fold that of the father.

159

His body began to sway and his hand with it, and the lamp sent the shadows of Murphy and Pete across the ceiling like crouching demons leaping through space. The room for the moment became strangely silent, with all the figures motionless and stiff. Then Matt, shouting another warning to Murphy, flung the silence into pandemonium.

As his fist crashed between Rose Angela's eyes Murphy sprang. He hurled himself on Matt, or more correctly where Matt had been, for Murphy's hand slid off Matt's twisting shoulders as if they were greased and he measured his length with a thud on the floor.

Pete did not move, but his unblinking eyes never left Matt; not even when James's swaying body rocked towards Matt did he remonstrate. Not until Matt threw the lamp did he spring. Then, like an enraged monkey he hurled himself sideways across the table, knocking Rose Angela flying as she stood swaying and moaning, her hands covering her face. Still with the antics of a monkey, he caught the lamp, and fell to the floor with it, balancing it upright like some circus clown.

Murphy, rising to his knees, clawed wildly at Matt's legs as he rushed towards the door, but he did not succeed in checking him . . . It was James, looking more weird and grotesque than ever, his long, wasted legs sticking like props from beneath his shirt, who blocked Matt's way. Once more he and Matt confronted each other, and James's anger was even greater now than it had been on that faraway night, but his strength was as a child's. As his feeble hands were raised to strike, Matt's foot shot out, aiming at his stomach, but catching him on the thigh and sending him sprawling against the wall.

The way clear now, Matt flung himself out on to the landing and went down the stairs, rocketing against the walls as he went, and through his brain rocketed only one regret – the lamp had missed her! All through that blasted dwarf! As he neared the hall he knew by the thundering on the stairs above that they were after him, and in the yard, where no vestige of light showed, not even a glimmer from the street lamp, for that had been put out, he knew himself to be running for his life, and that every man's hand was against him. By a stroke of luck he found the alleyway, but in the street, shadows that seemed darker than the night loomed at the end by which he had entered, so he turned in the other direction.

He was running as he had been wont to do years ago, with long loping strides, springing from one foot to the other. He became conscious as he ran of a strange and new feeling of freedom; his body seemed light and young once more . . . he would beat them yet . . . When had he last felt like this? The night he had run home to see Bridget and saw the black swine for the first time . . . Bridget, Bridget, why did you do it? It was as if the years

160

were being flung off with each flying step until he was back to that very night, walking the black streets and crying like a child as he walked, 'Bridget, Bridget, why did you do it?'

He was now in a maze of buildings, warehouses mostly, and this told him he was near the river. If only he could find an alleyway. He paused in his running and listened. Yes, blast them, he could hear their feet pounding the cobbles . . . Where was there a damned alleyway? He groped along one wall and laughed in relief as the wind, rushing up the alley, brought him the tang of the river. Once on the bank, he could make his way to the Mill Dam; he would slope them yet. His legs became infused with revitalised life; he was young again, really young. He had done something he had wanted to do for years – he had bashed that one's face. And now he was going to tell his Bridget that the nigger was alive, but was less than useless. He wouldn't trouble her, but it would put paid to Mister Tony, and his Bridget would be alone again, and would turn to him. Oh, Bridget, Bridget! His running cut through the wind like the keel of a ship through the water, and his head filled with the wind. It swelled and swelled, making his body so light that he was no longer on the ground. The wind became a whirlwind; until finally the roaring of it culminated in a bang and his head burst into stillness.

He came to a sudden stop on the very edge of the wall that hemmed in the river, and below him he could hear the lap-lap of the water against the wall. He put out his hand and felt the walls of the warehouses that closed him in on both sides. He put out his foot and there was nothing. This last action conveyed only one thing to the hollowness of his mind – he must not jump down there because he couldn't swim. He lifted his hand to his brow and his fingers groped at the emptiness under them. What had he been thinking when he was running? Had he been running? Yes, he had been running . . . but what had he been thinking? He must try to remember what he had been thinking. The sound of the pounding feet came to him again, and they carried another single thought into the hollowness . . . he must hide. But there was only the river, with the sheer wall down to it.

It was impulse that made him lower himself over the wall. Alongside the warehouses the shelf of the wall was scarcely more than a hand wide, but the finishing stones had been left in parapet form and to these he clung, and edged himself a foot or so out of the line of the alleyway. His legs were in the water up to his thighs, and when his toes, scraping against the wall, found a niche where a brick had been washed out, he thrust his feet in, and this lifted the weight from his hands; and he hung there, listening to the footsteps, their coming and their going, and he began to laugh softly.

CHAPTER THIRTEEN

THE FEET OF THE BELOVED

It was ten o'clock when Rose Angela stumbled over the last sleepers towards the clearing, and the white-painted door and windows of the house shone at her like welcoming beacons. Never had she loved the house as she did at this moment; nor needed its comforting warmth and colour so much; and once inside, with Michael's arms about her, all her mental and physical pain would be eased.

She pressed her hand to her brow, where the pain was most acute. How would he take the sight of her face? She must tell him everything . . . everything but how she came by the blow. She would say that she fell – she must not tell him Matt did it, for not even to him must she say that she had seen Matt last night, for as yet she did not know what had happened to him. Hour after hour she had sat waiting by the side of James for Murphy or Pete to come back with some word, but they hadn't come. Nor yet had any of the neighbouring men looked in, or the women, and this augured bad, so she must not say she had seen Matt.

The terror of last night would remain with her, she thought, until she died, and after, and the terror had not ceased when Matt had flown, for the scarlet blood pouring from James's mouth had been equally terrifying. But this morning he seemed better, yet she knew that last night's events had precipitated his end, and she had been loath to leave him even for the short time it would take to tell Michael the reason for her absence. Oh to be with Michael just for a few minutes, to rest against him and have his sympathy flow over her. She broke into a run, and when she rounded the narrow shingled path to the back door she could not restrain herself from calling his name aloud, 'Michael! Michael!' If he was up in the studio he would hear her and come bounding down the stairs, to stand horrified for the moment at the sight of her face – yes, she knew her face would shock him.

She turned the handle of the door and, finding it locked, called again, 'Michael!'

He mustn't be up yet, and it was after ten. Likely he had been working most of the night. Automatically her hand went to the beam that supported the roof of the porch, but her fingers, groping behind it, did not come in contact with the key. When she had tried the other side, and been met with the same emptiness, she turned and looked at the blue boat bobbing forlornly against the side of the wharf. She was nonplussed. If he was not down in the morning the key would still be behind the beam, where she left it at night. Again her fingers traced the key's hiding place; then panic seized her. If he had gone out, he would have left the key. Perhaps he had been taken ill and couldn't get downstairs . . . perhaps he was dead.

'Michael!' She battered with her fist upon the door. 'Michael!'

When she heard his steps in the kitchen only the tight painfulness of her face prevented her from laughing with relief, and he had barely opened the door before her hands went out to him. But they found no answering grip. His arms did not pull her to him, exclaiming in horror at the sight of her face, nor did he demand in his impetuous way where she had been until this hour. After staring fixedly at her face for a moment, he merely turned from her and put the width of the table between them.

As she stared at him in astonishment her whole body began to shake, and her voice, too, trembled as she asked softly, 'What's the matter?'

He did not answer her immediately, but continued to look at her with eyes so coldly blue that she appealed to him as a child might, saying, 'But what have I done?'

She watched him pass one lip over the other, and his voice was so quiet when it came as to be scarcely recognisable at his.

'Are you living in Holborn, Rosie?'

The racing of her heart warned her of what was to come, and she answered with difficulty. 'Yes, but I was going to tell you . . . I . . .'

A small deprecatory movement of his hand checked her hesitant words.

'With an Arab?'

'No. No!' She screamed the words at him; and again he checked her, asking sharply, 'Last night you never went to the fifteen streets, you got off that tram and went back to Holborn, didn't you?'

She was unable to answer him – her eyes were fixed on his face like a fear-paralysed rabbit.

'That Arab I chased was waiting for you, wasn't he?'

Still no words would come, and he went on, 'I see he has thrashed you for your duplicity. He has that to his credit, anyway.'

'Michael' – she gasped his name fearfully – 'I'm not living with him. It's true he was waiting for me. He's . . . he's a friend. He takes me into Holborn. I'm living with my father . . . the Negro, the one that you painted.'

163

She watched his eyebrows rise, then draw into a thick furrow. 'Your father, eh? My God!' He shook his head as if at his own gullibility. 'Rosie, I wouldn't have believed you capable of such barefaced lying.'

She leant across the table towards him and cried beseechingly, 'Believe me, oh, believe me, I'm not lying. I know it looks bad, but I'm not lying.'

'Be quiet!'

At his low-growled command she straightened herself and tried to draw on what little pride and strength she had left to face up to this man, who was now neither master nor lover. But it was no use. Under his contemptuous glance she not only bowed her head but her body also, and she leaned her hands on the table for support as he went on, 'May I ask where your mother comes in, in this scheme of things? Why isn't she with your father?'

'I can explain—' She made to raise her head.

'Wait. If I remember rightly, you told me your mother was a widow, and that your father died when you were a child.'

Yes, he remembered rightly, and she could remember his question 'Is your father out of work?' and her answer, to save explanations and more humiliation, 'He's dead. He died when I was a child.'

She spoke with difficulty from under her breath, 'That was a lie, but it's the only one I've told you.'

'Rosie!' His tone as he uttered her name was quiet but heavy with scorn. 'Don't make matters worse. Look at those.' He placed two letters on the centre of the table. 'Do you recognise the writing?'

She shook her head.

'They are anonymous letters about you.'

'About me?' Her head came up with a jerk, and her mouth hung agape in amazement.

'Why do you appear so surprised? Everyone isn't blind, you know; I happen to be an exception. One of those letters, I know, is from Bessie, who tells me it's about time I found out I was being fooled. Apparently she had her own ideas of why I kept you on. The other is from someone, I should imagine, who knows you very well. One sentence interests me very much. It says you can assume a cloak of timidity and fear so as to hoodwink people. I once said to you that I wasn't sure whether you were so full of humility as not to be a woman or so full of the wisdom of the serpent that you were being amused by me, and, my God, how you must have been amused! What was your game, anyway? Did you think you could get off with it?'

'Please M—' She could not now speak his name. 'Please don't say any more . . . you're wrong. Those letters are full of lies.'

'Yes?' He picked up one of the letters. 'This writer points out that you have always been a great source of worry to your mother, and that she tried to stop you from going into Holborn. But you wouldn't listen to her. Is that a lie?'

'Yes . . . no . . . She did try to stop me, but . . .'

'Why didn't you tell her then about . . . your father?'

'Because he didn't want me to . . . he was ill, as you know and changed.'

'How was it I didn't notice any tender relationship between you during his visits here? Throwing my mind back, I never once remember you even looking at the man. Why, in the name of God, must you bring him into all this?'

'Because I've told you . . . he's my father.'

Stanhope scrutinised her for a moment, then said softly, 'And the Arab is just a friend? He waits for you each night and takes you home?'

Knowing her answer would bring down his contempt on her head, she hesitated before saying, 'Yes.'

'What do you take me for? If it had been a white man I would have had my doubts, but an Arab! And to term him a friend. You know as well as I do that no man, black or white, could be merely a friend to you, and an Arab least of all.'

Oh God! It was like the scene of her frequent dismissals over again, only intensified a thousandfold. She had often wondered what her master would be like were he in a real rage. Then, she had thought, his bellow would reach such volume as to scare even the bravest. She had never imagined that his rage would produce no bellows, that his voice would be low-toned and even. Nor had she imagined that his eyes could express such disgust and a disdain that would make her feel unclean, unmerited as it was.

The terrible coldness of his manner was having a numbing effect on her already failing senses, and as his voice went on she had to grip the edge of the table for support.

'And your face . . . the Arab didn't do that?'

'No, he didn't.'

In spite of her faintness her words carried conviction. But when he asked, 'Who did then?' and she answered, 'I fell on the stairs,' he made a sound like a laugh.

'Do you take me for a fool altogether? In my young days I used to box, but had I never given or received a blow between the eyes I would know that it was a fist that had hit you.'

Rose Angela knew that there were levels of pain she had not yet probed. What she was suffering now would be nothing compared to the agony that would be produced by the emptiness of a life separated from this man's . . . She must tell him about Matt.

'It was a fist. My uncle did it – the one that wrote that letter. He's always hated me and lied about me.'

'Oh, your uncle, now! Is he lying when he says you have been turned out of situation after situation because of your double-dealings with men, and that you've never kept a job more than a few weeks?'

Rose Angela stared at Stanhope without seeing him. What was the use? Living or dead, Matt's work went on. She could do no more; yet through all the turmoil of her feeling ran a thread of bewilderment at what appeared to her a determination on Stanhope's part not to believe anything she said, for only last night hadn't he told her it was her honesty that had altered his opinion of women?

Then, as she stood swaying on her feet, his voice, losing its levelness and sinking into his throat with bitterness, brought her sharply back from the oblivion that was upon her; and she knew part of the reason for his unrelenting attitude towards her, for, as much as he hated her at this moment, he hated and loathed himself even more.

'Last night I asked you to live with me, but after you had gone I knew that wouldn't be enough . . . I must marry you and make sure of you. Make sure of you . . . that's funny, isn't it? And when this morning I received these two letters it was history repeating itself, for all this has happened to me before. When I was about to be married, twelve years ago, I received such a letter as that.' He flicked Matt's letter with his nail. 'The girl was as beautiful as you, and as practised a liar.' He paused for a while, and ran the side of his finger across his lips as if wiping something distasteful from them. 'I felt a young fool, then, but now I feel an old one. And that I find harder to stomach!'

Now she knew the uselessness of trying to convince him. The giddiness swam over her again, and his voice came to her as if from the end of a long corridor, saying, 'There's a week's wages in lieu of notice. And you may keep the brooch. It is of some value, as doubtless you expected when you asked for such a simple gift.'

When the mist cleared from her eyes she found that she was alone. She hadn't heard him go. His movements, like his voice, were now quiet and final. She leant over the table, her body trembling. Her hand went to her throat, and, groping at the brooch fastening her blouse, she undid it and placed it on the table near the money he had laid there. Then unsteadily she left the kitchen.

Outside, she stood watching the sun's watery rays reflected on the river. It was over – just like that . . .

She walked on, almost blindly, over the rails and sleepers and she wondered vaguely why she was shedding no tears, for inside she was crying as she had never cried before: in many ways at one and the same time, like a child that had been misjudged, and like a girl who had been spurned, and like a woman who had drunk bitterly of humiliation. The child was crying, 'It's always the same. Oh, I wish I was dead! Oh, I wish I was dead!' And the girl was crying, 'He believed everything in that letter, about the men an' all.' But the woman's cry overshadowed the others, for she was crying, 'It's my colour. If I'd been all white he would have let me convince him, in spite of that other girl. Last night he said colour didn't matter, but I know, I know. It will always matter, and balance the scales; it's still like when I was a child.'

She drew to a halt and stared at the river. The fitful gleam of the sun had vanished, leaving the water a broken mass of steely grey. There was a way out – it was deep by the broken wall, and once in she would never get out. There was only her da to really mourn her; and then not for long, for he would soon go . . . Mourning. All her life had been one long mourning; mourning because she was what she was. She was tired, so tired, and her face was like a sheet of hot pain. She had been born to misery, so why had she imagined that anything might come right for her? And of all things, Stanhope's love! She had been like a child, firmly believing that a fairy-tale could become reality.

She started to run over the sleepers, tripping and stumbling like someone drunk. She passed the railway carriage and was deaf to Murphy's voice calling after her. And she had actually mounted the broken wall before she was pulled to a halt.

'Here, here! Steady on. What is it, lass? What you running like that for? . . . Look, stop it!' Murphy put his arms tightly about her, restraining her until she suddenly became still. 'That's better. What is it? What's happened to you?'

She leant against him, her head resting on his greasy muffler, and he held her gently until she murmured, 'It's him.'

'Him? Who?' asked Murphy.

'The guv'nor.' She used Murphy's own term for Stanhope. 'He won't believe me. He won't believe I'm not living with Hassan.' She was speaking slowly, with the dull simplicity of a child, and Murphy stared at her perturbed as he repeated, 'Living with Hassan? God Almighty! What put that into his head?'

'Matt. Matt sent him a letter; and Bessie too.'

'Why, blast the pair of them for lying skunks! Look, lass, come inside the cabin a minute and get yourself warmed; you're all in.'

She allowed him to lead her back and into the railway carriage, where he sat her on the backless chair before the fire and began clumsily to chafe her stiff hands, talking all the while and trying to break through the strange light in her eyes. And he looked apprehensively at Pete when she broke in on him, saying dully, 'He was going to ask me to marry him, and I would have been Mrs Stanhope then, Murphy.'

Murphy pursed his lips and jerked his head approvingly. 'Aye, fit to marry anyone, you are, Rosie . . . you'll marry him all right, won't she, Pete?'

Pete nodded, sparing his words as usual.

'Not now,' she said, 'because it's all happened before.'

'There, there then. Are you warmed? . . . I'll brew some tea. There ain't any milk, but it'll be hot. Been through a bit too much, you have. Lean back against the wall . . . he'll marry you all right, don't you worry.'

'No . . . he wouldn't believe about Matt . . . about him always being bad.' Murphy's hand became still for a second as he measured the tea into the black can, and his eyes darted towards Pete's; then he turned the thread of her thoughts by saying, 'Not that Pete and me want you to marry and be skedaddled off to some place else, do we, Pete?'

Pete shook his head.

'Best friend we've ever had, you've been. Not many like you about. No wonder yer da dotes on you. It'll be a bad day for all of us when we lose you, I can tell you that.'

Bad day for all of them when they lost her . . . best friend they'd ever had. She felt a momentary glow of comfort . . . there were kind people in the world – these men were kind. And they believed in her, they who had known her so short a time. Not like her mother, who knew her even before birth, and him who last night had told her he adored her from the moment he set eyes on her and would continue to do so every moment of his life.

The crying and inward sobbing began to mount. It was Pete's unused voice that caused her pent-up tears to break, betraying himself by look and word as he said briefly, 'Nobody's good enough for you . . . the Stanhope bloke nor nobody else.'

This was a long speech for Pete, and as Rose Angela looked at the dwarf his love penetrated the mist of her mind, and all the pain within her gathered itself into her throat, and as it found release she covered her face with her hands and sobbed, great tearing sobs that convulsed her body.

The men stood helplessly by, gazing at her bent head. When the sobs, gathering on themselves, threatened to choke her, their hands hovered towards her but did not touch her. It was as if they both realised that this safety valve must not be checked. Twice the crying died down, only to burst out afresh, and it was only when her body sagged almost double that Pete intervened by motioning to Murphy to give her the tea.

Clumsily Murphy straightened her hat, saying, 'Come, Rosie, lass, and have your drop of tea.' He took the mug from Pete's hand and held it to her lips. 'There now, drink that, and we'll get you a drop of water, for your face and hands are in a mess.' His voice was placating, he was humouring her as if she were still the strange distraught child he had pulled from the wall.

But after she had sipped the tea she spoke to him, and her voice was as he knew it. 'I'm sorry, Murphy.'

Murphy's face showed his relief. 'There, there, it's all over now.'

She sat in silence, the two men watching her. Was it all over? Wasn't there more to come?

'Where is Matt?' She asked the question as she stared down into the mug of black tea.

After a pause Murphy muttered, 'We don't know.'

She cupped the mug in her cold hands and the steam rising from the tea wafted about her face. 'What happened last night?' Her voice betrayed her premonition.

There was another pause before Murphy said, 'We chased him and he went down the drop alley.'

'The drop alley?' She looked quickly up at Murphy. 'But there's no way out of there but the river.'

Pete's eyes were fastened on the floor, and Murphy turned his head aside as he replied, 'I know. Me and the fellows waited to see if he'd come back, and Hassan and Pete went along to the sculler steps to nab him if he came up that way. But he didn't come . . .' He paused, and then went on hopefully, 'He could have swum along the river and come up somewhere, though, and is hiding out, trying to scare us.'

Rose Angela looked through the carriage window to where the river was moving swiftly in black and grey patches. 'He couldn't swim,' she said flatly.

Neither Murphy nor Pete made any comment or movement, and she went on fearfully, 'There'll be an enquiry if they find him, and if there are any marks on his body . . .'

'Honest to God, we didn't touch him, Rosie,' Murphy put in. 'We never got near enough to him, or I don't know what we might have done at the time . . . but we never laid a hand on him, did we, Pete?'

Pete gave the usual reply with his head.

'If there are enquiries, you'll have to be careful.' She was talking quietly now, as if it were an ordinary, everyday topic. For the moment all the turmoil seemed to have been swept away on the flow of her tears, and being thus quiet she asked herself questions, and the answers brought no pain. She asked herself did she hope Matt was dead; and the answer came: Yes, oh yes! She asked herself why she had pleaded so much with Stanhope. Had she stormed at him, as most women would have done under the circumstances, would she have convinced him? Her head shook slowly from side to side. No. Anyway, she could never have stormed at him.

All her life she had been humble because openly and in covered ways she had been given to understand that her mixed blood was like a poster advertising some inferior form of human being, and she had never used the argument, 'Is it our fault we are what we are? Must we go around searching for others like ourselves to form a world apart? The blame lies with them that bred us.' To have taken this view would have meant criticism of her mother and her da. Yet in this moment she dared to wonder what life would have been like had each stuck to his own kind, for it was borne in on her that Stanhope's unrelentlessness, whether he realised it or not, was due not so much to the fact that he had been duped before but that this time it had been done by a half-caste . . . The thought laid hold of her. Last night when he said that colour did not matter it was because he wanted her – men would say anything to get what they wanted. Life had taught her that lesson thoroughly. Last night he and God were colour-blind; now there was, as before, only God.

She surprised Murphy by rising abruptly and saying, 'I'll go now. Don't come . . . I'll be all right,' and adding calmly, 'If you are questioned you'd better say you were in with us till ten o'clock. And Hassan too . . . we must all say the same thing, mustn't we?'

They did not answer her, and she turned from them and went out of the railway carriage, and together they moved towards the door and watched her walking away with a step that had in it some quality that reminded them strongly of James. And as she walked, Rose Angela herself had the strange feeling inside her, in some depths where no white mind could reach, that most of her father walked with her.

Murphy watched her until she disappeared from view, then he turned to Pete. 'What do you make of it?'

Pete shook his head.

'She was ready for the high jump then, all right. Think she'll be all right now?'

Pete nodded.

'Can't understand the guv'nor taking notice of them letters, can you? He don't take no notice of what nobody says as a rule. What do you think we best do?'

Pete brought his eyes from where in imagination they were following Rose Angela, and said briefly, 'Tell him about Hassan?'

'Aye, that would be the best thing.'

Murphy pulled the door of the railway carriage to, then they set off walking slowly over the sleepers – slowly, as if they did not relish coming to the end of their short journey. Murphy did not speak again until they reached the wharf, when he said, 'What if he's mad?'

Pete's answer was to indicate the door with a motion of his head, which said plainly, 'Knock and find out.'

Murphy knocked four times on the door, but received no answer. It took courage to go round the house and ring the front door-bell; but even this brought no response, and only when they came to the back door again and knocked once more was the studio window thrust up with a bang; and Murphy and Pete stepped back and looked up at Stanhope. No word was spoken for quite some seconds, for Stanhope's expression froze Murphy's tongue. He was used to hearing the guv'nor going off the deep end and to see his face become furious with sudden temper, but the man up there was not in any way connected with the guv'nor he knew. His face was white, almost livid, and he did not yell at them, as usual, with, 'Well, what the devil do you want?' but stood waiting for them to speak.

In keeping with the unusual that seemed to be the order of the morning, it was Pete who spoke.

'Can we have a word with you?' he said.

Murphy looked swiftly from Stanhope to Pete and back to Stanhope again, who asked curtly, 'What about?'

'Well' – it was Murphy starting now – 'it's like this, guv'nor. Y'see . . .' His Adam's apple jerked swiftly and he swallowed and brought out, 'It's about Rose Angela.'

'What about her?' The words seemed to take their time in reaching them; they were weighed with something that chilled Murphy and curbed his ready tongue.

'Well, there's been a mistake made, guv'nor' – he dared not say 'You have made a mistake,' and went lamely on – 'about Hassan. The Arab fellow, y'know.'

'Yes?' This word came sharp now, like a rapier.

'Well, she said you . . . Well . . . you've got the idea—' Murphy hesitated. 'It's a bit of a mix-up, guv'nor.'

'And she sent you along here to explain it away?'

'No, no. But we thought you should know . . .'

'She's living in Holborn, isn't she?'

'Aye, she is.'

'Who with?' Again the words were heavy.

Once more Murphy brought his gaze down to Pete's. Here was a complication they hadn't given themselves time to foresee. If they said Jimmy, one thing would lead to another and before they knew where they were they would be talking of Matt; then of last night; and the less who knew about that affair the better.

But Murphy was not required to answer this particular question, for Stanhope threw another at him. 'Who gave her the black eyes?'

'What's that?'

Murphy's mouth was agape as he stared up at him. It was as if he hadn't heard, or having heard, the question did not make sense to him.

This pose of stupidity seemed too much for Stanhope. In a moment he became the guv'nor they recognised, only more vehement than they had ever seen him before.

'Get the hell out of it, the pair of you! Get!'

It was as if he would topple out of the window on to them with the force of his passion.

'But look here, guv'nor . . .'

'I'll give you a minute to get going. If you aren't gone by the time I come down I'll throw the pair of you in the river!' His voice rose to a yell, and before he had crashed the window down they were off the wharf, for they were too experienced to attempt to reason with anyone in the state he was in.

'What do you think we'd better do?' asked Murphy as they returned to the railway carriage.

'Wait and tell him the morrer.'

'But what will we tell him then?'

'The lot.'

'The lot?' Murphy stopped in his stride. 'Oh, I think we'd better see Jimmy afore doin' that.'

'Aye,' Pete assented with a nod.

'Will we go now?'

Again Pete nodded.

'But how about taking a look round first in case he's . . .' Murphy did not add 'come up'. And once more Pete's head inclined agreement, and without further words they walked along the river bank, their eyes turned towards the water.

CHAPTER FOURTEEN

COLOUR

The quietness was still with Rose Angela as she mounted the stairs to James, but it was now a frozen quietness, and she knew that when it melted there would be pain to bear greater than ever she had known before.

James's eyes, burning in their great sockets, fastened on her from the moment she opened the door, and his voice came as a hollow, cracked whisper from the bed, saying, 'You not long.'

'No.' She went straight to him and took his hand. 'How do you feel now?'

'Oh, a lot better . . . heap better.' He stared up into her face, his eyes searching hers. 'What wrong now? Something more wrong now? They find him?'

'No.'

'Well, what wrong? You been crying mightily.'

'Don't talk any more. Now lie quiet.' She put his arms inside the clothes, then turned from him and took off her hat and coat.

'Your face pain?'

'Yes.'

'Rose Angela . . .'

'Yes, dear, what is it?' She turned at the entreaty and bent over him.

He stared at her in silence for some time before answering, 'I feel in here' – his hand was moving under the bed-clothes with its old gesture of patting his chest – 'things not right with you . . . Painter . . . Mr Stanhope, he all right . . . him not mad at you staying off?'

She had to prevent her eyelids from closing to shut out the pain, for now the quietness was melting, and it was a moment before she answered, 'Yes, he's all right.'

'And you hear nothing about . . . the other one?' James could not bring himself to pronounce the name.

'No.'

'Sure?'

'Yes. Now don't talk, dear; I'm going to make you a drink.'

'I got to talk. It won't make no difference, one way or other. Sit down by me.'

She was lifting a chair to the bedside when a tap came on

the door, and to her 'Come in' Hassan entered, and she saw immediately that he was disturbed.

'You've heard something?' she asked hesitantly.

He shook his head, but said nothing, only continued to stare at her, and James called feebly, 'Hassan! Here!'

Hassan went to the bed and James motioned him to sit down. 'What happen?'

'Nothing.'

'No sign of him?'

'No.'

'Perhaps him get back home somehow.'

'No; they're looking for him.'

'You been up?'

'I sent up.'

There was silence in the room for a time until Rose Angela came to the bed with a drink for James and she said to Hassan, 'Could you stay for a short while? I've got to get some oil and things.'

He nodded, but still he did not speak to her, only stared up into her face.

She put on her hat and coat again, and saying, 'I won't be more than a minute or two,' she left the room.

She had hardly closed the door when James hitched himself up on his pillows and said urgently, 'Something wrong with her – something more wrong. She come in and she been cryin' sore. You know what 'tis, Hassan?'

Hassan looked away, and James urged, 'If you know, you tell me – I not long for top and I want her be happy.'

'Jimmy' – Hassan leant forward and took James's hand – 'I want to marry Rose Angela. You know that, don't you, without me telling you?'

James stared fixedly at the Arab without answering, and Hassan went on, 'I can make her happy. I know I can.'

James shook his head.

'I tell you I can. What have you against it? You married a white woman.'

Again James shook his head, and his voice rose above its whispering quality, and for a moment there was the echo of the deep timbre note in it again. 'It very wrong thing for black man marrying white woman. It bad enough for man, for him sore inside all his days, but for white woman it hell. And bigger hell for children. What you think the real reason I no let my wife know I'm here? It because I know she happy with white man. That's as should be – colour to colour. But me . . . I not blaming you, Hassan, for wanting my Rose Angela, for only when fellow near death can he be wise. When life leaps inside him no man wise.'

'But Rose Angela's different . . . she's not all white.'

174

'She is' – James was sitting up now in agitation – 'she's white. I tell you she is white.'

'All right, all right, Jimmy,' Hassan said soothingly. 'Outside she may look more white than black, but inside she's all you – and that's a good thing.'

He smiled into James's troubled eyes, and James leant back and said between gasps, 'You say kind things, Hassan. I always like you, but I near death and I must speak truth. I no want my Rose Angela marry you. Anyway, the . . .' James looked down on his hands, almost transparent in their thinness, and went on lamely, 'I think she loves painter fellow.'

'Yes, and he's turned her out.'

Hassan had risen to his feet, his voice harsh and angry, and James's eyes darted up his thin frame to his face. 'What you say?'

'That fellow Matt wrote and told him she was living with me, and without any evidence he believed it. That's the kind of white god he is. And he turned her out, and she nearly threw herself . . .'

Hassan pulled up too late, and James said fearfully, 'Go on.'

'It's all right. She was a bit overdone – I'm sorry I said anything. She's all right now.'

James bent over and gripped Hassan's arm. 'She try throw herself in river?'

'She's all right now. Don't you worry.'

'My God! You say don't worry. Go after her. Don't leave her, and bring her back.'

'But she wants me to stay.'

'Go now – go.'

Hassan turned from the bed; then swung round again. 'If I ask her and she will marry me, what then?'

James closed his eyes. 'I said my say, Hassan.'

When Hassan had gone, James lay back weak and exhausted, and for some time he did not move. Only his fingers clutched and gathered up the white Marcella bedspread. After a while he moved his head to one side on his bank of pillows so that the knob of the bed should not obstruct his vision, and now he could see the three statues standing on a shelf to the side of Rose Angela's shake-down. There was a statue of St Joseph and one of the Virgin, and another of Jesus. Years ago he had bought them at the door of the church because the man there, who said he was a brother of St Vincent de Paul, also said that many blessings went with these statues. He remembered Rose Angela, from when she was a tiny child, claiming them as hers, and they were among the few possessions she had brought here. Now, in his mind, he began to talk to the statues, as he had often done of late, but this time with added urgency. 'You not let this come about, you not let the painter fellow believe this. You can't do this. You not let her marry Hassan, or kill herself in river.' He hitched himself a little farther to one side and appealed across the distance, 'I not want to die till she fixed up right. You can understand that. Don't let me die till she fixed up right.'

He waited in his thinking, and a narrow shaft of sunlight, the only shaft in the day that ever found its way into the room, fell across the face of the figure of Christ, and for the moment obliterated it in light; and James became still inside in wonderment.

He lay quiet and at peace now, watching the streak of sunlight narrow before it disappeared altogether. When it had gone he shook his head at himself. 'Me, I imagine things. All my life I imagine things.'

He lay staring at the statues until the drowsiness which was becoming more frequent of late took hold of him, and as he dozed off he wondered whimsically if, when he went into the long sleep, he would meet the people the statues represented.

He did not know what he would find in the coming long sleep. Perhaps he would see God, perhaps not. Perhaps God died when the brain could function no more. Perhaps he had done his work then. But if, on the other hand, he did meet him, what then? What had he to show for his life? Drowsily he shook his head again. Only a kindness here and there . . . and loving. Yes, he had loved. Love had been the driving force, the force that had brought him to this way of dying. Then perhaps it had to be . . . perhaps he had followed the pattern cut out for him. But it did not matter either way. He allowed himself to slip farther down the bed. All that mattered was that his Rose Angela should know happiness, happiness such as he knew existed but which had escaped him. If his daughter could have this happiness, then the pattern of his life had been a good pattern; and working it out was like paying in advance for another life – Rose Angela's life.

Hassan guessed that Rose Angela had gone to a little group of shops off Commercial Road, and he made for there. But as he turned the corner of the street he actually ran into her, and in her surprise at seeing him she clutched at his arm, exclaiming, 'He's not . . . ?'

'No, no – he's all right. He asked me to come and help you with the basket.'

She looked at him in disbelief. 'What's wrong, Hassan? There was something the matter when you came in.'

She started to walk rapidly towards the house, and he took the oil-can from her hand and said without looking at her, 'There are two men I'd like to kill, and one's that painter.'

She stiffened, and he went on, 'I must talk to you, Rose Angela. Will you come to the café for a minute?'

She shook her head. 'I must get home.'

'Just for a minute.'

With the appeal of his voice she turned her head towards him and said kindly, 'You know I can't leave him for long.'

They were crossing the yard now, and it was empty of people, as was the dark hallway, and inside he brought her to a halt. 'Listen just one minute, Rose Angela. Tell me, are you afraid of me?'

'No, oh no, Hassan!' Her answer was so spontaneous that it brought a smile to his face.

'Thank you, Rose Angela. Do you . . . do you like me?'

'Yes, I like you. No-one could help liking you, Hassan.'

'You are not afraid of me and you like me.' He took the basket from her hand and laid it, together with the oil-can, at the foot of the stairs. Then he gathered both her cold hands in his. 'Will you believe me when I say I can make you love me?'

She stared into his eyes and saw there the released fire of his feelings.

'Will you believe me?'

'Oh, Hassan!'

She bowed her head, and he pulled her to him. 'I love you so much, Rose Angela, that I would give my life for you. You cannot believe it at this moment, but there would be no pain with my love as there would have been with his.'

She made a movement to withdraw her hands, and he gripped them closer. 'Listen. All your life you will be colour-conscious. I know, for I have watched you. You feel inferior. Inside you feel inferior . . . you, who could be a queen. And could he take that inferior feeling away? No. And however he might have over-looked it, his fine friends would not, and he has plenty of fine friends. But with me you will never feel inferior. Instead of knowing you are looked down on, you will be looked up to – adored, worshipped; and you will want for nothing . . . Oh, Rose Angela, look at me. Tell me, Rose Angela.'

She did not raise her head, for his words were finding resting-places in her mind. He was right. Always inside she felt inferior, but never so much as she did at this moment; and as he said, with him it would go. She could believe this, for he did not feel racially superior to her. With him she could stop fighting; once joined to him she could allow the stamp of her colour to rise to the surface and she could accept what she was, and with acceptance would come release.

For a moment the face of Stanhope came before her eyes, as it had been last night, saying, 'What are you going to do about it?' He hadn't thought her good enough to marry, then; only this morning in the midst of rejecting her he could say he had been going to marry her. It was easy, then, when there was no possibility of its taking place. Into the pain and despair that seemed to be finding pas-sage through each vein of her body was mingled a feeling of bitterness against him, and against her mother. Bridget was also in her mind at this moment, for was she not another, the only other one that mattered, who had so readily believed the worst of her? And if she were to marry Hassan she would not have to suffer the shock of breaking it to her, for that had already been endured. And yet another worry that Hassan could relieve her of was money, for she had only a few pounds she had saved up to provide extras at Christmas. All her wages had been spent on James and the room. If she was to support him she must find work; for the short time left she must find work – or else. She raised her eyes to Hassan. He had said, 'You will want for nothing.' Well, she had never wanted very much from life, and the little she had got, which amounted to food and a few clothes, was acquired only through long hours of labour at the beck and call of others. And these had always been punctuated by the fight against men. So what had she to lose if she married Hassan?

Hassan sensed the change in her, and he pressed his point. 'Tell me, Rose Angela.' And although he was urging her answer, when it came he was rendered dumb with surprise.

'Give me time, and I'll try.' And as she said it there swept over her a wave of sound, full of her father's voice, crying, 'You not do this.'

It was done, but as Hassan leaned forward to place his lips on hers she recoiled, saying, 'No, no, not yet.'

'All right, I can wait.'

There was pain in his eyes, and she turned from him and picked up the basket and the oil-can, and went heavily up the stairs.

CHAPTER FIFTEEN

PAYMENT

After Stanhope had rushed down the stairs to carry out his threat to Murphy and Pete, and found he was not called upon to do so, he again locked the back door; then he stood and glared around the kitchen. He looked at the delft rack. The dishes she had washed yesterday were all arrayed neatly and gleaming, and his anger was such that he had to place the utmost restraint on himself not to raise his arm and sweep the lot on to the floor.

He flung out of the kitchen and into the drawing-room. The cold deadliness of his feeling was passing and he was wanting to storm. He caught a glimpse of himself in the mirror, and was brought to a halt. He looked as he felt, wild with temper.

He sat on the couch and, resting his elbows on his knees, he gripped his hair with both hands as if he would pull it out by the roots. God, why had he let himself in for this? The first time was bad enough, but nothing compared with this. She had got into his blood and maddened him, and in spite of her lies, this raving ache would go on and on . . . The lies, the bare-faced lies! He might have questioned the truth of that man's letter if she hadn't actually admitted she was living in Holborn. To think he had put her on the tram and she had doubled back into Holborn!

Anyway, it served him right, at his age, falling for a bit of a girl! . . . But she wasn't a bit of a girl; she was mature, with the knowledge of life in her eyes; and by God, she must have it, too, living in Holborn! And he had been such a fool as to fall for her simplicity. Living with her father in Holborn!

He lifted his head and let out a staccato laugh. That black he had painted! Why on earth had she to pick on him? Had there been the slightest resemblance between them he would have noticed it . . . wouldn't he? It was a pity the painting had gone . . . His thinking brought him upright, and before the thought ended he was up the stairs and into the studio. He pushed aside a number of files that stood against the wall, until he came to one with the word 'Hulk' written across it. This he lifted on to the table and flicked over the loose sheets it contained, most of them being rough sketches of a boat rotting in the mud. And when he came to the sketches of the Negro he became still, devouring each line of the drawings. This one was a quick sketch, done when he first saw the man. It was made up of only a few lightning strokes, because, finding he was being sketched, the Negro moved off. Then this one, a side view, showing that enormous ear. And this, just his mouth. Was there any resemblance between that mouth and hers? . . . None! But he had done one full-faced. He flung over more drawings, depicting hands and feet. Then he came upon it: the ear, the pock marks, and the emaciation, all there. But out of this, James's eyes, almost alive, stared up at him, and for a moment the man became submerged in the artist, and he thought, with a sense of awe, of his own achievement: I got those eyes. Then, still looking down into the charcoal eyes of the Negro, he began to place odd pieces of paper over the face. In all positions he placed them, until only the eyes were left, and as he stared an uneasiness grew in him; and he protested, speaking aloud, 'It isn't so. I would have known; I would have detected it.'

He looked around the room, at the various paintings hanging there, as if they would confirm him in his belief . . . 'I would have known.' Yet the eyes looking up at him were the eyes of Rose Angela.

My God! Supposing she was speaking the truth! But the Arab . . . he was waiting for her all right. And her face. Who had really done that to her?

He was still staring down into the eyes when a faint tap, tap came to him. There was someone at the back door again, blast them! Murphy come back, perhaps. No . . . Then Her? He gave himself no answer, for it would not be her; she would not come here again – his reception having blasted her as far as another continent from him.

Well, who the hell was it, then? He marched to the window, and, flinging it up, looked down on to the wharf and into the upturned face of a woman.

'Mr Stanhope?'

He found himself answering quietly, 'Yes.'

'I'm Mrs Paterson. I've come to see my daughter.'

For a long moment he stared at her. Then he said, still quietly, 'Wait a moment, I'll be down.'

He would not allow himself any pondering as he went hastily down the stairs. But when he unlocked the back door he was made to wonder what this woman's visit could portend.

Bridget and he appraised each other for some seconds, and it was she who spoke first. 'Can I see my daughter, please?'

His reply was to step aside and say, 'Will you come in?'

Silently Bridget passed him and walked into the kitchen, into the blue kitchen that Rose Angela had described so vividly. She stood stiffly waiting, and he pulled a chair from the table and said, 'Please sit down.'

She sat down, and looked towards the door that led to the hall, as if expecting Rose Angela to make an appearance.

Stanhope looked at this woman, the mother of Rose Angela, the woman who had married a coloured man. She was a fine-looking woman with a stately bearing, but there was a stiffness about her that wasn't a veneer of the moment. It seemed to emanate from within her.

She looked up at him and asked, 'Is Rosie in?'

'No.' He turned from her and looked out of the window towards the river. 'I'm afraid, Mrs Paterson, she is not here.'

'Not here? You mean she's gone?'

He nodded.

'When?'

'This morning.'

'This morning,' she repeated. 'Mr Stanhope' – she was on her feet now, looking at his back – 'do you know where she's gone?'

'No.'

He heard her swallow in the silence that followed his answer. Then she burst out:

'Mr Stanhope, you know something, you know where she's gone. Has she gone into . . . Holborn? Is she living there altogether?'

He did not answer her, and she went on, 'Has she been working here all along?' And he said, 'Yes, up to yesterday.'

'And is she not coming back?'

'No.'

Slowly Bridget sat down again. 'If I'd only come yesterday.' She was talking softly as if to herself. 'I knew something was wrong. Mr Stanhope' – she entreated the forbidding solidness of his back – 'you know more than I do, for God's sake tell me!'

He remained for a moment longer staring at the river. Then turning slowly, he pulled a letter from his pocket and handed it to her. 'Read that.'

Wondering, she took the letter from him, and he watched her closely as she began to read it. He saw the colour of her face change; and before she had read very far she turned to the back of the letter in search of the signature. Then she said in an awed whisper, 'My brother wrote this.'

She read a little farther, then again she stopped, and the glisten of tears was in her eyes. 'Oh, it's lies, all lies. She was the best lass in the world, she never caused me a moment's trouble. Not until . . . these last few weeks. But this about having to leave her places, it's a pack of lies. She left because she wouldn't . . . well, the men wouldn't leave her alone, and her mistresses . . . It wasn't her fault. Matt, my brother, has always hated her.'

She read on to the end of the letter, then folded it slowly and handed it back to him. 'There's not a line of truth in it, except . . .' She bit her lip and pulled at the fingers of her thin black gloves. 'He . . . Matt, my brother . . . he said he saw her with an Arab. And then she said she was going to lodge in Holborn. But somehow, knowing her, the more I thought of it the less I could believe it, in spite of what I did.' For an instant her eyes flicked away from his. Then she murmured in perplexity, 'But if she's left here and is . . . in Holborn . . .'

Stanhope pushed his hand through his hair. 'I don't know, I don't know what to think. An hour ago I would have said she was with the Arab all right. Now I'm not sure. And if I'm wrong . . .' The enormity of his thought brought his movements to a stop, and he stood, his hand in his hair, staring at the table, as if lying there for him to see was some disastrous result of his doubting.

'Mrs Paterson' – he dropped into a chair opposite to her – 'I think I'd better tell you . . . You see, I loved Rosie. I was no better than any of her other bosses, but not up till last night did I tell her . . .'

'Not till last night? Then she wasn't . . .?' Bridget caught herself up.

He shook his head at her. 'No, she wasn't living with me.'

'I'm sorry I . . .'

'Don't be. Last night I was quite willing that that's how things should be; but then, on reflection, I knew I must marry her. I went with her to the tram and saw her get on it – as I thought, to go home. Prior to this I had chased an Arab away from outside. Then this morning I received this letter. And not only this one, but another from Mrs Grant. Then Rosie came. You can imagine how I was feeling.' He looked away from Bridget towards the window again. 'But I can see now that the distress she was in was genuine. And her face, her beautiful face, was scarcely recognisable.'

Slowly Bridget rose up from the chair. 'What about her face?'

'It was disfigured.'

'Disfigured? With a knife?'

'No, no, not with a knife; the blow had been done with a fist, right between her eyes. She said her uncle did it, but I didn't believe her; I thought the Arab had done it.'

'Oh, my God! What's it all about?' Bridget clutched at the front of her coat. 'Matt always said he'd spoil her face. I went in fear for years that he'd do it. And yesterday morning he went out, and hasn't been seen since. My other brother's been looking for him half the night; and this morning we had to tell the polis. Oh, Mr Stanhope, I'm afraid of our Matt and what he'll do to her. Was she alone last night when he caught her?'

'I don't know.'

'Have you any idea at all where I'll likely find her?'

'Apart from knowing she's in Holborn, I can't say. She said she was . . .' He stopped and stared at Bridget. 'Mrs Paterson, is your husband alive?'

Bridget stared back at him, and murmured, 'I don't know.'

'It's some years since you saw him?'

'I saw him last when Rosie was four years old. He had a fight with my brother and he thought he'd killed him, and he ran away. I haven't seen him since.'

'Sit down, I won't be a minute.' Stanhope left the kitchen, and in a matter of seconds was back with a single sheet of paper in his hand. He put this face downwards on the table and, leaning towards Bridget, said gently, 'Mrs Paterson, this may come as a shock to you . . . or it may mean nothing. Do you recognise this man?' He turned over the drawing for her to see. He watched her eyes widen and her lips slowly drop apart; then he saw her body fold up as if it had been released from a spring, and she slumped face forward over the table before he could reach her.

Lifting her limp head he urged, 'Come on, Mrs Paterson,' but she made no response. He hurried into the drawing-room, and when he returned with some brandy she was raising herself up. And her face was blanched.

'Drink this.'

He put the brandy to her lips, and she sipped it and shuddered, then said, 'I'm all right.'

'Take another drink.'

She shook her head. The drawing was still on the table, and she looked down on it again, but did not speak. Nor did Stanhope, for he was seeing Rose Angela's face as she said, 'I'm living with my father . . . the Negro . . . the one you painted.'

Every word she spoke had been true, then, and he had kicked her out. He closed his eyes.

Bridget's voice, low and trembling, was saying, 'This is my husband. He's changed . . . but it's him. Where is he?'

'If that is your husband, then, Mrs Paterson, he's in Holborn. And he's been living there for some time. And Rosie is living with him. That is the explanation of it all. The only thing I can't see now is why she had to keep it secret.'

Bridget took her handkerchief and wiped the moisture from her face. Her conscience was suggesting one reason why James had remained hidden. She stared at the drawing again. The eyes were as she remembered them, but that ear and the pox about his chin and the hollowness of his cheeks all spoke of hardship. Remorse and pity rose in her! Oh, Jimmie, Jimmie! And Rosie knew. All the time she knew and stayed with you, and put up with everything rather than let on in case Matt found out. Yes, that would be one of the reasons why she had kept quiet . . . in case Matt found out. Oh, Rosie, lass!

Stanhope touched the outline of the drawing with his finger. 'He was a very sick man when I drew that . . . You should know he was dying with consumption.'

'Consumption?'

'I'm afraid so. And after I'd finished painting him he seemed to disappear. Murphy and Pete, two friends of his, never mentioned him again, and I took it for granted he was dead.'

Bridget gripped the edge of the table and brought herself to her feet. 'Now I know!' She turned startled eyes on Stanhope. 'Matt knew about him' – she nodded to the drawing – 'about Jimmie being here. He's been queer for the last week or so; he's been queer for some time. But lately he's been saying strange things; I thought he was going mad. Only yesterday morning he said' – she paused as if to recall each word – 'he said, soon he'd be able to tell me something and I'd be really free; he said there wouldn't only be one funeral. You see, me father's ill. He had an accident and burnt his hands; then he got soaked sitting on the . . . being out one night, and he took pneumonia and we thought he was going to die. But my mother's pulling him through.'

She paused again, and Stanhope could see her mind probing, and for the moment, he knew, she was no longer with him but back in a number of yesterdays, piecing together what well might be a tragedy.

Since coming downstairs this morning his life had been changed completely. Yesterday he was lord of all he surveyed – the house, the wharf – and last night, Rose Angela. In spite of the torment of his growing passion for her his days had been full and smooth; he had his work and material, for it swarmed about him. But now, after a few hours, he was being drawn rapidly into the maelstrom of lives, each converging to a climax that had its beginning when this woman married a Negro. That she foresaw tragedy he could see by her expression – the terror in her face conveyed itself to him – and he thought, I likely could have prevented anything further happening if I hadn't been such a blasted fool and had listened to Rosie.

'If they meet, Matt'll kill him,' Bridget spoke again. 'He always said he would. I must find Rosie. When I find her I'll find him.'

'Likely they have met already. When your brother hit her he must have cornered her somewhere, for it's not likely he'd try it on in the street.'

'But he hasn't come home! You don't know Matt; he'll keep at a thing until it's done.'

'But where are you going to start to look for her? You know the people in that quarter – they can be like oysters if they choose . . . Wait! What am I thinking of? Murphy, the man who lives in the railway carriage, he'll take us. I'll get my coat.'

When he returned, Bridget said, 'But it's putting you to a lot of trouble.' And he answered soberly, 'Trouble, Mrs Paterson? If I can't gain Rosie's forgiveness, then I'm only at the beginning of my trouble.'

They stood for a second longer looking at each other and understanding each other, as if this was but one of many meetings during which their hopes and fears had been laid bare.

He opened the door for her and she went out before him, and as they hurried over the sleepers he took her elbow to help her, and this action thrust her painfully back into the past – Jimmie had done things like this . . . Tony didn't. His loving showed itself in other ways; like the men of the fifteen streets, he practically ignored women in public, at least when it meant doing any service that would qualify him for the name of 'Sloppy' and bring derision on him and the recipient of his affection. But, she remembered, Jimmie had not minded. He, like this man, had done these little things naturally. Her heart began to ache with an intolerable ache. Poor Jimmie! She should never have married him; she should have had the courage to have the bairn. But he had wanted her so. And she was young and silly, and ignorant.

And now he was dying; and he'd been living in the town and hadn't troubled her; and Rosie had stood all that scandal about living with an Arab rather than give him away. Would Rosie ever forgive her? What must she have felt when everybody turned against her! Oh, Rosie, lass, Rosie!

Stanhope's tongue, clicking with impatience, brought her thoughts from Rosie. He was looking through the railway-carriage window.

'They're gone!' He turned a disappointed face to her. 'The thing is now, where to look for them, for they may have gone across the water. Yet there's the chance they may still be knocking around the market place or the ferry.'

So, for an hour or more Stanhope and Bridget walked about the market and the ferry and beyond them, but saw no signs of Murphy and Pete. Then Stanhope suggested that Bridget, who was looking very tired, should return home and that as soon as he found Murphy he would send her word.

But Bridget was reluctant to comply with his suggestion, even when he pressed the point that they would likely go on for hours without success. At last, when he intimated that he stood more chance of finding something out if alone, she agreed; and, as he had put her daughter on the tram for home last night, now he did her, reassuring her once more that as soon as he had any news he would send for her.

Alone again, he hurried down the Mill Dam bank; but stopped before turning into Holborn. It would be a good idea to leave a note at the railway carriage telling Murphy, should he return, to wait there for him. Forgotten now completely was the fact that a short while ago he had threatened to throw him in the river.

He was going through the narrow cut, when, to his surprise and relief, he saw Murphy entering it from the river end. Murphy had, however, seen him first, and was already making a hasty retreat when Stanhope shouted. 'Hi there! Murphy!'

Murphy did not stop, so Stanhope broke into a run, calling, 'Just a minute! What's the matter with you, man?' And when he came abreast of him he demanded, 'Are you deaf? Couldn't you hear me?'

Murphy looked at him out of the corner of his eye and cautiously answered the latter part of the question, 'Aye, guv'nor.'

Then, remembering the reason for this caution, Stanhope said, 'I'm sorry about that; I was a bit mad. But something's happened since then, and I want your help, Murphy.'

'Aye, guv'nor.' Again Murphy looked sideways at him.

'I want you to take me to Rosie.'

'What?' Now Murphy was fronting him. 'Take you to Rosie! Oh, well, guv'nor.' He rubbed his chin with the palm of his hand. 'Well, it's like this. I can't do it . . . not right away I can't. I'll have to have a talk with . . . Well, you see . . .'

He stopped, and Stanhope said, 'It's all right; I know who Rosie's father is. Her mother has just been to see me.'

'To see you,' repeated Murphy. 'But God, guv'nor, she don't know nowt about Jimmie being here!'

'She does now.'

'How?'

'By the drawing I did of him.'

'But he don't want her to know.'

'She knows, anyway, and it's right that she should. And she's worried about Rosie. I'm worried about Rosie, too, Murphy.'

Murphy had never before detected such a tone in Stanhope's voice, and he moved from one foot to the other, saying, 'Well, guv'nor . . . I dunno . . . I suppose it'll be all right.'

'It will be, I assure you.'

'I wish Pete was here.'

'Where is he?'

'Gone along the river looking for a sign of . . .' He stopped; it wasn't likely the guv'nor knew anything about Matt. 'Seeing if there's anything doing,' he ended.

'Take me now, Murphy,' Stanhope urged. 'If you don't, I'll find them anyway. It will take me longer, but I'll find them.'

'Aye, there's that in it.' Murphy again looked sideways at him, and his next words would never have been spoken had he given thought to them. But as he stared at this big, blustering man, they seemed to be drawn to his lips. 'You're a bloody funny bloke,' he said, and his mouth fell agape at his own temerity.

After a moment they laughed together, then turned and went through the cut and into Holborn.

Hassan came thoughtfully down the stairs. His first love offering had just been refused. When previously he had left Rose Angela he returned to his café and had there packed a basket of delicacies for James, and for her he had selected, from a small hoard of such things, a ring, a very valuable ring. Although he had given a lot of money for it, he knew he had paid only about a third of its real value. Rose Angela, however, had merely glanced at it and shook her head, and instead of allowing him to place the ring on her finger she had placed her fingers on her lips to ensure his silence so as not to disturb James's sleep. And when he left the ring on the table she picked it up and followed him on to the landing and whispered, 'No, Hassan, I can't take it. Not yet, anyway.' And he simply said, 'All right,' and told himself that he must go carefully, and that time was young. Give her a few weeks to recover and she would turn to him; she would be his . . . he would make her his; only let her not see that painter and she would forget.

It was at this point that he reached the foot of the stairs, and, as if his thought of the painter had conjured Stanhope up, he saw him. Through the open doorway he saw him and Murphy enter the yard, and as fire will sweep over oil, so a flame of hate swept over him.

He stood guarding the foot of the stairs; and when Murphy, coming first through the doorway, said, 'Watcher, there,' he made no reply. He did not even look at Murphy, but kept his eyes riveted on the breadth of the man protruding behind him.

Stanhope, coming abreast of Murphy, faced Hassan, and he recognised in this thin tall Arab the man he had chased from the house last night. Also, even before Hassan spoke, he knew him to be the Arab whose name was coupled with that of Rosie, and immediately guessed that if rumour was wrong it was not this man's fault.

'What do you want?' Hassan pointedly addressed Stanhope.

And Stanhope tried to override his own dislike, for, after all, this was a man, and if his feeling for Rosie was to be compared with his own, then, whatever his race, he was to be pitied. So, with unusual calmness for him, he replied, 'Don't you think that's my business?'

'No, I do not.'

The English was precise and clipped, not the pidgin kind, and this too impressed Stanhope that he was not dealing with the ordinary run of Arab who manned the cargo ships running back and forth from the Tyne. So again he curbed the hot retort on his tongue and said, 'Well, whether you do or not is beside the point. Now, if you'll move . . .'

'I'll see you in your own particular hell first!'

'Why, Hassan, man' – Murphy was gaping open-mouthed – 'what's come over you? Look, the guv'nor just wants to see Rosie and . . .'

Hassan turned on Murphy and repeated, 'Just wants to see Rosie! You fool!'

Murphy stood dumb with amazement. Never before had Hassan taken this line with him. To him Hassan was a warm man, and a very decent bloke, better than many whites, for he always had a civil word and would sit and crack with you. But now he was speaking to him as if he was a dog. And no coloured man, however decent he might be, was going to speak to him like a dog! After all was said and done, what was he but an Arab, even if he had money. No, by God, he'd soon let him see who he was speaking to!

'What the hell's up with you! The guv'nor's come to see Rosie, and he's goner see her!'

Murphy's tone now brought Hassan's gaze back to him, and his anger for a moment was touched with sorrow: Murphy was no longer Murphy, he was a white man, taking another white man's part against colour. And Jimmie, in his wilful ignorance, thought Rose Angela could entirely escape this!

Hassan's voice was quieter now as he addressed Murphy, but bitterness lay deep in it. 'A few hours ago you saved Rose Angela from jumping in the river, because of this man's treatment of her. Now you bring him to her. Well, it's too late, she's going to marry me.'

'What' – the loose goose-flesh skin of Murphy's neck rippled – 'marry you!' He turned and looked at Stanhope; but Stanhope was showing no surprise at this preposterous statement, for inside he was sick with this new knowledge, that because of him Rosie had tried to drown herself.

'Marry you!' gulped Murphy. 'Why, man, you must be mad.' He knew that Hassan was fond of Rosie, but so was he, and so was Pete. Aye, by lad, Pete was very struck on Rosie. But would any of them think they could marry her? Yet here was Hassan saying he was going to. Why, it was enough to make the guv'nor bash his face in. He looked again at Stanhope, who was looking at Hassan . . . not as he should do, in one of his mad tears, but quietly, and what was more puzzling he was speaking quietly too. Funnily quiet, Murphy thought.

'I am here to see Rosie, and I am going to see her! As for what she does, that is for her to decide.'

'You're so sure of yourself, aren't you? You think you only have to see her again and tell her you know now she wasn't living with an Arab and everything will be all right!' Hassan's lip curled back, miming the scorn against himself the last words implied.

And Murphy thought, I shouldn't have told him. I want me head look'n.

'Will you get out of my way?'

Hassan's reply was to remain staring down at Stanhope from the vantage point of the bottom stair. There were now spectators on the scene, some on the stairs above and some in the doorway. Stanhope was not aware of them; he was only aware that his tolerance had reached its limit. With a lightning stroke for one so heavily built his hands shot up, and the Arab and he changed places. In almost the wink of an eye he had swung Hassan bodily from the step. But like lightning, too, Hassan's hand moved behind to his hip pocket in a movement that spoke plainer than words to the onlookers, for whereas before no-one had uttered a word, now there were cries of, 'Don't be a fool, man!' 'You know who'll get the worst of it, don't you?' and 'None of that, now; do you want to bring the polis on the house?'

Hassan's fingers still gripped the handle of his knife as Stanhope turned from him and walked up the stairs, followed by Murphy. And now the people in the hall and those on the stairs came and closed round Hassan, urging him, for his own sake, to be sensible and reminding him of the too swift justice that followed when a coloured man attacked a white.

As Murphy tapped gently on the door, Stanhope stood taut, waiting. His mind was in a turmoil; all he wanted to do in this moment was to savour the thought that he was about to see her again, but the scene just past and the significance of the Arab's statement that she was going to marry him, combined with the thought that but for Murphy she might have succeeded in drowning herself, all added to his confusion. And when the door was softly opened and Rose Angela stood there, a warning finger on her lips, all he could do was to stare at her.

As her hand dropped to her side, Murphy whispered, 'What did I tell you, eh, Rosie? Here's the guv'nor; he wants to see you.'

When neither she nor Stanhope spoke, Murphy went on, 'Is Jimmy asleep? Well, that will do him good.' The silence being too much for him, he moved from one foot to the other, then sidled past her into the room.

Stanhope said, 'I must talk to you, Rosie.'

With a backward glance towards the bed, Rose Angela stepped out on to the landing and pulled the door to behind her. And now they were within a foot of each other. He looked into her face, discoloured and bruised from cheek-bone to cheek-bone, her eyes swollen level and their expression without life; and his love at this moment became purified and selfless. All he wanted was to ensure that never again would she know fear or want; and so deep was the sadness in her eyes that he felt that not in a lifetime could he erase it. That he had put

189

most of it there he knew, and the responsibility lay like a weight on his tongue, making him inarticulate. 'Rosie . . . what can I say?'

She did not help him, she only looked at him, into his eyes.

'Oh, Rosie, if you had only told me at the beginning. Can you forgive me?'

He took her hand, and it lay passively in his. 'Can you?' His voice was deep with his feeling.

Slowly she inclined her head, and he sighed. 'Oh, Rosie, I'll never forgive myself . . . never.' He looked about the landing. The other two doors were closed, but he felt that behind them were straining ears, and he whispered, 'Come back with me, I must talk to you.'

She shook her head.

'But we must talk.'

He looked at the door behind her, and for the first time she spoke. 'My father is very sick.'

'Can I see him?'

'I would rather you didn't.'

The listlessness of her voice perturbed him, and he said, 'There's bound to be some way in which I can help.'

Again she shook her head, and it seemed to him she was growing more lifeless each moment.

'Rosie' – he meant the demand in his voice to stir her – 'go back to last night; try to forget what has happened in between. I will make you forget. I'm to blame, at least for this morning . . . Will you?'

Still looking into his eyes, she answered him, 'A short while ago I promised Hassan . . .' But what she had promised Hassan she could not go on to explain. Instead she shook her head pitifully and Stanhope's brows gathered into a furrow and his jaw stiffened. 'You can't do it! You didn't mean it. You did it on the rebound, you know you did. And perhaps, naturally, to hurt me.'

'No. I did it because' – she looked away from him as if she was seeing the reason for her action beyond the walls of the house – 'because I'm tired of fighting.'

'Tired of fighting?' He echoed her words in perplexity.

She nodded, her gaze penetrating the future. 'With him there'll be no need to fight; I won't be ashamed any more of being what I am.'

'Rosie, you're mad! You don't know what you are saying. You, ashamed of what you are! You're tired and ill. You're not thinking rationally because of all you've been through.'

She turned and looked at him again. 'It's strange, but my mind is clearer now than ever before in my life. I've always been fighting inside myself because I felt inferior. I've always felt inferior and tried to hide it; and only Hassan could see it, for he, too, knows what it is like to be looked down on. But now there won't be any need to hide it.'

'Stop it!' Stanhope's voice had a touch of the old arrogance in it. 'You cannot compare yourself with him.'

'You don't like Arabs, do you?'

'No, I don't!'

'Yet I'm coloured too.'

'Rosie' – he swallowed hard and inhaled deeply in an endeavour to retain a hold on his calmness – 'why all this talk of colour? What's come over you? Last night you didn't take this line.'

'No, I didn't; I was still hiding from myself. But now I know it was because of my colour that you believed the worst of me.'

'My God, Rosie, you can't believe that! It never entered into it. Can't you see it was because, as I said, when I was to be married before, I found out about this girl, and the circumstances were pretty much the same? Rosie, Rosie, for God's sake get that out of your head!'

'But I kept telling you the truth, and you wouldn't listen to me.'

'Yes, I know, I know. But I was mad with jealousy because I loved you so much. Look' – he pulled her to him – 'you're not going to do this. You wouldn't only be wrecking your own life, but a number of lives. There's your mother – she's worried to death.'

Her face was close under his and she whispered, 'My mother?'

'She's been to see me. She knows about your father, and she's worried because your uncle hasn't returned home. And she's afraid he'll do you both further harm.'

'My mother's been to see you, and she knows?'

'Yes.'

He felt a sigh of relief pass over her, and the despair for a moment left her eyes.

'She's coming here?'

'Yes, as soon as I can get word to her.'

She looked towards the door of the room in which James was lying. 'I must warn him.'

'Rosie, let me speak to him.'

She hesitated a moment, then said dully, 'All right.'

'And Rosie' – he pulled her closer – 'listen to me. I love you and I'm willing to spend my life trying to convince you of it, but I'd rather see you dead than married to that Arab. You love me, don't you? . . . Look at me. You can't look at me and say you don't. Look at me.'

But she did not look at him. Her eyes, wide and staring from her head, were looking at something beyond him. And he flung round from her, expecting to be confronted by the Arab. But he faced a man whom he had never seen before, and who was staring with a diabolical stare, not at him, but at Rosie. And before he had time to think, the man had sprung past him and at Rose Angela, and they were borne to the floor together.

*　　*　　*

Matt had lain all through the night and most of the day concealed between the wall of a warehouse and a rubbish dump. He had slept fitfully through the night, and each time he had woken he had groped at his head. Once he woke up laughing and punching at the air. When daylight came he kept awake, but did not move from where he was. He could not tell himself why he was staying here, but instinct was telling him that he must hide. There was a pile of shavings among the rubbish, and after a while he burrowed into this and lay trying to find something to hold on to in the hollowness of his head. He could not remember his name, nor where he had come from; he only knew he had been running . . . running, running. But when he thought of himself running he felt disappointed, and groped at the feeling, but the reason for this, too, evaded him.

Although a drizzle of rain was falling, he did not feel cold, only hungry. But he was loath to move, until the fading light of the afternoon urged him to get up. And he had to struggle out of the shavings, for his limbs felt heavy. He gazed about him, but did not know where he was. The river meant nothing to him, and he turned from it and walked with dragging step to where an opening showed in the wall beyond the refuse heap. It was an alleyway, and at the farther end he could see people passing in the street; and, strangely, he did not fear them now, but had an urge to be near them. Yet, once in the street, he walked close to the wall, keeping his head down. He turned the corner and crossed a road as if he knew where he was going, and he had walked quite some distance before he stopped. He was beside a short passage leading into a yard. Some way beyond, on the pavement, two men stood talking to an Arab. He turned his back on them, and as though he had done it before he lifted his eyes to the tin plate nailed above the arch and read 'River Court, 1, 2, 3 and 4'. Then he went along the passage and into the yard, and looked from one to the other of the four doors leading from it.

In the centre of the yard a woman was emptying slops down the drain, and as she banged the bucket to dislodge some filth she turned and glanced at him, and he hung his head. She took no further notice of him, but went to a tap near the wall, rinsed the bucket, threw the water on to the yard, then went through an open doorway.

Matt looked around the yard, selected a door, and went towards it. As he reached it his hand went to his head again, and his fingers moved over his scalp. Two children coming through the doorway looked up at him, then continued on their way; and he walked into the hallway and up the stairs without meeting anyone. But when he reached the second landing he heard voices, and he stood still, listening. First a man's voice, then a woman's. The woman's did not come often, but he waited for it. It was soft, scarcely above a whisper, and his mind clung to it, and he knew that he knew it. It began to form a substance in the hollowness, yet he could not pin it down, for when he groped at it it evaded him, moving away swiftly, almost becoming lost in the void again, until the whisper was renewed. Then he could feel it, the something that would bring him back. But when, for a seemingly long time, the woman's whisper did not reach him, he began to mount the stairs, pausing on each tread to listen. He was half-way up when he saw the feet through the banisters. They were close together, the woman's and the man's. He mounted still farther, until now he could see the back of the man's head. Then he was at the top of the stairs, and the woman moved her head and he saw her face, and he knew.

Now he knew what he had been trying to remember: his life that had been wrecked, his days bare and his nights empty, and all because of her. And he had come back to level things off. Once he had done this he would be happy, and the remainder of the void within him would be filled again. The woman saw him and became petrified, so petrified that she could make no sound, and at the sight of her fear he experienced a feeling of pure glee. And when the man who was shielding her with his body turned, the way was clear, and he sprang.

His hands clawed at her flesh, and he felt her body under his as they went down together. He heard the rattle of pails and tins as they were scattered about them. Then he was no longer on the landing but swinging into the air. And as he fell the second time he clung to the thing that had lifted him and bore it with him. He was fighting now like a mad-man, with his teeth, his fists and his feet, until fresh hands tore at him and fresh faces milled around him . . . white faces, dark faces; and hands, thousands of hands; and voices, crying and screaming. Then as suddenly as the void had begun to fill, so it emptied again. He still fought and struggled, but now only to get away, because he had become afraid of something, not of the pain from the blows, but from something welling inside him. Above the noise and stamping of feet he heard a high scream; then the struggle ceased abruptly.

He was on his knees, and the front of his coat and shirt were ripped away, and on his bare chest there were spatters of blood. Someone was holding his arms, and someone else had hold of his hair and was pulling his head back. The strain on his neck was excruciating, and from this angle all he could see was an Arab standing some distance from him. His eyes strained from the face down the man's side to the knife clutched in the brown hand.

Then the grip on his hair eased, to fall away altogether. And now his eyes were looking at the floor and the dirty boards spattered with blood, and he felt a rising gurgle of laughter moving up through his stomach. But before it reached his lips it changed. He saw it changing. It was in the centre of the great empty void that was him. He saw it disintegrate, then form again. And it formed into a sorrow that he knew was his life. And the weight of it became so great inside of him that he felt he must tear it out. But he had no means of doing this, and he knew it. Then into the stillness came a terrifying sound. It was the thing that had frightened him, the thing that he feared. It was the sound of his own weeping.

Stanhope looked from the sobbing man to his arm. The long gap in his greatcoat, coat and shirt looked like a series of jagged red lips. He was feeling no pain; from the moment when a red hot needle seemed to rip his skin the arm became numb. His main feeling was one of amazement. Even in the heat of the fight he had felt this amazement, when he realised that the Arab was trying to knife him. When he first saw the knife gleaming in the Arab's hand he wanted to protest against its use on Matt, but the milling of six bodies, for by then Murphy and two other men had joined the fray, made it impossible. When the knife slit the front of his coat he thought it was an accident, but not when he felt the prick of it between his shoulder-blades. He had untangled himself from the arms that were trying to hold Matt down and turned, filled with fury, yet still amazed, to where he thought the Arab was, for in the dimness of the landing it was fast becoming difficult to distinguish one figure from another. Almost at the same moment as he heard Rose Angela scream he felt the knife go down his arm, and he was thrown against the wall by the force behind the blow.

And now there was quiet on the landing; even the people crowding the stairs were quiet; and Stanhope thought he must be light-headed when, in a matter of seconds, the stairs were emptied of people as if a hand had wiped them away. Doors on the landing, which had been open and filled with shouting women, were now closed. He saw the two men who had been very prominent in the mêlée glide like vapour down the stairs. And now there remained only Murphy, who was holding the kneeling Matt by the arms, Rose Angela, who was pressed tight in the corner of the walls, the Arab and himself.

He looked at the Arab, whose face appeared a dull grey, its expression a mixture of hate and bitterness, and he thought, The dirty greaser! He tried to do me in. And he'll try to pass it off on to the madman there. A flame of intense anger swept over him, and he knew that if he himself had a knife handy at this moment he would ram it home into the Arab's chest. His anger impelled him from the wall, and, shouting a gabble of words, he lunged at Hassan. But before he could reach him, Murphy was between them. He struck at Murphy with his good arm until, without any warning, his strength left him and he had to lean on Murphy for support. The sweat ran into his eyes, blinding him for the moment. Then again he was looking at the Arab. But the Arab was now staring at Rose Angela, and she at him. For a seemingly long time he watched

194

them stare at each other, until he pulled himself from Murphy's hands and stumbled towards them.

Hassan, turning his eyes from Rose Angela to Stanhope, seemed to be on the point of saying something; but, instead, he allowed his curling lip to convey the contempt he was feeling. Then, unhurriedly, he walked across the landing and into the black well of the staircase.

There seemed to be nothing left now but the sound of the crying. It was like the crying of a lost child, with snuffles and breaking sobs. And again, from the support of Murphy's arm, Stanhope gazed down in stupefaction at the man sitting on the floor, his clothes torn from his body and his face and chest spattered with blood. He could not reconcile this whimpering heap with the maniac he had been fighting, and to his disgust he felt a faintness overcoming him, and he retched.

James lay with his eyes closed. His heart was beating rapidly, but not so rapidly as it had done two hours ago. Then he had thought that each beat would sever the slender line with which he was holding on to life. His heart was pounding now because of what was to come, for at any moment the door would open and Bridget would be in the room.

He had thought he did not want to see her, but now he knew he had been lying to himself by way of comfort. What she had done with her life since he left her did not hurt him any more, nor was he worrying about what effect his changed appearance would have on her; not for much longer would he suffer from vanity or pride or whatever it was that had made him hate the idea that she should see him looking anything but . . . the big fine Negro man.

The murmur of whispering voices floated to him; Rose Angela's and the painter's. He was a man after his own heart, that painter, stubborn and generous. The doctor had been stubborn man too; he say the painter must go to hospital, and the painter, he say he not go. The painter was worried in case Hassan come back, but Hassan no come back, and that good thing. Yet he was sorry, very sorry, for he liked Hassan, and he wished things had worked out different, for he no want Hassan or any man to hide like he had to hide. But now Hassan think that painter put polis on him, and he lie low for time. Yet painter generous, for he had the chance when polis ask him who stab him, and he say he not see man who did it. And when polis ask could it be Matt, painter still say he not know.

James had always felt that life was full of strange contradictions. Things had puzzled him, and when he groped into the deep depths of himself in search of answers, he had only become more puzzled. Yet he would have stood by the theory that once you love, you always love, and once you hate, a groove is seared in the mind, a groove that can be filled with nothing but itself. He would have rejected the idea that he could allow pity to fill the groove, yet the groove of his hate for Matt had been filled with pity when he watched him for the last time through the open door and saw him propped against the banisters, crying, ceaselessly crying. There was something improper in a man crying like that, but instead of arousing his scorn, pity for this man who had directed his life into tragic channels rose in him; for, to all intents and purposes, Matt was a dead man. He was gone now; they had taken him away. And the doctor was gone. And Murphy was gone too . . . to fetch Bridget.

Life was strange. A man wanted something, and he got it; and he thought it make him happy; and he thought all things that came of it must be good things because it made him happy. He had wanted Bridget, and he had got her. And he was happy for a time. But it was not good. For sixteen years he paid for that bit happiness. And others paid too . . . Rose Angela, she paid; she paid too much. And Bridget, she paid; just how much he did not know. But she paid all right. And now Hassan, he pay. And Matt; yes indeed, he pay; he was bound to pay in some way. Everything in life must be paid for, but some things were charged too big a price. He had wanted the painter for his Rose Angela, but this, too, would have to be paid for, and by her.

The hoodwinking of himself, the pretence, the day-dreaming, all fell away, and in a moment of illuminating truth he knew that because of his folly his daughter must pay and go on paying, for, as Hassan said, inside Rose Angela was black, and the tragedy of his race lay buried in the blackness. In what way she would be called upon to pay he did not exactly know: perhaps with babies who would be black outside as well as in.

She had a saying that the priest had told her. It went: God is colour-blind. He had always had his doubts about this saying; he thought it would be better if God could see colour, for then he would see the black man as the white sees him, and seeing him so, and being God, he would certainly have given the black man some power wherewith he could command of the white and of all races their respect; for surely it was an indignity for a man to desire the flesh of his flesh to be a different colour from that of his own. God should not allow a man or a woman to be born to despise the seed of their body like that; he should not ask such a price for a life.

He raised his tired lids and looked at Rose Angela. She was bending over the painter as he sat in the old armchair by the fire. The strained look was gone from her face, but the sadness still remained. He watched the painter's hand go up to her cheek. Then she saw him rise and come towards him. He looked up at this man into whose keeping Rose Angela was going, and he knew a measure of contentment . . . if anyone could, he would make the payment easier.

He put out his hand, and the painter grasped it, and they gazed deep at each other – the need for words was past.

As the sound of a car came to them from the street below, Rose Angela bent over him, and softly and tenderly and with love she kissed him. Then with the painter she left the room, smiling at him before closing the door. And, his heart pounding again, he lay watching the door, waiting for it to open into his past.

THE END

THE UNBAITED TRAP

Contents

PART ONE

DINNER AT EIGHT

CHAPTER ONE

THE ROOF

John Emmerson brought his speed down to twenty as he neared the bottom of the Avenue. Although it was only six o'clock on the November evening, there was already a tendency to frost, and he knew from experience the road would be wet near Handley's Place. There was a spring somewhere up on one of his fields and nothing could be done about it. Twice last year he had skidded on the same spot, and around this time of the year, and he didn't want this to happen tonight, not with his new acquisition only a week old. He'd had a Rover car for years, changing it every so often, but this last change had brought with it a thrill, and he had long since felt that thrills were things that happened to other men, and youths. Yes, thrills were the prerogative of youth. But the Rover 2000 had stirred something in him. It was a small stir, but nevertheless, because such emotional happenings were rare, it loomed as something large. The effect of the car on him was, he imagined, like that caused by a few pep pills.

As he turned into Lime Avenue his headlights picked up the line of trees. Stiff and stark, they marched into the distance, their blackness shades darker than the night sky.

A short way up the road a headlight crossed his own and he swerved to the right, and as he did so he tooted his horn twice, and received the same reply from the other car. Later tonight the driver of that car would be coming to dinner, and this time next year his only daughter would be his own daughter-in-law.

His house was on the opposite side of the road, number 74, 'The Gables', and was quite a way from number 7, 'Syracuse', since each house stood in about quarter of an acre of land.

He had lived in Lime Avenue ten years, moving here when he became senior partner of the firm. It was in a way the insignia of his success; and no little success, he having bought out Ratcliff, Arnold & Baker. Now to all intents and purposes he was Ratcliff, Arnold & Baker, the leading solicitors of the town. And that state would continue, he supposed, until Arnold Ransome bought him out. The junior partner, Boyd, did not come into it at this stage – junior partners had long, long roads to travel.

7

He turned into his drive, made the S-bend, and came to his front door. Ann had forgotten to put the light on. She was careful about lights, economical about silly little things, and wildly extravagant about things that cost a great deal of money. But in just under two hours' time she would have the house ablaze to greet the Family Wilcox. Her dear friend, May, her future daughter-in-law Valerie, and the scion of the local Bench, James; dinner-at-eight, the same old routine, the same old crowd.

He went under the glass-covered porch and inserted his latch-key in the heavy oak front door, and before he turned to close it he switched on the lobby lights, when he passed into the hall he again switched on the lights. The burnt orange shades of the wall lights warmed the white walls. He could stand the white walls at night, but in the daytime their starkness chilled him. About two years ago Ann had taken this craze for the stripped look; the lounge had become white, the dining-room a pale French grey; the staircase and landing white; her bedroom pale lilac and white. He had checked the attack on his own room, but he had done it gently, as he did everything when dealing with Ann, or anyone else for that matter, but particularly when dealing with his wife. And so his room was left to its overall greenness, and it was the only place in his home that didn't cause his eyes to blink and water.

He went into the cloakroom and hung up his coat and hat, and having washed his hands he bent his tall, heavy body towards the mirror, and, moistening a finger, rubbed it over the hair at each side of his ears. Then he stared at himself, as was his habit. The blue eyes that looked back at him looked slightly washed out and weary. He now drew his finger and thumb down his long nose, then nipped its point before dropping his index finger to the bristle on his upper lip, which he daily prevented from becoming a moustache. But the movement of his finger was like that of a man stroking his moustache. These were private actions, almost unconscious, indulged in daily over the years until now he neither saw nor felt himself doing them any more. The only way he would have become aware of this habit would have been if he had found himself being observed. It was as if some compassionate part of him looked kindly at the whole, like a mother giving praise to the runt of her litter. Last of all, he stroked his hair back. It was very thick and grizzled and was the only strong-looking thing about him.

He now tugged at his waistcoat and went into the hall again, and he was making for the stairs when he heard his wife's voice coming from the kitchen. After a moment's hesitation he went towards the door and pushed it gently open.

His wife was standing at the table. Her hair was done up in a pale blue chiffon scarf, and she was enveloped in a long overall. On his

8

entry she looked up and gave him a thin smile as she said, 'Hello, dear. You're early.'

'Yes, yes. The case was finished much sooner than we expected. I came straight on from Newcastle. My, my! aren't we busy.' He joined his hands together in front of his chest as if he was greeting himself, and smiled his tight smile as he turned towards the woman standing at the stove. 'Well, Mrs Stringer, something smells good. What are you hashing up for us tonight, eh?'

He was always hearty when in the kitchen and speaking to Mrs Stringer. He felt it was expected of him, a form of appreciation for services rendered; and it pleased Ann, for she was always saying she didn't know what she would do without Mrs Stringer. Yet he always felt something of a fool whilst adopting this pose.

Mrs Stringer's conversation always took a staccato form. 'Oh, sir, going to town tonight,' she said 'Aw, yes. But it's not me. I haven't concocted nothing; all praise to the mistress here. Dead beat she'll be afore eight o'clock. What she should do is have a bath and lie down . . . Yes an' I told her.'

'There now. Sensible advice. What about it?' He looked towards his wife, and when she made no rejoinder he stood awkwardly staring at her. She could do this, could Ann, refuse to make comment. She could carry on with what she was doing in a silence that screamed, and it didn't seem to affect her. That was wrong; it affected her all right. He could almost hear her nerves jangling in her body. As he continued to stare at her, he thought she was still good looking; in spite of everything she had kept her looks . . . and poise. The latter perhaps owed a lot to her tall thinness, that thinness that had always been able to carry clothes like a fashion plate. And her face, too, had hardly altered since he first met her, except for her mouth, which drooped noticeably at the corners now. But her complexion was still as clear as a young girl's, and she forty-five this year. Poor Ann. He jerked his head on this last thought and the compassion that the words released in him.

As he turned away, being unable to find any more small talk with which to fill the void, she said suddenly in her crisp way, 'Just a minute; I'm coming.' As she pulled off her overall Mrs Stringer took it from her hand, saying comfortingly, 'That's it, Ma'am. That's it.'

He stood aside and held the door open for her, then followed her across the hall into the lounge.

A log fire was burning on the new hearth that stood two feet from the ground, its funnel-like chimney protruding into the room like some accoutrement in a farmyard – a corn shute he always likened it to. He supposed this was one of the smartest lounges in the town. It should be, too, for the alterations and furnishings had cost him a staggering sum. The new teak floor glowed reddishly along all its

9

thirty-five feet, which took in the dining-room as well. The dividing doors were open and the long dining-table was gleaming with glass and silver. Beyond the table, dull gold velvet curtains shrouded one wall completely, and in the lounge itself the curtains broke the white expanse of wall in three places. If there was an emotion in him strong enough to be called hatred, then he could say he hated this room.

He looked towards her as he said now, 'Would you like a drink?' His voice, no longer hearty, had a tentative sound to it.

'No. No thanks.' Her body made a nervous movement. Then sitting down abruptly on a mushroom-coloured couch, she leant her head back and after a moment said, 'Yes, I think I will, after all. Just a small one.'

He went into the dining-room and beyond the table, and to what looked like a corner cupboard with a carved counter roughly hewn out of a length of oak standing in front of it. When he opened the door of the cupboard, there was displayed a sparkling array of glasses and bottles. The bottles started from floor upwards, and the glasses from above his head, all graded sizes and all standing on their particular shelves. He took down two and placed them on the counter; then lifting up a bottle of sherry, he filled the glasses and carried them down the room to the couch. After handing her a glass, he stood with his back to the fire and again the silence descended on them. With the second sip from his glass, he asked quietly, 'What are we having tonight?' It didn't really matter to him what they had, he wasn't very interested in food – he'd had to learn to eat less and less to keep his bulk down – but she spent a lot of time thinking up menus for her dinners, and again he felt it was expected of him to be interested.

'Oh, nothing elaborate.' She shook her head. 'Sole with wine sauce, and pineapple ham and apple rabbit, with the usual accessories; then French pears.'

Nothing elaborate, she had said. There'd be about six vegetables, and a sauce with everything, and wines in their right places, and a platter with eight different cheeses. Nothing elaborate! And all for the Wilcoxes, whom she saw at least every other day.

The Wilcoxes had been her friends for years, long before he knew her. She and May Wilcox had gone to school together and had remained inseparable since, but a battle for social supremacy had grown up between them, and the giving of little dinners such as was to take place tonight was part of that battle. Nothing elaborate! If May's dinners started with shrimp cocktails or hors d'oeuvres you could be sure that in his house those items would not be allowed on his table for many months.

In this covert and genteel battle his wife, John knew, had always been on the winning side, whether it was planning a meal, or being re-elected chairman of a committee, or organising the coffee mornings. That was, until James Wilcox promoted himself from the position of assistant accountant in the firm of Baxter and Morton, to starting a business on his own. This was achieved by the sudden death of his father-in-law, a widower who had dabbled more than a little in property. Following this unexpected rise in their fortunes it became obvious that May Wilcox could no longer be tactfully patronised, so the battle between the two friends had become more balanced.

But the battle, John had thought of late, had reached a point where a definite cease-fire must be called, for the implements of it had moved from dinners to interior decorating, and he had the strong feeling that the next choice of weapons was going to be headed mink. Yet he was aware, from experience, it was one thing to decide the line he must take, and quite another to carry it out, for he knew, and she knew, oh yes she knew, that he owed her this one outlet.

As he emptied his glass there came the sound of a deep laugh, a guttural, jolly laugh, from the direction of the hall. John did not look towards the door but kept his eyes on his wife's face. At one time her face had brightened when she heard that laugh. It was as if a light were shining under her skin and illuminating her eyes, yet since the wedding date had been fixed between their only son and the daughter of her dearest friend the light in her face had dimmed. She could have been overjoyed that her son and her closest friend's daughter were going to cement their parents' friendship, but she wasn't. She had never said one word to him that would betray her feelings for her future daughter-in-law, but he knew that she didn't like the girl. But there, would she like any girl who would take from her the one thing that had made life bearable?

When Laurance Emmerson came into the room he was still laughing. 'Hello there,' he said. He included his father in the greeting, but only just. Then without pausing he went on, 'Stringy's priceless. Talk about the honour of the house. "No-one can do pineapple ham like the missus." ' He was mimicking now. ' "Are you suggesting that my future mother-in-law is not a good cook?" said me. "Ain't suggestin' anything, merely telling you." '

His laughter rose as he flopped onto the couch beside his mother. Then gradually it faded away. But his face still showed his merriment as he bent towards her and kissed her cheek, saying, 'How are you?'

'Oh, all right.' She kept her eyes on him.

'Tired?'

'Just a little; nothing that a bath won't cure.'

He turned his head and looked towards the dining-room. 'Looks wonderful.' He was gazing at her again, his eyes tender and full of concern. 'You are tired,' he said. 'Go on up now and have a rest. You've got a good hour-and-a-half; go on with you.'

As he pushed her gently his father went out of the room, and he turned and looked towards the door, after which he sighed and lay back, his head leaning towards his mother's.

He always felt better, more relaxed, when his father wasn't about, although nowadays his presence didn't affect him as it used to, for he had come to the conclusion that there was nothing in his father to be affected by. He was too colourless, too inane – too gutless. Yes, that was the word that summed up his father. It was hard to believe that a man so big could make so small an imprint on others. Yet they said he was good in court, that he talked well. It was a pity he didn't make use of his legal versatility at home; it would make things a little more lively for his mother. He wondered how she had stood it all these years. The big bulky quietness of him, his soft voice, and that soundless laugh. Why didn't he laugh, really laugh? It was odd, but he had never heard his father laugh outright in his life.

He now put out his hand and picked hers up from where it was lying by her side as if waiting. Without moving she said, 'What kind of a day have you had?' She was sitting with her eyes closed.

'Oh, the usual . . . You know, between you and me old Wilcox is a pompous beast; he makes me sick at times.'

'Ssh! Ssh!'

'Well, no-one can hear us.'

'It doesn't matter. If you think it, don't say it.' She moved restlessly. 'It's a pity you ever went into his office. But then, you didn't know he was to become your father-in-law, did you? Perhaps you should have gone in for law after all.'

'No. No.' His cultured, pleasing voice was gruff now. 'Not law for me.'

She remained quiet for a moment. It was as if he had said, 'What! Be like my father.'

She moved restlessly again. 'Once you're married he may offer you a partnership.'

'I'm not banking on it; if that was in his mind he would have broached it before now. He loves to be top-dog and have a lot of little puppies running round his heels.'

'Ssh! Ssh!'

'Don't keep saying Ssh! Ssh!' He wagged her hand, and they laughed softly together.

'Does Valerie know how you feel about him?'

'I think she guesses.'

'He's very fond of her. When once you're married she'll likely persuade him to . . .'

'Oh, no, she won't.' He sat up and turned to face her. 'Look.' He wagged his finger like a pendulum before her face. 'I don't want any favours through my wife. Don't forget that where Papa Wilcox is today is solely because of Mama Wilcox's favours, and she's never let him forget it.'

'Oh, Laurie, don't be silly. And don't call May Mama Wilcox; you might come out with it some time without thinking.'

'Oh, that would be too bad. But I'm not being silly, and you know it. He's the big boss in the office, but out of it . . . Oh, boy! Who wears the trousers in the house, and who keeps the finger on the purse strings? I know what I know, dear Mama.' He nodded at her, smiling broadly now. 'Anyway' – he pulled himself up from the couch – 'there are other jobs. If he doesn't make himself plain about my prospects at the end of another year, well I can always move.'

'You wouldn't leave . . . leave the town?'

He turned to her where she was sitting on the edge of the couch staring up at him, and he put his hand out and gently touched her cheek. 'No. Don't worry, I won't go far away. There are at least four other accountants' offices in the town . . . Anyway, I may set up on my own. All I need to do is pinch a few clients and rent an office.'

She lowered her eyes and dropped her head as if in shame.

'Come on.' His voice was cheerful, bracing. 'Upstairs you go, and get ready for the fray.'

He still had her by the hand as they entered the hall, and there saw his father crossing it with a briefcase in his hand.

'I'm . . . I'm going back to the office for a little while.' John looked at Ann and she looked up to the half-landing at a clock encased in a gold-starred frame, like the home of the eucharist in a Catholic church. 'It's twenty-to-seven,' she said.

'I won't be more than half-an-hour. I want to collect some papers. The case was finished today; I told you. And I . . . I want to tidy up.'

'They'll be here about quarter to.'

'Oh, I'll be back before then.'

'You're not changed.' She looked him up and down.

'It won't take me long. I'll give myself half-an-hour. I'll be back on time.'

As he went out of the door into the lobby, he knew that they were both watching him. He got into the car and drove out of the drive onto the road, not taking so much care of the frost now, which was much harder.

After turning out of the avenue, he drove down the lane which still clung to the country, then on to the main road, past the park; past Brampton Hill, that mansion-studded hill, a relic of bygone days, a hive now of building speculators, who vied with each other to see how many flats they could get out of a house; past the old town, bordering on Bog's End; past the new town, with its brash shopping centre; over the main bridge that spanned the river; and to Greystone Buildings.

Greystone Buildings consisted of five four-storied houses. They had been built by one Arthur Greystone, in 1874, primarily as dwelling houses for better-class citizens, men say, who worked in Newcastle and could afford to drive there by coach and pair. The only remaining evidence of this particular splendour was the coach houses at the back now making admirable garages. Four of the houses in Greystone Buildings were taken over as offices; only number ten still carried out its primary use, and this had been turned into four flats.

John's office was in number eight, and somewhere within him, unacknowledged but nevertheless known to be there, was the fact that this house spelt home to him more than did 'The Gables', 74 Lime Avenue.

His fingers trembled as he inserted the key in the Yale lock. The hall into which he stepped was the usual office hall, bare but for a list of slotted names in an oak board attached to the wall, and it had that dreary air that seems to permeate most solicitors' offices, at least the entrance to them. He went up the brass bound stairs, past the door marked Enquiries, up another flight, past a number of doors here, one with a nameplate on which said 'J. A. Ransome', and another 'M. O. Boyd'. Then up a third flight of stairs to the top floor.

There were three doors on the top floor. One bore his own name, a second led to a storeroom, and the third to an antiquated lavatory with an equally antiquated wash-basin.

As a young man he had been put on this top floor, and together with two other clerks he had shared the one large, chilly room. When, in the course of years, he received promotion and the staff was moved round, he asked to stay on the third floor. There had been nothing unusual in that request, for he was still not very important, but now, as head of the firm he should have been occupying a room on the floor below, the one his junior had, but he had stated a preference to remain on the third floor. This had been considered odd, and, what was more, not good for business. Influential clients were used to lifts; there were no lifts in Greystone Buildings and never likely to be.

Yet people climbed the stairs to the top floor and business grew so much that at times he passed work on to his less fortunate colleagues in the town.

The room he entered was warm from the central heating. It looked what it was, an office, but a comfortable one. It had a good carpet on the floor, four large leather chairs, and a great mahogany desk. One of the walls was covered by a high glass-fronted bookcase, and round the remaining walls were a collection of prints, some sporting, some so faded that their pictures were hardly discernible.

He switched on the metal angle-poised desk light, then returned to the door and switched off the main light.

After this, he lowered himself slowly into one of the chairs; then, with his hands covering his face, he sat perfectly still. He shouldn't have done it, come back here. And so little time. But he felt he would have gone mad had he stayed in the house. After he had changed he couldn't have stayed upstairs until the others actually came, and if he had gone downstairs, there they would have been, the two of them, holding hands, or laughing with each other, or talking over his head. He couldn't stand it much longer, he would go mad. Would it be better when he was married and out of the house? No, it would be worse, because then she would be entirely lost and he'd feel her agony and not be able to lift a hand to ease it.

But he shouldn't have come out tonight. He knew what stock she laid on these dinner do's. That's all she asked of him: to be there at the head of the table when she gave her dinners. He knew, too, that in her own way she was grateful to him if he smiled and talked and generally made himself agreeable. And he always tried, knowing that the one fear of her life was that the state that existed between them should ever become public knowledge.

He was sure that even May Wilcox knew nothing whatever about the pattern of their real life. The Wilcoxes just considered him a quiet, withdrawn sort of fellow . . . Did Laurie talk to Valerie about the situation in the house, a situation that had not altered from when he was a small child? No; somehow he didn't think that Laurie would discuss his mother with anyone, not even his future wife. At least he would say nothing that might cause her to probe his mother's façade, that well-bred, cultured, ready-for-any-situation façade that effectually hid an intolerable situation. Instinctively he knew that his son was as protective of his mother's image as was she herself.

But he must get home. Why the devil had he to come out tonight of all nights? He'd take the papers and do some work later after they had all gone.

His hand dropped from his face to the arm of the chair, and he went to rise; then stopped, one leg stretched out, one shoulder forward. Slowly now he brought his hand towards his ribs and held it there, and after a moment, during which he remained still, he asked himself how long it was since he'd had a turn. About two months. But this could be indigestion; that lunch had been too heavy . . . He'd get into the air; he always felt better if he could get into the air. But he couldn't drive the car like this. Get up, get up, he said to himself. Take it slowly. But he remained stationary, and it was some time later when he moved.

15

He hadn't taken his overcoat off, just his hat, but he did not pick it up, nor yet put the desk light off when he got to his feet.

On the landing he slowly turned the key in the lock, put the key case in his pocket, and went towards the stairs. There was a good light over the stairs, it picked out every step down to the next landing, but as he stood with his hands on the top of the balustrade he knew he couldn't go down them. He closed his eyes and went back to his door and stood leaning against it for a moment, his breathing short and sharp now. He would have to get air, he wanted air. The roof. Why hadn't he thought of it before? Of course the roof. He went slowly past the storeroom door, past the lavatory door and towards eight steps wedged in the corner of the passage, which mounted up to a fanlight. He had only to stand on the bottom step to release the bolt that secured the glass frame. When he stood on the second step his hand pushed the frame upwards, and from the third step his head came into the open, and the frame dropped back onto the roof none too gently. He leaned his arms on the flat roof now and bowed his head as he gulped at the air, and after a while he slowly drew himself up to the roof proper. That was better; that was better.

He knew the roof as well as he knew the room down below; it had been a sort of bolt-hole to him for years. In the summer he kept a deck chair up here. Sitting with his back to the chimney, he could look over the town to the river, and beyond to the fells, to that part which hadn't as yet been encroached on by housing estates. He considered the view from the roof one of the pleasantest in Fellburn.

But there was no chair up on the roof tonight, so he stood leaning with his back to the chimney breast for a moment before making his way to the low stone parapet that was the only barrier between the houses. Then sitting on it, he bent over and rested his elbow on the top and cupped his head in his hand.

There was a wind blowing, a gusty, rough, iced wind, but it didn't affect him, for he was sweating. He could feel the moisture running down under his shirt.

He became aware that there was a noise coming from somewhere, a strange noise for up here, like people laughing, and singing. It could be coming from the street; yet it wasn't, it was too muffled. It was likely coming from the flats. Yes, from the flats. All the years he had used the roof he could count on his two hands the times he had seen anyone else up here. That was, except for the warm summer a few years ago when his clerks and typists discovered the building had a roof; as did those in the offices of Wallace & Pringle, and the wholesale firm in No. 1.

He wanted to lie down; he would have to get back. It had been mad to come up here, but he'd wanted air. If he lay down he could be here all night. Well, would it matter? No. No, not one jot. Best way in fact. Yes, the best thing that could happen. And when they found him, they couldn't say he had tried anything, could they? Not like before. He was tired, oh, so tired of it all.

He heard the music again and the laughter. It was still distant, still muffled. Then as if someone had turned the volume of a wireless to its full pitch a voice screamed over his head, 'LOVE ME, LOVE ME OR I DIE.'

He slid down onto the flat of the roof with his head leaning against a low parapet, and as he did so he thought he heard a child's voice shouting, 'Mam! Mam!'

There was a blank space in his thinking, as if his heart had stopped and he had died, and then he felt someone lifting his head up and a frightened voice from a long distance, saying, 'Is he dead?'

Now there were different voices all floating around him, and some part of his mind was trying to put faces to the voices. He was very sensitive to voices; when he met clients for the first time and they opened their mouths, he came to decisions about them, and he was very seldom wrong.

'Is he dead?'

'No, no. And get out of the way.'

'I saw his hand, Mam, in the light from the stairs, hanging over the wall. Eeh! I got agliff.'

'Be quiet, Pat, and get downstairs. Can you get him on his feet, Ted?'

'He's a big fellow, I'll try . . . No, it's no good; I could never get him over the parapet on me own. What about old Locket? Give him a shout.'

'No, no, he'd have a heart attack. He couldn't get up here anyway. Look, we'll manage him together.'

'Wait a minute, he's coming round.'

'How are you feeling?' It was a soft, warm voice. He opened his eyes and whispered to the dark figure, 'Better, thanks.'

'Do you think you can get to your feet? We'll help you.'

'Thanks.'

They sat him on the wall, and it was the woman who lifted his legs, one after the other, over the low parapet. The man started backwards down the steps, similar to those up which John had come from his own landing and the woman held the shoulders of his coat tightly in her fists to steady him from above.

He was swaying and blinking as they brought him across the landing and into a room, which was crowded with people, at least so it seemed to his fuddled mind.

Now he was lying down and the woman was loosening his collar and tie. It was years since anyone had touched his neck. He felt shy and wanted to protest. The voices started up again, muted and soft now, but each different, forming mental pictures in his mind.

'Aw, he looks bad.' This was an old voice, a thick North-country voice, a workman's voice. 'Reckon he could peg out any minute.'

'Don't talk daft, Bill. Trust you to say something sensible. What if he hears you?' Another thick voice, a woman's, but kindly. He put a fat figure to this voice.

'Do you think we could give him a drop of brandy, Ted?'

This was the voice he had first heard. He wanted to open his eyes and look at the source of this voice.

'Don't see that it could do much harm. Of course, it all depends what's wrong with him. I think we should get a doctor.' A clipped, precise voice this. North-country too, yet different from the other man's. This was a voice that was used to talking.

'Why, I know him.' The high exclamation caused him to flicker his eyelids. 'He's Mr Emmerson, the solicitor from next door. You know, I've told you, my people's daughter, Miss Valerie, is going to marry his son. You mind, Cissy, me tellin' you about their engagement?'

This voice was thin and fussy, and brought him to himself. He opened his eyes and looked at the faces around him. They were all slightly blurred, but the nearest one he knew belonged to the woman with the nice voice. Yet she wasn't quite a woman, and yet she wasn't a girl either. And beside her stood a thin, dapper man. He was the one who had helped him down the ladder; he had the voice that was used to talking. At the foot of the couch stood an old couple. They were likely the owners of the North-country voices. And to the side of them stood another two women. The thin, small one was smiling at him. She, he felt, was the one who knew him. Her companion was equally small, but fat with it. And then standing to the side of this fat woman was a boy. He was slight and thin and very fair and looked about nine years old.

'Do you feel better?'

'Yes. Yes, thank you.' He looked up into a pair of warm dark brown eyes in an oval face, the cheeks flanked by two long strands of fair hair.

'Would you like a drop of brandy?'

'Thank you . . . please.'

No-one spoke until the brandy was brought to him, and as he tried to sip it, it spilled down his chin and onto the front of his shirt.

'Drink it all up, it'll do you good.' She held her hand round his to steady the glass.

In a moment or so he felt better, stronger. His heart wasn't beating so fast, although it was still thumping hard.

'Look, I'll put a cushion behind your head.'

She put a cushion behind his head, then said, 'Will I phone for your doctor?'

'No, no thanks. I'll . . . I'll soon be all right. I'm so sorry . . .'

'Oh, don't be . . .' He felt she was going to add, 'silly', but she smiled and changed it to bothered, and repeated, 'Don't be bothered about anything . . . Look.' She sat down on the edge of the couch near his legs, and bending forward, asked softly, 'Will I phone your house?'

This question was like an injection, giving him life. He pulled himself a little way up on the couch and said quickly, 'No, no, please. I'll be all right. If I . . . if I could just stay a moment longer.'

'Oh!' He watched her throw her head upwards, an action suggesting that her whole body was relaxed, loose. 'You're welcome to stay as long as you like.'

'Thank you.' He looked from one to the other of the company now, and it came to him that they were a mixed group . . . this wasn't a family. And his voice was troubled as he said, 'I've interrupted something?'

'You haven't. You haven't.' Again she tossed her head, smiling widely now. 'They were all about to go, weren't you?' She looked round the company, and one after the other they nodded and said in their own particular ways, 'Yes, yes, we were just going.'

Then the old woman spoke to him. 'It was Cissie's party,' she said; 'we just came up for a cup of tea, but as always happens when we get in here we forget to go. We need a reminder.' She nodded at him.

'Oh, Mrs Locket!' The young woman looked at the old woman, and again she said, 'Oh, Mrs Locket!'

'It's true, Cissie; we always stay too long.' Mrs Locket now took her husband by the arm, and she nodded towards John before making her way to the door, almost on tiptoe, as if afraid to disturb him further.

Now the little fat woman and the little thin one made to depart, and the little thin one looked at him and wagged her head as she whispered down on him, 'I hope you'll soon be better, Mr Emmerson.'

The man, called Ted, followed them. Then came the sound of a door closing, and the man came back. 'How are you really feeling?' he asked gently, bringing his face close to John's.

'Much better. Much better. Thank you.'

He did feel better, but so tired. He wanted to sleep, and he felt he could sleep, he was so comfortable and so relaxed. He had put these people out, broken up their party and yet he didn't feel disturbed by the fact, which was strange. His eyes were now drawn to the boy who was standing staring at him. He could see he had a nice face; it was like the young woman's. He connected them as mother and son. They had the same colouring, the same shaped face, the same brown eyes. In fact, they were replicas of each other.

The young woman was saying, 'Do you think you could manage a cup of coffee?'

'That's kind of you. Yes, I think I would like a cup of coffee.'

'I'll make it, you stay where you are.' The man put out his flat hand towards her, then disappeared round the head of the couch.

John blinked rapidly, then tried to focus his tired gaze on the young woman again. She was sitting down, but even so she looked tall. He said to her, 'Your husband's very kind.'

The laughter of the boy brought his head slowly round and he looked from one to the other. They were exchanging broad smiles. He watched her put out her hand and push at the air between them, as if to stop the boy's laughter, the action also indicated that they were sharing a joke. She said soberly now, 'He's not my husband; that's Mr Glazier from the ground floor flat.'

'Oh, I'm sorry.'

'Oh, you weren't to know. He's a traveller. He's very rarely here, but he always comes up and sees us when he comes home.'

He inclined his head towards her but made no further comment.

She now bent slightly towards him and began to identify the late company to him as if it were important he should know them. 'The old man and woman,' she said, 'are a Mr and Mrs Locket. They live on the second floor, No. 3 Flat. They're old-age pensioners, and they get lonely at times. I often ask them up for a cup of tea.' Her head moved as she spoke. 'Then the other two, the one who knows you, she's Mrs Orchard. She works as a daily for Mrs Wilcox, and she lives with Miss O'Neill, that's the fat one. Miss O'Neill's a cook in the school canteen. They live on the first floor.' She pointed her finger downwards. She paused here, then looked towards her son and smiled again as she said, 'And up here among the gods, there's Pat and me.'

Pat and me, she had said; no mention of a husband. She could be a widow, or perhaps not married and the child illegitimate. Yes, very likely, for she had the kind of personality that attracted people seemingly; old and young, cooks and commercial travellers.

'I'm tiring you. You don't want to hear about all us here, but I thought I would explain. Look, wouldn't you like me to ring your home?'

'No, no thank you very much.' He moved restlessly now, and as if coming out of a drugged sleep he stretched his eyes wide and asked, 'What is the time, please?' As he did so he fumbled for his watch, and she turned her head and looked at a grandfather clock in the far corner and said, 'Twenty minutes to nine.'

'Twenty minutes to . . . !' With a jerk he was sitting upright. 'It . . . it can't be.' He looked at her as if he were begging her to tell him she was wrong. 'I came to the office just before seven and . . . and I was out again within ten minutes . . . at least I . . .'

'You must have lain on the roof for some time?'

'No, no.' He shook his head. He had lost an hour, and he had lost it in the office, not on the roof. It wasn't the first time he had lost an hour when this had happened to him. He'd have to see about it. But now he must get home, and at once. What would she say? He felt very tired again as he thought she would say the same if he went home now or in another hour's time, or tomorrow morning, because he hadn't been home at eight o'clock. He'd have to tell her about these turns he was having, then perhaps she would understand . . . But no she wouldn't; she would never forgive him for this. He couldn't do even this one thing for her, she would say. And she would say it quietly, and the echo of that quietness would seep deeper into them for months ahead; the fact that he had conformed to her pattern of social etiquette for years would bear no weight. He had missed conforming this once, and it was always the once that mattered.

'There.' The man came to the couch with a tray in his hand. 'I've made it strong. Do you like plenty of sugar?'

'One spoonful, please.' As he took the cup from the man's hand he said, 'I must get home. I wonder if you'd be kind enough to phone for a taxi as I don't think I'll be fit enough to drive my car?'

'You've got a car downstairs?'

'Yes.' He nodded at the man.

'Well then, I tell you what I'll do. I'll drive you home and Cissie here can come on behind in my car and bring me back. How's that?' He looked at Cissie now and she said quickly, 'Yes, that's the idea.'

'Can I come with you, Mam?'

'Yes, yes, of course.' She smiled at her son.

'I'm putting you to too much trouble.' John made to move his legs off the couch, and when she bent down to assist him he became hot with embarrassment. He wanted to say, 'No. No, don't do that, please,' but that would have made things awkward, so he let her bring his feet to the carpet.

'By the way, what is the make of your car?' asked the man.

'A Rover 2000.'

'Really? Oh, boy! I'm going to enjoy this. I used to have a Rover; but a Rover 2000! I hear they're spanking. You don't mind me driving her, do you? I'm a good driver, that's part of my living.'

'I'm sure you are, and you're very welcome to drive it . . . particularly tonight.' He smiled weakly.

They had the room to themselves now, as the young woman and the boy had disappeared, getting dressed he surmised, and the man took this opportunity to praise his hostess. Bending down to John, he said in a confidential whisper, 'She's a good sport, is Cissie, none better. They don't come like her the day. A good sport.' He jerked his head and winked his eye.

21

The nod, wink, and information could have suggested many things, but he was in no frame of mind at the moment to analyse them.

He stood up now and steadied himself on his feet. He still felt a bit rocky. He was aware of his overcoat being creased, and he smoothed it slowly downwards with his hands, then buttoned it up to the neck.

The boy and his mother now returned to the room, and the boy, coming up to him, said, 'Wasn't it lucky I went up for the ice-cream?'

He looked down on the fair head and smiling face and repeated, 'Ice-cream?' He was unable to follow the child.

'We had two blocks of ice-cream. I keep things up there in the winter, I haven't a fridge.' She was pulling a hat carelessly onto her head as she spoke, tucking the strands of hair behind her ears. She looked like an overgrown schoolgirl, not the mother of the boy. 'So it was lucky we went up, wasn't it? How are you feeling now?'

'Oh, much better.' He did not comment on her reference to luck. But for two blocks of ice-cream he would have lain up there all night, and that would have been the finish. He had wanted it that way, but two blocks of ice-cream had baulked his intention. It was odd how things, little things, could interfere with one's life, or the desire to be rid of it.

'Careful how you go.' Ted had him by the arm now, steadying him firmly, as if he were an old man, down one step after another until they reached the street. There John handed him his car keys and he felt the man's excitement when he took the wheel of the car. He tried to explain the mechanism to him. 'It's a bit different,' he said. 'Quick off the start compared to . . .'

'Oh, I'll get it, never you fear. There's never been a car yet I couldn't drive. There, that's it.' He pressed the starter, then turned his face to John, saying, 'You can hardly hear her, she's a beauty. I've read a bit about her. I bet you what you like I'll not rest until I have one. There'll be some second-hands coming along shortly . . . Now, where to?'

'Do you know Lime Avenue?'

'Oh yes. Yes, I know Lime Avenue. Nice houses there. What number?'

'Seventy-four.'

He looked through his mirror and said, 'I'll just wait a tick until Cissie comes round the corner . . . Aw, there she is. Now off we go.'

John thought the man handled the car as if he had driven it for years. He was a natural driver, and he didn't talk while he was driving. As the journey neared its end he wondered about asking them in. It might ease things, help to explain without words. They were in the drive now, going round the bend and into the blaze of light from the windows. And there was Wilcox's car right opposite the door. They always came by car; the comparatively short distance down the road was not to be walked when going out to dinner. He said to the man, 'This is very kind of you.'

'No, no, not at all. Sad world if we can't help one another. Anyway, it's put me in your debt, and what's more it'll likely put me in real debt afore I'm finished.' He laughed. 'For as I said I'll not rest until I have one of these.' He patted the wheel.

'Would you care to come in?'

The man hesitated, then said slowly, almost shyly, 'Well, not tonight, if you don't mind. I'm off early in the morning. I leave around six and I've got things to see to.'

John was out of the car now and he looked towards the gate, from where he could see the reflection of the headlights of the other car. She hadn't got out and he didn't feel able to go to her and thank her. He said, 'I would like to thank Mrs . . . what is her name?'

'Mrs Thorpe.'

'Will you tell her . . . ?' His voice trailed away on a feeling of weakness.

'Don't you trouble about her; she doesn't need any thanks. Get yourself inside. Good night now.' He pushed him gently towards the porch. 'Sure you'll be all right?'

'Yes, thanks. I'm all right, and I'm very very grateful.'

'Go on, go on.' The man spoke as if he were addressing an old pal; then added, 'I won't be back for another few weeks or so. Going down south this time, but I'll be interested to know how you get on.'

John nodded, there was nothing more to say.

He fumbled in his pockets and found his key, and as he opened the door he heard the man's steps crunching away down the gravel drive.

He drew in two deep breaths, then opened the lobby door into the hall and there, confronting him, were the guests of the evening, together with his wife and son and partner. They all stood as if transfixed, staring at him, all silent. And he stared back. At least he stared at his wife. Her face looked like a piece of alabaster and as stiff, and expressionless, all except her eyes. The first glimpse they'd had of him had swept the fear from them, and now deep in them he saw a white anger, that quiet anger that he knew so well. Quiet people were always more forceful, more dangerous than noisy ones.

James Wilcox was a noisy man, a fussy little man. He showed it now by crying, 'Well, well! This is a nice kettle of fish. What happened to you?' He did not add, John, which would have tempered his demand for an explanation. 'Come on. Come on, man;

don't stand there. What's all this about? Everyone of us distracted here. Poor Ann nearly out of her wits.' He flapped his hand upwards over his shoulder to indicate Ann.

'I . . . I went to the office and I didn't feel very well.' Even to his own ears the truth sounded inane. Silence, full of disbelief, met his statement. And then May Wilcox spoke.

May had a pseudo-refined twang. She was a petite-looking woman with greying hair, tightly dressed over her small scalp. Everything about May was tight and small. John had always thought that she and James were well matched. Couples nearly always paired off together, he had found that. It was an oddity of human nature that you should choose for your mate someone who reflected yourself, as you saw yourself, or your mother, or your father. Yes, it was odd. He brought his eyes fully to bear on May as she said, 'Arnold—' she inclined her head with a genteel movement towards his partner—'Arnold went to the office. Ann phoned him; she was very worried. There was no-one there, not at the office . . . was there, Arnold?'

Arnold Ransome swallowed hard and pushed his hand over his well-oiled hair, then he moved towards John as he said, 'Perhaps you had gone by the time I got there. It was about half-an-hour ago.' He was looking him straight in the face, and his eyes were saying, I'm trying to work in with you; whatever this is about I'm trying to work in with you. And he nodded as John said, 'I had left before that.'

He turned from them now and unbuttoned his coat and dropped it over a chair, and when he turned towards them once more they were all eyes again, all staring at his neck. With the realization that his tie was hanging slack and his collar was open, he felt the colour rushing to his face like a wave of guilt. As his hand went to his neck he looked again towards Ann, but he was more aware of his son than he was of her at the moment. Laurie was standing by her side, his face looking grim and pugnacious, as if he wanted to hit out at him. He'd felt that often about Laurie lately, that he wanted to hit out at him. He turned from them all and made his way towards the stairs, his gait slightly unsteady, and as he did so he saw his wife go into the lounge and his son follow her. When he passed James Wilcox he heard him sniff audibly a number of times, like a dog which had caught a scent, and he was halfway across the top landing when there came to him the scarcely muffled whisper: 'Well! What do you think of that? Did you smell him? He's been drinking . . . brandy!'

Down in the hall, Arnold Ransome shook his head and repeated, 'Brandy? He doesn't drink brandy.'

James Wilcox drew in his lips, thrust out his chin, and said in no small voice, 'I know the smell of brandy. He's drunk.'

'But John doesn't drink brandy; it isn't his drink,' Arnold Ransome persisted.

'Well, it mightn't have been before tonight, but it certainly is now. I tell you he's been drinking brandy. What is he up to, does he think?'

Arnold looked back at the little man. He had never liked Wilcox, or his wife, or his daughter, and so he couldn't keep the sharpness out of his tone as he said, 'How should I know? As he said, he felt ill. Likely when he left the office he went for a drink.'

'And loosened his collar and tie? Did you see the condition of his overcoat?' It was May Wilcox speaking now, and with an exaggerated, gracious movement of her hand she indicated the overcoat lying on the chair. Then picking it up, she held it for their inspection. 'It looks as if he had been rolling in the gutter, doesn't it?'

She was right there. Arnold Ransome moved uneasily. There was something behind all this, but he hoped whatever it was it wouldn't afford these two any more satisfaction. Self-righteous prigs, both of them. And him on the Bench. How in the name of God had that come about?

'Well, we'd better go in to Ann and see if we can sort this thing out.' May Wilcox now marched towards the lounge, her husband following her, and reluctantly Arnold Ransome followed them. But before he entered the room he glanced towards the stairs and thought, 'What if he is bad, he's looked off colour for months now? Somebody should go up to him.' But it wasn't his place to say so.

Laurie walked Valerie round the bottom of Lime Avenue and up the lane that led to Handley's small-holding. The ground was hard and slippery, and as he was holding her arm they slithered together. They walked to the end of the lane, turned the corner, and stopped at the back of Handley's barn.

There had been silence between them since they left the house, but now as she stood within the circle of his arms she gave a small laugh and said, 'Well, what do you think of it all?'

'You mean father?'

'Who else could I mean?'

There were shades in her voice which at times indicated undercurrents he could not fathom, and this had the power to nettle him, as now.

'It could have been as he said. He felt bad, and then went out for a drink.'

'Oh, Laurie, don't be naïve. You don't come in like that, collar and tie awry . . . And look at his coat. You don't get like that by going for a drink. Imagine loosening your collar and tie in The George, or at the club.'

'He needn't have gone to The George, or the club.'

'But would he have loosened his collar and tie in any bar . . . your father, in his position?'

'Oh God Almighty! He could have loosened it in the car coming back.'

'All right, all right.' Her voice was controlled. 'I thought you might have seen the funny side of it.'

He peered at her through the darkness. He could just see the outline of her face. He knew that there would be laughter lurking at the back of her round dark eyes. He had never been quite able to make Val out; that was part of her attraction for him. She had quite a bit of her mother and father in her makeup, yet she laughed at them, criticised and scoffed at them on the quiet. This did not displease him at all, especially when it was directed at her father. Yet he couldn't bear the thought of her taking the mickey out of his own parents. He might think what he liked about his father, but the situation changed when other people began to express their opinions of him, for any adverse criticism of his father reflected, he thought, on his mother.

'I was sorry for Aunt Ann, as it was her turn to score.'

'Score! What do you mean?'

'Oh, Laurie, for heaven's sake don't pretend you don't know what I mean about this an' all. You play dumb on so many things. What's the matter with you? You know for a fact that mother and Aunt Ann have been scoring off each other over these dinners-at-eight for years.'

'Oh, that! But I don't see it as competitive. They put on good meals, and . . .'

'Oh, be quiet. Kiss me.'

He kissed her, his mouth covering hers, one hand under her arm pit, the other across her buttocks. It was a long kiss, the length extended by her rather than him.

After it was over there was no breathlessness about her, and she said evenly, 'There'll be no dinner-at-eight for us, I'm a stinking cook.'

'I'll have to eat, so you'll have to learn.' He pulled her closer to him.

'Learn to stand two days in the kitchen preparing a meal? Can you see me? No, darling, that's not for me. Except for drinks and perhaps a snack, our guests will be invited out.'

'That'll run into something, won't it? How often do you think we can do that?'

'Oh, we'll be able to manage it . . . between us.'

He stiffened inside. 'Between us.' That was something else that irked him. She was earning more than he was, at least at this stage of their careers. She had been teaching for two years now in the

26

High School, and she intended to go on teaching after they were married. There was to be no family for the first five years; they had talked it all out. He sometimes wondered if he was a little bit square, for this kind of cold-blooded discussion was distasteful to him. He was all for family planning in principle, but these things could be arranged without a lot of discussion, at least without making a debate of it. Her raw outlook on many things surprised him so much at times that he wondered if there wasn't some prudish trait in him, inherited from his father. Not that he could actually pin such a trait on his father; but he wanted to find no facet in himself that touched on sexual weakness; that was inefficacious.

'You shivered; are you cold?'

'No.'

'You are. Let me warm you.'

She jerked him to her, flattening herself against him.

This was another thing. She always took the initiative, she never waited for it to come from him. There were so many things he liked about her, loved about her. She was cute, smart, and clever, but he wished her cuteness stopped short at this particular line. This was his line. This was the line where he should take the lead, be the master.

'What's the matter with you tonight?' Her voice held a sharp note now.

'Nothing. What could be the matter?'

'What happens to them doesn't touch us. They're living their own lives, we've got ours to live. Let's get on with it.'

There was a space while she held him tightly. Then releasing her hold, she said bluntly, 'Don't you want me?'

He paused before answering, 'What do you think?' Then he pressed his body against hers as if aiming to push it through the barn wall. But quite suddenly the pressure eased and he asked, 'Did you and young Clark have this?'

Her two hands on his chest, she pushed him slowly away from her and he knew that her face was screwed up as she asked. 'Why do you want to know?'

'I just wondered.'

'You've never wondered before. At least, you've never asked.'

'Well, I just wanted to know now.'

'Why? Why now?'

'I just wanted to know if I am the first . . . or not.'

'God!' He heard her laughing in her throat. 'You're funny. What difference does it make? I love you, I want you.'

'You loved Tony Clark.'

'Tony's gone, married, dead to me. That was two years ago. I could ask you if you've been with Susan Lumley. You knocked about with her for years.'

'Not years, and just on and off.'

'You went with her for about four years. When I came back from college on vac I remember seeing you both together several times. So I'm asking you now, did you have her?'

'No, I didn't. And now you answer my question.'

'It's the same as yours. No, I didn't.'

They both knew they were lying.

'Do you want me or don't you? I'm getting cold.'

Oh, God. It was like a groan within him. Slowly he fell against her, and let his hands move over her. But as the minutes passed there rose in him a feeling bordering on panic when he realised that the whole process was tasteless.

CHAPTER TWO

THE FAMILY

Ann got out of bed, put on her dressing-gown, then drew the curtains. As she finished, the clock on the stairs struck eight. She walked towards the dressing-table and sat down, and the reflection she saw in the mirror annoyed her. She put her fingers over her cheekbones, then stretched the muscles of her face, trying to get rid of its stiffness. Except for fitful dozes she hadn't slept. The anger was still boiling in her. He had to fail her in the one thing left she asked of him. She would never forget last night as long as she lived, nor would she forgive him.

There came a tap on the door and Mrs Stringer entered, bringing in her early morning cup of tea.

'Good morning, Ma'am.'

'Good morning, Mrs Stringer.'

Mrs Stringer did not, as was usual on these occasions, begin, 'Well, what did they say, Ma'am? Did they say they enjoyed it? Hard to please if they didn't.' She was silent this morning.

As was usual on dinner nights such as last night, Mrs Stringer had stayed and served the meal, and washed up before going home, so she knew all that had transpired, and all she said this morning was, 'Drink that up while it's hot, Ma'am.'

Ann nodded, and Mrs Stringer left the room.

As she sipped her tea she listened for movements from across the landing, but she heard nothing. He was sleeping it off. She took a quick mouthful of the tea and it scalded her throat, and she had a hand to her neck when the telephone bell rang.

She sat on the end of the bed and lifted the receiver from the table.

'Ann? . . . That you, Ann?'

'Yes, yes, it's me, May.'

'Well, I thought I'd better phone you straight away. Mrs Orchard's just come in, and you know what she's just told me?' There was a pause, and Ann waited. Then May's voice went on. 'He was ill last night. John was ill. He went up on the roof and collapsed. The people in the flats took him in. I thought I'd tell you; fair's fair after all . . . Are you there?'

'Yes.'

'Well, that's what she said. She lives there, down below, and the young boy went onto the roof for something and saw him lying there. They were all up in the top flat, there was a birthday party or something going on, and they carried him down. One of the men drove him back.'

'Oh, May . . .' Ann was still holding her neck. 'But . . . but James, he said he could smell brandy on him.'

'Well, yes.' May's voice was crisp now. 'He did smell of brandy; they likely gave him brandy. And you must admit he looked a sight. What was anyone to think? It was natural. Anyway, that's what Mrs Orchard says happened and she was there.'

'Thanks, May . . . Thanks for telling me.'

'I'll come along presently, dear, as soon as we have breakfast over.'

'Yes, do. Thanks, May.'

She put down the receiver and sat gripping it. He was ill and nobody had been near him; he could be dead. She hurried across the room, out on to the landing and to the far door. Discarding her usual procedure, she entered her husband's room without knocking; then she stood with the door in her hand and looked towards the bed. He was awake and he didn't move as she went towards him. When she came to the foot of the bed she stopped and her mouth opened. She was about to say, 'Why didn't you tell me you were ill?' But he had told her. She said instead, 'How are you feeling?'

He blinked. Then his eyes widened slightly as if he hadn't heard what she said. She knew he had; it was her concern that had surprised him.

She said now, 'I'll get the doctor.'

'No, no.' His voice was low, weary. 'I'm all right now; just a bit tired. I think I'll have the day off. Would you phone Arnold for me, please?'

'Nevertheless, I'll get the doctor.'

'No, Ann.' He pulled himself up onto his elbows and leant towards her, saying, 'Please don't bother, I'm all right.'

She put her hand up to her lips and patted them a number of times and her eyes dropped before she spoke again. 'I'm sorry I . . . I didn't really understand that you had been ill.'

He looked puzzled, and she raised her eyes to his and explained. 'May's just phoned. She told me about you being found on the office roof. Mrs Orchard apparently was one of the people in the flats.'

'Oh!' He lay back and he could not prevent the slow smile spreading over the lower part of his face, even though it was a facial expression of his which he knew annoyed her. She'd have to have outside proof that he was ill. He hadn't presided at her table, so the evidence before her eyes had been ignored.

She said now in her usual clipped tone, 'You can't blame me for last night. You didn't explain anything, and coming in like that. You could have got the people to let me know.'

He closed his eyes; then said softly, 'It's all right, Ann. It's all right.'

'It isn't all right. You're putting me in the wrong and it isn't fair.'

He opened his eyes and after a moment during which he didn't look at her, he asked, 'Do you think I might have a cup of tea?'

'Yes . . . yes, of course.' Her voice was polite now, as if talking to a guest. 'I'll bring you some breakfast up.'

'No. No, thanks. I just want a cup of tea.'

She remained staring at him. Then with an impatient movement she went out, but she closed the door quietly after her.

Laurie was crossing the landing towards her bathroom and she beckoned him silently into her room.

'What is it?' he asked under his breath.

'Close the door,' she said. She turned and faced him now, her hands fastening and unfastening the bow of her dressing-gown. 'He was ill . . . he is ill.'

'What?'

'May's just phoned. Apparently he was on the roof and collapsed, and the people from the flats found him.' She jerked her head, and her voice rose slightly as she said, 'But he should have explained, he should have told me. He's put me in the wrong.'

When he made no comment she turned and said, 'Shouldn't he?'

His face was straight, his heavy brows drawn together, and he ran his hand through his hair before he replied, halting. 'Well . . . when you come to think of it, he didn't get much chance, did he? We all stood gaping at him as if we'd never seen anyone drunk before.'

'Well, you'd never seen him drunk.'

'No, that's right.'

'You're blaming me for . . . for what happened?'

'No, no I'm not.' He went swiftly to her and put his arm around her shoulder. 'Don't be silly, dear. Of course I'm not. I felt I could have slain him myself when he didn't come back to dinner after all the work that you'd put in.'

'It was James, James that said he was drunk. The whole situation put him in his element, it gave him a handle.'

'A handle?' He seemed to be picking up the conversation from last night when Val had said, 'Poor Aunt Ann. It was her turn to score.'

'Well, anyway,' she stretched her thin neck and tilted her chin upwards, 'he's found his mistake out this morning. I hope he feels silly.'

Laurie patted her shoulder and turned away, saying, 'I suppose I'd better go in and see him.'

'Yes. Yes, do.'

31

Out on the landing he paused. It was true what she had said: old Wilcox had acted as if he'd got a handle over them when he thought his father was drunk and had been in a scuffle. He'd likely seen it as the beginning of the steep road down. He could almost hear him in the club, commenting on it. 'Pity. Pity. But I've expected it for a long time. He's always been an odd bloke, has Emmerson. Deep, I could almost say furtive. And he's had cause to be for he's been on the secret drinking line for years. But now it's out . . . The one I'm sorry for is Ann. Fine woman, fine woman. She was one of the Coopers, you know, Bailey & Cooper. Yes, yes, the shipbuilders. Of course the Coopers have gone down over the years, dropped out of the firm some time ago, but still they were people of note in the county at one time. And what did she do? Marry Emmerson, a farmer's son. Oh yes, quite a decent farm, but after all they were only tenants of her father. It never pays. It never pays. I've seen it again and again.'

Laurie rubbed his hand tightly over the side of his head, shutting out Wilcox's voice, then pressed his fingers on his eyeballs for a moment. He was all at sixes and sevens this morning; he hadn't slept well last night, in fact he hadn't got to sleep until two o'clock, for he had been troubled about another member of the Wilcox ménage. He had been thinking about Valerie and himself, funny thoughts, odd, disturbing thoughts. He drew in a long breath, then walked slowly towards his father's door, knocked gently, and went in.

He felt awkward, as awkward as he used to be when, as a boy, he tried to talk to this man. It was a strange facet in their relationship that when he was away from him he could think and speak of him as his father without feeling unduly disturbed, but when he was physically close to him, as now, he was filled with feelings of resentment, and dislike, above all with the knowledge that he despised him as a man.

'How are you feeling?'

'Oh.' John smiled at his son, the same smile that he had given to his mother, the smile that rarely spread his mouth beyond the edge of his teeth. 'I'm all right. There's nothing wrong.'

'You want a holiday.'

'It's only two months since I had one.' The smile remained stationary.

'What I mean is, a long one, six months.' He heard himself speaking in an abrupt manner. It was always like this.

'Yes, yes.' John nodded. 'I'll take a year off some time.' It was meant to be funny, and with anyone else Laurie would have picked it up and said, 'Well now, that's what you want to do, take a year off. And you can you know. The business won't drop to bits because you're not there.' Instead, he said, and politely, 'Can I get you anything?'

'No. No, thanks.'

'I'd stay in bed today.'

'Yes, I'm going to.'

'I'll look in and see you later.'

'Thanks.'

On the landing. Laurie pulled at the collar of his dressing-gown as if it was tight, then went on into the bathroom. He wanted to be sorry for him but he couldn't. Did that mean there was something lacking in himself? Because this man could stir no good emotion in him, no feeling that should be between a father and son – a good father, because by all the rules of the book he was a good father – did it point to the fault being in himself?

He slipped off his dressing-gown and stood looking at his naked body in the long mirror, and not for the first time he was thankful that he did not see before him a replica of the man across the landing. He was two inches shorter than his father, being five foot eleven. His body had no bulk about it or superfluous flesh as was on his father's. He was cut to a symmetrical pattern; his shoulders were broad, his hips were narrow, his whole body looked hard and compact. There was hair between his breasts, and a little on his legs. The hair on his body had remained fair, while that on his head had turned from blond as a boy, to light brown as a youth, and was now shades darker. He opened his mouth and drew his fingers down one cheek, then the other, feeling the heavy stubble on each. He could never understand why, with a mother as beautiful as his, he hadn't inherited one feature of her face, but he hadn't. His face was the same shape as his father's, and his features almost identical, yet, on his father's face they resulted in a soft, insipid look, while, on his, the combination looked pugnacious. He'd always been thankful that was so.

The tinkle of the breakfast bell came to him, and brought a picture of Stringy standing at the bottom of the stairs, the bell in her hand. He was still staring at himself in the mirror when he said aloud, 'Once I'm married I won't hear that.' He could see them scrambling their breakfast at a service counter in the kitchen; then Valerie would dash into her Mini and away to school, and he'd take a bus down to the office, for they wouldn't be able to afford two cars; and he'd as likely as not have to clear up before leaving. He didn't like the picture at all. His life up to now, under his mother's management, had been ordered and gracious. They lived as few people lived today, and, once he left this house, the pattern of his life would alter drastically. Valerie could scoff at 'Dinner-at-Eight', but, for himself, he was more than partial to it, and all it embraced. This might not be as important as the issue made plain to him beside the barn last night, but it had its place.

33

CHAPTER THREE

MOTHER AND SON

'Mam, I heard a funny one yesterday.'

Cissie Thorpe, standing at the sink, with her hands in the soapy water, stopped rubbing at the hardened yolk of egg on a plate, and, letting her head fall back on her shoulders, opened her mouth wide before she called into the next room, 'Tell it me. Come on, tell it me.'

There was a scrambling sound, and the boy came into the kitchen in a hunched position, attempting to tie his shoe lace as he walked. Just within the kitchen door he dropped onto the floor and hastily knotted the lace, then getting to his feet, he came to her side and looked up into her face and laughed. 'Well, it was like this,' he said. 'There was a Catholic priest fell off a six-storied building, a big high one.' He demonstrated with his hands. 'An' he prayed all the way down past five of the stories that he'd be saved, but as he passed the last one he made the sign of the Cross – you know, Mam, like Catholics do' – he demonstrated again – 'and he said, "Oh, my God! Now for the blooming bump!" '

'Ooh! Pat.' She had her arms about him and he had his arms about her, tight round her waist, his head down and pressed into her stomach, and they rocked together. Then leaning against the sink and pushing him from her, she said, 'Tell it again, I must remember this one for Ted. You know I forget half of them you tell me. Who told you that one?'

'Barry Rice. An' he's a Catholic an' all, Mam . . . Well, like I said, there was this Catholic priest . . .'

She was still laughing loudly when she turned to the sink and started to rub at the plate again, and she said now, 'But you shouldn't say my God! It's like swearing.'

'Well, I don't say it, Mam, just when I'm tellin' the joke.'

She raised her eyebrows and smiled to herself as she looked out between the frilled curtains of the window to where she could see a silver streak beyond the roofs and chimney tops, the river with the sun shining on it. It was a grand morning, crisp, frosty, bright. She tossed her head back to get her hair from the front of her shoulders, and asked, 'What you going to do this morning?'

34

'I was going round to Mr Bolton's to see if he wanted any jobs done.'

She looked at him over her shoulder, her face straight now, saying, 'You'll get wrong, you know. You're not supposed to work yet, so be careful.'

'He always keeps me in the back, weighing up, nobody sees me.'

'Well, that's all right. And Pat,' she turned round as he was making for the room door, 'what you doing this afternoon?'

'I was going to play football on the pitch.'

'Will Tim Brooks be there with the others?'

'I suppose so.'

As she watched his chin move downwards, she hastily dried her hands and went towards him, and, dropping onto her hunkers, she held him by the shoulders, her face level with his as she said, quietly, 'Pat, you're not going round with him again, are you?'

'No, Mam. 'Struth.' His head went lower and his eyes screwed up tightly against her scrutiny, and his voice mumbled as he said, 'He comes up to me and talks, and hangs on. I dodge him . . . I dodge him all the time.'

'Well, go on dodging him.' For the first time there came a stern note into her voice. 'Now listen to me.' She shook him gently. 'Go on dodging him. Don't be seen talking to him. Just remember what nearly happened. That boy's bad.'

'Ah, Mam, he's—'

'Don't tell me what he is, Pat. He's bad. You just take my word for it, he's bad . . . Promise me you'll steer clear of him.' There was pleading in her voice now.

'All right, Mam, don't worry.' He smiled, and the smile had an adult quality about it. It could have been a smile of understanding on the face of someone twice his age. 'I'll do what you tell me.'

'Good boy.'

She bent forward and kissed him, and they clung together for a moment before, pushing him on the side of the head, she said, 'Go on now. And mind, don't stuff yourself with bruised fruit. Remember your tummy last Saturday night.'

'Oh, aye. Coo! yes.'

She walked behind him, through the long room and into the hallway, and from a narrow wardrobe she took out his coat and scarf, and as he put them on he grinned up at her and said, 'I'll eat nothing but the best the day, so I won't have the belly ache.'

Again she pushed his head, then opened the door, and he was away.

She listened until the sound of his footsteps faded at the bottom flight of stairs. Then closing the door she sighed and lifted her arms high above her head and stretched. Aw, Saturday morning. She loved Saturday mornings. To lie in, do what she liked. She could lie in on Sunday too, but Sundays were different. The shops weren't open on a Sunday, and there were few people about, whereas Saturday was a live day. She liked live things.

She went into the long room again and looked about her. Everything that met her eyes gave her a feeling of satisfaction, and she sighed. Then stretching her arms above her head again, she planned her day. She would finish the dishes, then tidy up. Not that there was much to do. She had worked at the place until after twelve last night. That was her usual Friday night routine so that she could have Saturday free for herself and Pat. Then she would have a bath and go out and do some shopping. What would she get for dinner? She stood with her back to the fire, legs apart, her hands joined behind her head, and looked up to the ceiling. He liked sausages. But he was getting too many sausages; she'd get something more substantial this weekend. Chops, chump chops, and a bit of kidney, and one of those small chickens for tomorrow, yes. She swung round swirling her dressing-gown into a tent, and as she gathered up school books and magazines from the couch and banged up the cushions she began to sing: 'I love you because you understand me and all the little things I try to do.'

She was singing while she had her bath. She was singing as she put on her make-up and dressed herself; and when the bell rang she didn't stop singing as she went to the door to answer it, for it would be either old Bill Locket, or Clara, or Miss O'Neill. It wouldn't be Mrs Orchard, because she always worked up till one on a Saturday, and it wouldn't be Ted because he wasn't expected back yet.

But when she opened the door it was no-one of these.

She gazed at the tall, heavy man with the grey hair. Then her mouth falling open, she exclaimed, 'Why! Why, I didn't know you. Come in. Oh come in. Are you better? Well, you look better.'

As she closed the door he said, 'Yes, thank you, I'm quite recovered.'

'Come on in. Come on in.' She was walking sideways away from him now, her arm extended towards the room, and he followed her. But within the room his step was checked with amazement at what he saw. He couldn't remember any part of this room, although he knew he had been there.

'Sit down, sit down.' Again her arm was extended, but towards the couch now. 'I was just going to make a cup of coffee, would you like one?'

'That is very kind of you. Yes, yes, I would.'

She turned away, almost at a run, then turned back again, saying, 'Oh, I am glad to see you looking better. My, you did give us a scare that night, you looked so ill. Have you been in bed since?'

'Yes. Yes, for the last few days; the doctor thought I should have a rest.'

'I'd say you needed it.' She shook her head slowly at him, then said, 'I'll just put the milk on, I won't be a tick.'

She was the same as he remembered her. He hadn't been able to get her face straight in his mind, and yet now he knew her image had been there all the time. But he had remembered her voice clearly, that airy, bright, warm voice. A caressing voice. A deluding voice, because it had that quality about it that made others think they mattered to its owner. During the last few days the memory of her voice had stayed with him, the tone, one of concern for a sick man. Yet he was no longer sick, and the quality he remembered was still there; it hadn't been imagination. And now this room. He hadn't remembered anything about the room, and if he had, and had remembered it as he was seeing it now, he would certainly have put that down to his imagination. He looked at the walls, papered deep blue, a sort of midnight blue he supposed they would call it, and dotted all round the room were pieces of antique furniture. Almost opposite to him at each side of one long window was a pair of Sheraton mahogany card tables with satinwood bands down the legs. He turned his head to where she had disappeared into the kitchen and saw a double-pillared dining-table with a set of Hepplewhite chairs around it. On a small grand piano in another corner stood a pair of inlaid tea caddies he took to be Regency.

It was fantastic, the whole room seemed full of antiques. He knew about these things, he had been brought up among similar things. A number of pieces like these were still in the family. Some in his elder brother's house in Oxford, and others in his sister's in Dorset; but to see stuff like them here, in a top-floor flat and belonging to this girl . . . woman . . . young woman – he hadn't got her right in his mind yet with regards to age – seemed utterly out of place, out of character. Yet why, why should it?

'There, it won't be a minute.' She came hurrying towards him, as if she wanted to hurry towards him. And when he rose to his feet she said, 'Oh, please, sit down.'

She did not sit on the couch but on a pouffe near the fire, and then she said, 'Now tell me all about it.' And as she did so she lifted the tongs and took a large piece of coal from a bright copper coal scuttle. 'There.' She dusted her hands as if they were dirty, and gave him her whole attention. 'What was it? A heart attack?'

He smiled at her. 'Well, a little lead-up I should say. The doctor wasn't quite sure himself, as I was better when he came.'

She shook her head at him. 'I thought about you all night after you'd gone. Just imagine, if I hadn't put the ice-cream up on the roof. You could have been there all night and died, it was bitter.'

'I suppose so.' His head moved slightly.

'You suppose so! I'm sure of it.'

'Well, I've got you to thank for saving my life.'

37

'Oh, I didn't mean that.'

'I know you didn't. Nevertheless, I'm grateful. That's what I came to say.'

'Oh, but you shouldn't have bothered about that. Oh, not that I'm not pleased to see you, I am, but you know what I mean.'

Again they nodded.

'The coffee will be ready now.'

He turned his head and watched her this time as she went towards the kitchen. She was tall, almost as tall as himself, slightly taller than Ann he thought, and somewhat of her build, even thinner, but so different, oh, so different. She was mobile. Yes, that was the word that described her, mobile, every part of her body, while Ann was all repose, repose without rest. Repose that frightened you and stretched your nerves to screaming point.

'I've done milk 'cos I like it white; perhaps you prefer it black?' She was hurrying towards him again, carrying a tray.

'No, I like half and half.'

When he took the cup from her hand he said, 'You've got a very beautiful home.'

'You like it?' Her wide mouth stretched, showing large white teeth, apparently all her own, for one at the side was overlapping another, and one at the bottom showed a sign of stopping.

'Yes, I . . . I don't think I've seen so many pieces of antique furniture together in one room before, except in a sale room.'

'Perhaps it is a bit overdone.' She looked around the room now, her face unsmiling, and he put in hastily, 'Oh, no. No, I wasn't inferring that; I think the pieces are beautiful and the arrangement equally so. Oh, please believe me.'

'Oh, I do.' The smile was back again. 'But I sometimes wonder myself about there being too much. But I like old stuff, I love it.'

'I can see that.'

She took a sip from her cup then leant towards him, her mouth twisted slightly as she said, 'I bet you're wondering how I came by it all.'

For the first time since entering this room he found himself reverting to his professional training, and the process surprised him because he hadn't realised that he had been acting and talking naturally, spontaneously, talking without first stopping to think. But now he said in his professional manner, 'No. No, I hadn't really thought about it. But if I had, I should have supposed that they were left to you. These things usually are . . . passed down.'

'You're right.' She stretched her eyes wide. 'But not in exactly the way you mean. I didn't inherit them from my father, and he from his, not like that, yet I did get them from my father. You see, he was a second-hand dealer.' She looked away from him towards a small Georgian mahogany sideboard and said slowly, 'Ours was a rubbishy shop, not what you could call an antique shop, all bits of odds and ends. But he came across nice pieces in his travels, which he never put inside the shop, he always fetched them home.' She brought her eyes back to him once more, and laughing gently she said, 'My mother used to play war with him, because, she said, there was the profit all stuck round our walls, but me dad looked upon these pieces as a sort of investment.'

'And he was certainly right; they would bring some money today.'

'Yes, yes, I think they would too. In fact, I'm sure they would. I've had dealers after them more than once. But I'll never sell any of them. When I don't need them any longer they'll go to Pat. I think that's the kind of profit on his investment Dad would have liked best.'

'I hope when your son is an old man you're still surrounded by your beautiful furniture.'

'Oh.' Her head went up and back. 'There's not much chance of that . . . Will you have another cup of coffee?'

'No. No, thank you, I feel I have intruded on you long enough.'

'Oh, but you're not intruding.' Again her head moved from side to side, and the action seemed to sweep away all opposition. 'I look upon Saturday as my day. I make it a lazy day, I haven't to go to the office, I enjoy Saturdays . . . Not that I don't enjoy my work. I suppose it's unusual these days for anybody to say they enjoy their job, but I do. I suppose it's because I've got a good boss.' Without pausing, she went on, 'I work for Holloways, the wholesalers. You know, in the market. I've been shorthand-typist there for thirteen years.'

'Yes, yes, I know Holloways.' He inclined his head. 'We handle their business.'

'Well I never! But, of course . . . Ratcliff, Arnold & Baker. I've written to them often. But to a Mr Ransome.'

'He's my partner.'

'Well I never! It makes us sort of connected.' She leaned towards him, and he was forced to laugh, and was not a little surprised by the noise he made – he couldn't remember when he had last heard it. Then, his eyes crinkling with enquiry, he said, 'You did say you had been working for them for thirteen years?'

'Yes.' She nodded.

'But . . . but you must have started very young?'

'No, I was seventeen when I went there. It was my first job after the secretarial course . . . I'm thirty. I was thirty the night you put in your appearance.' She dropped her head slightly towards her shoulders, but there was nothing coy about the action.

He stared at her. Thirty! He couldn't believe she was thirty. Of course, her boy must be nine or more. He was curious about the boy. If she had worked for Holloways for thirteen years it pointed to her not being married.

The next minute she startled him by saying, 'I was married when I was nineteen, but I kept my job on and went back shortly after Pat was born.' It was as if she had been reading his mind and he felt a warmth on his face which deepened when she added, 'My husband was killed when Pat was three. He was driving a lorry and a bus ran into him on the Low Town bridge and he went through the parapet into the river.' Her voice was now flat, unemotional, her face straight.

Low Town bridge. A lorry plunging into the river. He remembered. Yes, of course. The contractors sued the bus company. The bus had slithered onto the wrong side of the road. The widow of the deceased driver had been awarded quite substantial damages. Yes, he remembered.

There came a little embarrassed silence between them. He supposed she was dwelling on a painful memory. He broke it by saying, 'Have you always lived here?'

'No, no. I've only been up here about six years.'

'It's an unusual flat; this room is so large, larger than any in our office. But then in the old days they built largely, didn't they?'

'I understand this was two rooms at one time. Would you like to see round?' She was on her feet, looking down at him. And he noticed again how all her movements seemed to flow. Although quick, they weren't jerky.

'It's very kind of you but I feel . . .'

'Now I've told you, you're not putting me out. Look, this is the bedroom. I have two.' She preceded him into another large room, and here again there was old furniture on which the patina was soft to the eye. A bow-fronted tallboy stood corner-wise near the window, and what was evidently a Queen Anne cabinet stood in the opposite corner. The only modern article in the room was the bed, but flanking it, looking like bedside cupboards, were two small Georgian Davenports. He recognized these particularly because in his mother's bedroom at home there had been one. It had known some rather rough wear yet his brother had been offered a hundred pounds for it recently.

'I had to have a modern bed. I bet you wouldn't believe it but Dad had a four-poster. Mam kicked up over that. Oh, but there were some laughs over that four-poster. Mam said she was always afraid of dying in it. And she did die in it, and Dad wasn't long following her, and in the same bed. I think that was the reason why I just couldn't sleep in it. And it was a pity for it fitted in with the rest of the stuff, while this . . .' She waved her hands towards the plastic-headed double divan. 'It sticks out like a sore thumb, don't you think?'

'Oh no. I think it's feminine, nice.' They were smiling at each other, and she turned away and walked into the long room again and across it to another door.

'This is Pat's room.'

'Yes, this is a real boy's room.' He looked about him, and saw that even here there were pieces that would have graced a drawing-room, one being a sofa table, another a four-tiered whatnot which was being used for a display of miniature aeroplanes. The walls he saw were plastered with pictures of aeroplanes in all situations.

'I see your boy is very air-minded.'

'Oh, he's crazy about aeroplanes.'

'Is he heading for the air force?'

'No, not particularly. He wants to be an engineer. He's very good at maths, he's at the top of his form, and his teacher says he should get through to the grammar school next year. He's only ten now.'

'Oh, that's excellent.'

'He's a good boy.' She was looking straight at him, her face unsmiling as she said this, and when she turned from him she again said, 'He's a good boy.'

He felt he detected something in her voice. Was it a trace of anxiety about the boy?

She showed him the bathroom that held a pink bath with matching basin and which was half-tiled in black. It was startlingly modern and in sharp contrast with the rest of the house. The modern pattern was repeated in the kitchen, but here the colours weren't black and pink, nor yet the stark clinical greys and white of his own kitchen. Here various colours met and mingled, blue, lilac, primrose, soft green.

'What a lovely kitchen!' he said.

'I did it myself.'

'You did?'

'Yes. I went mad with eight colours. There's eight colours in here. And look,' she said going to the window, 'you can see the river from here. Just a little bit of it, but I love to see the river gleaming in the sun.'

As he followed her pointing finger he said, 'I often go on the roof to have a look at the river, and the air always seems fresher up here.' He turned to her now. 'That night I took ill, that's why I went up there, I wanted air.'

She looked back into his eyes, her own soft with innate kindness, her voice expressing it too, as she said, 'And you were ill, weren't you. As I said, I couldn't get you out of my mind all night, and I kept wondering about you. I nearly phoned, but I didn't like to. I had a call from Ted last night and he asked after you. He'll be pleased to know you are better.'

'He was such a help I remember. I would like to see him and thank him.

'Oh, that's all right, Ted doesn't need thanks. He's a good sort, a real good sort, but you've got to get to know him. He might appear a bit brash at first but he's not, he's a good man at rock bottom.'

Ted had extolled her virtues, and now she was extolling his. It was good to hear people speaking well of each other. There was likely something between them. And why not? Again, why not indeed?

'Well, I mustn't keep you any longer. I have really outstayed my welcome.'

'Not a bit of it.' She led the way out of the kitchen. 'You've made a most interesting break in my day, something different, you know what I mean?' She glanced over her shoulder. 'I generally know exactly what I'm going to do on a Saturday. I usually do some shopping and then . . .' She swung round towards him. 'You wouldn't believe what I do on a Saturday afternoon.'

He smiled, waiting.

She leant towards him. 'I go round the junk shops.'

They were laughing again loudly, and again he was surprised at the sound of his own voice, and as he laughed he gazed at her. He had never met anyone like her, oozing life. That was the only word he could find in his mind for her, life. She personified it. Some time before the war, right far away back he must have felt life like this, lived it, while being unaware of living it, expressing it in every moment, walking, eating, smiling, sleeping. Yes, some time in his existence he must have unconsciously expressed life as she was doing now, but in one searing moment it had been burnt out. That moment was with him yet, and would remain with him until he died.

He took his eyes from her as if unable to bear the sight of her. And he felt descending on him the sadness that would portray itself on his face and translate itself to others as inanity. He must get away from her before it showed. He had felt happy here, different.

In his conventional manner he now held out his hand and said, 'Thank you for the coffee, and for being so kind to me. Goodbye.'

'Goodbye.' She seemed a little nonplussed by his change of manner. She handed him his hat from the hallstand and held the door open for him.

When he had passed onto the landing he turned to her, his eyes not looking into her face now but lowered towards her feet encased in high, spindle-heeled shoes, and again he said, 'Goodbye.'

'Goodbye.'

She watched him until his head disappeared from her view down the stairs; then she went in and closed the door, and after a moment she walked across the little hall and to the sitting-room door, and there she stood looking round the room. He had been impressed by it, very impressed. He knew old furniture. He was a nice man, oh such a nice man. A gentleman. Oh yes, a gentleman. She could tell. But there was something about him she couldn't quite fathom, a sort of sadness or something, as if he was lonely. That was daft . . . him lonely! The leading solicitor of the town, living in the posh end where he did, and bags of friends . . . Lonely!

She walked towards the fireplace and moving the pouffe with her foot she sat down on it and held her hands out towards the blaze, and her own action seemed to interpret him in some way which she couldn't explain. And again she said, don't be daft. Him a big pot in the town. Fancy thinking he looks lost and lonely. She moved her hands in front of the blaze. It was funny about him calling. She had felt happy and full of life this morning, and even all the time he was here, right up to those last few minutes. And now she felt flat.

Aw well, this wouldn't get the shopping done. She jumped to her feet. It had been a very nice break anyway, and he was a very nice man, and it was good of him to call. Now she would get her things on and go out and everything would go as usual.

But when she was dressed for outdoors she paused before leaving the hall, and there came to her, as she termed it, a funny little thought. The usual Saturdays were finished it said. You're crazy, she said; you get the daftest ideas.

After she had closed the door she started to sing as she went downstairs.

CHAPTER FOUR

A LITTLE PERFUME

John finished his breakfast and went to renew his cup with more coffee when he realised that Ann was sitting at the table. He could never get used to her being down for breakfast. She had done this two or three times of late. Why, he didn't know, except perhaps that with the approach of Christmas she had had so much to do that she'd needed more time, and today being Christmas Eve she had more than the usual preparation to contend with in connection with tomorrow's dinner. Yet she hadn't put in an early appearance other years and the arrangements had been the same.

He handed her his cup, and as she filled it she said, 'I'll have to leave my car in, there's something wrong with the brakes. Could you run me into town this morning?'

'Oh! Well . . . Yes.' There was a pause between each word. Then he added rapidly: 'I can drop you on my way to the office, I won't be going for another hour or so.'

He was drinking his coffee when she said, 'Arnold doesn't go in Saturday mornings, is it necessary for you to do so?'

He blinked a number of times before looking at her, then said, 'Arnold doesn't happen to be responsible for my clients.' Without rising he pushed back his chair, and the action made a screeching sound as the legs scraped over the polished boards.

'Excuse me.' He now rose to his feet but did not look at her, yet he was aware that the sound of the scraping chair had brought her face into a grimace. He went past Laurie, who had his head bent over the morning paper, and out of the room, across the hall and up the stairs, and when he reached the upper landing he pursed his lips and whistled the first bar of Mozart's Sonata No. 3.

Back in the morning room, Ann looked towards Laurie, and he was looking upwards. The sound of the whistle had been as startling to them both as if a ship's siren had suddenly let blast in the hall.

It was close on eleven o'clock when John reached the office. He entered the room in a hurry, threw his case onto a chair, then went to the seat behind his desk and, sitting down, removed his hat, rubbed his two hands over his head, then looked at his watch. He had about five minutes, he never went up before eleven, although she wouldn't have minded what time he went up, he was sure of that. He leant back in his chair unaware that he was smiling, his lips wide, exposing all his teeth. How many times had he been up there since that first time? Five, six, seven? He had lost count. It seemed now that every Saturday morning in his life he had mounted to the roof, gone over the parapet and down her stairs. Yet he would never have gone down those stairs a second time if it hadn't been for the chance meeting in the market square. He had been passing the electric showrooms when he saw her standing gazing in the window. He could have passed on but he hadn't. He had raised his hat, and with what appeared to most people old world courtesy had bowed slightly towards her as he said, 'Good morning, Mrs Thorpe.'

She turned a delighted face towards him, and her 'Fancy seeing you!' did not grate on him. 'I'm looking at fridges,' she said; 'I should have got one years ago.' To which he replied, 'Don't you think it's as well you didn't?' And she laughed outright, a high, infectious laugh.

'What do you think about that one?' She pointed to a small refrigerator in the middle of the window. 'I would like one of the bigger ones, but you see it's the room. That's why I haven't had one before. What with my washing machine, and the spin dryer, and then my stove and the sink, that wall is all taken up. You see?'

He saw. And together they admired the small refrigerator, and he commiserated with her when she said, 'The cupboard behind the door will have to go, and where I'm going to put the china I haven't the least idea. And it's good china, Coalport, and I've some pieces of Dresden . . . just a few.'

What about her lovely china cabinet, he had suggested, for her overflow of china?

But that was full. He had seen it was full. But perhaps he hadn't noticed. Why should he? She was silly. Again her high laughter.

They walked a little way round the market square until they came to a café, where she stopped and said, 'I've got to go in here. This is where Pat comes and picks me and the shopping up after he's finished at the greengrocer's.' To this he wanted to say two things: 'Well I could do with a cup of coffee, and what's to stop me running you and your shopping home?' But the training of years checked such indiscreet spontaneity, and again he raised his hat and inclined his head towards her and bade her goodbye, and the morning once again became November, raw, bleak, with no break in the overhead leaden sky.

It was the following Saturday morning that he had gone up on the roof. He knew what had taken him there; and it wasn't to get the air. When she pushed open the fanlight he imagined his thoughts had drawn her from the room below. And from his side of the parapet he watched her hand reach out to the meat safe, then become stationary. He watched her face light up. As he stepped over the dividing wall she exclaimed, 'Well, I never! you're up here again. Aren't you afraid of getting your death?'

He assured her that he wasn't, explaining that he had come up for air and to enjoy the view.

She had pointed to the wire-mesh-fronted box, saying, 'Well, this is the last time I'll be using this, I've got the fridge coming on Monday. And I've got something else, guess what?'

'I haven't an idea.'

'Another china cabinet.'

'No!'

'Yes.' And to this she added, 'Come on down and see how you like it.'

And like a boy climbing into a cave, into an Aladdin's cave, he went down her steps and into the long room again, and, of all things that morning, she had finished up by playing the piano to him.

He had noticed the open piano and the music on the stand and had remarked, 'You play the piano, Mrs Thorpe?'

'Oh, play it,' she said in her airy way; 'I should be able to, I learned long enough. My mam put me to it when I was five, and I passed all my exams up to the advanced stage of Trinity College, but to tell you the truth I've no touch. Technically I'm all right, but my teacher used to say my fingers were like hammers. She used to say they were all right for Beethoven, but, you know, I don't like Beethoven, I like Mozart or Chopin. You always like the things you're not fitted for, don't you?'

She hadn't to be coaxed to play; she had played for him and given to the music her own interpretation. Perhaps her touch was slightly hard, perhaps an authority on music would have writhed and tried to shut his ears to certain passages, but as he sat on the couch, his head resting in the corner of it, his eyes focused on the mantelpiece where stood, in artistic isolation, the jade figure of a Chinese lady, her playing had soothed him, stimulated him, and excited him. Here was this girl who not only lived with beautiful furniture, but who knew and appreciated it, who could sit down at the piano without any fuss and play. What else could she do? She appeared to him at that moment like an uncharted island, mysterious, alluring . . . This girl whom Ann, without a moment's hesitation, would have dubbed common.

That particular morning before he had climbed the ladder to take his departure she had looked at him, her expression and whole manner serious, as he was finding it could be at times, and she said to him, 'Don't think this is cheek, or that I'm being forward or

46

anything, Mr Emmerson, but you're welcome here any time you've got a mind to drop in. I'm always in on a Saturday.'

He had thanked her for her invitation with a gravity similar to that with which she had made it, and although during the following week he had told himself that he must not go into her house again, the next Saturday morning found him, like some furtive lover, kneeling on the roof, tapping at her fanlight.

During his first three or four visits they had been alone together, and he couldn't now recall anything they had talked about. Then one Saturday morning the old man, Mr Locket, came up, and this had made him ill at ease, but only for a short time, because he realised that Bill Locket had not been at all surprised to find him there. Yet this fact, when he came to think about it later, disturbed him.

Bill had stayed about half an hour, drunk four cups of treaclish tea, given him an insight into the workings of the gas works, by which company he had been employed until his retirement. Together with his version of why the last war had gone on for so long, and lastly a whispered appreciation of their hostess, who left the key for him under the mat, so that when his wife was out he could slip up and make himself a pot of tea.

This generosity on Cissie's part, and the necessity for Mr Locket to avail himself of it, was explained by Cissie after the visitor departed. Clara, Mrs Locket, had to make ends meet, but, in her efforts she not only made them meet, but managed to make them overlap. Clara was careful. She bought a certain quantity of tea each week, and that had to last them. The irony of it all, Cissie had explained, was that Clara's saving was to enable her to leave something to her only son, who was in Canada and apparently comfortably off. People were funny, weren't they, she had said to him. And he agreed heartily with her . . . people were funny.

Then last week Mrs O'Neill had dropped in.

Mrs O'Neill's presence really had disturbed him; women always put the wrong construction on things. Mrs O'Neill was jolly and laughed a lot, and on that occasion she had seemed determined to outstay him. And he hadn't imagined it was because she enjoyed his company.

He had come across Cissie again this morning, in Danes' store, at the perfume counter of all places. She had been profuse in her greeting as if they had known each other for years. 'After Christmas boxes?' she had said. Yes, he had replied, that was what he was after. She said she liked lavender water, it was so refreshing; and he agreed with her; and this after receiving very little change out of a ten-pound note for a bottle of perfume.

The thought of the perfume brought his eyes to the chair, and he rose and took the small package out of his case. As he stood looking

47

at it lying in the palm of his hand he hoped she would like it. He didn't know what perfume she used; there was always a fresh smell about her, but he didn't associate it with anything in particular.

He went hurriedly into the wash room now, washed his hands, smoothed down his hair, stroked his nose, moved one finger to each side of his upper lip, and he was ready.

He had to make his way carefully over the roof. Heaps of last week's snow were still lying frozen hard in the corners, and the roof itself was like a sheet of glass.

There had been no arrangement for leaving the fanlight open, no arrangement whether or not he should come down if he heard voices, nothing surreptitious about his visits, but he tapped gently on the fanlight before opening it, and when he stood in the hall he called gently. 'Are you there, Mrs Thorpe?' She was still Mrs Thorpe, and he was still Mr Emmerson.

'Yes. Come on in. I won't be a minute.'

He went into the long room which now held an enchantment for him. There was something about it that cried to him of home as no other room had done since, as a boy, he sat before the fire in the big farm kitchen surrounded by the close unity of his family.

She put her head round the kitchen door and smiled widely at him as she said, 'Sit yourself down. I'm trying to turn a blancmange out without breaking it; I won't be a tick.'

He had taken off his hat, but he never took his coat off until she asked him. He sniffed at the air. There was a Christmas smell pervading the room, and as he sat down he called to her in a soft voice, devoid of the heartiness that he used to Mrs Stringer, 'Something smells nice. Are you roasting your goose?'

'No, no,' she called back, 'not till tomorrow. And it's a turkey. I've been making brawn this morning.'

'Oh, brawn.' He was looking towards the fireplace, his eyes on the leaping flames. She made brawn. He had never heard of anyone making brawn since his mother had made it; he thought everybody bought that kind of thing now, there were at least three cooked meat shops in the main street.

'There.' She came hurrying towards him. She was wearing a deep mauve coloured woollen dress, and round her waist she had a pink apron. Her fair hair was tied back, young-girl fashion, this morning, with a ribbon; her arms were bare past the elbow. The whole sight of her hurt him.

'Well, it's nearly here. I've done as much preparation as if I'd ten bairns. Anyway, it only comes once a year.'

Because it was she who had said the threadworn phrase there was nothing trite in the remark.

'Why don't you take your coat off? I'm always telling you.' She put her hand out, and he rose from the couch and took off his coat.

48

But as he gave it to her he exclaimed hastily, 'Just a minute; there's something in the pocket.' When he withdrew the small parcel he looked at it for a second before handing it to her and saying, 'I hope it's right. A Merry Christmas.'

'For me? Mr Emmerson, you shouldn't, now you shouldn't . . . Oh, but thanks.'

'You haven't looked at it yet, it might be a cracker.' He watched her intently as she undid the brown paper, then the expensive-looking coloured tape with which Danes' always wrapped up their goods, and when she came to the plain oblong box with the simple word 'Chanel' written across it she stared at it for a moment, then looked up, her dark eyes moist, her whole face drooping in soft lines. 'Oh!' she exclaimed under her breath. 'Oh, you shouldn't have done it. Not Chanel, it costs the earth. Oh, Mr Emmerson.'

He saw her body sway slightly towards him, and for a second he thought she was going to kiss him. It was a terrifying second. The anticipation checked his breathing, and when the movement of her body stopped it was her hand that touched him, and there swept over him a feeling of relief, yet mixed with it a sense of loss and a wide emptiness. But it wouldn't have done. No, it wouldn't have done, the little voice was piping at him. If she had kissed him that would have been the end of their association. He wanted this to go on for ever, the way they were now, but it couldn't have gone on if she had kissed him, because he would . . . What would he have done? What? . . . Told her? Yes. Yes. Strange, but he could have told her. She was the one person in the world he had met whom he could have told, and in the telling he knew that he wouldn't have been enveloped in shame.

'I've never had Chanel. I've always wanted it, mind you, and I could have bought it for myself many times over, but I wouldn't afford it. It must have cost the earth; look at the size of the box.'

'Nonsense.' His voice was a little hoarse as if it had been affected by the raw fog from outside. 'It's a very small appreciation for all your hospitality and kindness.'

'Oh, that.' She folded her arms around his coat while she held the bottle in her hand, and she gazed into his face as she said, 'Anything I've done for you you've repaid a thousandfold. I'm going to say it now . . . I've never met anybody like you, not to talk to. What I mean is, outside of business. I meet men like Ted, who prattles, and my husband wasn't much of a talker. No.' She shook her head now and repeated, 'No he wasn't much of a talker.' He felt her words conveyed something other than what they said; her face was in its rare unsmiling state. 'And there's been the music. I've never had anyone to listen to me before. I play for myself sometimes, but it's different when you're playing for somebody else . . . And then the books. Oh, I've read novels of all kinds but I've never read an autobiography until you mentioned they were your favourite reading.'

'I'm glad,' he said. 'Perhaps I should have got you a book or two?'

'No. No.' She flapped the hand at him that held the scent. 'I can get them from the public library.' Her head went back and she laughed, and clutching the bottle to her again, she cried, 'Oh! my scent. Oh! won't I smell lovely.' Then, 'You're so kind,' she finished. Solemnly she turned from him and went into the hall with his coat, and he watched for a moment before sitting down again. One small present – and compared with what he gave Ann it was small – yet what a difference in the reception and the thanks.

'What are you doing over the holidays?' she asked as she came back into the room.

'Oh, the usual thing. Tonight we go to my son's fiancée's place. That's been the usual procedure for years, even before they got to know each other . . . at least well. Then tomorrow we don't have dinner until the evening, when we have a few personal friends in.' He felt somehow as if he were excluding her by saying that, and he put in quickly, 'I must admit I don't enjoy it very much, I mean dinners and things.'

'Do you go to many cocktail parties?' Her head was on one side.

'For my sins I have to attend a few, but if I can get out of them I do.'

'I suppose you're kept at it every night at this time of the year; I've never known such a town as this for parties. Everybody seems to want to throw parties. I'm going to one on Boxing Night; one of the girls in the office is having a do. I don't care very much for parties. Too many people saying nothing, if you know what I mean.'

'I do. I do. And I go to one on Boxing Night too,' he inclined his head towards her. 'My partner's having a do, so we're both going to suffer, though I must say that Mr Ransome's do's are more bearable than most.'

She sat down on the pouffe at the side of the couch and said musingly, 'You know, I think Christmas is overdone, it's just become a racket for the shops. Would you believe it?' Her eyes widened. 'I've spent over twenty-five pounds on Pat.'

'Twenty-five pounds!' he repeated. 'That's a lot of money.'

'But, I've bought him things that'll last, like a set of encyclopedias.'

'Oh, that's sensible.' It came to him at this point that he'd forgotten to buy the child anything, and he said, 'I didn't know what to buy him but I thought a little extra pocket money wouldn't come amiss, not if I know boys.'

'Oh, Mr Emmerson, you mustn't. No, you mustn't. After buying that scent, no, you mustn't.'

He was about to protest again that it was nothing when there came the sound of a door opening and Pat came in from the hall in a rush.

'Oo! Mam. Coo! it's cold. Hello, Mr Emmerson. Oh, Mam, I'm freezin'. How long's dinner going to be? I've got to go back to Mr Bolton's this afternoon, he's up to his eyes in orders. He let me off at eleven 'cos he had to get the place cleared afore I could do any more, and . . .'

'All right, all right.' She hadn't moved from the pouffe, and when he came round to her side she put her arms about him and pressed him to her as she said, 'One thing at a time, and I'll answer one thing at a time.' Again she hugged him to her, and bouncing her head at him and laughing she said, 'Yes, it's cold, and dinner won't be ready for another hour, and I'm glad you're going back to Mr Bolton's this afternoon. Go on now into the kitchen and have a sausage roll; that will fill up the space until dinner-time. But, mind you' – she pushed him from her – 'no more than two. I said two, mind. I've counted them.'

The boy grinned at John, and John grinned back at him, and as he ran towards the kitchen he cried, 'You said two and two, that's twenty-two, twenty-two sausage rolls.'

She looked at John and shook her head and was about to make some comment when Pat's voice came from the kitchen door, muffled now with food, saying, 'Forgot to tell you, Mam, Ted's back . . . Saw his car outside the stables.'

'Oh is he? Oh, that's great. He said he'd try to make it. Now he won't be stuck in some hole by himself for Christmas.' She looked at John. 'He gets lonely. Commercial travellers do, you know. People wouldn't believe it, but by what Ted tells me it's one of the loneliest occupations on earth.'

He watched her face intently as she talked. She was pleased that the man was back; what were they to each other? It was not the first time he had asked himself the question, and he gave himself the same answer now as he had before. It was nothing to do with him. She was a young woman, free, and could live her own life. Nevertheless, as before, the answer increased the loneliness within him.

'I'm off to play for a bit, Mam,' called Pat. 'All right?'

'All right,' she said. 'But don't be long.' Then turning back to John, she continued, 'That'll mean we'll have a bit of fun over the holidays. Ted being back. They're all coming up, the others you know, Miss O'Neill, and Mrs Orchard, and Mr and Mrs Locket; but it wouldn't be the same without Ted; he makes things go, he's got that way with him. As I said, he prattles, but he's funny in company.' She leant towards him. 'I . . . I suppose you wouldn't like to come in one evening when . . . ?' She straightened up and ended quickly, 'Of course you wouldn't. You'll have all your spare time planned over the holidays.'

He caught her statement as an excuse and said, 'Yes. Yes, my wife generally works out all my spare time.' He widened his eyes and shook his head as if it was funny, and she smiled understandingly back at him.

Quite candidly he told himself that even given the time he would never accept an invitation to join in one of these gatherings, informal and natural as they were – and there was a craving in him these days for the informal and the natural. The small voice told him he was going beyond the bounds of propriety in visiting her at all. In the beginning he had hoped to keep his visits secret, yet he had acceded to this in one way only, by coming over the roof. Even this, he felt, was proving more clandestine than if he came boldly up the stairs, for his visits were known to the other inhabitants in the flats. And what if they put the wrong construction on things? It wasn't the first time he had put this question to himself, and again he shied from giving himself an answer.

In his work he dealt with all types of cases, among which divorce was frequent, and slander not infrequent. The latter, in nine cases out of ten, was dealt with privately. Slander always started in a whisper. That was no legal phrase, he had first heard his mother use it. He wondered now if there was already a whisper going through the building. He had been vitally aware from the morning Ann had come into his bedroom, after hearing through May that he had really been ill the previous evening, and not drunk, that Mrs Orchard could quite easily start a whisper about him. Yet he felt certain that if she had said anything to her mistress, May would have passed it on to Ann quicker than a shot from a gun.

For the past few weeks he had been holding his hands out towards a flame; and that was all he told himself he ever meant to do, just hold his hands towards the flame and feel the comfort of it. Yet how many people would believe him? And could he expect anyone to look upon his motives as altruistic? He would find it hard to take this view were he surveying such conduct in someone else. If a client in the same position were to say to him, 'I didn't stop seeing her because my conscience was clear. There was nothing between us but friendship, just friendship,' he would smile at him, his professional smile, and reply quietly, 'The public don't want to hear about clear consciences, they don't want to know about the good people, they're only interested in the bad, and once they get a smell of any kind they follow it, hoping at the end they'll find something rotten. That is human nature.'

'You look miles away.'

'Yes.' He blinked his eyes. 'Yes, I think I was. This . . . this couch is very comfortable.' He moved his head against the back of it. 'It induces one to relax. But you were saying?'

'Oh, I forgot what I was saying. I suppose I've been thinking too. Yes, yes I was. I was thinking we're going to have a jolly Christmas. I've got a tree for Pat.' She was whispering now. 'He doesn't know yet. I've got the lights and things, and I've had to keep moving them so he wouldn't find them. I'm going to have it all ready for when he comes in tonight. I don't like trees set up days before Christmas . . .'

She was interrupted by a sound from the direction of the outer landing, of someone singing 'Good King Wenceslas', and he watched her spring up from the pouffe, her face alight with laughter, and fling out her hand towards him in her characteristic way, saying, 'That's Ted larking on.'

He watched her as she ran towards the hall, then heard the door open and her crying in mock indignation, 'No carol singers the day, thank you'; then the man's voice, deep and pleasant-sounding, singing now, 'I wish you a merry Christmas, I wish you a merry Christmas, I wish you a merry Christmas and a happy New Year.'

'Get in. Get in. Oh, you are a fool, Ted. Go on with you. Mr Emmerson's here . . . Get in.'

Ted came into the room. He had a wrapped bottle in the crook of one arm and a number of parcels in the other, and he cried to John, who had risen to his feet, 'Well, hello there. I'm glad to see you better.'

'Thanks. It's nice to see you again.' John felt his own greeting sounded too polite and formal. But Ted had turned to Cissie. 'Here,' he said, thrusting the bottle into her hand; 'that's to be kept exclusively for Irish coffee.'

'Oh, thanks, Ted, thanks, Irish coffee! It's a long time since we had Irish coffee.'

'And here; these are for the Christmas tree.' He piled the parcels into her arms. 'Those two are for you, and those three are for his nibs. And mind, nothing to be opened until tomorrow morning. I was going to play Santa and visit all the beds in the house, but then I thought that if I got into Millie's and Maggie's downstairs I would never get out.'

He laughed heartily, and Cissie laughed with him. And John thought, the usual prattle of commercial travellers.

'Oh, it's good of you, Ted, but you shouldn't have bought all these things.'

'Aw, go on with you. I'm looking for a free dinner. Anyway, you don't know what's in them, so don't get all effusive until after you've opened them.' He pushed her, then came towards the couch. 'Well, well, I wouldn't have known you. You feeling all right now, Mr Emmerson?'

'Yes, thank you. Yes, I'm quite recovered.'

'By, that was a night, wasn't it? How's the car behaving itself?'

'Oh, splendidly.'

'By, I'd give me ears to have one like that.'

'Would you like a coffee now?' Cissie was leaning over the back of the couch between them.

'Would I like one? . . . Two, but Irish.' Ted stretched out his hand and touched her nose. 'Have you any cream in?'

'Yes, I got a pot fresh this morning; I must have known you were coming.'

'That's the ticket . . . Do you like Irish coffee?' He leant towards John.

'Yes, yes, at times, but I'm afraid I'll have to be going.'

'Oh, nonsense, Cissie won't be a tick brewing it, will you, Cissie?'

'No; and do stay, Mr Emmerson. Go on.'

Looking up into her face, he inclined his head and said, 'Since you insist, I will.' He couldn't help but be aware that his form of speech always sounded stilted, sort of old-fashioned, as if he was of another generation. Well, he might be compared with her, but not with the man.

'Aw, it's nice to be back.' Ted stretched out his legs and buried the back of his head in a cushion. 'You know, I often think of this room when I'm stuck in some dreary hotel. It's funny but I never visualise my own place downstairs, although it isn't bad, but this room has something special, don't you think?'

'I do indeed. Yes, indeed, it's a beautiful room. I've never seen so many good pieces of furniture in one room before. I've told Mrs Thorpe so.'

'Yes, yes. But if they were just egg boxes I'm sure Cissie could do something with them, make them home-like. You know what I mean?'

'Yes, yes, I do. Do you travel much in your work?'

'Yes, length and breadth of the country. I didn't used to when I worked for Randalls, but I changed over last year. This is a new paint firm I'm working for and I'm pushing it, it's all very uphill but the prospects are good. They're pleased up top with what I've done this year and they're talking about me training representatives.'

'Oh, that's good; it should make you feel very pleased.'

'Aw, I don't know. Do you smoke?' He pulled out a packet of cigarettes.

'No thanks; I gave it up about a year ago and I'm trying not to start again.'

'I wish I could. But as I was saying, it's funny the things that please you. If this opportunity had come up ten years ago I would have been over the moon, but now . . . well. You've got to have somebody to work for.' He turned his head towards John. 'Don't you agree?'

'Yes, yes, you're right there.'

'I used to work like stink when I was young, but I picked the wrong job.'

'Oh, I wouldn't say that, you seem to have made a go of it.'

'Well, I suppose I have in one way, although I've had to pay for it. It's cost me my family.'

John made no comment on this and Ted went on, 'You, being a solicitor, come across my case every day in the week I suppose: wife left too much on her own, goes after other blokes. But it wasn't quite like that in my case, until me daughter married.'

'You have a married daughter?' There was genuine surprise in John's voice.

'Yes, she'll be twenty-one this month. And I've a son nineteen. After the girl married, Gladys, that's my wife, told me bluntly she'd had enough. Of course, I knew she'd had enough for a long time, and I knew what had been going on, but when you have two kids and want to keep a home together and give them some sort of a chance you close your eyes to lots of things. The boy went into the air force; then, as I said, Claire got married, and what was there left for us? But she said nothing about a divorce until a few months ago, and now that's going through. So there you are.' He spread his hands wide. 'As they say, that's life. But, you know, they can have it for me. I'm forty-six and I've been on the road since I was nineteen . . . life! . . . Still' – he sat up and pulled at his waistcoat – 'here and there you meet one of the rare ones.' He now thumbed over his shoulder towards the kitchen. 'The best there is.' His voice was a whisper. 'They don't come any better. You take my word for it.' He now leant towards John. 'You believe me?'

'Yes, yes, I do.'

'She's rare.'

'Yes, as you say, she's rare.'

It did not appear ludicrous to him that he was discussing the qualities of this young woman with this strange man. For weeks now he'd had a personal view, an unprofessional view, of how the other half lived, and in this moment he felt an active participant in their way of life, and the candour, the honest unpretentiousness of it, appealed to him.

Cissie now came into the room with the tray, and John got to his feet, and she said to him, 'Sit down, sit down.' But he took the tray from her and put it on a side table.

'I'm going to let you put your own cream and brandy in it.'

'Good idea. Let me get at it,' cried Ted.

When they had each helped themselves to the brandy and the

cream, they sipped at the coffee in silence, their eyes moving from one to the other. Then John said, 'Excellent, excellent.'

'Haven't tasted better.' Ted winked at Cissie and jerked his head. Then putting the cup sharply down on a small table she had placed to the side of the couch, he cried, 'Aw, I've got a funny one for you, priceless. It's about two spiritualists . . .'

Perhaps it was something in John's face that checked his flow, for now he turned to him and said, 'Oh, it's all right, it's clean. It's funny, real funny, but clean. I'm not the kind that ladles out muck to women.'

John wanted to say that he was sure he wasn't, but he remained silent, his face slightly flushed, as Ted, addressing himself solely to Cissie, began:

'Well, it was like this. There were these two spiritualists, and they made up their minds, a sort of pact, that whoever died first would try to get in touch with the other, because they believed that they would change form once they died and they wanted to pass on the gen. Well, Johnnie was the first to go, and Bill set about his stuff. He tried, and he tried, and it was a long time before he made contact with his pal, but one day, after saying, "Are you there, Johnnie? Can you hear me, Johnnie?" he heard Johnnie's voice coming through, saying, "Yes, I can hear you, Bill." "Aw, good," said Bill. "By! I've had a hard time contacting you. Where are you, Johnnie?"

' "Oh, I'm in a wonderful place, Bill," said Johnnie, "wonderful. It's hard to describe to you, but it's simply wonderful."

' "No kiddin'," said Bill.

' "No kiddin'," said Johnnie. "The weather's perfect. Sun all the time. You've never seen anything like it. And the food, man . . . there's lashings and lashings and lashings of it . . . As for the women. Oh, boy! Dames never ending."

'Bill could hardly believe his ears, and in an awe-filled voice he said to his late pal, "Johnnie, it sounds marvellous. And it's done something to you; you sound changed. What are you really now, Johnnie?"

' "Well . . ." said Johnnie. "I'm a bull in the Argentine, Bill . . ." '

John watched Cissie's head go back as she laughed. He himself knew that he was expected to laugh, to roar; he made a good pretence at it, widening his mouth and covering his face with his hand. And as he did so he listened to Ted's rollicking mirth and his voice choking on 'A bull in the Argentine! A bull in the Argentine.'

The inference of the joke, its masculinity and virility, touched him on a spot that was painful. He hadn't ever cared much for jokes; and jokers, the type that spouted the tales that bred the club-room guffaw, had always been distasteful to him. As he looked at Cissie

56

again he felt that she hadn't really enjoyed this joke either, and he was glad. He understood that women, when they got going, could out-do men in their relating . . . of good ones. He had never been able to imagine women telling each other dirty stories, yet he knew that they did. But, as Ted had said, this wasn't a dirty story, yet he felt it was unsuitable for mixed company.

'Going to have another coffee?' Ted was leaning towards John now, and John knew that the man was aware of his feelings about the joke.

'No thank you. No thank you. It was delightful, and the brandy very good indeed' – he nodded towards him – 'but I must be getting along.'

As he got to his feet Cissie also rose, saying, 'It's a shame you've got to go so soon.' But as she spoke she went towards the hall, adding, 'I'll get your coat.'

After some seconds, when she didn't return to the room, John held out his hand to Ted, saying, 'Well I hope you'll have a good Christmas and enjoy the rest.'

'Thanks, and the same to you; the same to you.'

As John reached the room door Ted's voice came at him loudly, 'Mind, if ever you want to get rid of that beauty of yours, remember me, won't you?' and John looked over his shoulder, smiled, and said, 'Of course, of course.'

Cissie was standing in the hall near the door, which seemed to indicate that she wanted him to leave by this way, and he felt strangely hurt, she had never done this before. She held his coat ready in her hands, and he made a small movement of protest when she went to help him on with it. Then handing him his hat she said softly, 'Thank you for your present. I still feel you shouldn't have done it, but thanks all the same. And I do hope you have a good Christmas.' Her hand came out to his and he took it. It was the first time they had shaken hands. It was also the first time he had consciously touched her. His eyes were blinking rapidly, and he said under his breath as if he was whispering some endearment, 'And you too.' He relinquished his hold on her hand and she opened the door, and again they looked at each other.

'Goodbye, Mr Emmerson.'

'Goodbye. Goodbye.'

As he went down the stairs he pulled on his trilby. It was a good job he had been holding it in his hand, for if his two hands had been free he would surely have clasped hers with both of his. Yes, it was just as well he had been holding his hat.

Back in the hallway Cissie stood looking at her hand. For such a soft-spoken, quiet man he had a firm grip. She laid great stock by handshakes. She never trusted the jelly-like handshaker or those who tried to wring your fingers off. The latter were usually big-heads. But his handshake had been firm with a kind of tenderness about it. She liked him. Oh, he was a nice man, such a nice man.

She went into the room to Ted. By, it was going to be a nice Christmas.

CHAPTER FIVE

THE JOKE

There were three Christmas cards on the mantelpiece. They had been chosen for their lack of ostentation. The only other indication of Christmas that Ann had allowed play in her lounge were three red candles. These were arranged within a floral display, termed, apparently because of its meagreness, Chinese.

There were no crackers on the long dinner-table, such signs of low-class frivolity would have been quite out of place. The table displayed the usual glass and silver, the latter supplemented on this occasion by two candelabra. The candles they held were of a delicate cream colour, their wicks as yet unsinged.

The men stood around, with drinks in their hands, waiting for the ladies to come downstairs. The male company was made up of James Wilcox, Arnold Ransome, and the junior partner, Michael Boyd, together with Laurie, and John himself. On occasions such as this it was very often Laurie who enquired of the guests their different tastes; then passed round the drinks; but tonight his father had forestalled him.

When they all had glasses in their hands, and had told each other how boring they had found Christmas, which attitude seemed to be the right one to take with regard to this festive season, there fell upon the company, as is often the case, a quietness. It was the kind of quietness which tells a man that he must do something. So when young Boyd and Arnold Ransome spoke together it was as if they had combined to create a unique witticism, so loud was the laughter that ensued.

'Go on.' Still laughing, Arnold nodded towards Michael Boyd, and the young man, knowing his position, shook his head, saying, 'No, no, it was nothing. You first.'

'Oh, well, I was just going to say I heard old Rawlins speak the other night at a dinner in Newcastle and wondered if you had heard him, John?'

'Yes.' John nodded. 'A long time ago. But never at a dinner, mostly from the Bench, and I dreaded being on the receiving end of his rapier tongue.'

'I bet, I bet. I've never heard him in court, as he's been in London

59

for years, but I can imagine it. He had the whole place roaring. And can't he imitate dialects. He told the case of an Irishman who had been brought up for fighting on St Patrick's Day and assaulting a policeman. And he talked as broad as any Irishman I've ever heard. Apparently a priest had come to speak up for the man . . . Oh, if you had heard him doing the priest. I could never imitate him, but he went something like this: "Yer Honour, Shane O'Grady is a peace-lovin' man; he's at his duties every week, an' he's sober in his habits. But you must remember, yer Honour, that this happened on St Patrick's Day, and for anyone to question the land of your origin on such a day is an insult."

' "Would you enlighten me?" said old Rawlins.

' "Well, it's like this," the priest said. "When a countryman of his, who had not long since landed, asked him if he was English green or Irish green he saw red. For your information, yer Honour, I'll explain. There are Irish Catholics and English Catholics and as God knows they both adhere to the green, but it's the Irishman that knows that the dye in the green of the English Catholics is not to be compared with the real thing, if you know what I mean. So the doubt put upon his true colour was too much for Shane, and he up with his fists and down went his countryman. But there were no hard feelings, it was just unfortunate that the polis man should come along at that moment, and that he shouldn't happen to be of either dye, an' blood, as you know, is thicker than water, and green, yer Honour, whatever its shade, is thicker than blood." '

They all roared.

Still laughing, Laurie took a sip from his glass. He could tell a story could Arnold. What was that one he had heard the other day about the tax inspector and the brewer. He was searching his mind rapidly for the telling point of the story when he heard his father say, 'I heard a funny one too about an Irish priest the other day.' Only in time did he stop his mouth squaring from his teeth, but his eyes narrowed as he gazed in astonishment at the man standing with his back to the high hearth looking down into his glass as he began to tell the story. His father, to his knowledge, had never told a yarn in his life; he would have said he wasn't capable of telling a story. There were men who could tell stories, and there were men who couldn't, and his father was one of the latter.

'Well, there was this Catholic priest who fell off a six-floor building, and as he dropped rapidly past five of the stories he prayed like nobody's business to be saved, but when he came to the sixth he suddenly made the sign of the Cross and shouted, "Oh, my God, now for the bloody bump." '

James Wilcox was laughing. He didn't want to laugh, but he was laughing, while in the back of his mind he was saying to himself, 'Ah, I was right about that night. He may have been ill but he'd had a skinful nevertheless, and he's been at it again today or I'm a Dutchman . . . Emmerson telling a joke!'

Arnold too was laughing, and he too was saying to himself, Fancy old John telling a joke, and in the back of his mind he thought, he's changed lately; he's more relaxed, easier. And he recalled the two Saturday mornings when he phoned the house to have a word with him, and Ann had said he was in his office, and when he had phoned the office he had received no reply. He had made no comment on this, but the second time he had thought it odd.

Michael Boyd was thinking, That was very funny, the way he told it. Now for the bloody bump! I must remember that one. Fancy the old man telling a yarn. He had always thought him very stiff and strait-laced, sort of old-school. Yet there was nothing in the story; it wasn't one of those, it was the kind that could be adapted to any kind of telling. But fancy the old man telling a story at all. He didn't seem that type.

Laurie had laughed at his father's joke. He had not wanted to laugh, but not to laugh would have seemed odd. His father had stood there in company and told a joke, and yesterday morning he had heard him whistle. There was something different about him lately. Was it a defiance? No, no, he couldn't call it that. Yet he was changed. Nothing that happened would surprise him after this . . . his father telling a joke.

The sound of the men's laughter had penetrated the bedroom upstairs, and on hearing it Valerie, turning to Mrs Boyd, who was only a year or so older than herself, said, 'I think we are missing something, come on.' And looking over her shoulder she added, 'We're going down, Mother . . . Auntie Ann.'

'All right, dear, we won't be a minute.' May Wilcox turned from the dressing-table seat and beamed on her daughter, but she made no attempt to rise.

After the two young women had left the room, Ann stood looking down on her friend and she asked softly, 'What do you mean, May, I'm not wearing it? You don't expect me to wear a mink stole tonight, do you?'

'Don't be silly, dear.' May slapped her arm. 'I wasn't meaning the stole, I was meaning the perfume . . . the Chanel.'

'Did Laurie tell Val that he was going to buy me Chanel? He bought me these.' She flicked a treble strap of pearls encircling her thin neck.

May screwed up her face in a puzzled way. Then her eyes dropping to her hands, she turned round to the mirror and, patting her hair into place, said quietly, 'It's been some mistake. I'm sorry I spoke.'

Ann looked at May in the mirror, but May would not meet her eyes. 'What's this about Chanel?'

'Now look, I don't want to cause any trouble, Ann.' May looked up now.

'Tell me what this is all about, please.'

'Look, Ann, you've got a dinner facing you. There are people downstairs, not just James, Valerie and Laurie. We'll talk about it after.'

'We'll do no such thing.' With a quick movement Ann placed her hand on May's shoulder, and said below her breath, 'You'll tell me now. What do you mean about this perfume?'

'Oh my God!' May shrugged herself from Ann's hold and, rising to her feet, put her hand to her brow. Then turning on Ann she said, 'Well if you must know, you must. It happened that Millie, Mrs Orchard you know, rooms with a Miss O'Neill, and this Miss O'Neill happened to be in Danes' yesterday morning when John was there at the perfume counter, and he was buying a bottle of Chanel, a large bottle, nearly ten pounds she said it cost. Well naturally . . .' She spread her hands wide. 'I thought it was for you. I knew it wasn't for Val, as he had bought her and Laurie the joint present of the chair, and you don't go round buying ten pound bottles of Chanel for . . . Oh what am I saying?' She beat her forehead with the palm of her hand, then ended, 'Aw, don't look like that, Ann. Come on, pull yourself together.'

Ann had her eyes fixed tightly on May's face, and when she tried to speak her voice made a croaking sound. Then she gave a little cough to clear her throat and said, 'May, you're not to mention this to anyone, James, or Val, or anyone. Promise me?'

'All right, all right.'

'Don't just say all right, all right. May, I want your solemn promise you won't mention this to anyone.'

'All right, Ann, I promise you. Now don't get upset.'

'Not to James?'

'I won't mention it to James.'

'Nor to Val?'

'I've told you, I've told you. Now come on, pull yourself together; we'll talk about it after.'

'I'm all right, I'm all right.' Ann turned towards the mirror, but she couldn't see herself, only the fuzzy outline of her face. But May was waiting, and her guests were waiting, so she walked with apparent calm out of the room and down the stairs. And just as she entered the lounge she heard young Boyd's high voice exclaiming, 'A Bull in the Argentine!' Everybody was laughing. Her husband was laughing; for the first time in twenty-six years she heard the sound of his laughter. It stood out against all the other sounds in the room.

CHAPTER SIX

PAT

Oh it was hot, more like a summer day than one towards the end of spring. Cissie dropped her shopping bag and handbag onto the landing floor while she took the key from under the mat and opened the door; then picking up her things again, she went inside.

When she reached the room door she went to call Pat's name but checked herself, her mouth half open. He wouldn't be in with the key under the mat. But what had happened to him? He had never failed to turn up at the café before. Perhaps Mr Bolton had been busy and kept him on; even so he had been busy other Saturday mornings, but things had always slackened off before quarter past one, the time he was supposed to meet her.

She put her shopping away, then went into the bathroom. Standing in front of the mirror, she lifted the hair from her forehead. She was sweating, it had really been hot walking from the market, and it would be this morning that that little monkey hadn't turned up. Wait till he came in. She washed her hands, applied a little fresh make-up, then returned to the kitchen again.

Where could he have got to? Oh, stop worrying, she said to herself, and get on with the dinner He'd likely come dashing in in a minute and not a thing ready . . .

An hour later she was standing at the window looking down into the street. From this position she could see Albany Road and Cromwell Street. He would come down one or the other. Five minutes later she saw him, and her hand went to her throat and gripped it, for on one side of him was a policeman, and on the other a man in a fawn mackintosh.

'Oh my God! Not again. No, no, Pat, not again.' She found she was shouting her thoughts aloud.

She was waiting for them when they reached the top landing, and it was she who spoke first. In a gabble she said, 'What's the matter? Where've you been?' She put her hand out making to grab Pat and shake him, but he stood stiffly between the two men as if petrified. It was the man in the mackintosh who said, 'Mrs Thorpe?'

'Yes, yes, I'm Mrs Thorpe. You know I'm Mrs Thorpe.' Her voice was rising.

'Can we come in a minute?'

'Yes, yes, come in.' She stood aside until they were in the hall, then closed the door and said, 'Go into the room.'

In the room she stared at the plain-clothes man and asked, 'What is it? What is it now?'

'Now don't get distressed, we're only making some inquiries.'

'He wouldn't do anything, he wouldn't. He promised. Anyway he didn't do it before . . . Pat?' She appealed to him, and of a sudden the boy flew to her, and, putting his arms round her waist and looking up into her face and fighting his terror for a moment, he gasped, 'I didn't, Mam, I didn't do anything. I swear, I swear I didn't. I've been at Mr Bolton's all mornin'. I was just talkin' when they came. I didn't, I didn't.'

She held him tightly to her for a moment before pushing him aside. Looking from the policeman to the other man, she said, 'What is it this time? He's never been near Woolworth's or Smith's, I would swear on it.'

'Sit down, missus.' It was the policeman speaking again.

'It's a little more serious than Smith's or Woolworth's this time I am afraid, Mrs Thorpe.' The plain-clothes man's voice was flat, and unemotional. 'It's to do with a little girl.'

'A little girl?' Cissie screwed her face up at the man.

'Yes, a little girl was interfered with this morning in a shed round by the old dump, the car dump near the children's playground.'

'My Pat in-ter-fere . . .' She looked from him down at her son as she said, 'You're mad . . . Pat' – her voice was a whimper – 'you didn't?' She was appealing to him now.

'No, Mam, I swear; I swear I didn't. I know nothin' about it.'

'You see, you see. Don't you believe him?' She was confronting the men again.

The plain-clothes man now looked at her coolly, and said, 'We've got another two of the boys. There were four of them in this altogether, and after questioning they admitted that your boy was one of the gang.'

'Who said that – Who said he was? Tim Brooks?'

'Yes. Yes, it was the boy Brooks.'

'I knew it. I knew it. That boy hates Pat, he hates him. He got him into trouble before; he planted those things on him. He knew what he was doing.' She was wringing her hands.

'Listen a moment. Listen a moment. We have more than Tim Brooks's word that your son was involved in this . . . You see the little girl has made a statement.'

'She said she saw him then?' She turned to Pat. 'She couldn't, oh you didn't . . .' Her voice cracked, and he whimpered back at her, 'I didn't. I tell you, Mam, I didn't. Honest, honest I didn't.'

'She didn't exactly see the boys' faces, Missus,' said the policeman now. 'They were wearing stockings, gangster-like.' He nodded slowly at her. 'But she recognized Brooks by the clothes he was wearing and his unmistakable hair. She also recognised your son by the tie.'

Before Cissie could repeat 'The tie?' the plainclothes man put his hand in his pocket and drew out a blue and red striped school tie.

'Is this your son's?' He handed it to her and she held it across her two hands, saying, 'Yes it is. It was. That's the one . . .'

She again turned her eyes towards Pat and he cried, 'It's the one that was pinched, along with me pullover, a fortnight ago after gym. You remember? You made me go and report it, an' I did. I did. I've never seen it since.'

Cissie was turning up the corner of the tie and she pointed to some loose threads. She tapped at them quickly before she brought out, 'Look. Look, his name's been taken off. I put a name on everything because of the pinching. His name's been taken off.'

'Yes, the tag's been taken off, but there's a faint trace of his name in ink further up the tie.'

She looked towards the middle of the tie where it narrowed and saw the faint outline of Patrick Thorpe. She had put that on ages ago, and then she had bought tags because she thought it looked better, and nicer, especially on his shirts. She had marked all his things. She said slowly, 'It was planted; it was planted by Tim Brooks.'

'I can understand you wanting to think that, Mrs Thorpe, but if that was his intention he was more likely to leave the tag on, don't you think? However, the little girl happened to come by the tie when she was struggling with . . . one of the boys.'

Cissie lowered herself into a chair, and she closed her eyes before saying, 'Was she . . . ?' She didn't finish the question, but with lowered head she said, 'What are you going to do now?'

'We would like you to come down to the station with us.'

She looked slowly towards her son. His eyes were staring out of his white face as he stood gripping the back of a chair. His gaze held hers and screamed at her for protection, and she said to herself, 'Oh my God! Oh my God!' Aloud she said quietly, 'Go and wash your face and hands.'

It was some seconds before he released his grip on the chair; then he turned from them, and he staggered as he went towards the bathroom.

She looked at the plain-clothes man again and said, 'Was the child harmed?'

'Yes, she had been interfered with.'

She dropped her head deeply on her chest and groaned aloud; then quickly she raised her face to the two men and her voice was strong and firm again, even hard, as she said, 'If Christ himself came down this minute and told me my Pat had anything to do with it I wouldn't believe Him, and I'll prove it to you. He couldn't have done it, he wouldn't.'

'Well,' said the plain-clothes man, non-committally, 'we'll be very pleased for you to prove it.'

It was five o'clock when Cissie returned home. For the second time that day she unlocked the door; but now, pushing Pat roughly into the hall, she said, 'Now you stay there and don't move until I come back.'

'But Mam, Mam' – he was crying bitterly – 'where are you goin'?'

'It doesn't matter. Just you stay there.' Turning from him she locked the door and ran down the stairs, to be met at the second-flight by Miss O'Neill.

'Is there anything wrong, Cissie? Anything wrong?' she asked.

'No, nothing, nothing, Maggie.' She didn't stop, and Maggie called after her, 'Are you sure? I'm only too willing to help. You know that, Cissie. Anything, anything.'

Out in the street, Cissie hurried across the road and ran towards the bus that had stopped round the corner. Five minutes later she alighted almost opposite Mr Bolton's greengrocer's shop. This was her second visit here in the last hour.

As she went into the shop Mr Bolton turned surprised eyes towards her, then moved his shoulders impatiently as he handed a customer her change. Not looking in Cissie's direction he called across the shop to another customer, 'What can I get you, missus?' then went fussily on attending to the order.

Cissie was standing near the potato bin when he came to fill the scoop, and he said to her under his breath, 'Look, I don't want to get mixed up in this.'

'Well, you're going to be whether you like it or not, Mr Bolton.' She, too, was speaking under her breath.

His words came hissing from the side of his mouth now. 'Don't you take that attitude with me.'

'Then you speak the truth and there'll be no need for attitudes.'

The three customers in the shop were giving them their attention and Mr Bolton banged the scales and blew out bags and clashed the till with a minimum of talk, until there was no-one left in the shop but Cissie and himself. Then confronting her, he said, 'Look. I told them all I'm goin' to tell them, or you. Kids come round here lookin' for jobs. I set them on when they're fourteen and not under.'

'You're a liar and you know it.'

'You prove it, missus. You prove it.'

'You know what could happen to my boy just because you're afraid of being pulled over the coals for employing children under age?'

66

'Look.' He turned his hands, palm upwards, towards her. 'It'll blow over. He was in this scrape. It isn't the first time that kids have had a bit of a lark together, and it won't be the last. And likely she asked for it. They all ask for it the day. If you saw what I see at times outside the back of this shop your hair would stand on end. And them still at school, I tell you it's done all the time.'

'It isn't done, not by my son. I don't care how many do it or who does it, but he didn't do it. He wasn't with them. He was in this shop at the time that child was attacked, and you know it.'

'Look, I said I saw him out there knocking around among the boxes. There's a back way around here. All the kids come the back way and mess around. "Can I weigh up your taties, Mr Bolton?" they say. "Do you want any rounds made, Mr Bolton?" they say. "I'll do so-and-so for a bob," they say.'

'You gave my Pat three bob this morning. You don't give lads three bob for nothing. He was out here early on; he left the house just after eight. Where was he from then until dinner-time? He's been coming here week after week.'

'They all come week after week. He's just one of the rest.'

'You're a stinking liar. And, by God, I'll make you prove it if it's the last thing I do.' Her teeth were clenched, her eyes black with anger.

'You'll have a job.' He squinted at her and his mouth moved into a crooked smile. 'As I said to the polis, when they were all here a while ago, he could have been here an' he couldn't have been here. They looked out the back for themselves and what did they see? Half-a-dozen kids among the boxes and the refuse out there.'

'My Pat didn't get as far as the boxes and the refuse, he was in there' – she pointed to a small room to the side of him – 'where you do the orders. I'm going to get a solicitor, Mr Bolton. And you know something? You might be sorry you didn't just speak the simple truth and admit that Pat was here between nine this morning and one. If you'd said you saw him between twelve and one that would have been enough, but no, you wouldn't say anything because they might start asking questions and you'd be out of a few bob. Well, Mr Bolton, lots of things come to light once people start using a rake. So remember that.'

She turned from his grim face and walked out of the shop down the street and into the main thoroughfare. The sun was still shining, people were busy shopping, everybody seemed to be smiling and happy, and here was she on the point of losing her son, the only thing she had in life that she cared about. What could they do to him if they proved they were right? An approved school. And then? and then? She stood stockstill, unaware of the buffeting of the crowd. She must have help. She had told him, Mr Bolton, she'd get a solicitor, and she would, yes. Mr Emmerson. Yes, Mr Emmerson, he would help her. Without looking right or left she stepped onto the road, almost under the wheels of a car, and made her way to a phone box.

When she had got the number from the directory she lifted the phone and inserted the four pennies, and when a woman's voice said 'Felburn 289', she pressed the button, wetted her lips and said, 'Can I speak to Mr Emmerson?'

There was a considerable pause before the voice came again, saying. 'Who's speaking?'

'I'm Mrs Thorpe. I would like to speak with Mr Emmerson, please.'

'I'm afraid Mr Emmerson is busy. Could I give him a message?'

'I'm sorry, no. This is important, very important. Would you tell him it's me, Mrs Thorpe? I'm sure he'll see me . . . speak to me.'

Again there came a pause, and then Cissie heard the receiver being laid down. She heard the faint sound of footsteps receding away, and it was a while later when John's voice came to her saying, 'Yes. John Emmerson here.'

'Oh, Mr Emmerson, I'm sorry to trouble you.'

'That's all right, Mrs Thorpe, quite all right. Is there anything wrong?' His voice sounded different.

'Yes. I'm in great trouble. It's about Pat, Mr Emmerson. Do you think I could see you?'

'Pat? Something's happened to him . . . an accident?'

'No, not that . . . much worse. Could . . . could I see you?'

'Yes, yes, of course I'll come round right away.'

'Oh, thank you. Thank you, Mr Emmerson. Goodbye.'

'Goodbye.'

When John turned from the telephone table he saw Ann standing in the lounge doorway. There was a curious look on her face and he felt obliged to give her an explanation of the call, so he said, 'I've got to go out for a little while. It's a client, she's in a little trouble.'

As he went up the stairs he was aware that she was still standing in the doorway watching him, and it recalled to his mind that first night he had returned from Cissie's, when they had all stood watching him going up the stairs. He hadn't felt guilty that night, but he did today. There were times when he wished she knew about his visits to Cissie's. There was one way to enlighten her and that was to tell her, yet he knew he would never be able to bring himself to do it. She would never understand his need of a person like Cissie, and it was as well that she didn't, for otherwise the personal affront to her would be terrible, and he had no desire to hurt her further.

Up in the bathroom, he washed himself, combed his hair, drew his fingers down his nose, then along each side of his upper lip and was ready to go . . . go to Cissie's, to see her twice in one day. He thought of it as going to Cissie's. He never called her anything but Mrs Thorpe, but he never thought of her other than as Cissie.

He found himself almost running down the stairs, not quickly like Laurie did, but at a much faster pace than usual. As he stood in the lobby putting on his hat and coat his attention was brought to the glazed door and to the outline of Ann standing in the middle of the hall. She was apparently looking towards the closed door. This fact made him uneasy; she had been acting rather strangely of late. She came down to breakfast every morning now, and time and again in the evening he would look up to find her eyes on him. He had thought, just after Christmas, that perhaps she wanted to talk, and he had made a strong effort to open up a conversation with her, something that he had given up attempting many years ago. But apparently her attitude hadn't changed; she wanted nothing from him, not even small talk, except when they were in company, or in the presence of Mrs Stringer, when appearances had to be kept up.

Having to reverse the car out of the garage, which was to the side of the house, he swung it round at right angles to the front door, looking in his mirror to take care that he didn't hit the porch, and, as he did so, he was more than surprised to see reflected, as if in miniature, Ann standing to the side of the lounge window just beyond the edge of the curtains watching him.

He was blinking rapidly as he drove out of the drive.

PART TWO

LAURIE

CHAPTER ONE

THE IMPOSSIBLE

Ann was lying in bed, and Laurie was sitting by her side holding her hand. He had been holding it only a few minutes when, with an impatient movement, she withdrew it from his grasp and, pulling out of her closed fist a fine lawn handkerchief, she began to straighten it out on the silk coverlet, tugging at the lace edge and forming the whole into a small square.

He watched her in silence, nipping at his lower lip as he did so; then he closed his eyes, as if thinking deeply, before saying with gentle insistence, 'Now look, dear, you've got to tell me what's troubling you. I've never seen you like this before.'

She didn't answer straightaway, and when she did it was as if she was repeating a lesson. 'I've told you, I'm feeling run down. I had that cold and it's left me feeling run down. There's nothing more to it than that. Surely I can stay in bed for a couple of days.'

Laurie rose from the chair and walked to the window and looked down into the garden on to the groups of tulips, daffodils, and narcissi, and as he stood there he heard Valerie's car come onto the drive. He could not see it but he knew the sound of the engine and the way she skidded on the shingle when she drew to a stop. Turning now, he walked back to the bed and, his voice still soft, he said, 'I may as well tell you I went to see the doctor today.'

'You what!' She gathered the handkerchief again into a ball. 'You had no right to do that.'

'Someone's got to do it, and if I don't, apparently no-one else will.'

'Don't say that.' Her tone was so sharp that it caused his eyes to widen and his chin to move upwards. He was surprised that his inference that his father wouldn't trouble should have roused her, and now, his own tone sharp, he said, 'The doctor told me you haven't got a cold, you are suffering from nerves. And that didn't surprise me, but what did surprise me was that he inferred you're worrying about something, and you won't be any better until you air it. He tells me it's been going on for months.'

She was staring at him almost, unbelievably, in hostility, he imagined. Going quickly round the bed, he took his seat again, and

73

gripping her hands, whispered, 'Oh, my dear, I'm worried about you. You've never been like this before, you've always been so calm, reasonable. What is it? Look, you can surely tell me? What is it?'

Her head was bowed, her eyes tightly closed, and her lips were trembling as she replied, 'It's nothing, Laurie, nothing. Believe me. I'm just run down.' She moved her head slowly. Then raising it, she looked him in the face and smiled, a stiff, small smile. 'I'm not getting any younger and I suppose I'm going through what is known as . . . as the difficult period in a woman's life.'

He stared back at her. Perhaps. Yes, it could be that. But he should imagine that she had started that some years ago. He also should imagine that anyone of his mother's type would have taken such a thing in her dignified, reserved stride.

There was a sound of quick, soft footsteps on the stairs now, and when she turned her head towards the door he said, 'It's Val; she's bringing her work round tonight. I've got a pile, too. We thought we'd get at it downstairs.'

She made no comment, and when a tap came on the door he called, 'Come in,' and rose to his feet.

Valerie smiled at him and he at her; then she moved towards the bed, saying, 'Hello, Aunt Ann. How are you feeling today?'

'Much better, Valerie, thank you.' The tone was polite.

Valerie now said, 'It's been a marvellous day; it's a pity you couldn't get out. Are you thinking about getting up tomorrow?'

'I may.' Ann now looked towards Laurie and said, 'When you go down will you ask Mrs Stringer to come up; I'd like to see her.'

The request was also a dismissal. 'All right, I'll do that.' He put his arm around Valerie's shoulder and moved her towards the door, where she, half-turning towards the bed, said, 'You'll likely want to get to sleep; so I won't disturb you again. Good night, Aunt Ann.'

'Good night, Valerie.'

They went down the stairs in silence, but as he opened the study door for her he said, 'I won't be a minute. I'll just tell Mrs Stringer.'

When he returned to the room Valerie was lighting a cigarette, and she handed her case to him. He lit his before either of them spoke again. And then, as she often did when she meant business, Valerie spoke enigmatically. She said, 'Something should be done.'

'Something should be done? About what?'

'Your mother, of course.'

'Well, I know. I went to the doctor today.'

'What did he say?'

He pushed his hand through his hair and paused before answering her, wondering the while if he should tell her what the doctor had said.

'Well, what did he say?'

74

'He said he thinks she's got something on her mind, something worrying her.'

She dropped her head back on her shoulders and puffed the smoke towards the ceiling. 'You're telling me,' she said.

'What do you mean?'

'Now look, Laurie.' She flicked the cigarette ash towards a tray and took no notice when it fell onto some papers on the long desk. 'These evasive tactics of yours annoy me to say the least. You always play so dumb about your mother.'

'What do you mean, play so dumb?' His annoyance was evident.

'Just what I say.' She leant towards him, speaking under her breath. 'You must be blind if you don't know what's going on. I said to Mother tonight, damn it all somebody should do something, promises or no promises, and I said I was going to tell you.'

He got to his feet, looking at her while he stubbed his cigarette out.

'Well, tell me,' he said quietly.

Valerie drew in a long breath that brought her shoulders up; then when they had subsided she said, 'Do you mean to say you haven't noticed anything in the atmosphere of this house since Christmas?'

He could say to her 'Nothing more than usual', although when he came to think of it there had been a difference, and it could be summed up by the statement that his father had talked more and his mother had talked less. Odd that, but that is how it could be summed up. But it meant nothing. The situation in the house had been the same as it always was, but only he knew that, not Valerie, or her old nosey father, or her mother, even if she was his mother's dearest friend.

'There's no way to give you this, Laurie, but straight; your armour needs to be attacked with an axe. Either you know, and you're covering up, or you're absolutely stone blind to the fact that your mother is ill because your father's keeping another woman.'

It was some seconds before he cried, 'Father's what! What did you say?' He leant towards her as if he hadn't heard aright.

'Just what I said. Sit down before you fall down.' She pushed him in the chest with the tips of her fingers and he sat down.

'Do you remember Christmas night when your father went all jolly? Do you remember when he told us about the bull, the bull in the Argentine. He had told it twice and he laughed like I'd never heard him laugh before. And do you remember your mother sitting like a statue most of the night? You don't remember, you just didn't take it in did you, the unusualness of your father telling jokes. My father used to say it would take a landmine to move your father in any way, and that night he was laughing, and causing laughter, and the landmine was a woman, the one that saw to him the night he was taken ill. You do remember the night when he came back with

75

his collar and tie loose, the night that he forgot to turn up for the dinner, don't you? And father was right about him that night, too . . . He was blotto.'

'Hold your hand a minute, hold your hand a minute.' His face was turned from her, almost buried in his shoulder, and he was punching the air with his clenched fist. 'This is all surmise; you're just looking for one thing to explain another. It's all guess work.'

'You listen to me.' She pulled at his arm and brought him round to face her. 'It was on Christmas night that mother, up in the bedroom here, asked Aunt Ann why she wasn't wearing the Chanel perfume, and your mother asked her what she was talking about. And then it all came out. You see Millie – you know our Millie. Well, she lives with a woman named Miss O'Neill. They live on the first floor in number ten Greystone Buildings, and she, this Miss O'Neill, happened to be in Danes' when your father was buying a bottle of Chanel which cost nearly ten pounds. So she tells Millie that she saw your father buying the perfume, and Millie says to mother in all innocence that she knows what Mrs Emmerson's going to get for her Christmas box. A bottle of scent, a great big bottle of Chanel. Naturally mother asked Aunt Ann about the scent, and your mother was so taken off her guard that she gave herself away and she made mother swear that she wouldn't tell father or me. And she didn't at first, not until she started pumping Millie and learned that your father visited Mrs Cissie Thorpe at least once a week, on a Saturday morning. Mrs Cissie Thorpe is a typist and has Saturday mornings off. They thought nothing of it the first time, because he came to thank her for looking after him the night he took ill. But when it becomes a regular habit . . . well they are only human, as Millie says, and they start talking and prying. Miss O'Neill, who happens to be off on Saturday mornings too, goes upstairs to visit her friend and happens to find your father there, and the funny part about it is he hasn't come up the stairs to get to the top flat. Nor did he leave by the stairway, so they could only surmise he came over the roof. If they wanted any more proof, the old couple underneath this lady's flat gave the show away, because, not only had the old man been up there and seen your father but they could hear them talking on a Saturday morning, and, as the old lady said, they stopped going up because they didn't like to disturb them . . . Ha, ha.'

Valerie now dropped her bantering tone, and, getting up and putting her arms around Laurie, she said, 'I'm sorry. Don't take it like that. But I just had to tell you, and in such a way as to make you believe it, because you know' – she pulled him tightly towards her now – 'you just will not face up to things, you pretend you don't see them.'

Laurie wiped the moisture from his upper lip, then asked quietly, 'What did you say her name was?'

'A Mrs Thorpe. Millie calls her Cissie, and by the sound of it she's a right Cissie at that. There's a commercial traveller who lives on the ground floor; he's a regular visitor. And at one time, as far as I can understand, young Holloway – you know the wholesaler in the market, his son used to visit her.'

'I can't believe it.' He shook his head slowly and spoke as if to himself. 'Him running a woman? It's impossible. Of all people, him!'

'Yes, my reactions were the same when I first heard it, because there's no getting away from the fact that he's one of the most inane creatures . . . I'm sorry, Laurie, but I can't think it possible that he's your father. Oh, I know he is, you look alike, that's the odd thing about it. You've got all his features, but thank God they don't make you look like him. Yet it isn't his looks so much as his manner that makes him so utterly watery . . . Then the latest is that the woman's in trouble . . .'

'You mean . . . ?'

'Oh no. No, not as far as I know anyway. Not that way, no. It's her boy. He's been in the courts before – he was up before father – and now he's coming up for interfering with a girl, and him only ten. I tell you they're a real bad lot. But I wouldn't like to be that kid when he comes before my dear papa next week, for he feels very strongly about this business and if he can strike a blow in the defence of Aunt Ann he certainly will. As he said, there's more ways of killing a cat than drowning it.'

Laurie got to his feet, pressing her gently aside. He didn't heed what she was saying about the woman's son. He was thinking of his mother lying upstairs, on the verge of a nervous breakdown. That's what the doctor said. 'You must persuade her to get away, take a long holiday,' he had said. 'Is there any trouble at home? I mean . . .' and before the doctor had finished he had assured him there was no trouble like that, none whatever. 'Then get your father to take her away on a holiday, a sea trip. That might do the trick. Get her away from the house and all her present associates, this often works wonders.'

Get his father to take her on a sea voyage! He was walking blindly to the door when Valerie said, 'Where are you going?'

He turned back towards her and sat down. The numbness, the shock, was wearing off, but taking its place was a feeling of anger, of rage. It began to burn inside him as if a fire had suddenly been lit. The evidence of his feelings was pouring down his face in sweat, and it was as if Valerie's voice was coming from another room when she said, 'Now look, don't let it disturb you like that.' When she wiped his forehead he pushed her hands roughly aside, saying, 'Stop it. Don't do that,' and she stood back from him, her voice huffy now. 'Well, you needn't take it out on me. Don't be like that with me. I told you because I thought it was for the best.'

'Well, you should have told me earlier, months ago when you first knew about it.'

'My mother had promised.'

'And she kept her promise, didn't she?'

'Now look. Don't take it out on me, Laurie. I'm telling you.'

Instead of her tone giving him warning, it only increased his anger, and he rounded on her, crying, 'If she knows' – he thumbed towards the ceiling – 'that your father knows and you know, she'll go mad. Why couldn't Aunt May have kept it to herself, or told me on the quiet?'

'Look.' Her voice became cool, reasonable. 'My father is a magistrate, he's used to keeping secrets.'

'Huh!'

'Now don't use that tone when speaking of Father, Laurie.'

'Well, don't make him sound infallible because he's a magistrate; you said only a minute ago that he was going to take it out on that boy, that woman's boy whoever he is, for something he hasn't done.'

'The boy has done something. He helped to interfere with a girl. Isn't that something?'

'But your father won't be judging him for that, he'll be judging him because his daughter's future father-in-law has slipped up.'

She took a step backwards and her pert face became stiff, and she surveyed him with cold eyes for a full minute before she said, 'You're an ungrateful sod.'

She said the word sod in such a way that it was deprived of some of its coarseness, but nevertheless it caused the muscles of his face to twitch. She often used that word sod and he didn't like it, and she knew he didn't like it. She now grabbed up the papers that she had placed on the desk and stalked towards the door, saying, 'I'll see you when you're in a better frame of mind.'

He heard her pause in the hall to pick up her coat, but he made no effort to follow her. He sat bent forward, his hands between his knees. The feeling of rage was increasing in him. His father would be the laughing stock of the town; they'd all be a laughing stock. But if this had been going on for months, as it must have been, his father supposedly didn't mind being a laughing stock. Nor, apparently, did he mind jeopardising his position in the town, but the contemplation of such an eventuality was driving his mother to the verge of a mental breakdown.

That his mother should be thrown over for some loose piece and become the object of pity to her friends was unbearable to him. There were those who would say, 'Poor Ann,' but who would glory in her downfall, and among those who would derive private satisfaction from the situation he included her dear, dear friend,

Aunt May. It was very odd, but at this moment, this particular moment, he loathed the Wilcox family more than he did his father, and that was saying a great deal. And this did not come as a revelation, it was something he had been trying to disregard for a long time. But now he was facing it.

He sat on in the same position, waiting, listening for his father coming in. He felt sick at the thought of seeing him. He'd want to hit him; he pictured himself pushing his father's big flabby body up against the wall and slapping out right and left at his pale face. How in the name of God had he the nerve to go after a woman . . .

When seven o'clock came John hadn't come in; nor yet when the clock reached half-past. During the last half-hour Laurie had walked between the lounge, the study, the dining-room and the kitchen a countless number of times, finally ending up in the kitchen.

'What is it, Mr Laurie?' asked Mrs Stringer. 'Are you worried about Madam?'

'No, Stringy. Look.' Turning to her with an impulsive movement he said, 'I know you should be off but can you stay a little while longer?'

'Yes. Long as you like.'

'I have to go out and I don't want to leave Mother alone. I may be only half-an-hour, but it might be a little longer.'

'Don't hurry. Don't matter what time you get back as long as you run me home.'

'I'll do that, Stringy. Thanks.'

Without bothering to don a hat or take up his light overcoat, he hurried out through the side door into the garage. Getting into his mother's car, he drove into the town, finally bringing the car to a stop opposite number eight Greystone Buildings. Afterwards he remembered that apart from wanting to confront his father and hit out at him, there was in him a deep curiosity to see what type of woman it was who had fallen for the big lump of inanity.

Getting out of the car he looked towards the door of number eight. It was locked. That squashed any possibility of his father still being in his office. He walked now towards number ten. In the hall he saw the names of the tenants. Mrs Cecilia Thorpe's was at the top of the list. As he mounted the stairs his nostrils twitched with distaste against the mixed odours of cooking, and when he came to the last flight he paused for a moment, looking upwards, then went swiftly to the top. Without hesitation he rang the bell.

'Yes?' She looked surprised as if she had been expecting someone she knew.

He looked at the woman. But she didn't look a woman, more like a young girl. She had long sandy-coloured hair tied back from her shoulders; she had dark brown eyes, was tall, and extremely thin.

'Yes, what is it?'

'I'm Laurance Emmerson. I would like to see my father.'

His tone expressed his deep hostility and she appeared to stretch herself upwards before it as she answered, 'Mr Emmerson isn't here.'

'I'm afraid I don't believe you. Tell him I want to see him.'

Her mouth dropped open, then snapped shut again.

'I've told you he's not here. Come in and see for yourself.' She pulled the door wide. 'And what's more, Mr Emmerson, I don't like your tone.'

He stood still, glaring at her. That's who she had expected. Well, he had got this far and he would wait too. He passed her, and she closed the door behind him with a bang that vibrated through the flat. 'Go on in. Go on in. Search.'

He moved into the room, just within the doorway, and then stood stock still. And what he saw proved to him how right Valerie was. He could see for himself she was a type and she was certainly living in style. You didn't collect this sort of stuff on a typist's salary.

She pushed past him and walked towards the middle of the room before she turned to face him, and from there she said, 'I know what you're thinking Mr Emmerson, but you're wrong, quite wrong.'

For answer he said, 'You're expecting my father?'

'Yes, I'm expecting him.'

'Then I'll wait.'

'Do, but let me tell you something. And get this clear. You're on the wrong track. I'm not going to say I don't know why you're here, I do, but you're on the wrong track . . .' She turned abruptly from him, and looking towards a door at the far side of the room and to a boy standing with his back to it, she said, 'Go back to bed, and stay there.' When she turned to him again he said, but under his breath, 'Do you deny that my father visits you?'

'No, I don't. There's no point in denying it, everybody in the house knows it. You can't keep anything secret in flats not even if you want to, and I can assure you neither I nor your father went out of our way to keep anything secret . . . Yes, he visits me. What of it?'

'And I suppose you talk art.' His tone, still low, was an insult in itself, and it brought the colour rushing into her pale face.

'Now look, I'm warning you. You be careful, because you're going to be sorry for what you're saying.'

He walked farther into the room now, looking around him, his stare insolent. He looked at the card tables flanking the window, then at the small baby grand, its lid closed now. Then he turned and without invitation seated himself, and looking up at her he said, still quietly. 'I know your type, and this set up, a sort of unbaited trap, until they get inside . . .'

Cissie put her hand to her throat. She wetted her lips and closed her eyes for a second before she ground out, 'If . . . if you weren't his son I'd call Mr Glazier up and have him throw you out.'

'Mr Glazier?' He nodded at her. 'He's the one in the bottom flat, isn't he? I've heard about him.'

'Oh my God!' Her hand still to her throat, she turned from him and walked across the room and looked down into the street for some minutes before she said, 'Mr Emmerson, I'm in trouble, I'm very worried over my son. Your father's seeing into it for me. I'm expecting him up any minute . . . Now,' she turned to him, 'if I swear to you that you are wrong, will you go? I don't want any disturbance. He'll . . . he'll explain it to you.' She made the characteristic wide sweep with her hand. 'But there's really no explaining to do, nothing, nothing.' She joined her hands now in front of her and walked slowly towards him. 'Your father comes here. We have a cup of coffee, we talk . . .' She suited her step to each word, her body swaying slightly as if to a rhythm. 'He likes music, and furniture, and . . .'

'You needn't press it. What do you take me for? Do I look green?'

'Stop it! Stop it!' Her voice coming as a scream startled him. And at that moment, there came sounds from the hallway, like a small door closing then quick footsteps and when he turned there stood his father in the doorway.

He rose to his feet and looked at this big now florid-looking man for his father's face was suffused with a deep red, almost purple tinge. It was evident that he had received a severe shock and was trying to rally against it.

'What are you doing here?'

It didn't sound like his father's voice. It had a strength about it that he didn't associate with the man before him. But here he was seeing a different man to the one he saw at home. Of course, this house was where he led his different life. He had been clever, he had used two distinct personalities. They said he was good in court, he wasn't a solicitor for nothing. This kind of thing had likely been going on for years. It explained too why this undeniably attractive piece should fall for him.

He watched him come forward into the room, slowly, heavily. He watched him ignore himself and go towards her. He saw him look at her with a look he had never seen on his face before, tender, loving, with a sort of mute adoration. When he heard him say softly to her, 'I'm sorry about this, very sorry,' and she answer 'I've tried to explain', it was too much. And his wrath burst from him, uncontrolled for the moment. His voice filling the room, he yelled at them, 'You're sorry. You're both sorry about being found out. But what about my mother? I suppose it's news to you that she's on the verge of a nervous breakdown?' He was glaring at his father.

'I went to see the doctor today; you couldn't, you were otherwise engaged. The doctor told me she'd something on her mind, something worrying her. She'd been like it for weeks. Is it news to you that she's known about your carrying on all the time?'

John opened his mouth to speak but found he couldn't. There was a racing feeling underneath his ribs. His brain was racing too. Ann had known about this? No, no, she couldn't. She would have said something, something mild, slightly sarcastic, telling him that she valued her good name, her position in the town. But that is all she would have said, because that was the only way it would have affected her. Yet if she had known, why hadn't she spoken of it? The racing feeling accelerated, bringing with it a pain, a pain so sharp that it brought his shoulders down. He was still looking at Laurie, trying to say something. The last thing he remembered was Cissie's arms going round him, and her voice spiralling upwards, crying, 'Oh, Mr Emmerson. Oh, Mr Emmerson.'

'See what you've done. See what you've done.' She was kneeling on the floor supporting John's head on her knees. Laurie, too was on the floor, kneeling at his father's side looking into the lifeless face.

'You've killed him. You've killed him.'

'Be quiet!' He tore at his father's waistcoat and put his head down to his chest. Then looking up at her, he said, 'He's not dead.'

'It isn't your fault.' She poked her face at him as she spoke, and then, the tears bursting from her eyes and spilling down her face, she cried, 'You! You!' and after gulping two or three times she shouted at him, 'Don't sit there like a dummy, go and get a doctor.'

Obediently he scrambled to his feet. His own face was white and drawn and he felt a fear within him. Although his father's heart was beating, he looked dead; he might die at any minute. She was shouting at him. 'There's a doctor round in Cromwell Road, a few doors down. Bell, Doctor Bell. Go and get him.'

He took the stairs two at a time, almost over-balancing an old man who was coming up. He ran into the street and down Cromwell Road, and stopped at the door with the plate on it.

The woman who answered the door said, 'The doctor has finished surgery.'

He gabbled at her that his father had had a heart attack in Greystone Buildings. Reluctantly she went and brought the doctor, who as soon as he saw Laurie said, 'Oh, hello. What's the trouble? You're young Emmerson, aren't you?'

'Yes, yes, Doctor; my father's had a heart attack.'

'Where is he? In his office?'

'No, next door, in one of the flats.'

'I'll be with you directly.'

It was just a matter of minutes later when the doctor, following Laurie at some distance up the stairs, puffed his way into the room. Cissie was still in the same position, still holding John's head on her knees.

'Put him down,' said the doctor quietly, 'and get a pillow.'

A short while later the doctor looked up from the floor towards Laurie and said, 'Ring for an ambulance. Mention my name and tell them to be smart about it.'

Fear had entirely replaced his anger now, and once again he was dashing down the stairs, only to stop in the street and wonder where he would find a phone box. And then he remembered having seen one round near the garages at the back of the building.

After he had made the call he stood in the box and leant his elbow on the top of the directory and rested his head on his hand for a moment. What had he done? WHAT HAD HE DONE? What had possessed him to go to her house? He should have waited. Oh yes, now he knew he should have waited. When it was too late to alter anything he knew he should have waited.

He walked slowly back to the house and up the stairs. His father was still lifeless on the floor. The doctor was standing near the head of the couch looking down at him. The girl was standing near his father's feet, her hands joined tightly under her chin as if she were praying. As he walked into the room the doctor was saying to her, 'How did it happen? Anything to cause it? Was it sudden?'

She looked up, not at the doctor, but towards him, and after two gasping breaths that sounded like a child sobbing, she said, 'Nothing. It was sudden.'

The doctor now turned and looked at him and asked, 'You got through?'

He nodded his head but didn't speak.

'Has he had these attacks before?'

'I don't know,' he said. 'No.'

'Yes, he has; he's had them before.'

The doctor turned slowly round towards Cissie. He didn't know who she was, only that she wasn't Mrs Emmerson, but she seemed to know more about the man on the floor there than the son did. There was something fishy here. 'How many?' he said.

'I know of one, a bad one, but . . . but not like this.'

'How long ago?'

She considered a moment, then said, 'Last November.'

The doctor raised his brows, looked down towards the floor again, then turning sharply towards the window said. 'That's them now . . .'

When John had been placed on the stretcher the doctor followed the bearers out of the flat, and Laurie followed him. At least he followed him into the hall, but there he paused and looked back towards Cissie, where she was standing in the middle of the room. And he watched her press her lips together and fling her head from side to side before crying under her breath, 'You! You!'

CHAPTER TWO

THE REASON

It was turned twelve when Laurie brought his mother home from the hospital. His father had regained consciousness but the doctor thought it unwise that she should see him, such was the state she was in.

Since earlier in the evening, when he had dashed from the hospital back to the house and told her what had happened, at least that his father had had a heart attack and had been taken to hospital, she, too, had seemed on the point of collapse. During the time they had sat in the waiting-room she had hardly spoken. In fact, during the first two hours of waiting she had sat in a coma of dumb misery, and it wasn't until towards eleven o'clock, when the door had opened and that woman had come in, that she had come to life.

He had walked towards the straight grey-coated figure and under his breath had said, 'What do you want here?' She had looked past him towards his mother, and he had turned and seen the recognition in his mother's face. Then she had said, 'You know why I'm here, I came to enquire about your father.' There was dignity about her bearing, a quietness about her tone that maddened him, that made him want to go for her, expose her for what she was. What he would have done had the night nurse not come in at that moment he didn't know, but he glared at her as she said to the nurse, 'Can you tell me how Mr Emmerson is, please?' And having been told there was as yet no change in John's condition, she had then looked back at him with one long, penetrating, disdainful stare before leaving the waiting-room.

It was after the nurse had gone that his mother had spoken for the first time. 'How did she know he was ill?' she said.

When he hadn't answered she had turned on him, her voice deep and harsh in her throat, and said, 'Well?'

He had sat down in a chair before saying. 'It happened at her house.'

'And you were there?'

He moved his head downwards once.

'Why? Why were you there?'

'Mother.' He had appealed to her under his breath, 'Don't let's go into it here. Wait till we get home. Please.'

And now they were home.

He opened the front door for her and she stormed past him. The calm reserved woman was gone. Her fingers were moving agitatedly, her head was jerking all the while, first to one side and then to the other. She tore off her coat as she was crossing the hall; she flung her bag on the table and her hat after it; and then she went into the lounge.

He followed her slowly, wondering what the outcome of this was to be. He had never seen her het up like this, never imagined her letting herself get into this state.

'Well now!' she turned on him. 'Tell me. Tell me about it; explain how you managed to be with him when this happened?'

'Look, Mother, sit down and calm yourself.' He went towards her, his hand outstretched, but she backed away from him. She had never moved away from him in her life before, but now it was as if she didn't want him to touch her.

'I want the truth. Do you hear? I want the truth.'

'All right then.' He found himself shouting back at her. 'I'll give you the truth. You know what's been going on for a long time.'

'What do you mean?'

'You asked for the truth, didn't you?'

When she didn't make any reply to this he said, 'I didn't know about anything until this evening, when Val told me.'

'Val? What does she know? She knows nothing.' All her body was jangling, her hands, her head, her legs, as if she was about to go into a dance.

'Aunt May knew, didn't she? Well, could Aunt May keep anything? Everybody knew he was having an affair with—'

'He wasn't having an affair.' Her voice was thin, the words pinging as if off stretched wires. For a second her body became still, and she remained poised, her head half turned to him, and when he looked away from her and said slowly, as if tired by her gullibility, 'Oh, my God, Mother,' she screamed at him, 'He wasn't having an affair. He wasn't! He wasn't, I tell you.'

'All right, all right.' Again he was shouting back at her. 'If you want to look at it like that, he wasn't having an affair. He was just visiting this girl but he wasn't having an affair.'

'That's right, that's right.'

'Look, be your age. What are you getting all worked up about if you think he wasn't having an affair?'

'He wasn't having an affair. I tell you he wasn't. HE WASN'T.' Her voice rose to a screech, and now to his amazement he saw her grip her hair on both sides of her head. He saw her face become contorted, her mouth open wide as if gasping for air, and then on a loud cry the tears gushed from her eyes and her nostrils, and the saliva ran from her mouth. Then, almost bringing him from the floor, she let out one piercing scream after another. After a moment's hesitation he had her by the shoulders, shaking her, shouting, 'Give over, Mother. Stop it! Stop it!' He tried to draw her into his arms to smother her cries but she fought him, struggling and pushing at him.

'Stop it!' he begged her. 'Don't scream like that; they'll hear you down the road.'

When she opened her mouth for yet another scream, he screwed up his face, paused a moment, stepped back from her, then struck her with the flat of his hand. The blow did not knock her off her feet, but like a deflating balloon she subsided onto the couch.

Gasping and sobbing now, she lay back staring up at him, and he, panting as if he had been in a fight, stood looking down at her. He had heard that slapping the face was an effective cure for hysterics, but had he been told he would ever use it on his mother he would have sneered at the ridiculousness of such a suggestion.

'I'm sorry.' Although he sounded sorry he did not sit beside her or take her hand, or show her any comfort; this wasn't, he felt, the time for softness. He went towards a chair and sat down beside a little table a distance from her, and he waited, not speaking until her breathing returned somewhat to normal. But when at last she spoke to him, her tone calm, saying, 'He wasn't having an affair with her,' he thought, Oh my God is she going to start all that again? But he said nothing, he just let her go on.

'Don't look at me like that, Laurie. I'm telling you, your father couldn't have an affair with . . . with anyone . . . anyone.'

'What! Do you mean he's . . . ?' He didn't say impotent, but it was as if he had, for she shook her head. Then she pulled herself a little way up on the couch, and with both hands she smoothed her hair back from her brow, stroked down the front of her dress, then turned towards the high stone fireplace and said, 'We were only married a week when he was called up. I fell with you right away.' He felt surprise at her using this natural kind of expression. 'Your father did three months' training before being sent to a unit. The second day at this new place they were handling some ammunition in a shed and it exploded. Seven of the men were killed outright, about ten others injured . . . The bottom of your father's stomach was shattered . . .'

He felt something jump within him, like a live thing. It leaped from his groins up through his stomach and into his throat and checked his breathing.

'He was in hospital for nine months. He tried to take his life twice during that time, and they sent him to an asylum.' Her voice was unemotional.

Almighty God! He never went to church; he didn't think about religion in any way, it was mostly bunkum; yet in this moment he cried to something outside himself, something that understood pain, the strange pain he was experiencing now, and the years, the eternities of pain suffered by the man he had despised.

'You were a year old before he saw you. By that time I knew that you were all I had, or would ever have, of comfort. He saw that I was wrapped up in you. Sometimes I thought he was glad that this was so; other times I knew that he suffered, and I couldn't do anything about it. And the years went on and on. He had his work and I . . . I had you.'

He sat staring at her with the strangest emotion coursing through him. This elegant but now slightly dishevelled woman was his mother. He had always loved her, championed her, adored her, but in this telling moment no vestige of these feelings remained. Yet there was feeling in him for her, but what was it? Hate? No! No! No! How could he hate her? Did he despise her? How could he despise her? All this reversal of feeling was ridiculous and would pass. But at this moment he knew that if she were to touch him he would shrink from her hands, because whether she had intended to or not she had made him despise the man who was his father. From as far back as he could remember, and without saying a word against him, she had held him up as something as pulpable as unleavened dough, something lukewarm, spineless, inane, until her picture of him had become fixed in his mind. She had said she'd had only himself, and with her every breath she had secured him to her while alienating him from the man who was of no use to her.

With a feeling now that seared him he conjured up the picture of his father, the big flabby-fleshed blinking man, the eunuch hiding behind the fixed smile. God! God! He had the unusual desire to lay his head on his arms and cry. He knew now with a certainty that if his father were to die remorse would gnaw at him for the rest of his days. He turned his head slowly and looked at the woman who in the past few minutes had shattered his emotions, the emotions that she had guided, and he said to her, 'If you knew that nothing could happen between them why have you made all this fuss?'

Unmoved, he watched her as she closed her eyes and bit on her lip before saying, 'You don't understand. I couldn't expect you to. But . . . but lately, this last year or so, not just since I knew I was going to lose you. No, no,' she moved her head emphatically, 'before that. I felt . . . I felt. Oh! I can't explain.' She dropped her chin onto her chest. 'Perhaps it was remorse for the way I had treated him, for having shut him out. I don't know. I only know that for some time I've wanted to get near him, to take that awful lost look from out of his eyes. It had been there for years, but somehow I noticed it more of late. And then . . . then at Christmas when I got the first inkling of this business, I . . . I knew it was too late. I knew I had lost him. I think I knew from the very minute it started. He had never sought companionship of any kind from man or woman; then this . . . this thing I could have had, that would have been far more lasting than anything created by sex, this thing that was there for my taking, and which I scorned, and belittled him even further by doing so, he gave to someone else.'

Her lips parted and he saw her tongue wobbling in the dark cavity of her mouth, and for a moment he thought she was going to lose control again. But she didn't. She snapped her mouth closed, pressed her fingers against her lips, then said, 'I told you you wouldn't understand. I don't expect you to, because I can't understand it all myself. If anyone had told me three or four years ago that I would be jealous of him, that I would be nearly driven mad with the thought of him being happy in another woman's company, I would have laughed. Yes, even two years ago I would have laughed. I'd never had a normal married life, so what was there left to be jealous about? But even so I've gone through hell. I've been terrified of anyone finding out, terrified at the humiliation, of people feeling sorry for me. But now, funny, it doesn't matter any more what they know. I feel he's going to die, and I'll remember that the only happiness he's had in the last twenty-six years is what that cheap-looking girl has given him. For he has been happy lately. That's what's been so hard to bear; I've known he's been happy. There's been a lightness about him and he's tried in vain to hide it. Just last week I heard him singing softly to himself in the bathroom. It was like a knife being driven through me.'

She became quiet, one hand was resting on her lap, the other lying palm upwards on the seat of the sofa. He sat staring at her unable to go to her, or even to offer her a scrap of comfort, for there was nothing left in him for her. With her confession she had scraped him bare of sympathy; she herself had smashed the picture of a beautiful, not quite-of-this earth creature tied by law to a bloodless individual.

He saw her now like a leech sucking all his affection from him, leaving nothing that could be spared for the man who had created him, and whom he had needed, yes needed . . . And now, because the despised, crippled creature had found comfort – other than physical. And there was the rub, other than physical – with someone else, she suddenly realised that she wanted him, that she needed him. After twenty-six years of isolation, of freezing him out, she had thawed towards him, only to find it was too late.

Yet, he now asked himself, was he blameless in this matter? Couldn't he, as he grew older, have made some kind of effort to look at his father through his own eyes? Why hadn't he stopped to think of what others saw in him? Men like Arnold Ransome and

Michael Boyd; they both held him in high esteem. And they weren't the only ones . . . But no, he had only allowed himself to see what she saw. He was, in a way, as much to blame as she. Strip out the childhood, when he hadn't much say in the matter, and come to these last few years . . . even at this late stage, he could have given this man a form of companionship, the rare form that exists between a grown son and his father.

When he saw her rise from the couch he made no move towards her. She said softly, 'I'm going up.' Then she stood looking at his averted face and added, 'You're blaming me, aren't you? You're shocked.'

He, too, rose to his feet, and with his eyes averted from hers, he said, 'It's no use apportioning blame now, but to tell you the truth I do feel a bit shocked. I . . . I feel he's had a rotten deal all through.'

The force of her stare brought his eyes to her, and he saw that she looked tired and ill, and even old. Her chicness had gone; that calm, suave veneer was stripped from her; she looked more like an ordinary woman than ever he had seen her before. Yet the change evoked no softness in him. He would need time he knew before any such feeling would return; he was still stunned by her cold-blooded, diabolical treatment of a human being, whom, and this was a telling point, she had made feed, clothe and house her in style for years.

She left the room without speaking again, and when he heard her muted footsteps overhead he looked up towards the ceiling. Women were vicious, cruel. If such a thing was to happen to him, say, if tomorrow morning he went out and was hit by a car and his sex life was finished, how would Val react? Say they were married, how would she react? In exactly the same way as his mother had reacted. He nodded his head in affirmation. Only Val would go a step farther; she would either divorce him or get her satisfaction elsewhere; she wouldn't starve of the thing she needed most.

Slowly he rose to his feet and went out of the room and up the stairs. As he crossed the landing he looked towards his father's room and a feeling of remorse, so weighty that he bowed his head under it, descended on him. And when he reached his room he did not switch on the light but groped his way towards the bed and dropped onto it and, his hands clutching at the pillow, brought it pressing hard against his mouth.

At half-past eight the next morning the Wilcox family came en masse to the house. Ann was up. She had been downstairs since six o'clock, when she had phoned the hospital. And now James and May were closeted with her in the lounge, while Valerie was having it out with Laurie in the study.

Laurie stood with his hands on the desk leaning slightly forward, letting her go on as she had for the last few minutes.

90

'. . . And when would you have told us? Tonight? Tomorrow? Can you imagine what we felt like when Millie came in and told us he was in hospital . . . had been picked up from that woman's place and that you were there? Why did you have to go? At least why didn't you tell me you were going?'

Laurie turned his head to the side and did not speak, and Valerie continued, 'Father's furious. He says you're a damn fool and should have minded your own business and—'

'And what do you say?' His voice sounded patient, cool. His head was still turned from her.

'Well, if you want to know, I say the same. It's bad enough your father's name being bandied round the town in connection with her without you going out of your way to give it more publicity. And Millie says you were fighting with her. Miss O'Neill heard you. The whole place was raised. Are you mad?'

Now he turned on her, his voice no longer quiet, his lips squaring away from his teeth. 'Yes, I'm mad. But I'll be madder if you don't shut up. And another thing I'd like you to remember is that your father might be my boss at work but he has no say about what I do in my own time. As yet I can go where I like, talk to whom I like. Yes, and row with whom I like . . . As yet I can even go into Bog's End and stay the night at Bella Pickford's and enjoy all she has to offer. As yet I can do all that, and don't you forget it.' He was now pressing his finger into her chest. But she did not move away. Her cool gaze appraising him, she said, 'Yes, yes, you can do all that. As for Bella Pickford, I've no doubt you're well acquainted with her.'

'No doubt,' he said, making a deep obeisance with his head. 'No doubt.'

After glaring at each other for a moment longer he turned towards the desk and began to gather up some papers. And now, her voice almost soft, she said, 'Oh, Laurie, I'm sorry. But you must admit it's shattering. Even if we weren't going to be married, our families have been close for years and this happens, and you don't let us know . . . we've got to hear it through the daily woman.'

'And by all accounts, she gave you a graphic description of the events. She's missed her vocation, that one; she should have been a reporter.'

'There wouldn't have been any need for us to learn the news from Millie if you had acted like an ordinary human being . . . But look. Let's stop this bickering and tell me, what's she like?'

'What's who like?' He turned his head towards her, but kept his eyes averted.

'That tart up in the flats.'

Looking fully at her now he said quietly, 'From outside appearances she looks no more like a tart than you do.' He did not know if this was his real opinion of the woman or he was saying it to annoy Val. He was still so churned up inside from what he had learned last night that he couldn't think straight.

'I beg your pardon.'

'You asked me what she looked like and I've told you.'

'Thank you. Well, for the present moment let's skip appearances. What did you say to her?' She was striving to control her rising temper.

'I can't remember.'

'You can't remember what you said to her? You went to tell her to lay off your father and you can't remember?'

'No, I can't remember. I can only remember what she said to me . . .'

At this point there came the sound of a door banging, then James Wilcox's voice, crying, 'Where are you, Laurie? You there, Val?' The study door was thrust open now and the little man bristled in.

'Ah, there you are. Now I've just had a talk with your mother. I've told her to leave everything to me.'

'And what did she say to that?'

'She said the same as all women do, that she can manage her own affairs. But you know how far that takes them . . . Well now, about this piece you saw last night, this so-called Mrs Thorpe. What was your impression of her?'

Laurie looked at his future father-in-law, wetted his lips, told himself to count ten, but got no further than five before saying, 'My impression of her was that she was an extraordinarily good-looking woman, with tastes beyond the usual, and somebody not easily frightened.'

James Wilcox screwed up his small eyes and surveyed Laurie through his pin-point vision, then looking towards his daughter he said, 'You two been having a row?'

When neither of them spoke he went on, 'Well, that's neither here nor there, there's something much more important to be tackled at the present moment. Now, Laurie.' He pointed his hand, fingers held stiffly together, gun-fashion towards him. 'If your father gets better there's a strong possibility that he'll carry on with this game. Who knows; he might even want a divorce. Once these Thorpe types get their claws on a decent man he hasn't got a chance. Well now.' He pushed out his little chest. 'It's fortunate, as I see it, that her boy's in trouble. Yes, I say fortunate, and I mean fortunate.' He bounced his head towards Laurie. 'I've had them before me on another occasion, and on this one I intend to make the town so hot for that lady that she'll be glad to go somewhere else to cool off.'

'Are you going to try the boy or her?'

'What do you mean?'

'Just what I say. Before the boy comes up you've already decided on your verdict. Is that right?'

'Now look here, Laurie; I want none of your altruistic theories. I know my job as a magistrate; I know the types I have to deal with in this town, and I act accordingly. And I don't need any lessons in justice.'

'No?'

'NO! And don't forget who you're talking to.'

'Father.' Valerie took hold of his arm, and when he turned towards her she said, 'Leave this to me, will you? Please.'

'Huh!' The sound that Laurie made brought their attention to him. They watched him push papers into his despatch case, lock it, then walk past them into the hall.

'Where do you think you're going?'

'I'm going to the office.' Laurie was now putting on his coat. 'You have reminded me more than once in the past that unpunctuality keeps a man's feet on the first rung of the ladder. Isn't that so?' He picked up his hat and walked out, ignoring Valerie's voice, high and sharp, saying, 'Laurie!'

He would not use his mother's car, as he sometimes did. His father's he had never used, and he would not have used it today had it been here, but it was still where he had garaged it last night, in the stables behind the office.

Having reached the road he did not immediately board a bus but walked to the nearest telephone box, and from there phoned the hospital.

There was little change, the sister said, but he was holding his own. And yes, he could visit him at any time. After replacing the receiver he stood looking down at it. Somebody should be with him, sitting with him. Blast old Wilcox and his job. Blast the lot of them. He picked up the receiver again, put another four pennies in the box and gave his own number. When Mrs Stringer answered he said, 'Tell Mother I want to speak to her for a moment,' then asked, 'Is Mrs Wilcox still there?'

'Yes, Mr Laurie.' Mrs Stringer's voice was very low.

'Then just tell mother she's wanted on the phone. Will you do that?'

'Yes, Mr Laurie.'

A few seconds later he heard his mother's agitated tone saying, 'Yes! yes?'

'It's me . . . Laurie. I just wanted to know if you were going straight to the hospital. If not, I'll go and sit with him.' There was a short pause before she answered. 'I'm going straight along now.'

'All right; I'll come in at dinner time.'

'Very well.'

'Goodbye.'

'Goodbye.'
They were like strangers.

Laurie's office was one of four small rooms going off a dark corridor; the other three being occupied by two typists and James Wilcox's private secretary.

The door of James Wilcox's office was directly opposite the corridor, and although he was a bustling man, noisy in speech and manner, it was rarely he banged his door, and so the staff, in their cubby holes, seldom had any indication of the boss's arrival. But this morning was different; the boss's door banged and almost instantly the bell rang in his secretary's room. A minute later the secretary knocked on Laurie's door, and on being told to enter she came in, closed the door swiftly behind her and hissed, 'His nibs wants you. Hair's standing on end. Did you hear his door banging?'

Laurie had worked with Miss Patterson for years; there were no secrets between them with regard to their opinion of the boss.

'OK, Patty.' Laurie nodded to her, and she swiftly departed. He did not immediately follow her but stood gnawing at his lip, asking himself what line he was going to take if the old fellow became impossible. Tell him to stick his job. No, he couldn't do that; there was Val. Val! How he wished he could push the last year back. This thought propelled him out of the room.

He went along the corridor, knocked at the door, and entered the office, there to be met by James Wilcox's back. He knew quite a lot about that back, having had to gaze at it on many occasions: the hands joined over the buttocks, the short legs astride, the shoulders hunched high, cupping the head. It always meant trouble. An odd thought came to him as he stared at it. He was glad he had never called this man 'Uncle'. It had been quite easy to say 'Aunty May' but something had stuck in his gullet at the thought of calling James Wilcox 'Uncle'.

'Well now, Laurie.' The voice was studiously polite. 'We've got to have a little private discussion, haven't we?' This was delivered as Mr Wilcox turned his body slowly about and walked to his desk. Then sitting down, he pointed to the chair opposite.

After a moment's hesitation, Laurie seated himself and, his eyes unblinking, he watched James Wilcox go into action.

'Now,' the shoulders, still hunched, were bent over the table and the finger was wagging with ominous slowness, 'don't you remind me that I've always said it's bad business to bring your private woes into the office. There are exceptional circumstances, and I consider this business comes under that heading, so we'll start from there, eh? Valerie tells me you've been awkward in more ways than one lately. Now, now.' The finger beat became more rapid. 'If my daughter can't talk to me who is she going to talk to? Anyway, we're soon to be one family, and such being the case there should be no secrets between us . . . Well, well, I won't go as far as that because every man has his secrets.' The wisdom of this statement brought his head down in a deep sweep, and when it rose again he continued, 'But about the simple fact of letting us know your father had collapsed. Such a thing as this doesn't come under the heading of secrets but of ordinary human behaviour. Then going off to that woman's house and not saying a word. And see what it brought about? Your father wouldn't be where he is this minute if you hadn't bulldozed in there. These things can always be handled better by finesse. It's no use using the bull at a gap tactics with women on the side, women like this Thorpe piece. Legality is what you want there; they're frightened of the law. They're all loud-mouthed, big noises until you mention the law, and then they come cringing. I've seen it over and over again. Now, that said I'm going a step further.' Mr Wilcox's body swayed backwards and forwards between his chair and the desk. 'As I said this morning it's ten to one, if your father recovers, this thing will go on, and it could lead to divorce. And we're not having that, are we?' He did not wait for an answer but continued. 'So . . . I want you to promise not to interfere in any way. Leave this business to me, and don't go near this woman, or speak to her. That's vitally important.'

'What made you think I'm going to?' The words were rapped out.

On this occasion Mr Wilcox did not take umbrage at Laurie's tone, but said evenly. 'You went last night, didn't you?'

'I had my reasons.'

'You could have your reasons again, but I'm warning you.' The finger was once more in slow operation. 'You leave this to me. Don't go near the woman. Those types are dynamite.'

Looking across the desk into this little man's face, Laurie had an overwhelming desire to take the flat of his hand and push it back, not strike it, just push the face as far back as possible. A blow, being a spontaneous action, could be said to have some dignity attached to it, but what he wanted to do to this man was something that would carry with it the insignia of indignity. He had a mental picture of pushing him slowly backwards, his head going down and his feet coming up – he could see him lying in a ludicrous heap on the floor. It came to him, with no touch of humour, that since last night he had for the first time lived up to his looks. He had wanted to hit his father, he had actually slapped his mother, and now it was all he could do not to put his desire into action and lay hands on his boss.

He rose to his feet and said coolly, 'I don't think my father would want you to deal with this matter, sir.' The insolence attached to the sir wasn't lost on James Wilcox.

'Now look here, my boy.' He was on his feet, his head wagging like a golliwog's. 'Don't you take that tone with me, I'm warning you. And anyway, you've no say in this matter, it's your mother who will decide what's to be done. I don't know why I'm talking to you.'

'I think my mother's answer will be the same as mine; she won't wish you to interfere in my father's affairs.'

'You'll go too far.' Mr Wilcox put his hand to the back of his neck and flexed it, as if trying to relax the muscles, and as he did this he kept on talking. 'You forget yourself, you're not being wise, in fact I would say very unwise. No man who wants to rise in this world bites at the hand that is stretched out to help him, so to speak. I tell you, you can go too far, too far.'

'Is that all, sir?'

James Wilcox, his face bright red now and choked with his indignation, swung round, walked to the window, put his hands behind his back and placed his feet in the straddled position. It was as if he hadn't moved since Laurie had entered the room.

Back in his own office, Laurie sat with his head resting on his hands. He wouldn't be able to stick it, he wouldn't. He had known for a long time things were coming to a head. To be married to Val, to have the families even closer, to come in here each morning and see him; to have a partnership dangled on the end of a long, long pole before his nose, its shortening depending entirely on his subservience to the little man's whims. He just couldn't do it. But how was he going to get out of it?

He knew now that what he had felt for Val wasn't love, never had been. Perhaps, if from the beginning she hadn't continually and blatantly extracted from him all he had to give, he might have felt differently. He didn't know, he just didn't know. His head pressed harder on his hands. He was in a mess and he couldn't see how he was going to get out of it.

CHAPTER THREE

FATHER AND SON

John looked at his son sitting at the side of the bed and he was pleased he was there; he seemed to be part of the great stillness that was filling him. This stillness that he mustn't disturb, a stillness wherein his heart was beating faintly. He was strangely at peace in this stillness; except for one thing, one little niggling thought, that would keep drifting to the forefront of his mind, then drift away again. It always drifted away when they gave him his pills, but it was some time now since he'd had them and the niggling thought was back, and with it the gentle urge to do something about it. And he felt that Laurie could help him.

He remembered thinking earlier in the day that if he had known that his imminent death would have brought his son closer to him he would have done something about it a long time ago. He did not have to ponder, or reason, or recognise that the young man who sat evening after evening by his side was not the same person with whom he had lived for years; this man was his son, he could feel it; after all these years he could feel it. The bastion that had grown up between them, mounting as the years mounted, was no longer there. It had vanished. It was as if it had never been. Yet it had been; he had watched its erection brick by brick. Oh yes, it had been. But now it was no more. But about this thing? He moved his hand slowly on the coverlet towards Laurie, and as slowly he said, 'Laurie, will you do something for me?'

'Yes, Father, anything. Tell me.' Laurie leaned towards him.

'Mrs Thorpe. She's . . . she's in trouble . . . The boy's case is coming up. I . . . I was seeing to it, but . . . but Arnold won't talk business. I . . . I want you to go to her, get her to tell you everything about . . . about Bolton . . . the greengrocer.'

Laurie stared back at his father. The last thing on earth he wanted to do was to come face to face with that woman again. Doubtless she was all they said she was, but with regard to the situation between her and his father they had been wrong. Everybody had been wrong, but only his mother and himself and the two concerned would ever know . . . That was a thought. Did the woman know? It wasn't likely. Then if she didn't, why . . . ?

97

'Will you go . . . Laurie?'

'Yes. Don't worry, I'll . . . I'll see to it.'

John's hand came on his, and the fingers made a slight pressure. 'Thank you. Thank you . . . Bolton, he's the man. He's . . . he's frightened. You see . . . Mrs Thorpe. She'll . . . she'll explain.'

'All right, all right. Don't worry. Now don't worry; I understand.'

He watched his father pull at the air, dragging it into his chest, and he held his hand tightly as he said, 'Leave it to me; everything will be all right, don't worry.'

'Laurie?'

'Yes, Father.'

'She's . . . she's a good woman. Very, very good.'

He had to lower his eyes.

'There was nothing . . . nothing between us to . . . to hurt your mother.'

'I know.'

They were looking at each other.

'Don't worry. I know. I know all about it.' His voice was gentle, as if he was speaking to a child, a sorrowing child, trying to convince it he understood all its unspoken problems.

John's head pressed back deeper into the pillow, as if to put more distance between his face and that of his son's, to get him into focus . . . So that was it. Ann had told him. It wasn't because he had nearly died, or was dying, it was because he knew. God, after all these years. But . . . but what did it matter? If it had created this feeling between them, if it had brought them together at last, what did it matter? In a way he felt it lightened the shame of his inadequacy; it took some of the weight of the burden from him . . . But there were others . . .

John's hand began plucking agitatedly at Laurie now. 'You won't . . . you won't let that go any further? You wouldn't . . . tell?'

'No! No!' The syllables came rumbling up from his throat like a torrent from an underground passage, so powerful was the denial of any idea of betrayal of the knowledge that he possessed, and John was convinced and his agitation subsided.

To convince his father still further, Laurie said, with a half-smile on his face, 'You've never liked the Wilcoxes' ménage have you, Father? Well, I'm going to let you into a secret, neither have I.'

There was a crinkling on John's face that tended towards a smile, and a light in the back of his eyes that spoke of his amusement, but there was also bewilderment in his look.

'And . . . and there's something more.' Laurie paused. 'I can't go on with the marriage, Father.' He paused again, watching his father's face, then exclaimed, 'Oh . . . oh, I'm sorry. I shouldn't have mentioned it. Don't let it disturb you.'

There came a pressure on his hand now while they stared at each other. Then John said quietly, 'I'm glad.'

'You are?'

'Yes, she – she wasn't for you, never.'

'Keep it dark, won't you? You see, she doesn't know yet – I mean Val. And I wouldn't want to upset Mother. It'll all come out in good time and then . . . oh boy, the fireworks. I . . . I must admit I've got cold feet. I haven't got a notion of how I'm going to do it . . . I – I shouldn't have told you. I'd no intention when I came in.' He lifted one hand expressively. 'But . . . but I thought you'd understand, and I felt I must tell someone.'

Again the pressure on his fingers. Then John said, 'It won't be easy . . . they'll put you through the mill.' He gasped and began pulling at the air again.

'You've talked too much. It's my fault. Lie quiet now, lie quiet. No more talking.' Laurie smoothed the side of the pillow.

They stayed for some time in silence, until John, his words more spaced, said, 'Don't . . . wait for . . . for your mother coming. Go and see . . . Cis . . . Mrs Thorpe now. Will you?'

'Yes.'

'Now?'

'Yes.'

'It'll . . . it'll rest my mind.'

'Don't worry. I'll see to everything.' He stood up. 'I'll look in in the morning and tell you how things have gone.'

John nodded slowly. Then reaching out his hands, he caught at Laurie's, muttering, 'Thanks. Thanks for everything . . . everything, Laurie.'

The gratitude, the humility in his father's tone was too much for him. He turned swiftly and went out of the room, down the corridor that housed the private patients, into the main vestibule, out into the street and along to where his father's car was parked. Yesterday his father had said, 'Use her, don't let her rot.' He had put it as if asking a favour.

He sat in the car now making no attempt to move off. He felt uneasy to say the least. What would he say to her? How would he begin? Would he wait until it was dark before he went? All those nosey-parkers on the stairs, especially dear Mrs Orchard and dear Miss O'Neill, private eyes of the Wilcoxes. Well, what was he going to do? He just couldn't sit here indefinitely. If he went home Val would descend on him; she would be on the watch as she had been for the past three nights.

He beat a tattoo on the wheel with his fingers, then pursed his lips into a whistle, but made no sound. Aw, he might as well go and get it over with. But God, how he hated facing her again. Talk about crawling in the dust; she'd make him do that all right.

Outside Greystone Buildings he parked in front of his father's office, in exactly the same spot he had left his mother's car five evenings ago, then walked to number ten. Making his tread as soft as possible, he mounted the stairs and made the journey without meeting anyone. And for the second time he rang the bell of Flat Four.

When the door opened there stood the boy he had caught a glimpse of the other evening. He looked down into the big-eyed, pale face, with the mop of fair hair topping it. Michelangelo's angels could have been designed from such a face. And this was the boy who was accused of interfering with a little girl. But didn't all little boys interfere with little girls, and mostly by invitation? And the little girls, as they grew up, didn't alter much, except to get worse. He could hear Val saying, 'What's the matter? Don't you want it?' IT. IT. It wasn't only the infringement on the male prerogative that got him down, it was the crudity of the approach. Where that was concerned education meant damn all; a low type pro would have more delicacy at times than Val had. He wondered where she got it from. Her mother? The old man? How could you tell by how people looked. Val, he supposed, would even look prim as she faced the girls in class. The thought of the girls recalled his attention to the boy again, although he hadn't taken his eyes from him. 'Is your mother in?' he said.

'Yes.' The boy didn't move.

'Who is it?' He heard her steps coming across the room.

She stopped at the doorway leading into the hall and looked at him; then came hurrying forward and pushed the boy backwards before saying, 'What do you want?'

'I want to talk to you.'

'I've got nothing to say to you. Now get away; I want no more trouble with you.'

He felt the colour draining from his face. 'My father sent me,' he said quietly.

He watched her concern. He watched her wet her lips, look round to where her son was, then grudgingly, 'Come in.'

In the room she walked swiftly towards the fireplace. Then turning to him, she said, 'Well?'

He was standing some distance from her, to the side of the couch, his hat in his hand. He felt utterly nonplussed. He looked from her towards the boy who was standing as if he were looking out of the window, then said quietly, 'My father's worried about . . .' He inclined his head towards Pat. 'He tells me he was taking the case. He wasn't able to explain it all to me; he wondered if you might give me the details. Something about a greengrocer, a Mr Bolton.'

He stood looking at her, watching her rapid breathing. Her body was swaying slightly from side to side and she was moving her hands in long stroking movements up and down her hips, the whole attitude showing her extreme agitation, and it came over in her voice as she said, 'I don't see what you can do. Mr Ransome's dealing with it.'

'Mam. Mam.' The boy turned and came towards her, his voice as agitated as hers. 'He said he had written to him. That's all, that's all, Mam. It's no good just writin' to Mr Bolton, he'll just write back. I told you, I told you. You've got to go to him. I told you.'

'I've been to him, haven't I? I've been to him twice. You know what he said, if I went to him again, I . . .' She closed her eyes for a moment, shook her head, then pushed at the boy, saying, 'Go on, get yourself out and leave this to me.'

The boy looked from her to Laurie. Then, his head drooping, he walked listlessly across the room and out into the hall. But the moment she heard the flat door opening she was running across the room, calling, 'Don't go away, just round the block mind. Be back here in ten minutes. Do you hear?'

There was no answer to this, and then she returned to the room, and as she walked past him, said, 'I've left the door open; there's nothing you can do.'

'Is it any use saying I'm sorry?'

'No, it's no use saying you're sorry.' She rounded on him, her voice bitter. 'You come into my house and insult me, you show me up in front of all my neighbours, but worst of all, you cause your father to have a heart attack, and then you think you can get over it by saying you're sorry. You don't know the meaning of being sorry for anything, not your crowd.' She began to move about the room, throwing her words at him. 'You're so cock-sure about everything, you're of the chosen few. You've been set up in the world, you've got a position in the town, and because of it you think you can kick people around. Have a good address, belong to the right societies and clubs, and you're infallible. You can carry on how you like but nobody can point a finger at you; they can't come into your house and insult you . . . Oh no, because you are the right people.'

He followed her movements as she upbraided him, and he was reminded of his mother the other night, only he didn't think this girl would lose her head. He said quietly, 'You're wrong; you've got it all wrong.'

'Am I?' She was confronting him squarely now, standing still. 'Look, I've been in business for years and I've met your type. You said you knew my type, well, I know yours. I meet them all the time, and they're ten-a-penny little upstarts. They're in their jobs because of their father's money, or their mother's money, or because they've got friends at court. If they had to rely on their own brains they'd be on the dole, half of them . . . three-quarters of them, and I'm telling you.'

'Did you think that way about my father?' There was an edge to his voice now.

'No, I didn't. Your father's different, a different breed altogether to you and your kind. Your father's a solicitor, I know, but in his mind he's still a simple man, living in the farmhouse where he was born. Besides, your father's a lost, lonely man, and he's out of his element; there's nothing brash about him. He needs ordinary things, ordinary people. He's lonely . . . lonely.' There were tears in her voice now, and in the back of her eyes, and she swallowed twice before she went on. 'I've never met anybody in my life so alone, so lonely, as that man. And there's a cause for it; there must be a cause for it. I didn't know what it was, but after having seen you and your mother, it isn't far to seek.'

'Thank you. Do you feel better?'

Her eyes widened, her mouth opened, and she gulped before she said, 'There you go, expert at the cool, smart answer. It puts everything and everybody in their place, doesn't it?'

'Look,' he said, 'forget personalities for a moment. You say you liked my father, then ease his mind by letting me do something about this business.'

'You can do nothing more than is being done at the moment, and as much as I would like to please your father I don't want any help from you, is that final?'

'Yes,' he said; 'I think it is.' He was staring at her and she at him. Then, only because he couldn't stand the pained look in the depth of her eyes, he looked away from her and around the room. It was a wrong move, as he found out when she cried at him. 'Go on and ask me how I came by all this.'

He screwed up his face in question but made no comment, and she went on. 'But there's no need, is there? You know how I've got all this stuff. It's the men I have, dozens of them. At times they queue up on the stairs. That's what you think, don't you?'

'Please don't talk rot.'

'Rot, you say? I'm talking rot? When you entered this house the other night you treated me as if I were a prostitute from Bog's End. Rot! Now look.' She put out her arm at full stretch, the hand vertical. 'Don't say any more. I don't want to hear your excuses, I just want you to go. And I'll thank you not to come back here. Is that clear?'

Slowly he turned his head to the side and looked towards the floor, and as slowly he turned round and walked out. As she had said, the door was open.

As he neared the first landing he heard a door click closed and it wasn't the one he had just come through. He realised that the private eyes were on duty, but the knowledge aroused no ire, for he felt numb. It was a humiliating numbness. He'd been given the treatment he had wanted to hand out to Wilcox. Metaphorically he was lying on the floor in a heap, and the indignity of it was weighing heavily on him. Wilcox had dressed him down, but that was different, very different.

He was getting into the car when he heard someone say 'Psst! Psst!' and looking to the corner round which led to the back of the buildings, he saw the boy beckoning. He paused a full minute before going to him, and when he did the boy put out his hand and pulled him into the shadow of the wall, and looking up at him he said, 'She's not going to let you, is she?'

'You mean help?'

He nodded.

'No; she doesn't want me to help.'

The boy now rubbed the nails of his thumb and first finger up and down the sides of his front tooth; then sticking his four fingers in his mouth he bit on them hard before looking up at Laurie again and saying, 'I didn't do it, I swear. I swear I know nothin' about it.'

'That's the truth?'

'Yes, it's the truth. Oh yes, it's the truth.'

'Come here.' Laurie drew him further up the alleyway that led to the garages, and when they stopped he stared hard into the boy's face before saying. 'Tell me exactly what happened on that Saturday morning.'

'Well, it was like this.' Pat sucked in his lips, swallowed and went on, 'I go to Mr Bolton's every Saturday to help make up the orders, taties and things. I get there on nine and I leave about one, and then I go to a café near the market where I meet me mam and help her carry the groceries back. I've been doin' it for a long time like that. Mr Bolton sometimes gives me two bob and sometimes three, depending, but I keep out of the way in the back 'cos I'm not supposed to work 'cos I'm just on ten, see, and he can't set them on until they're fourteen, an' he tells me to keep out in the back an' if anybody comes, strange like, to make on an' just play about like I was one of the lads come scrounging for bruised fruit in the boxes outside. It's near the dump you know, the car dump. You know where it is?'

'Yes.' Laurie nodded.

'Well, on Saturday mornin' I finished the orders an' I said to Mr Bolton are there any more and he said no, and I said it's five to one and he gave me three bob, and as I went down the street I remember the Town Hall clock striking one. Then I was passing the dump and Barrie Rice, a boy I know, and Tim Brooks, another boy, he's older than me, nearly fourteen, came running down the side, dodging like, and Tim Brooks grabbed me by the shoulder and pulls me with him, and I say, "Leave over! leave over! What's up with you?" and he pulls me beyond a car, and I thought they were having a game, or being chased by the other gang or somethin'. An' I said again, "What's up?" an' I said I had to go because of me mam was waitin' but Tim Brooks, he kept hold me and he made Barrie do the same, though Barrie told him to let go. Then they pulled me to the dugout, that's a place beyond Tollington's factory, and they wouldn't let me out, at least Tim Brooks wouldn't. And he kept saying to me, "You're in this, Pat Thorpe. You're in this." An' I got frightened 'cos he had got me into trouble afore. You see he used to lead a gang I was in, an' one day he swopped me a ball-pen and a key case for some medals I had, and then he swore he never did and that I had pinched them from Smith's. When the gang went round on Saturday they had a sort of game to see who could pinch most from Woolworth's, or Smith's, or Craig's, but I never did 'cos of me mam. But he said I did, and he said I never gave him no medals. Well, anyway, there I was in the dugout, and then the polis came, an' I didn't know what it was all about and I told them, but he said – Tim Brooks, that is – he said I was just playing dumb and I was in it, and then the polis said was this my tie, and he said didn't I tell you so. He said that to the polis. An' it was my tie, but I hadn't worn it, I'd lost it last week, with my pullover; it'd been swiped when I had stripped for gym. Then the polis asked Barrie Rice had I been with them an' he said yes. He's frightened of Tim Brooks, an' he had to say yes . . . An' that's the truth, mister, that's the truth. I would have never have done such a thing, I wouldn't hurt me mam; 'cos she was upset the last time and frightened. I wouldn't upset her again. Anyway I'd never do a thing like they said.'

When he hung his head Laurie said, 'Were you wearing a tie when the police spoke to you?'

'No, just an open-necked shirt.'

'Where does this Barrie Rice live?'

'In Portland Street, number four.'

'And your mother's been to see Mr Bolton?'

'Yes. She's been twice, but he takes no notice of her because she's a woman.' He moved his head slowly as he repeated, 'She's a woman, you see.' This statement conveyed his opinion of why his mother had failed to make any impression on Mr Bolton.

As Laurie looked down on the boy he saw him standing in front of old Wilcox. He heard the magistrate's voice leading off, his holier-than-thou attitude well to the fore. 'You and your kind are a menace to our community and I intend to make an example of you. You are depraved and the only hope for you is strict supervision. I am assured that this would never have happened if you'd had the proper parental control . . . ' At this point he saw her face as Wilcox carried out his intention of making the town too hot for her.

'Where's his shop?' he said.

'Cox Road.'

'Does he employ anybody else?'

'No. Not now. He used to have bigger lads, but he got wrong once about something that happened in the shop. I don't know what it was, but after he didn't have any help for a long time.'

'Well now, listen,' said Laurie. 'You go upstairs and look after your mother. Don't tell her you've seen me or told me anything, understand?'

'Yes.' He nodded.

'And I'll see what I can do.'

'Thanks. Thanks, Mister.' He went to move away. Then turning and looking up into Laurie's face, he said, soberly, 'Me mam isn't bad, she isn't. She isn't a bad woman. She's good. I'm in the house all the time. Me mam isn't bad.'

God! this was dreadful, terrible. Laurie's gaze dropped towards the ground. Then raising his eyes again to the boy's face, he said softly, 'You go on thinking that way about your mother.'

'But it's the truth.' The nervousness had disappeared from the lad's voice, there was a touch of aggressiveness in it now. 'Everybody likes me mam. She's jolly, she's happy, at least she was . . . and funny, fun to be with I mean. Except this last week, and this business, and since Mr Emmerson took bad. She likes Mr Emmerson. But she's good. She could get married the morrow but she doesn't want to. Ted, Mr Glazier, him that lives at the bottom, he's getting a divorce and wants to marry her but she told him no, I heard her. He's going to live down south, but she doesn't want to marry anybody, ever. And nobody ever stays in our house at night . . . She's good.'

Ten years old and defending his mother. 'Nobody ever stays in our house at night.' He bent down until his face was on a level with Pat's. 'Don't worry about it. I believe your mother's good, I do. Go on now; go on, keep her company.' He pushed him away gently, then said, 'Wait. Where am I likely to find you if I want you?'

'I go to Remington Road School.'

'Very good. Pat.' He reached out and touched the boy's shoulder. 'If I need you I'll come there after school.'

Pat nodded solemnly, then walked into the street, and when Laurie reached the pavement he saw him entering the flats.

He got into his car, drove down to Cox Road, and there drew up opposite the greengrocer's shop. It was closed, and he sat in the car looking across at it. It was a double-fronted shop and had been newly painted, as had the windows above it. These were nicely curtained and looked like a flat. To the right side of the shop window was a door painted a vivid red, the private door to the flat, he supposed. It could be that Mr Bolton lived above his shop.

He got out of the car and crossed the road, and after a moment's hesitation he rang the bell. The door opened slowly, but no-one confronted him until a voice from the top of the stairway shouted, 'Yes, what is it?'

He put his head back and looked up to see a woman with her hand on a pulley.

'Does Mr Bolton live here?'

'Yes, who wants him?'

'I wonder if I could have a word with him?'

'He's busy bookin'.'

'Well, I wouldn't keep him a minute.'

'Who is it?' A man had now joined the woman, and he bent forward and looked down the stairs as he asked, 'What you want?'

'I . . . I just wanted to have a word with you about the boy, Pat Thorpe.'

He watched the woman move back on the landing as she said under her breath, 'I knew it was about that, I knew. You tell him where to go to.'

'Look.' The man bent his knees and heaved further forward, but made no attempt to come down the stairs. 'I'm havin' nothin' more to say about that little nipper. What I'd to say I've said to the polis.'

Laurie stepped into the passageway and looked up to the man. 'You still mean to say you didn't employ him on that particular Saturday morning?'

'Not on that particular Saturday mornin', or on any other mornin'. I've got me work cut out to keep the little bastards out of the back shop, thieves and scroungers the lot of them.'

Laurie let a moment elapse before he said, 'You remember the boy, Pat Thorpe, don't you?'

'Aye, I remember him all right because I was always tellin' him where to go to. And look . . . I don't know who you are, and I don't bloody well care, so get goin' an' shut the door behind you.'

Laurie kept Mr Bolton under narrow scrutiny for another few seconds, then he turned around and closed the door after him.

As he drove away he thought: Types. My God! the types, and he was a liar. His short acquaintance with him had convinced him of that.

Bolton. Bolton. The name kept repeating itself in his mind. Bolton. Bolton. He had an orderly mind for names, he rarely ever forgot a name. Bolton. Bolton. Was he on their books? Not on his. He didn't do any work for anyone of that name. But he had seen the name Bolton on a file somewhere. Now where would he have seen that, except in the office? Bolton. Bolton. There came a little click, Bolton. Wilcox. That's where he had seen Bolton's name, in the old man's files. He had a number of clients whom he attended to himself. He couldn't remember how long it was since he had seen the name, definitely before the old man started locking things away. It could have been years ago, and Bolton could have transferred his business elsewhere, but there was a chance he hadn't. There came another click in his mind which told him he was sure he hadn't. He was in the Wilcoxes' dining-room, where every weekend, summer and winter, was displayed a great bowl of fruit. James was so fond of fruit, he could hear May Wilcox remarking, and he had thought more than once that they spent a lot on fruit, and this had seemed out of line with Aunt May's cheese-paring budget. The only time she went to town with regards to food was for the 'dinners-at-eight'. Of course, he could be barking up the wrong tree. It could all be surmise, wishful thinking. But anyway he'd look into it tomorrow. Long shots sometimes paid off.

And now for this Barrie Rice's abode.

When he reached number four Portland Street, he hesitated before getting out of the car, because, standing at the open door, her arms folded on the top of her stomach, was a woman of more than ample proportions. Moreover, she was in loud coversation with another woman. She might or might not be the boy's mother, but he felt chary of approaching her. Still, as he had stopped the car and was now under scrutiny from the two women he thought it best to make the approach.

Stepping across the pavement, he addressed himself to the large woman, saying, 'I'm looking for a Mrs Rice.'

'I'm Mrs Rice.' The arms still remained folded.

'I wonder if I could have a word with your son, Barrie?'

'You from the polis?'

'No, I'm not from the police.'

'Then you can't have no word with him.'

'Well, you see I'm from a firm of solicitors.'

'Thompson and Curry, they're the solicitors we've got. You one of them?'

'No, no, we're not that firm.'

'Well, then, Mister, whatever you want to know you'd better go and ask the polis, that's my answer to you. What you want to know you go and ask the polis.' Mrs Rice nodded at him, then to her friend, and without more ado he turned round, got into the car and drove away. He knew when he was beaten.

When he came downstairs before half-past six the following morning he wasn't surprised to find his mother already up. She had been down before him every morning since his father had taken ill. He wondered if she slept at all, but he didn't enquire. The wall that had stood between his father and himself hadn't fallen into disuse; it had re-erected itself now between him and her.

When they spoke to each other it was quietly, as if each were

107

considering the other's feelings. It seemed strange when he remembered that he hadn't touched her or held her hand for days, nor had he kissed her goodbye, which had been the usual morning procedure. Could the tie that had held them together be severed so completely?

Although he wasn't due at the office until nine o'clock he left the house at eight-fifteen, and scooted down the avenue as if the devil was after him, part of the evasive tactics that he knew only too well must soon come to an end.

Thursday was court day and consequently a day when there was a slackening of routine and nerves in the office, but this morning he felt no benefit from this. For one thing he had a thick head, having had a session at the club last night in order to evade going home and being waylaid by Valerie. He had even driven up Handley's rutted lane and come into the avenue by the top way. And then there was the Bolton business. If it wasn't that today was the only time he'd get the chance to investigate the files he would have left it over.

He heard the girls come in; then a few minutes later when he heard Miss Patterson's firm tread along the corridor he went out of his office and followed her into her room.

'Can I have a word with you, Pattie?' he said.

'Yes, of course, but let me get my things off.' She laughed coyly at him over her shoulder; then patting her greying hair into place she said, 'You're here bright and early. And it Thursday an' all. Now, what is it? By the way, you look tired; you been on the tiles?'

'Well, not exactly on the tiles, Pattie. Just indulged a little last night.'

'Oh, naughty boy. You won't be able to do that much longer.'

He slanted his eyes at her, and she giggled. Then he said, 'I want your help, Pattie. I want a little information. First of all can you tell me if the old man does Bolton's, the greengrocer's accounts?'

'Bolton's? Yes. He's done them for years. His stuff came in only last week.'

'Do you think I could have a look through them?'

'I don't see why not. But . . . but wait.' She flapped her hand at him. It was another coy movement. 'He might have them locked away, he does with some of them. I don't do all the work on all of them you know. I couldn't, could I? Just the working out of the fees and covering letters and such.'

'Will you have a look?'

'Yes, yes, I'll do that. But what do you want to know?'

'Just a little thing.'

'It won't cause trouble?' She looked apprehensively up at him.

'Oh, no, no.' He shook his head at her. 'And I won't keep it long. If you could bring it into my office, it would be better, for who knows he may pop in and I wouldn't want him to find me along there.'

'Oh, my, no.' She laughed her high thin laugh. 'We don't want any high jinks on a Thursday, do we? All right.' She winked at him. 'I'll go along in a minute and have a look for it.'

'Thanks, Pattie.' He smiled at her warmly, then went out.

Back in his office he sat thinking. Since he had been first articled to this firm certain names had become synonymous to him with success, or failure. Year after year he had watched the rise or fall of the businesses to which these names were attached. When he qualified Wilcox had handed over to him a number of clients, and with time the number had risen, but he had always been aware that there were, on the books, names about which he knew nothing. Bulky parcels would arrive addressed to 'Mr Laurance Emmerson', and underneath 'James Wilcox, Chartered Accountants'. And bulky packets would arrive addressed to 'James Wilcox, Esq., Chartered Accountants', and marked 'Private'.

He didn't think the old man was up to any fiddle; he was too wily for that. But there were many things an accountant could do to lighten a client's burden, such as not asking too many questions, while praying that the tax inspector would be of like mind. And there were always ways of being paid in kind; it went on all the time. Still, it wasn't with the idea of getting anything on old Wilcox that he wanted to see Bolton's file. It was simply with the hope that he'd get a clearer picture of Bolton and perhaps in some way get a handle with which he could turn the truth out of the greengrocer. The whole thing was just a hunch, but he had always believed in hunches; and a hunch might make all the difference to the fate of that boy. He hadn't been able to get him out of his mind. Nor had he been able to get the woman out of his mind. The more he had drunk last night the more clearly he had seen her as he had left her in that room.

The door suddenly opening, Miss Patterson tripped in, whispering, 'Here they are. He's never touched them yet. But mind you, if I hear him come in I'll give you a buzz, and you make them scarce.' She nodded, as one conspirator to another.

'Thanks. Thanks, Pattie, I won't keep them long. Thanks.' He smiled at her, and she tripped out.

Knowledgeably, he sorted out the contents of the large packet. Under the heading of 'replacements' was the price of a new van, and set against it was what had been deducted for the old one. There'd been alterations done to the shop which amounted to £200; the bills were there all signed. There was a thick sheaf of wholesalers' weekly receipts. Then there was a book marked 'Wages'. The first knowledge he gained from this was that the greengrocer paid his wife ten pounds a week for serving in the shop. Fair enough;

she would have to pay tax on it. Then under a heading of 'Casual Labour' was 'Van driver: Saturdays 1 p.m. to 6 p.m. £2.15.0.' Beneath this was given the year's total. Then below this there was a statement that brought Laurie's teeth onto his bottom lip. 'Two boys packing orders: Saturday 9 a.m. till 1 p.m. 30s;' and under this, too, was given the year's total . . . '£78'.

He was still biting his lip but smiling as he put the papers back into the envelope. Funny about this hunch. Damn funny.

He took the envelope back into Miss Patterson's office, and, placing it on her desk, said, 'Put that back where it belongs, Pattie. And remember, you never gave me that envelope, I must have gone into the office and got it myself.'

'There's not going to be trouble about this, Mr Emmerson, now is there?' She poked her face up to him.

'Not for you, Pattie, not for you.' He grinned broadly at her. 'Just remember you know nothing at all about it.'

'Oh, I'll remember that all right. He'd go mad if he knew I'd . . . Oh, I'll remember that all right.'

'You do, Pattie. And thanks, thanks.'

Back in the office again he got through to Arnold Ransome, and the first thing Arnold said was, 'How's your father?'

'Oh, much improved this morning, Arnold; the sister seemed very pleased with him.'

'Good, good. Oh, I'm glad to hear that. I got a shock when I saw him on Tuesday night.'

'He's worried about this Thorpe case, Arnold. You know, the little boy from the flats next door.'

'Yes, I know, I know. I'm dealing with it; there's no need to trouble him further with it.'

'Have you seen the greengrocer?'

'No, I've written to him.'

'He's a wily type, Arnold, and he's a liar. I believe the boy when he said he worked there. Father was on to something and I've taken it from there.' He lowered his voice. 'This fellow Bolton told the police that he never employed any boys, yet on his income tax returns he's got down thirty shillings every week for two boys working from nine till one on a Saturday.'

'Are you sure of this, Laurie?'

'I've just seen it with my own eyes.'

'Oh, oh.' Laurie could imagine Arnold tapping the desk with his fingers. Then his voice came again, saying, 'That's all very well but one's got to prove it in court, and we'd have to get old man Wilcox to show the statement, and I can't see him doing that; he would consider his client's affairs as being private. And another thing, he's got his teeth in this case, and you know why, Laurie?'

'Yes, I know why all right.'

There was a short silence, then, 'I can't see it's much use really,' said Arnold.

'You mean that?'

'Yes. Yes, I do. If this fellow sticks out and says he doesn't employ anyone, and we've got to bring proof that he has done, it's going to take time.'

'But it could be done?'

'Oh yes, of course it could be done, but by that time the boy will be wherever old Wilcox decides to put him, for I can't see us getting a remand on such slender evidence, which after all will be merely hearsay if we can't produce his tax returns. And about that we'd have to be very careful, for he – the greengrocer – could turn the tables on us.'

'I see what you mean.'

'Of course the case can always be reopened.'

'Yes, yes. It comes up a week today, doesn't it?'

'The preliminary hearing, yes. Wilcox tried to push things through for today but the little girl is still suffering from shock and the mother said she couldn't appear, so it was put back for a week.'

'Well, that's something. Thanks, Arnold.'

'You've got a point, Laurie; I'm not saying you haven't. I must give it some thought; and given time it might alter the whole case. In fact I'm sure it will. But it's time, it's time we want . . . And Laurie. This is going to upset Wilcox, you understand that?'

'Yes, I understand.'

There was a pause. Then: 'Oh well, as long as you understand. Goodbye, Laurie.'

'Goodbye, Arnold.'

He sat looking down at the desk. The law was meticulous, finicky, and slow. Arnold said it was time they wanted, and in the meantime Mr James Wilcox, J.P., would see that that little fellow got time in an appropriate place, and he would scathe the mother not only by this act, but with his public censure of her. As he'd said, he'd make this place so hot for her she'd have to find some place to cool off.

At dinner time he had lunch in the town as he had done all the week, then he went on to the hospital, and it was as he was going in the main entrance that he saw Cissie coming out. They passed in the open doorway and she looked through him and beyond him, not flicking an eyelid in recognition.

As soon as he entered his father's room he knew that she hadn't been there, for he was lying as he always was now, propped up against the pillows, calm, quiet, almost serene, and he didn't think that if he had seen her he would be like this. She had likely been to the desk to enquire.

'How are you?' He sat down by the bed.

'Oh, better, much better. Your . . . your mother's just gone.'

'Just gone?'

'Well, about a quarter of an hour ago. Did . . . did you do what I asked?'

'Yes, yes, Father, I saw her.'

'And she told you all about it?'

'Yes. Yes. She told me everything.'

'Did you see the boy?'

'Yes, I saw Pat.'

'No, no.' John shook his head. 'The Rice boy.'

'No, but I will.'

'And Bolton?'

'I'm seeing him tonight.' He did not mention his fruitless visit last night.

'Bolton's crafty, Laurie, and he's a bad lot. He's been cautioned about employing boys under age. Also, something much more serious with regards to them; it wasn't proved absolutely. They are frightened of him around there. Anyway that's . . . that's why he won't come into the open about Pat.'

Laurie leant towards him. 'He'll come into the open now if I know anything.'

'Yes?'

'I think I've got him where I want him. Just you wait. I'll likely have news for you tomorrow. Just leave it till then.'

John smiled. It was the most his face had stretched in days. Then, the smile sliding away, he said, 'She'll die if that boy's taken away from her. He's all she's got. And the boy's innocent. I'd swear my life on it.' He raised his hands and his lips twisted slightly, 'For what it's worth.'

'It's worth a lot yet, you'll see. Just take things easy.'

'You think so?'

'I do.'

'You know, Laurie, it doesn't matter much.'

'Oh, don't say that, please.' Without embarrassment he took up the pale limp hand and held it firmly, thinking as he did so how strange it was that he should feel so intensely for this man now, and that the feeling should contain so much remorse and guilt, for up till a week ago he would have said that he had done nothing in his life to elicit these levelling emotions, for he was no better or no worse than any of his contemporaries. And what did that mean? He suddenly thought of Val and Tony Clark, and all the others before him. She had started early, he knew that. And then himself and Susan Lumley, and Betty Fuller, and Kitty Frost. His faculty for remembering names took him back down the years to the first one, Henrietta Jacobson. She was fifteen and he was thirteen. She had terrified him. She chased him for weeks; then raped him, and his fear fled. Girls were easy after that, too easy, but they all seemed the same, always rushing things, always pressing, demanding, usurping the male prerogative. And Val had beaten them all at this. At times she had sickened him. You could have too much of a good thing . . . Oh yes, he had learnt that early. He had also learnt that it had nothing whatever to do with love. This thought brought his attention back to his father. His mother was right. What his father felt for Mrs Thorpe was likely something bigger than any feeling that stemmed from the sex urge.

As he looked at him, there was added to his emotions yet another, and it surprised him most of all, and after a moment he discarded it with an inward deprecating laugh. Jealous of his father. Jealous of this man he had despised for so long. What was happening to him anyway? He was getting so damned mixed up he'd soon have to see a psychiatrist.

'Have you told Val yet?' asked John.

'What? Oh that. No. No. I'm jibbing.'

'The longer you put it off the harder it will be. Are you sure you want to break it off?'

'I'm not sure about many things, but I'm sure of that. Oh yes, I'm sure of that.'

They looked at each other, their faces straight, no smile between them. 'That's all right then,' said John softly. 'And I would get it over.'

CHAPTER FOUR

MR BOLTON

It was just turned five o'clock when Laurie entered Mr Bolton's shop, and the greengrocer turned from sorting some fruit in a box and said, 'Yes, sir, what can I . . . ?' His voice trailed away and the set smile left his face, and he ended, 'You again. Now I've told you.' The last words were drawn out and took the shape of a threat.

'Yes I know, but now I've got something to tell you, Mr Bolton. Would you like us to talk quietly, or otherwise? It's all the same to me.'

There was something in Laurie's voice that stayed Mr Bolton's next remark, but he stared fixedly at him for some time before saying, 'Come in here, and make it snappy.'

He pushed a door open and let Laurie pass him; then going to the stairs that led out of the packing-room, he shouted, 'Gladys. Shop.'

Almost immediately Mrs Bolton came down the stairs, to stop dead the moment she saw Laurie. She cast an apprehensive glance at her husband, and he said, 'See to things; I won't be a minute. And I mean a minute . . . Well now, spit it out.'

'You told me last night,' said Laurie, coming straight to the point, 'that you never employ boys. You also told this to the police. That right?'

'Right.'

'You're lying, Mr Bolton.'

'Now, I've warned you, chum.' Mr Bolton did some contortions with his face. He widened his eyes; he thrust out his lips seemingly in an effort to meet his nose. The whole effect was comical, but there was no-one to laugh at it.

'You have your returns done by James Wilcox, do you not?' Laurie now watched the face slowly iron out, leaving the mouth dropping slightly. 'In your returns there is an item. To quote: Paid to two boys for casual work Saturday mornings, 30s.; Total for year £78. Right, Mr Bolton?'

'You bloody sneaking bastard.'

'I would save your breath, Mr Bolton. You haven't heard it all yet; but I think that's enough to be going on with. It'll be enough anyway, for the magistrate whether he be Mr Wilcox or not.'

'Who the hell are you anyway? And wait till old Wilcox finds out about this.'

'I happen to be his accountant.'

'Well you won't be that much longer, laddie; he'll skin you alive. You open your mouth about this and he'll skin you alive.'

'Why should he? He's not to know that you're fiddling your returns. He's checked them in good faith hasn't he, Mr Bolton? You've got signed receipts, one from your casual driver?' This last was a shot in the dark, but he saw it had struck home.

'You're a smart bloody Alec, aren't you? But wait till I tell old Wilcox.'

'I shouldn't worry too much about old Wilcox if I were you,' said Laurie with aggravating coolness. 'It's the police I should worry about. But anyway you won't tell Mr Wilcox that I've been here.'

'Won't I, begod!'

'No, you won't. I'm going to make a deal with you, Mr Bolton. I'd much rather go straight to the police and tell them you've been lying about the Thorpe boy and show them your returns to prove it, but it won't suit my purpose. This is what I want you to do, Mr Bolton. I want you to go to the police, you yourself, and tell them you made a mistake. Tell them that you were rushed that particular Saturday morning, but now you remember that you did employ Patrick Thorpe, up till one o'clock. Therefore he couldn't have been with that gang of boys when they attacked the little girl. And for once you'll be speaking the truth. They mightn't be too lenient with you, as this isn't your first offence in this and other directions, is it, Mr Bolton?'

Mr Bolton gulped. He gulped three times before he said, 'I'll see you in hell's flames burnin' afore I do.'

'It's up to you. You'll likely get fined and a strong reprimand, but that would be a flea-bite to what the tax inspector will do to you, because there's not only the case of the casual labour on a Saturday, is there, Mr Bolton?'

This was another shot in the dark, based on the fact that if a man fiddled in one way he was more than likely to do it in other ways.

That his second blind shot had found its target was evident when the greengrocer, after grinding his teeth and wiping the sweat from his brow with the back of his hand, growled out, 'You're a dirty blackmailing swine.'

'What?' It sounded like a polite enquiry.

'I'll not do it.' Bolton's voice rumbled deep in his throat. 'I'll not be got over by a bloody young punk like you.'

'I wouldn't speak too hastily, Mr Bolton. I'll give you twenty-four hours to think it over. Talk it over with your wife; women have a way of seeing these things sensibly. One warning though. Speak a word of this to Mr Wilcox and I don't hold my hand. I'll go straight to the police and I'll kill all your birds with one stone, and I wouldn't be a bit surprised if you'd have to sell up all this' – he waved his hand about the room – 'to pacify those dreadful Inland Revenue people. And don't think that you can tell Wilcox about this visit and he'd keep his mouth shut. He couldn't; you see I know him very well; he's shortly to become my father-in-law.'

He now felt a desire to laugh as he saw the surprise on Bolton's face. 'You can get me at my office any time tomorrow. Ask for me personally, Mr Laurance Emmerson.'

As he went through the shop he fully expected some heavy implement to hit him on the back of the head. He was shaking slightly when he started up the car, and he fumbled at the gears before he got her going. He was smiling to himself, but nervously, and when he had travelled some distance he pulled into the side of the road and, leaning back against the seat, wiped his face with his handkerchief. He had started something, and if it went the way he thought it would the boy would be all right. But what about himself?

In the shop he had been not a little proud of the way he handled the man; cool, tough, James Bond fashion. But the play-acting was over. He had to face the fact that he had made an enemy of Bolton and he'd have to look out.

CHAPTER FIVE

VAL

'He's a lot better.'

They were having their evening meal. There were only the two of them, but everything was set as usual. He glanced up at her and swallowed the food in his mouth, then said, 'Yes.'

'Laurie.'

'Yes, Mother.'

'I feel we should talk.' She laid down her knife and fork. 'You've turned a complete somersault in a week.'

'What do you mean?'

'You know what I mean, dear.' She shook her head at him. 'Your father was all wrong before and I was all right; now he's all right and I'm all wrong. You know, there's never any real black or any real white.'

'I'm sorry if you see it like that.'

'You know it's true, and I . . . I never thought that when I told you the truth that it would turn you against me. I – I don't think I would have told you if I'd known it would have come between us.'

'It hasn't, it hasn't.' He stopped eating and leant towards her, trying to convince her, and himself as well.

'I'd like to think that but I can't, Laurie. But anyway, what – what I want to say now is that perhaps we could start from here. Everything's in the open now, there's nothing more to hide, or at least from ourselves, and – and it would be nice if we could get along on a sort of friendly footing until you . . . you were married.'

He watched her breaking some bread, her eyes cast down towards it, and he said, 'I'm not going to be married.'

'You're not . . . you mean? Oh, Laurie.'

For the first time in days he took her hand, saying, 'Don't be upset, please.'

'I'm not, I'm not, not for me. But why?'

'Oh, so many reasons. I just can't stand the old fellow. And Aunty May either, for that matter. Oh, I know.' He lifted one shoulder. 'I wouldn't be marrying them but . . . but they're all bound up together, and we've done nothing but fight for months now.'

117

'They say that isn't unusual with an engaged couple, although your father and I—' She bowed her head and he passed over the allusion quickly by saying, 'But this is different. They're not just rows we've had or differences of opinion, it's our whole outlook.' He paused. She still had her head bent when he ended, 'I'm sorry.'

'Oh, don't mind me, Laurie.' She was looking up at him, her expression tender and understanding. And there was relief in it too, and he saw this.

'You never really liked her, did you? Val, I mean.'

'No, Laurie, I didn't. But . . . but that doesn't mean that I'm glad about it, because, well, because I think you should marry.' She raised her eyebrows. 'That might seem strange coming from me, but I feel now that you should marry, and, and get away from us both.'

They stared at each other, she waiting for a comment on her last remark, but she didn't get it. Instead, he said, 'You know, for days now, weeks in fact, I've been longing to be a free agent again, to come and go as I please without having to clock in at Syracuse, either by tooting the car horn, or waving, or stopping. It's odd the few times you can pass that house without somebody seeing you.'

He had risen now and was standing at the french window of the morning room, looking out into the garden, when she asked guardedly, 'Is there anyone else, Laurie?'

Slowly he turned towards her. 'Anyone else? No, no. Good Lord, haven't you been listening? I've just told you I want to be free. And who else could there be?'

'But you've left it so late and May will go mad. Then there's your father. You'd better not tell him.'

'He knows.'

'Oh, Laurie.'

'It did him good. It acted like an injection on him.'

'You really mean . . .' She nodded her head, then said, 'Yes, yes, I suppose it would. He's never had any room for them.' She paused awhile before adding softly, 'There'll be trouble, Laurie; I doubt if Val will take this quietly . . . or James.'

'I doubt it too. But I've got to go through with it, or through with the other, and the other is for life, and I know I just couldn't stick it.'

He moved from the window now, saying, 'Are you going to the hospital – I can run you there and look in on him; then I've got some business to do and I can pick you up later, any time you like.'

'That would be nice, yes.' She sounded grateful that he wanted to go with her to the hospital . . .

Ten minutes later she stood dressed in the hall and he said to her wryly, 'I hope we can break through the lines.' She turned an enquiring glance towards him, then gave a small laugh. 'Oh, yes, yes. Oh, Laurie.' She shook her head.

But they passed Syracuse without seeing any of the Wilcox family. They got out of the car in the hospital foreground, crossed through the hall, went up the private corridor to No. 7 and Laurie, pushing the door open, went to hold it for her, to allow her to pass in, but the next minute he had let the door swing closed almost in her face, and, taking her arm, hurried her back along the corridor, round to the side of the entrance hall and into the waiting room.

The room was empty, and he stood facing her now, holding her by her shoulders, saying, 'It means nothing. It doesn't mean anything, I tell you. He told me, and she told me. It means nothing.' He watched her close her eyes and press her lips tightly together.

'Let me sit down,' she said. When she was seated he gripped her hands in his, saying, 'It looks bad, but she could just have been saying goodbye to him. Anything. Anything.'

'Yes, yes.' She moved her head slowly, but he knew she didn't believe that the woman kissing her husband was saying goodbye to him, more like setting a seal on the future.

'Stay there,' he said. When he reached the hall it was to see Cissie leaving by the main door and he glared after her; then, returning to the waiting room, he said, 'It's all right. Now listen. Don't let him know you saw anything. If they heard the door open they would think it was a nurse. They didn't see me. I tell you it's all right, take my word for it. Come on, come on.' He touched her chin with the old tenderness. 'Don't let him see you're upset, it would make him worse.'

She was dry-eyed, but she breathed deeply before saying, 'I'm all right. Are you coming in?'

'No, I'll see him when I get back. As I said, I have some business to do. How long do you want to stay?'

'An hour or so. It doesn't matter; don't hurry.' Her voice was flat, dead sounding.

He left her at the corridor, squeezing her arm before parting from her. He felt something of the old feeling for her; he was also deeply indignant on her behalf.

He had intended to go to that one's flat in any case to tell her what had taken place with regard to Bolton. He had waived, in his mind, what her reception of him might be, thinking only of easing her worry over the boy, and now he was so blazing angry inside he could slap her from here to hell. He could see the picture of her; bending over the bed, her arms around his father, her loose towy hair hanging like a sheath covering their faces. He could hear her again as she went for him the other night, defending herself, putting on the innocent act, making him feel an out-and-out swine . . . Wait till he saw her.

When he arrived at Greystone Buildings he knew that she couldn't have reached home yet, not by bus, and that suited him. He would act as a reception committee for her. He went up the stairs, not bothering to step softly now. He didn't care about the private eye, or who saw him. He felt a hatred of her, cheap little get-up that she was. Good woman! Of course his father would want to think of her as good, he was ripe for being gulled. Well, she wouldn't gull him. He would make it plain that his mother would fight her every inch of the way; and if she were to win there wouldn't be much money left in the kitty for her. This fact, he felt, would be the main deterrent.

When he reached the top landing the door was open and the boy was standing there.

'I thought at first it was me mam,' he said. 'She's out.' He looked up at Laurie.

'I know, I would like to wait for her.'

'Come on in.' The boy left the door open and followed him into the long room, and as he did so he said eagerly, 'Did you see anybody? I mean Mrs Rice or Mr Bolton? Did you do anything?'

As he stared down into the boy's face, he thought, old Wilcox was right where she was concerned. Perhaps after all he did know about her kind and how to deal with them.

'Well did you?'

'Oh, yes, yes, I saw them both. Not the boy, the boy's mother, Mrs Rice. She wasn't very communicative, I mean helpful, but I think it's going to be all right. I saw Mr Bolton. I'll . . . I'll know by tomorrow for sure.'

'You mean . . . you mean he'll tell the truth?'

'I hope so, but you mustn't say anything about this to anyone, you understand?' His anger didn't touch on the boy. He still felt sorry for him.

'Oh, yes, yes, Mister. Oh, yes.'

'Do you think your mother will be long?'

'No, she should be back at any minute. She was just going to the hospital to see . . . to see your father.'

'She wasn't going any place else?'

'No. No, she told me to stay put, not leave the house an' she'd be back directly. Won't you sit down?' The boy made the same movement as Cissie did, his arm extended towards the couch by way of invitation.

'No, I like walking about.'

And he walked about, looking from one piece of furniture to the other. She had invested her money all right.

When he came to the piano he said to the boy, 'Do you play?' He wasn't interested whether he played or not, but the boy was standing watching him with a set look on his face.

'I'm learnin', I've just been at it a year, but me mam plays lovely, she can play anything, all the hard stuff. Beethoven and Bach.'

She could play more than Beethoven and Bach if he knew anything about her.

They both heard her on the landing. The door closed and neither of them moved.

Cissie came into the room and stood just in the doorway. She looked from her son to Laurie, then kept her eyes on him. As she threw down her bag and took off her coat she still kept her gaze tightly on him. Then without looking at Pat she said, as she had done last night, 'Go into your room.'

'But, Mam, Mr Emmerson . . . Mr Emmerson's got news.'

'Go into your room, Pat.'

The boy went slowly into the bedroom, and not until he had closed the door did she come forward. Snapping her eyes from him, she went to the fireplace, switched on the electric fire, kicked the pouffe to the side with her long pointed shoe, then sitting down and endeavouring to pull her skirts over her knees, she said coolly. 'Why don't you start? I'm waiting.'

When he didn't speak but continued to glare at her, she said, 'I'm surprised you're stumped. I'll give you a lead, shall I? I'm a bitch. I'm all the things you think I am. You've just had proof of it, haven't you? You came into your father's room, and found him in my arms and me kissing him.' When she saw his eyelids flicker she went on, 'Oh, yes, yes I knew it was you and your mother. You weren't quick enough in closing the door. And you know something else? I'm not going to give you any explanation.'

To say the wind was taken out of his sails was putting it mildly, but the anger in him was intensified. 'What do you hope to get out of it?' he said. 'If you think that my father would ever leave my mother for you you're vastly mistaken.'

'Am I? Well now, Mr Know-all, I'll tell you something. If I had wanted to I could have made your father leave your mother weeks ago, months ago, like that.' She raised her little finger slowly upwards.

He said disdainfully, 'You're suffering under a great delusion, woman. There are things you don't know about my father. If you did you'd know that your cause was absolutely hopeless.'

'There's nothing, Mr Emmerson, that I don't know about your father. NOTHING. NOTHING. You understand? You don't want me to explain further, do you?'

He felt the blood draining from his face. His father had told her that. There had been so much between them that he could tell her that.

'You don't want me to go on, do you?' She rose abruptly from the pouffe and went to a cabinet in the corner of the room and dragged the doors open, took out a bottle of whisky and a syphon, put a dash of whisky into a gill glass, then squirted in a long drag of soda, almost filling it to the top, and with the glass in her hand she walked back across the room, saying, 'I won't offer you a drink because I might be tempted to put something in it.'

'Your type's good at one other thing, and that's cheap prattle.' He sent the words at her with his upper lip pulled back in a sneer, and the next minute he was gasping and spluttering as the contents of the glass enveloped him. He had taken it full in the face. Some had gone into his mouth and was causing him to choke; the rest had drenched his collar and shirt, the front of his head, and was running down his face.

His eyes were stinging, and when he squeezed the liquid from them and blinked hard he saw her standing immobile, one hand pressed tightly across her mouth, the other hand still holding the empty glass. She was no longer looking fierce, her expression was now one of amazement as if she had seen someone else do this. Then he saw the glass drop to the floor and watched her long body crumple as she threw herself onto the couch, and as he listened to her sobbing he went on slowly wiping his face down with his hand.

He was still standing in the same place when the boy rushed past him and to the couch, crying, 'Oh, Mam, Mam.'

He took a handkerchief out of his pocket and began drying his face as he continued to look at her. The sound of her crying was a strange sound, not high and hysterical but a deep strangled sound, more like the sound a man would make, or like someone not used to crying. The boy, too, was crying, talking through his wide open mouth. 'Oh, Mam, Mam, give over. Oh, don't cry, Mam, don't cry.'

Then quite suddenly the boy was standing in front of him, his attitude threatening, the tears spilling from his chin like rain. He was shouting, 'My mam's good, she is. She's good, she is.'

Perhaps it was the sound of her son's championing of her that brought Cissie up from the couch. Groping blindly towards Pat she pulled him away from Laurie, and pushed him before her to the bedroom, and there she said, 'It's all right. It's all right. Go on in. I won't be a minute, stay there.' She closed the bedroom door; then came slowly back across the room, crying still, and as she came near him, her head bowed now, she said, 'I'm sorry I did that.'

'Can I have a towel?'

Without lifting her head she went to the kitchen, and returning with a towel she handed it to him.

He put his sodden handkerchief in his pocket, and wiped his face and neck, the front of his hair, then rubbed down his coat and waistcoat.

She stood away from him now but looking towards him, the

shuddering sobs shaking her body, and after a time she said, 'Why had you to come? There's always trouble.'

'I . . . I had news for you about the boy. I thought it might ease your mind.'

He was amazed at his change of attitude. His anger had gone, seemingly washed away on the wave of whisky and soda. He said, 'I think I can make Bolton tell the truth. I'll know by tomorrow anyway.'

She swallowed deeply, her eyes watching as she looked at him. Then she whispered, 'You can?'

He nodded, still amazed at himself as he said, 'Whichever way he turns, I've got him. I don't think you need to worry any more.'

'And . . . and you came to tell me that?'

'Well . . .' he closed his eyes and turned his head to the side for a moment. 'That was primarily my intention, and on the way I dropped my mother off at the hospital.'

Now she lowered her eyes from his face and said contritely, 'I was saying goodbye to your father. It was the first time I had kissed him. The first time that there had been any endearment between us, but . . . but he had been talking . . . telling me about . . . about his life. About the war and what happened to him, and he told it to me for a purpose, and I loved him in that moment more than I have ever loved anyone in my life. And . . . and I can tell you now, quite quietly, that . . . that if he'd asked me to stay with him and it was for his happiness I would have done it, but he didn't. He's – he's got a sense of responsibility to your mother. And I'll also say this to you now, she's not worth it. A woman . . .' She gulped in her throat, and there was the dry harsh sobbing sound again. 'A woman who could live with a man for years and years, twenty-six years, and make him as lonely as your father is, isn't up to much, not in my opinion.'

He looked down towards his feet as he repeated the words his mother had said to him earlier on, 'There's nothing really white, and nothing really black, in any of us.'

'Oh, it's all very well saying that, but I think her treatment of him was a subtle form of cruelty. Not that he's ever said a word against her, he's hardly spoken of her till this morning, and then it was kindly, but I know women, as I know men, and he didn't have to tell me what had put that look in his face. It had puzzled me since I first met him, but not any more.'

'Your boy said a moment ago you were a good woman; I can say the same of my mother. She's a good woman.'

'It all depends on what you mean by good.'

They were talking quietly now, as if they were discussing something abstract. When they both stopped speaking and the room became filled with a silence that yelled at them, he wanted to get out, away from her, but he remained still and watched her go to the fireplace again and stand with her foot on the raised hearth, her hand on the mantelpiece. She stood like this some time before she asked quietly, 'How did you get Mr Bolton round?'

'I would rather you didn't ask.'

After a moment she said, 'Well, it doesn't matter how you did it as long as you did it. And . . . and believe me . . .' There was another pause before she finished, 'I'm grateful.' She half turned her head towards him now. 'It mightn't appear so . . . but what's just happened is another thing, isn't it? Nothing to do with Pat and the court business.'

Solemnly he agreed with her, saying, 'Yes, another thing entirely. I'll be going now.'

She turned from the fire and went towards him. He face had a deep look of sadness on it, and her tone was laden with remorse. 'I'm truly sorry; I've never done anything like that before.'

'There's always a first time for everything. That's what they say, isn't it?' At the back of his mind he thought he couldn't have made a more trite remark if he had tried. 'Goodbye,' he said.

'Goodbye.' She inclined her head towards him but didn't move. He went out of the room and let himself out of the flat and drove back to the hospital.

When he went into the room he saw his father talking in his slow, laboured fashion to his mother. He had hold of her hand and seemed to be trying to impress something on her.

He felt awkward as he said, 'How are you?'

'Oh, I'm feeling well today, quite well,' said John. He smiled at Laurie. 'I was telling your mother I'll be home in a week or two.'

Ann exchanged a glance with Laurie as she said, 'The doctor advises a sea voyage; we were just talking about it.'

'Oh, that would be fine,' said Laurie. 'The very thing to put you on your feet.' They talked a little more; then Laurie said his goodbyes and went towards the door. He did not wait to see if they kissed or not.

In the car they said little, but once they were alone in the lounge he said to her, 'It's all right, you've got no need to worry.'

'What do you mean?'

'I've seen her. It – it was . . . Well, she was saying goodbye to him and – and that was the first time it had ever happened – I mean anything like that between them.'

'Laurie! You haven't been to that woman again? But why?' There was a note of fear in her voice.

'Her boy's in trouble. Father was taking the case. Arnold took it over and was going about it in a legal way, naturally, but you can't deal legally with men like Bolton . . . Oh.' He raised his hand. 'Forget all about that, that's got nothing to do with you; only I can assure you,' he took her hands in his now, 'you've got nothing to worry about. Do you know what she said? She said Father loved you . . . There.' It was easy to stretch 'responsibility' to 'love' and it did no harm. What was vital at the moment was she needed reassurance and comfort.

'How did she know?' The note of fear was now replaced by one of indignation.

'I don't know, but that's what she said.' As he looked at her walking away from him, pulling at her handkerchief, he thought she was an entirely different creature from the mother he had known a week ago. The lady with the cool façade and slight hauteur of manner was gone, and the woman in her place was more human, more, he would say, of a woman.

'Now everything's going to be all right. Don't you worry any more, just take things as they come, eh?' He was speaking to her back, and at that moment the front door bell rang, and he knew that particular ring. When she turned towards him he said, 'Out of the mouth of babes. Take things as they come, I said.'

She came to him and caught at his hand. 'Go gently with her. It's an awful thing for a girl.' She shook her head slowly from side to side. 'I didn't tell you but she was over last night, Mrs Stringer left a message.'

'I'll be in the study,' he said, then went quickly out and across the hall and into the room where the battle was to take place.

Awful thing for a girl. Valerie was no girl. His mother was still living in this century; Valerie was a twenty-sixty-four female if ever there was one. She was an Amazon, a five-foot-three Amazon, and his maleness resented being dominated by an Amazon of any size. He heard his mother say, 'He's in the study, Valerie,' and her voice was gentle.

Then Valerie came in. He was sitting at his desk as if he had been there for some time; he had a pen in his hand and he looked up at her as she stopped with her back to the closed door. She returned his scrutiny and, to his surprise, she smiled at him before saying, 'I'm going to make no reference to Mohammed and the mountain.' She moved towards him now. 'Been busy?'

'Yes. Yes.'

'Girls!' she began abruptly. 'Oh, how I get sick of the sight of girls. Beseeching eyes, moist lips, groping minds.' She flung herself into the leather chair and stretched out her shapely legs. Then looking at him out of the corner of her eyes, she said, 'You'd never believe it but one's got a pash on me; she brought me a box of chocolates today. It's half mother-instinct I think. She's sixteen and already five foot seven.' She laughed.

At this point he knew he was expected to make some witty quip, and when he didn't and she made no comment on his blank reception of this biological tid-bit, he knew she was working to a set plan. She had likely talked it over with her mother and been advised to play it cool so to speak. Not that Aunt May would have used that term, and not that Valerie needed any advice, tactical or otherwise. She was the kind that walked the road she had mapped out, and stepped over the corpses in her way. She didn't believe in by-roads.

'Feel like going out?'

'Not tonight.'

'Well, I don't much either. I could have brought my work up but I've had a bellyful today.'

He rubbed his hand across his brow, then leant his elbow on the desk and supported his head with his finger tips. This was going to be harder than he thought, damnable in fact.

'Oh, I forgot to tell you. We've got another wedding present. My cousin from Bromwich; you know, in the electric business. A toaster. I bet it was a throw-out. I'd also like to bet we'll get half-a-dozen before we finish.'

He did not raise his head.

'Did you hear what I said, Laurie?'

He knew by her tone that her control was slipping. It was going to be as difficult for her to follow the path of mediation as it was for himself to do what he had to do.

'Yes, I heard what you said.'

'Well, why the hell don't you answer?' She was on her feet looking down at him now. 'I came round here fully prepared to forget the last few days because I knew you were worried about your father and all this rotten business, but what meets me? A blank wall, and I don't take to blank walls, Laurie. Now, look . . . whatever's on your mind, spit it out and let's get it over with.'

He placed his forearms on the desk and joined his hands together and looked at her for a long moment before saying, 'I can't go through with this, Val.' He moved his head in small jerks. 'I just can't go through with it.'

He felt an overwhelming sense of pity for her as he watched her rear up with the shock, stretching herself to the limit of her height. And he felt himself to be something so low it could have crawled out of a sewer when, placing her two hands flat on the table, she leant towards him, opened her mouth twice, then said, below her breath, 'Are you telling me, really sitting there telling me you can't go through with it? You mean, our marrying?'

He bit hard on his lip, then gave her a small nod.

Slowly she straightened up and from the top of her brow to where the curve of her small full breasts disappeared behind the square neck of her dress her flesh looked stiff and cold. 'You're telling me quite calmly that it's off?'

'I don't feel calm about it, Val, I feel damned awful.'

'Really! Well, it's nice to know you are a little troubled. And now would you mind explaining why, at this stage of our acquaintance, you have decided that you are going to drop me?'

'Look, Val,' he moved his head desperately. 'I . . . I just don't think we're suited, we wouldn't make a go of it.'

She stepped back from the table and pressing her forearm into her waist she cupped her elbow in her hand and surveyed him for some time before she said, 'and you've just found that out?'

'No, no. I've got to be honest with you . . .'

'Oh, yes, let's be honest, let's be honest. Go on . . .'

'Please, Val, please. It's just that I should have told you sooner but I didn't want to hurt you.'

'You didn't want to hurt me! You leave it until now and you say you didn't want to hurt me. Six weeks' time, the date's fixed for the 12th July, remember? We're in the process of buying a house, we've got most of the furniture, and you can sit there calmly and tell me . . .' She gulped as if overcome with the enormity of his nerve. Then in a slow ominous tone she went on, 'Oh, no, you don't, Laurie. You don't do this to me. You're not going to show me up before everyone in this town. Remember, I work in a girls' school. Seven hundred girls, a good proportion of them sixteen, seventeen and eighteen; you don't know girls in the horde, Laurie. But apart from that you're not doing this to me. I'll make you go through with this even if we get a divorce within three months. But you're not standing me up . . . You're not standing me up.' Her body now snapped forward. Her hands again on the desk, she brought her face within an inch of his. 'We're getting married on the 12th of July.'

'You can't force me to marry you, Val.' He gave a short laugh, but there was no mirth in it, it was merely a gesture to hide his nervousness.

'Can't I? You don't know your Valerie. Our community wouldn't hold a man who jilted his girl on the eve of their marriage and her going to have his baby.'

She drew back from him and surveyed his gaping face with one long, long look; then she marched from the room.

After a moment he sat back in his chair and put his hands across his eyes.

CHAPTER SIX

MR BOLTON REMEMBERS

It was eleven o'clock the next morning when Mr Bolton phoned Laurie. 'Is that Emmerson?' said the voice on the other end of the phone.

'Yes, this is Mr Emmerson.'

'It's Bolton, here.'

There was a pause, during which Laurie remained silent.

'You can have it your way.'

Another pause.

'Well, I've said it, haven't I?'

'Have you been to the police?'

'No, not yet.'

'Well you can phone me again when you have; I'll be here till six o'clock.'

'Blast you!'

'The same to you, Mr Bolton . . .'

It was just on half-past five when the phone rang, and picking it up, he expected to hear Bolton's voice, but it was a woman who said, 'I would like to speak to Mr Emmerson.'

'Mr Emmerson here,' he said.

'This, this is Mrs Thorpe . . . I don't know how to begin but . . . but the police have been round, and Mr Bolton's been to the station and said he's made a mistake and that Pat was with him until one o'clock on that Saturday . . . Are you there?'

'Yes, yes, I'm here. I'm very glad.'

'They say this is a big factor in clearing him and . . . and if the other boys would own up he'd be cleared altogether. There's no hope of Tim Brooks doing that but Barrie Rice could. I'm going round to see his mother now.'

'I doubt if you'll make any headway with her.'

'Oh. Why?'

'I called on her the other evening, she strikes me as another Mr Bolton. I'd leave her to Mr Ransome.'

There was such a long silence now that he was about to ask, 'Are you there?' when her voice came to him softly, saying, 'It was very kind of you. You've been so kind and . . . and

' after what happened last night, it makes me feel awful.'

'Think no more about it. I'm . . . I'm sure everything will be all right now. Mr Ransome will be getting in touch with you. I've had a word with him. He thinks even as things stand your boy'll be cleared.'

'Oh, thank you. Thank you. I . . . I would like to express my thanks more fully but I can't I – I don't know what to say.'

'There's no need to say anything.'

'Goodbye, Mr Emmerson.'

'Goodbye, Mrs Thorpe.'

So that was that . . .

When he reached home Mrs Stringer met him in the hall. 'Missis told me to tell you that she wouldn't be back till 'bout seven, Mr Laurie, but Miss Valerie's in the lounge.'

'Thank you, Stringy.' His voice was level. He took off his hat and coat, dropped his case onto a chair, went into the cloakroom, washed his hands, took a long drink of cold water, then went into the lounge.

Valerie was sitting on the couch. Her face looked a little paler than usual, but that was the only change visible in her. There was no nervousness showing, no sign of hysteria. He closed the door firmly behind him and took a seat near the empty fireplace; then looking towards her, he said, 'Well?'

'I thought I'd pop in to tell you that the mistresses are wondering what to buy us for a wedding present. Miss Becker came and asked me today. I said I would consult you.'

He got up from the chair and walked the length of the room and into the dining section, and he stood with his stomach pressed against the back of a dining chair as he said, 'You're not going to have any baby, Val.'

'How can you prove that at this stage. Only I know if I'm going to have a baby or not. And if I wasn't going to have one you couldn't be blamed for not trying, could you?'

His back still to her, his face screwed up with distaste.

'I've said nothing about this to anyone, as you will have already gathered, because had I mentioned it to father you would have been eaten alive by now.'

He turned towards her, and over the distance he said, 'You can mention it to him as soon as you like, Val, the sooner the better, because more than ever now I know that I can't marry you.'

'What if I sue you for breach of promise. I could skin you alive, and I would you know, because if there's got to be publicity I would make it pay. I would rub your nose in the mud, and not only your nose.'

He moved swiftly towards her and, standing over her, said thickly,

'Do whatever you like, Val, whatever you like. But just get it into your head I'm not going to marry you.'

He had never seen Val in tears, or near to them. He didn't associate her with tears, but now they were in her eyes. But they were tears of rage, and the rage brought her springing up from the couch to stand close to him. Her voice full of venom, she cried at him. 'I could tear you to shreds. I could claw your face to pieces. Talk about your father being inane and gutless; you mightn't look like him outside but you're him inside, every inch of him. I could spit on you.'

He thought for a moment she was going to do just that, and he felt himself flinch and shrink inwardly as if from the ignominious assault. As he looked down at her he felt her hate coming at him like hot steam. He watched her turn about and move across the room. She went slowly as if her rage was weighing her down, and at the door she turned and looked at him once more, then from between her clenched teeth she said, 'You dirty sod. You weak-kneed dirty sod.'

When the banging of the front door reverberated through the house he went to the couch and sank onto it. Weak-kneed, dirty sod. Well, the sod had cleared the first hurdle, but by the end of the course there was no doubt he'd be in the mud, as she had said, and in ribbons. Weak-kneed dirty sod.

He was still sitting on the couch, his eyes closed, his head back, when his mother came in. 'What is it?' she asked quietly. 'Are you ill?'

'No.' He opened his eyes slowly. 'Val's been.'

'Oh! . . . Has she accepted things?'

'I don't know about accepting things. If she does what she threatens to do, and I haven't a doubt but she will, there'll not be much left of me by the time she's finished.'

'You'll survive, dear.' She sat down beside him. 'She can't kill you, nor can she take your credentials from you.'

'True, true.' He sighed. 'But she can strip me of every penny I have, and she knows what that is. She'll be totting up at this moment what Uncle Robert left me, plus what I've saved in the last few years. That's on the monetary side. On the moral side she'll make my name stink; she'll be the wronged, innocent girl and she'll play it to the finish. She threatens breach of promise and she'll make a three-act play out of her wrongs. I can see her doing it.'

'It may not come to that, but if it does it isn't the end of the world, and if you've got to leave your job, well there's plenty of others.'

'If?' He turned and looked at her. 'There's no if about that, that's a dead certainty from both sides. And with the pull he's got in this town I can't see me getting another.'

'Oh!' Her voice was high. 'There's Newcastle . . . dozens of places you could go to.'

'Yes, yes.' He smiled wearily at her, then asked, 'What about you and Aunt May? I'll break that up too.'

She rose from the couch, patting his hand as she did so, saying, 'It's been long overdue. I won't be sorry.'

'You're sure?'

'Absolutely. May has bored and irritated me alternately for years . . . Now have you had anything to eat?'

'No,' he said. 'But I don't feel like anything.'

'You must eat, and it'll be all ready,' she said. 'I told Mrs Stringer to set it in the morning room; I thought it would be more cosy than in there. Come along.' She waited for him to rise, then added, 'The Avenue won't hold May and me after this. I'm going to look for another house.'

He looked slightly startled. 'But there's been so much spent on this. And Father . . .'

She cut him short by saying, 'Your father's always hated stucco walls, he'll be glad to change.'

As he followed her out he thought, She must have known that when she had the place decorated. And there came back to his mind the Thorpe woman saying, 'I think her treatment of him was a subtle form of cruelty.' Like a door opening from a dark passage showing a lighted room, he knew why his father had been drawn to that woman. There was no cruelty in her, subtle or otherwise – she was kind . . . Yes, even if she had drowned him in whisky and soda! . . .

Laurie left the hospital at about a quarter-to-nine. His father had looked extremely tired tonight. The sister said it was nothing unusual in cases like this; doubtless he would be much better tomorrow. Not till he was seated in the car did he decide to go to the club. The thought that he wasn't answerable for his movements to anyone brought a little relief to his worried mind. There was no use in trying to put a good face on the situation to himself for he knew there was trouble in front of him, and change, but the latter didn't matter. He had been tied to the town by his mother's need of him. But with her change of heart he was no longer absolutely necessary to her. This had been revealed clearly to him when she said: 'You should marry and get away from us both.' It was as if at last she was throwing him out of the nest. He felt no hurt at this, only relief. If he was honest, an overwhelming relief. He hadn't realised before how much the home ties had irked him. He had taken compensation from the standard of living under her management, but now he saw all her actions towards himself like local injections. He had been living under sedation for years. Well, it was over, finished. Many things were finished.

The Rover was almost jammed in between two other cars that

hadn't been there when he parked, and he had to nose his way gently out, feeling as he did so that the fellow in front in the grey Ford could have helped him by driving a few yards forward, but apparently he was against co-operation.

He noticed, through his mirror, that the car moved away almost immediately after he had passed it. Example of the considerate driver, he commented to himself.

In the club he had a small whisky and a lager, and a long chat to Harry Belham, whom he hadn't seen for several months. It would be more correct to say that Harry Belham had a long chat with him. Harry was a keen fisherman, and an authority on fishing rights, river boards, and the crazy, mad, ignorant nincompoops who took their holidays in motor cruisers and sailing craft, and selected for their enjoyment all the best rivers in the land, so it wasn't until quarter-past ten that he left the club. His car was parked in the private car park by the side entrance. There were not more than half-a-dozen cars there, and as he went to insert the key into the lock of the Rover a voice behind him said, 'Have you a match, chum?' . . .

What he remembered later was turning round, then doubling straight up as a fist was rammed into his stomach, then being dragged up straight by the shoulders and another fist meeting him under the chin. As the world spun round, he felt himself choking, then slowly dropping to the ground as if he was floating down.

Following this he was vaguely aware of something sharp being repeatedly jabbed at his hip. The fact that it was the toe of a boot didn't get through to him until he felt the car stop. He hadn't realised he was in a car. There were hands grabbing his shoulders again and he was being hauled from the floor of the car, then pushed against something hard. Vaguely he became aware of his surroundings as he was pushed up against the wall, then the fists came at him from all sides, into his stomach, his chest, his face . . . Oh, his face. Once more he was floating down and then there was nothing.

When he next regained consciousness he thought he was on a rack, for his arms were being dragged out of his body. Only faintly he realised he was being pulled along by his arms. And then he was on his feet, but they kept flopping against something. Flop, flop, flop, flop. As he groaned out a protest something hit him in the face and the blackness came down on him again and he sank into it as if never to return.

'Oh my God! Oh my God!' The words were swirling round his head as he crawled up through the layers of blackness towards the surface. 'Oh my God! Oh my God!' They kept repeating themselves over and over again. They were like rumblings heard through the dentist's gas. When with a gasp he thrust himself into the light and tried to open his eyes he groaned and joined his voice to the other one, crying, weakly, 'Oh! Oh! Pol-ice! Pol-ice!'

'It's all right, it's all right. Oh my God! Who's done this to you?'

'Help!'

'Try to drink this. Come on, come on.'

When the raw whisky reached his throat, he coughed and the effort caused excruciating pain in every part of his body. 'Oh God!' He spluttered into the whisky.

'Try, try to drink it all up.'

'Wh . . . where am I? What's?' He opened his eyes as wide as he could and saw her above him with that hair hanging down each side of her face. 'Wh-where?'

'Lie quiet . . . Is that kettle not boiling yet? Bring the water, Pat.'

'It's here. It's here.'

The warm sponge on his face was soothing, but the rest of his body felt terrible, and he was going to be sick. He tried to push her away and retched, and she said, 'It's all right, it's all right.' She held his head and he turned on his side and vomited into the bowl on the floor at her knee. When he had finished she wiped his mouth and laid his head gently back on a cushion.

'Oh God!' He lay panting, trying to understand what had happened to him. Then looking at her he said with the simplicity of a child, 'Why?'

She shook her head. Her voice and her body were trembling. 'I don't know, I don't know.'

'How . . . how did I get here?'

She gulped and blinked her wet eyes. 'I . . . I was in bed. The bell rang, and when I opened the door, there you were.'

He wanted to shake his head at her but he couldn't. It didn't make sense.

'You must have the doctor,' she said, 'you're in an awful state. Pat!' she called softly. 'Get your things on.'

A few minutes later, when the boy was standing by her side, and he said, 'Doctor Bell, Mam?' she answered, 'Yes, and be quick.'

At this point Laurie protested. 'Wait . . . a minute. Don't go. Not a doctor. I'll . . . I'll be all right. Help me up.'

With her arms about him she got him to his feet and onto the couch, and as she did so she thought, first the father and then the son.

She pillowed his head, then knelt by his side and muttered coaxingly, 'Let me send for the doctor. You're in a bad way.'

'No, no. No fuss, only cau-se trouble . . . more . . .' He was finding difficulty now in moving his lips. 'If . . . if I could get home.'

'You could never get home like this.' She shook her head at him. 'You're in an awful state.'

'You drive?'

'Yes.'

'My car . . . Don't know where it is. Would . . . ?' He looked towards Pat and she said, 'Go downstairs and see if Mr Emmerson's car is by the garages.' She looked down on Laurie again and asked, 'Is it your father's?' and when he made a slight movement with his head, she said, 'It'll be a Rover. You know, a big blue one. Take the torch.'

When the boy had gone she said, 'You'll never get down the stairs.'

'You help me.'

She stared at him, all the pity in her body showing in her face. Then her head dropping, she murmured, 'Oh! oh!'

'Could . . . could you get me some black . . . black coffee?'

'Yes, yes.' She put out her hand and gently touched his distorted, swelling face; then she flew to the kitchen, but was back within seconds. And again by his side, she said, 'It won't be a minute.'

He put his hand to his thigh now and as he gasped she said, 'What is it?' He made a motion with his head that indicated he didn't know.

'Will you try to sit up and I'll get your coat off.' Again he made a motion with his hands to be left alone.

Then Pat came back hurrying into the room. He stood at the bottom of the couch and whispered hoarsely, 'There's no car there, Mam, and the garages are all locked up.'

Laurie looked at the boy as he tried to sort things out. He had to get home. He was in a bad way, and he was going to get worse, he knew that. He had to get home. He said to her now, 'Can . . . can you get word to . . . to my mother?'

'Yes,' she nodded swiftly. 'I'll get someone from downstairs to go and phone.'

He put out his hand, caught hers and groaned at the sudden movement. 'No, don't let this . . . this get about. Don't want any fuss. Pat . . . Pat could phone.'

'He can't use the phone, I'll go.'

Of a sudden he was fearful of being left alone, of dropping into that blackness again . . . or worse still, of someone coming at him again. His hand tightened as much as it could on hers, and he whispered, 'Don't . . . don't leave me.'

He watched a tenderness suddenly flood her face. She turned from him and spoke to her son. 'You know where Lime Avenue, is, don't you?'

'Yes, Mam.'

'If you hurry you might get the last bus, the one that goes to the corner of Newton Road . . . What's the number of your house?' She was bending over him.

'Seventy-four. Right-hand side. Near – near the top.'

'Seventy-four. Near the top,' she repeated to Pat. 'Go on now, and if you miss the bus run all the way; you can do it in quarter of an hour or less. That's a good boy. You're not frightened, are you?'

'No.'

'Go on then . . . Wait a minute.' She went after him and led him towards the door. 'Ring the bell and ask for Mrs Emmerson. See her yourself and tell her . . . tell her to come here. Tell her to bring the car. Tell her Mr Emmerson is ill. All right?'

'All right, Mam.'

Laurie lay with his eyes closed. He heard her running towards the kitchen, then it seemed only a second later that she had her arm under his shoulders and was holding a cup to his lips. 'I've made it ready for drinking,' she said.

He took a sip, and then another, and then two long drinks, and she put the cup down and he lay back.

His mind was clearing a little. He was trying to think, think what had hit him, who had hit him, and why. There had been two of them, but he never saw their faces. Not even the face of the man who had asked for a light. Yes, that's how it had started, a man had asked for a light. That was the only time he'd heard anyone speak. No, no it wasn't. Some time after when they propped him up against the wall. One of them had said . . . What had he said? . . . Tax collector . . . Something about a tax collector . . . 'That's one for the tax collector!' But he couldn't have said that, he was imagining it. It was because his head was going round and round. But no. No. 'Have you got a light, mister?' 'That's one for the tax collector . . .' It had been the same voice. Bolton had promised him something and he had kept his promise.

'Bolton.' He wasn't conscious of speaking aloud.

'Who? Bolton? Bolton's done this? Yes, yes, of course. Oh my God!' And again she cried, 'Oh my God! . . . and all because of us.' She was touching his blackening, swelling face with her finger tips and he peered up at her through his fast-closing eyes. She was kind. His father said she was kind, and her son said she was good. She was also beautiful, in spite of that towy hair she was beautiful. 'Don't cry, don't cry,' he said.

She gasped out now between her catching breath, 'I . . . I never meant it. It was the last thing on earth I meant to do, but, but I've brought trouble to you both, both you and your father.'

He put his hand out. It touched her hair, but he could see nothing for the blackness was descending on him again, and without protest he was sinking into it. The last thing he remembered at this time was that she held his hand tight in both of hers and buried it between her breasts.

＊　　＊　　＊

Pat caught the last bus. He was one of two passengers, and the conductor, looking at him, said, 'You're out late, sonny. What's your mother about?'

Pat said, 'There's someone ill; I'm taking a message.'

When he alighted from the bus, he ran up the lane leading to the avenue as if someone was after him; it was very dark in the lane and he was frightened. In the avenue he paused before numerous gates, peering at their numbers. When he came to No. 74 he ran swiftly along the shingled drive towards the house.

There was a car standing outside the front door, and a light shining in the porch, but before he had passed the car and entered the porch he heard the sound of an angry voice, like someone fighting, he thought, which was very puzzling to him, for people that lived in houses like this didn't fight.

As he paused with his finger hovering over the bell he heard a man's voice say, 'I'm waiting. If it's two o'clock in the morning when he comes I'll be here to greet him,' and a woman's voice, angry sounding too, replied, 'If John were here you wouldn't act like this.'

'Oh, don't make me laugh, Ann. John! John! You faced up to the fact years ago just how much spunk John had, so don't come that over me now.'

'Shut up you! Shut up . . .'

It was a row. They were really rowing in there. The surprise jerked his finger onto the bell, and almost immediately he heard the sound of the woman's voice, high now, crying, 'No, you won't, this happens to be my . . .' Then the man's voice saying, 'Get out of my way, Ann.'

The next minute Pat was looking up into the red, angry face of a man he had seen before, and for a moment he was swamped with terror and had the desire to turn and flee. Although he knew that Mr Bolton had told the truth and things looked better for him now, he knew that this was the man he'd have to go before next week. He had seen his face in nightmares during the past week, and it had looked just like it did now.

'What do you want?' Apparently the man did not recognise him, and Pat, looking at the woman who had come to the door, said in a small voice, 'Are you Mrs Emmerson?'

'Yes, I'm Mrs Emmerson.' He saw her put her fingers to her lips, and he glanced towards the little man again before saying, 'Me mam sent me. She said would you bring the car, Mr . . . Mr Emmerson's took bad.'

'W'what! Mr Emmer . . . You mean . . . Who are you?'

'Pat . . . Pat Thorpe.'

'Thorpe?' James Wilcox almost screamed the name. 'Yes, yes, I thought I recognised you. Yes, of course, Thorpe. And your mother

wants the car because Mr Emmerson's taken bad? Well, well.'
He turned on Ann, his fury almost lifting him from the ground.
'It's clear now. Oh, it's clear now. This is what you were trying to
hide, and no wonder, father and son drinking from the same
fountain.'

'How dare you! Be quiet.'

'Don't you tell me to be quiet, Ann, because I haven't started yet
. . . Bring the car, Mr Emmerson's taken bad . . . How bad is he,
young man? Is he drunk?'

Pat moved his head back on his shoulders away from the red face,
and he shook it slightly as he said, 'No, no he's not. He's been beaten
up.'

'O . . . O . . . h!'

Pat looked quickly up at the woman as she groaned, then back
towards the little man, who was standing straight now, his head
wagging from side to side on his shoulders and a funny expression
on his face, as he said, 'Beaten up? Well, well, now the situation is
becoming interesting. Likely another of her gentlemen friends didn't
take to the new arrangement.'

'My mam's got no gentlemen friends.' As Pat's fist shot out and
caught James Wilcox in the thigh it was a question of who was the
more surprised, he at the assault, or Pat at his own daring.

Ann now held Pat by the shoulders, pulling him to one side, and
she was talking in a strangely quiet voice. 'Get out, James,' she was
saying. 'And I'll thank you not to come back here again.'

'I'll be back again, Ann. Oh, I'll be back, if only once, for I mean
to have my say to that white-livered son of yours. And he's finished,
you understand, finished. Not only in my firm but in this town.
And he may think that he can go farther afield and find a job, but
he's mistaken. If I have to spend the rest of my life putting spokes
in his wheel I'll count the time well spent . . . As for you, young
fellow, we'll meet later.'

Pat, wide-eyed, watched the little man almost throw himself out
into the porch, so furiously did he move his body; then he watched
the woman close the door, lean her back against it, cover her eyes
with her hands for a moment and inhale deeply before she looked
at him again. Then she took him by the arm and led him into a big
white room, and staring down at him, she said, 'Tell me what this
is about.'

He looked up into her face and said hesitantly, 'We . . . we were
in bed, and there was a ring at the door and I heard me mam
get up, and I waited. And then she told me to get up quick, and
when I went into the room Mr Emmerson was lying on the floor.
She said she had found him outside the door on the landing.' He
shook his head slowly at her now. 'His face was all battered, he's
bad.'

He watched her hand go across her mouth again; then he said, 'Me mam wanted to send for our doctor but he said no, he wanted you, and to get home.'

Ann was still staring down into the boy's face. He was a good-looking boy; the mother was a good-looking woman; why was it she had come into their lives? She had taken John from her. Yes, she had, although she was on a better footing with her husband than she had been since Laurie was born, she knew that she had lost part of him, and would never be able to retain it because it had been given to this boy's mother. And now her son had become involved with her. How had this come about? Why? They were leading people of the town, highly respected, and they had become involved with this cheap woman. Because she was cheap; you had only to look at her, her good looks couldn't hide it. Why was it that nice men were always attracted by cheap women?

'Aren't you going to come?'

'Yes, yes.' She put her hand across her brow, then said, 'I'll get a coat. Come along.'

A minute later he stood aside and watched her lock the front door. Then going to the garage, she beckoned him silently into the car beside her.

Within half-an-hour the car was back on the drive and Pat was once more seated beside 'the stiff lady' as he thought of her in his mind, while in the back seat were Mr Emmerson and his mother, and without looking round he knew that his mother was trying to keep Mr Emmerson up straight.

'Unlock the door.' The lady was thrusting a key into his hand and he scrambled out of the car and ran to the front door. After a moment of fumbling, the key turned and he pushed the door wide, just in time for them to pass, his mam on one side of Mr Emmerson, the stiff lady on the other. Mr Emmerson looked awful, like people, he imagined, when they were going to die. He took his eyes quickly from the blue-black distorted face, then from beneath lowered lids he watched them go slowly up the stairs, and when they had disappeared across the landing he stood with his back to the thick oak post from which the banisters started, and looked about him, and although he couldn't quite make it out he connected what he saw with the stiff lady.

Upstairs Ann went to lower Laurie into a chair, but he made a movement towards the bed, and when they sat him on the edge he fell sideways, and it was Cissie who lifted his feet up, shoes and all, onto the grey satin quilted cover.

'We should get him undressed.' She spoke under her breath as she looked at Ann Emmerson, and for the first time since their meeting Ann looked fully into her face. Her own expression had a startled quality about it as if Cissie had suggested something improper. 'I can manage quite well now, thank you.'

It was a curt dismissal, and Cissie felt the heat of indignation sweep over her body as she stared unblinkingly back into the cold, pale face, before her. She wanted to make some protest against all this woman's look was saying to her, but this was neither the time nor the place, so she turned swiftly about and went towards the door, only to be stopped as she opened it by a weak voice from the bed muttering, 'Cecilia.'

She turned her head quickly over her shoulder, thinking for a moment he was speaking to his mother. She couldn't remember anyone calling her Cecilia; no-one had ever given her her correct name. She still thought he was addressing his mother until she saw his hand lifted towards her; then she went back to the bed. And she took his hand and held it, and when, through his distorted and broken lips, he muttered, 'Thanks, thanks,' the only thing she could do was to nod towards the two narrow slits which was all she could see of his eyes. Then she turned from him and passed the woman who was standing at the door.

Ann followed her down the stairs, and in the hall, in the manner of someone who knows her duty towards her inferiors, she said, 'I'll phone for a taxi to take you home.'

'There's no need, thank you very much, we can walk.'

Cissie's tone was bitter; and she added, as she held out her hand towards Pat, 'It's a doctor you want to phone for, and quick. And don't try to cover this up by not getting a doctor or you'll likely have something much more serious on your hands.'

Ann drew herself up and her flat chest took on shape as she exclaimed with chilling haughtiness, 'I don't need you to tell me where my duty lies, Mrs Thorpe. And were there more serious consequences of tonight's business who, I ask, should be held responsible for them?'

Cissie was near the hall door now, and she turned quickly as she said, 'You, Mrs Emmerson, you and no-one else. If I hadn't known your husband I wouldn't have known your son, and I leave you to work out how I, a common individual, because that's how you consider me isn't it, came to be acquainted with a man in Mr Emmerson's position. Just you work it out, Mrs Emmerson. Good night.'

Pushing Pat before her she went out into the lobby, then through the front door and round the drive into the road, and when they had left the avenue and turned down the dark lane Pat stopped and, flinging his arms around her waist, pressed his head into her ribs, whimpering, 'Aw, don't cry. Ma, don't cry.'

PART THREE

BREAD-AND-CHEESE
AND BEER

CHAPTER ONE

THE PROPOSAL

John came in through the lower gate from the field path and began to walk round the garden. It was the last time he would ever walk round this garden, and he asked himself if he was sorry, and the answer came: No. No, not at all.

Tomorrow they were starting on a three months' holiday, going first to Denmark, then round the Kattegat and up the Baltic to Finland. On the return journey they were leaving the boat at Stockholm and were staying there for a time. Ann had planned it all. She had been wonderful really, because neither he nor Laurie had been able to see to a thing. She had even done the whole business of the new house. He thought he was going to like the new house; it wasn't as big as this and it was more homely. She had discussed the decorations with him. Her taste had changed quite a lot, for she had suggested having patterned wallpaper. He would have further to travel back and forth to the office from the new house – it was more than three miles beyond the town boundary, and it was rather isolated, but he didn't mind that, not in the least. It was on a rise and had some splendid views; a most interesting feature was a piece of woodland with a stream at the bottom. All the garden had been set out in a natural way, mostly with shrubs, no stiff borders. Yes, he felt he was going to enjoy the new house, and there would be only the two of them. Would he enjoy that? Why not? He stopped in his walk. It would be like starting a new life. Everything was different now. Yes, quite different.

He moved on again; past the greenhouse and the potting shed, and through the arch in the privet hedge that separated the vegetable garden from the lawns and flower beds, and up the side path that led to the terrace that flanked the french windows of the dining-room.

There was a small rose pergola here that formed a wind break, and he sat down in the wrought-iron chair that stood beneath it and looked over the garden, but now without seeing it. The phrase, new life, had set his mind working, pushing queries out along paths that he didn't want to explore. For some time now he had kept telling himself to take things as they came, that everything would work out;

the main thing was not to hurt anyone. It was odd, but he hadn't thought until recently that it was in his power to hurt anyone, but now he knew it was, and the possession of this power brought him no gratification.

To check his trend of thought he was about to rise from the chair when he heard a door open in the room at the other side of the pergola, and then Ann's voice speaking to Laurie. Again he was about to rise when the tail end of what she was saying kept him still. 'You can't evade it any more. There's not much time left.'

Then Laurie's voice answering her. 'There's nothing to discuss, nothing to talk about, I've told you . . . Oh, for God's sake, Mother!'

'How can you say that when she's been on the phone this very minute?'

'Well, she didn't ask for me, did she?' The words were hissed.

'No, but she hoped you would answer.'

'Look, Mother.' Laurie's voice was patient sounding now. 'I was in a devil of a mess, as you know, when she found me. She's phoned three times in a month to find out how I am. I don't consider she's overdone it.'

'Stop hedging, Laurie. I'm going away tomorrow and I can't leave with my mind in this state; I've got to know what's between you and her. Can't you understand how I feel? First your father, and now you . . . It's terrible to me, and disgusting . . . Yes, disgusting.'

John was leaning forward, his forearm resting on the iron table in front of him, his eyes riveted on a piece of grass growing between the slabs of the crazy paving on the terrace. The voices from the room became indistinct. He knew that Ann was still talking and Laurie answering her, but what they were saying he couldn't hear for the noise in his mind made by the whirling names: 'Laurie and Cissie, Laurie and Cissie.' He felt the beat of his heart quickening to the repetition of 'Laurie and Cissie. Laurie and Cissie.' And then he pressed his fist to his chest, saying to himself, 'Steady, steady.' And the noise in his head faded away and he heard Laurie speaking again, his tone low and harsh.

'I've . . . I've seen the woman four times, and each time we've rowed, except the last time, when I was in no position to do anything, and from that you've got me living with her. You've convinced yourself that I've taken over where father left off, haven't you?'

Out on the terrace John's head drooped lower. 'Taken over where father left off.' Then he raised it slightly again as Ann said in a dull, flat tone, 'It was because of her that you gave up Val, wasn't it?'

'Oh my God! Now don't get me mad. Now look, I'm telling you, don't get me mad.'

'And don't treat me as a child, Laurie, asking me to believe that you've only seen her four times and that you fought with her. If that is so, well, all I can say is that your manner underwent a great change the night she helped to bring you home.'

'What do you mean?'

'You don't hold a woman's hand and call her Cecilia, and she doesn't cry over you after four meetings in which you fought all the time.'

'Cecilia? I held her hand and called her Cecilia? You must be bats. I didn't even know she was called Cecilia, I've never called her anything but Mrs Thorpe.'

'Laurie, Laurie.' She was almost shouting now. 'Be quiet. I don't want to hear any more. If there was a doubt in my mind before over your association with the woman you have certainly dispelled it.'

'I . . . TELL . . . YOU . . . MOTHER . . . !'

'Please, please, Laurie, don't protest any more. I don't want to think of you as a liar too. But let me tell you this. Wilcox has ruined your career, that man Bolton has ruined your looks, but that woman will ruin your life. She's gone a good way already. And I'll say one more thing, one more thing . . . you'll have to choose. I mean it, Laurie, I mean it. If you continue your association with her I never want to see you again. Do you understand what I'm saying? Don't think I will soften, for the very thought of her makes me physically sick.'

As the sound of a door closing came to John he pulled himself up from the chair, went hastily from the terrace along the side path, and through the arch in the privet once again, and going into the tool shed, he shut the door behind him and sat on an upturned crate.

'Cissie. Cissie.' He was saying her name aloud, his voice, sad and tender, was yet threaded with reproach. Slowly he rested his elbows on his knees and bowed his head over his hanging hands. He had been a fool, a fool. He could have had her and all she meant to life; gaiety, warmness, understanding and kindness. Yes, he could have had Cissie. He knew that morning she came to him in hospital that she was his for the asking, and because of this he had told her about himself. It had been quite easy to tell her, but he had not been prepared for the effect of the telling. When she had kissed him on the mouth he had wanted to hold her and never let her go. But he knew that he could not lay the burden of his deformity on her. He had watched Ann become crippled under it and he could not let the same thing happen to Cissie, although she would have known what she was taking on . . .

But Laurie had denied his mother's imputation. Perhaps he was right and there was nothing in it. How could there be seeing her only four times. But he himself had only seen her once, well twice, and it had happened to him. But he had been lonely and ripe for such an affair, if you could call the relationship between them an affair . . . And he himself had sent Laurie to her, begged him to go.

He felt the old feeling of aloneness return, and it was more poignant now than at any time over the long bleak years, for then he'd had really nothing to lose, but during the last few months, whilst he had known Cissie, life had come back into his living, and when having lost her, as it were, he had found his son, he had thought that things usually balanced themselves out . . . And now, before he had hardly found Laurie, he was to lose him too, for if there was anything in it, it would be as Ann said, Laurie would be cut off from them. She wouldn't bear to see him because of the girl, and he wouldn't dare to see him . . . because of the girl.

'Oh, there you are, dear. Why are you sitting in here? You are not feeling ill again?'

'No. No.' He pulled himself upwards and took the hand she held out to him, and as it gripped his firmly he thought what a sense of wonder it would have brought to him if it had been held out this time last year; but now between their hands would always be Cissie's; no matter what happened it would always be there . . . No matter what happened.

At twelve o'clock the following morning Laurie stood on the quay and watched the boat move slowly from the dock. High up above his head on the first-class deck stood his mother and father. He did not raise his hand until his father raised his, and then he waved back. His mother did not wave until the boat was some distance from the quay, and then it was a small movement of her hand conveying over the distance to him her worry and anger. Her last words to him had been, 'You will go to your uncle's, won't you, Laurie? You'll go straight away, they're expecting you.'

And he had said, 'Yes, yes, of course,' knowing full well that he had no intention of going to his uncle's.

She had bent forward then and he had kissed her, and he had smiled at her and said, 'Now forget everything and have a good time.'

He had left her in the special suite which was filled with flowers, and going out on deck he had walked with his father to the gangway, and there for a moment they had stood facing each other. He had smiled at him too, and had been about to say what he had said to his mother, 'Now forget everything and have a good time,' when John muttered abruptly, 'I have something to say to you, Laurie, and we haven't much time. And please don't be offended.' John had glanced downwards for a moment before looking back into his face and adding under his breath, 'I happened to be on the verandah last night when you and your mother were talking.'

He had closed his eyes and brought his teeth down onto his lip. The attitude was one of striving for patience, but he could not keep the weariness from his voice as he said, 'Now look, Father, let me say this . . .'

But John cut in on him, 'No, Laurie. No. Don't give me any reasons, just listen to me for a moment. What I want to say to you is, follow your heart. Do what you want to do. Don't, don't, I beg you, sacrifice yourself for anyone, not for your mother . . . or me. You'll get no thanks for it in the end and I've brought enough harm to you already.' His eyes had moved swiftly over the discoloured face.

'Father. Will you listen just a moment?' He had stood with his elbows pressed tight against his sides, his hands spread out in front of his chest, but John, ignoring the plea, went on, 'I know how you feel. I'm well aware of the fix you're in . . . I've been in it myself, so I know all about it. One thing I ask of you: give her a message from me, will you? Tell her . . . tell her that she's got to take happiness, grab it with both hands. Tell her I'm happy for her, will you; will you tell her that?'

He had remained silent as he returned his father's fixed stare. It was no good, it was no good protesting, one way or the other. The only thing to do was to let them think what they liked, only time would prove them wrong. But in the meantime they would both be as miserable as hell. Well, he had done his best. All the talking in the world wouldn't convince them. It was just one of those unbelievable things that happened; surmise became stamped with truth because he had apparently spoken her Christian name. He put out his hand, and John took it and held it fast for a moment.

'Get well,' he said.

'Don't worry, I'll be all right.' John smiled at him as he looked into his face. 'Goodbye, Laurie.'

'Goodbye, Father. Goodbye.'

He had turned away, then stopped as John's fingers touched his arm. 'You'll write and tell me how things go?'

He drooped his head slightly before half turning it over his shoulder and nodding. Then he was running down the gangway and onto the quay.

Their faces were now getting smaller. His father was waving all the time, his mother intermittently. Soon it was no use standing any longer. He turned slowly away and, going to his car, drove back to the house.

When he got into the hall Mrs Stringer came from the kitchen, saying, 'Well, they got off then, Mr Laurie?'

'Yes, Stringy.'

'Did they have a comfortable room?'

'Marvellous, almost as big as the lounge. Home from home.'

'You're jokin'.'

'I'm not. It's a fact. Bathroom, shower, the lot, and the place swamped with flowers.'

'Aw, how nice. I hope it will do them both good . . . Well now, I've set your lunch in the breakfast-room, Mr Laurie, and I've put all your clean things out on the bed ready for packin'.'

As she was talking he bent forward over the hall table and looked at his face in the oval mirror. Even after a month it hadn't fallen back into shape. He doubted if it ever would. He touched his left eyebrow with his fingers as he looked with a sideways motion at Mrs Stringer through the glass and said, 'I won't be going tomorrow, Stringy.'

'Oh now, now, Mr Laurie, it's all arranged; your uncle's expecting you and the missus was on the phone not ten minutes afore she left telling them what time you'd get there.'

'I'm going to ring them now, Stringy.'

'But why, Mr Laurie?'

'I'll explain in a minute.' He sat down on the gold-coloured cane chair near the telephone table and picked up the receiver.

'Hello,' he said after a moment. 'Is that Uncle Ron?'

'Yes, Laurie. What's the news?'

'They got away all right,' he answered. 'Splendid cabin . . . They'll be living it up for weeks.'

The heavy voice from the other end of the line now asked, 'When're you setting out? We're all waiting for you. The girls have got you booked up for the next three weeks, God help you.'

'Uncle?'

'Yes, Laurie.'

'Uncle, I'm sorry I won't be able to come.'

'What's that? Did I hear you say you won't be able to come? What's the matter, you haven't taken bad again, have you? Ann was on the phone to Susan first thing this morning telling her you'd be leaving in the morning. What's the matter? What's happened?'

'It's just this way, Uncle. I'm, I'm going into hospital; I believe I'm going to lose the sight of one eye.'

'God almighty! But your mother . . . why . . . ?'

'She didn't know. Neither of them knew. I didn't tell them. They wouldn't have gone, and everything was booked up, and Father needed to get away.'

'But an eye. Is it certain?'

'They think so. Anyway it won't matter, for I've hardly been able to see anything with it since I . . . I was hurt. It was a blow on the temple apparently that caused it.'

'Oh, lad, this is terrible. Look, do you want Susan to come down there and see to you?'

'No, no. You see, I'll be in hospital, and I don't know for how long.'

'Well this is a shock. I don't know what Susan's going to say, she's out at the moment. Oh, I am sorry about this, Laurie. And do you know something? I think you should have told your father.'

'It couldn't have helped, and I didn't want to give him any more worry at this stage.'

'No, no. I see your point. But oh my God, boy, I'm right sorry for you . . . Look, when it's over will you come through?'

'Yes, yes, I'd be glad to.'

'And you'll keep us informed?'

'Yes, I will, Uncle.'

'But what if you go to this new house? When is that going to take place?'

'Oh, not for another three weeks, and Stringy's here to see to things as usual. She's doing all the packing and going over there and putting things to rights. She'll have everything more than ship-shape by the time they come back. In the meantime, she's looking after me fine.'

'Laurie, I don't know what to say; you've knocked the wind completely out of my sails.'

'Oh, don't take it like that, Uncle, I feel I've been lucky; it could have been both of them.'

'Yes, yes, that's the way to look at it I suppose. But nevertheless it's a tragedy. I'll get your aunt to phone you as soon as she comes in, eh?'

'All right, Uncle.'

'Goodbye, lad.'

'Goodbye, Uncle.'

When he put the phone down he heard a small sound from the kitchen door and there stood Mrs Stringer with her two hands cupping her face, her compact body swaying slightly from side to side.

'Oh, Mr Laurie. Oh, Mr Laurie.'

'Now, now, it's all right.'

'And for you to let them go and not tell them.'

'It's better this way, isn't it?' He put his arm around her shoulders and led her back into the kitchen, saying, 'There, there. Now don't you start howling.'

'Oh, Mr Laurie.'

'Look,' he said; 'I'm hungry and I want some lunch. Come on.' He pushed her playfully towards the stove. 'Give me the dishes, I'll carry them in.'

As she handed him the vegetable dishes she looked up into his face and muttered again, 'Oh, Mr Laurie. Oh, Mr Laurie.'

A few minutes later, sitting in lonely state eating his lunch, he put his elbow on the table and rested his head on his hand, bringing his fingers as he did so over his left eye. Oh, Mr Laurie. Oh, Mr

Laurie. It was funny what sympathy did to you. It probed the soft spots, the fear spots, and there were more than one of those under his skin at the present moment. The only way for him to tackle this thing was on the side, so to speak, treat it as something unpleasant but necessary, that had to be done, like having a tooth out. There were two things he had to steer clear of, sympathy from others and resentment against the source and cause of his condition.

It was funny, the little things, the little decisions and actions that led up to losing an eye. That was the way to look at it . . . philosophically, as if it had had to be and nothing he could have done would have prevented it. That was the only line to take.

It was as he finished his meal that he heard the doorbell ring and Stringy go to answer it; and then her voice, high and indignant, saying, 'The family's all gone, Mr Wilcox. There's no-one here, they've all gone.'

'All but one, Mrs Stringer, and I'll thank you to get out of my way.'

Laurie rose to his feet and went to the morning-room door, and from there, looking across the hall, he said evenly, 'It's all right, Stringy. Let Mr Wilcox in.'

James Wilcox came in, his step slow and heavy like that of a man twice his size. He kept his eyes on Laurie even while he passed him and went into the room, and there he continued to stare at him, seeming to derive satisfaction from what he saw.

During a long tense moment in which Laurie returned the older man's glare neither of them spoke. Then James Wilcox, clearing his throat, began, 'You knew I wouldn't let you get away with this, didn't you?'

'I've been expecting you.'

'Then you're not disappointed, are you? I thought I'd wait till they got off, so you wouldn't have any skirts to hide behind.'

As Laurie ground his teeth Wilcox went on, 'I blame her as much as anybody, she's spoilt you since you were born and she suckled you until you went into long pants . . .'

'I'm going to give you a warning, and take heed. I'm past taking anything more from you. Just another crack like that and I'll take you by the scruff of the neck and throw you out of the door . . . And I mean it.'

'I would like to see you try it on, young man. Like all your breed you're gutless.' He tugged at his waistcoat and drew in a deep breath. 'Well, I came here to tell you what I think of you and to pass on two items of news that you'd better pay heed to . . . The first one is that my daughter has broken off her engagement to you . . . You understand, SHE'S BROKEN OFF HER ENGAGEMENT TO YOU because of your carry-on with the Thorpe woman . . .'

'Oh . . . Oh no, you don't.' Laurie's face was scarlet, and digging his index finger towards Wilcox's chest, he cried, 'You set that tale about and I'll have you up in court before you know where you are, and on the wrong side of the Bench this time.'

'Try it on, try it on, and we'll see who wins.' Mr Wilcox's head was wagging as if on wires. 'It's public knowledge now that your father was visiting that woman for months, and now everyone knows that you were seeing her on the side too. It's a public scandal . . . and, and my daughter finding this out wouldn't stand for it. That's the story, and you try to alter it in this town and see how far you get. It's also current news that one of her fancy men beat you up and deposited you on her doorstep.'

Laurie only just stopped himself from springing on the older man, but he moved towards him, and his fists clenched and held stiffly by his sides, he growled at him, 'Nobody's fancy man beat me up. It was Bolton's thugs who beat me up, and you know why . . . Or don't you?' He thrust his scarlet face down towards the now slightly surprised countenance of Mr Wilcox. 'He had me beaten up because I exposed his little game. I went through his returns . . . among your files, and found out he was doing some twisting, as you knew he'd been doing for years and shut your eyes to it. He said he had never engaged the Thorpe boy on a Saturday morning, but he'd been putting thirty shillings on his returns for employing two boys on a Saturday morning for years. I went and confronted him with it and forced his hand. I made him go to the police and clear the Thorpe boy. That's news to you, isn't it?'

'You! . . . you went to my files and . . . ?' Bubbles of saliva spurted from Mr Wilcox's lips.

'Yes, I went through your files.'

'You . . . You mean to stand there and tell me . . . ?'

'Yes, I mean to stand here and tell you, and if you hadn't anything to hide you wouldn't mind who went through your files.'

'The client's business is private, you know that.'

'But YOU have a section that is specially private, haven't you?' He paused for a telling moment before going on, 'So now I'm warning you. You drop your fancy man business or it isn't too late to do what I should have done the night I got this.' He pointed to his face.

Mr Wilcox swallowed deeply. He was definitely flustered now as his voice showed. 'You've got no proof that it was Mr Bolton who instigated the . . . that.'

'I've got all the proof I need.'

'Well, why didn't you use it? I can't see you having a trump card in your hand and not playing it.'

Laurie stared down into the mean little face, then he stepped back from him as if the proximity of this man was distasteful to him, as it was. And he said slowly, 'Yes, you would think that way because that's how you would have acted, isn't it? Well, I'll tell you now why I didn't play my card. It was because if I had accused Bolton I would have had to give my reasons for the attack, and I couldn't have done that without bringing up the matter of how the boy Thorpe was cleared and that would have involved you. Funny, isn't it, me considering you.'

'I need no consideration from you, young man; my business can stand scrutiny of the closest kind.' Mr Wilcox was bristling again.

'Doubtless, doubtless, you would have been able to prove that you knew nothing about his little fiddles on the side, but you know and I know that Her Majesty's Inspector of Taxes has just got to get the tiniest inkling that there is some laxity with regard to the scrutiny of the returns of privileged clients and they're on to you; they'll watch you like a hawk until the day you retire.' Laurie wiped the sweat from around his mouth with his hand, then shook his head as he said, 'It's funny. As much as I hate your guts, and I'm telling you to your face I do, I didn't want to do this to you.'

Mr Wilcox too wiped his face, but he did it with a large white handkerchief, and when he had finished he was smiling, a twisted, sarcastic smile. He spread his lips wide, revealing his neat dentures, as he said, 'A very noble way of putting it. But it would have been nearer the truth had you said that you held your hand because your conscience was troubling you concerning your treatment of Val and your association with that woman.'

'Look. I'll tell you once again, I had no association with . . . that woman, as you call her.' Laurie's whole attitude now was one of taut aggressiveness. 'But if I'd known as much the night I got this,' he touched his cheek, 'as I do now I wouldn't have hesitated in taking the whole matter to the authorities . . . But mind, as I've said, it isn't too late; so I'm warning you.' He again dug his finger towards Wilcox, 'you start any rumours going about fancy men and me having an affair with Mrs Thorpe and I'll bring the whole matter into the open . . . Now.' His voice dropped. 'You've had your say; you've acted, as you would put it, like a man . . . the little mean man that you are. Now get out.'

James Wilcox's lips met and were drawn in between his teeth. His portly body quivered; he tugged with both hands at the points of his waistcoat; he was about to go but he had to have one more shot. 'You're finished in this town, you know that, don't you?' He now lifted his body around almost with a jump and made for the door, and Laurie followed him. He followed him across the hall and he stood behind him as he fumbled with the latch of the front door. And when he had succeeded in opening it; Wilcox turned to him once again and, nodding towards his face, said under his breath, 'Well, whoever did that, they made a pretty mess of you, and I'm going to say now, and frankly, that I wish I'd had a hand in it.'

Laurie remained quite still, and his voice was deceptively calm when he replied, 'Thank you, your honour. And I'm sure that if you had I would have lost the sight of both eyes, instead of just one.'

In the moment that he paused before banging the door in Wilcox's face he saw the startled look of surprise spreading over it.

When he again entered the morning-room his body was shaking and he felt slightly sick. He stood for a moment with his hand to his head, before turning about and going into the dining-room and pouring himself out a stiff drink . . . Her fancy man! He knew that all his brave talk about what he would do if Wilcox spread that rumour was mere wind, for it would already be in circulation – Val would have grabbed at the whole business as a face-saver. He wondered that old Wilcox had bothered to come and tell him. What he had really come for was to act the man, the enraged parent, and shout his mouth off.

His father had started something, hadn't he? The old feeling against him revived with a surge, swamping that more liberal one that had emerged during the past weeks. He walked back into the lounge and, standing before the high hearth, finished his drink at a gulp, then hurled the glass into the empty grate.

The same evening Laurie went to see his doctor, who told him that he would get him into the hospital towards the end of the following week. He'd had a report from the specialist, but he was afraid there was nothing to add to what he already knew. In the meantime he would give him a prescription for more drops . . .

It was as he stood to the side of a partition of baby foods waiting for his prescription to be made up that he saw Cissie go up to the counter; and as he stood looking at her back he felt a galloping racing emotion within him that could have been fear. If there had been a door to the left of him he would have sidled out, but any move from where he stood must bring her attention to him, and so he stood still.

She was wearing a plastic mac over a brown suit, she was hatless and her long wet hair hung in separated strands onto her shoulders, and the undisciplined sight of it irritated him. He heard the assistant say to her, 'Will you take a seat, it'll be a few moments.' When she turned to where the seats were she was directly in front of him and as his own face reddened he watched hers light up. For a moment he saw her eyes shine with a warm brightness, as if she was seeing someone she had never expected to see again.

'How are you?' She was standing close to him, looking into his face and her eyes, after moving from one feature to the other, came to rest on the dilated pupil of his left eye.

'Fine,' he said; 'fine.'

'Sure?' Her face had suddenly dropped into straight solemn lines. 'You don't . . . I mean, it hasn't . . . ?'

'Oh, this.' He patted one cheek and then the other. 'Oh, that'll disappear in time.' As he continued to look at her he thought she would never know the extent of the trouble she had caused him. Nevertheless, what little he knew of her, he gauged she was the kind of person who would not wittingly bring trouble on anybody. He believed now, as his father had impressed on him from the beginning, that she was kind. Whatever else she might be, she was kind. She had dropped her eyes from his and was standing to the side facing the counter now, and she said, 'I've got Pat in bed with a cold.'

'Oh, I'm sorry,' he said. Then: 'The other business was cleared up all right?'

'Oh, yes, yes.' She turned her head quickly towards him, nodding in small jerks. 'When Barry Rice knew that Pat could prove that he had been working all that morning he told the truth. He also told the names of the other two boys . . . But you know all this, I suppose. Mr Ransome would tell you all about it?'

'Your drops, sir.' The chemist handed Laurie a small wrapped bottle, and he thanked the man, pocketed the bottle and looked at Cissie with the intention of saying goodbye.

She had been looking at the bottle; now she was looking to the one side of his face and she asked under her breath, 'Is there anything wrong with it, your eye?'

'No, no.' He shook his head. 'At least nothing that can't be put right.'

'You're sure?' Her voice sounded anxious and he nodded again, 'Yes, perfectly sure. Good night.' His accent was exaggerated, rebuffing.

'Good night.'

Outside it was raining heavily and he paused for a moment in the shelter of the shop doorway looking towards his car parked against the kerb before hurrying to it and unlocking the door. Inside, he pushed in the ignition key and pressed the self starter, but then he sat back making no move towards the gears. 'Don't be a blasted fool. Get going.' It was as if the voice with no high-hat accent now was coming from the back seat, and his head drooped under the derisive condemnation of the tone. 'Get going,' it said again. 'For God's sake, man, have sense and don't prove them right.'

As he put his hand towards the gear lever she came out of the shop. She was on his right-hand side and he could see her without having to turn his head. He wound down the window and spoke to her across the pavement, saying, 'Get in.' There was impatience in his tone now, as if he were speaking to a wife who had been dawdling.

'What?' She came towards him, bending down until her face was level with his, and the rain from her hair splashed onto his shoulders. 'Get in,' he said; 'I'll run you home.'

'Oh, no. No, thanks. I can get the bus.' She backed away and straightened up, and he bent over the wheel and looked up at her and said again, 'Don't be silly. Come on, get in.' He leant away from her and opened the other door, and when he sat up again she was still standing on the pavement, and now she bent towards him again and hissed quickly under her breath, 'It would be silly, you know that . . . But thanks all the same.'

'Look. Don't argue, get in. You're getting wet.'

He watched her turn her head to the side and look down at the grey shining pavement, then slowly raise her head again and look at him. 'You know what you're doing, don't you?' she said.

'I know what I'm doing. Get in.'

Once she had entered the car he didn't speak, but when she couldn't get the door locked he leant across her and flicked the handle into place, and he was aware as he did so that her body was pressing tightly against the seat away from contact with him, and he had the strongest desire to turn on her and say brutally, 'It's all right. It's all right. You've got nothing like that to fear from me; I should say not!'

They had covered some distance when her voice, tentative now, asked, 'How is your father?'

'When I saw him this morning he was in fine fettle. They left Newcastle for a three months' holiday, mostly by sea.'

'Oh, oh. I'm glad. That should do him good . . . the world of good.' Then she added, as if to make polite conversation, 'You should have a holiday yourself; I'm sure you could do with it.'

'Yes,' he said, swinging the wheel round as they took a corner. 'I feel I could do with a change. I'm going to Oxford shortly to stay with an uncle of mine. I don't suppose I'll come back here again.'

'You . . . you've left your job?' There was a high note of surprise in her voice.

'Oh, yes. Yes, I've definitely left my job.'

She had her face full towards him and her words tumbled over one another. 'B . . . but I thought you were g-going to be married.'

He swung the wheel again. 'I was, but I am no longer.'

Her face still towards him, she asked in a frightened tone, 'All this business . . . me . . . am I anything to do with it?'

'Not a thing.' Glancing swiftly towards her he asked sharply, 'What makes you say that? Why should you? Why should you think you have anything to do with it?'

Even in the short glance he gave her he saw the blood rush to her face, and he added. 'Well, what I mean is, how could you?'

'I know that, I know that, I-know-all-about-that. But people's tongues . . . they say . . .'

'Well, what do they say? What can they say in this case?'

'I know, I know.' Her voice was high and agitated. 'But some folks are wicked. They'll take your name away if it's the last thing you've got left; they'll not be satisfied till they've stripped you.' She stopped abruptly. Then hanging her head, she said, 'I didn't mean it, I wasn't referring to the other day or, or what you said, or anything.'

'I couldn't blame you if you were.'

He brought the car now to an abrupt stop outside the flats and immediately she fumbled with the door handle, and once more he had to lean across her to open it, and almost before he had released the handle she was standing in the road. The door still in her hand, she looked at him and her face was again showing concern. 'I hope you get on all right,' she said.

He did not answer her. With his hand still on the wheel he stared at her as she banged the door, but still not hard enough to close it, and for the last time he leant forward and adjusted the handle. As he started up the car he saw her enter the doorway, and she didn't turn round.

The following day he helped Mrs Stringer to pack. From early morning until after tea he packed articles ranging from clothes to kitchen utensils. Then in a room that was already beginning to look unlived in, he had his evening meal, and later took Mrs Stringer home. It was eight o'clock when he returned, and from then until eleven o'clock the time seemed longer than the whole of the day.

The pattern was almost the same the following day, and returning to the empty house after depositing Mrs Stringer he had such a longing for company that he played with the idea of going to the club. But even while he did so he knew he wouldn't go because he was afraid to, afraid of the power of Wilcox's malice, afraid of someone making an excuse that he had to go and meet the girl friend, or that he was expected home, or had a business appointment, and so he sat and looked at the television. And as he looked he suddenly thought, if I never see her again, I'll never forget her. Then getting to his feet and switching off the set he said aloud, 'Blast her!'

It was half-past eight when he got into the car and drove into the town and to the flats. He glanced at her name on the board in the hallway before he mounted the stairs: Mrs Cecilia Thorpe. He did not go quietly up the stairs, and he hoped that someone would come out of their doorway, preferably Mrs Orchard, but he met no-one, and when he reached the top landing he immediately rang the bell.

When she opened the door he saw that she was startled and that his presence made her afraid.

She stood with the door in her hand blocking the entrance, and she said simply, 'Yes?'

'Aren't you going to ask me in?' His voice was as aggressive as his look.

She gulped in her long throat. 'What do you want?'

'I want to talk to you.'

She glanced behind him, and suspicion rose in him and he thought, Ah! Then she stood aside and he went past her, across the little hall into the long room. But there was no-one to be seen.

The electric fan was reflecting on imitation logs. There were some magazines on the couch and the indent in the cushions where a head had been. He glanced about him, still expecting to see someone, and the reason for his interest wasn't lost on her. With a touch of harshness in her voice that dispelled the suggestion of fear she said, 'I'm on my own, except for Pat, and he's still in bed.'

'What makes you think I . . . ?'

'Oh, I know what you were thinking. Suspicion dies hard, doesn't it? Look . . . I don't want to be angry with you, I want to forget about everything, all I want is a quiet life. Why have you come here?'

'Because I'm lonely.' His voice was rough, coarse sounding.

'Lone . . . ? But what has that got to do with me?' She screwed up her face at him. 'Why come to me?'

'Because I think you owe me something.'

'Owe you something!'

'Yes, just that. You owe me something.' His manner changed. He threw his hat onto a chair and undid the buttons of his raincoat, and there was a hint of wry amusement in his voice as he went on, 'I'm out of a job. I'm estranged from my parents, I've lost my future wife, and my home has been sold over my head, and last but not least the town's so hot for me I'm having to leave it.'

She was gaping at him, her mouth and eyes stretched wide. Her whole body appeared to be swelling; her voice spiralled: 'And you're blaming me for all this?'

'Yes. Yes, everything.' One side of his lip curled inwards at the corner.

She joined her hands together and held them against her waist; her face tightened, and a wary, defensive look came into her eyes as she said quietly, 'And you expect me to do something about it?'

'Yes, just that.'

'And what, may I ask?'

'Oh well, I'll leave that to you.' He was grinning engagingly at her now.

'Get out!'

'Oh look. Look.' His manner changed completely and he put his hand out towards her. 'It was meant to be funny. I'm sorry.'

'Funny!' She cried. 'You can't get it out of your head that I'm loose, can you? You've just said it again. Things have happened to you and you're blaming me, and I've got to pay you, pay you in a way you think I pay most people . . . It's true. It's true.' She wagged her hand quickly in front of her as if warding him off; yet he hadn't moved. 'You've only got to come here and say you're lonely and I'll comfort you like I've comforted others. That's what you think, don't you?'

'Listen to me a moment, just a moment, please. Why do we always get off on the wrong foot?'

'You call it the wrong foot! You say what you do, you make suggestions, and you call it—'

'Listen!' The word was a bark. Then bending his body towards her, he asked more quietly, 'May I sit down?'

'No, you can't.'

He bit on his lip. 'Well, it's going to be harder saying what I have to standing up.' He paused, staring into her hostile eyes. Then lowering his gaze from hers he began to talk. 'You see, I'm in a hell of a state inside; have been for the past month. It's all connected with you and I can't get it straight, and I don't know why. The last thing I meant to do was to insult you, yet I thought there was somebody here when I came in . . . I thought that because I feared that, and I found I was furious with you. Does that surprise you? Yet, believe me, the last thing I want to do is to upset you. Can you understand what I'm getting at? Why should I want to upset you when my main aim is . . . is to get you to like me?' The last words had dropped to a whisper, and in the silence that followed he saw her put her hand across her mouth, and the pressure of her thumb and fingers sent the blood upwards and towards her eyes.

He said again, 'May I sit down, please? I feel a bit wobbly.'

When she gave neither her consent nor a refusal, he walked towards the couch and sat down on the far end of it, and looking towards her he said, with touching gentleness, 'Come and sit down and let me talk.'

As if under hypnotism, Cissie went to the couch and sat down, but at the extreme end, away from him.

Looking towards her, his voice still very low, he said, 'I was three weeks in the house without going out, and every minute of it, night and day, I couldn't get you out of my mind, and I didn't know why. I thought it was a sort of delirium and it would pass, but it didn't. And then I tried to reason it out. The few times we have met we have fought. To all intents and purposes you have been having an affair with my father . . . Please, please.' He put up his hand. 'Hear me out. Then as the days went on I realised why you attracted me and I didn't like it. It was because I've a great deal of my father in me. The things that attracted him appealed to me.

'All my life, right up until he took ill, I repudiated the thought that there was anything of him in me, any trait that I couldn't crush that is, and then, lying there with time to think, I discovered I liked the kind of people he liked; I wanted the same kind of things, the same kind of responses. The first words he ever said about you to me were that you were good and kind. I knew then that I wanted someone kind, warm and kind. This was the sort of person I needed. I must have known this even before I met you because that was one of the reasons why I gave up my fiancée. She wasn't a kind person, and I knew that one rarely grows to be kind, you must be born kind.'

He was now looking at her bowed head, and his voice had a touch of hoarseness to it as he went on, 'I gave up all idea of trying to see you; I felt that during our slight acquaintance you had brought sufficient havoc into my life to last me all my days; and then a few days ago I learnt that we were irrevocably linked together, at least in this town. Does it come as a surprise to you to know that we're supposed to be having an affair? That the reason why I was beaten up was that one of your admirers objected to our association?'

Her head was up and she was gaping at him now. 'It's a fact.' He nodded slowly. 'So much so that my parents believe it.'

'Your father?'

'Him most of all, I should say. He gave me a message for you a moment before he sailed. He said you had to take happiness, grab it with both hands. He said to tell you he was happy for you. Oh yes, he believed it.'

Again she had her hand across her mouth and her head was moving in utter bewilderment, and through her spread fingers she muttered, 'People are cruel, cruel. I don't mean your father . . . but the things people say. And now—' her voice cracked, 'and now they'll believe they're right . . . you coming here. They'll have seen you and . . .'

'Does it matter very much?'

'Yes. Yes, it does.' Her tone was vehement. 'I don't want to be thought of like that. All my life I've had to fight it. People think I'm cheap. Oh, I know what they think, but I'm not, I'm not.' She poked her head towards him. 'I could have married over again if I'd wanted to, but I don't want to.'

'Why haven't you?'

'Because I swore I'd never marry again.'

There was a long pause before he asked, 'Were you so very happy with him that you couldn't bear to put anyone in his place?'

'Happy? Happy did you say?' Her lips were showing all her upper teeth, the twisted one at the side. 'I was seventeen when I married.

He was twelve years older than me, and I had three dirty, filthy years with him. Dirty and filthy in every conceivable way. There are so many ways in which a man can be nasty, from his eating, to his sleeping. I was so very young in all ways when I married, but I was full of life, and I died for three years. But when he was killed – he was killed when his lorry went over the Low Town bridge – I came alive again. From that day I was reprieved. It was as if God had given me another chance. I had Pat. He was only a few months old; he was all I wanted; and I promised myself never again, never, never . . . again. And then I met your father . . . He was so kind, so good . . .'

'Don't! Don't!' He pulled himself up abruptly and walked towards the electric fire and stood looking down at it.

'Well, you've been pouring yourself out, why not me?'

'Because I can't bear to hear you say it. It's another thing I've been fighting, the fact of him being so,' he substituted the word placid for inane, 'so placid yet having the power to attract you.' He turned round and came back to the couch and sat down nearer to her now, within an arm's length of her. 'Tell me something. Did I call you Cecilia the night you and mother brought me home?'

She made a little movement with her head, then said, 'Yes.'

'My mother said I did, but I couldn't believe her. I didn't even know that I knew your name.'

'No-one's ever called me Cecilia before. Cissie's a bit common, I know, but I've always been Cissie. Cecilia's so starchy and that's not me.'

'I told my mother I didn't even know your name and she was wild. It seemed to stamp me a liar in her eyes for good and all, but I didn't remember calling you by your first name. So it just goes to show; you must have hit me even before you drowned me in whisky.' As he smiled at her now she turned her face from him and said, 'Please don't go on because . . . because I don't want to take up with anybody.'

'But you would have with my father.' His tone was low, but not nasty.

She jumped to her feet and stood looking down at him. 'Don't keep on about that. That's over, but it won't stop me liking him, I'll go on liking him as long as I live; he was something nice that happened in my life and I want to remember it just like that, something nice.'

'Other nice things could happen to you if you'd let them.'

'If I'd let them.' She bent her thin body towards him. 'Look, let's get this straight once and for all, and let's put it in plain language. You're lonely, and you want an affair . . . well, you've come to the wrong shop.'

'I don't want an affair.' He was on his feet facing her. 'Who's talking about an affair?'

'What else could you be talking about, we haven't met more than half-a-dozen times? We know nothing about each other, only that we go for each other like cat and dog. I've never in my life argued and fought with anybody like I have with you . . . no, not even my husband, because he didn't use words.'

Into the significant pause he said quietly, 'I'm asking you to marry me.'

She was no more surprised than himself when he heard the words. This was jumping the gun with a vengeance. He'd had no idea of saying such a thing . . . well, not yet. He'd just got out of one trap, so to speak. But this was different. There was no bait in this trap, of sex, or money, or promotion, or family ties. Then what was attracting him? Her. Just her. All of her. He wanted to have her belong to him. Have her near him all the time. See that light in her face that would mean she wanted him, that she cared what happened to him, like the night he lay on the floor with his head on her knees. He wanted to marry her. Yes, he wanted to marry her. As if he were the recipient of a revelation he felt himself uplifted by a great surge of feeling, and now he whispered softly, 'Say something.'

Slowly she sat down on the couch without taking her eyes from him. 'You're mad,' she said.

'Why? Tell me why.' He brought his face down to the level of hers.

'Oh,' she twisted her body back and forwards from the waist, 'there's a thousand reasons, but the main one is it wouldn't work . . . you in your position . . .'

'I haven't any position. I'm one of the unemployed, and likely to be . . . And look, don't belittle yourself so much. About your name and everything. You're doing it all the time in different ways. There's no difference between us.'

'No?' She raised her eyebrows at him. 'Say that to your mother. I'm as low down the social scale in your mother's eyes as a kitchen maid to the Colonel's lady. As for my name, the likes of her wouldn't give it to the cat.'

'You're talking rot . . . Anyway, this doesn't concern my mother, because I know now that whatever happens I won't live at home again. The ties between my mother and me are broken, finally, so let's forget about her and her social status, which after all exists only in her own mind . . . Let's forget about both of them, eh, and concentrate on us.'

She now turned her eyes from him and ran the fingers of both hands through her hair, lifting it from the scalp.

He sat slowly down on the couch again, his knees almost touching hers, and watched her as she repeatedly combed her hair with her fingers. And when she stopped she looked up at him and, her face now soft, as was her voice, she said, 'I couldn't. I'm sorry, I . . . I would have to care for somebody very much before I could marry him.'

He could only see her face with one eye, but she looked to him at this moment like a picture set in a deep frame, all toned down, soft and tender. He asked quietly, 'Could you like me?'

Her lips parted, and her eyelashes sent shadows across her cheeks as she lowered them. 'Oh, I could like you all right. I . . . I don't find it hard to like people, it . . . it's loving that's difficult.'

'Well, what about letting us start at the beginning: I'll put up with the liking.' He put out his hands and caught her fingers and, as if she were being burnt, she snatched them away and held her hand tightly pressed to her chest. Then pulling herself backwards and upwards away from him she said, 'No, no, it's no use, don't let's start anything. It's madness and it'd come to no good.'

'All right,' he said quietly, looking up at her, 'don't be alarmed, I was just suggesting that we could be friends.'

'It wouldn't work. You know it wouldn't.'

'I don't see why not.' He smiled wryly, sadly. 'We could discuss music – Pat told me you played beautifully – or antique furniture, you definitely know about that, or the latest book, or we could . . . Oh, Cecilia, don't, don't cry like that, please. I'm sorry. I wasn't meaning anything. What have I said?' He rose and moved quietly to her, and he put his hands on her quivering shoulders and pleaded again, 'Aw, don't, don't cry like that. I'm sorry.' Gently now his arms went about her and for a second he held her pressed against him, and for a second her body relaxed against his, and while it did he buried his face in her tousled hair. And then it was over. By a thrust that nearly knocked him onto his back, they were apart, and she was standing half the length of the room from him. Her face streaming with tears, she was shaking her head violently, crying, 'No! No! No!'

'All right, all right,' he said. 'Don't distress yourself. I'll go.' He went slowly towards the chair and picked up his hat with a shaking hand. Then turning towards her, he asked quietly, 'May I come and see you again?' And immediately she answered with another violent shake of her head. 'No. No. Don't come back here . . . ever. I don't want to see you, understand . . . I've had enough trouble. Don't come again. I'm telling you.'

When he went out of the flat and closed the door behind him she was still talking.

He started the car up immediately and drove fast through the town. As he went up the avenue the Wilcoxes' car was at the front of their drive, and from habit he almost tooted his horn.

Strangely, it was Val he was thinking of as he entered the house

162

and what she must have felt like when he turned her down. He had said to her he was sorry, and he had been sorry for her, but he hadn't known what she felt like; he had a good idea now.

He took off his outdoor things, then looked in the hall mirror. He stood straight staring at himself. She had thrown him off her as if he were a reptile, as if bodily he was offensive to her. But he was a man; he looked a man, whereas his father looked like a big flabby . . . He swung away from the mirror and went into the lounge. And there, her voice in his head seemed to reverberate through the room, crying, 'It was as if God had given me another chance, and I promised myself never again, never, never again . . . And then I met your father. He was so kind, so good . . .' And on that alone she would have taken him, knowing he had nothing else to give her, nothing, she would have been satisfied with that as long as it was from him.

He thought again of the girls he had known before Val. How they had poured themselves over him and how he had tired of them, as he had tired of Val . . . Perhaps if things had gone as he wished tonight the pattern would have been repeated. Unconsciously, he flung his arm out in a wide sweep rejecting the idea, then began to pace about the room. She was different from anyone he had ever known. And the point was, she wasn't a girl, she was a woman. She was older than him; he knew that, he worked it out from Pat's age. She would be three, nearly four years older. What of it? The feeling he had for her was different, new; he had never experienced anything like it before. If it was love it was not blind love, for there were things about her that annoyed him, irritated him. Her silly name for instance, Cissie; and that hair, like tow flopping all around her face. And the way she dressed; no sign of taste. Stiletto heels and her skirts up to her knees; it might be all right for some but she was too tall. Had his father picked these points out of her? Damn his father. He had started all this; because of him he was losing the sight of his eye. 'She's a good woman. She's worried about her boy. Go and see this Bolton chap.' And the result: half vision, and a deep craving to touch, hold, and possess Mrs Cecilia Thorpe. Having seen her only half-a-dozen times, yet knowing from the start that she'd got into your blood like disease and you'd die of her.

Did every man who met her feel like this? No, not like this; they couldn't. Only two men felt about her this way; he and his father, because under the skin they were one.

CHAPTER TWO

THE SEARCH

After almost two weeks of rain and high winds which made people say, 'Well, we'll soon have winter on us, and autumn hardly started,' summer returned. For three days the sun shone. Women went back into sleeveless dresses. The leather jackets of youth were flung open, some showing bare chests. It was hotter than it had been all summer; in fact, hotter than it had been for years.

Cissie had been across the town to Holloway's new office. Being such a lovely day she had decided to walk both ways, but before she reached the main gate she was regretting not having taken a bus, for she had developed a skinned heel.

She was limping as she crossed the yard, and immediately she had passed into the small hall, from which a staircase led up to her office, she whipped off both her shoes and walked up the wooden stairway in her stockinged feet.

The door to the office was open, as was the window, and she lowered herself gratefully into her chair and, letting her head drop back on her shoulders, sighed.

The clatter of typewriters came to her from the other office, where the three typists worked. Her adjusted ear told her that only two of the typewriters were busy; then only one. She heard the girls chattering, and then the other machine stopped and she heard Susan's voice saying, 'That's likely why she's been off colour lately; it's not like her to be snappy.'

Then Jean's voice. 'I've been here six years and I've never known her like she's been these past few weeks.'

Then Susan's voice again, low and disjointed: 'Well, I suppose being saddled with someone blind's no joke. Seems like retribution on him for doing the dirty on the Wilcox girl. Then she had Pat in that trouble, and although he got off she was worried to death. You remember?'

Cissie was standing now looking towards the wooden partition and frosted glass door that divided the two offices; then after a moment she moved swiftly and noiselessly forward and, pulling open the door, looked at the three girls.

Startled, they stared back at her.

'You were talking about me?' she said.

'Oh, Mrs Thorpe, we didn't mean any . . . we . . .'

'It doesn't matter about that.' She wagged her two hands. 'It was me you were talking about, wasn't it?'

They glanced at one another now, and it was Susan who said sheepishly, 'Yes. Yes, we were.'

'About . . . about someone being blind?'

'Well, we didn't mean anything, Mrs . . .'

Again she wagged her hands at them. 'That doesn't matter. Just tell me; was it Mr Emmerson you were talking about being blind?'

'Yes.' Susan screwed her face up as she answered. 'We thought you . . . well.' Again the girls exchanged glances.

'Jean.' Cissie was bending over the middle desk, addressing herself pointedly to the eldest girl. 'What . . . what do you know about Mr Emmerson being blind?'

'Well, it was just what I heard, Mrs Thorpe. Well I thought you knew and that's why . . . well you've been a bit upset lately. And we were just saying . . .'

'All right, all right.' Her tone was level and controlled as if she was talking to a child. 'It doesn't matter about that, only just tell me what you know.'

'Well, just that he had to go to hospital because he was losing his sight.'

Cissie straightened up and continued to stare at Jean; then she looked at the other two girls, and they looked back at her. They watched her turn slowly round and their eyes dropped to her stockinged feet as she went into her office and closed the door.

'Oh no! Oh no! Oh, my God. No.' She was sitting with her elbows on the desk now, her two hands pressing against her cheeks. 'Why hadn't he said? He must have known. That night he must have known; that's why he had come. He said he was lonely. Yes, he would have felt lonely . . . and frightened. If he had told her, would it have made any difference to her attitude?' As she read the answer in her mind she thought, if only he hadn't said that bit about discussing music and furniture, and books, and me thinking his father had said something and he was taking the mickey. But blind! Oh my God! Bolton . . . he should do time, he should, he should. But it was my fault, in the first place it was my fault. Ooh! . . . She thrust out her hand and grabbed the phone and dialled his number.

Within the next half-hour she dialled the number countless times before finally getting through to the exchange and being told that that particular number was no longer in use.

Hastily now she went to the first-aid box attached to the wall outside her office door, and, taking out a sticking plaster, applied it to her heel, Then, her shoes on again, she opened the communicating door, to be met immediately by three pairs of eyes, and,

speaking to Jean, she said, 'Take my calls, Jean, will you? And if
Mr Holloway should come in tell him I had to go home, but I'll be
back in the morning.'

'All right, Mrs Thorpe.'

'Oh, and should he ask for the Williams contract it's in my desk
drawer, I've just brought it back from the bottom office. But I don't
suppose he'll call in today; it's just in case.'

'All right, Mrs Thorpe, I'll see to it. Don't worry.'

After the door had closed on Cissie the three girls listened to her
heels clicking down the wooden stairs before they spoke again, and
then it was the youngest member of the group who, laying her hands
flat on top of her typewriter, said breathlessly, 'Well, and would
you believe that! I thought she was living with him. Everybody said
they were, and that was why the Wilcox girl threw him over and he
lost his job. And it must be all lies 'cos she didn't know. What do
you make of it?'

For answer Jean contemplated her typewriter as she said, as if to
herself, 'It could be lies an' all about her throwing his father over
for him. Eeh! The stories that get about.'

Lime Avenue looked detached and aloof, much more so in the hot
sunshine than it had done in the dark. The houses resting behind
their green façade had a disdainful look. Cissie kept her glance
directed ahead away from them as one does from the passengers
when passing through a Pullman to get to the second-class. These
houses, like the occupants of the Pullman, spoke of money, position.
They didn't awe Cissie, but they were coupled in her mind with
the cold white face of Ann Emmerson.

When she came to number 74 she stood staring at the board above
the gate. It was like something desecrating the road, bringing it
down to the ordinary level of commerce. 'For sale', it said in large
letters. 'This desirable residence comprising . . .' She did not finish
the description but, quickly pushing open the gate, she went round
the drive and looked at the gaping windows. Quietly she walked all
round the house, then out into the avenue again and down the lane
that looked as if it was in the country, and out into the main road.
She had noticed a telephone kiosk as she got off the bus, and she
now hurried to it almost at a run.

He would be in the Newcastle Eye Infirmary.

She got the number from the directory and picked up the phone.
'Could you tell me which ward Mr Emmerson's in, please?'

'Has he just come in?'

'I don't know . . . No. Some time ago, a week or two.'

'Just a moment.'

As she waited she heard the familiar click of the switchboard and
the murmur of two people talking.

'Are you there?'

'Yes.'

'I'm afraid Mr Emmerson's left.'

'Oh!' She stared into the mouthpiece, wetted her lips, and then asked, 'Could you tell me the extent of his trouble . . . his eye trouble?'

'I'm sorry I can't, but I can put you through to the sister.'

'If you would, please.'

After a moment a crisp tone said, 'Yes?'

'I was enquiring about a Mr Emmerson, but I find he has left. Could you tell me how . . . how bad his eyes are? Is . . . is he blind?'

'No. Oh, no. He's losing the sight of one eye, but the other is quite all right.'

She drew in a long breath, then said, 'Do you think you could give me his address?'

There was a pause at the other end of the line, then the crisp voice said, 'Well. Well, just a moment.'

In her duty room Sister Price stood looking down at the telephone receiver lying on her desk. The request for a patient's address was rather unusual, but then Mr Emmerson himself had been rather unusual. He was the first patient she'd had for many a long year who hadn't had one single visitor all during his stay, and people with eye troubles needed visitors. More than anyone else they needed human contacts. The last one in that position she seemed to remember had been an old tramp, and he had died in hospital. She had at times thought that Mr Emmerson wouldn't have cared if he had died too, although there hadn't been anything physically wrong with him except the sight of the one eye, and when it could have been both eyes he should have considered himself lucky. Flicking over the pages of her admittance book she picked up the phone again and said, 'There are two addresses. The one on admittance was 74 Lime Avenue, Fellburn, but on his discharge he gave his address as Meadow Mere, Hill Lane, Bromford. Have you got that?'

'Yes, yes.' Cissie repeated the address, then said, 'Thank you. Thank you very much.'

Bromford was on yon side of the town, quite a way out.

She stood outside the box now considering what to do. She could likely get his number from the exchange as she had the name and address, but no, no, she would go there. But what would she say to him when she saw him? She walked slowly up the road towards the bus stop. She would know what to say when the time came. At present all she could think was: Thank God it's only the one eye.

In the market place she got on a bus that was going to Bromford. Half-an-hour later the conductor put her off at Hill Lane and, pointing up the steep winding path, he said, 'You can't miss it; there's only one house up there.'

Her heel was paining again and she felt inclined to limp, but she made herself walk straight. Then she reached the end of the lane and saw the house. It was a lovely house, small, low and white, with a verandah running along two sides of it.

She was shaking with nervousness, and sweating too when, leaning forward, she knocked on the open door. When she heard a man's heavy tread crossing bare boards in a room to the left of the hall, her heart began to pound against her ribs.

The man who came into the hall was a painter. He had a can in his hand. 'Oh, hello,' he said. 'I didn't know anybody was there.'

'Is Mr Emmerson in please?' She was shaking, not a little with relief at the respite.

'Oh, no. There's just Mrs Stringer here. Will I get her?'

She hesitated, then said, 'Yes, please.'

She saw him go along a little passage off the hall and heard him speak to someone; then, coming towards her, she saw a woman in her fifties enveloped in a large overall. She had grey hair and a round face and looked motherly.

'Yes?' she asked, looking straight at Cissie.

'I . . . I've called to see Mr Emmerson.'

It was as if a skin had dropped over the motherly countenance. Cissie saw the mouth tighten and the eyes narrow.

'Mr Emmerson isn't here. They're abroad on holiday.'

'I mean young Mr Emmerson.' She knew that the woman was well aware which Mr Emmerson she was asking for.

'Oh, I'm afraid he's away too.'

'Could . . . could you give me his address?'

'I'm afraid I couldn't. You see . . . you see I don't know where he's gone.'

Cissie looked into the woman's face. She was a working class woman. If you were speaking of levels you could say that she would be considered as far down in the social scale from herself as she was from Ann Emmerson. Yet this woman was an ally of Ann Emmerson. She was not only tied to her in servitude – the latter she would have denied strongly – but all her loyalty was to her mistress; she might be of the lower working class and talk their language, but her ideas, her way of looking at life, her condemnation of all those who didn't conform to a particular pattern, would be the same as Ann Emmerson's.

Cissie knew all this instinctively, yet she felt that she must get behind the hard core of this woman. Her voice low, she said, 'It's . . . it's so important that I should see him. It's for his own good, believe me.'

'That's a matter of opinion, Miss, but as I said I can't tell you 'cos I don't know.'

Cissie took her finger tips and wiped the sweat from her brow, lightly pushing her lank hair back from her face as she did so. She was hot and tired, and she felt at the end of her tether, like a child that had been for a long walk and calls at a house and says, 'Can I have a drink of water, missus?' She wanted to ask just that: could she have a drink of water? But she wouldn't ask this woman for water, nor would she plead any more or cringe before her. She managed to lift her head and straighten her shoulders as she said, 'Thank you. Good afternoon.'

'Good afternoon.'

She knew the woman was watching her walking away and she kept her steps steady and her back straight until she was out of sight of the house. Then sitting on the grassy verge of the road in the shade of the hedge, she took off her shoe and stocking and straightened the plaster on her heel. And when she had done that she wiped her face with a handkerchief, then said to herself, 'Don't. Don't. You've likely got a long way to go yet and crying is not going to help you.'

The next morning she phoned the office of Ratcliffe, Arnold and Baker and asked to speak with Mr Ransome.

'What name is it, please?' asked the secretary.

'Mrs Thorpe.'

It was a full minute before she heard a man's voice, saying, 'Ransome here. Goodmorning, Mrs Thorpe.'

'Goodmorning, Mr Ransome.'

'What can I do for you?'

'I wonder, Mr Ransome, if you could give me Mr Emmerson's address.'

A long significant pause now, then Mr Ransome's voice saying pleasantly, 'Oh, I'm afraid it's beyond my power, Mrs Thorpe. You see they're on a cruise . . .'

'I mean Mr Laurance Emmerson, Mr Ransome.'

'Oh! Oh, Mr Laurance. Well, that's just as difficult. I'm afraid I can't help you, Mrs Thorpe, because I don't know Mr Laurance's address.'

Cissie waited a moment, then said, 'Mr Ransome, please, please if you know Mr Laurance's address, please tell me. It's very important.'

'Believe me, Mrs Thorpe, I would if I knew it, but I don't. The only place he might be that I can think of is in Oxford with his uncle.'

'Well, could you give me that address?'

'Dear, dear. Now, I don't really know that either.' Mr Ransome sounded flustered. 'The name is Emmerson, as it's Mr Emmerson's elder brother, but that's as far as I know.'

'What do you call Mr Emmerson, I mean the one at Oxford, I mean his Christian name?'

'Ronald . . . Ronald I think.'

'Thank you, Mr Ransome; you've been very helpful.'

When the phone clicked, Arnold put down the receiver. 'Helpful?' This was all very puzzling. He was under the impression that if anybody knew where Laurie was it would be Mrs Thorpe. It was all over the town that he was living with her in her flat. John's departure abroad was put down to this fact, more than his need for recuperating after his illness. He hadn't set eyes on Laurie for weeks. But that was understandable; he'd been so knocked about that he didn't want to be seen . . . But this was very odd, her not knowing where he was . . . If he wasn't with her then where was he? . . .

It was later in the morning when Cissie got through to Ronald Emmerson's house in Oxford, and when a hearty voice greeted her she asked directly, 'Is Mr Laurance Emmerson there please?'

'Laurie? No. Who's speaking?' the voice asked.

'I'm . . . I'm a Mrs Thorpe.'

'Are you a friend of Laurie's?'

'Yes . . . Yes I'm a friend of his.'

'And you expected him to be here?'

'Well . . . well, I thought he might be.'

'So did we, but he changed his plans. We expected him to come on after he came out of hospital, and then we got a letter from him saying he'd got some kind of job. He wouldn't explain what and was very brief, very brief, but he said he would be getting in touch with us. We're rather worried about him; we feel that after this eye trouble he should have somebody to look after him. John and Ann are away on a cruise, you know, and we promised Ann we'd see to him. It's all very worrying . . . You say you're a friend of his, Mrs Thorpe. When did you last see him?'

'Oh, just before he went into hospital.'

'Was he all right when he came out? I mean as right as he could be; you can't feel very right losing the sight of an eye.'

She hesitated before saying, 'Candidly, I didn't know he was going into hospital. I saw him just before but he didn't tell me.'

'Stupid boy. Stupid boy. He did the same with his mother. She doesn't know a thing about it. Myself, I think he's going through a very bad patch, mentally disturbed, you know what I mean. Something went wrong when he broke off his engagement. We were coming through for the wedding, everything was settled . . .'

The voice went on and on. This was John Emmerson's brother but he sounded so different. He was a chatterer. She broke in on the voice, saying, 'Could you give me his address, I mean from where he wrote last?'

'Oh, that was from their new house, Meadow Mere, Bromford way, but he said he wouldn't be going back there, having got this job, and as I said before he promised to write us later, and he hasn't.'

'Thank you, Mr Emmerson.'

'I wish I could tell you more. We are very worried this end.'

'Yes, yes, I understand. Thank you. Goodbye.'

'Goodbye.'

Cissie sat staring down at the desk. It was as if he was trying to lose himself, trying to break contact with everyone he knew. The only one she felt who could help her was the woman up at the new house, but it would be easier walking through a stone wall than getting any information out of her. It was some days later when the thought struck her that perhaps he had to attend the out-patients' department at the hospital. After she had phoned she sat with her head in her hands. Yes, they had said, he attended the out-patients' yesterday. No, he wasn't due to come again . . . at least not to this hospital. No, they didn't know which one he might attend.

The weather changed abruptly and autumn came with a rustling stride. There was hard bright sunshine some days with warm patches, but all the evenings were cold, and when the north-east wind blew it seemed to go straight through the body.

Every Saturday and Sunday, whatever the weather, Cissie, Pat with her, would take a trip out to Bromford village where they would look round the church, and have tea at the only café in the main street, then walk back up the road that passed Hill Lane, looking, always looking, for a blue Rover car. Sometimes they even ventured up the lane and came within sight of the house.

Pat knew whom his mother was looking for. She had explained to him enough to make him understand that because of them Mr Emmerson had lost the sight of an eye, and he was as anxious as she was that they should meet up with young Mr Emmerson again, even, he thought, if he did make her cry, because for a long time now she had been different, and he didn't like her being different.

There were nights, before it got too dark, when she would leave him in the house to do his homework, with the strict order not to go out, and she would take the bus to Bromford.

Her visits to the village became so frequent that people began to wonder about her, for evidently she didn't come to see anyone, for she just went into the church, then walked up the road. Perhaps, some of the old ones said, she went into the church to pray for someone belonging to her who had died, perhaps along the road there, at the toll bend. Two people had been killed there last year. Yet no-one asked her why she came to the village, not even Mrs

Bailey in the tea-shop. Customers' affairs, she said, were none of her business; serving tea was her business, and the blonde young woman was always good for a tea and left a respectable tip.

Then one Saturday, late in October, as they came out of the teashop, Cissie saw the blue Rover, but driving it was John Emmerson, and sitting beside him was his wife . . . They were back.

She didn't go to Bromford any more after this, for the thought of meeting up with John embarrassed her greatly now.

It was almost a month after she had seen John in Bromford that he phoned her.

'Mrs Thorpe.' His voice, quiet as ever, brought a tightness to her throat, and she had to clear it before she could say, 'Yes, Mrs Thorpe here.'

'This is John Emmerson.'

'Oh, hello, Mr Emmerson.' There was a slight pause now and she added, 'I hope you are better.'

'Yes, I'm quite well again, thank you.'

'Did you have a good holiday?'

'Oh, yes, a splendid holiday.' Another pause, and now John said, 'I wonder if I could see you?'

Oh, no. No. She hadn't spoken the words aloud. She gathered the skin of her neck into her fist and waited.

'Are you there?'

'Yes . . . Mr Emmerson . . . I – I think it would be better if . . .'

'This is nothing personal, Mrs Thorpe . . . You understand? Nothing personal.' His words were rapid but scarcely audible.

She made no comment on this and again she waited, and he went on, 'I heard only yesterday – it was during the course of a conversation with Mr Ransome – that . . . that you had been enquiring after Laurie. It is that I would like to see you about. I . . . I can't discuss it over the phone, you understand?'

'Yes.' Her voice was as low as his.

'Would you care to meet me?'

'Yes.'

'Where?'

'Oh. Oh, I don't know.' Not at home. Not at home. Never again.

'I could be walking through the market about half-past five, say on the Education Office side.'

'Yes, yes, that will do. I'll be there exactly half-past five.'

'Very well. Goodbye, Mrs Thorpe.'

'Goodbye, Mr Emmerson.'

She sat with her hands tightly clasped on the desk before her. During the last few weeks her mind had settled down into a state of acceptance: if a thing had to be, it had to be; if it hadn't, it hadn't. She had done her utmost to make it possible and it wasn't to be, that was all. She had lost her chance. Everybody was given one chance, sometimes two. She had only been given two and she had made a hash of the second but she wasn't really to blame because the chance had been presented to her in such a way that she hadn't recognised it.

It was going to be awkward meeting Mr Emmerson. The way things were she just didn't know how she was going to face him, and no matter what the result of their meeting would be she knew that she would feel she had let him down, and that he would feel this too, and in a way blame her.

She saw him coming towards her just past the Education Offices. He was wearing a grey overcoat and trilby and was carrying a despatch case under his arm. His skin looked healthier, browner, but the expression on his face was one she remembered from when she first met him. He stopped in front of her and raised his hat, and as they stood looking at each other the embarrassment was high between them. And then he said, 'I would rather we could have met at some place more congenial than this but . . . but you understand?'

'It's all right.'

He stood blinking and peering at her; then he said, softly, 'You're looking tired.'

'It's the cold; I don't like the cold weather.' She shrugged her body beneath her coat. 'The nights are drawing in, I think it's always colder in the twilight.' She looked over the roofs of the market stalls housed in the middle of the big square. The fading light was merging them into one. Then looking back at him she waited, and after blinking rapidly again John said, 'Well . . . About Laurie. Did you know he had lost the sight of an eye?'

'Yes, I did, and . . . and I feel responsible.'

'No. No, you mustn't feel like that. Any blame must be attached to me. I sent him to Bolton.'

'But it was about Pat's business.'

'These things happen. You mustn't blame yourself. Tell me, when you last saw him did you know his eye was bad?'

'No.' She shook her head.

'And when you found out that was why you wanted to see him?' It was a question asked softly.

As she stared at him through the dim light two women with prams pushed past them and they had to move towards the kerb, and the movement seemed to give her time, and courage, to say to this man, who was the last person in the world she would want to hurt, 'Not exactly.' She bowed her head and into the silence that fell between them she whispered, 'I'm sorry.'

'Oh, don't. Please don't be sorry, because if you're sorry it'll make me be sorry for something I value, for a period in my life that I'll cherish to the end of my days.'

She was staring up into his face. 'Don't talk like that.'

'Why not? Why shouldn't I value something good that I experienced? Life for most of us is humdrum routine, so why not welcome the breaks?' He was speaking lightly. 'What we must face up to is that these episodes are merely breaks, they can't go on . . . It couldn't have gone on.' His voice lost its light tone. 'I realise that now; that period had something of a fairy-tale quality about it . . . You know, as you grow older you often find yourself reading the books you enjoyed as a child, and groping back into the world of fantasy because you remember nice things, unusual things happening in that world. It was like that with me.'

Again they were staring at each other in silence. And now John, wetting his lips, said, 'But I wanted to see you to tell you about Laurie. It . . . it was a great shock to us when we returned to find he'd had an operation on his eye. We had a further surprise when we found he'd taken up a new way of life. He's taken on a dilapidated farmhouse with four acres of land attached and is working it as a smallholding. It had been a smallholding before, I understand, with pigs and poultry, but he's turning it into a nursery for flowers and such things.'

He stopped speaking and she said haltingly, 'I'm glad; it'll do him good to work outside. Perhaps he's taken after you, you being born on a farm . . .' Her voice trailed away.

'I don't know about doing him good. Laurie has changed. He doesn't seem to want people about him any more. It . . . it has upset his mother greatly. She . . . she doesn't often see him now.' He paused here and his eyes held hers, and by his look he tried to tell her what he found too difficult to put into words, the rejection of his son by his wife. At one time their close association had been unbearable to him. The irony of it was it didn't matter any more, for the pain and the jealousy had been transferred to his son's association with this girl. But he hadn't realised until he was talking to Arnold that they weren't together. He had never stopped imagining they were. This seemed to be confirmed when after their return they received a letter from Laurie telling them, in so many words, that he didn't expect them to visit him. He said now, 'Would you like his address?'

'Yes. Yes, please.'

He was fiddling with his despatch case. 'It's quite a way off, between Rothbury and Alnwick. The best way to get to it, if you're going by rail, is to go to Alnwick and get the bus back towards Rothbury. The place is called Slagbottle Farm. Not a very pretty name, and it doesn't do justice to the surrounding country. It's . . . it's beautiful in parts, but rather wild and isolated. Look, I'll put it down for you.' Tucking his case further under his arm he put his hand in his pocket and took out a diary, and after writing in it at some length he said, 'There, that should help you to find it. I . . . I would advise you to start rather early because after getting to Alnwick there's quite a journey by bus, and they're not very frequent, I understand . . . I haven't been to the farm, but, but I know where it is. I – I took a run out there one weekend.' His face was scarlet as he finished.

She took the flimsy piece of paper from his fingers, and now her hand impulsively gripping his, she said, 'Thanks. Thanks. I've . . . I've always thought it, and I'll go on thinking it, there'll never be anyone quite like you.'

His fingers remained slack and still within her hold, and then his hand was free and he was hitching his case up again under his arm, and his voice had a businesslike, brisk sound now. It was a tone she hadn't heard him use before. 'When you see him, tell him I'll take a run over one of these days. Now I must go.' He hunched his shoulders up under his coat. 'Goodbye, and . . . and I hope you find the place all right.'

She moved her head in the characteristic way he had come to know so well and enjoyed watching, and not as a father might a quaint mannerism of a favourite daughter, but that is how he must think of her from now on, as a daughter. Yes, a daughter. But how did one take to oneself a daughter when he didn't want a daughter? Well, the years ahead would tell; he'd have plenty of time for practice . . . All his life he had been practising law, restraint, to live without bodily expression, without love, to smile – that had almost been the hardest, and would certainly be so in the future. To smile for Ann, who, of a sudden, needed his smiles to prove to her that he was happy, that she was making him happy, for now he was not only at long last her husband, but also her son, her lost child. A stronger man would have run from this new burden of affection, but he wasn't a strong man, he was a vacillating man, a weak, kindly man. He wondered at times how he got by in court. Perhaps because in court he was dealing with other people's emotions, emotions which he knew couldn't impinge on himself. In court he stepped out of the weak man and acted a part. He was fortunate, he supposed, in having this form of outlet; other weak men had to be content with dreams . . . Dreams! Now he, too, would have to resort to dreams; for the rest of his life he could only be with Cissie in dreams. He had been a fool, an utter fool. He could have made her happy; even as he was he could have given her more than Laurie could ever dream of. For the young only took, but he would have given, and she had wanted what he had to give. She wanted more than mere sex; but even there he would have satisfied her, there were ways and means. During all the long twenty-six years with Ann he had never thought along such lines. There had been no incentive.

You don't look for ways of loving an ice-coated wall. But with Cissie
. . . Oh, Cissie.

'Are you all right?'

'Oh yes. Yes.'

He had been staring at her so long, sort of holding his breath, she
thought he was going to have another attack. 'You sure?'

'Of course. Now I really must go. Goodbye.'

His abruptness now disturbed her. She tried to smile at him but
couldn't. 'Goodbye, Mr Emmerson,' she said. 'And thank you.
Thank you so much.'

When he passed her and walked away she should have walked in
the opposite direction, but she turned and watched him until he
stepped off the pavement and went towards the market stalls and
disappeared into the gloom. She had the unnerving desire now to
run after him and catch him by the arm and say, 'Come on home,
John.' She wanted to lift that look from his face. That lonely look.
That lost, empty, hungry look that had first caught at her sympathy.
And it had all been there again as he stood staring at her . . . But
in the hospital he had said . . . what had he said? Only, 'I've nothing
to offer you, Cissie, and you're young.' But it wouldn't have
mattered about what he hadn't got to offer, she'd had all the sex
she wanted in her lifetime. This being the case, then why had she
been breaking her neck to find Laurie?

'You can't have them both.' She came to herself with a shuddering
shock, not only from the context of her words but the fact that she
had spoken them aloud in the street.

CHAPTER THREE

THE FARM

She set off early from Fellburn the next morning for Newcastle, from where she took the train to Alnwick, and it was just on twelve o'clock when she reached there. On enquiring, she found there was no bus passing Slagbottle Farm but that she could be set down near a road which led to it.

Out of Alnwick the change in the aspect of the country both surprised and awed her, and this wasn't helped by a low rain sky. There were few houses to be seen, only great stretches of fell land rising to bare-looking hills. Eventually they came to a little hamlet, followed by a long stretch of deep, black-looking woodland, then open country again, and it was while passing through this that the conductor said, 'There's your stop, missus. Go along the road there.' He pointed to a track. 'Fork to the left over the hill an' you can't miss it.'

'What time do you come back?' she asked.

'Oh, around half past three, a minute here or there.'

'Is that the last one?'

'No, there's another around six.'

She thanked him, and he rang the bell, leaving her standing, seemingly alone in a vast wilderness, for wherever she turned she could see nothing but rolling fells.

She set off on the rough cart track, which went uphill for some way. Then over the brow she came to the fork in the road that the conductor had spoken of, and now she found herself going gently down hill and looking across a wide valley. She could see in the far distance the wood she had passed in the bus and, nearer, were small copses. The land here looked less gaunt; altogether it had a gentler aspect.

Then she saw the farmhouse. It lay in a hollow on the hillside. It was as if a giant hand had scooped out the earth to make a place flat enough to build a house. After staring at it a moment or so she went on down the hill and came to a five-barred gate. After passing through and closing it she walked along a footpath that skirted a deep rutted field. And again she was going uphill. At the edge of the field some of the earth had been dug and made ready for

177

planting. She walked now between stacks of seed boxes, then past a greenhouse that was in the process of being erected, and all the time she looked around her. But she saw no-one, not even an animal.

Then she was walking up a flagged path, bordered on each side by a tangle of weed and bramble that had once been a garden. And so she came to the back door of the grey stone house. She noticed that the weather boarding on the bottom of the door was rotten and that the door had not been painted for years. She shivered, not only from the cold, which had become intensified in the last few minutes with a thin drizzle of rain, but with a foreboding of fear as to what she would find when the door opened.

She put her hand out and tapped on the door, two small knocks. She imagined she heard a movement inside, but when no-one appeared she tapped again, louder this time, and the next minute the door was opened and there he stood, at the top of the three steps, his face at first expressionless until the colour suddenly flooded over it.

Her whole stomach jerked as it hadn't done since Pat first kicked at her from within the womb. 'Hello,' she said softly.

Still with the door in his hand he didn't move. She was shocked at the change in him. He was older, much older, and although his face was flushed to a dark red, his skin indicated pallor. There was an oddness too about his looks. Both his eyelids moved but only one side of his face seemed alive.

Her voice trembling, she said gently, 'Aren't you going to ask me in? I've – I've come a long way.'

As he half glanced over his shoulder she was reminded of the last time she had seen him, when she had half glanced over her shoulder. He had thought then she had someone with her. Now the same fear attacked her making her feel faint and sick, and it sent flying the doubts she had had about the reason for her visit here. When with a jerk he stepped aside and pulled the door wide she walked past him and entered the house.

She had taken no more than three steps into the room before she was brought to a halt with shock. The place was stark and bare, reminiscent of most of the land outside. The floor was made of great uneven slabs of stone. There was a big open fireplace with the remnants of a dead wood fire on the hearth, and in the middle of the room an old wooden table and one chair. On the table was a board on which stood a loaf, some butter, still in the paper, and a piece of cheese, it, too, lying in its wrapper, and towards the edge of the table lay a knife and plate, and beside it a half-empty bottle of beer and a glass.

She turned her eyes from the table and looked at him. He was standing with his back to the door, his hands hanging by his sides. She didn't know what to say. She had thought she would have known, once she saw him, but she didn't. She hadn't expected it to be like this. She hadn't expected him to look like this. He had always looked cocksure, but now he looked ill, yet aggressive. She made herself smile as she said, 'It's . . . it's grand country; I've never seen such scenery.'

He seemed surprised at her choice of words and she watched him clutch at them as if with relief as he spoke to her for the first time. 'Yes,' he said, 'it's wonderful.' He cleared his throat then moved stiffly towards the table. 'It makes you wonder why you ever stayed in town.'

'May I sit down?'

'Yes, yes.' He pointed to the chair; then his hand, continuing the movement, covered the table, and he gave a hick of a laugh. 'I'm living rough; I'm not settled in yet, there's so much to do.'

'Yes.' She nodded. 'There's always a lot to do on a new place.'

He scraped his foot, which was encased in a thick, heavy boot, over the stone floor, and then he looked down at it, and she looked at it too. He had changed, all of him. He was wearing dirty corduroy trousers and an old leather jacket on top of a pullover, and his hands were rough, his nails broken. She remembered having admired his hands and the way he dressed. As yet she couldn't understand the reason for the complete change in him. Would losing the sight of his eye do this?

His voice startled her, bringing her eyes up to him. 'Why have you come?'

'I wanted to see you.'

'What for? We have nothing to say to each other; you pointed that out very forcibly the last time we met and you were quite right. I know now you were quite right. Oh yes.'

She leant over the corner of the table towards him. 'Please! Listen. I . . . I hadn't had time to think.'

The seconds piled up before he answered, 'You . . . you wouldn't have needed time if it had been my father, would you?' Now she saw it all, the reason for this self-imposed isolation, the way he was living, the whole disintegrating of him, it was almost tangible. This thing that was eating him was not the loss of his eye, this thing that might take her a lifetime to conquer, this thing that would well up at times and make them blaze at each other, this thing that would be secreted in some corner of his mind for as long as she was alive, was jealousy of his father.

Still leaning towards him she almost convinced herself she was speaking the truth, so emphatic did she sound when she said, 'It had nothing to do with your father. He didn't come into the picture at all, not in that way. I was mad at you, that's why I said what I did . . . and, and I didn't believe you would want to marry me.'

Again some time elapsed before he spoke. 'If my father was free and you had to choose between us you would have him now, wouldn't you?'

'No! No! I wouldn't.' She shook her head wildly. 'He's nearly twenty years older than me, another generation. He . . . he could be my father.' Somewhere inside her she was apologising to John, begging him to understand.

'You've changed your tune.'

'Look, be reasonable. Just think for a minute . . . I didn't know you when I met your father. If I'd met you first, well . . .'

'He still wants you.'

'He doesn't. He doesn't.' She was shouting now as if he were at the other end of the house. 'He sent me . . . Aw, please.' She rose to her feet and pressed her hands over her face and begged, 'Don't let's start again, don't let's row . . . Please.'

'He sent you?' His lips scarcely moved as he spoke. 'You've been seeing him?'

'No. No.' She closed her eyes. 'He phoned me yesterday and told me where you were.' She knew better at this stage than to say she had met John. 'He had just learned the day before that I had been looking for you, and I have, for months and months, from shortly, shortly after that night. I, I went to the hospital, then to your old home, then to the new place. The woman there wouldn't tell me where you were. I got in touch with your uncle at Oxford. I . . . I went back weekend after weekend, and sometimes of an evening, to Bromford, hoping that I might see you, at least see your car, and when I did see it and your father and mother were in it I stopped going. I phoned Mr Ransome and begged him to tell me where you were. He said he didn't know, and then he must have told your father about me enquiring and' – she spread out her hands to him – 'and here I am.'

As she finished speaking she felt a faintness coming over her and she turned from him, groping at the back of the chair, and sat down again.

He looked intently at her but did not go towards her.

'Could I have a drink of water?'

Without a word he went out of the room, his boots clattering on the stone floor, and in a minute he came back carrying a cup. He did not put it into her hand, but on the table to the side of her, and she took it up and drank it nearly all. Then, wiping her mouth with a handkerchief, she said, 'It was a long walk.'

'Would . . . would you like a glass of beer, and some bread and cheese?'

'Yes, yes, I would, please I . . . I've had nothing since breakfast; perhaps that's what's made me feel faint.'

'Help yourself, my hands are not too clean.' Brusquely, he pushed the board, with the loaf and butter and cheese, towards her; then he went out of the room again and returned with a bottle of beer in one hand and a box in the other. He put the bottle to her hand, saying, his manner unchanged, 'I'm afraid you'll have to use the cup, I'm short of glasses at the moment.' Then taking the box to the other end of the table he sat down and poured the remainder of his beer into the glass.

The food was sticking in her throat; she was cold both inside and out, and the beer wasn't helping. There was an unreality, she felt, in their sitting together like this, eating together in this awful room, in this awful silence. 'What kind of farming are you going to do?' Her voice was small.

'It isn't farming, nothing so glorified as that; there's only four acres. I'm going in for flowers, building my own greenhouses.' He moved his head towards the door but he kept his eyes on his plate. 'I'd like to try orchids; there's money in them and this spot is amazingly sheltered.'

'The house looks old,' she said, her voice still under-toned.

'It is. It's over three hundred years. They hauled the stones over the hills from the quarry, and there're timbers in some of the rooms that were once part of the old wooden ships on the Tyne.' His tone was stiff, his flow quick, but he was talking.

'Would you show me round?' she asked gently, and when his eyes flicked towards her before returning to look at his plate, she said. 'My bus doesn't go until half past three.'

'Half past three?' He nodded, then added, 'They don't run very often.' Then finishing his beer, he said, 'It won't take all that long, there's not much to see, only the skeleton of the house. I'm concentrating on the outside first, getting the greenhouses up. They're the most important.'

'Yes,' she said, 'they would be.'

He rose from the box and walked across the room and she left her unfinished bread and cheese and quietly followed him. At the door he flung his arm back and said, 'This is really part of the hall. The stairs used to go from here but they shut them off to make another room, but later on I'm going to have the partition down and it'll make a fine hall.'

They were standing now in the other part of the room, from which led a shallow black oak stairway. There was another door in the far wall, which she took to be the front door, and to the side of it a window which stretched from floor to ceiling, giving a view across the valley.

'It could be very nice.' She looked around her, and he nodded and said, 'Yes, when I get down to it; it'll look all right.

'This is the kitchen,' he said. 'It's a bit old-fashioned but there's plenty of time to alter things. At present I cook with calor gas but

I'll get that old range going one day; there's not a thing wrong with it.'

She looked at the great black open range taking up almost one wall of the big room, which was also flagged with stone. There was no furniture at all in this room, no table or chairs, nor even a working surface. The cold bareness, that in itself indicated loneliness, made her ache with compassion. His father had been lonely, but that wasn't his fault. But this kind of loneliness, this self-inflicted loneliness, spoke of a sickness of the mind.

'There's another room on this floor,' he said, as she followed him out of the kitchen. 'But I won't use it much, as it'll take too much heating.' He opened a door and she saw a long, low, beautifully shaped room, it had a wooden floor, the boards, worn with use, were over a foot wide.

'It'll be a pity if you don't,' she said, 'it's a lovely room this.'

'Yes, I suppose so.' He turned abruptly away and walked back into the hall and up the stairs. On the landing he said, 'There's five rooms here. Mind your head.'

She had to bend down to go into the first room. It had a dormer window and the walls were plastered. The next three rooms were larger but much the same. The fifth door he didn't open, and as he passed it he said, 'That's just the same,' and she guessed it was where he slept.

As she followed him down the stairs, her eyes on the back of his head, she thought what a dreadful place to be alone in. There flashed into her mind a picture of her flat, and she almost groaned aloud at the comparison.

Downstairs again he walked through the room by which she had first entered the house, saying, 'There's a big cellar underneath. It's full of rubbish, but it'll do for a storage place when I get going.'

He was still walking, in silence now, and she was still following, and when they reached the other side of the house she saw, to her surprise, a large courtyard with two stables going off and a thatched barn that was used as a garage. The thatch was rotten and there were gaps in the roof, and inside the garage stood a van.

'You've got a car?' she said.

'Oh, it's just an old van, but it's a necessity up here. I bring all my stores from Alnwick once a week, and of course I'll need even a bigger one when I get going.'

'Yes, yes, of course.' She nodded.

He walked past the barn now and along a tangled pathway, saying, 'This was a sort of vegetable garden.'

'Has the house been long empty?' she asked.

'No, it has never been empty.' He spoke over his shoulder. 'An old couple lived here. The old man died and she went down into the town. It's too far out for most but it suits me, just what I wanted.

Moreover, it was going cheap. Twelve hundred she was asking, that was all. Amazing these days. When I get the house finished it'll be worth six times that, let alone the land.'

It was just talk. He knew it, and she knew it. He would never get the house finished, not without her he wouldn't. Without her he might work out part of his sickness on building the greenhouses, and when they were completed he would move on. This could be a temporary resting place for him, or it could be a home for life. It all depended on her and how she handled him within the next hour. She couldn't just say to him, 'I'll marry you;' it wouldn't be enough, she knew she would have to convince him that he meant more to her than that, that there was nothing he would ask that she wouldn't do for him. Even more than that, that he would have no need to ask.

He was saying now, 'The old man was born in the house and he was eighty-four when he died, amazing.'

She could imagine old people having lived in the house for a long time. It looked like it, and smelt like it. She would alter all that.

Her back was straight and her head was up. Then she stumbled over a bramble. He turned quickly but he did not touch her. Instead he looked at her shoes and she felt he was about to criticise them; but when he saw they were flat-heeled, he said, 'I must get the paths cleared.'

'It's all right,' she said. 'I wasn't looking where I was going.'

When they came to the greenhouse she said, 'It's very clever of you to be able to build it on your own.' And to this he replied, 'Oh, there's nothing in it, it all comes in sections. The difficult part of the job is getting the stuff carted up here, cement and things for the foundations.'

She was surprised he knew how to handle cement. Likely he hadn't at first, as two burst bags of hardened cement indicated.

'Later on I mean to make up the track to the main road; it'll be easier on the van.'

As he led the way back to the house he looked up at the sky in a casual manner and remarked, 'I think we're in for another shower.'

In the room again she could not control her shivering, for it seemed colder inside the house than it did out. He was aware that she was cold and he walked towards the fireplace, saying as he went, 'I usually don't light up until the evening; I – I'll get it going. Would . . . would you like a cup of tea?'

'No, no thanks.' She paused, then asked, 'Is there a telephone box on the main road?'

'Yes.' He nodded. 'About a hundred yards along from the bottom of the lane.'

'I'll have to make a phone call,' she said. 'Pat is staying with the mother of one of the girls at the office. I would like to get in touch with her. I'd better be getting down,' she said.

He turned from her towards the fireplace again and she saw his left shoulder twitch; then as quickly he turned back and stared at her. His distress was too much to bear without going to him, and the time was not yet. When she moved to the door he muttered thickly, 'If you'll wait a minute I'll take you down in the van.'

'Thank you; it would be a help.'

He went past her, almost knocking her aside, and she watched him hurry along the side of the house. A minute or so later she heard him starting up the van, and then he appeared at the corner, shouting roughly, 'You'll have to come this way.'

She went quickly towards the courtyard where the van was now standing, and he opened the door for her but did not help her up the steep step. And then he was sitting behind the wheel and thrusting in the gears.

Going down the rutted lane she was bumped and jostled, and twice she fell against his arm, until she found that by bracing herself with her feet she could curtail her movements somewhat.

He had not spoken during the journey down but when they neared the road he said gruffly, 'They don't like you parking on this stretch, it's narrow and on the bend. There's the kiosk along there.' He pointed across the corner of the field.

Out of the van, she would not let herself look at him. She must burn her boats completely before she made the final move. She said under her breath, 'Thanks,' then walked down the road conscious that he was watching her.

It was a funny thing about the burning of boats, you were always frightened; even if you wanted to burn them you were still frightened. She had once before burnt her boats when she ran away from home and married Harry. The result of that burning was her loathing of sex, the abhorrence of even the thought of physical contact. Yet within the next few minutes she was going to set the seal on another episode of physical contact – and not under the sanction of marriage either. She was going to do what she had been suspected of doing for years, and perhaps she would never be really able to convince him that she hadn't. Well, that was as might be, but at that moment she knew instinctively that the only way to help him was to give him her love . . . unreservedly. That's what she had come to do, but she had never imagined he would need it as much as he did.

She lifted the receiver and got through to Jean's mother. Yes, Mrs Watson said, Pat was fine; eaten a big dinner. And, no, no, of course she wouldn't mind having him for the night. Was she herself fixed up for the night? Oh, that was good. Some of those country people did you well.

As Mrs Watson continued to talk Cissie was startled by the distant sound of the van starting up. She twisted around, the phone still to her ear, and saw the van turning in the road . . . She said 'Yes, yes,' to Mrs Watson, then gabbled, 'I'll have to ring off. There's a bus coming.'

She jammed the receiver down, but moved no further than the door, and from there she watched the van bounding and bumping up the hill. She closed her eyes for a moment, then walked heavily towards the track, and just as she reached it she saw the bus winding its way towards her from the far distance. Another two minutes and it would be here. Perhaps that's what he had thought; the bus would be along in a minute, and it was no use prolonging the agony. When the bus passed the bottom of the road she was a few hundred yards up the track.

Before she reached the fork in the road it was raining heavily. When she reached the house door she was very wet, tired, and sad.

She didn't knock this time but, lifting the latch, she pushed the door open. She watched his head jerk up from his arms on the table. His face looked ghastly, and she did now what she should have done when she first entered the house. She went to him and put her arms about him.

His face buried in her breasts, his body shook convulsively and she muttered over him, 'There now. There now. It's all right.' It was like talking to Pat until, after a while, she brought his head up and, bending to him, placed her lips on his. After a long moment he pulled himself up and held her tightly to him, and, both their faces awash now, they looked at each other. And then she said, 'I – I was just phoning to say I wouldn't be home tonight.'

She saw the greyness seep from his face. And now, her voice high and cracking between laughter and tears, she gabbled, 'We can go in tomorrow and clear the flat, and collect Pat . . . You won't mind Pat?'

For answer he held her face tightly between his hands, and after searching it with his limited gaze he muttered, 'Oh, Cissie, Cissie.'

Not Cecilia, she noted, but Cissie.

'You'll have to marry me some time . . . doesn't matter when, just to make it right with Pat.'

'Oh, Cissie, Cissie.' He gathered up handfuls of her hair as he kept repeating, 'Oh, Cissie, Cissie.'

She put up her hands and caught his and pressed them to her head.

It was funny. She was about to throw her hat over the windmill, so to speak. Well it was done every day, but she had always resisted it, not alone, she knew now, merely because she had been sickened of sex, but because in giving way to it she'd really be doing what people expected of her. So she had lived a way of life that belied her looks, just to keep her self-respect. But now that didn't matter any more; nothing mattered, except his peace of mind and happiness, and she could give him both . . . Yes, she could do that so long as they didn't talk about his father. And as long as she herself stayed shut away in this wild separate world and didn't see him . . . Oh John, John I'm sorry.

THE END